EVE

THE AWAKENING

JENNA MORECI

Printed in the United States of America

First Edition, 2015

ISBN-13: 978-1507886571
ISBN-10: 1507886578

TABLE OF CONTENTS

CHAPTER 1: THE YOUNG CHIMERA   1

CHAPTER 2: WELCOME TO BILLINGTON   27

CHAPTER 3: JASON A. VALENTINE   51

CHAPTER 4: SNOW GLOBE   81

CHAPTER 5: THE LACE PANTIES   111

CHAPTER 6: NIGHTMARES   132

CHAPTER 7: DEEP BREATHS   153

CHAPTER 8: STARRY NIGHT   177

CHAPTER 9: THE LIST   209

CHAPTER 10: ONE OF US   243

CHAPTER 11: A NIGHT BEST SPENT IN BLACK AND WHITE   273

CHAPTER 12: FLORENZA GALLO   317

CHAPTER 13: THE QUEEN OF DIAMONDS   348

CHAPTER 14: THE ALIBI   380

CHAPTER 15: GO TO HELL   422

CHAPTER 16: LIGHT 'EM UP   457

CHAPTER 17: NEVER UNDERESTIMATE YOUR ENEMY   500

CHAPTER 18: GOING HOME   541

CHAPTER 1: THE YOUNG CHIMERA

Every detail of that day was vividly imprinted on her memory. The breeze was gentle, the air ripe with the scent of freshly cut grass and the heat of Indian summer. The sun was setting in the distance, painting the sky with streaks of pink and orange like the swirls of her favorite sherbet ice cream.

Eve was only eight years old: a little girl with bouncy brown curls and a fresh California tan. She sat in her front yard, the blades of grass tickling her toes as she hunted for ladybugs, snails, and any other critters she could find crawling through the sod. Her aunt was watching her from the kitchen window, as she did every weekday afternoon until her parents arrived home from work. They would be home soon—with pizza, no less—and in that moment, Eve knew it was going to be a good evening.

A single ladybug crawled down her arm, across her palm, and onto the tip of her index finger, where it launched itself into the sky, quickly fluttering away with the breeze. Eve's eyes followed the insect until they caught sight of something else: a small blue car gliding up the street. Her parents were coming. She sprang from the lawn, her knees and bottom stained green from the turf, and skipped along the sidewalk toward the corner of her block, where she stood and waited. The car stopped at one stop sign. Another. She could make out her mother in the driver's seat—her mom waved and smiled. The moment was *perfect*, as if taken straight from the pages of a children's picture book. If she could have frozen time in that instant, she would have done so in a heartbeat.

And a split second later, a fiery red truck hurtled through the intersection and smashed into the little blue car.

The crash sounded like a thunderclap in the middle of the street—a turbulent, ear-piercing explosion. Her parents' car flipped once, twice, three times, then slammed into a nearby telephone pole and wrapped itself around the wooden post. With a deafening boom, the truck landed upside down atop the wreck, crushing what remained of the car until it was nothing more than a mangled, aluminum carcass.

As suddenly as it began, it was over; there was nothing left but silence.

Eve was motionless. She stood at her corner and gazed at the destruction, her body paralyzed, her eyes vacant. Her heart and lungs were frozen and heavy in her chest, and though she knew what had happened, though she had seen every detail, she remained still and unresponsive. In those few, agonizingly long seconds, she was hollow, a shell of the person she'd been just moments before. All she could do was stand and stare at the distant scrap pile of metal, rubber, and blood.

Movement: a bloody arm dangled from the shattered window of the truck, finally bringing life to the crumpled heap. It frantically searched for the door handle and, with an arduous tug, swung the door open. A man tumbled out of the truck and landed face-first onto the pavement, his body limp and pathetic as he struggled to get up. He forced himself to his feet—his clothes were tattered, his face smeared with blood—and as he stumbled away from the wreckage, his eyes darted around desperately until finally locking on to Eve.

"Don't you tell anyone, little girl," he slurred, staggering toward her. "Don't you tell a goddamn soul, y'hear me?"

It hit her then like a ton of bricks; her senses were abruptly brought to life, working at once with adrenalized, feverish intensity. Her heart pounded as if it could escape from her chest, and an uncontrollable pulsing surged in her brain. It was a pain she had never known, a torturous throbbing that spread through her skull until her entire field of vision was consumed with darkness. Her limbs shook as tears poured down her face, and with what felt like every ounce of energy she had within her, she let out a gut-wrenching scream.

And as she screamed, something happened—something that Eve could not predict or explain. The contorted truck lurched from its resting spot, seemingly coming to life in an instant, and shot high into the sky like a horrifying rocket. It disappeared from sight, then, just as quickly, reappeared, plummeting down to the ground and crash-landing only a few yards away, right on top of its driver, smashing his body into the rubble beneath him.

Eve sprinted toward her parents' car, her cry echoing down the street. Her hair was plastered to her wet face as she howled for her parents, desperate to see their faces, but all she could see were scraps of metal and a stream of smoke oozing from the mutilated car hood. She hadn't noticed the truck's sudden resurrection or the death of its driver. She hadn't seen her neighbors pouring from their houses, nor did she hear their shrieks: "*It was her!*" they cried. "*She killed him!*" She didn't feel her aunt snatch her up and grip her tightly. All she felt was the heaving of her lungs, the rawness of her throat, and the strange, defiant pulse in her brain.

"*Did you see what she did?*"

"*She's one of them!*"

"*She's so young...*"

Their words reverberated in the background, fading away until all she could hear was the sound of her own piercing, terrorized scream.

Eve's eyes shot open, and she gasped for air. She propped herself up atop her mattress, cradling her aching forehead in her hands as her breathing slowly normalized. It was a nightmare—an all-too-familiar nightmare. The same nightmare she had been having every night for the past eleven years. She turned to her side and checked her clock: 7:53 a.m. With an obscenity-riddled grumble, she dragged her body out of bed and began her morning routine.

Eve stumbled across the studio apartment and parked herself in front of the bathroom mirror. She wasn't a little girl anymore: she was nineteen years old, nearly a grown woman. Her corkscrew curls had softened into long waves of coffee-colored hair that cascaded down her freckled, olive shoulders. The spitting image of her late mother, she had large brown eyes, full lips, and an angular face, with sharp cheekbones and a pointed nose. She was slender, gangly, and awkward, with legs that extended endlessly, her height clearly inherited from her late father. As she hurriedly brushed her teeth, she stopped for a moment and stared at her reflection—at the subtle hints of her parents looking back at her—and then quickly spat in the sink.

The abrupt ringing of her phone interrupted the silence. Eve checked the clock—8:02 a.m.—and rolled her eyes, ignoring the noise, letting the call go to voicemail. Without the slightest hint of urgency, she rummaged through her measly closet and pulled out a grey hooded sweater, a pair of cutoff shorts, and her favorite black combat boots, then shimmied the clothes onto her body and combed her hair into place with her fingers before heading for the door. She grabbed her skateboard, yanked at the doorknob and stopped; her phone still sat on her nightstand, its message light blinking brightly as if to torment her, and she sighed with irritation as she shoved the device into her pocket and slammed the door behind her.

San Francisco was sunnier than usual. Normally, Eve wouldn't even fathom wearing shorts in the middle of June, but the sky was a little bit more blue than grey, and streams of sunlight perforated the clouds. She dropped her skateboard to the ground and pushed off, gracefully gliding down the street and swerving around the pedestrians meandering across her path. The wind tossed her hair across her shoulders and the sunshine warmed her hands and cheeks, but even in that moment of peace she couldn't help but notice them: the disparaging faces of those who watched her speed by, their mouths twisted into grimaces, their eyes beady and scornful. She pulled her hood over her head as she skated down the road, though she knew it wouldn't do her much good. They still watched her. They always did.

Eve reached Haight Street, skating by a group of lost tourists who gazed disappointedly at their less-than-impressive surroundings. She passed the rows of alternative boutiques and hole-in-the-wall restaurants, and still the scathing stares followed her. It was of no consequence to her—that was a lie of course, but one she told herself so frequently that she nearly believed it—and besides, she would only be there for a short while.

She found her spot: Bob's Pawn Shop, right in between the Chiquita Taquería and the Shang Wu Holistic Pharmacy. Bob himself sat outside smoking a pipe with his old German shepherd, but aside from that the entire block looked startlingly unfamiliar. A line of police cars circled the corner, their lights flashing as the officers cluttered the sidewalk. The pharmacy was a mess: the windows were bashed in, and caution tape covered the entire storefront. The owners, an elderly man and woman, were crying as they gave the police their statements, their voices frantic and distraught. Suddenly, they stopped and stared at Eve, and soon the officers followed suit, their faces wearing the same look of disdain that had haunted her since she'd left her apartment. Without a moment's hesitation, she tucked her skateboard under her arm and made her way into the pawn shop.

The shop was dingy, poorly lit, and layered with so much dust that she could feel it in her lungs. A few patrons were scattered across the room; they talked to one another, giggling at the obscure artifacts, until they heard the door close behind Eve and saw her walk into the room. Their faces dropped—there it was again, that horrible, ugly scowl—and the room became eerily quiet aside from the slight hum of the vintage radio. One of the patrons, a regular whom Eve had seen before, pointed her nose in the air and, with her little finger raised, turned up the volume of the radio.

"The chimera population has plagued us with disorder and mayhem since they first appeared nearly forty years ago. It's an atrocity, really—one that this country is clearly unprepared to deal with."

Eve's phone rang from within her pocket, bringing her back to reality. She stared at her phone, frowned, and immediately silenced it.

A paunchy, balding man scurried from the back of the store, his face riddled with anxiety, beads of sweat forming at the top of his shiny head. He was Stuart, Bob's son and the true heart and soul of the shop, though Eve questioned whether he had either. He waddled behind the glass counter and glared at her.

"What do you want, Eve?"

She nodded her head toward the door. "What happened at the pharmacy?"

"There was a raid. Interlopers tore the whole place apart."

Eve flinched slightly, her fingers tense as they dug into the side her skateboard. "Interlopers?" she said. "Why?"

"Apparently the owners were running an underground medical clinic. For chimeras."

The shop felt small, too small, and suddenly Eve remembered the other patrons staring at her. She turned—they were still staring, of course—and picked at her cuticles nervously.

"Look, whatever you want, make it quick. I've got customers," Stuart spat.

Eve plopped her board onto the counter. "I want to sell you this."

Stuart eyed the skateboard, running his hands along the nose of the deck. "Is this a *vintage* Flip skateboard?"

"Yes. Released in 2019."

"Jesus Christ, it's made of wood and everything." He lifted the board and examined it closely. "Good pop. The artwork is limited edition. This brand doesn't even exist anymore. Why have you been *riding* it?"

"I have to get around somehow."

"Well, your 'getting around' has been devaluing this piece." He rested the board back on the counter and wiped the sweat from his bald head. "How'd you get your hands on this thing in the first place?"

"It belonged to my grandpa. He gave it to my dad. Now it's mine."

He scowled. "You know, I still think it's terrible what you're doing, selling your parents' stuff off, God rest their souls."

"Well, I'd love to get a job so I wouldn't have to sell any of their things, but for some odd reason, no one will hire me," Eve grumbled, her tone laced with sarcasm. "How about you, Stu? Do *you* want to hire me?"

Stuart looked away uncomfortably. Eve's phone rang again, and she quickly sent the call to voicemail.

"If this board was in mint condition, it'd be worth thousands, but the grip tape is wearing off and the tail is scuffed down pretty bad." He folded his arms and dipped his chin. "I can give you four hundred fifty."

"Are you *insane?*"

"That's the highest I can go."

"I've done my research, and boards in worse condition are going for three times that amount."

"Yes, but did those boards once belong to *Evelyn Kingston?*" he hissed. "Look, if people ask me where this came from, I'm going to be honest. Your name alone drives down the price."

Eve glared back at the man—at his round cheeks, bright red nose, and the gross sweat that dripped down his temples. She could feel her hands tremble—she resisted the urge to ball them into fists—and she could sense her vision start to haze over into a deep, overpowering blackness, but she stopped herself.

"You're a real dick."

He smiled smugly. "And yet I'm the only one who will buy your shit."

Eve nodded at the cash register, biting her lip resentfully. "Fine," she muttered.

Stuart fiddled with his old-fashioned register, pressing his stubby fingers against the touch keys in such a way that made Eve cringe with disgust. The register drawer flung open, and as he counted out four hundred and fifty dollars in twenties and tens, Eve's phone rang yet again. She impatiently silenced the device, shoving it back into her pocket as Stuart watched her out of the corner of his eye.

"You're awfully popular today. Didn't know you had friends."

"My school keeps calling," she explained, apathetically. "They want to know if I'm coming to my graduation. I'm the salutatorian—I'm supposed to make a speech."

"When's your graduation?"

"Today."

"When does it start?"

The faintest hint of a smirk graced her lips. "Twenty-seven minutes ago." And again, her phone let out a ring, and still she ignored it. She could hear one of the patrons clear her throat and then raise the volume of the radio even higher.

"*To disregard the threat that chimeras pose to this nation is moronic—and downright dangerous. Are we just supposed to sit back and watch without taking any steps to control them? To contain them?*"

Stuart plopped the wad of cash onto the counter and let out a long, aggravated breath. "Look, I've got to put my foot down. You can't come back here. You're—"

"Bad for business, I know, you've told me a thousand times." She scooped up the money, counted it, and shoved it into her back pocket. "Fortunately for you, you'll never have to see me again. I'm moving; leaving for college in two months."

"College? Where?"

"Billington University."

"*Billington?*" He laughed, his entire face turning an obnoxious shade of pink.

Eve growled. "What's so funny?"

"You're telling me a tall tale, Eve, I know it. There's just no way you could ever get into that school."

"I'm smart, you know. I'm the salutatorian of my class, remember?"

"I'll believe it when I see it."

Eve yanked her phone from her pocket and furiously tapped at the screen, activating the image database. A large holographic picture appeared above the screen; it was a digital acceptance letter, the text twitching and colors fading from green to grey to blue, the quality poor and hardly functional but the message as clear as day:

Evelyn Janine Kingston,

On behalf of the esteemed Billington University, it gives me great pleasure to offer you a place for admission in September 2087.
Sincerely,
Finnegan Furst
Acting Dean of Admissions and President of Billington University

"Look legitimate enough for you?"

Stuart ran his fingers through the hologram, expanding the flickering image. "Wow, your phone is *really* old."

"*All* of my things are really old."

He ignored her retort, his eyes wide as he reread the letter. "It's impossible... Smarts aside, the tuition must be astronomical. You could never afford it."

"I got a scholarship. It covers my freshman year."

"Then what? How will you pay for the rest of college?"

"I'll find a way. I always do."

"I can't get over it." He finally tore his gaze from the letter and looked at Eve. "*The* Billington?"

"The one and only, down in SoCal."

"I know where it is, I'm just—"

"An ass." She offered him a patronizing sneer and shoved her phone back into her pocket. "Pleasure doing business with you, as *always*."

She headed for the door, but just as she reached it, she stopped; she could hear the radio far behind her, the volume raised once again, now to its highest level.

"Now, to those out there who say, 'Heck, give these people a break,' I must correct you; chimeras aren't people. Just because they look like us doesn't mean they have the right to be regarded as people. They are aberrations. They are creatures."

The back of Eve's neck became hot, tingling with a fire that surged down her spine and illuminated her entire body. Her vision faded to darkness, a thick black that pulsed with each beat of her heart. She didn't bother to stifle it this time, despite the nagging voice that begged her to stop, that insisted she walk out the door and never look back. As she took one last breath, she allowed the power to flow through her, making its presence known with the slightest flick of her wrist.

The patrons gasped in horror as the radio dial spun furiously as if suddenly possessed. It flipped from one channel to the next, finally stopping at a booming rock anthem, the heavy bass and thumping drums echoing throughout the tiny shop.

Eve turned to look at Stuart and the others. Their faces were drained of color, their eyes gaping with fear.

"Looks like your radio is broken," she mumbled. "You should probably get it fixed."

And with that, she left the shop, wincing as the sunlight stung her eyes and poured across her face. She cursed to herself; she had made a mistake, clearly. What she did—the looks on their faces, the terror in their eyes—was hardly constructive, and yet she couldn't shake the feeling of prideful retribution that festered deep within her chest. It was too much, sometimes, to hear the opinions of others. To hear that she was an atrocity—a *creature*. After all, she certainly looked human. Her skin, blood, and bones were human. She walked, talked, laughed, and cried like a human. But Eve was not like other humans, because she was a chimera.

To be fair, the correct term was *humanovus*: the new human. They were the first of their kind, an advanced breed with all of the same traits and DNA as the standard human, except that, for some reason modern science couldn't yet dictate, their genes were simply *better*. No amount of research could pinpoint a specific cause. The genetic makeups of humans and humanovi appeared identical, and scientists of every field remained frustrated by the mystery of the humanovus, for despite their physical similarities, the two beings were clearly so very different. The new humans were physically stronger with unparalleled muscle memory and stamina. They were faster, their energy boundless, their bodies rarely in need of replenishing. Their immune system and healing properties were unimaginably resilient, causing doctors to speculate that the average life expectancy of a humanovus could easily surpass one hundred and fifty years, though no one yet knew for certain.

But above all else, the most extraordinary feature of the humanovi was the power they held in their minds. There was no proof that they were inherently more intelligent than normal humans, but each humanovus possessed one particular brain function that no other human had ever been able to attain: the power to manipulate and move objects with the force of their thoughts. *Telekinesis*—it was a term linked to countless pieces of fiction, and yet it was now *real*, a mere fantasy come to fruition. Yes, the humanovi were, in fact, telekinetic, though the title itself seemed so frivolous and romantic, and thus people began referring to it as "the gift."

As is common with any sudden change in modern society, the appearance of humanovi was met with fear and apprehension. Some theorized that humanovi were simply the next step in the human evolutionary chain. Others found them to be miracles, a gift to rid the human race of disease and weaknesses. Still, others believed that the new human was brought forth by evil; they were powerful, *too* powerful to be good or pure. Thus the debate began—as did the riots, the protests, the persecution and prejudice. Panic ran rampant across the globe as human beings began to feel increasingly threatened by the presence of humanovi.

Humanity's fright ultimately led to the creation of a colorful new term. The general public decided to regard these new humans as *chimeras*, a particularly interesting choice of word in Eve's opinion. In the sixth grade, she'd learned that the chimera was a creature from Greek mythology: a fire-breathing lioness with the head of a goat on its spine and a snake serving as its tail. During vocabulary discussions in high school, she'd discovered that a chimera was also a fantasy or delusion of sorts. And through her own research she'd found that a chimera was also a random, arbitrary blend of different tissues: a mutant. And from that, she understood how society truly saw her—as a fantastical blend of monstrous parts.

A freak.

Eve was especially freakish in the eyes of her peers. The typical chimera was hard to diagnose initially; a child with great muscle memory could simply be labeled a superb athlete, and a teenager who never caught a cold was just seen as the winner of the perfect attendance award. The only obvious distinction between humans and chimeras was the gift, and ironically, a public display of the gift was considered as crude and taboo as strolling the streets in the nude. Most chimeras kept their gift to themselves, locked away indoors where no one else could see or judge—if they could even control it at all, which many could not.

In fact, a majority of the public was ignorant to the details of emergence—the deliverance of the gift. Once chimeras reached their early adulthood, their gift would develop suddenly, in what felt like a random instance of mental anarchy. Shooting pain, loss of vision, a sense of displacement, and, of course, the erratic misfiring of the gift—they were all associated with emergence. Scientists maintained that age and maturity brought the deliverance of the gift, although there was an exception to the rule: the emotional intensity and exaggerated brain function triggered by extreme trauma could also precipitate emergence, at any age. That, unfortunately, is exactly what had happened to Eve, approximately twelve years too early, at the age of eight, after witnessing the gruesome death of her parents.

Eve stopped in front of the pawn shop, almost too angry with herself to take another step, though her feelings of regret soon subsided as her attention drifted elsewhere: back to the pharmacy, or what remained of it. A uniformed officer was sweeping up the shards of glass, leaving behind streaks of a yellowish substance across the sidewalk. She peered inside the building and saw tables, cabinets, and chairs all overturned and destroyed, along with a sea of papers, vials, and herbs scattered from wall to wall.

"Can I help you?"

Eve winced; she hadn't even noticed the policeman approach her, and wished that, for once, she could be the slightest bit inconspicuous.

"Just looking," she answered, slowly stepping away from the scene. "I'll get out of your way."

"Not so fast." The officer extended his finger, beckoning her forward. He cocked his head toward the pharmacy. "You know anything about this?"

"About what?"

"The chimera medical clinic."

"No." Eve crossed her arms, her shoulders tense, her stance defensive. "Why would I know anything about it?"

"Look, I know what you are."

What she was: as if she were an animal or an object. No matter how many times she heard it, it still stung just as much as the first.

She sneered, offended. "Then you should know that I don't have much of a need for medicine."

"Clinics like this are illegal, you know. If you were in any way involved—"

"Don't you have more important things to worry about?" she interrupted. "Like the Interlopers?"

"We handle raids like this every week. You let *us* do *our* job."

"I most certainly will. In fact, I'll leave *right now* so you can get back to work."

"Hold it right there, I'm not done talking to you—"

He didn't have time to finish—a raspy cry captured their attention, followed by a series of crashes, from deep within the pharmacy. Suddenly a short, stocky policeman ran out of the pharmacy door, scuttling through the taped-off crime scene with a trail of blood oozing down his forehead.

"It's here," he panted, his face white with terror. "I don't know how we missed it. HOW THE HELL COULD WE HAVE MISSED IT?"

"Missed what?" another officer asked.

His question was soon answered. Another noise sounded inside the pharmacy: a loud boom. Again. And then again, the pounding followed by a shrill screech. Eve knew what was coming—she could hardly believe it, but there was no other explanation—and then it stormed from the pharmacy, its enormous wings breaking through the shop's frame, leaving a gaping hole in the building.

The thing stood over seven feet tall, yet its body was lean and gaunt. Its skin was grey and slick like rubber, puckering at its joints and around its bones, which protruded grotesquely from its flesh. Long, spindly limbs hung limply from its hairless body, and each hand and foot—if they could be referred to as such—was adorned with sharp talons. Two immense, bat-like wings expanded from its back, wavering slightly with each fervid breath it took. Finally, its face—its bald, wrinkled skull; its large, black eyes; its mouth filled with hundreds of foot-long, needle-like fangs in a glistening silver—yes, its face was the most horrifying sight of all.

It was an Interloper.

The creature shook the debris from its back, letting it fly across the street like specks of dandruff. It arched its shoulders, stretching its skin far across its bones, and then, with a deep breath, it let out a guttural roar.

Eve jumped, staggering backward with the horde of policemen who scattered across the street like frightened children. One lifted his gun, his hand shaking so severely that the firearm nearly fell from his grasp, and fired two poorly aimed bullets at the creature. The Interloper hardly reacted; instead it swiped its wing dismissively at the policeman, knocking him over with a single blow and sending him toppling into what was left of the pharmacy storefront. It stomped forward, its inky eyes scanning the terrified faces until it abruptly stopped—when it saw Eve.

Eve had seen an Interloper before, but never this close—close enough to hear the air puffing from its slit-like nostrils and feel the slight tremor of the ground as it paced from side to side. She wanted to run away, but her feet were firmly rooted to the concrete as if unresponsive to her screaming thoughts. She was scared, yes, but not as scared as she should've been. After all, the Interloper was staring right at her.

It inched forward, tilting its head slightly as it eyed her up and down. It took a step closer, and yet Eve still could not move. Its teeth—God, its teeth were like awful knives, and she could see her faint reflection in each and every one of them.

And then, unless she was mistaken, she could've sworn she saw the creature smile.

Six gunshots resounded in Eve's ears, and the Interloper lurched back-ward. Another gunshot, and another, and then finally a swarm of bullets showered the Interloper, sending yellow fluid bursting from its perforated skin. It swatted at the balls of lead like they were pestering insects and un-hinged its jaw, roaring loudly as strings of saliva sprayed from its teeth. With one last breath, it glared at Eve, undeterred by the bullets still burrowing into its flesh, and then it finally bolted into the sky, beating its wings until it soared out of sight.

"SONOFA-GODDAMN-BITCH!" a policeman cried, his face beet red as he kicked the rubble at his feet.

"Can *someone* check on him?" another ordered, pointing at his comrade who was still lying in a heap on the ground.

"I swear to God, those things are like raccoons. Giant, ugly-ass raccoons. Vicious shits with a knack for picking fights and digging around in the garbage."

"I *hate* those freaks. I *HATE* them."

"How could we have missed it? We covered the entire pharmacy three times. How the *hell* did we not see it?"

The ramblings of the officers faded into the background, becoming noth-ing but a distant haze in Eve's mind. Her eyes were still set firmly on the sky—she wasn't sure what she was looking for, as the Interloper was long gone, but for some reason, she couldn't help but watch the clouds above. Maybe because she knew that it was up there, watching her.

The Interlopers had arrived when Eve was just a baby, and though she had never known a life without them, the slightest mention of their existence still sent a chill through her body. If Eve was a monster, then the Interlopers were the offspring of Satan himself, though neither was true. The Interlopers were aliens: creatures from somewhere beyond this world, surely of another name and possibly from another galaxy altogether, but there was no way for Eve or anyone else to know for sure, because they were simply impossible to engage in conversation. Sure, they could speak—a multitude of human lan-guages along with their own dialect, surprisingly enough—but communicable and friendly they were not. Regardless, they had made their intentions more than clear: they came to Earth seeking one thing and one thing only.

Chimeras.

What horrendously terrible luck for people like Eve. Already the entire globe had been up in arms about the chimera population—and then the

Interlopers arrived, and the majority opinion was solidified: chimeras were intolerable. A curse. Damned. For not only had they brought fear into the lives of humans across the planet, but they'd also brought a flurry of winged aliens who terrorized their homes.

Goddamn chimeras.

Fortunately—as if a silver lining was even possible to find—while the Interlopers were terrifying enough, they had yet to prove themselves inherently dangerous. They were nothing more than scavengers searching for data, blood samples, and anything else that could tell them more about chimeras. Some speculated that they sought the chimeras' health and strength, though that possibility was widely rejected; the aliens were already nearly impossible to kill, and although bullets and blades tore through their skin, the damage appeared to be insignificant to them. Many assumed they were after the gift, and that they destroyed facilities like the Shang Wu Holistic Pharmacy in desperate search of something, *anything* that could reveal the key to the power they insatiably desired. And while initially people revolted and rebelled, they soon learned to simply stay out of the Interlopers' way. After all, not a single unprovoked Interloper had ever attacked a human or chimera. The provoked ones, however—well, that was a different story entirely.

"Can someone get her the hell out of here?"

Eve blinked; she was still standing in the middle of Haight Street amid the chaos. Spectators were beginning to gather—and the last thing she needed was people watching her.

"He was looking at *her*, you know," another officer added.

"Probably wanted to take her with him."

"We should've let him. Would've done us all a favor. Hell, I would've shook his hand—er, claw. Whatever the hell it is."

Eve ran down the street as fast as she possibly could—which, for the record, was very, *very* fast. She had to get away—from the police, from the onlookers, from everyone. From San Francisco. Her heart beat loudly in her chest, and the cool breeze suddenly felt like ice clawing at her face, but still she kept running, her body fueled with an unparalleled energy that didn't cease even when she reached her apartment. She rarely grew tired, at least physically, though her mind was exhausted from the day's tribulations: the stares, the pawn shop, and of course the Interloper. She closed the door behind her and then, against her better judgment, pulled her phone from her pocket and pressed the *play* button. A hologram, though barely functioning, appeared from her phone, displaying the image of her high school principal.

"Hello, Miss Kingston? I see you're unable to answer your phone; I can't fathom why. It's eight o'clock, and you should be here by now."

She deleted the holomessage, and the next one played.

"Evelyn, I'm not sure if you're trying to pull some sort of stunt here, but it's not funny, nor is it mature. Not only are you our salutatorian, you're also the only student of ours to ever be accepted to Billington. Come to the auditorium immediately."

Deleted. The next one appeared, and the next, and the next.

"Evelyn, where in God's name are you? Do you realize we're going to have to rearrange the entire ceremony because of you?"

"Dammit, Evelyn, you're not even going to attend your own graduation?"

"I hope you're SATISFIED with yourself. I can't imagine what the Billington officials saw when they accepted you, but I can tell you what I've seen since the moment you entered my school: a deplorable CHIME."

Eve flung the phone across the room, sending it crashing into the wall and shattering into tiny pieces. This act of defiance didn't help—not even the fact that she had done it with her gift alone. The phone was of little importance to her—besides, she had no one to talk to anyway—but her principal's voice echoed through her mind over and over again, repeating like some form of cruel punishment. *Deplorable chime.* For some reason, those words seemed so much more foul than the Interloper she had seen only moments prior.

It would all be over soon enough: she was moving to Billington in two months. She would be living four hundred miles away from this place—away from the lingering stares and a past she cared not to remember, in a home that never felt like home in the first place. That was all she wanted: to start over with a clean slate in a city where no one knew her name or what she truly was. A chance to live a normal, anonymous life—the life of a human. She would have all of that, soon enough.

She would have that at Billington.

* * *

"Evelyn, do you want some water?"

Eve held her head low, her tangled curls hanging over her face. She didn't answer.

"I know you're sad, sweetie, but we're going to have to ask you a few questions, okay?"

Eve remained motionless.

The officer placed a paper cup in front of her. He rested his hand on her shoulder and glanced at another officer, who was pacing back and forth at the opposite side of the room.

"Now, Evelyn, I need you to tell me what happened today." He paused to gently rub her back. "I need you to tell me about the accident."

Eve whimpered softly; she finally looked up at the officer, her eyes glistening with tears. "Are my mommy and daddy dead?"

The officer scratched at his mustache and sighed. "I'm afraid so."

Eve was silent. Her lip trembled as a tear slid down her cheek.

"I know it's hard, honey. But we need you to tell us what happened."

"This is useless," his partner muttered, adjusting his belt under his protruding stomach.

"Can you just tell us what you saw?"

Eve wiped her face and breathed in deeply. "He crashed his car into my mommy and daddy." Her voice wavered as she spoke. "He just... just crashed into them."

"And then what happened?"

"Then..."

She paused and looked down at the paper cup on the table. Her mind drifted to the scene of the accident and then faded into darkness. She flinched. For a second, she thought she saw the cup moving in front of her, but she was mistaken.

"I don't know," she murmured. "It was really fast, I... I can't remember."

"That's BULLSHIT!"

The second officer kicked at a nearby chair in a fit of rage. Eve shrieked aloud as he charged toward her and shoved his round, sweaty face in front of hers, his lips quivering with disgust.

"You listen here, you *chime*. You're going to start talking *right now*."

Eve looked up at the first officer in desperation. He was leaning casually against the wall, his formerly soft, kind eyes now hard and cold.

"I... I don't know—"

"YOU TELL US RIGHT NOW!" The second officer grabbed her shoulders and shook her violently until she burst into tears. "You killed that man, didn't you? You killed him and you did it on purpose! And you're going to tell us how you did it and why, this very second!"

Eve screamed and cried as tears poured down her raw cheeks. She yelled out for her mother and father, knowing all too well that there was no way they could help her. No one was going to help her.

Eve jumped in her seat, knocking her head against the window beside her and sending the nearby passengers into a fit of giggles. She rubbed her aching temple and muttered profanities under her breath as she tried to regain her composure. It had been another dream, of course. The air in the bus was thick and hot, enough so to lull her to sleep, and she wondered if the weather outside could be any worse than the swamp-like atmosphere within the cramped shuttle. Suddenly, the bus lurched to a sharp stop, sending every unsuspecting body swaying forward in unison. Eve looked out the window; she had arrived.

The gated entrance of the university was large and foreboding, like the solid black bars of a prison. The resemblance was unintentional, and probably one only Eve would discern, but still she wrinkled her nose in distaste as she peered out at the campus. So, this was Billington—the nation's highest ranking and most widely acclaimed university, centered in the heart of upscale Southern California in the city of Calabasas. It was a gem among pebbles, a stallion among asses, or whatever other clichéd metaphor its backers could conjure up. But the hype, for the most part, was accurate: the courses were difficult, the competition was fierce, and the admittance process was god-awful.

Eve had known that getting into the school in the first place would be a near impossibility, but she'd thrown her name into the hat despite her doubts and cynicism. And now, so many months later, here she stood, immersed in the beautiful Southern California weather—*God*, was it hot out—staring at the infamous Billington University campus, the mecca of innovation and enterprise, the place where brilliant young minds were molded into lawyers, doctors, soldiers, and CEOs.

Eve didn't care about any of that. In fact, she thought there was something almost pretentious and off-putting about the whole thing. No, Eve was there for one reason only: anonymity. The chance to live as a human—not as an outed chimera. If any place could change her fate, it had to be Billington. And even better, she was there on a scholarship—well, at least for her freshman year.

Eve clung to her belongings—two awkward duffel bags and a lumpy suitcase stuffed to the seams—and with an effortless swing, she hoisted them over her shoulder and made her way through the gleaming gates.

Eve entered the pristine courtyard, where perfectly manicured maple trees stood like statues atop the immaculately groomed lawn, creating a sea of green for what seemed like miles into the distance. Each leaf, twig, and blade of grass had been cut with the utmost precision and exactness; the meticulous nature of the courtyard created a painfully sterile atmosphere that left Eve with an overwhelming feeling of discomfort, and so she hastened her stride.

As she walked, she watched the other new students moving into their prospective buildings. Most were accompanied by their families: mothers cried as their precious babies moved out on their own, and fathers beamed as their strong, capable sons and smart, accomplished daughters became real men and women. The whole spectacle was all so touching—in the most sickening way, at least to Eve. She rolled her eyes and continued on her trek to Rutherford Hall, west of Hutchinson Hall, wherever that was.

She paused for a moment. Had she passed it already? It was hard to tell. The architecture was so uniform and consistent, it was nearly impossible to tell one end of the campus from the other. Feeling overwhelmed, her eyes darted across the pathway in front of her, and she spied a tall, lanky boy with a face filled with cystic acne. Like her, he juggled several musty duffel bags, and, like her, he was alone.

"Excuse me." She tapped him lightly on the shoulder. "Do you know where Rutherford Hall is?"

The boy raised his eyebrows, looking her up and down with a critical eye. "*You're* looking for Rutherford Hall?"

"Yes, why?"

"You definitely don't look like the Rutherford type."

She scowled impatiently. "Can you just tell me where it is?"

"Make a left at the student union and go straight. You won't miss it. Trust me," he answered, tilting his head to point her in the correct direction. Eve gathered her bags and hurried onward, eager to finally find the room she would be calling home for at least the next year.

At last she spotted it: just as her pimply-faced guide had stated, it was impossible for her to miss. One giant dormitory stood before her, its grandiose appearance a lone exception in a blanket of uniformity. The building was stately, almost majestic, with a tower atop it that extended at least ten stories above the others; barred balconies adorned the front like rows of bows across an already liberally decorated gift. The two front doors of the building were jet black, much like the front gates of the university, with golden embellishments and sparkling door handles. Above the doors in gleaming gold letters read the words *RUTHERFORD HALL*.

Eve stared in disbelief at her new home. *There must have been a mistake*, she thought. She observed the other students who made their way into the dormitory and, indeed, they were very much like one another and not at all like her. Each and every one of them seemed to carry the same designer luggage in various colors, and many were accompanied by sharply dressed drivers and obedient-looking servants. As she watched, a sleek, white limousine pulled up alongside the building, and a team of uniformed workers began unloading an endless array of pink leather bags and carrying them into the hall. Elsewhere, two muscular bodyguards wearing suits and sunglasses were escorting a young man through the front doors, while another guard barked orders into a radio earpiece.

Eve pulled a crinkled piece of paper out of her back pocket. The words *"FALL SEMESTER 2087"* were printed at the top, and underneath was a list of her classes and her dormitory plan. Sure enough, no matter how many times she read the fine print, the words *"RUTHERFORD TOWER, ROOM 1226"* were still neatly printed across the bottom of the page. She half expected to find a disclaimer—"Kidding, moron!"—splattered underneath, as if the school were trying to play a cruel joke on her. However, no such prank could be found, leaving Eve perplexed as to why the deans of the school found it necessary to house her in a building with students who, for whatever reason, needed limousines, pink luggage, and bodyguards.

"Lost, hon?"

Eve flinched, startled by the strange girl who'd suddenly appeared at her side. She was much shorter than Eve, which ultimately meant she was of average height and build, and had shimmering red hair that was perfectly waved and pinned to the side with a pearl barrette. Her mint green sweater blouse subtly matched her emerald eyes—the pairing was most likely intentional—and she smiled at Eve with the largest, toothiest, and phoniest smile Eve had ever seen.

"Uh…" Eve stuttered for a moment, fumbling to unfold her fall itinerary once more. "I'm not sure, actually. It says here that this is where I'm staying, but—"

"Oh, you're Evelyn Kingston!" The girl peered over Eve's shoulder and briefly read her itinerary. "I remember you from the face database."

"It's Eve." She paused. "What's the face database?"

"It's a categorized list of all the students here at Billington." The girl flipped her wrists as she spoke, her perfectly manicured fingers almost as expressive as her plucky voice. "I like to peruse all the newcomers to Rutherford Hall. I have great intuition, you know. I can read a face and instantly tell you everything about that person. That's why I *love* the face database." She pointed to a slender boy with auburn hair and at least a million freckles. "See that guy? Thomas Cooper. Schemer. Troublemaker. Double-crosser."

Eve raised a single eyebrow. "And you can tell that all by his face?"

The girl cocked her head and grinned. "Among other things. You were a standout in the database, you know."

"Oh?" Eve hesitated. "And why is that?"

"Well, for starters, you didn't have any background information. How *mysterious*. I figured you had just forgotten to submit a personality inventory."

Eve flashed an insincere half-smirk. "You caught me."

"And when I took a look at your picture, I just felt like, oh, I don't know..." The girl stopped for a moment, her grin spreading even wider across her cheeks. "Like I knew you from somewhere. Tell me, Eve: have we met before?"

"Not that I can remember."

"Are you sure? Because I could've sworn I recognized you from somewhere."

A pang of discomfort burned in Eve's stomach, but she remained calm and tried to appear unfazed. "I think I would've remembered meeting someone like you."

"Hm. Oh well." The girl shrugged, her eyes quickly glancing over Eve's itinerary once more. "It looks like we're going to be neighbors. Well, practically."

"I'm sorry, I didn't catch your name."

"Heather McLeod—Room 1230. Just starting my sophomore year." She pointed toward the twelfth story of the tower. "See that balcony right there, with the flower box? That's my room. I planted those daisies myself." She beamed with pride.

Eve shaded her eyes as she stared up at the massive tower, completely underwhelmed by Heather's green thumb. "I don't understand. This place looks more like a hotel than a dormitory. Isn't it, I don't know, excessive?"

"Excessive? Maybe, but I like to think of it as *architectural panache*. Rutherford Hall has everything you could want in a dormitory: comfort, class, a hint of opulence, not to mention privacy, especially if you live on the fifteenth floor. That's where all the luxury suites are."

"*Luxury* suites? Who's so important that they need a luxury suite in *college?*"

Heather nodded toward the group of bodyguards huddled by the front doors. "See all that mess over there? They're here for the president's son, Marshall Woodgate," she whispered. "Really standoffish guy, but you didn't hear it from me."

"Damn..."

Heather giggled. "Everyone staying in Rutherford Hall is here for a reason. You either have a lot of money, a lot of power, or you're really, *really* smart." Her eyes scanned over Eve's clothing and faded duffel bags. "You must be really smart."

Before Eve could respond, Heather squeezed her hand excitedly. "Here, let me grab one of your bags and I'll show you around a bit."

With a playful skip, Heather plucked Eve's lightest bag from the ground and dashed up the front steps of Rutherford Hall. Eve had no choice but to follow.

The large doors swung open, and Eve stepped into a stunning lobby. Plush red couches and ebony tables sat atop a black-and-white checkered floor, and portraits of ex-presidents in gold leaf frames lined the walls like guardians watching over the bustling students. Before long, the girls had reached a fork in the lobby as two separate hallways were divided by a single set of elevators.

"To the left is the dining hall," Heather explained. "It's privately catered. You can request your meals in advance if you want something extra special."

Eve peered past the open double doors at an elegant room filled with sable-colored tables, each one adorned with a flower centerpiece and sparkling gold china.

"Dining hall? Isn't that what the cafeteria is for?"

"Oh, Eve," Heather sighed, lightly patting her on the back. "Don't you want to feast on freshly prepared cuisine in an immaculate dining room with fellow Rutherfordians? You don't want to eat the garbage at the cafeteria with everyone else, do you?"

With everyone else—the phrase sounded dirty and demeaning leaving Heather's lips, and even worse was the term *Rutherfordian,* a title Eve wasn't sure she wanted to bear. She grimaced and continued to follow Heather.

The two girls headed to the right of the elevators, squeezing their way into a smaller, though much livelier, room. A row of tables—ping pong, pool, air hockey and the like—were lined against the back wall, all of which were surrounded by laughing and cheering "Rutherfordians." A giant holovision screen covered the entire front wall; the screen itself displayed a wooded landscape, the image so crisp and clear that, for a brief moment, Eve couldn't help but feel as if the room had been transported into an eerie forest. Creatures weaved around the trees—zombies, most likely—their grotesque figures scurrying back and forth until, one by one, their arms, legs, and then their entire bodies protruded from the HV screen and wandered into the room. Suddenly, the holographic forms fell to the ground, lurching from side to side before fading into the floor and ultimately disappearing into nothingness. It was a hologame—a very popular one at that, as Eve had seen it advertised for months now—and she watched as several students aimed small plastic guns at the holographic zombies, spraying them with virtual bullets until they vanished from sight.

"This is the rec room," Heather stated, her voice unusually flat. "It's the prime location for mindless entertainment, if you're into that *juvenile* stuff." She cocked her head back toward the elevators. "Let's head up, shall we?"

Eve filed into the elevator, awkwardly pressing herself against the wall as other Rutherfordians crammed inside the small metal box. The room became silent, aside from the muffled beeping of the elevator as each floor was passed, and Heather quickly resumed her tour-guide duties.

"The second floor is home to our study hall and tutoring center. We have private tutors, mostly other Rutherfordians studying for their master's and PhDs, and believe it or not, we have our very own vintage library. *Books,* Eve—real books! I hadn't seen one in person until I came here. They smell funny, did you know that?"

Eve tried to feign interest but instead let out a hardly convincing grunt.

"The third floor is extra special. It's home to our event center and ballroom."

"*Ballroom?*"

"Every once in a while someone throws a big party—birthdays, weddings, cotillions—and you just have to hope you're invited." Her eyes sparkled with delight as she spoke. "I wish you could've come to my cotillion. It was the best. *Ever.* Don't let anyone tell you otherwise, because, well, they're simply lying."

The elevator finally reached the twelfth floor, and Eve and Heather filed out, stopping in the center of a brick hallway. Along either side of them were two long rows of dorm rooms, each one marked with a cherry red door and a golden room number, and ahead of them sat two sets of large, silver doors.

"Those are the washrooms," Heather said. "The boys' dorms are to the right, and we're on the left. We're not supposed to go into any boys' rooms and vice versa, but some of the people here can't control their indecent urges." She sneered at a few passersby before turning the corner toward their prospective dorms. "Tacky, if you ask me, but they can get away with it, because no one really checks up on us."

"No resident assistants? No staff members?"

"Someone complained about them, so they were fired."

"What a sweet story," Eve mumbled.

"We don't need incessant supervision. We're not a bunch of *animals*. We're here because—well, we're special." Heather finally stopped in front of a red door with a golden *1226* nailed to its front: Eve's room. She turned to Eve and grinned. "Enjoy the privileges and amenities. We *deserve* them."

Eve's nostrils flared as if she smelled something rotten.

Heather carelessly plopped Eve's bag onto the floor. "Looks like we've reached your room! Mine is only two doors down, so if you ever need anything, feel free to pop your head in and say hello." She leaned in toward Eve and lowered her voice. "If you ask me, we really got the luck of the draw. Our rooms have a perfect view of the entire campus; it's great for people-watching. You wouldn't *believe* the excitement I've witnessed, what with all the commotion around campus these days."

"Commotion?" Eve repeated, wrinkling her brow. "What kind of commotion?"

Heather chuckled. "Oh, to be a freshman again—so uninformed and naïve." She skipped toward her room and stopped for a moment, turning to face Eve one last time. "You should keep your door locked if you can."

With that, Heather disappeared into her own room and slammed the door behind her.

Eve muttered to herself, juggling her cumbersome bags as she stumbled into her dorm. A part of her feared what she might find inside, but the room proved to be boring at best. Two twin beds sat on opposite sides of the space, both with plain white sheets to match the bland, cream walls. The balcony opened up at the back of the room, its glass doors covered in soft, sheer linens that gently grazed the hardwood floors. Next to the front door were a compact end table and a large, wooden wardrobe, completely untouched and vacant aside from several plastic hangers and two sets of room keys. Eve was so focused on examining her new home that she almost failed to notice the girl sitting on the bed to her left.

"Hi," the girl squeaked. She had an unusually small frame, thin, pin-straight blond hair, and fragile legs that delicately hung over the edge of the bed, her toes barely touching the floor.

"Hey, I'm Eve." She extended her arm for a handshake, but the girl remained motionless. Eve awkwardly put her hand back to her side. "I'm your roommate."

The girl's large grey eyes stared blankly back at Eve. "No you're not."

Eve looked around the room, perplexed, and fished her itinerary out of her pocket once more. "Um, I have a piece of paper here that says this is my room."

"I know that. That's not what I meant. This is your room, but *I'm* not your roommate. Madison Palmer is."

"Oh." Eve hesitated, even more confused than before. "So... why are you here?"

The girl wiggled her nose and twirled a limp strand of hair between her fingers. "Madison is my best friend. She asked me to come by her room, sit on both beds, and save the softest one for her." She looked down at her hair, examining the split ends, then back at Eve. "This bed is taken."

"Lovely..." Eve muttered, tossing her belongings onto the free—and apparently less comfortable—bed. The girl's eyes slowly moved from Eve to her faded bags.

"Are you poor?"

The door was suddenly flung open, and in stormed another blonde with three pink tote bags in hand. Behind her were several servants carrying an endless supply of pink leather suitcases—the very same suitcases that Eve had seen earlier outside of Rutherford Hall.

You've got to be kidding me, Eve thought to herself.

"Maddie, you're here!" The girl's voice sharpened into a high trill, but her vacant facial expression remained. "I saved you a bed."

Madison sat atop the mattress and groaned. "If the people here think I can sleep comfortably on *this* piece of crap, they are cuh-ray-zee," she moaned, looking over at Eve. "I mean, you know what I mean?"

Eve mumbled in apathetic agreement, leaning against the wall as, one by one, servants bombarded the now-crowded dorm room, stacking countless pink bags in what little space was left.

"This is your roommate. I forgot her name…"

"Oh my God, Hayden, that is so incredibly rude!" Madison shrieked, waving her hand toward the door. "Can you, like, leave? Why are you still here?"

Hayden quickly scurried out of the room, along with the servants, finally leaving Eve alone with Madison—and her luggage.

Madison let out a long sigh. "You know, that girl used to be so excited to see me. I don't know what's changed."

Eve subtly took in her new roommate: she was a textbook bombshell, her body ample and voluptuous in all the right places, and clearly she knew it. Her breasts were pushed forward, spilling out of the collar of her pink dress like two creampuffs, and her hips swayed from side to side as she shimmied around her rows of suitcases. She turned to Eve and smiled. Her sapphire eyes, rosy cheeks, and snow-white skin were luminous, though hardly warm or disarming.

Eve finally mustered a polite smile. "I'm Eve."

"My God, do they really expect us to share a *closet*? I mean, is this college, or is this prison, am I right?" She laughed to herself, pleased with her wit. "What's your name again?"

"Eve."

"Oh my God, your name is *so* pretty," Madison chirped. "I'm Madison Palmer."

"Nice to meet you, Madison."

Madison stared back at Eve as if waiting for her to speak. Instead, Eve began unpacking her belongings, still very aware of Madison's unrelenting gaze. Her eyes followed Eve with each movement she made, piercing like daggers, until finally, the buxom blonde cleared her throat and broke the silence.

"Just in case you were wondering, yes, I am *the* Madison Palmer," she gloated, flipping her voluminous hair across her back.

"Oh…" Eve avoided eye contact. Baffled, she replied, "I'm sorry, I'm not really sure what you mean by that."

Madison's mouth gaped open. "You've *never* heard of Madison Diamonds?" She pointed to a glittering diamond bracelet that hung from her wrist. "It's *only* the largest distributor of diamond jewelry and accessories in the *world*."

"Oh," Eve muttered. "Yeah, that sounds familiar."

"God, Eve, for a second there I thought you were clueless!" She lovingly tinkered with her bracelet. "Daddy named the company after me. If that's not an expression of complete devotion to your daughter, I don't know what is."

Eve fought to muffle her laughter, setting aside her now half-empty duffel bag and taking a seat on her bed. "You're very lucky."

"I know, right?" Madison was quiet for a moment as she looked Eve up and down. "You're pretty."

"Thank you."

"Well, I mean, kind of. In an awkward, lanky, weird way. You're weird-pretty."

"...Thanks."

"You're *really* tall."

Eve chuckled and nodded her head.

"You know what? I think you and I are going to be good friends. Pretty girls have to stick together, even if one of them is kind of funny-looking." Madison pulled a diamond-encrusted nail file out of a small, pale pink clutch. She pointed the nail file at Eve. "Do you have any friends here?"

"Not really. I just met some girl named Heather—"

"Heather McLeod?" she gasped. "That girl is a *vulture*. God, Eve, you are *so* lucky to have met me!" She dashed over to Eve's bed and sat beside her. "Wow, this bed is *way* worse," she mumbled to herself. "Listen to me carefully, okay? I've gone to private school with that *slophole* ever since I was in the first grade and she was in the second. Let me tell you, she is the absolute *queen* of gossip. She knows everything about everyone, and she's *more* than happy to spill the beans. Do not, I repeat, do *not* tell her anything in confidence." She grabbed Eve's hand and clutched it tightly. "Got it?"

"Got it," Eve answered, surprised by her roommate's sudden intensity.

"And whatever you do, do *not* tell her anything about *me*."

"My lips are sealed."

Madison smiled. "Eve, do you know what I just did here?"

"Um..." Eve glanced back and forth across the room as if the answer were somewhere to be found. "No?"

"I just saved your life." She beamed with pride. "Well, your social life, at least."

Madison began to quickly file her nails, and Eve watched as a cloud of filings lightly floated onto her bed, forming a pile of dust on her sheets.

"I told you we're going to be good friends."

CHAPTER 2:

WELCOME TO BILLINGTON

"Holy shit, that was intense."

The man grabbed Eve's hand and tugged her forward, shuffling through the hallway so quickly that her little legs struggled to keep up.

"I know," his partner muttered. "I was expecting involuntary manslaughter, *maybe* manslaughter, but not this."

"Yeah, they're really trying to nail her to the wall."

The men hastened their stride, and so Eve's brisk walk turned into a run. They made their way through the courthouse, past the winding corridors, and into the marble entryway, and all the while the man yanked Eve from side to side with so much force and disregard that at times her feet barely even touched the ground. In that moment, she felt so small—so insignificant.

"We don't have to find an attorney for her, do we?"

"Of course not," the second man hissed as he fiddled with his phone. "The court will appoint someone. And for God's sake, will you get ahold of her aunt?"

"We've contacted her seven times already, even showed up at her house twice. She's dodging us."

"Well, keep trying. We have to get her out of the state's custody. No one will be willing to foster her if it ever comes down to it."

"No kidding." The man gripping Eve's hand looked down at her as if noticing her for the first time, though she didn't bother to meet his gaze and instead stared blankly ahead. He wrinkled his forehead and glanced at his partner. "She okay?"

His partner shrugged. "Probably as okay as she can be, given the situation."

"God, I can't believe it. An eight-year-old chimera charged with *second-degree murder.*"

The words stung Eve as they left his lips. She didn't fully understand them, but she knew the severity they carried.

His partner tossed his phone into his briefcase and led the way down the staircase. "Believe it. This trial is going to be all over the news."

"The *news*? But she's a *minor*. She's protected by *law—*"

"Nationally, yes. But locally?" He laughed. "There's no way this story isn't leaking, and we've got front row seats to her public lynching. Speaking of which—"

The next thing Eve noticed was the sound of faraway voices that, with each step down the staircase, grew louder and louder. Then, she saw the row of glass doors—the exit to the courthouse—and the crowd of people forming behind it. They wore blazers and ties and held cameras and microphones, and soon she could hear their shouting much more clearly: *"Young chimera likely to be charged as an adult," "The hottest case to hit San Francisco in nearly a half-century,"* and *"We have to get a shot of her—we have to see her face!"* Panic suddenly consumed her; she dragged her feet, desperate to stay as far from the horde as possible, but the man pulled her down the steps without relenting. His partner turned to them both and smirked.

"Brace yourself. There's a shitstorm outside."

The alarm went off, and Eve immediately sat upright in her bed. Morning had arrived. With a calming breath, she tore herself from her sheets and began preparing for her first day of school.

Eve zipped up her slim black pencil skirt and slipped on a pair of pointed heels. She had to look her best, whether she cared to or not—the Billington dress code required that all students wear full business attire, a rule that forced her into buying whatever suits and blouses she could find with the last four hundred and fifty dollars she had to her name. She grabbed a palm-sized mirror and held it in front of her; her loose waves were somewhat tamed, parted to the side and delicately draped over her shoulders. Her white blouse was simple and standard, fitted snugly across her chest and buttoned all the way to the collar where it was adorned with a petite, black bow tie. She frowned; her reflection looked to her like an impostor, a costumed figure who was practically unrecognizable. With an audible sigh, she rolled her sleeves and cuffed them around her elbows, desperate to create some sense of casualness, however minor or inconsequential it may be.

Conceding defeat, she weaved through the countless pink suitcases that littered her floor, plucked her shoulder bag from the corner of the room, and headed for the door—only to be halted by a small pink pillow that smacked her across the back of her head.

"Where the hell are you going?" Madison pouted. She was still sitting at her vanity applying her makeup.

"Uh, to class?"

Madison turned to Eve and glowered. "Best friends walk to class together, dummy."

Eve sighed and took a seat on her bed. Yesterday, Madison had determined that she was her "good friend," and today she had been promoted to "best friend." It was a title any girl would've dreamed of—that is, any girl but Eve. But there was no use in fighting it; she had a new image to uphold, one that was very foreign to her. She was now a human—an agreeable one, the kind who blended in with the crowd, who didn't attract attention, create friction, or raise questions. If that meant she had to tolerate her roommate's eccentricities, she would do it—with rancor, but still, she would do it.

Madison kicked on a pair of stilettos and took one last look in her mirror. Her outfit shimmered just as brightly as the diamonds on her wrist; her blouse was golden, clearly hand-stitched by an extravagant designer in some far-off country that Eve had never been to. The sleeves were capped at the shoulders and enhanced with silk ruffles that matched the appliqué at the bottom of her snow-white skirt. Her tie was large and tethered into a thick bow across her neck like a decorative ribbon on a beautiful package. As she turned from the mirror, she glanced at Eve, examining her from head to toe.

"Well, we can't *all* wear couture," she smirked, strutting out the door.

The two girls dashed through Rutherford Hall and out into the courtyard in search of the business building. An ocean of suits clouded Eve's vision: skirts, ties, and trousers in grey, black, and blue stretched as far as the eye could see, and while some, like Madison, made an effort to stand out, Eve for one was happy to blend in with the monotonous majority. She could hear the pitter-patter of Hayden's feet as she scuttled behind them, desperate to keep pace as they located their lecture hall. Eve's first class of the day was Leadership Principles with Professor Clarke, and she had the unfortunate displeasure of sharing it with Madison Palmer and Hayden Von Decker. As the threesome found their seats, the professor approached the podium and began his lecture.

"How many of you want to be here right now?" he asked.

The class was quiet aside from the indifferent mutterings of a few students, and a scant number of hands slowly and reluctantly reached into the air.

"That's what I thought," the professor chuckled. "And to those of you who raised your hands, you're liars." He stepped away from his podium and sat on the edge of his desk. "Look, I get it, I really do. You're here because this class is required. No matter the major, the concentration, the special circumstance or whatever else, you all *have* to be here. And it sucks."

Eve studied him for a moment; he was a young man in his mid-thirties with kind brown eyes and flawless, chocolate skin. His words were strong and firm but laced with a friendly, almost gentle undertone.

"Does anyone know *why* this class is required?" he asked.

Again, the room was silent.

"How about a history lesson. Can someone tell me why Billington was constructed in the first place?"

A single student in the front of the class glanced across the room and awkwardly sank lower into her chair. "Interlopers?" she mumbled.

"Interlopers," Clarke repeated, nodding at the girl. "But more specifically, our *reaction* to the Interlopers. You see, to put it simply, we're not getting anything *done*. The people in Washington? They're stumped. Progress is at a standstill. We're in a state of chaos, class."

The professor ran his fingers across a palm-sized controller, and as he did so, words appeared along the wall at the front of the class, projected as holograms that illuminated the room like light bulbs:

Necessity Breeds Innovation.

"With few other options, our government created Billington: a place where young minds can be molded into visionaries and pioneers. A place where our youth can grow into the kind of people who can restore this country to what it once was. Other schools have history and pedigree, but here at Billington, we have *intention*. We have a specific, calculated purpose. *That's* what makes us special."

His words were motivating, maybe even inspirational—at least, they probably were to someone, somewhere in that room. Eve looked over at Madison—she was yawning and drawing penises all over her desk. Eve rolled her eyes and turned her gaze back to the projection.

"Now, I realize that's a hell of a lot of pressure on your shoulders, but *you* signed up for it. Whether you realized it or not, when you enrolled in this institution, you told the world that you're a leader. *That's* why this class is required—because every single one of you has what it takes to be a leader."

The sound of smacking and slurping broke Eve's concentration; Madison was gnawing at a sticky piece of bubblegum, her lips flapping with each noisy chomp, while Hayden guzzled down juice from a dainty children's juice box. Eve laughed under her breath—*leaders*, she thought to herself. Perhaps not all of Billington's students were as qualified as Clarke assumed. Just when Eve thought her gawking had gone unnoticed, Hayden's eyes shot toward her and squinted into a piercing glare. Eve quickly turned away and focused her attention on the lecture.

Clarke approached his podium. "Activate your scratchpads, and we'll start with chapter one."

The class groaned as they fiddled with their bags and one by one pulled out small cubes of various colors. They placed their cubes on the desks before them, pressing the center button and then watching as the metallic sides pivoted and unfolded into the shape of a large, flat computer screen. Eve sighed; her scratchpad was bulky and thick, an older version that had come out over a decade ago and desperately needed to be renovated. Her peers, by contrast, had sleek, almost weightless scratchpads that were as slender as a sheet of paper but a thousand times more durable—and exponentially more stylish. Eve glanced over at Madison; her scratchpad was lined with diamond flecks that reflected beams of light across the ceiling in prism-like patterns.

Professor Clarke delved into the history of leadership—"*those who triumphed versus those who failed*," as he put it—and Eve found herself immersed in a topic she was hardly interested in. As she flipped through the pages of her digital textbook, she caught a glimpse of her two unwanted comrades out of the corner of her eye—Madison continued to decorate her desk with phallic artwork, and Hayden still scowled in Eve's direction.

Time was soon up. The students gathered their belongings, and Madison scoffed at Eve's large, clunky scratchpad as she deactivated it and shoved it into her shoulder bag. They headed down the steps of the lecture hall, and just as she made her way to the front of the class, Eve locked eyes with the eloquent Professor Clarke. He nodded at her and smiled, as she assumed he did to every student, and with a forced half-smirk she quickly scurried out the door.

"What's your next class?" Madison asked, staring at her cuticles as they strolled down the hallway. "Is it a total suckgasm like that last one?"

Eve took a look at her itinerary. "Business Math," she read.

Madison grimaced. "Yuck. Who's your teacher?"

"Professor Richards?"

"Dr. Dick?" Hayden turned to her, and for the first time all day, her glare lifted into the slightest hint of a grin. "You're going to die, Eve."

"What?"

"Eve, hon," Madison cooed condescendingly, "a professor doesn't get a nickname like 'Dr. Dick' for no reason. Prepare to fail."

"How do you know this?"

"How do you *not* know this? *Everyone* knows about Dr. Dick. His class is a *nightmare*. Let me see this." Madison snatched Eve's itinerary from her hands. "Strategic Communication with Professor Gupta. Sounds boring." She stopped suddenly, her face twisted into a disgusted scowl.

"You're taking *Hand-to-Hand Combat?*" she gasped. "Tell me this is a joke."

Eve grabbed the paper and shoved it back into her shoulder bag. "What's wrong with that?"

"Well, number one: you're a girl. Number two: you're not a guy. Number three: ew?"

"Maybe she has violent tendencies," Hayden added. "I mean, what do we really know about her?"

"Oh my God, just shut up, Hayden," Madison said, waving Hayden away as if she were a pestering fly. "Eve's not violent... Right, Eve?"

"Seriously? Of course I'm not violent." She paused for a moment as she stared back at the two girls, racking her brain for a believable explanation.

A lie.

"I just like a good workout, that's all."

"Well, if you start to develop manly muscles, we won't be on speaking terms."

The girl was unbearable, as was her devoted lackey. Eve was no expert on friendship, but if this was any indication of what it was like, she needn't bother with the stuff. Still, a nagging voice in the back of her mind urged her to remain quiet. *No friction*, it said. *Friction leads to questions, and questions reveal the truth—your truth.* She clenched her jaw and said nothing.

Before she could waste any more time stewing over the topic, she found herself distracted by a faint glow coming from the other side of the corridor. A brightly lit screen hung from the wall, its display covered in flashing headlines and keywords: *room for rent, holovision for sale,* and *calculus tutor needed* were just a few that caught her attention. Below each heading was a large red button that read *click to download to scratchpad.* She was staring at a digital bulletin board.

"Eve? *Eve!* Are you even listening to me?" Madison whined, making her way to Eve's side. "What are you doing?"

Eve kept her eyes on the streaming text. "Looking for something."

"For what?"

"A job."

"A *job?*" Madison snarled in disbelief. "Have you lost your *MIND?*"

"What? I need work. My scholarship only covers this year."

"So? Get your parents to pay for school. That's what they're for."

"My parents are dead."

Madison faltered. "Oh. Awkward."

Hayden cocked her head. "Is that how you got the scholarship?"

"Don't you *dare,*" Madison spat, swatting Eve's hand away from the many red buttons. "Barista? Server?" She read over the job listings, her eyes wide with horror. "*RETAIL?* You know they make you fold clothes, right? Do you really want *folding* in your future?"

Eve bit her bottom lip, her patience waning. "How else am I going to get the money?"

"Maybe find a way that isn't degrading, perhaps? Sell your blood, or your hair, or even your eggs! Just please, *please* don't make me the poor Rutherfordian who's rooming with a *working girl.* I'll never survive the humiliation."

As Eve fought to suppress the biting witticisms lingering on the tip of her tongue, she caught a glimpse of something peculiar. A young, burly man dressed in military fatigues was strolling through the hallway, his hand firmly gripping a rifle at his side. He looked over at her, their eyes locking for a moment before he turned away and exited the building. She furrowed her brow—was there a military base close by? She couldn't fathom why an armed soldier would be roaming the halls of a university, and even more strange was the fact that no one else seemed to notice, mind, or care.

Suddenly, a heavy weight smashed into Eve's back like a wrecking ball, sending her stumbling forward and falling directly into Madison's cushy breasts.

Madison pushed Eve from her bosom, her nostrils flaring with annoyance as she straightened her blouse. "God, Eve, if you can't walk in heels, you shouldn't wear them," she moaned.

Eve growled—she had had enough. She spun around in search of the bull-in-china-shop culprit and found a young man in a grey blazer, hunched over as he gathered his belongings from the floor. He looked up at Eve—at her scornful scowl—and his cheeks reddened the slightest bit.

"Sorry," he chuckled as he stood to his feet. He was taller than Eve, with chestnut-colored hair and a cleanly-shaven, chiseled jaw, and she thought for a moment that he belonged on the cover of the Billington University catalog.

"It's okay. Sometimes I forget how to walk, too," she scoffed, her words lathered with sarcasm.

"It was an accident. Just roughhousing with the guys."

"Well, lucky for you, this campus is loaded. I'm sure there's a playground somewhere. Maybe you should go roughhouse *there*."

The boy laughed, his eyes wide with surprise. "Ouch," he mumbled, staring back at her curiously. He smiled and rested his hand on her arm. "Please accept my sincerest apologies." He winked.

"How kind." She rolled her eyes. "Don't kill anyone on your way to class."

"I'll try my hardest."

She turned away from him—she could hear him tell his friends some nonsense about her ripping him a "new one," but she ignored it. Consumed with irritation, she hurried to her next class, hoping to leave Madison, Hayden, and the clumsy, bumbling whoever-he-was far behind, only to realize that the two girls were instead frolicking right beside her.

"*Eve*," Madison gasped, playfully smacking her shoulder. "You didn't!"

"Didn't what?"

"Do you *know* who that was?"

Eve wrinkled her nose. "Am I supposed to?"

"*That* was Jason Valentine!"

"...Should I know that name?"

Madison huffed. "Eve, just once can you at least *pretend* to have some knowledge of the elite social pyramid?"

Eve stared back at her, her gaze empty and apathetic.

"Jason Valentine is the son of *Senator* Valentine. From New York? Ring a bell?"

"Not really into politics, Madison."

"Politics, schmolitics, that's not the point. He comes from a very influential bloodline, and more importantly, he comes from *money*. Not *my* kind of money, but money nonetheless." She pointed her chin in the air. "Our parents summer together all the time. He's one of my top ten potential husbands: number three, to be exact. It's not easy to break into the top five."

"Well, congratulations to Jason..." Eve mumbled, unimpressed.

Madison shoved her hands onto her hips. "You weren't flirting with him, were you?"

"*What?* I talked to him for two seconds—"

"I bet she was flirting," Hayden added, flashing Eve a look of blatant skepticism. "He touched her arm."

"Friends don't do that, you know. They don't flirt with each others' husbands."

Eve laughed aloud. "So now you're married?"

"It's not funny, *Eve*," Madison snapped. "Do you see me laughing? Are you laughing, Hayden?"

Hayden crossed her arms and wiggled her nose. "I'm not laughing."

"She's not laughing."

Eve sighed. "Look, I don't know the guy. I don't care who he is, or who he's related to, or how much money he has. You can have him."

Madison stared at her for a second longer and then finally smiled.

"God, Eve, it is *so* refreshing to meet a girl I can actually trust."

"But—he touched her arm..."

"Shut up, Hayden!"

The twosome sauntered down the corridor, finally leaving Eve behind—then stopped, just for a moment, and turned in unison.

"We're having dinner in the dining hall at seven," Madison instructed. "You're sitting at *my* table. Be there—that is, *if* you survive Dr. Dick's class."

The heiress and her minion turned the corner, bickering incessantly until they made their way out of sight. Eve exhaled loudly; to be rid of them was a gift, even if it was only for a few hours. But Eve's sense of relief was quickly replaced with a badgering anxiety as she recalled which class was awaiting her: Business Mathematics with the so-called Dr. Dick.

Eve reluctantly entered the classroom and scanned her surroundings; she saw no familiar faces, though they all seemed to wear the same expression of grim dread. Maybe there was some validity to this "Dr. Dick" rumor after all.

But she didn't have much time to speculate on the topic, because as soon as she sat down, her professor barged through the doorway and trudged toward his desk, plopping his papers and briefcase down with a slap.

"We're starting with cash flow," he groaned, leaping straight into the lecture without so much as an introduction. He was a forty-something-year-old, sloppily dressed man with his shirt partially untucked and his faded yellow tie askew. His ashy hair was greasy, thin, and uncombed, and his face looked tired and droopy.

"Get out your scratchpads and pull up page five in your manual."

Eve activated her small computer and flipped through her digital textbook, stupefied by the algorithms and formulas that covered the screen like a thick, black blanket of symbols. A faint hum filled the lecture hall as the students mumbled among themselves, completely perplexed by the calculations in front of them.

"QUIET DOWN," Professor Richards barked, causing the entire front row to flinch suddenly. "You're adults now. Better start acting like it."

And so the lecture began, his voice droning on endlessly like water surging through an opened floodgate. Within minutes, Eve found herself lost in a maze of numerical nonsense that she couldn't seem to decipher or comprehend. She glanced across the room, only to see that her classmates looked equally as hopeless and forlorn as she felt, and just when she thought that the class couldn't get any more intolerable than it had already become, she noticed what she could only describe as a terrible, regrettable decision on someone else's part: a single raised hand in the front of the class.

The professor stopped, zeroing in on the sacrificial lamb before him. "Yes?"

The girl lowered her hand somewhat apprehensively before she spoke. "Professor, would you mind slowing down a bit? You're going pretty fast."

Professor Richards paused. He stared at the girl for a moment, his eyes beady, his lips parted foolishly, almost in disbelief.

"Repeat yourself," he finally said, his enunciation sharp and disdainful.

The girl cautiously looked from side to side and then back at the professor. "Can you just... slow down? Please?"

Richards curled his fingers around his palm-sized controller and gripped it tightly. Eve could barely hear him muttering under his breath.

"You think you can teach this class better than *I* can?"

The girl wavered. "What? No, I just—"

"You just what?"

"I thought—"

"You *thought?*"

"I—"

"Duck."

"What?"

Without hesitation, Richards hurled his controller at the girl, hitting her straight across her eye with a painfully loud clap. The entire class gasped, their mouths gaping with shock and transparent fear as the girl clutched at her swelling eye.

The professor resumed his casual pacing at the front of the class, seemingly indifferent to the scene he had created. He shrugged. "I thought you wanted to teach the class. Just giving you the tools to do so."

He strolled toward the girl's side, leaning in closer as if to examine his victim. His voice came out in a hiss. "This is the part where you *leave my class.*"

The girl sprang from her desk and raced out of the room as if chased by the devil himself. As the door slammed behind her, Richards turned to face the rest of his students, a devious grin plastered across his oily, wrinkled face.

"Anyone else want to tell me how to do my job?"

"Damn, this guy is no joke."

Eve heard the hushed whisper coming from the student sitting beside her—a boy, tall and skinny, with curly blond hair and a face covered in freckles. He was leaning to his side and talking out of the corner of his mouth with his short, stocky friend.

"Seriously. I've heard stories about him that would make your skin crawl."

"I bet that girl was a chimera. He *hates* chimeras—at least, so I've been told."

Eve perked up in her seat; she subtly kept one ear on their conversation as she typed away at her scratchpad.

The portly boy chuckled softly. "Then he must be thrilled with what's been going on the past couple of months."

"Bet he celebrates every time another one is taken."

"Wait," Eve interrupted before she could stop herself. "Who's taking what?"

Both of the boys looked at her apprehensively, unaware that she'd been eavesdropping. They quickly glanced at one another, their eyes wide and fearful.

"You don't know?" the freckled one finally whispered back. "You must be a freshman."

"Definitely a freshman," the stocky one added. "Freshmen are clueless."

Eve exhaled impatiently. "You caught me," she scoffed. "Now, care to elaborate?"

"I..." the freckled boy stuttered, nervously looking back and forth between Professor Richards and Eve. "I can't."

"You can't what?"

"Tell you."

"Why?" Eve glanced over at the professor, who was still immersed in his lecture. "He can't hear us."

"It's not *him* I'm concerned with."

"Then what's the problem?"

"You really don't know anything?" the second boy sneered. "Haven't you seen them?"

"Seen who?"

"The patrolmen," he said. "They're kind of hard to miss. Angry guys walkin' around in uniforms, holding big guns?"

"Oh." Eve thought back to the man in military fatigues whom she'd seen roaming the hallway. "Yes, I saw one earlier today."

"And that didn't get your wheels turning?"

Eve frowned. "Look, are you going to tell me what's going on or not?"

The freckled boy's face dropped as he looked across the room one more time. He was anxious, that much was clear, and the more panic-stricken his expression became, the more Eve felt herself become tense with worry.

"The Interlopers," he said at last, his voice as soft as he could possibly manage. "They're taking people."

He paused, his shoulders curling forward as he leaned in closer to Eve.

"They're taking *chimeras.*"

Her heart stopped, frozen in her chest like a block of ice. "What?" she muttered. "No, that can't be right. Interlopers don't do that."

"They do now."

"But they're—"

"Not violent?" he answered. "Times have changed."

She leaned back in her chair, staring blankly at the projection in front of her. Interlopers at Billington.

"*Unbelievable.*"

It was an understatement. In nearly two decades, the Interlopers had never changed their behavior. Even worse, they chose Billington, of all places, to stage their new advances. Eve's fingers tightened around her scratchpad. The Interlopers were here—in her new home, the home she had worked so hard to escape to, the place where she'd planned on starting anew. Could things have possibly gone *this* wrong, this quickly?

She released her scratchpad and dropped her hands to her sides. She was being too obvious—too responsive. Still, she needed to know more, and with the steadiest voice she could muster, she approached the boy again.

"What do they do with them?"

"Look, I already told you too much," he hissed, his nervousness intensifying. "Besides, I don't really know anyway."

"There has to be a mistake. I haven't heard anything on the news—"

"Which is exactly why I shouldn't be telling you this." He turned to face her, looking her in the eye for the first time since their conversation began. "And if you're smart, you won't tell anyone, either."

"HEY!"

Eve flinched—Richards was staring directly at them.

"Am I interrupting your little conversation?" he barked. "Would you like me to step outside so you can continue?"

"No, sir," the boy answered, his voice cracking.

"Am I boring you? Is that the problem?"

"No, sir."

"Professor," Eve added against her better judgment, "it was my fault. I started the whole thing."

Richards squinted at her, his body rigid and lips tight with anger. He leaned forward as if studying Eve, scrutinizing her every pore and hair, creating a detailed image to forever hold in his mind. Finally, after what felt like unbearable hours of silence, he folded his arms and glowered.

"I'll definitely remember that when I'm grading your work."

The students near her giggled. Eve had been put on Dr. Dick's radar, and apparently that was a terrible place to be.

When class was finally dismissed, it wasn't formulas or equations that were on Eve's mind—the only words she remembered were the ones uttered by her classmate. *The Interlopers were taking chimeras*: chimeras like Eve. She cursed herself, not for moving to Billington, but for allowing herself to think that things might be different, normal even. Endless questions flooded her thoughts, and though she tried to appear calm, she felt as if the wondering and doubt could eat her alive.

As she searched for her Strategic Communication classroom, three men in military fatigues marched past her. She glanced at them briefly—*So, these are the patrolmen.* One of them looked as if he was not much older than her; his posture was confident, but his eyes were frightened, as if he knew some grave secret that was slowly gnawing away at him.

Eve reached her class and reluctantly walked through the door. Her professor was already present, juggling his controller and preparing his projection. He was an older man with tanned skin and a thick wool sweater covering his round belly. The room itself was the slightest bit smaller and more intimate than her previous classes, and Eve took a seat in the back row, eager to blend in or fade away.

Professor Gupta turned to face his class and flashed a bright white smile. "Communication is so much more than merely conversing," he began, his tone upbeat, his stomach bouncing as he spoke. "It is an art form. My job is to teach you all how to be glorious artists of communication.

"We will be covering each of the different facets of communication: the art of proper conversation; how to perfect debating and form the occasional constructive argument; and of course, we will conquer the beast that is public speaking."

Eve's classmates groaned. The girl sitting next to her pretended to gag.

"Where's your excitement, class?" he asked. "I guarantee that if you engage yourself, you will be victorious. If you work hard, I will work hard *for* you. I want to see all of you triumph."

"He's so adorable," the girl beside Eve murmured. "I bet we'll be hearing these inspirational quotes all semester."

Eve forced a smile but didn't respond. Her mind was elsewhere—on the Interlopers—and she simply had no interest in meaningless conversation.

"He can be as articulate and impassioned as he wants," the girl continued, "but at the end of the day, he's still just teaching us how to talk. The underlying theme here is that we're learning how to make people *like* us. Kind of manipulative, right?"

Eve shrugged and kept her eyes on her notes. "I suppose so."

"I guess it's a useful skill for all of those politicians-in-the-making." The girl nodded her chin at a group of students sitting in the front of the class, all of whom wore navy blue blazers or sweater vests and khaki pants. Their fingers raced across their scratchpads as they jotted down every last word that left Gupta's lips.

"The future presidents of America right there, God help us. And look—" She pointed to a boy sitting on the opposite side of the room. "Baby Woodgate won't even associate himself with them."

"*Baby* Woodgate?"

"You know, the president's son. Marshall Woodgate."

Eve had never seen Marshall Woodgate in person—and had only bare-ly noted his occasional HV appearances. He was very tall with dirty blond hair and twirled an old-fashioned pen in between his fingers as if completely bored by the lecture.

The girl leaned back casually in her seat. "I have three classes with the guy, so either I'm unconsciously stalking him, or he's stalking me."

Eve chuckled but quickly returned to her notes.

"I'm JinJing Zhou," the girl said, "but everyone calls me JJ."

Eve discreetly examined JJ out of the corner of her eye. She was petite, almost an entire foot shorter than Eve, and a little rough around the edges. Her soft, ivory skin was a stark contrast to her jet-black hair, which was short and choppy with jagged bangs and uneven layers. Her brown eyes were lined with black, coordinating perfectly with her purple lipstick, which in turn matched the purple and black chain necklaces that peeped out of her unbut-toned collared shirt. Her entire ensemble appeared deliberately disheveled, as her striped tie was undone and hanging around her neck, her trousers were rolled up past the ankles, her wrists were adorned with rows of beaded bracelets, and a pair of dusty, unlaced sneakers—in purple, naturally—loosely hung from her feet.

"Nice to meet you, JJ."

"So, you're not going to tell me your name?"

Eve sighed. "Eve," she finally mumbled. "My name is Eve."

"All right, Eve. What are you here for?"

"God, you make it sound like a prison sentence."

"Well, it kind of is, at least for me," JJ explained as she kicked her feet onto her desk. "My parents are waiting for me to '*come around*.' You know, be a good girl and make them proud. This is their version of boarding school, or boot camp. Lord knows they've already tried all that crap."

"Well, it's sort of the opposite for me," Eve said.

"You trying to escape something?"

Eve hesitated. "I guess you could say that."

"Dynamic. I can respect that." She paused. "You never answered my question, you know. Everyone's here for a reason. What was *your* golden ticket?"

"I'm just smart."

"Ah, yes, the nerd-type. There are plenty of you guys here."

Eve took a step, albeit a minuscule one, out of her comfort zone. "You?"

JJ grinned smugly. "You could say I'm good with computers."

Eve could feel JJ watching her, staring her up and down the same way Madison had when she'd first met her. She felt tense and uneasy and wished for once that she could simply be left alone.

"You know, you and I should be friends," JJ blurted out matter-of-factly.

Eve wrinkled her nose. "Why?"

"Because I think we'd get along."

"Where would you get that idea? You don't know anything about me."

"That's not true. I have great observation skills. I know tons about you."

"Like what?"

"Well, for one, you clearly have no interest in making *any* friends, which leads me to believe that you're antisocial and probably cynical about people in general."

Eve smirked. "And that makes you want to be my friend?"

JJ raised her eyebrows. "Do I look like the kind of person who likes people?"

Eve took another glance at JJ's outfit. "I guess you have a point."

"Two, you've got rings around your shins," JJ continued. "That tells me the heels you're wearing aren't your normal shoe choice, which means you're probably not all that girly. Let me guess, combat boots?"

Eve paused. "Wow. I'm not sure if I should be impressed or disturbed."

"Which leads me to three: you're sarcastic, which I'm sure is some type of defense mechanism to keep people at a distance. It also means you don't readily take shit from anyone."

For the first time since their conversation began, Eve turned away from her notes and looked up at JJ. But she instantly found herself distracted— through the window in the back of the room, she saw something much more intriguing than any frivolous classroom chatter.

JJ snickered. "And lastly, you keep looking out the window, which means you don't give a single shit about what that bobblehead in the front of the class has to say. Probably don't care about what I'm saying either. I guess I can get over that."

Eve was quiet. She hadn't heard JJ's latest ramblings. Puzzled, JJ turned around, eager to see what had captivated her classmate. There, just outside the window, stood a single patrolman.

"Interested in the patrolmen, huh? Either you've got a thing for men in uniform, or you've heard about the Interlopers. My money's on the latter."

Eve's eyes flicked back to JJ. "Do you know anything?"

"They're taking chimeras. They go off-campus with them, somewhere secluded. They use a new location for each abduction. Keeps the patrolmen guessing, I suppose."

"The patrolmen," Eve whispered. "That's what they do? They find the missing chimeras?"

"They're *supposed* to prevent the abductions. But they never have, not yet at least. It's just perpetual damage control. They're always one huge step behind the Interlopers. By the time they find them, the chimeras are already—"

"Dead?"

"No. Something else."

Eve leaned in closer. "What are they *doing* to them?"

JJ shrugged. "That I don't know, not for certain, anyway."

"Then you at least have an idea, right?"

JJ glanced around the room before continuing. "People think they're looking for an on-switch: some biological trigger that makes the chimeras... well, chimeras. Guess their old methods aren't working."

"What happens after the abduction? After the chimeras are brought back?"

"They go straight to the Billington Medical Ward—some for longer than others—and then they're released."

"That's it? Don't they tell anyone what happened to them?"

"Of course not, and there's two reasons for that. One, because they're outed chimeras—no one wants to talk to them anyway. Two, because their pockets are heavy."

"Their pockets are heavy? What does that mean?"

"Hush money." JJ played with her bracelets as she spoke. "Keeps them quiet. If this shit gets out, Billington is royally screwed. No one wants to back a school that's overrun with aliens."

Eve shook her head. "I don't understand. How do the Interlopers even know who to look for? Chimeras look like everyone else."

"Don't know, but whatever their system is, it's pretty brilliant. They've revealed more closet chimeras than daytime talk shows. And you know the craziest part? Over half the kids they've nabbed didn't even *know* they were chimeras yet. Hadn't hit emergence." JJ took one last look out the window and watched as the patrolman strolled away, disappearing from view. "They probably have some kind of technology that's able to detect that sort of stuff. Bet the government is jealous as hell. I'm sure they'd *love* to track chimeras like that."

A range of emotions flooded through Eve, forming a tight knot in her chest. The Interlopers were no longer scavengers—that much was certain. They were brutal, savage, aggressive; they were evil, and yet no one outside of the Billington gates had any idea of it.

She stopped—she couldn't do this, not here. She had to remain calm. She turned to JJ and smiled.

"Thanks for filling me in," she said. "I asked some guy about this stuff earlier... he didn't want to tell me anything."

"People don't want to talk about it. They're afraid they'll get expelled. That's the rumor. Talk, and you're out of here."

"Then why are *you* talking about it?"

JJ winked. "'Cause I'm not scared of *shit*."

Eve thought back to her previous class—to the freckle-faced boy and his thickset friend—and recalled their useless information and mocking retorts. She turned to JJ.

"How long have you been here?"

"I'm a freshman. Today's my first day."

"Oh," Eve murmured, dubiously. "Then how do you know all this?"

"Guess I just know the right places to look."

Eve took in a deep breath; while certainly bothersome and relentless, JJ was at least informative and maybe even funny at times.

JJ grinned with self-satisfaction and playfully punched Eve across the shoulder. "Do you see what we're doing right now?"

Eve furrowed her brow. "Whispering?"

"We're bonding over a common interest. That's what *friends* do."

Class was soon over, and the lecture hall emptied into the congested corridor. Eve tried to behave casually, as if the Interlopers were of no consequence to her—as if she were human, and thus unaffected. It was a hard part to play:

the role of an average college student without the lingering worry of judgment, of hateful misconceptions, of abduction and God knows what else. She
made her way out of the classroom and through the hallway, her thoughts still
clouded with uncertainty, and JJ followed close behind.

"So, *friend*," JJ teased, "where you headed now?"

"The gym. I have combat class."

"Combat? Didn't see that one coming. You're kind of a beanpole."

Eve let the slightest half-smile slip, though this time it was genuine. "I
think I can handle it."

"Well, if you live to see another day, you should introduce me to *your*
friends. We can paint each others' nails and talk about boys or whatever the
hell girls do."

"I don't have any friends."

JJ laughed loudly. "With your winning personality? How could that be?"
She poked Eve in the ribs. "You're probably the biggest recluse in your entire
dorm. Let me guess, Clarence Hall? I'm in Hutchinson—we call it the Hutch—
but I haven't seen your tall ass around there. Maybe you're in Langley? You
look like the Langley type. They're all a bunch of hermits down there—you'd
fit right in."

"It's Rutherford," Eve corrected. "I live in Rutherford Hall."

JJ stopped, her body suddenly paralyzed, her eyes and mouth gaping
open.

"*You* live in Rutherford Hall?"

"Yes?" Eve answered, reluctantly. "Why? Does it matter?"

"Of course it matters, Eve." JJ's lighthearted attitude had abruptly turned
hard and stoic. "You can't possibly pretend you haven't noticed the caste system here at the glorious Billington penitentiary."

"Well, yeah. Rutherford Hall is a little extravagant."

"A *little*? Rutherford Hall is a *little* extravagant like I'm a little *little*." JJ
shook her hands as if to wave Eve away from her. "You can go on without me."

"Wait, I don't understand. You're mad at me?"

"You're right, you don't understand: I'm not *mad* at you. I'm merely deciding that I dislike you."

Eve grimaced. "Because of where I *live*?"

JJ ignored her retort, taking one last critical look at her. "Have a nice life,
princess. Enjoy your false sense of superiority."

Eve watched in shock as JJ—the *friend* who had forced herself upon her and just as quickly shunned her—walked away. She recalled how Heather had proudly dubbed her a Rutherfordian; it truly was an ugly term, just as she had feared, and she knew that being a chimera was no longer the only burden she had to bear.

There was no time to dwell on the situation. She marched off to the gym, her mind overwhelmed with bitterness as she dissected every malicious word she wished she had said. She hurried into the women's locker room—she was the only one there, though she'd half-expected that to be the case—and angrily yanked at the buttons of her blouse, almost ripping them from the seams. She flung open her designated locker and found her combat uniform—a solid black tank top and a pair of matching cargo pants—which she quickly shimmied onto her body, along with her favorite combat boots, before finally heading to class.

The air in the gym was moist and filled with the thick stench of perspiration. The immense space felt barren; every footstep seemed to echo, bouncing from floor to ceiling, making her entrance far from discreet. A group of roughly forty boys had congregated in one corner of the gym, no doubt engaged in casual conversation about school, sports, tits—whatever it was that boys discussed amongst themselves. It was a small and, as Eve had suspected, all-male class, which made her presence even more noticeable.

The boys' talk simmered to a quiet hum and then to an uncomfortable silence, as one by one they turned around to gaze at the one spindly female who had joined their group. Her classmates were large and brawny with bulging arms and legs that were nearly as thick as her own waist. She stood quietly in front of them and watched them watch her, as if she were some strange creature lying dormant under a microscope. A few of them whispered to one another, and a couple even snickered, as if they had never seen a female before, and Eve felt her aggravation begin to brew inside of her once more.

Before the situation could grow any more uncomfortable, the gymnasium door slammed shut, and one last person made his way toward the group: an older man, a bit shorter than Eve but much larger in build, with broad, heavy shoulders and leathery skin that looked tight over his protruding muscles. His face was covered in deep stress lines and grey whiskers, which matched his full brows and buzzed, salt-and-pepper hair. He stood before the group, his presence commanding a level of attention that not even Eve could compete with, as his authority seeped through the room like pheromones oozing from his pores.

"Line up."

Eve and her classmates quickly scurried into formation, their bodies spurred to action by the man's booming voice.

"I am Captain Ramsey. You *will* refer to me as Captain Ramsey—not Mister, not Sir, and most certainly not Buddy or Pal, because I am *not* your friend."

The atmosphere of the gym had changed abruptly. Eve saw that her classmates had become tense, their false confidence ripped away by this sudden intimidation, yet she remained poised and at ease.

"I served in the United States Navy for over twenty-five years. I've paid my dues, and now it's time for you to pay yours. You will take orders. You will follow instructions. I am God and you are my loyal servants. Is that understood?"

Eve was silent. A few of her classmates muttered, "Yes, sir."

"Yes, *Captain*," he corrected, his face still wooden and unvarying. He held his hands behind his back and walked down the line, looking each of his students up and down with a critical stare.

"You're not ready to fight. None of you are."

He stopped in front of a chiseled student with perfectly combed light brown hair, hazel eyes, and a chin dimple.

"You have any experience, son?"

"Sir—"

"Captain Ramsey," he interrupted.

"Captain Ramsey, I've been playing football for thirteen years and I'm here on an athletic scholarship."

"I didn't ask if you can chase a ball around, son. I asked if you have experience."

The boy stammered and fumbled over his words. "Well, I, I mean—"

"Do you have experience in a combat situation? Have you trained in any form of fighting, self-defense, or martial arts? If we were ambushed here in this gym right now by fully armed men, would you know what to do to survive?"

The boy with the chin dimple lowered his head, his cheeks flushed with embarrassment. "No, Captain," he began, "but I can fight. I promise you that."

"Well, ain't that somethin', 'cause your promise means so *goddamn* much to me."

Ramsey shook his head and moved along, continuing down the row of sinewy bodies as if he were inspecting an assembly line. Eve could feel the anxiety festering in the room, but she herself was unconcerned.

Ramsey stopped beside another student. The boy was massive, his frame looming over the ex-seaman, and yet he stared at the ceiling, too intimidated to look the captain in the eye.

"How about you?" the captain asked once more. "Any experience?"

"Muay Thai," he barked abruptly.

"How many years?"

He hesitated. "One."

Captain Ramsey let out a loud, discouraged sigh. The rest of the students dodged his gaze, attempting to fade into the background as he marched along the line. To Eve, the entire display was pitiful—she felt as if she was in the presence of beastly-looking cowards who shrank away at the first sight of strength. However, her disparaging opinions soon were pushed from her mind, as the daunting Captain Ramsey stopped directly in front of her.

"And you?" he inquired, his voice rough and gravelly. "You have combat experience?"

Before she could answer, another voice chimed in from the other end of the line.

"'Ey Captain, you better tell her that catfights don't count."

A chorus of laughter erupted around Chin Dimple, and he grinned smugly, pleased with his own comic genius. Eve refused to move, to turn the boy's way or show emotion, to give him any sense of satisfaction; and though her fingers instinctively curled into tight fists, she said and did nothing.

The captain was not quite as contained as Eve. His head shot swiftly toward Chin Dimple, his face red with anger.

"Is something *funny*?"

Chin Dimple looked down, but was barely able to mask his smile. "No, sir."

"No, *Captain*," Ramsey spat, now tromping toward the football player. "You dare to disrespect one of your comrades?"

"Comrades? I don't even know her—"

"These people are now your greatest allies, and when you're here, you *will* treat them as equals."

Chin Dimple hesitated, his smirk still faintly visible. "Yes, Captain."

Ramsey paused for a moment, his face inches away from the football star's cleft chin.

"At the end of the day, you're a grown-ass man and you can do what you damn well please." He nodded toward Eve. "If you want her to be your enemy, then *so be it*. But you should *never* underestimate your enemy, boy. Remember that."

Ramsey faced the class, his expression dripping with disapproval.

"We won't be doing any combat today. Or tomorrow. You're all soft, and you need to toughen up. You'll be working your asses off until I've decided you're ready to do some *real* training. Outside. *Now.*"

The group scampered out of the gym and headed toward the football field. When they arrived, Ramsey flashed a mischievous smile.

"You will run for the remainder of this class. We've got, what, thirty-five minutes? Whoever finishes last will stay here and run drills for another hour."

Chin Dimple sneered tauntingly in Eve's ear. "Sorry about your drills. I'm sure the hour will fly by."

Without warning, Ramsey blew his whistle, and the entire class took off down the track. Her supposed comrades sprinted like a herd of wild buffalo, their cumbersome, hulking figures stomping along the pathway and kicking up dust and sand. Amid this clumsy stampede, Eve felt graceful and serene; she could hardly feel her feet move as she placed one in front of the other, and yet she sped past her peers without any struggle.

As she ran, her mind wandered to her past classes; to JJ; her new, slimy title as a Rutherfordian; the campus attacks; the Interlopers. *Can I really stay here?* she asked herself. Of course she could—in fact, she had to, because she'd spent her entire savings on the move to Calabasas. She had nowhere else to go. Interlopers or not, she was stuck at this university, pretending to be someone she was not.

Eve's mind shifted back to reality—she was out at the front of the pack, already about to lap the stragglers. Her eyes grew wide and darted back and forth across the field until she spotted Ramsey. He was standing by the bleachers staring directly at her, his eyes small and focused. Eve gritted her teeth and, despite her overwhelming urge not to, slowed her pace, allowing the stampede to swarm around her once more. For the remainder of the long, tedious run, she kept herself in the middle of the pack, all the while resenting the mediocrity she was forcing herself to fake. It was for the best, she told herself. No one could know who she truly was, and if that meant feigning weakness, she would do it.

The whistle blew, signaling the end of the run as well as the end of the class.

While her peers appeared to relish the prospect of water and rest, Eve instead felt unfulfilled and sick with self-loathing. As the boys mopped the sweat off of their sore shoulders and drained faces, she gathered her things and headed for the door—but not before she caught wind of their conversation.

"Did you see her? She was blowing us out of the water for a minute."

"She's not even *tired*."

"Come on, man. She's a girl, not a machine."

"Seriously, look at her. She's not sweating. At all."

"Girls don't sweat."

"*Bullshit*."

It had begun—her act had been for nothing. Despite the intolerable heat, she threw her hooded sweatshirt over her perfectly dry shoulders and headed off, eager to escape the whispering behind her.

Suddenly, an obstacle blocked her path: Captain Ramsey stood in front of her, his face donning the same intense expression he had worn during her laps.

"Is there something I can do for you, Captain?" Eve asked. This time, it was her turn to avoid eye contact.

The captain stared at her, his eyes piercing her like daggers.

"No, Kingston. You may proceed."

Eve hurried past him with her head hanging low. Even as she left the field, she could still feel Ramsey and her classmates watching her. She had to be more careful—*much* more careful—if she was going to maintain this façade. Anonymity was already starting to feel like such a struggle to achieve, but she would have it; she would be normal, *human*, for once in her life. As she imagined a life unlike her own, one of peace and solitude, she became reinvigorated with a sense of purpose, so much so that, for a moment, she almost forgot the lingering threat of the newly hostile and dangerous Interlopers.

Almost.

CHAPTER 3: JASON A. VALENTINE

A swarm of orange jumpsuits stampeded around her, knocking over lunch tables and metal chairs like wild animals released from a cage. They were fleeing—to where, she didn't know, as there was no place to go, and so they pressed their bodies against the walls, their eyes frantic, their skin pale with terror. Guards in black uniforms dispersed throughout the space, desperate to subdue the chaos at hand, but their efforts were futile. They were too late.

Eve stood in the center of the room, her feet rooted to the cement floor. As small as she was—probably the smallest, and certainly the youngest person there—she felt large and towering, as if all eyes were focused on her, which she knew was more than a paranoid assumption. Her body shook; she couldn't tell whether it was fear or power quaking within her, because she was too inexperienced and naïve to know the difference. All she could do was stare at the floor in horror.

She could feel him standing a few yards in front of her: a teenage boy, much bigger than her and nearly twice her age, though his once intimidating appearance was now feeble and weak.

"You did this." His voice trembled as he spoke. "You know that, right?"

He clutched something in his fist: a toothbrush, whittled at the end into a sharp point. A shiv covered in blood—the same blood that was spilled at Eve's feet, a pool of red that she couldn't tear her eyes from.

The blood spread slowly across the ground until it lapped at her shoes. Another boy was lying in the center of it, face down, limp, still. He had been no more than ten years old—upright, talking, smiling only minutes prior—and now, nothing but an endless sea of red. All she could see, all she could feel was the boy and the blood. So much blood. So much red.

"*You did this.*" The teenager repeated. Eve had almost forgotten he was still there, staring at her, his gaze fearful. Petrified.

"This is all your fault."

Eve's eyes flicked open, her entire being forced awake in an instant.

It was Saturday morning; Eve had survived her first week of school. The sun was shining through the sheer curtains, and she could tell that it was going to be a beautiful day. How unfortunate, then, that she would be spending her time in the study hall, burying her face in the digital pages of her scratchpad and catching up on her endless array of work.

She glanced at the other side of her room; Madison was already gone, her bed disheveled and her clothes strewn across her luggage like the debris from a pink tornado. Eve took a brief moment to bask in her coveted solitude before tearing herself from the comfort of her sheets and preparing for what was sure to be a dull day. She tossed a loose blouse over her head, pulled on a pair of denim shorts, and strolled out of her dorm, only to be abruptly stopped at her doorway.

"Eve! *So* glad I ran into you!"

Heather, the vivacious redhead from move-in day, was waiting just outside Eve's room, lightly tapping her perfectly manicured nails along the door.

Eve grumbled, "Well, you *are* standing in my doorway."

Heather flashed her trademark smile. "Where you off to?"

Eve struggled to squirm past, but Heather didn't step aside.

Eve sighed. "I'm going to the study hall."

"Not anymore!" Heather linked arms with Eve and yanked her toward the elevator. "You're coming with me to the Billington Medical Ward!"

"I am?"

"You know, community service looks stellar on resumes. I thought I'd get a head start and apply to do some volunteer work at the medical ward. They're holding a meet-and-greet today for anyone who may be interested."

"Well, that's nice and all, but I'm *not* interested." Eve looked around for someone, anyone to save her from Heather's grasp, but the halls were empty. "Does that mean I can just go to the study hall?"

"Eve, darling, don't you care about your future?"

"I do, I just don't care about the medical ward—"

"Eve!" Heather gasped. "There are sick people *suffering* over there. Don't you feel the slightest bit obligated to lend a hand?"

Eve felt the pressure of guilt creep through her. "Well... I guess—"

"I'm *kidding*," Heather giggled. "The truth is, the medical ward is such a great place to people-watch. If one of your classmates gets a bad case of mono, you're the first to know. If someone breaks their leg in a drunken stupor, you see it before everyone else! And best of all, we'll get to see all of the attack victims."

"Attack victims?"

"Oh come on, Eve, you *must* have heard about the Interloper abductions by now." Heather playfully squeezed Eve's hand. "I'm *dying* to know what's happening to them—the chimeras. It's exciting, don't you think?"

Eve scowled with disgust. "Thrilling."

Eve had never been to the Billington Medical Ward—she had heard of it, sure, as it was the most prestigious teaching hospital in the country—but she had hoped to stay as far from the place as possible. Nevertheless, she soon found herself standing in the middle of the lobby, its plain white walls and linoleum floor feeling like the lining of a very stale and very sterile tomb. Despite the bland surroundings, the ward itself was far from dull, as eager volunteers hustled through the empty space and winding hallways.

"Wow. Didn't expect to see so many people here," Eve mumbled.

"Well, *clearly* other people care more about their future success than you do."

Eve scanned the room until her gaze landed on a huddle of doctors and nurses in a faraway corner. They whispered to one another, their brows and palms sweaty, their eyes darting across the crowded space.

She flinched as Heather slapped a piece of paper against her chest.

"A little jumpy, are we?" Heather teased. "Here, fill out this form while we wait in line for our blood tests."

Eve stopped, her body suddenly cold and numb.

"Blood test? Why do we need a blood test?"

"It's standard procedure, hon. We'll be working in a hospital. Naturally they have to make sure we're healthy."

"...I'm not taking a blood test."

"And why not?" Heather stared back at Eve, her green eyes wide with intrigue. "Is there a problem? You don't have anything to hide, do you?"

Eve looked at Heather—at her steadfast gaze and phony smile—and she could've sworn she saw the vulture Madison had so vehemently warned her about.

"Of course not. I just don't like needles."

"Oh, Eve," Heather squealed, "you're adorable, do you know that?"

They parked themselves in line, and Heather immediately began tackling her form. Eve kept her paper by her side and stared blankly at the bustling crowd, her mind racing into a state of panic. She knew exactly what the tests would disclose: negative to all infectious diseases, viruses, and bacteria. Her results would implicate her as the healthiest person in the building—*too* healthy, at least for a normal human being, but not too healthy for a chimera. She couldn't take that blood test. The thought of revealing her identity—of proving without a doubt that she wasn't human—was utterly unbearable.

Eve looked over her shoulder at the injection lab; she was only third in line and would need to figure something out quickly. She could excuse herself to use the restroom, maybe feign a sudden illness, but neither option seemed believable. She could simply faint, pretending to be scared of the sight of blood, though such an act of weakness seemed so demeaning.

Suddenly, an alarm sounded through the overhead speakers, and the ward stirred into action. Volunteers nervously glanced about the lobby while the staff's faces filled with fear. The small group of doctors and nurses in the back of the room dashed toward the doorway, shouldering their way through the mass of students and ushering aside all those who blocked the entrance.

"What's going on?" Eve asked. "Should we leave?"

"Not a chance," Heather insisted. "We're next in line."

Eve looked back at the injection site. A lab technician flagged her over, patting an open seat, his friendly smile appearing ominous in her eyes. It was too late for her to turn away now; each step she took felt like one step closer to her worst fears being realized.

"MOVE! OUT OF THE WAY!"

A patrolman burst through the lobby doors, his hands wrapped around a massive firearm. Eve turned toward the commotion—five, seven, ten more patrolmen barged into the lobby, clearing an aisle down the main hallway toward the ICU. Eve scampered out of the injection lab toward Heather, who was peering past a patrolman at the scene in front of them.

"Stand back, ladies," the man ordered. "Don't come any closer."

"What's happening?" Heather asked, straining her neck over his shoulder.

"Medical emergency. We're bringing in an attack victim."

Heather's eyes brightened. "A chimera?"

"Don't come any *closer*," he repeated.

The front doors swung open. Countless paramedics spilled into the lobby, their navy scrubs covered in sweat and blood. The scene unfolded in slow motion as doctors cried for assistance and patrolmen barked orders over the chaos. More paramedics, their eyes filled with terror, pushed a rattling metal gurney through the entryway. Eve could see a young man with messy brown hair and tattered jeans lying on the stretcher; she instantly recognized him as Jason Valentine, the boy from her first day of classes and the supposed owner of Madison's heart. His face was ghostly pale, his eyes wide with shock; he panted for air, his breaths short and shallow. Eve scanned his filthy body when she saw it, an image she knew would haunt her for the rest of her life: Jason's chest had been split open, his flesh and muscle torn down the center and savagely spread apart like the pages of a book. The incision was clean and precise, as if executed with meticulous exactness, with time and care, by someone or something so evil, so heinous that the thought alone sent a wave of nausea through Eve's body. She could clearly make out the sheen of his ribs and the mess enclosed within: his crimson heart quaked within its cavity, and his pink lungs throbbed rapidly and violently.

"Oh my God," Eve stammered, appalled. "They *dissected* him?"

Jason's eyes rolled to the back of his head as he drifted in and out of consciousness. A doctor shined a small flashlight in his face as they raced through the corridor.

"Jason! Can you hear me, Jason?"

Jason blinked, then glanced around in a daze until his gaze finally made its way to his chest—his open, bloody chest and the internal organs now fully exposed in front of him. Panic set in; his eyes widened, his hands trembled, and his lungs surged as he helplessly gasped for air. Then, with a sudden swell of energy, he clutched at the rails of his gurney and let out a deafening, horrified scream.

Eve jumped—his scream sent her own heart pounding in her chest, and though she prayed to God it wouldn't occur, the unthinkable happened before her eyes. A nurse running alongside the stretcher suddenly flew into the air, her body torn from the ground and tossed across the hallway like a limp rag doll. Immediately after, a doctor was jerked from the floor by some invisible force—some power that pulled her off her feet and sent her body colliding into the wall. One by one, bodies were thrown about the room like leaves being scattered by a turbulent breeze. Another nurse was flung across the hallway, and then another, his body landing in a heap upon a row of chairs.

Eve watched in complete shock at the mayhem before her; it was all so surreal, and yet so familiar to her.

One last doctor was hurled into the air, his limbs flailing erratically as he quickly plummeted back down—right toward Heather McLeod, who stood paralyzed in his path. Without a second to think, Eve bolted forward and grabbed Heather's shoulders, spun her around, and slammed her against the wall just as the doctor fell to the floor.

"EVE!" Heather yelped, her body still pressed into the wall. "What just happened?"

Eve released her, backing away from the girl as she watched the ICU doors slam shut behind Jason's speeding gurney.

"He just developed his gift," she answered almost unconsciously. "He can't control it."

"Have you ever seen anything like that before?"

Eve's mind wandered to the death of her parents—to the terrible wreck, the pain in her skull, the truck that flew into the sky.

"No."

The lobby was a mess. Eve stood in the center of it, shocked and nonplussed, oblivious to Heather's unwavering stare as she hovered closely behind her.

"That was unbelievable."

"I know," Eve said. "His chest... all that blood—"

"No, I meant you," Heather corrected. "How you caught me. How you moved me away right in the nick of time." She folded her arms, suddenly calm and collected. "You're so fast, Eve. It's almost like you're... I don't know, *super*. Like you're not even human."

Eve looked at Heather—at her adorable white sundress and despicable smile, at her cheeks that were once pale with fright but were now suddenly back to their usual rosy glow. With a heavy sigh and a resentful glare, Eve headed for the exit.

"Where are you going?"

"Away from here. Away from you."

"But the blood tests—"

"*Screw* the damn blood tests, Heather," Eve spat. "Screw the medical ward, and screw *Billington*."

"Well, *you're* awfully perturbed. Was it something I said?"

Eve stopped in front of the doorway and turned; she had a perfect view of the destruction—the overturned chairs, the blood-spattered linoleum floor, the frantic, tear-streaked faces—but this time, all she saw was the redheaded girl before her.

"Someone was just *dissected*, Heather. You may not give a shit, but I do."

And with that, Eve stormed out of the ward, pushing her way through the throng of bodies, pleading with herself to please, *please* remain calm. *Don't look back.* Patrolmen were scattered in front of the ward, cornering terrified volunteers. "You saw *NOTHING*," they ordered. "*Do you understand?*" Eve charged ahead, keeping her eyes forward, blinding herself to the surrounding chaos. She couldn't ignore it any longer: the attacks were real. Jason's butchered, dissected chest was real. As the initial shock slowly dissipated, reality soon set in: no chimera was safe at Billington—not even Eve.

* * *

The blue car resembled a piece of mangled tinfoil wrapped around the telephone pole. A thin trail of smoke oozed from the hood and crawled up the mutilated frame, disappearing beneath the colossal truck that sat atop the car's remains. Eve watched as the truck's driver fumbled for the door handle, and she realized that she had been here many, many times before—but for whatever reason, this time something was different. She looked down at her hands—they were smooth and mature, with long, slender fingers and a faded, pencil-thin scar heading straight across her right palm. She had gotten that scar during a fight in the seventh grade when one of her classmates had threatened her with a knife. *"I'm gonna cut that gift right out of you, chime,"* he'd said to her through gritted teeth. Suddenly, she knew what was so strange about her dream; she touched her face and felt her sharp cheekbones and pointed nose. The accident was so real, so accurate, but for the first time in eleven years, the dream had changed: Eve was no longer a child. She was seeing the nightmare through the eyes of her nineteen-year-old self.

"Don't you tell anyone, little girl. Don't you tell a goddamn soul, y'hear me?"

Eve's heart raced as she resisted the urge to kill the man with her own two hands. What good would that do? After all, this was only a dream, and he was already dead. Still, she couldn't slow the heavy beating in her chest. After years of being haunted by this recurring vision, she had grown accustomed to it, desensitized even; and now that it had changed, she felt herself panicking once again.

She closed her eyes—*Maybe I'll wake up*, she thought to herself. *When I open my eyes, everything will be back to normal.* With one last moment of hesitation, she opened her eyes. The drunk driver was gone, and in his place stood Jason Valentine.

He looked exactly as he had on the hospital gurney: his chest was carved open, and his flesh and muscle hung limply at his sides. Eve stared in horror at his pulsing heart, at the blood that drizzled down his stomach, past his navel, and onto his jeans, while his eyes looked back at her with an empty, lifeless gaze.

"We're all going to die."

His voice was calm and unwavering. Eve's legs began to shake; she wanted to run, to wake up, to find a way to escape Jason's presence, but she couldn't stop herself from staring deep into his unblinking, expressionless eyes.

"We have to stop it. We have to make it end. Or everyone dies."

Eve lurched up in her seat, and a couple of nearby students giggled and whispered to one another as they watched her catch her breath. She was in the Rutherford study hall, trying to tackle her assignments from the day prior but failing miserably. Her eyes panned down to her scratchpad; her digital textbook read *Page One*, and she cursed under her breath. It was Heather's fault—her sleepless night, her tossing and turning, the new, horrible nightmares that tormented her. With a sigh, she admitted defeat, gathered her belongings, and headed for the door.

Eve hopped in the elevator and pressed the button for the first floor. It was nearly seven o'clock, and dinner would soon be available in the dining hall. The idea of eating there with the Billington elite, and even worse, with Madison and Hayden, made her cringe. She would much rather eat by herself—being alone was her comfort, her refuge, the only thing that felt familiar and safe—but it was a luxury Madison had ensured she would never enjoy again.

The elevator doors opened to reveal a sight Eve hadn't expected: the lobby was filled with students, all madly dashing in the same direction—straight to the rec room. Curious, Eve followed suit, peering over their heads and shoulders as they squeezed their way through the tight space. The room was crammed with Rutherfordians—many sat cross-legged on the floor, while others shared the scant chairs, and some even teetered atop the tables—but every last one of them had their sights set on the wall-sized HV screen.

The news was on. A sharply dressed anchorwoman's hologram paced the floor, walking through a few of the students who sat too close to the projection. She stopped and faced the room, her tone somber and urgent.

"In our top story of the day, controversy tears through Billington University. According to what we believe are reliable sources, Interlopers have invaded the esteemed college. Even more disturbing are reports that the Interlopers are not just occupying the campus—they are, in fact, abducting chimera students and performing live dissections on them."

The students surrounding Eve nervously murmured to one another, but she remained silent.

"An anonymous source within Billington has informed Channel 4 News that as many as nine chimera abductions have taken place at the university over the past several months, and that Billington officials have resorted to extreme measures in order to keep these attacks out of the headlines. The most recent abduction and dissection, occurring just yesterday, is certainly the most shocking of them all: Channel 4 has confirmed that Billington sophomore Jason Valentine, son of New York Senator Donald Valentine, is the latest attack victim."

A small photo of Jason appeared in the top corner of the screen. His smile was friendly and sincere, but Eve felt a chill run through her body.

"According to our anonymous insider, Jason Valentine suffered life-threatening injuries to the chest and abdomen and is currently in recovery. Sources speculate that no one within the Valentine family, including Jason, was aware of his status as a chimera. Senator Valentine took an anti-chimera-rights stance during his campaign, and thus far, has not released any statements regarding his son's condition or the attacks at Billington in general."

A few students snickered to one another as they pointed at Jason's photo. For a brief moment, Eve thought that she heard one of them mutter, *"Chime."*

"This tragic discovery at Billington University marks a turning point that many have feared: the US Government has now officially declared the Interloper population a physical threat to chimeras."

"What are you doing?"

A sharp voice rang in Eve's ear, breaking her concentration. She jumped—then looked to her side and saw Hayden's grey, beady eyes staring back at her.

"God, Hayden, you can't just sneak up on people like that."

"Madison sent me to look for you. You're late for dinner."

"I'm *late*? Is she my roommate or my mother?"

"Less talking, more walking." Hayden scanned the room, her face vapid and expressionless. "Let's go."

Eve followed Hayden toward the dining hall, shoving her thoughts of the Interlopers to the back of her mind as best she could. As they made their way past the long rows of tables and chairs, she saw Jason's mangled body flash before her eyes, and she blinked furiously to rid herself of the images. With little time to calm herself, she finally found Madison's table and sat in front of her.

Madison trailed her fork through her salad, tossing bits of lettuce across her plate like a child playing with her food.

"Ugh," she moaned. "This salad is the worst. These cherry tomatoes taste like barf." She looked up at Eve and growled. "Where have you been?"

"I was in the rec room watching HV. Haven't you seen the news? They're talking about your *beloved* Jason."

Madison plopped her fork in the middle of her salad and grimaced. "Don't even remind me of Jason. *So* disappointing to hear he's a chimera. *Gross.*"

Eve winced. "Gross?"

"Totally! Just think, if we were to have babies, they'd be *tainted*, like crossbreeds, or *mutts*. Plus, I'm sure his chest looks like a vomitosis mess now that it's been ripped open and sewn back together." She wrinkled her nose and pushed her half-eaten salad off to the side. "I can't even eat just thinking about it."

Eve bit her lip and shoved her hands deep into her pockets, attempting to keep her anger out of sight as she dug her fingernails into her palms.

"So, I'm guessing he's been cut from your list of top ten future husbands?"

"*God* no. He's been demoted, but not removed completely. He's down to number ten now—barely hanging on by a thread. But he's still rich and pretty. That counts for something."

Eve rolled her eyes. "I can't think of anything that matters more."

"I don't know what she sees in him," Hayden added, slurping her juice and glaring pointedly in Eve's direction. "I don't know what she sees in a *lot* of people."

"Ladies! Fancy seeing you here!"

A bubbly voice trilled behind Eve, catching her off guard. She cringed— she knew exactly to whom it belonged.

"Heather!" Madison beamed, much to Eve's surprise. "Hon, you look fabulous!" She hopped up from her seat and gave Heather a firm squeeze.

Heather glanced back and forth between Madison and Eve. "I didn't know you two knew one another," she said, her eyes lighting up with delight. Eve was familiar with the look—and she didn't trust it.

Madison smiled. "Oh, we more than *know* each other. We're roommates and instant friends. Attached at the hip, really."

Eve looked briefly at Hayden; the blonde angrily scowled back at her and downed her juice like it was a shot of vodka.

"Well, isn't that special." Heather's eyes danced across Madison and landed on the large, glittering orbs that hung from her earlobes. "Madison, I must say, those are some beautiful diamond earrings."

"You noticed!" Madison shot a quick glower at Hayden and Eve. "These two bottom feeders haven't said a word about them."

"Are they a gift from Daddy?"

"You know me too well, Heather." Madison cupped the dangling gems, stroking their platinum settings affectionately. "They're new, you know. You can't buy them in stores yet, and they're already sold out in presale, but those sort of restrictions don't apply to *me*, obviously."

Heather cocked her head. "They're awfully sparkly."

"That's because they're Everlasting Diamonds, the latest thing in synthetic gems."

"Synthetic?" Hayden asked. "So... they're fake?"

"They're the *future of fashion*, you idiot," Madison snarled. "Natural diamonds are scratch-resistant, but they're not shatterproof. Everlasting Diamonds are totally indestructible." Madison flicked her wrist nonchalantly. "It's chemistry or something, I don't know. But I do know that it's the first of its kind, a diamond to surpass all diamonds. Nothing like this has ever been made before."

Eve squinted her eyes, blinded by the shimmering monstrosities. "I don't understand. Why would anyone need a shatterproof diamond?"

"Why would anyone need a needle lace dress hand-stitched by Finnish nuns? Because it's extravagant and dynamic and above all else, it's a *statement*."

"A statement of what? Wealth?"

"*Exactly*. Besides, the toughness is what makes these bad boys so twinkly, and really, that's all that matters." Madison turned to Heather, her eyes glowing with self-regard. "My daddy even let me come up with the commercial slogan: your heart will never break, and neither will your diamonds."

"Well, aren't you the little marketing maven. So much so that you've sold me," Heather cooed. "It's a shame they're not available for purchase."

"I know, it's a real pain in the crotch, but what can you do?"

"What *can* you do?" Heather repeated, stroking her chin almost comically. "That's a phenomenal question. If only someone had special access to these Everlasting Diamonds. I know if I did, I'd give some to my friends." She stared at Madison, her eyes fiercely focused. "My closest companions. The ones who knew my *deepest secrets*. You know, out of the goodness of my heart."

Madison looked back at Heather, her cheeks suddenly morphing from pink to white.

Heather folded her arms. "But that's just me, of course."

Madison sprang to life, immediately digging through her golden clutch like a dog tracking a scent. She yanked a velvet coin purse from her bag and poured out its contents: three small diamonds.

"An Everlasting Diamond for *each* of you," she said, placing one into the palm of each girl's hand, "because that's how much you all mean to me."

Eve eyed the jewel; it was small, the size of a pea, and yet she knew its value likely surpassed even her most lavish estimates.

"Madison, you are *so* generous!" Heather chirped, admiring her gem in the light. "How unfortunate that I have two ears and only one diamond."

Madison forced a pained grin and reluctantly pulled one last gem from her coin purse. "Now you have two diamonds," she managed to utter through poorly concealed gritted teeth. "Just for you, my oldest friend."

"But what about—"

"Shut up, Hayden," Madison snapped. She turned to Eve, who had remained quiet throughout this odd display, and scowled resentfully. "I know you're not too familiar with the finer things in life, but that diamond is worth more than you are. If you lose it, I'll gut you like a fish."

"Speaking of guts..." Heather placed her diamonds in her handbag and turned to Eve, gently resting her hand on her shoulder. "How are you holding up, darling?"

Eve grumbled and shook the girl's hand from her shoulder. "I'm *fine*, thanks."

Heather leaned in toward the girls. "We were in the medical ward yesterday when the whole..." She paused and looked from side to side. "...*situation* happened."

Hayden's eyes lit up with curiosity and Madison gasped.

"Eve!" the heiress yelped. "How come you didn't tell me?"

"It's something I'd rather not talk about. Ever."

Heather took a seat facing Eve. "You know, I had a class with Jason during the first semester of our freshman year. I never would've suspected that he was one of them." She turned to Madison. "What about you, doll? You've known him for quite some time, haven't you?"

"No one is more shocked than *I* am, that's for sure." Madison pouted melodramatically. "I feel lied to—betrayed, really. He should've said something. He should've *told* me—"

"He didn't know."

The table fell silent, and Eve felt all eyes on her. *For God's sake, learn to keep your mouth shut,* she thought to herself, and yet she couldn't help it. She looked up at the three girls beside her.

"They said so on HV."

Heather frowned. "You seem so tense, darling. Are you sure you're okay?"

"I said I'm fine."

Heather giggled. "Oh, Eve, so tight-lipped and full of mystery. I swear, you're like an onion—you have to be peeled back layer by layer." She stood from her seat and patted down the pleats of her skirt. "It's been so lovely catching up, but I have places to be and things to do. Thank you for the diamonds, Madison." Just as she stepped away from the table, she stopped and turned toward the girls one last time. "Oh, and Eve, my little enigma, do take care of yourself. I certainly can't wait to see each and every one of your layers. They're fascinating, I'm sure."

The threesome watched Heather scamper away, completely silent until she had turned the corner and left the dining hall.

"Thank *God* she's gone," Madison hissed, slumping in her chair with relief. "That could've been a suckgasmic mess."

"What was *that* all about?" Eve asked, dumbfounded. "The compliments, the diamonds. I thought you hated her. You told me she was a *vulture.*"

"Yeah, well, she can't know that."

"Why not?"

"Eve, don't be so naïve," the heiress sneered. "That slophole has ruined too many reputations in her lifetime. I can't risk getting on her bad side. You know what they say: keep your friends close and your enemies closer."

Eve caught herself before she rolled her eyes. In fact, she realized that her disapproval was almost hypocritical. After all, she was eating with Madison and Hayden, two girls she couldn't stand to be around, and for what? For safety. For survival. That was what she had told herself each day as she tolerated their company. In her desperation to coast by anonymously, she was becoming what she despised: a fake. *Keep your friends close and your enemies closer*—the words echoed through her mind, and she knew they described her current situation. Maybe Eve was no better than Madison. Maybe Eve was a phony, too.

***

The days came and went, and despite the news of Jason's abduction, school continued in a startlingly normal manner. Most of the student body appeared unfazed, even blasé about the whole thing, and though they spoke of the dissection, it was with no more seriousness than they spoke of the latest dirt on who-is-dating-who. Besides, the wellbeing of a chimera was of little importance to many; much of the talk about Jason was speculation over the appearance of his chest and possible resulting deformities.

In fact, Eve had been hearing for days that Jason was actually only one of two or three chimeras already in the medical ward. In some ways, there was really nothing special or unique about his situation, apart from his influential father. So perhaps it shouldn't have been surprising that before long, the dramatics surrounding Jason Valentine had been reduced to "old news."

But Eve didn't feel that her day in the medical ward was simply "old news." In her eyes, everything had changed.

It was a Monday afternoon, two weeks into the semester, and Eve was nearly half done with her classes for the day. She typed up the last of her notes and shoved her scratchpad into her shoulder bag; Professor Richards's class was wrapping up, and she was eager to escape the confines of the prison-like lecture hall. She glanced at the professor out of the corner of her eye—as much as she hated to admit it, Madison was right, he truly was a *dick*—and stealthily slipped from the back of the room and into the mass of students heading for the door, desperate to blend in with everyone else. There was no need to draw attention to herself, especially after the catastrophe on her first day of school, and as she moved closer and closer to the exit, she felt the slightest swell of relief inside of her.

Suddenly, her path was blocked only inches before the door, stopping her and everyone behind her in their tracks. Before her stood a glowering Dr. Dick.

"Are you Evelyn Kingston?" he asked.

Her stomach churned; she was sickened by the sound of her name leaving his lips. In a room filled with countless students, how could he possibly know who she was?

"Yes?" she replied reluctantly.

He stared at her in silence, aside from the sound of his congested breathing.

"Did you need somethi—"

"Just wanted to put a face to the name. You're the girl from the first day of class, aren't you?"

Shit, she thought to herself. *Shit, shit, SHIT.*

"Um—"

"Figures. You can leave." He stepped to the side and pointed at the door. "Go."

He needn't tell her twice. Eve quickly left the room, her face flushed and body stiff as she hurried down the hallway. Anxiety trickled through her veins. *He knows my name. Why does he know my name?* The feeling lingered even as she reached her Strategic Communication class.

As she fought to rid her thoughts of Dr. Dick, Professor Gupta took his place at the podium, his face bright with excitement and belly bouncing with sprightly delight.

"Hello, my brilliant minds. Another day of betterment and learning, yes?"

A knock sounded at the classroom door, immediately silencing the professor and his students. The door opened, and a bookish, gawky boy with jet-black hair and tanned skin scuttled in and handed a note to the professor. As Gupta read the note, his smile faded into a grim, somber stare. He hesitantly looked up at his students.

"Evelyn Kingston? Is there an Evelyn Kingston here?"

Eve groaned. *Again?* As she reluctantly raised her hand, she felt her peers turn and stare at her, their gazes maddening and intrusive.

Gupta flicked his fingers, beckoning her forward. "Please, Evelyn, come to the front of the class."

Eve clenched her jaw and bit her tongue as she made her way to the podium. Gupta stared down at the floor, unable to look her in the eyes.

"You have been called to the dean's building. Dr. Furst would like to see you."

An eruption of murmurs spread across the classroom. Eve could distinctly hear JJ's condescending laughter among the whispers, and she squirmed with discomfort.

"Am I in trouble?"

Gupta remained withdrawn, his eyes still pointed to the ground. "He would like to see you immediately."

With a heavy sigh, Eve gathered her things and left the classroom, leaving the irksome whispers behind. She made her way across the campus grounds, plodding slowly, as if each step took her closer and closer toward an eerie unknown. She was familiar with Dean Furst: he was a well-respected man, one of the founders of Billington, and easily the most esteemed figure at the university. What could a man of such importance want with someone like her?

The dean's building was small and discreet, but beautifully decorated with ivory adornments and immaculate landscaping. Its lobby was just as elegant, featuring perfectly polished hardwood floors and lines of ebony doors that extended across either side of the room. As Eve entered, the receptionist—a stunning woman with golden blond hair—looked up from behind the check-in desk and smiled.

"Evelyn Kingston, I presume?" she cooed. "Follow me, dear."

The woman glided from her seat and led the way toward the back of the building, finally stopping in front of a black door with the name *Dr. Finnegan Furst* emblazoned across it in glittering gold letters. The receptionist rested her hand on Eve's shoulder.

"Have a wonderful day," she simpered.

Eve felt her breath catch short. She lightly slid her fingers across the golden doorknob, almost scared to turn it, to find out what was on the other side. With a surge of conviction, she opened the door and stepped into Furst's office.

Furst was a small man—much smaller in person than he appeared in photos, Eve thought. He looked older, too, most likely in his early seventies, with a tired, round face and white hair that thinned toward the top of his skull. His attire, on the other hand, was fresh and dapper: he wore a rich brown suit, vibrant red tie, and glasses—it was so very strange to see someone wearing glasses these days—lined in gold with a designer emblem on either temple.

Eve waited patiently at the back of the room while Furst remained at his desk, looking over a stack of papers and ignoring her very obvious presence.

"You wanted to see me, Dr. Furst?"

Furst continued to skim through his documents without so much as a grunt in response, and so Eve stood in silence, waiting for something to happen. Just as she'd resorted to counting the tiles on the ceiling, the dean scribbled something on the last page of his never-ending pile of papers, pushed them to the side, and finally glanced over in her direction.

"Please, have a seat."

Eve awkwardly sat down in the burgundy leather chair in front of her, eyeing the line of awards and plaques that adorned Furst's desk.

"Am I in trouble?"

"Have you broken any campus rules?"

"Not to my knowledge."

"Then why would you be in any trouble?" He scowled at her over his glasses. "The truth is, Miss Kingston, I've called on you for a favor."

Eve's eyes widened with surprise. "A favor?"

"Yes." He began shuffling through more stacks of paperwork, avoiding direct eye contact with her. "You see, Miss Kingston, the world is an unfair place. It is full of lies, deception, and false promises, even from those with the best of intentions. This university, unfortunately, is no exception. We admit the brightest of the bright and promise to mold them into the leaders of tomorrow. But, well…" He put his papers down and looked up at her. "For some, that just won't be happening."

"What do you mean?"

"There are countless students roaming these halls who are more than qualified to be leaders. Visionaries. Innovators. They are gifted, driven, and extremely intelligent. They possess all the ingredients they need to lead this country and become legends—all ingredients but one."

"And what's that?"

"Connections." Furst pulled out a handkerchief and began cleaning his glasses. "All the knowledge and skills in the world are useless without the means to leverage them. Of course money helps, but truly, connections are imperative." He rested his glasses on his nose and glanced at Eve. "And that brings me to our second group of students at this fine university: the well-connected. They have at their fingertips all the power, money, and support they could ever need. Now, whether or not they are intelligent is beside the point. These students *will* become leaders, not because they're qualified, but because the path has already been paved for them. The hard work has been done by someone else: a mother, a grandfather, an uncle."

"You're right, that isn't fair," Eve said, crossing her arms.

"Yes, well, again, such is life. The fact remains that these well-connected students have greater odds of becoming not only successful, but monumental. And because the odds are in their favor, it is our job to make sure they become strong, cultivated individuals so they can be capable leaders. Do you understand?"

"Yeah, I get it. They're guaranteed the job, and you just have to make sure they don't suck at it."

Furst cocked his head and smirked. "What you lack in eloquence you make up for in brutal honesty."

"So, what does this have to do with me?"

"Ah, yes, the favor." He smiled. "You're aware of our campus attacks, yes?"

Eve sank lower into her chair. "Isn't this topic off limits—at least, for me?"

"Times have changed. Are you familiar with the victim of our most recent attack?"

"Oh, God." She winced as she recalled the scene. "I'm more than familiar. I was there when they brought him in. I saw him... I saw his insides, too, actually."

The dean fiddled with his pen, seemingly unaffected by the dark turn their conversation had taken. "His name is Jason Valentine, though I'm sure you know that by now. His father is a New York senator, so, as you can imagine, his abduction has received a great deal of attention." He paused for a moment and looked Eve straight in the eyes.

"I need you to tutor him."

Eve barely contained her laughter, completely taken aback by the dean's statement. "Wait—*what?*"

"All of the higher-ups here at the university have discussed the best course of action to take with Mr. Valentine, and it has been decided that you must tutor him."

Eve's face dropped as she realized that Furst was, indeed, serious.

"I'm sorry, I don't understand. He's a sophomore; I'm a freshman. I mean, we don't have any of the same classes—"

"You will not be tutoring him in his classes."

Furst paused and leaned in closer.

"You will be teaching him how to use his gift."

Eve's mouth hung open. In an instant, she felt her blood pumping through her veins like fire, heating her entire body and burning within her chest. Her fingers gripped the arms of her chair, her nails digging into the leather as she attempted to control her visible shock and anger. *This isn't happening,* she thought, though she knew it was a lie. After what felt like hours of silence, she took in a deep breath and finally managed to speak.

"*What* did you just say?"

"Jason Valentine is the son of a senator. There is a good chance that he will be a politician someday. With a path like that in front of him, it's very important that he not only understands his gift, but learns how to control it."

"How did you know about me?"

"We all know, Miss Kingston."

"Who's *we?*"

"The staff here at Billington University."

"How is that possible?"

"Applicants are screened for any potential items of interest. Being a chimera is obviously especially interesting to us."

"That—" Eve stuttered as she struggled to stifle her now boiling anger, "that is *none* of your business. There have to be laws against that—digging through peoples' history. That's an invasion of my *privacy.*"

The dean chuckled. "Privacy, ah, yes. I remember when that actually existed."

"All right." Eve finally released her grip on the chair. "So you know my whole damn story. Wonderful. What difference does it make to you?"

"My dear, how do you think you got *in* to this institution?"

"I graduated with the second-highest GPA at my high school. My college prep test scores were in the ninetieth percentile—"

"And we have rejected students with greater marks. Even those few who have been lucky enough to make it here on such credentials... well, they're certainly not living in Rutherford Hall."

"So you're telling me that I was accepted *just* because I'm a chimera?"

"Not just any chimera."

The dean remained emotionless as he held her gaze.

"You are the single most powerful chimera in the entire world."

Eve stared at him in disbelief. The rage seething within her drained away as she tried to make sense of what the dean was saying.

"What do you mean?"

"You harnessed your gift at a remarkably young age. Eight years old, correct? That is the earliest documented shift on the entire planet. And your abilities are sharper, more developed, more controlled than any other chimera that we've heard of. There are plenty of chimeras in this world, but no one quite like you, and that, my dear, is a fact."

"How," Eve stammered, "how do you know this?"

"The government has access to all types of data, and this is a government institution. We are kept well informed, especially with regard to our students. Receiving your application was quite a treat for us." Furst relaxed into his chair, looking pleased with Eve's obvious confusion. "Do you understand what this means? *You* are the best."

Eve sat in silence, overwhelmed by the range of emotions and questions that flooded her mind.

"You are much stronger than you realize."

"I know what I can do, okay?" Eve finally spoke, shooting a glare at the dean. "No one knows that better than I do."

"I don't doubt that. And that is exactly why you must tutor Mr. Valentine."

Eve shook her head and sighed. "This is unbelievable."

"You will tutor him five days a week, Monday through Friday. If he is slow to catch on, we will increase it to six. Possibly even seven."

"Wait, do I not have a choice?"

"No, my dear. I'm afraid you do not."

"You have no *right* to force me—"

"If you're worried about your schoolwork suffering, I can assure you that that will not be a problem," Furst interrupted. "Your professors are fully aware of this arrangement. They will make special accommodations for you to ensure that your tutoring duties remain a top priority. If that means you must miss a few classes here and there, then so be it. You will not be penalized."

"Don't you think people will start to notice? Won't people wonder why *I'm* the one tutoring this Jason guy?" Eve picked at her cuticles nervously. "People are going to know something's up. I've been harassed my whole life for being who I am. You're just going to go ahead and put me on the radar like this?"

"It is a risk you must take for the good of—"

"The good of what? Your reputation? Your relationship with some New York senator?"

Frustrated, the dean sighed. "You *will* tutor Mr. Valentine. And we will make the process as comfortable for you as possible."

Even though she'd just learned that she was the strongest chimera in the world, Eve felt completely powerless. She had envisioned her college years as a time for her to take control of her destiny—and yet all her control had been wrested away from her in an instant.

A thought came to her mind.

"What's in it for me?"

"Pardon?"

"You can't possibly expect me to do this for nothing in return. There has to be some type of payoff."

"Ah, yes. You are a very smart girl." The dean pulled out yet another stack of papers and began flipping through them. "You're here on a scholarship, correct?"

"Yes."

"And what does that scholarship cover?"

"My freshman year," she answered.

"And how do you intend to pay for the remainder of your education?"

Eve hesitated. "I don't know. I was going to get a job, I guess."

"An after-school job? How quaint." The dean messily jotted down notes as he spoke. "This favor you provide for the university will not go unrewarded, despite the protest of some of our professors here."

"Wait, who?"

"Miss Kingston," Furst continued, "assuming you honor your commitment to Mr. Valentine, the tuition for your sophomore, junior, and senior years here will be covered. Consider this tutoring job a means to graduate."

Eve was silent. She tried to comprehend Furst's claims, both the good and the bad: that she was incomparably powerful, that she was now forced into a job she didn't want, that that very job would pay her way through school. It was all too much to digest at once, and though she tried to speak, she couldn't seem to find the words she was looking for, or any words at all.

"Now, we are willing to cover your next three years, nothing more. That means no messing about—none of this second- or third-year senior nonsense. You *will* graduate in four years. Any additional semesters spent at this university will have to be paid for out of your own pocket."

Eve stuttered, finally breaking her silence. "I—I can't believe this."

"Yes, well, I'm glad you find the terms suitable."

"I'm still pissed that you invaded my privacy."

The dean chuckled. "You *are* a stubborn one." He handed Eve a small plastic ID badge. "This will give you access to the medical ward. Your tutoring sessions start tomorrow."

"Wait, doesn't he need more time to recover? He's only been in the hospital for a week."

Furst shook his head in disagreement. "The staff at the medical ward says that his has been the most miraculous recovery they have ever seen. His wounds practically mended themselves. Nine days is more than enough time for a chimera to regain his strength. *You* of all people should know this."

***

Tuesday morning crept up on Eve like a predator stalking its prey. It had arrived wearing a cloak of dismal tedium, but Eve knew the monotony was just a façade. She tried to behave as if it were any other morning—she muttered obscenities under her breath at the sound of her horrid alarm and faked an air of camaraderie with Madison and Hayden as they sat through Leadership Principles—but Eve knew that it would be anything but a normal, boring day for her. She had a new job to attend to and an unwanted student to meet.

Eve reluctantly headed for Business Mathematics, dreading the class almost as much as her upcoming tutoring duties. She cautiously tiptoed to a desk toward the back corner of the lecture hall, her eyes frantically scanning the room in search of the very conspicuous Professor Richards, though he was nowhere to be found. His name alone made her grimace, and after their brief interaction the day before, she was determined to make her presence as unnoticeable as possible.

A loud boom thundered in front of her, and she flinched. She looked up to see a large stack of papers sitting on her desk and a pasty hand resting atop the mound—the hand of Dr. Richards.

"Test time," he growled. "We do 'em old-fashioned in my class, with pencil and paper, no scratchpads. Less cheating this way." He folded his arms and snarled. "Pass 'em down, *Kingston*."

The class groaned in unanimous dread at the first unannounced test of the semester, but Eve had other, more complicated anxieties: the way Richards had looked at her, with his furrowed brow and death gaze; the way he'd said her name, as if the taste of sewage lingered on his lips. His actions spoke volumes, and what they said left her with a sinking feeling in the pit of her stomach.

Eve read and reread the first question of her exam: *A finite random variable X has the following probability of Professor Richards hating you.* She stopped—her mind was playing tricks on her, and so she read it again, this time correctly, and scribbled her work across the page. She had to focus; focus was key, and yet it seemed nearly impossible. Her eyes wandered up to Richards—he was staring right at her, and she quickly looked back down at her test once more.

The slight click of the classroom door opening sent the entire room in a stir. Out of the corner of her eye, she saw a boy—the same shaggy-haired boy from Gupta's class the day prior—scamper toward Richards, his fingers clasped around a small piece of paper. Richards snatched the slip from his hand and read over it, then let out a long, irritated sigh as he dropped his arm to his side.

"*Kingston*, come to the front of the class."

Eve cringed. The time had come: her moment of dread, the beginning of her karmic punishment. She rose from her seat and made her way down the lecture hall stairs, dragging her feet like heavy bricks. Each step was punctuated with hushed whispers and wide-eyed glances from her curious classmates, all of whom suddenly knew her name, unfortunately. The whole scene was déjà vu, an all too familiar experience extracted from the timeline of her life, and all she wanted was for it to end. She wanted to find herself lying in bed, waking from another dream, but as she stood in front of Dr. Dick, she knew without a doubt that this was real.

"You've been summoned to the medical ward."

"Oh," Eve mumbled, her eyes darting back and forth between her murmuring classmates and the professor. "But, my test..."

"Right, your test. Looks like you won't be able to finish that, huh?"

Eve lowered her head. *Shit*, she thought to herself. *He's going to fail me.*

"Is that it?" Richards asked, pointing to the crinkled packet in Eve's hand. "Yes, but—"

Richards snatched the papers from her grip and scanned over her formulas.

"Mr. Richards—"

"*DOCTOR* Richards," he barked. A few of her classmates chuckled, and

Eve felt as if she could die right there in the middle of the classroom.

"*Doctor* Richards, I only got through the first three questions..."

"Really? Three? Then I guess I'll just have to grade what you have here."

Eve winced as the professor's red pen streaked across her paper like blood. She was about to fail the test, and that would surely signal the beginning of her failing the entire class. She shut her eyes tightly as Dr. Dick slapped her test down onto his desk.

"Well, look at that! You got a hundred percent!"

Her eyes snapped open and shot down toward her test: all three questions were marked with obnoxious, sloppy stars, and a giant A-plus was written across the top of the page.

"But, I didn't finish—"

"I graded you based on what you provided here for me: three out of three, Kingston. You do the math—you *can* do math, right, Kingston? After all, you did the math correctly for these first three problems."

Eve stared at the professor in shock. Was she wrong about him? Rather, was the entire school wrong about him? Was the *Dr. Dick* persona just a front?

"Hey, that's not fair!" one of her classmates yelled from the back of the room, causing the other students to angrily chime in. Richards grinned sadistically.

"I'm *so* sorry class, but unfortunately, my hands are tied. There's not much I can do about a student who requires *special treatment*."

He handed the test to Eve and shrugged innocently at her classmates. Suddenly, his intentions were more than clear. The rumors were true, and Dr. Dick was going to torture her in the most creative way possible.

"Well, Kingston, thanks to your *unique* situation, you may be the very first student to ever receive an 'A' in my class." He tucked his pen back into his shirt pocket and shot a glare in her direction. "I hope you're proud of yourself."

"I'm going to destroy the curve," she muttered. "They're all going to fail because of me."

"All conveniences come with a price. You should never feel entitled, Kingston. That's a horrible trait."

Richards turned away and began flipping through the papers in his brief-case. Eve looked over at her classmates, all of whom scowled back at her. Without hesitation, she dashed out of the classroom, eager to escape what felt like a witch hunt led by the infamously intolerant Dr. Dick.

Sunshine poured across Eve's shoulders as she burst through the doors of the business building, though the warmth and solitude were small consolation for the embarrassment she had just endured. She forced herself to concentrate on the task at hand: her tutoring session with Jason, the son of a senator, tenth in line to being Madison's unfortunate groom, and now the proverbial thorn in Eve's side. She plodded along the pathway at a glacial pace, delaying her inevitable fate for as long as possible. Unfortunately, the medical ward was only a few yards in front of her.

She took a deep breath as she walked through the doors of the ward, the smell of hydrogen peroxide invading her nostrils until it stung ever so slightly. The lobby was still and nearly empty. Eve blinked once, and instead of the present blandness, she saw uniformed patrolmen and blood-soaked paramedics hauling Jason's stretcher past a crowd of onlookers. She saw Jason's shaking body, his carved-open chest, his lungs expanding and contracting, and then she heard his blood-curdling scream.

She blinked again, and once more the lobby was calm and banal, free from any hint of chaos.

Eve made her way to the elevators and watched the doors close in front of her. Jason was waiting for her on the fifth floor in the isolation wing—a separate, secure unit for high-profile patients. She looked down at her ID badge; the palm-sized card was her key to the wing, and for a moment she considered dropping it down the elevator shaft. Was it wrong of her to feel this way—to feel so inconvenienced by Jason, by Dean Furst, by her newfound status as the strongest chimera in the world? She was getting a free ride through college out of the deal, and yet the entire scenario troubled her. Too many people knew who she was; more than ever, she realized that anonymity was all she truly longed for.

The elevator doors opened, and Eve immediately recognized her destination. The isolation wing was visible down the hallway, marked by a very tall, very large security guard who stood menacingly in front of a massive door. To the right of the guard, tucked away in the corner, was a small clerk's desk, and sitting at that desk was a familiar and unwelcome face.

"Eve, darling!" Heather squealed, skipping toward her.

"Heather!" Eve gasped, her surprise obvious. "What are you doing here?"

"I should be asking you the same thing, silly! I told you I'd be volunteering here."

"Oh, that's right," Eve mumbled. How could she have forgotten?

"I specifically asked for this desk, right in front of the isolation wing. It's kind of the crème de la crème of locations, don'tcha think?"

Eve sighed; the school vulture now had the perfect perch from which to observe her comings and goings five days out of the week.

"It's fantastic, I'm sure."

"So, you still haven't told me."

"Told you what?"

"Why you're here."

"Oh." Eve faltered, racking her brain for a good lie and then finally settling on a mediocre one. "I'm thinking about volunteering here, too."

"How exciting! You and I will get to work together! I can show you the ropes!" She grabbed Eve's hand and held it tightly. "But, what are you doing on this floor?"

Eve smiled nervously. "Just taking a tour. Trying to get a feel for the place."

"Then by all means, let *me* show you around."

"That's not necessary—"

"But I *insist*—"

"Heather," Eve interrupted, taking a step closer to the wing, "I'm actually almost done here. Just got one more place to check out."

Heather looked over her shoulder. "What, the isolation wing? No one will let you in there," she snorted matter-of-factly.

"I think I'll take my chances."

"You have to have a—" Heather stopped short as she looked down at Eve's hands. "Oh, you have a badge. How'd you get that?"

"What, they didn't give *you* a badge?" Eve took another step backward, slowly inching her way toward the wing. "I thought they gave these things to everyone."

"No, they don't. They're actually *extremely* hard to come by. You have to be important, or..." She paused. "*Special.*"

"Is that so?" Eve asked cynically. "I've never been special before. Guess I should be flattered." She nodded her head toward the wing. "Look, I'd love to chat, but I've got some touring to do."

Eve turned to face the guard; he was almost a foot taller than her, and three, maybe four times as wide, and yet his hulking figure was a much more welcome sight than Heather's critical sneer. She waited impatiently as he ran her badge through the reader, then promptly unlocked the door beside him. "Proceed," he commanded.

Eve took one last look at Heather. She was standing in the middle of the hallway, her arms crossed and head cocked, and she smiled the same devious smile she had worn so many times before. As the door slowly closed, Heather craned her neck, eager to get a glimpse of the isolation wing, until the door sealed shut, locking Eve in like a prisoner.

Eve examined her new surroundings: though hidden from view, the isolation wing looked like every other wing of the hospital. A few nurses weaved in and out of the various rooms, although a couple stopped and stared at her, their brows wrinkled as if the presence of a visitor was unusual—and, indeed, it probably was. Eve quickened her pace, searching for Jason's room, and found it much sooner than she had hoped to. With a deep breath, she opened the door and stepped inside.

It was the largest hospital room Eve had ever seen, and yet it was also so bleak and depressing. Despite the obvious similarities to any other hospital room, the special touches were plentiful, if hardly helpful in softening the dismal ambiance. A large HV adorned the wall beside the door, though it appeared dusty and stagnant as if it had never been touched. A compact refrigerator sat in the corner next to a long desk covered in wilting flower arrangements and uneaten fruit baskets. Piles of gifts were scattered beside an old folding chair, but the shimmery paper and bows couldn't counteract the darkness that permeated the room. The blinds were drawn low, most likely for privacy purposes, or so Eve told herself, and her eyes strained to adjust to the dimness. Next to one window was a stack of medical equipment, and even it seemed sad and lonely as if begging to be needed—but alas its cords hung lifelessly, dangling across the floor. Finally, Eve saw the large, cushy hospital bed, and in that bed sat Jason Valentine.

Jason remained stoic as Eve closed the door behind her. He stared at the wall, his face expressionless aside from a slightly furrowed brow and clenched jaw. His chest was bare, exposing his grisly T-shaped dissection scar. Thick staples covered the red, puffy incision line that stretched across the top of his chest and down between his ribs, ending directly above his navel.

"What do you want?" he finally spoke, his body still motionless.

"Excuse me?"

"A quote? An interview?" His eyes remained fixed on the wall. "A photo?"

"I think you have the wrong idea..."

"I thought you people weren't allowed in here."

"Jason," Eve answered, slowly stepping forward, "I'm not a reporter, or a stalker, or whoever else you're thinking of. I'm your tutor." She paused. "Did no one tell you I was coming?"

He finally looked at her; he had deep brown eyes, just like Eve, and his face was stubbly from lack of maintenance.

"Tutor?" He nodded at a scratchpad on his desk. "Someone already uploaded my homework for the next month. No one said anything about a tutor."

"So, they didn't tell you." She sighed and shook her head. "Of course."

"Look, I know the higher-ups here love to advocate hand-holding, but I think I'm capable of studying by myself."

"I'm not that kind of tutor, Jason."

"Then what kind of tutor are you?"

Eve locked eyes with Jason; she held his gaze but concentrated her mind on the right side of the room. She remembered seeing a small gift sitting by the folding chair, one covered in shiny, royal blue paper with a glittery white bow. The image of the gift pulsated in her brain, meshing into the corners of her mind until it consumed her. Within seconds, she was ready; she folded her arms and watched as the gift delicately floated up from the floor and glided through the room, gently landing on Jason's lap.

"I'm here to teach you how to use your gift."

Jason stared blankly at the present. His entire body was still, his limbs limp at his sides and his neck bent forward. Finally, he looked up at Eve.

"Is this some kind of *joke*?"

Eve was taken aback. "What do you mean?"

Jason flung the gift onto the floor and buried his face in his palms, sifting his fingers through his unkempt hair. With a deep breath, he lifted his head and shot Eve a scathing glare, his entire body suddenly emanating a palpable anger.

"I was attacked a few days ago. By *ALIENS*. And this school thinks they can just patch me up"—he pointed at his scar—"good as new, and then *train* me to use the very powers that put me on that table in the first place?"

Eve's eyes widened with shock. "What you experienced... no one should have to go through that. I know it sucks—"

"It *sucks*?" he spat. "Finals suck. Blind dates suck. I was *dissected*." He closed his eyes and grimaced. "I felt *everything*."

"Jason, I'm sorry—"

"Like hell you are! You don't *know* me. You're just here doing the school's dirty work. It's *pathetic*."

Eve stammered in disbelief. "I... I just—"

"And now what? I'm just supposed to forget that I was nearly killed and *embrace* this whole thing?" He shook his head, his lips curled with disgust. "This *gift* that I didn't even know I have, and now I'm stuck with. Tell me, why exactly do they call it a 'gift'? 'Cause if you ask me, it feels a hell of a lot like a *curse*."

"A *curse?*" It was Eve's turn to raise her voice, her words dripping with offense. "What the *hell* is your problem?"

Jason raised his eyebrows. "*Excuse* me?"

"You've suffered, I get that. But all that angst you're feeling right now— that's *your* issue, not mine. And it doesn't give you the right to be a *dick*."

"Are you *serious* right now?"

"Look, Jason, do you think I *want* to be here? I didn't sign up for this burden."

"Your life must be *so* hard—"

"Says the poor little rich boy with his mountain of *presents*." She cocked her head toward his gifts. "Am I really supposed to pity you?"

Jason's chest heaved with each livid breath he took, and he squeezed his fists tightly. "So, that's what you see when you look at me: my parents' money."

Eve ignored his retort. "You know, without that awful *curse* you seem to hate, you wouldn't be alive right now. Did you ever think about that?"

"Are you really telling me I should be *happy* that this happened?"

"I'm telling you to appreciate your power."

Jason laughed sarcastically. "Okay, sure. I've changed my mind. I *appreciate* my gift. I'm perfectly fine with my skin being sliced open by Interlopers. I'm happy that the whole entire world is going to *hate* me from this point forward—"

"Oh, so *that's* what this is about. It's just a popularity contest to you."

"A popularity contest? *Seriously*? Look, when a vast majority of an entire planet fears you, that's a lot worse than simply being *unpopular*."

"So, basically you're scared?"

Jason clenched his jaw. "*Scared?*"

"Scared of what others think. Scared to fulfill your potential." She crossed her arms and smirked. "Scared to be different."

"Oh, *God*—"

"You don't even realize how lucky you are!" She pointed at the blue present on the ground. "What I did there? That isn't easy. It takes a *lot* of practice. I had to learn all of that on my own, just like every other chimera, but *you* get a tutor. And you're *upset* about it?" She rolled her eyes. "You're unbelievable."

"All right, I'm done with this conversation."

"Great," Eve yanked her shoulder bag off of the floor and flung it over her arm, "because I was just leaving." She strutted toward the door with her head held high and tugged at the doorknob, more than eager to be rid of her defiant protégé. But before she slammed the door behind her, she turned to take one last look at Jason.

"And by the way, since you didn't bother to ask, my name is Eve. It was an absolute *pleasure* to meet you."

CHAPTER 4: SNOW GLOBE

A heavy fog loomed over Eve, weighing on her chest and pushing her deep into the weak springs of her mattress. This morning felt unlike the rest; she reflected on her brief time at Billington and became consumed with disappointment. Her wish to escape—to rid herself of her demons, to be someone, anyone other than a chimera—had been compromised a mere two weeks into her first semester. Instead of the invisible, unnamed human she'd wanted to be, she was now the strongest chimera in the world, not to mention teacher to an unwilling student. *This isn't how it's supposed to be*, she thought to herself. Nothing was going as planned.

There was no need for self-pity though—and she was too proud for such emotions anyway. She fiddled with her tweed skirt as she waited for Madison, who was sitting in front of her vanity, brushing her golden locks over and over again.

Madison set her brush down with a huff. "I guess this will have to do."

"You look fine."

"*Fine* is for ugly girls," Madison pouted, stomping out of their dorm room like a sulking child.

Eve locked the door behind her and joined her roommate in the corridor. As they ventured through the narrow hallway, she felt eyes following her. Everyone she crossed caught her gaze, their stares as scathing as laser beams. She kept her chin low and hoped Madison wouldn't notice.

"God, my hair must look worse than I thought. Everyone's staring at me."

Eve sighed; Madison *had* noticed.

"They're not staring at you, Maddie."

Eve turned around to see Hayden, looking so demure in her pastel blue shirt-dress, shuffling toward them.

"They're staring at Eve."

Madison raised a single eyebrow. "Eve? Do tell."

Eve shrugged uncomfortably. "I don't know why they're looking at me."

"Rumor has it that Eve was spotted in the medical ward yesterday."

"So?" Madison sighed. "Are you sick or something? If you're contagious, you are *not* sleeping in our room tonight."

"She was visiting the isolation wing," Hayden added, struggling to keep up with the two girls.

"Isolation what? This story is getting really boring, *really* fast."

"Only *important* people are admitted to the isolation wing. High-profilers. People with power. People with *money—*"

Madison stopped in the middle of the hallway, her mouth gaping in shock. "Eve! Is this true?"

Hayden flashed a victorious smile. "*And* she had a special ID badge and everything! They just let her in!"

"I think you've said enough, Hayden," Eve muttered.

"And when she left, she looked *pissed*. Like, *really* pissed."

"How the hell do you even *know* this?" Eve spat.

Hayden shot her a dirty look and wiggled her nose. "Heather McLeod told me. She told *everyone*."

Of course she did, Eve thought to herself. She held her breath and closed her eyes—the gossip was already spreading, just as she'd suspected it would.

"Eve!" Madison squealed. "Why didn't you tell me about this? I thought we were best friends?"

"I thought *I* was your—"

"Shut up, Hayden," Madison snapped. She turned back to Eve. "It's, like, the number one rule of friendship. We tell each other *everything*. Now, spit it out!"

"Spit *what* out?"

"Who were you seeing in the ward?"

Eve paused. "Family?"

Madison laughed. "Get real, Eve. If you expect me to believe that someone *you're* related to is in the isolation wing, you're seriously disturbed. I've *seen* your clothes; they reek of bargain-bin poverty."

Eve sighed. "There's nothing to tell. I was thinking about volunteering there. They gave me an ID badge so I could take a tour. That's all that happened."

Madison rolled her eyes. "Okay, Eve, number one: ew. Volunteering is for slopholes. Number two: I can spot a liar a mile away, and your pants are definitely on fire."

"Yeah, *Eve*." Hayden grinned with delight at the mess she had created. "*Liar.*"

"Ladies, it really isn't as big of a deal as it seems."

"If that's the case, you shouldn't have a problem telling us."

"The story is dull, at best."

"Then just tell us who you *know*."

"I hardly *know* him at all—"

Madison gasped and wildly smacked Eve across the arm. "So you admit it!"

Eve grimaced—she had said too much.

"It's a *he*, too," Hayden chimed in.

"You're not a high-end escort, are you?"

Eve flared her nostrils. "I'm going to pretend you didn't just ask me that."

"Is he cute? He's obviously rich, but *cute* rich boys are hard to come by."

"Madison, it's a school thing." Eve hurried her stride as she made her way up the steps of the business building. "I told you, it's volunteer work. Nothing more."

Class was already in session, and Eve cringed as the other students turned and watched them take their usual seats in the back of the room. She wondered: did they stare because of their late interruption, or had news of her medical ward visit spread past the confines of Rutherford Hall?

"You know," Madison whispered, not easily deterred, "if it's really so unimportant, you wouldn't mind giving me every teeny, tiny detail, right?"

Eve growled under her breath. She had always considered herself an honest person—too honest, most of the time—yet with her newfound desire to remain unknown came the endless fictions that spewed from her now duplicitous lips. She hated that about herself.

"Madison, I already told you everything you need to know."

Madison's face dropped into a scowl. "I don't believe you. You're hiding something."

Eve glared back at the girl—she couldn't help herself—and lowered her voice to an authoritative whisper. "It's not a big deal, Madison. Let it go."

Suddenly, the classroom door opened, and Eve cursed aloud and hung her head in defeat. She knew exactly what would happen next, and she closed her eyes, hoping that her blackened vision would transport her somewhere far away.

"Eve Kingston?" Professor Clarke said.

She opened her eyes. The skinny messenger boy was standing beside the professor at the front of the class.

"Eve," Clarke beckoned her with his index finger. "You've got a message from the medical ward."

Reluctantly, Eve packed up her things as Madison chuckled to herself.

"Not a big deal, huh?" the heiress smirked.

Just as Eve stood from her seat, Madison grabbed her wrist.

"Tonight, you're going to tell me *everything*."

Eve ripped her arm from Madison's grasp and plodded toward the front of the classroom, her demeanor as enthusiastic as that of a rotting corpse. Professor Clarke flashed her a sympathetic smile.

"You've been summoned for jury duty," he snickered. "I'm just kidding, that was a bad joke. It's time for your tutoring session."

Eve grumbled, "Wonderful."

"I'll have my TA forward the rest of the lecture to your scratchpad, okay?"

Eve smiled. Clarke seemed so kind—so unlike Dr. Dick.

"Thanks for being so understanding about this whole thing."

The professor patted her lightly on the back. "Hang in there."

Without the slightest sense of urgency, Eve left the classroom. She didn't take a second look back at her peers, knowing they were probably already concocting new rumors about her. As she walked through the hallway and out of the building, she heard the cumbersome clomping of feet running behind her.

"Miss Kingston! Eve, wait!"

The messenger boy was jogging toward her, his arms flailing as he scurried to her side. Eve looked down—she could tell that even had she taken her heels off, he still would've been much shorter than her, though his gangly build told her that he still had a lot of growing to do. A mane of coarse black hair covered his head, matching his two thick eyebrows, and his clothes hung loosely over his small figure.

"Sorry," he panted. "I'm supposed to walk you to the ward."

"Walk me? Why? I know where it is."

"You left early yesterday. I guess they weren't sure if you'd show up today."

"Jesus," Eve groaned. "So you're my babysitter, basically?"

"Sort of. I guess."

They walked together in silence. Eve listened to the sound of her heels clicking against the pathway, and her new supervisor stared at the ground with his hands behind his back.

"So, what's your name?" Eve asked, eager to end the awkward quiet.

"Armaan Tavana."

"Do you work at the medical ward?"

"Yeah." He kept his eyes down. "Volunteering there looks good when you apply for medical school."

Eve eyed her new companion and smirked. "You look a little young to be prepping for med school."

"I'm seventeen."

"Damn. Seventeen years old and already a freshman at Billington?"

Armaan hesitated. "I'm a junior."

Eve laughed. "Wow, now *that's* impressive."

The boy shoved his hands into his pockets and sighed. "Impressive, maybe, but it doesn't matter. No one sees me. I'm too quiet, too small." He stopped for a second. "Not sure why I just told you that."

Eve smiled. "Well, I can see you just fine."

Armaan blushed but didn't respond.

"So you're going to be a doctor?"

"That's the plan."

"What field?"

He bowed his head even lower. "Humanovus General Medicine. You know... for chimeras."

"...Oh."

Again, the pair became silent. Eve anxiously picked at her cuticles and sighed. *Oh hell*, she thought to herself. She finally spoke.

"You know I'm—"

"A chimera? I kind of figured."

In an instant, her entire body became tense. She listened to the steady sound of her breathing, avoiding eye contact with the boy for as long as she could manage.

"I don't care." He raised his chin, finally looking her in the eye. "I mean, it doesn't bother me."

Her shoulders relaxed, and she exhaled. "Thanks, Armaan."

"I think you guys are pretty dynamic, actually, especially your gift." His eyes darted from side to side before he continued. "I'd *kill* to see it in action."

"Is that a hint?"

"Well, if you don't mind," Armaan whispered. He looked around—a few students were sitting in the courtyard studying, but most were at the dormitories or still in class, nowhere to be seen. "I know it's sort of personal and intruding, but you don't have to do anything huge. Just do something, I don't know, subtle. Please?"

Absolutely not. That's what she should've said, but instead she said nothing. She glanced at the path ahead and spied a single feather resting only a few feet away. Disregarding her reservations, she let her mind drift and sent the feather spiraling upward as if caught by the light breeze, though the two of them knew otherwise. The feather danced in the air, looping back and forth like a car on a tiny roller coaster, then gently landed in the palm of Armaan's now trembling hand.

Armaan laughed and gasped in awe. "That was *so* dynamic!" he yelped, his eyes filled with excitement. "You totally just made my day!"

Eve gave him a wink. "It'll be our secret."

"Oh, don't worry, I won't tell anyone."

The nervous tension between the two softened as they made their way through the medical ward. Had Eve found an unlikely ally? Possibly, though even so, she could hardly believe she had mustered the gall to gift in front of him, much less in a public setting. It was foolish and in poor taste, but she smiled to herself, pleased with her own brazen behavior. Armaan wasn't so bad—he was a fan of her kind, and that alone made him someone worth knowing, at least to Eve.

As they exited the elevators, Eve glanced nervously at the clerk's desk—Heather was nowhere to be found, and she breathed a sigh of relief. Armaan walked her to the door of the isolation wing and stopped in front of the large security guard.

"Well, this is where I leave you." He shook her hand vigorously, all the while keeping one apprehensive eye on the guard. "Don't leave early this time."

Eve waved goodbye and scurried into the isolation wing, staring down the long hallway as if it were the passageway to a menacing labyrinth. She suddenly felt ill—it was the dread of the unknown, the anticipation of how Jason would be receiving her this day. She reached his room and stopped; a nurse walking down the hallway watched as Eve stared at the door in front of her.

"Need any help, dear?" she asked.

"Got any sedatives?" Eve muttered. The nurse looked confused and Eve forced a smile. "Just kidding." She held her breath and, with one final surge of courage, opened the door.

The room was dimly lit and overwhelmingly depressing—again. Jason was sitting in his bed as he had been yesterday; his hair was still disheveled and his face prickly to match his attitude. Eve glanced at the staples protruding from his chest and quickly looked away.

"Hey," she mumbled, setting her shoulder bag on the floor. "Ready to learn?"

Jason didn't respond.

She slid the folding chair across the room and sat it next to Jason's bed. "Want to get started?"

Still he was silent.

"Look, I can't leave until we make some progress, so you're stuck with me."

He sighed and ran his fingers through his hair. "Fine. Let's get this over with."

Eve sat down and fiddled with her cuticles. "Honestly, I don't really know what I'm doing. I've never tutored anyone before." She looked up at Jason, and their eyes met. "Have you used your gift at all yet?"

"No." He looked away. "Just that day, in the lobby downstairs..."

"Your emergence?"

"*Emergence?*"

"The development of your gift." She recalled her own experience—the crash, the truck bolting into the sky and back down to the pavement—and shuddered. "It's terrible, really—like a surge of power you can't control." She looked back at Jason. "Do you remember anything from that moment? A rush of energy? Blackened vision? The worst damn headache of your life?"

"Sounds about right," he muttered.

"You're twenty, right? That's around the prime age to go through emergence, but it looks like your"—she hesitated, glancing at his scar—"*trauma* set it in motion."

"One of the nurses told me what I did—that I sent people flying across the room." He grimaced. "It's *sick*."

"It's not so bad, actually, if you look at the bright side at least."

"*Bright* side?"

"Moving people is difficult—*really* difficult, actually. Such a powerful onset of emergence usually means you have a pretty strong gift."

Jason grumbled under his breath, unimpressed. Knowing her day was about to get increasingly more difficult, Eve exhaled loudly and relaxed her shoulders.

"Okay, let's get started."

Her eyes scanned the room. She was looking for something small, but not too small, as a tiny object would be tricky to maneuver. However, if an object was too large and bulky, the weight alone made it hard to levitate. She needed something just right, like an apple, or—she paused and spotted a small snow globe sitting among Jason's presents. She felt her mind liquefy, and the snow globe gracefully popped off of the table and onto Jason's lap.

"You're going to pass that snow globe to me."

Jason grabbed the snow globe and studied it, running his fingers over the smooth surface. He looked back at her. "How am I supposed to do that?"

"You have to relax—not your body, but your mind." She flicked her wrist and sent the globe shooting from Jason's grip and into her hands. "It's called melting. Some people call it softening or dissolving, it's all the same. Your mind drifts into a state of freedom. Once you get really good at it," she paused as the globe floated up from her hands and into the air, "you'll be able to do it without even trying."

"So, how do I know if I'm melting?"

"You can see it, sort of like you're watching your brain through some type of third eye." The globe hovered in the air, and she closed her eyes. "I see darkness."

"*Everyone* sees darkness when they close their eyes."

"This is different. It's as if the black is pulsing and then," she stopped, sending the globe soaring toward Jason, "it starts to cascade downward, sort of like sand in an hourglass or water flowing from a faucet." The globe lingered in front of Jason for a moment and then plopped onto his lap. "And then it stops when I want it to stop."

"Very poetic," he jeered.

"I could do without the snarky commentary, thanks."

Jason ignored her retort and stared at the snow globe in front of him. "What do I do once I start melting?"

"Just envision the snow globe doing exactly what you want it to do. Navigate its movement with your thoughts."

"Sounds easy enough."

"You'd be surprised," she countered. "If your mind wanders, it'll change the path of whatever you're trying to manipulate. You need to think about the snow globe and nothing else, and you need to see it moving from your lap to mine."

Jason was quiet, focusing his gaze on the snow globe as he tried his best to melt. Nothing happened. Again, he took in a long, deep breath and centered his eyes on the globe, his stare intense and determined. Still it sat on his sheets, completely motionless. He sighed with annoyance and scowled at Eve.

She nodded. "Again."

He rolled his eyes and turned once more to the snow globe, glaring at it as if it were a palm-sized adversary. The globe didn't move, and Jason held his breath and squinted his eyes, straining to focus on his uncooperative assignment.

"You're trying too hard."

"I'm *trying* to concentrate."

"You're going to hurt yourself," Eve scolded. "You can't overdo it. You need to relax—"

"How can I *relax*?" he spat, angrily.

"Just let it happen. Just try again."

Jason cursed to himself, shaking his head as he prepared for his next attempt. A few seconds passed, and this time Eve saw his shoulders become limp and his eyelids grow heavy; he was melting, she was sure of it. The snow globe suddenly twitched in his lap, teetering awkwardly, then slowly floated up from the bed. Eve's heart raced as she watched the globe jerk and convulse in the air, staggering toward her until it stopped just a couple of feet in front of her face. She was puzzled; she looked at the snow globe, which trembled in place, and then at Jason. His breathing was rapid, his eyes clenched shut, and she immediately knew that something was wrong. The globe began to shake vigorously as his breathing intensified, sending the white flecks swirling through the glass orb like a turbulent blizzard. She knew what was happening—and she had to think fast. Without a second to spare, she ducked her head—just as the snow globe shot toward her like a glass bullet and hurtled across the room, plowing right through a framed picture on the table before smashing against the wall, sending glass and water flying everywhere.

"*What the hell was that?*" Eve yelled, jumping up from her seat and storming toward the shattered glass. "Were you trying to *kill* me?"

"It was an accident—"

"That thing almost hit me in the face!" She picked up the picture frame, which was now mangled and deformed. "*This* could have been my face!"

"I'm *sorry!*" he shouted. "I swear, I didn't mean to. I'm still learning!"

"Well, you seemed like you knew *exactly* what you were doing."

"I wasn't trying to hurt you."

"Then what *were* you trying to do? What were you thinking about? Because you certainly weren't thinking about what we discussed."

Jason faltered. "I don't know."

"You're lying."

"I *don't know*," he shot back, his eyes filled with anger.

Eve folded her arms and glowered. "Look, you're going to be seeing me for a very long time, and if we're going to get along, you have to be honest with me."

Jason paused and looked down at his hands. "I don't know."

"Bullshit."

"*I was thinking about my parents!*" he barked suddenly.

Eve looked at the mutilated picture frame in her hand and brushed away the broken bits of glass. It was a photo of Jason and an older man and woman at his high school graduation. The man beside him had the same nose and jaw as Jason, while the woman had his large, brown eyes, and Eve quickly realized that this was a photo of him with his parents.

"So, you have a problem with your parents?"

"I'm not talking about this."

"Look, I don't care if you hate your folks." She tossed the photo in the trash can and sat in her seat. "That's your deal. But don't put me in harm's way just because you have some petty beef with them. And the next time your parents stop by—"

"There won't be a next time."

"Oh, quit with the *dramatics*—"

"They've *never* been here," Jason snapped. "They're *not* coming. Not ever."

Eve stopped; she stared back at Jason, all the while struggling to comprehend his words. She must have misheard him—there was no other explanation—and yet the shameful look on his face told her otherwise. After all, the scenario was common: an outed chimera abandoned by all, including his own family.

Jason looked away self-consciously, his face red with embarrassment.

"What did you say?"

"Don't worry about it."

"You're in the *hospital—*"

"I *said,* don't worry about it."

"You were nearly killed," she continued, ignoring his command. "You were *dissected by Interlopers.* And your parents haven't come to see you? Not once?"

Jason's body became tense, as if her words were punches being thrown at his chest. "Pretty much."

"Why?"

Jason finally looked at her. His body remained rigid and defensive, but his eyes now appeared soft and kind, as if something about him, however slight, had changed.

"My dad's a senator. He ran a predominantly anti-chimera campaign." His nostrils flared with repugnance. "It doesn't look good for him to have a chimera son."

"So, what—that's it? They're just going to pretend that none of this ever happened?"

"It looks that way."

The air in the room suddenly felt thick and heated. An intense resentment emanated from Jason, filling the empty space and creating a palpable tension. Eve felt it too—the anger, the scorn. It was personal to her, because Jason was one of *her* kind, and through that, if that alone, they were connected.

"Wow." She furrowed her brow. "Your parents are assholes."

Jason's eyes suddenly darted toward her. "Excuse me?"

"They're *assholes,*" she repeated, this time much more firmly. "Frankly, they're probably doing you a favor, not coming here. I bet they're really awful to be around. They sound like it, at least."

Jason stared at her in silence. His eyes widened and his lips parted as if to speak, but he said nothing. Finally, after a moment of debilitation, he broke into a small fit of laughter.

"What's so funny?"

"You know, most people just say, 'Hang in there,' or 'They'll come around.'"

"Why would I say that?" she scoffed. "If anything, they probably *won't* come around, what with them being assholes and all."

His laughter turned into an uproar, and Eve gazed back at him in shock.

"Seriously, what is *so funny?*"

He calmed himself, though only slightly, and offered her a warm smile. "I think you might be the most honest person I've ever met."

Honest—it was something Eve hadn't been since she'd first started at Billington, and she suddenly found herself feeling exposed and embarrassed.

She shrugged defensively. "Sorry?"

"Don't apologize. It's a good thing... a nice change of pace."

Jason looked different, Eve thought—accessible and maybe even the slightest bit pleasant—but the change left Eve uncomfortable and restless. Eager to end the moment, she glanced at her surroundings for a new object to manipulate, and her eyes landed on the sink in the back of the room.

"Let's try again with something a little less life-threatening."

She abruptly melted, and a bar of soap soared onto Jason's lap.

"Now, do the same thing you did last time, except"—she shuddered—"try not to think about your parents."

Jason loosened his muscles and let his arms fall to his sides. Within moments, he was melting. Eve felt a surge of pride and surprise—pride because her student was progressing so quickly, and surprise because she was actually proud of him in the first place. She watched as the bar of soap quickly wiggled in place and then bounced up from the bed, slowly and clumsily bobbed through the air, and then finally plopped onto her lap. Jason glanced at his tutor and grinned.

"Better?"

"*Much* better!" Eve held up the bar of soap as if it were a trophy. "And you didn't kill anyone in the process."

Jason's once dark, empty eyes were now illuminated, consumed with a newfound dynamism as they eagerly scanned the room. "I want to try something else. Something harder."

"Ha," Eve laughed condescendingly. "Sorry, but that's not your call. You don't make the rules around here."

Jason ignored her; his eyes continued to pan across the room searching for something to play with. At last they landed on a tall floor lamp resting by the doorway.

"No, Jason—"

"Eve, relax."

She stopped for a moment, stunned that he had remembered her name. She shook her head and crossed her arms.

"It's dangerous."

Jason looked down at his stapled chest and back up at her. "Seriously? I think I can handle it."

"I said no—"

It was too late—without her blessing, Jason stared at the lamp and let his body go loose. His eyes were like daggers, willing the lamp to come to life, and within seconds it began to shake in place. As the lamp teetered across the floor, Jason's cheeks flushed and his shoulders became rigid.

"You're tensing up," Eve warned. "Ease off a bit."

Jason continued without relenting. His hands began to tremble at his sides, and he balled them into fists.

"Okay Jason, stop," Eve urged. "You're concentrating too hard."

Jason closed his eyes and clenched his fists even tighter, and the lamp began to bounce uncontrollably.

"Jason, *stop it.*" She clutched his arm. "Stop it *right now.*"

She felt something dripping onto her hand and looked down: one, two, three droplets of blood trickled down her knuckles and between her fingers. She looked up at Jason and gasped—his nose and ears were bleeding, each with a steady stream of fiery red that crawled down his face and neck. Her eyes frantically scanned his body, and she realized it was even worse than she had expected: pockets of blood were seeping through the staples on his chest, running down his abdomen and dripping onto his now spotted sheets.

"JASON!" she barked, violently shaking his arm.

Jason finally relented, ending his melt and forcing his senses back to reality. He looked down at the bloody mess he created and froze, his eyes large with shock.

"*Shit.* What did I just do?"

Eve rushed to the sink and grabbed a towel. "I *told* you not to overexert yourself." She ran the towel under the faucet and raced back to Jason. "Do you want me to get a nurse?"

"No." Jason raised his hand, urging her to stop. "I can take care of it." He wiped the blood away from his nose, smearing it across his face in the process.

Eve lifted her rag to Jason's chest, but he grabbed her wrist and stopped her, his body taut.

Eve looked him in the eye. "It won't hurt."

"Eve, I got it."

She rolled her eyes. "Don't be so stubborn. Let me help you."

Jason hesitated for a moment, his grip firm and his eyes focused, studying her like a book. He was skeptical—it was written all over his face, the doubt and suspicion. Eve recognized that look; it was one she had worn many times herself, but she was not going to fold under the weight of his stare. With a heavy sigh, Jason reluctantly surrendered, finally releasing his grasp on her wrist. He flinched only slightly as she slid the damp towel across his face and chest, delicately dabbing at the reopened wounds.

"I should've listened to you," Jason muttered. "I should've stopped when you told me to."

"Yeah, you should've," Eve grumbled.

Jason watched her hands—they were gentle and graceful as they glided across his skin, a stark contrast to her abrasive disposition.

"So, what exactly happened to me?"

"When you overdo it," Eve began, keeping her gaze on his bloodied chest, "when you try to push your power to a level you're not quite capable of, your body starts to rebel against your mind. That's when the bleeding happens." She could feel Jason's eyes on her and met his gaze. "It's not a big deal, just as long as you stop before it gets too serious."

"What would've happened if I hadn't stopped?"

She hesitated. "I don't really know, honestly. I don't think anyone's ever let it get to that point." She patted down the last staple, her towel now spotted with dark patches of blood. "All chimeras bleed at some point. Don't beat yourself up over it."

Jason glanced at the stained rag and then back at Eve. "Thanks," he said, "for being patient with me."

The statement was almost comical, as patience had never exactly been Eve's strongest virtue, but she could tell that he was being sincere. They sat together in silence. Jason was finally calm, his body relaxed and free from anger—and in turn Eve felt anxious. She suddenly noticed the blood-soaked towel still in her grip.

"This is gross. I should wash it."

She tromped toward the sink, clumsily kicking her shoulder bag over in the process. All of its contents scattered across the floor, including her Everlasting Diamond, which rolled to the center of the room. Eve tossed the rag into the sink and muttered under her breath as she shoved her things back into her bag, making sure to secure the diamond in a side pocket. As she stood to her feet, she looked back at Jason, who was staring at her with his nose wrinkled.

"What?" she snapped.

"Was that a diamond?"

"Yeah. So?"

"You just carry diamonds around with you?"

"I haven't found a safe place to put it, that's all."

He paused for a moment, his eyes darting to the spot on the floor where the diamond once sat. "Did someone give that to you?"

Eve scowled. "Are you implying that I *stole* it?"

"Wow, you're reading *way* too much into what I said—"

"It was a *gift*." She folded her arms. "From my roommate."

"Your *roommate?*" His eyes widened. "*Please* don't tell me you're rooming with Madison Palmer."

Eve fidgeted uncomfortably, refusing to answer him, but her silence was the only response he needed, and he laughed unapologetically at her expense.

"It's *not* funny!" she spat, her cheeks flushed.

"I knew it!" he chuckled. "Everywhere that girl goes she leaves behind a trail of diamonds."

"Stop laughing!"

"God, Eve, you really got the short end of the stick with that one."

Before she could say another word, she stopped herself. She wanted to be angry with him—to curse at him as she had the day before—but his laughter was so much more engaging than his angst, and she suddenly found herself a little bit amused. She leaned against his bed frame and smirked.

"So, you know my pain, huh?"

"I pity you, Eve."

Jason shielded himself as Eve jokingly swatted at his leg, their laughter echoing down the hallway of the isolation wing.

* * *

"Ms. Biello, this is what your sister and brother-in-law wanted."

The well-dressed man slid the documents across the table toward the woman. She was still shaking, her face pale and sullen.

"I know," she replied, her voice wavering, "but everything's changed—"

"Ms. Biello, she's just a child." He looked over at Eve, who was sitting on the floor in the living room with her back toward them. She pretended to play with her dolls but kept her attention on their conversation.

"She is *not* just a child. Don't you dare try to convince me otherwise."

The man let out an impatient sigh. "She's your flesh and blood. She's your late sister's daughter—"

"She's a *monster*—"

"She's your *family.*"

"I saw what she did. I was there, you know."

The man cleared his throat and gently rested his pen in front of her. "Sign the papers. Welcome your niece into your home. Try not to let her situation cloud your judgment."

"Her *situation*? Is that what they're calling it these days? Tell me, would you feel safe with someone like her living in your home?"

Eve winced, pained by the man's silence. She felt her eyes brimming with tears but quickly wiped them away, refusing to let herself feel the sting inside of her.

"I'd feel good knowing that I had fulfilled my sister's wishes. That's how I'd feel."

"There's no one else?"

"Ms. Biello, your parents are in an assisted living facility. Your brother-in-law's parents are deceased, and his only brother lives in London."

"Did you ask him?"

"Ms. Biello—"

"Did you?"

"Susan, please—"

"It's a simple question."

The man sighed once more. "His lifestyle isn't suitable for a child."

"So *he* doesn't want her either?"

"His job requires him to travel. Besides," the man leaned forward and pushed the pen closer to Susan, "your sister wanted *you.*"

Eve could hear her aunt softly crying, and she cringed at the sound of it.

"Fine." Eve's aunt grabbed the pen and gripped it tightly. "I'll do it for Janine. I *loved* my sister."

"And a short while ago, you loved Evelyn, didn't you?"

"Oh, don't try to make me feel guilty. Everything's completely different now."

Susan scribbled her signature across the documents and closed her eyes as a tear slid down her cheek. The man retrieved the paperwork and stood.

"Congratulations, Ms. Biello. You are now the legal guardian of your niece, Evelyn Kingston."

A sudden pain surged in Eve's side—a sharp jab to the ribs that nearly sent her tumbling from her chair. She grimaced and stretched her back, her mind still hazy from the nightmare, and noticed a pair of dusty, unlaced sneakers propped up on her desk.

Eve growled under her breath. "Did you just *kick me?*"

JJ chuckled smugly. "Rise and shine, princess. Class was dismissed early. I thought about letting you sit here, but it just seemed too cruel."

Eve looked around; she was in the Strategic Communication lecture hall, the room practically empty aside from the two girls and one additional body: Marshall Woodgate stood by the door, muttering to himself as he stared out the window.

"He's waiting for his bodyguards. Must suck, needing constant supervision. But then again, *you're* the one sleeping in class. Maybe you could use a babysitter to schedule a more convenient nap time."

"I haven't been sleeping well."

"I'm sorry, did I sound concerned? My mistake," JJ scoffed.

Eve rolled her eyes. "Why was class let out early?"

"Gupta got called to a meeting with Furst. Everyone did."

"Everyone?"

"The entire faculty."

"Why?" Eve paused. "Does it have to do with the attacks?"

JJ opened her mouth to speak but stopped herself. Instead, she glared at Eve and folded her arms. "And how the hell do you think I'd know that? Better yet, why do *you* even care about the attacks, Rutherfordian? Shouldn't you be off counting your hundred-dollar bills?"

Eve scowled; there was no use in trying to reason with the girl, and so without another word, she gathered her things and charged out of the lecture hall, leaving JJ and the president's son far behind her.

After a long and listless stroll, Eve reached the women's locker room, where she changed into her uniform before joining her combat class on the football field. They set off across the track, their boots pounding against the dusty pathway, the sound echoing in Eve's ears. A rigorous run would've been refreshing, but she knew all too well that *this* run—this pitiful, effortless trot—would leave her feeling unsatisfied. As much as it pained her to do so, she slowed her pace and allowed herself to be swarmed by her enormous classmates. They panted and groaned as they ran, their faces, chests, and backs dripping with sweat, and all the while Eve was breezy and unaffected. The only heat she felt was the fire burning inside her—a raging rancor toward herself, for the weak display she was forced to fake, for the nightly visions that haunted her without reprieve. She basked in her anger, hardly noticing that Captain Ramsey was calling her from across the field.

"Kingston! Can you even *hear* me?" Ramsey shouted.

Eve jumped and looked over at the captain, who was angrily pacing across the field. Chin Dimple, who had been trailing her for several laps, jogged up beside her, a snide smile plastered across his face.

"Time for your cooking classes?" he sneered. "Get lost, girl."

Eve gritted her teeth; no matter how much she wanted to act out, to show just what she thought of him, she resisted the temptation. As her classmates veered around her, she jogged toward the captain, her face bashful and apologetic.

"Sorry, Captain."

"God, Kingston, you deaf?"

"I was just in the zone, I guess."

"Psh, zone." Ramsey shook his head and stared off at the rest of his students. After a moment of silence, he looked back at Eve, his eyes fierce and penetrating.

"Kingston, you know what I hate more than anything else?" He leaned in toward her. "Slackers." He turned his head to spit on the lawn and then looked back at her once more. "Ain't nothin' worse than a slacker."

"Captain, I'm not sure what this has to do with me."

"You're holding back, Kingston."

"What?" Eve faltered. "I don't understand. My times are good—they're better than good, actually. I keep up with the boys, I'm holding my weight. I'm doing just as well as everyone else."

"I'm not asking you to do as good as those guys. I'm asking you to push yourself. Put your full effort in."

"But I am, Captain—"

"You're slackin', Kingston. You know it, and I know it."

"Captain, my times are *good*."

"Kingston." He fixed his eyes on hers. "I *know* what you *are*."

The words hit her like a ton of bricks. He leaned in even closer, and his tone became stern and forceful.

"Even before this damn tutoring shit. I could tell since day one. You think

I don't know what you're capable of?"

Eve looked down at her feet; she tried to speak, to defend her dismal efforts, but she said nothing and instead savored the bitter taste of shame on her tongue.

"Look, Kingston, if you want to pass this class, you're gonna have to give me one hundred percent, you hear me? There's no slacking allowed on my watch."

"But—"

"But nothing. We start drills tomorrow and sparring in a couple of weeks. I need to see a huge turnaround by then. You *will* give me everything you got, or you will fail." He didn't wait for her to argue and immediately nodded his head toward the gymnasium. "Time for your tutoring deal. Your escort is waiting by the lockers."

Eve desperately wanted to explain herself, but everything she came up with sounded weak and pathetic. Without a last word and with a troubling sense of defeat, she made her way to the locker room and quickly changed back into her business attire. She adjusted her vest and matching trousers and stared at herself in the mirror. She looked strong and professional, but inside she felt conflicted and contrived. Would the pretending ever get any easier? No one could answer that, certainly not Eve, and so she left the locker rooms and met with Armaan, who stood patiently by the double doors of the gym.

"Good day? Ready to tutor?" he chirped as the twosome headed for the ward.

Eve's response was lackluster in comparison. "You seem awfully cheerful."

"Of course, I've been looking forward to this all day!"

"That makes one of us."

"Come on, aren't you the least bit exhilarated?"

"*Exhilarated?*"

"This whole thing, it's exciting!"

"Wow," Eve murmured, "you're really hyped off this arrangement we've got going on."

"Eve, you have to understand—this is the best thing that's happened to me in my entire *life*."

"Walking *me* to the medical ward is the best thing that's happened to you? *Ever?*" She chuckled. "You need to get out more."

Armaan rolled his eyes. "Over the span of my academic career, I've skipped four grades. This is the only form of 'getting out' that I do." He frowned. "Sad, right?"

"Well, little man, I'm the one with the babysitter. Who's sad now?"

"You? *Sad*? Hardly!" Armaan rebutted. "If anything, you're the exact opposite—impressive. Awe-inspiring!"

"Flattery will get you nowhere, sir."

Armaan's eyes lit up with fervor. "What you did yesterday with the feather made me realize that I have a once-in-a-lifetime opportunity here!"

"And that is?"

"Chimeras are my *world*. I mean, I'm planning on focusing my entire career around you guys, so naturally I'm interested, intrigued—"

"Obsessed?" Eve teased.

Armaan continued with unrelenting excitement. "It may have been by chance—or, most likely, it's because people see me as an easy patsy—but being assigned as your escort could open new doors for me! I could learn so much from you. I mean, you *are* the most powerful chimera in the *world*."

Eve grimaced. "So I've heard. Tell me, did *everyone* know this little fact before I did?"

Armaan cowered. "Sorry. I just overheard it, that's all. People tend to talk around me as if I'm not there—as if I don't exist."

"Just—"

"I know. Don't tell anyone."

"Thanks."

"So, I'm curious," he continued. "How'd it go yesterday with Jason? Did he use his gift? Is he good at it?"

Eve looked away uncomfortably. "I'm not sure I'm even allowed to talk about this. Maybe I should be asking you, since you seem to know more than I do."

"Oh." Armaan stared at his feet. "Yeah, I guess that makes sense. Student-teacher confidentiality and all."

The two continued along the pathway in silence. Armaan's face was pointed at the ground, just as it had been the moment they first met, and all Eve could see of him was his thick mass of hair. She couldn't bear his disappointment any longer.

"He melted for the first time."

Armaan lifted his head, his face bright and radiant once again. "Really? How'd he do?"

"He did well." She smiled. "He moved a snow globe and a bar of soap."

"*So* dynamic," Armaan said, nearly skipping.

They crossed the campus side by side, like two lifelong acquaintances in the thick of a riveting conversation. It was unusual for Eve, and most likely for Armaan too, but she allowed herself to get lost in the ease of his company. He rambled endlessly about the magnificence of her capabilities, and although she certainly appreciated the praise, what she appreciated most was the fleeting moment of peace—of relief and even *happiness*—that she felt at his side.

As they made their way through the double doors of the medical ward, Eve's attention was torn from her friend to a scene just a short distance away: across the lobby stood Dean Furst, his face riddled with worry as he spoke in hushed whispers with a tall, uniformed man. Eve had never seen the second man before, but judging from his military duds and medals, she knew he must be a patrolman of high rank. He was fair in complexion, his skin practically blending in with his white-blond hair, and his eyes were fiercely blue like those of a husky dog. But one glaring feature stood out from the others: a scar, deep and textured, followed the left side of his jaw from his temple to his chin. The man was glaring at Furst, pounding his fist into his palm as he spoke, while Furst cupped his chin in his hands and listened intently.

"This was *never* supposed to happen," the patrolman whispered.

Eve stopped in the center of the lobby, halted by the cutting nature of his words. Her eyes fell on Furst—his gaze was cast down at the floor, his face drained of all color—and she could immediately tell that something was dreadfully wrong. A snap decision was made; hastily, she grabbed Armaan by the wrist and tugged him around a nearby corner, pushing both herself and him against the wall.

"What the—"

Eve pressed her finger against her lips, silencing Armaan instantly. Then she cocked her head in the opposite direction—toward Furst and the patrolman—and after a moment of confusion, he enthusiastically nodded, seemingly excited for the task at hand. Together they peered around the corner, trying their best to eavesdrop on the remainder of the exchange.

"This is all so much worse than we thought," the patrolman continued. "We need to take action *now*."

"And what sort of action do you propose we take?" Furst asked.

"We have to inform the students—"

"Absolutely not."

"We're *losing*, Furst." the man growled. "They're gaining momentum, and we don't even have a *specimen—*"

"Then we'll try harder."

"Furst, I don't think you understand the gravity of the situation."

"I understand perfectly, which is why I called the faculty meeting so urgently, but now is not the time for hasty decisions."

"There's no time to waste. They have everything: *Fairon has everything.*"

"Colonel—"

Furst stopped short as his eyes landed on their unwanted spectator: Eve. The colonel followed suit, turning abruptly to see what or who had caught Furst's attention. Eve's cheeks flushed and she quickly ducked back behind the wall, though her eavesdropping had already been made more than apparent.

"Follow me to my office, Colonel," Furst mumbled, and the two men left the ward together.

Eve turned toward Armaan. "Do you know who that guy was? The one in the uniform with Furst?"

He shrugged. "No idea."

They shuffled into the elevator and stood in silence. The image of Dean Furst and the colonel—with his snow-white completion and his jarring scar—filled her mind, and their words echoed in her thoughts.

They have everything.

Who were *they*? And who was Fairon?

As the pair reached the isolation wing, Eve's musings on Furst and the colonel were replaced by an overwhelming sense of anxiety. She couldn't help but groan aloud at the awful sight before her.

"Back for another *tour* of the ward, huh?" Heather barbed. She was sitting at the clerk's desk with an arrogant smirk plastered across her face. "Don't mind me, I'm just *observing.*"

Eve's face became hot. She looked at Armaan, who stared up at her with blank, puzzled eyes.

"Don't ask," she muttered. Refusing to give Heather a second glance, she hurriedly handed her ID badge to the security officer and grabbed at the isolation wing door.

"Hey," Armaan squeaked, halting her before she left, "I wasn't trying to make you uncomfortable earlier. You know, with all my talk about how dynamic you are."

Eve offered a reassuring smile. "No worries. We're fine."

"I just think we can really learn from one another."

She could feel Heather's scathing gaze; it was almost too much to bear. "Let's discuss this another time," she answered nervously.

"Oh, okay." His tone was meek and discouraged, and Eve felt her heart break for him just a little bit.

She squeezed his shoulder. "I promise we will."

Armaan's eyes lit up with his usual optimism. "We're friends, right?"

Friends—it seemed like such a foreign term. Her first few weeks at Billington had felt so lonely, not unlike the vast majority of her life, and despite her false camaraderie with Madison, Eve had yet to make a single friend in so many years.

"Yes. Of course we're friends."

Eve sauntered into the isolation wing, her spirits lifted, if only for a moment. Really, she wasn't quite sure *how* she felt anymore—lately, her varying emotions seemed to blend together into a massive knot that she fought to ignore. As she stood in front of Jason's door, she thought about what might be waiting for her on the other side: a dark room where Jason sat alone in his bed, staring lifelessly at the wall. Shards of glass on the floor, or maybe blood dripping from his stapled chest. The possibilities seemed endless, and the lift that Armaan had given her began to ebb. She bit her lip and reluctantly opened the door.

When she stepped into Jason's hospital room, Eve's mouth fell open, and she was sure her surprise was plastered across her face. The room was bright, almost cheery, with the soft hum of the sound system lightly filling the space. The bed was empty, its blue sheets messily flopped across the mattress, as Jason stood in front of his desk, his back facing her and his broad shoulders hunched over his scratchpad. He rubbed one foot against the opposite ankle, fidgeting with the hem of his flannel pajama bottoms as he flipped through the pages of his digital textbook.

As the door clicked shut behind Eve, Jason turned to greet her. His hair was combed, his face was clean-shaven, and he wore a somewhat unexpected smile that seemed to illuminate the room a bit more.

"Wow," Eve chuckled, her eyes wide with shock. "You shaved. You showered. You *actually* got out of bed..."

"Hey, in my defense, the nurses don't want me standing or walking around," Jason said, leaning against the desk behind him. "They don't want me to 'exert' myself. You're looking at a rebel right here."

Eve took a seat in her designated folding chair. "I'm looking at a changed man." She raised her eyebrows and stared him up and down. "Now, if only you could invest in a shirt."

He looked down at his chest and back at Eve. "The cotton rubs against the staples—it's itchy." He ran his hand lightly across his chest as if suddenly self-conscious. "Does it make you uncomfortable? The scar?"

Eve glanced over his scar: the incision was healing day by day as if weeks had passed. And beneath the scar, Eve couldn't help but notice the outline of Jason's firm chest and abdomen. Unlike the massive hulks in Eve's combat class, Jason was long, lean, and carved, with strong shoulders and a narrow waist. She hadn't noticed before; perhaps she'd been too distracted by the scar, or by the unpleasant ambiance, or possibly the initial tension between them.

"Don't be stupid," she quipped. She fiddled with her shoulder bag in search of a small object to manipulate. "Have a seat. We'll start where we left off last time."

A slight rustling caught her attention; she took a look at the corner of the room and saw Jason's pile of presents shaking as if it were coming to life. Suddenly, a small blue gift—the same one she had controlled during their first meeting together—darted from the mound and promptly landed in her lap. She looked back and forth between the gift and Jason, who met her gaze with a smug, toothy grin.

"Have you been *practicing?*"

"Maybe I have." He winked.

"Well, Mr. 'This-Gift-is-a-Curse,' you're certainly full of surprises today."

Jason took a seat on his bed and bowed his chin, jokingly paying his respects to his new tutor. "Just tryin' to make you proud, Teach."

Eve smirked. "All right, showoff, you've got the basics—rather quickly, by the way—but that doesn't mean we're going to take it easy. You'll be melting everything in this room today, starting with that, over there." She nodded toward his desk. "Your desk drawers—you'll be opening them one by one until you can drift into your melt without even thinking about it. And don't concentrate too hard like you did last time. The more relaxed you feel, the more control you'll have over your gift."

She turned her attention to Jason, expecting to see him preparing to melt, but instead found him staring back at her intently, his face donning a slight smirk as if he had a secret.

"Are you even listening to me?"

"I remember you."

Eve wrinkled her nose. "Well, you *should* remember me. You saw me yesterday and the day before. The Interlopers dissected your chest, not your *brain*."

"No, I mean before all of this—I remember you. We bumped into each other on the first day of classes."

"Oh." Eve's mind wandered to their encounter in the halls of the business building. "Actually, if you want to get technical, *you* bumped into *me*—gracefully, might I add."

"Ah, there it is: that familiar cutting sarcasm." He smiled. "You certainly know how to put someone in their place. Not sure how I could've forgotten you."

Eve looked away uncomfortably. "Well, you've been more than a bit preoccupied since then, what with being cut open by aliens and all."

"Wow. You put it so delicately."

"It's a gift."

"Seems like you've got a lot of gifts..."

"Speaking of which"—Eve ignored Jason's retort and snatched the package from his mattress—"you've got work to do."

"Why are you doing this?"

Eve let out a long, irritated sigh. "Are you going to keep stalling, or are we going to get to work?"

Jason laughed. "Come on, relax." He leaned back in his bed, propping his neck against the headrest. "I'm just curious. Why are *you* tutoring me? I mean, you said it yourself: you didn't sign up for this."

Eve's shoulders stiffened. "Does it matter?"

"No, not really. Do you always get this tense when people ask you questions?"

Of course not, Eve thought, though she knew she was lying to herself. She exhaled loudly and gave Jason a disgruntled look.

"I didn't have a choice. Dean Furst called me into his office—he said it was my job to train you, and that was that."

"Damn, an order straight from Furst himself?" Jason stopped short, distracted by a new idea. "You know, the man doesn't waste his time with just anyone."

"Yes, well, you're not just *anyone*. You're the son of a senator."

"I wasn't talking about me."

"Then what were you talking about?"

"Why you?"

"Oh, *God—*"

"Out of all the chimeras at this school, you were asked—no, *forced*—to be sitting here with me right now," he interrupted. "You must be special."

Eve pursed her lips, aggravated. "We need to get back to work."

"Eve, would you believe me if I said that I'm just trying to get to know you? Because like it or not, that's the truth."

She couldn't help but notice his eyes: he had a disarming stare that left her anxious, and yet she felt that maybe, possibly, he was truly being honest with her.

"You don't need to get to know me. I'm just your tutor."

"You're the only person I'm allowed to see—besides my nurses and doctor. Forgive me if I'm craving some genuine conversation about something other than sutures and antibacterial ointment."

Eve sighed; Jason was a pain in the ass. Unfortunately for her, he was a pain in the ass with a sound, logical argument. It couldn't hurt to tell him the truth—after all, he already knew her true identity, and it was an identity they both shared. If anyone could be trusted with this information, who better than a fellow chimera? And yet, all of the rationalizing in the world didn't make the words any easier to say.

"Apparently, I'm really... *good* at what I do."

"Why do I have the feeling that that was a significant understatement?"

"Because it was."

"So, were you planning on elaborating?"

Eve grimaced, stalling for a moment. "I'm kind of..."

Jason raised his eyebrows. "Yes?"

"Basically—"

"Just say it."

"I *am* saying it."

"Not really."

"I'm the strongest chimera in the world," Eve spat, annoyed by his badgering.

Jason stared at her in disbelief. "*What?*"

Eve faltered. "God, it sounds so weird even to me. There's no way to say it without, well, saying it just like that."

"You're the strongest chimera in the *world*?"

"Yes," Eve hissed, her cheeks rosy with embarrassment, "and it doesn't sound any less weird coming from you."

He smiled, his eyes still lit with the same fire—the same sincerity.

"It's not weird. It's incredible."

His reaction surprised her: *incredible*, he'd said. It *was* incredible, truly, but to hear it from someone else was so strange and unexpected. Try as she might, she couldn't think of the right words to say to him, so instead she stared at her hands as she always did when she felt uneasy.

"So, if you're the strongest chimera in the world, tell me: what can you do?"

"Can't we just melt already?"

"*Eve*," Jason groaned, "come on. Please?"

Eve grumbled. "Well, I'm fast. Really fast, actually. And strong, though I know I don't look it. Looks can be deceiving with chimeras."

"And your gift?"

Eve kept her gaze pointed at her cuticles. "I can move stuff, obviously— pretty much anything you could think of. A book, a couch..." She smirked. "A bus..."

"What else?"

"I can manipulate things. Anything you can do with your hands, I can do with my gift. You know, turn light switches on and off, open doors, tie shoelaces, hammer a nail."

"What about living things? What about people?"

"You sure are nosy."

"The correct word is *intrigued*."

Eve sighed, still resolute in her irritation. "Takes a lot more practice, but yes, I can move people. In fact, I could move a whole crowd of people—if I wanted to, at least. That's actually the hardest skill to master: melting multiple things at once. It took me years to get that down."

"Maybe an easier question to answer would be what *can't* you do."

Eve sat quietly, still fussing with her fingernails. She thought about his questions—his incessant, pestering questions. She didn't have to answer them; after all, this was none of his business. She was there to teach him, and nothing more. And yet, something inside of her, or possibly something inside of him, urged her to open up. Out of the corner of her eye, she could see him watching her, waiting for her answer with large eyes that looked so unthreatening.

"If it's rooted to the ground, I can't melt it. Like a tree or a building."

"Makes sense."

She hesitated for a moment, still staring down at her lap, avoiding his gaze.

"I can't fly."

Jason furrowed his brow. "Huh?"

"Let me rephrase. Right here, right now, I could make you levitate. I could have you soaring through the room doing flips and loops like it was nothing. But I couldn't do that to myself." She frowned. "Lord knows I've tried a million times."

"Anything else?"

Eve stopped. The answer was there, resting on the tip of her tongue, and yet it was so very hard to utter. It was a gamble—she knew this—but despite her greater sensibility, she decided to say it anyway.

"There are limitations," she began, slowly. "I mean..." She sighed. "I don't think you'd understand."

"Try me."

She growled slightly, aggravated by his resolve, but continued regardless. "I can do a lot of things with my gift. It used to scare me, how much I could do. It doesn't seem right, to have so much power trapped inside your mind."

Jason rolled his eyes. "You're starting to sound like my dad."

"You really don't get it." Their eyes met. "I could *hurt* people with my gift if I wanted to. I could hurl you against the wall, throw you high into the air and let you fall to the ground. I could melt a *knife* into your chest. It's sick, the thought of it." She stopped for a second, stirred by her own words. "But to answer your question, I can't just think about breaking your legs or your back and make it happen. I can't just melt an injury... or death."

She breathed in deeply before she continued, the words tasting bitter as they left her lips.

"What I'm trying to say is that, I can't just... *kill* someone. At least, not directly. Stop their heart from beating, snap their neck..." Her voice trailed off. "Nothing like that."

"Oh." It was Jason's turn to be quiet, and he looked away. "Have you... tried?"

"Of course not!"

"Then how do you know?"

Eve paused for a moment, almost unsure of the answer. "I don't," she finally said. "And I don't want to know, either."

"So, what you're saying is, you *won't* hurt or kill someone, but you really don't know if you can or can't?"

Eve stared at Jason, her back suddenly stiff and her eyes glossed over with a look of emptiness—of complete disconnection.

"Let's change the subject, shall we?"

***

Rutherford Hall wasn't much farther. Eve could see her balcony in the distance—the light in her dorm room was off, and maybe, just *maybe* Madison was already asleep, dreaming about diamonds and couture or whatever else her heart desired. Eve tried to remain optimistic—it was a change from her typical mindset, but today's tutoring session had left her feeling the slightest bit encouraged. Never had she ever been able to share her gift with anyone, aside from her small feather trick with Armaan, and though her opinion of Jason was far from decided, the arrangement itself was starting to feel a little less like a burden. He was intrusive—*God*, was he intrusive—but he was witty, and even kind. Yes, maybe Jason wasn't so bad, and maybe Billington University was the right decision after all. She rarely allowed herself to let go of her stressors, but she was beginning to think she could see a faint light at the end of the tunnel.

As she opened the door to Rutherford Hall, that light quickly flickered out. In front of her stood Heather, Hayden, and Madison, all three with their hands planted firmly on their hips as if ready for battle. Madison stood in the center as the leader, her pose threatening and her eyes filled with rage.

"You suckgasmic *ASS-sack!*" she spat, lunging toward Eve.

Hayden squealed and clapped her hands, entranced by the fuss in front of her. Heather remained silent, but a devilish smile spread slowly across her lips.

Eve staggered backward. "What *is* this? What the hell is going on?"

"Why didn't you *tell* me?" Madison barked.

"Tell you *what*? What are you talking about?"

"Oh, don't play dumb with me, you stupid little *shit.*"

"Jesus Christ, Madison, what the hell is *wrong* with you?"

The heiress thrust her face forward, close enough for Eve to taste her hot, foul breath. "I *know*, Eve."

"You know *what*?"

Madison bit her lip and balled her manicured hands into tight, quivering fists.

"I *know* you've been seeing *Jason*."

CHAPTER 5: THE LACE PANTIES

"Wake up, slophole."

Eve groaned and opened her eyes. Madison hovered above her bed, her arms folded, her gaze as critical as that of a disapproving parent. A week had passed since their confrontation in Rutherford Hall, but the heiress's resentment was still fresh and lingering, much like the scent of her overpowering perfume. The two girls had hashed out their differences with as much maturity as Madison could muster—which was hardly any at all—and the busty blonde had reminded Eve of her supposed betrayal every day since. *Time heals all wounds*—it was a common saying, but apparently Madison was unfamiliar with it, for with each passing day she wasted no time reopening the wound and jabbing at it with all of her verbal might.

"God, Eve, I don't know how you expect me to ever trust you again," Madison whined as the usual threesome marched toward the business building.

Eve rolled her eyes; the torture seemed never-ending.

"I mean, how could you keep such a huge secret from me? These private rendezvous with *the* Jason Valentine—*my* Jason Valentine—"

"Hold it right there—'private *rendezvous*?'" Eve interrupted. "I told you a thousand times, I'm tutoring him. It's as simple and boring as that."

"How do I know if I can even believe that?"

"You can't. She has *secrets*. Who knows what else she's hiding?" Hayden snarled.

"Shut *up*, Hayden," Madison grumbled. "Look, Eve—if that *is*, in fact, your real name—if your connection to Jason is as *simple* and *boring* as you claim it to be, then why cover it up? Why the lies?"

Madison had a point—she was smarter than she appeared. *God*, Eve hated that about her. Even more than that, she hated the deceit—the excuses, the fiction, the lies on top of lies on top of lies. Was the guilt and worry an appropriate price to pay for some peace and solitude? After all, she felt far from peaceful; in fact, she felt as if the whole campus was watching her, waiting for her to slip, to fall, to come clean. She asked herself: is it worth it?

Yes. It is.

"Answer me, *Eve.*"

She couldn't answer. Not because there was no answer to give, which certainly was the case, but because her mind had been transported elsewhere—about ten yards away, to the front of the business building, where a small swarm of students had begun to form. They huddled in clumps, their eyes panic-stricken and mouths racing, producing an incoherent jumble of words that Eve couldn't decipher. It was gossip, most likely—petty, inconsequential ramblings as was typical across campus—but the paleness of their skin told her that something was terribly wrong.

A tiny body wriggled its way from the group and glared at Eve; she had been caught staring, her gaping much more obvious than she had intended. Even worse, it was JJ who had noticed.

"Did you *need* something?" JJ glowered.

"What's going on?" Eve asked.

JJ raised her eyebrows. "I'm surprised you haven't heard. Guess the news hasn't traveled up to your pedestal yet, princess."

"Look, as much as I love the ridicule, an answer would be nice."

JJ looked straight through Eve, consumed with so much more animosity than usual—with hate. Her lips parted slightly before she spoke, and in that moment Eve sensed the slightest hint of fragility.

"Another chimera was dissected."

Like a punch to the gut, the words left Eve breathless, motionless, and stunned. She had forgotten the Interlopers, having been distracted by bickering blondes and tutoring duties, as if such disturbances took precedence; but there was a war going on, all across the planet—and Billington was the eye of the storm.

"Is he—"

"*She's* alive, but barely. Her chest was sliced open, just like that Jason guy."

Eve choked slightly, her face flushed and body hot. *"God—"*

"Do I detect some compassion?" JJ sneered. "And here I thought all Rutherfordians were soulless. How utterly *human* of you."

Eve didn't speak. Instead, she stared at the ground as she thought of the Interlopers, of chimeras, of people like her being ripped to shreds, of their screams and suffering at the hands, or talons, of such calculated cruelty.

A quick slap to the arm awoke her from her spell—it was Madison, of course, accompanied by Hayden, the two girls waiting less than patiently for their withdrawn third member.

"You done?"

JJ laughed, looking over the two blondes without a hint a subtlety. "Is *this* your gang?" She rolled her eyes. "Figures. Three pretty *harpies* all in a row."

Madison tugged at Eve's arm, dragging her away from JJ and through the double doors of the business building. And just like that, Eve was welcomed back to the pedestrian reality of her daily life—the pitiful triviality of being a Rutherfordian.

"Who was *that*?" Madison snorted.

"Yeah, and why did she call us all herpes?" Hayden mumbled.

"Is she another *secret* friend? God, I hope not. Did you *see* what she was wearing?"

Eve ignored their prattle. "Did you hear about the abduction? I had no idea..."

"Who *cares*? What, have your *dates* with Jason turned you into a chimera sympathizer?"

Eve yanked her arm from Madison's grip and glared at her dorm mate. "I've already explained myself to you, and I won't do it again. I'm *tutoring* Jason, and that's the end of it. From this point forward, we're going to forget about the whole thing and move on."

"You *would* like that, wouldn't you?"

A voice chimed in from behind Eve. Reluctantly, she turned to face the smug grin of Heather McLeod.

Eve didn't bother to mask her revulsion; it was, after all, Heather who had divulged her meetings with Jason. *Just some common sense and a bit of digging around* was her method of uncovering the truth, or so she'd boasted between self-satisfied smirks.

Eve scowled. "What do you want, Heather?"

"Me?" Heather pointed to herself, innocently. "Well, I don't want anything."

I'm just saying, how can we move on if we know you're not telling the truth?"

"Yeah, my point *exactly*," Madison snapped.

"Oh, for God's sake, Madison, you don't even *like* Heather."

"Another lie! God, Eve, you don't quit, do you?"

"What I don't understand is this," Heather continued. "How can you possibly be tutoring Jason? I mean, you're a freshman and he's a sophomore, after all."

"This is college. There are plenty of sophomores in my classes."

Heather offered another patronizing smile. "That may be true, but Jason Valentine *isn't* one of them."

And with that one statement, everything changed. The hallway grew smaller, darker, and suffocatingly enclosed. Heather looked so harmless with her pearl headband and polka dot dress, but within her eyes was a dangerous deceit.

"You see, volunteering at the medical ward has its perks. I have access to all sorts of documents and records, though I use the term 'access' loosely. I found your entire class schedule right away—sort of surprised to learn about Hand-to-Hand Combat, if I do say so myself."

"Don't get me started. *So* gross," Madison muttered under her breath.

"Of course, I had to compare it to Jason's schedule. The funny thing is, he doesn't have a *single* class with you."

Madison and Hayden gasped, and their mouths dropped open in unison. Eve clenched her jaw tightly, her entire body suddenly consumed with contempt.

"That doesn't—"

"Mean anything?" the redhead interrupted. "You're right, it doesn't. You could simply be tutoring him in a topic that happens to be your area of expertise, a possibility I naturally considered. It makes sense—you *did* get into Billington solely on smarts, right Eve?" She winked and chuckled to herself. "But I compared your majors and curriculum, and the answers I uncovered were *rather* disconcerting. You're a business major, and our Mr. Valentine? Why, he's majoring in political science, a concentration you haven't a single vested interest in."

"We've all seen him in the business building—"

"On his way to Leadership Development, a course required of all sophomores and one you're certainly unqualified to tutor for as a freshman." Heather folded her hands together. "And so, it appears we've come full circle, haven't we?"

Eve paused, her mind inundated with facts—facts that were most certainly true. Facts that Heather had meticulously investigated, and for what purpose? Eve felt her temperature rise and her face redden.

"Well, you've obviously done your homework, Heather."

"I'm anything but imprecise."

"You're anything but *mentally stable.*"

Heather giggled, pleased with Eve's obvious anger. "How do you explain all of that, Eve? I mean, how can you tutor someone if you don't even have the same classes, much less the same major?"

Eve wanted to speak; she wanted to curse and demean Heather, but she couldn't find the words. She had run out of excuses, as there was nothing left to tell—nothing but the truth, and she couldn't possibly reveal that. Rage and humiliation bubbled within her, so much so that she hardly noticed Armaan approaching. He stopped at her side and looked back and forth between her and Heather, completely perplexed by the scene in front of him.

"Um..." Armaan stammered. "Eve? It's time to go."

Eve neither moved nor responded. All she could do was stare at the despicable redhead in front of her.

"Looks like they're summoning you for your 'tutoring' session," Heather sneered. "Or *whatever it is* that you two *do* together."

Eve finally broke away from Heather's gaze and looked down at Armaan. "Come on, let's get out of here." She shot one last glare in Heather's direction and followed Armaan out of the building.

"This isn't over, Eve!" Madison shrieked.

"Yeah, this isn't over, Eve!" Hayden cried, her voice shrill and pitiful.

"Shut *up,* Hayden! *God,* I *just* said that!"

Eve marched in silence by Armaan's side, her fists still clenched and her mind racing. She was stuck in the exact place she had feared she'd end up since her sessions with Jason first began—and she had gotten there so much more quickly than she had anticipated.

"What was *that* all about?" Armaan asked, looking over his shoulder at the girls who were now far behind him.

"They know."

"They know what?" Armaan gasped. "Do they know you're a *chimera*?"

"No. Maybe. I don't know." Eve sighed. "They know something's up. They know I'm meeting with Jason and that it's not for school."

The stress was overpowering, feeding off of her strength like a parasite. Eve *appeared* composed—she had a knack for that—but inside she was frantic and scattered, a tangled mess of emotion and preoccupation. As she made her way across campus and through the medical ward, each face she encountered—Armaan's, the security guard's, even Jason's—seemed warped and disfigured until it managed to resemble Heather's. She tried to shake it— Heather would be so pleased if she knew she was lingering in Eve's thoughts, and that evil smirk was unbearable to imagine. No, she couldn't give Heather the satisfaction, she wouldn't. And yet, even with the strongest conviction, she couldn't help but think about the dramatics to come. *They're going to find out.* The phrase rang in her ears like an endless taunt. *It's only a matter of time before everyone knows.*

* * *

"Everyone knows."

"*What?*" Eve snapped.

"That Dr. Dick hates chimeras." Jason removed his eyes from his spoon, which was gracefully levitating in front of his face, and looked at Eve. "We were just talking about this."

"Oh," Eve mumbled. She was in the isolation wing, sitting in the folding chair beside Jason's bed, far away from Heather's prying eyes. She let out a long, relieved breath. "Sorry, I must've gotten distracted."

Jason sent his spoon soaring across the room and into the sink, his brow furrowed. "You okay, Eve? You've been acting funnier than usual."

Eve envisioned Heather's duplicitous smile and quickly forced the red-head from her mind. "It's just been a weird day..."

"Is this because of the abduction?"

Eve's eyes abruptly shot toward him. "You know?"

Jason hesitated. "I heard the alarm," he explained. "It echoes through the whole ward. Not sure whose genius idea that was. It's like some god-awful signal letting everyone know that another chimera has been sliced and diced."

Eve sighed; she hadn't even thought about Jason, about how the news affected him. It was incredibly selfish of her, she realized now, but it had been so long since she'd had to think of anyone but herself. As hard as it was for her to admit, she wasn't operating on her own any longer; she was bound to Jason, at first through force and now through—well, she wasn't quite sure, but he had grown on her in an unfamiliar way. Perhaps this was what friendship felt like.

"How are you..." She faltered, fumbling to find the perfect words to say. "I mean, are you scared?"

Jason smirked. "After *this*?" He pointed to his chest. "Nothing scares me." His voice, though strong, was laced with something else: something raw.

Eve glanced at his scar; after so many days together she hardly noticed it anymore, but there it was, slightly smoother than the day before, though still just as daunting.

"What about you?" Jason asked.

"What do you mean, what about me?"

"Aren't you worried? Aren't you afraid they'll come for you?"

Eve paused, staring off at the wall as she ruminated over the question. "You know, I haven't really thought about it." She sat still for a moment, her eyes distant and glossy until they finally made their way back to Jason. "No, I guess I'm not."

"Why not?"

She took one last look at his scar and then stared down at her hands. Her eyes landed on the pencil-thin blemish across her palm—the one she'd received from a seventh-grader wielding a knife.

"There are some things in this world that are worse than aliens."

"Well, I'm worried."

"You just said you weren't—"

"For you, Eve. I'm worried for you."

Their eyes met. Eve crossed her arms and quickly looked away.

"So, I was doing some research," Jason continued, "about chimeras." He paused for a second and smiled. "Did you know the average chimera goes through emergence between the ages of twenty-one and twenty-five?"

"Of course I know that," she scoffed.

"But you're nineteen."

"Yeah, so?"

"And you're also the strongest chimera in the world, right? Which means you must've had your gift for a while now."

Eve wrinkled her nose. "What are you getting at?"

"You're holding out on me, Eve."

"Dammit, Jason, are we doing this again?"

"I'm just curious—"

"And pushy, and invasive—"

"It's like pulling teeth with you, every time," Jason groaned. "You can talk about melting or school or the weather for hours, but if I ask *one* question about *you*, it's a problem."

Before Eve could form a rebuttal, she stopped herself; he was right, much to her chagrin. Where she came from, everyone knew her story—but to Jason she was a mystery, a well-kept secret, admittedly by her own choosing.

There was no use in hiding the truth—he already knew too much, anyway. She cleared her throat, stared down at her hands, and reluctantly spoke.

"My parents were killed in a car crash when I was eight years old. I watched it happen."

Jason was silent for a moment, his eyes wide, his body stiff.

"Oh God," he finally muttered. "I am such a *dick*."

"Jason—"

"I should've *never* asked. It wasn't my place."

"It's okay, Jason, I promise." She hesitated, nervously fiddling with her cuticles. "It was a long time ago."

He grumbled, still irritated with himself. "So you've had your gift since you were eight years old? It makes sense, then, why you're the best."

"Years of practice—practice *you* should be getting right now."

"With all due respect, we've melted everything in this room. There's nothing left to move, but—"

"Me."

Jason did a double take. "*What?*"

Eve grinned, amused by his surprise. "You're right. You've manipulated everything in here, and you've been good at it too. It's time for the next step in your training." She folded her legs beneath her. "You moved people during your emergence. You can move me."

"Yeah, but that was different. I was *freaking out.*"

Eve rolled her eyes. "I've told you this already: your emergence is a direct reflection of how powerful your gift will be."

He stopped and smiled. "What did *you* move during your emergence?"

"A truck."

"Dammit, Eve. Way to steal my thunder."

She smirked. "Come on, give it a shot."

"You sure this is a good idea?"

"No," she laughed, "but if you can move me just the slightest bit right now, only two weeks into your training..." She paused, her eyes bright with anticipation. "You're going to be unstoppable."

"What if I hurt you?"

"Don't flatter yourself." She winked.

With a chuckle, Jason cracked his back, loosened his shoulders, and prepared for the challenge in front of him. He let his hands fall to his sides, his palms facing up toward the ceiling, and Eve could see the far-off look in his eyes that told her he was melting. The excited pounding of her heart was distracting, beating in her eardrums and her throat, making it impossible for her to remain calm. *Please*, she thought to herself, *let this work.*

She didn't immediately notice when his eyes lost their faraway look, but she saw it now: his stare was intense and fixed on her, their eyes locked as if drawn together by a magnetic force. Jason lost his melt; he blinked and looked away.

"Sorry. Can't seem to focus," he mumbled.

"Close your eyes."

"Oh..."

"I mean," she stammered, "it'll probably help. That's all."

Again, Jason relaxed into a state of melting, this time with his eyes shut. Eve exhaled and squirmed in her seat, waiting impatiently for magic to happen right there in that room. The suspense was maddening, the quiet as torturous as nails streaking across a chalkboard, but she tried to pacify her anxious energy. Jason could do it—there wasn't a doubt in her mind, though the seconds felt like intolerable hours, and she couldn't stand to wait much longer. A faint prickling sensation coursed through her body: she assumed it was her nerves stirring within her, sending a tremor from the nape of her neck to her fingers and toes. She took a look down at the floor as the chill grew stronger, and suddenly she knew where the feeling was coming from.

"Jason, open your eyes."

His gaze slowly made its way from the floor to Eve, and a glint of awe lit up his face. Eve was hovering a foot above her chair. She was floating.

"Holy shit..." he murmured.

"You did it. You *really* did it."

Jason was still, his lips slightly parted as he stared back at her. Finally, he gently nodded his chin, following the motion of Eve's body as he rested her back in her seat.

"Thanks for the smooth landing," she quipped.

"Holy shit," he repeated. He looked at Eve as if he were seeing her for the very first time. "Holy. *Shit.* Did you see that?"

"I did."

"That was *unreal.*"

"Felt real to me."

He was quiet, his eyes panning from Eve's face down to his open palms.

"You're really powerful, Jason." Eve jumped from her seat, too inspired to sit still. "Most chimeras never use their gift. They're too scared. And those who do—they can melt pebbles, pencils, maybe books." Her smile was radiant. "You can melt *people.* That means something."

Eve's face suddenly dropped; Jason's excitement had faded into nothingness, his expression now bleak and somber.

"Jason, I'm kind of showering you with compliments here. This doesn't happen very often, you know."

He ran his fingers through his hair as he often did while deep in thought. "Can you imagine what we could do if we weren't *here,*" he growled, "stuck in this room?"

She frowned. "Got a case of cabin fever?"

"You have *no* idea." Jason wandered toward the window and peered between the blinds. "They keep telling me I'm not well enough to leave yet." He looked back at Eve, his eyes dark and feverish. "Look at me. I'm *fine.* I've been fine for *days.* But they're keeping me here anyway, and they won't give me a real reason why."

Eve sank into her chair; she watched him hover by the window, pacing back and forth like a caged animal, and realized that he was exactly that: caged, confined, and hidden from the world.

"I need to get out of here before I go crazy," he continued. "The only thing keeping me sane is—" He paused. "My sessions. With you."

An awkward silence filled the room. Eve could feel Jason's anxiety and his penetrating stare—she had to change the subject. Her eyes panned across the space until they reached the stack of gifts in the corner by his desk.

"I have a question for you." She nodded her head toward the pile. "Why haven't you touched those?"

He rolled his eyes. "They're not for me."

"Really? Because your name's written all over 'em."

"They're basically for my parents." He glared at the colorful stack as if it were mocking him. "Just a bunch of weak attempts to win favor with my dad.

Too bad he never stopped by to see just how many people are dying to kiss his ass."

"So, you're just going to leave them there?"

He shrugged. "I don't want anything to do with those people. I've never even met half of them."

Though he tried to conceal it, Eve could sense the bitterness in his words. She didn't blame him; the life he had lived was miles from hers—a life of comfort and affluence—and yet the jaded look on his face was one she herself had worn many times before. They were the same in that way.

With a spring in her step, she trotted toward Jason's pile of presents and rustled through the heap.

"There has to be something here from someone you know."

"You don't have to do that—"

"Come on, Jason." Eve smiled as she sorted through the packages. "It's like Christmas over here. You're stuck in this room all day. You should have a little fun."

"*Melting* is fun."

"I thought melting was a curse?"

"You're never going to let me live that down, huh?"

"Probably not."

"Okay," he folded, "you win. Hand me a damn gift."

Eve didn't know what she was looking for; none of the names were familiar to her, though she assumed that would be the case. And then she stumbled across it—the small blue box that had served as their plaything for the past two weeks. She removed a heart-shaped card from underneath the bow and scanned the text:

To: *Jason A. Valentine*

Lots of Love: *Madison Marie Palmer*

"*Madison* sent you a gift?"

"Oh God, put that one back. Better yet, burn it."

Eve ignored his request, tossing the gift onto his lap. "You have to open this."

"*Why?*"

"Just do it."

"Fine, I guess." He tore at the paper and revealed a box covered in diamond flecks. "Oh, *this* is very masculine..."

"What's inside?"

Jason slowly opened the sparkly box as if fearful of its contents. He stopped for a moment, his eyes bulged—and he laughed aloud, practically moved to tears by whatever was inside. With great reluctance, he reached inside and pulled out a scanty, bright pink lace thong.

"This is a joke, right?" he asked. "Did you know about this?"

Eve's jaw dropped. "She can*not* be serious!"

"You don't get to pick out any more gifts, Eve."

"Good God, I can't believe we've been levitating Madison's *underwear* this whole time."

"Told you we should've burned it!"

"It doesn't make sense," she stuttered. "She *demoted* you."

"Wait, demoted? What?"

"Nothing." Her cheeks flushed and she shook her head. "This was a bad idea." She hurriedly gathered her things together. "I have to go."

"Really? Already?"

"I have homework," she answered, pulling her shoulder bag over her arm and racing for the door.

"Oh..." Jason mumbled. "But you usually stay so much longer..."

She stopped by the exit, her hand hovering an inch above the doorknob. "I know, I'm sorry." Her eyes wandered back to Jason and then to Madison's pink skivvies tossed to the side of the room, and she cringed. "I'll see you tomorrow."

A half-second later, she was barreling through the isolation wing, desperate to leave Jason's room and Madison's panties far behind her. There was no explanation for what had happened there—at least, no rational one—and she quickly decided that she wouldn't bother trying to make sense of it all. Still, the image of Madison's underthings was ingrained in her thoughts like a foul branding, so much so that she completely forgot to even check the clerk's desk for Heather—she wasn't there, regardless—and instead kept charging forward. Just as Madison's pink thong flashed before Eve's eyes yet again, the elevator doors opened, revealing a friendly face waiting for her on the other side.

"Eve!" Armaan chirped. "What are you doing here?"

Eve grimaced as she stepped into the elevator. "Leaving. What are *you* doing here?"

"I'm trying to become a medical student—I'm *always* here," Armaan mumbled. "Are you done with Jason already? Don't you usually stick around a lot longer?"

"I have homework," Eve grumbled.

"Well, it doesn't matter. I was swinging by to pick you up anyway."

"Me? Why?"

"Dean Furst wants to see you."

"Furst? Really? What for?"

"How should I know? I'm just the *babysitter*."

Eve glanced over at her friend. His usually plucky spark was missing, and his face looked tired and drained.

"You okay?"

"Yeah, I'm fine," he sighed, leaning his back against the wall of the elevator. "It's just that everything is happening *around* me, and it's like I'm just... I don't know. Watching."

"What do you mean?"

"There's so much going on, you know? Like today, with the abduction." Armaan looked up at Eve, his eyes filled with sadness. "I could help, you know. I could do *something*."

"Armaan, that's what the patrolmen are for. That's *their* job."

"The patrolmen are a bunch of *hammers—*"

"*Armaan—*"

"I'm just saying," he moaned as the elevator doors finally opened, "I want to be a part of something *big*, Eve. Like you."

"Me?" She laughed. "I'm not a part of anything."

"But you're nursing an attack victim back to health."

"*Nursing?* God, you make it sound like I'm *breastfeeding* the guy."

"You're *involved*, Eve. And I'm nothing. I just... fade into the background."

She stopped and stared back at Armaan. She felt for him—it was hard not to.

"You want my advice, kid?"

Armaan shrugged. "Sure."

Eve leaned forward, struggling to reach eye level with her pint-sized escort, and put her hands on her hips authoritatively. "If you want people to see you, you have to *make* them see you."

He smirked. "Interesting suggestion coming from the girl who hates attention."

"Well, that's the difference between you and me, Armaan," she muttered. "I don't want to be seen."

Armaan left Eve standing in front of the dean's building, a location she had hoped she'd never have to visit again. She stared at the door as if it were an obstacle to overcome and cursed to herself as she finally made her way into the lobby. The striking receptionist was at her desk, and she raised her eyes slightly as the doors closed behind Eve.

"Miss Kingston—here to see Dr. Furst, yes?"

Eve nodded and promptly followed the golden-haired beauty down the hallway to Dean Furst's office door. Her mood had taken such a terrible turn, and the thought of their last visit only soured her spirits further. The first time they'd met, he had forced her to tutor Jason. And now, a new chimera had been abducted. Was history doomed to repeat itself?

The room seemed much quieter than the last time, almost unpleasantly still. Furst offered no smile nor welcome—just beckoned her toward him and pointed at the seat in front of his desk, instructing her to sit. As before, he scribbled across another never-ending stack of papers on his desk and ignored her while she impatiently shook her foot, waiting for the man to speak.

"Is this a bad time?"

Furst looked up from his paperwork, seemingly aggravated by her presence. "If it was, I wouldn't have called for you."

"Why did you need to see me so urgently?"

"I wouldn't call this meeting 'urgent.' Simply"—he paused—"convenient."

"Convenient for *you*," she mumbled.

Furst ignored her griping and flipped through his documents nonchalantly. "I'd like to discuss your tutoring services."

"I had a feeling. This is about the girl, right? The most recent attack victim?"

Furst finally glanced back at Eve, his forehead wrinkled, his glasses hovering at the tip of his nose.

"Pardon?"

"You know, one student is hard enough. I'm missing classes almost every day. People are *talking* about me, just like I thought they would," she rambled. "I'm sorry, but whatever you're offering—free grad school, a pony, I don't care—I can't tutor another chimera. It would solidify my fate. Everyone would know who I am."

Furst rested his pen and cocked his head, his gaze emotionless, almost bored. "Are you finished?"

"You don't even care, do you?"

"Whether or not I *care* is beside the point, Miss Kingston. You have clearly misconstrued the matter for which you are here."

Eve stopped short, confused. "Wait—you don't want me to tutor the girl?"

"No, Miss Kingston. The thought hadn't even occurred to me."

"Oh." Eve looked down at the ground and took in a deep breath. She assumed she would feel relief, but instead she felt puzzled, nonplussed, and even a bit angry.

"Why not?"

"Whatever do you mean?"

"Why am I tutoring Jason and not her? Does she have her own tutor?"

"No, Miss Kingston. She will not be tutored by you or anyone else."

"But why?"

"That is classified information—"

"So was the fact that I'm a chimera, and yet you found a way to put your strong sense of morality to the side on that one," Eve scoffed.

Furst glowered. "Jason Valentine is the son of a *senator*—"

"So I've heard."

Furst lifted his chin as if to deflect against Eve's cutting scorn. "Our most recent chimera is of a more... pedestrian livelihood."

"*Pedestrian?*" Eve sneered. "Of all the adjectives you could've chosen, you used *pedestrian?*"

"Well, what would you have *preferred*, Miss Kingston?"

"Well, I guess you could've taken the bold route and just come out with the truth—that she's unimportant. That her parents are mechanics or school teachers or whatever else—not *senators*."

Furst leaned back in his chair and crossed his arms. "Have you finished judging me?"

"Hardly."

"As much as I'd love to see the world through rose-colored glasses like you—"

"*Me?* See the world through rose-colored glasses? Has *hell* frozen over?"

"You 'root for the underdog,' as the saying goes," Furst cut in, his words stern. "It's an honorable trait, but, alas, it is unrealistic. My job requires me to be pragmatic, not *idealistic*."

Eve bit her bottom lip. "I guess calling it *pragmatism* makes it sound a lot less despicable."

"It's easy for you to label me as the villain, Miss Kingston," Furst coolly added, riffling through the documents on his desk once again. "After all, I did invade your privacy, as you so effectively indicated during our first meeting, and now there's this disagreement. But, as we speak, one hundred new patrolmen are stationing themselves across Billington at my request. We have refined our security and accelerated our defense efforts. And on top of that, I have made special arrangements for a new addition to our surgical team at the medical ward. You've heard of Dr. Dzarnoski, yes? He's the country's leading expert in humanovus medicine. He's here to treat our victims, and he's here because *I* asked him to be here. Now, Miss Kingston, do I still sound like a villain to you?"

Eve scowled. "Just tell me why I'm here."

"I'd like a full report on Jason Valentine."

"A *report*? What do you mean?"

"How is he doing? How is he coming along?"

"He wants to leave," she snapped. "He doesn't understand why he's still cooped up in the isolation wing when his chest is fully healed."

"Ah... so *this* is the source of your hostility. And I assume you want some type of explanation for that?"

"I don't, but he does."

Furst removed his glasses and rubbed his forehead, strained by her badgering. "The young man suffered serious injuries. You cannot possibly understand the severity of what his body endured. He may *feel* fine—"

"With all due respect, weren't you the one who told me that a week was, and I quote, 'more than enough time for a chimera to regain his strength'?"

Furst bowed his head and mustered a half-smile. "I had forgotten how sharp you are—too smart for your own good, if I do say so myself."

"So, what's the *real* explanation?"

"Miss Kingston, the world, for the most part, is familiar with the many qualities of chimeras: the gift, the muscle memory, the remarkable immune system. They've heard it in the news, read it in books, and so on and so forth. But few have actually *seen* these traits put to the test in a public setting."

"I don't understand what you're getting at."

"People are already aware that a chimera can heal at a much more accelerated rate than the average human being, but they do not get to see this healing process in action. Jason suffered trauma that no ordinary human could live through. People find it unsettling enough just knowing that he could survive that horror; can you imagine the fear, the *hysteria* that would ensue if people knew that he not only survived, but fully healed in only a week? It would create an uproar."

For once, Eve was at a loss for words. She sat in silence, her eyes like daggers. Finally, she spoke.

"How... *pragmatic.*"

"I know you think it's unfair, and to some degree it is, but it *is* for the greater good. Besides, Mr. Valentine is spending much of his days learning from you, and that is quite a privilege." Furst's words, though kinder than usual, were dripping with artificiality. "Now, on that note, tell me how the young man is *progressing.*"

Eve breathed in deeply and cradled her head in her hand. "He's..." She hesitated for a moment, her mind wandering to their sessions together—to his breakthrough earlier in the day, the tingling of her spine as she was lifted from her seat, and the warm, triumphant smile on his face.

"He's struggling."

Furst frowned. "Is that so?"

"Just needs more help with the basics, I guess."

"Well, I appreciate your honesty. I suppose we're going to have to address this issue pretty vigorously. You're meeting with him five days a week, correct?"

"Yes."

"Well then, we're just going to have to increase it to six. Better yet, we'll make it daily. You understand, yes?"

"Yeah," Eve stuttered. "I mean, if I have to."

Furst offered a condescending smile, pleased with Eve's sudden agreeability. "Splendid." He returned his attention to the paperwork on his desk. "I think we're done here, then. You're free to leave."

Eve refused to move from her chair. She stared back at Furst, her eyes scathing, and waited patiently for him to feel her presence.

Furst looked up from his work and removed his glasses yet again. "Did you hear me, Miss Kingston?"

"I heard you."

"I suppose you *want* something from me."

"Just a simple explanation."

"Well, please make haste with your question. My time is limited."

"*Who* has everything?" she asked, her tone strict and unwavering.

"Pardon?"

"And what *is* everything? And who's Fairon?"

"I don't believe I follow."

"Last week, you were in the medical ward with that patrolman," Eve explained, though she knew without a doubt that Furst recalled the interaction. "I want to know what you were talking about."

"Yes, I imagine you do. But that doesn't mean I'm obligated to tell you."

"It's the Interlopers, isn't it? You were talking about the Interlopers."

Furst pursed his lips with aggravation. "Miss Kingston, if you're concerned for your safety, I can assure you, there's nothing to fear."

"Look, it can't be *that* secretive if you and Colonel Scarface were talking about it out in the open like that. And if I have nothing to fear, you'd *tell* me what's going on."

"Miss Kingston—"

"I have a right to know," Eve boldly interrupted. "This affects me, too. It already affected Jason, that girl today, and God knows how many others. We *deserve* to know what we're up against. You need to tell me what's going on."

Furst remained unresponsive except for his eyes—they glared back at Eve, morphing into tiny slits that spoke volumes more than any words he could possibly utter. It was that penetrating stare which confirmed her greatest fear: that everything was far from okay, that Billington was most certainly in a state of turmoil. And with that realization, Furst finally broke his silence.

"My receptionist will see you out."

***

BANG BANG BANG.

Eve stared at the front door in silence. She could see the wood grain rattling with each loud, heavy thump. Someone was waiting on the other side; they were impatient, pounding at the door incessantly, as if their persistence would somehow bend her will, but it would do no such thing. She was accustomed to situations such as this, and she was *not* answering the door.

BANG BANG BANG.

She glanced around the entryway—her aunt was nowhere to be found, as was typical, though even when she was there she wasn't really, at least not to Eve. She turned back to the door—it looked alive, like a horrible monster, and in that moment, she could look at nothing else.

She flinched; a loud chorus of ringing joined the endless pounding, the two sounds transforming into a frightful symphony. It was too much—Eve sprang to life and hurried to the corner of the room, where she curled up into a small, tight ball, covering her ears and trembling in place as she kept her eyes firmly focused on the living, breathing, monstrous door.

Glass shattered, spilling across the living room and dangling from the window in sharp, jagged pieces, and Eve screamed. A small, silver object was flung into the room; she hadn't any time to discern what it was because shortly after it rolled across the carpet, a steady stream of smoke oozed from it, filling the room with an infinite mass of grey. Eve coughed on the smoke, her lungs raw in her chest, and soon her eyes stung so badly that tears gushed down her face. There was no other option, no escape, and so, against her better judgment, she ran for the door. It was what they wanted, after all—she knew this, even at such a young age, for she had experienced enough torment to know how it would end. In a fit of wild hysteria, she swung open the front door, took in one long, painful breath, and waited.

A hot, soggy mess splattered across her face, sticking to her cheek before it slid down her neck and dropped to the front step. She wiped her hand across her face—blood. A pile of, well, *something* was sitting at her feet—it was pink, slimy and stank of rancid flesh. Rotten meat—the entrails of an animal. Eve gagged, nearly choking on her own vomit, and dared to look out at her aunt's front yard.

There were people lined up across the lawn, though their faces were just a blur, as all she could see was a blanket of putrid guts. The people laughed menacingly, shouting *"chime"* over and over again as they flung the entrails at her, pelting her across her face, splashing her with blood and muck until it dripped down her nose and eyelashes. The stench was unbearable, but even worse was the wet slapping of the guts against her body. She screamed, the sound of her agony meshing with the despicable laughter until it faded into silence—until her vision changed from endless red to a quaking darkness.

Eve lurched up in her bed. It was a nightmare, and she flattened her hand against her chest as she felt her heartbeat slowly regain its normal rhythm. She checked her clock; it was three thirty-five in the morning, and she stared down at the light of the moon that trickled underneath her curtains, faintly setting her dorm room aglow. Madison was snoring like a fat man, tossing and turning beneath her heap of pink silk sheets, and for a brief moment Eve envied her.

There was no way Eve could go back to sleep, for each time she closed her eyes she saw nothing but red rain pouring down on her, a red that morphed into a pulsing, streaming black. It was decided, then—she tied her hair into a ponytail and slipped out of the room, desperate for a taste of the night and a hint of peace.

The elevator ride down to the Rutherford lobby felt longer than usual, and Eve nervously tapped her foot until she finally reached the ground floor. The lobby was warm and inviting, mostly because it was empty, and she basked in the solitude, comforted by the sound of nothing but her boots hitting the tile floor.

She sighed; a long stroll, she thought, was all she needed to clear her mind. She would find a spot, an isolated corner of the campus, stare up at the sky, and think about whatever the hell she chose to think about—certainly not her nightmares or the god-awful Interlopers, as they had already taken up enough space in her mind. She had to shake the anxiety, to rid herself of her demons. The gleam of the moon and the cool night air would be the perfect cure for her worry, and with a sense of hope, Eve barged through the front doors of Rutherford Hall.

Eve froze in her tracks. A rush of icy numbness shot up from her fingers and through her entire body, paralyzing her heart and lungs within her chest. She wanted to close her eyes, but they remained open, staring in disbelief at the grotesque display before her.

A large, metal construct in the shape of an "X" was propped in front of Rutherford Hall like some obscure statue, and a shadowy figure hung from it—a body, limp and broken. Dead. His arms and legs were pinned to the structure by large, needle-like rods, soaking his limbs in deep red blood that saturated his tattered suit. But his face was the most terrifying part of all: long, silver needles pierced through his eyes, securing his head to a metal sheet behind him. Streams of blood had dried on his cheeks like gruesome tears, his jaw hanging open as if his screams could still be heard.

Eve knew this face—she didn't need to see the dead boy's eyes to know that this was Marshall Woodgate, son of the current President of the United States.

As her paralysis slowly subsided, Eve's eyes made their way to the blood-bath at her feet. Huge streaks of ruby red were spread over the courtyard grounds, wildly smeared across the concrete beneath the X. Suddenly, she realized that the savage display was much more than just a horrifying mess—it was a message. Large letters painted in fresh, young blood detailed a hateful threat that could not be ignored:

STAND DOWN, OR MORE HUMANS WILL DIE.

CHAPTER 6: NIGHTMARES

"We will not stand down. This country does not fold under the threats of terrorists, nor will it accede to the demands of the Interlopers."

The Vice President and his podium were projected into the middle of the rec room, the hologram so clear and vivid that Eve could've sworn it was real. She and the Vice President were the only two figures there—the room had cleared out long ago, as this press conference was a rerun from days prior—but Eve couldn't seem to move from the spot where she stood. She watched the speech on repeat, playing it over and over again on every news station she could find, until she had memorized each word and hand gesture. It was almost a form of self-torture.

If she were honest with herself, she'd admit that there wasn't much need to watch the news anyway: the word of Marshall's death had spread like wildfire, and no one knew more of the gruesome details than she did. Still, even a week after she'd discovered his body, she could think of nothing but the bloody message and the needles protruding from his eyes.

The Vice President disappeared from the room, and a somber anchorwoman took his place. She cleared her throat before she spoke.

"The autopsy has confirmed that Marshall Woodgate was human, which would make this the first documented murder of a human being by an Interloper. Police have released a statement confirming that Marshall's death did not involve any type of dissection, and that it appears the Interlopers' only intent was to send a message to the American people. While their agenda is still centered on the chimera population, it is clear that the Interlopers are now willing to execute humans in order to meet

their goals."

Eve took in a deep breath, her blood as cold as ice. She listened intently to the broadcast, though it pained her to do so.

"Earlier today, the press asked the Vice President for an update on President Woodgate's stance on chimera relations. The Vice President declined comment."

Eve winced. *No comment*—she knew exactly what that meant. Her heart dropped in her chest, and though she thought gloom and defeat would overcome her, something else crept through her bones—something raw and empowering. It was the swell of anger that burned within her, inciting her to move, and so she did.

Her boots pounded against the floor as she stormed from the rec room and through the lobby, and just as the primal rage nearly swallowed her whole, she stopped short. The double doors of Rutherford Hall stood in front of her, and she breathed in deeply. She knew what was on the other side—what was waiting for her in the courtyard. With great apprehension, she glided her fingers down the wood grain, gripped the knob, and shoved the door open.

The crowd of protestors surged and roared, their bodies lumping together like a massive, multi-headed beast. They were ravenous and persistent, their fervor growing stronger and more heated with each passing day. Eve watched them for a moment, glancing across the scribbled signs they held above their heads.

SAVE THE HUMANS, CRUSH THE CHIMES

PROTECT THE HUMAN RACE, DESTROY CHIMERA COUNTRY

INTERLOPERS, YOU CAN HAVE THE CHIMES, WE DON'T WANT THEM!

With gritted teeth and no other options, Eve forced her way through the throng of people. They shouted at her, shoving their signs in her face as she shouldered her way through the maze of bodies. With an assertive push, she broke free from the pack and stumbled into the opposite side of the courtyard.

The faint, calming breeze of early October danced across Eve's face, though it was little consolation; the hatred was spreading until it literally waited for her at her doorstep. Eve turned to look back at the protestors, and instead she saw Marshall Woodgate's mangled body hanging in the center of the courtyard. She gasped, blinked twice, and he was gone.

Anger: it seethed inside of her yet again, reminding her where she was headed and why. She marched forward, shoving her hands deep into the pockets of her jeans in order to pacify her quaking fists. It was Saturday, and the campus was relatively empty, but Eve knew of one man who seemingly never left the gates of Billington. She was counting on him to be there, shuffling through paperwork as if doomed to do so for the rest of time, and so her fuming rage led her to the dean's building, where she was met by the surprised face of the receptionist.

"Can I—" She stopped short as Eve stomped right past her. "Miss? *Miss?* Where are you going?"

Eve headed down the hallway, paying no attention to the receptionist who scuttled behind her, wobbling on her stilettos and flailing her arms in the air.

"You can't go back there without an appointment!"

Eve barged through Furst's office door and marched to his desk, slapping her hands on his towering mound of paperwork.

"We need to talk," she growled. "*Now.*"

Furst was barely affected by the display. His eyes floated above the rim of his glasses as he looked up at Eve, and then behind her to his panic-stricken receptionist.

"Sir," she frantically stuttered, "I tried to stop her."

"It's all right, dear."

"But Doctor—"

"Miss Kingston is doing me a very important favor," he replied, casting a disapproving glare in Eve's direction. "The least I can do is humor her little interruption this *one* time."

The receptionist obediently bowed her chin and left the room, closing the door behind her. Eve wasted no time; she turned to Furst, thirsty for answers.

"Tell me what you know about the Interlopers."

Furst pushed his glasses back to the bridge of his nose and casually organized the trinkets on his desk. "I take it the Vice President's speech is still on the news." He nodded toward the burgundy leather chair in front of him. "Have a seat."

"I'd rather stand."

He sighed. "Perhaps that's for the best. My time is limited, and I'm sure you won't be staying for very long."

"You didn't answer my question."

"And that was intentional. Quite frankly, I'm surprised you're pursuing this avenue again, as it didn't garner much success for you the first time."

Eve crossed her arms, unimpressed with the dean's bitter tone. "What were you talking about with the colonel? What do they *have* that's so important? And for God's sake who—or *what*—is Fairon?"

"Miss Kingston, you're an intelligent young woman—too intelligent to possibly believe I would reveal *any* of this information to you."

"I need to know what I'm dealing with. We're all in danger—"

"And that's why we have patrolmen guarding the campus."

"Right, you beefed up security, and now the president's son is dead."

Furst grumbled, "I realize the events that have occurred are unfortunate—"

"Marshall Woodgate was *murdered*. It's not unfortunate, it's a *tragedy*."

"Everyone was deeply affected by his death—"

"Did *everyone* find his tortured body hanging in the Rutherford courtyard?"

Furst cocked his head almost patronizingly. "It was a terrible sight to witness, I'm sure, but the police won't be releasing your name to the public as the discoverer of Mr. Woodgate's body. You can take solace in that."

"I'm not *looking* for solace. I'm looking for *answers*."

"Answers I cannot provide."

"Don't you get it? The Interlopers got exactly what they wanted. Chimeras are public enemy number one now. *Everyone* is against us."

"An exaggeration, I'm sure."

"People are *protesting*, Furst, right where I found Marshall's body."

He sighed yet again, this time loudly. "Suppose I do answer your questions. What do you plan on doing with the information?"

Eve didn't respond. Instead she stared back at him, her jaw clenched and eyes squinted into a glare.

"Just as I suspected—you don't know."

"That's besides the point. We're easier targets for the Interlopers now more than ever." She leaned in closer to him. "The patrolmen can't defend us—that much is clear. I need to know what *you* know."

"What I know is that matters between the colonel and myself are none of your business—"

"*Dammit*, Furst—"

"I also know that security across campus has been increased to the highest degree possible without causing a sense of panic among students. The patrolmen are more than capable of keeping you safe, and aside from last week's hiccup—"

"Marshall Woodgate was a *hiccup?*"

"You have nothing to *fear*, Miss Kingston," the dean asserted, his gaze now just as firm as Eve's. "That is what I can tell you."

Eve stopped, her body heated, her lungs throbbing within her chest.

"So that's it? You're really going to leave me with nothing?"

"And what were you expecting?"

His face—the weathered lines; the fine, white hairs and limp skin—had taken on new form in Eve's eyes. It was a look she had seen before: in Heather McLeod, in Chin Dimple, in so many others from her past. She hated that face and all that it stood for. More than anything, she hated the anger still blazing within her.

"You *jackass.*"

"Miss Kingston, you *will* watch your tongue around me or—"

"Or what? You'll expel me? I'm sure your senatorial friend will be *so* upset to hear that Mr. Valentine lost his tutor because of you."

Furst's lips curled into an ugly glower. "There are *other* chimeras."

"But no one quite like me, and that, *my dear*, is a fact."

Without another word, Eve left the dean's office just as abruptly as she had entered and marched aimlessly across campus. Her hands trembled at her sides as her mind became flooded with anxiety and regret. She had behaved erratically—hell, she had called the university president a *jackass*—and to what end?

Her outburst was of little importance, or so she told herself, and she did her best to shake the confrontation from her thoughts. But just as Furst's deplorable face left her mind, she saw them—the Interlopers, Marshall Woodgate, the needles lodged deep into his eyes—and she was immediately overwhelmed with a sense of helplessness.

"Eve!" A voice shouted behind her. "Slow down!"

Eve stopped and turned to see Armaan running toward her. She waited for her pint-sized escort, all the while watching his shaggy mane bob back and forth atop his head as he frolicked across the courtyard.

"Geez, Eve, I've been looking all over for you," he panted, finally trotting to her side. "What were you doing in the dean's building, anyway?"

"Wasting my time, apparently," she muttered.

"Well, you're late for tutoring today. We need to hustle."

"They're making you escort me on weekends, too? God, Armaan, do you ever get a day off?"

He shrugged. "I don't mind, really. The more I'm at the ward, the better my chances are of getting into the medical program."

"Still, it doesn't seem fair. Just because I'm obligated to be there every day doesn't mean you should be, too. It's my burden, not yours."

Armaan glanced up at Eve. "Psh, yeah, *right*," he scoffed. "Your *burden*."

Eve's head spun toward him. "What's that supposed to mean?"

"Nothing."

"That wasn't '*nothing*.'"

"Yes it was."

"You meant something by it."

Armaan let a smile slip as if he knew a scandalous secret. "I just think that maybe you're enjoying your time in the isolation wing more than you're letting on."

"And why would you jump to that conclusion?"

"Word in the ward is that Jason is struggling with his gift, which is rather odd, seeing as you've been telling me how insanely dynamic he's been doing."

"So?" She crossed her arms. "Maybe they've got their facts mixed up."

"Or maybe you lied about him to Furst," Armaan countered with a wink. "But what do I know? I'm just a teenage genius."

Eve grumbled, "So I told a little white lie. I had the best intentions."

"Were those intentions to spend more time with Jason?"

"Do you think I *want* to tutor him seven days a week?"

"I don't *think* you do. I *know* you do."

She rolled her eyes. "Armaan, please."

"It's cute, Eve. Don't fight it."

She scowled at her friend, unamused by his quip. "Look, Jason's a lot stronger than I anticipated. I thought if we spent more time together, I could help him reach his full potential."

"So you lied to Furst in order to *help* Jason? It had nothing to do with his tight muscles or charming smile?"

"Okay, who supposedly has a crush on him—me, or you?"

Armaan paused. "Fair enough. I got carried away for a second."

The twosome entered the medical ward and headed for the elevators. Eve looked down at Armaan—his face still donned a silly grin, which irked her to the core—and she sighed loudly.

"Jason's gift is growing more powerful each day. A few sessions a week could take him to the next level. I thought that was a goal worth pursuing. Don't you?"

"I'm sorry, did you say something? I was too busy imagining your wedding day. You'll look *so* beautiful in white, Eve."

Eve glared at Armaan in silence, hovering over his tiny body in the elevator.

"I could punch you right now."

"Please don't, I'm very fragile."

The elevator doors opened before them, and Eve hurried down the hallway, eager to be rid of Armaan's dopey smile and wild accusations. She saw the isolation wing in the distance, and her eyes immediately shot toward the nearby clerk's desk—no Heather today, thankfully. She handed her ID badge to the towering security guard, and as the door swung open, she promptly made her way inside, catching a glimpse of her small friend as the door closed behind her.

He flashed her a smug grin. "Have fun with your *boyfriend.*"

Eve grabbed at the door handle and pushed her head through the opening. "He's *not* my boyfriend!"

With a childish pout, she charged through the wing and burst into Jason's room. Jason was sitting at his desk, his forehead wrinkled as he glided his fingers across his scratchpad, undoubtedly catching up on his studies. He turned to greet her and smiled, and though she wanted to cling to her lingering frustrations, she felt her spirits lift just the slightest bit.

"Notice anything different?" he asked.

Eve glanced at his chest, which for the first time since their sessions began was miraculously clothed. "You're not half-naked?"

"Very funny." He lifted the bottom of his t-shirt. "How about now?"

Her eyes scanned across his chiseled abdomen. She quickly looked away. "I'm sorry," she stuttered, "what am I looking at?"

"The scar, what else? They removed my staples."

"Oh." Eve had almost forgotten about his scar, but she saw it now—the pink incision line was surrounded by small puncture marks where the staples had once been. "How was it?"

"Hurt like hell. The doctor said they'd left them in for way too long. Guess it's harder to tell with people like us."

Eve plopped her body into her usual seat. "So, what now? Are you free to go?"

"I'm still here, aren't I?" He stood up and stretched his back. "They said they want to keep me here a little while longer for *observation.*"

Eve sighed; she knew what "observation" truly meant.

"Any news on Marshall Woodgate? The police didn't tell anyone, right? No one knows you found the body?"

The sound of his name alone sent a chill through her bones. "They kept my name anonymous."

"And the protestors?"

"Worse and worse by the day."

The room fell silent, though Eve knew it wouldn't remain so for long. Jason sat in front of her, his elbows resting on his knees, his eyes staring back at her with that all-too-familiar look—a look that would certainly lead to a question.

"Are you okay?"

"Jason, I'm *fine*," she growled.

"You found a dead body. You can understand why I'd be concerned."

"And *you* can understand why I wouldn't want to talk about it."

He sighed. "Look, I won't ask again, if that's what you want. You keep people at arm's length—I get that. I just hope that, by now, you know you can trust me."

Eve shrank back in her chair; his honesty stung like the rip of a bandage from her ever-resilient pride. She couldn't stand it: his disarming presence, that *quality*, whatever it was, that made her feel so completely at ease and uncomfortable all at the same time. Usually her intuition told her to trust no one, but in the case of Jason, her instincts were skewed, shouting mixed messages and conflicting data like a computer system gone haywire. She looked up at him.

"I see him—Marshall. I see him all the time."

Jason's head perked up. "Yeah?"

She stood from her seat and fretfully paced across the room. "The needles jutting out of his eyes. The blood pouring from his sockets." She stopped suddenly and parked herself beside him, sinking into his weathered mattress. "You know, I've seen more than my fair share of..."—she paused, struggling to get the word out—"...*death*. I thought it'd get easier. I was wrong."

Jason grabbed her hand and squeezed it tightly. It was shocking—like a pulse of electricity burst from his fingers into hers—and then it faded into warmth. Into exactly what she needed. She let out a long, deep breath.

"Thanks."

"For what?"

"For being so..." She hesitated. "So *you*."

"So *me?*"

"For giving a shit."

He chuckled. "I care about you, Eve."

The two stared blankly at the wall in front of them, and in that moment Eve felt strong, liberated, and *angry.* Rage was boiling inside of her once again as thoughts of Marshall and the Interlopers overtook her.

"You know what they're doing, right?" She turned to Jason. "The Interlopers—they're pitting us against one another. They're giving humans a reason to hate us, and it's *working.* They're winning through fear."

Jason's lips curled disgustedly. "All of this—everything that's happening—it's just the beginning. They'll kill again. Another human, or maybe—"

"A chimera. One of us."

A darkness hovered over the pair of them. Suddenly, Eve realized their hands were still clasped together; she quickly pulled hers away and folded her arms.

"I saw Furst today."

"What, why? What did he say?"

"It doesn't matter. He wouldn't tell me anything. Kept repeating some bullshit about having nothing to fear—about how the patrolmen will take care of us." She rolled her eyes. "What a joke, right? The patrolmen aren't doing anything."

Jason looked over at Eve, studying her closely. She had triggered something inside him—she knew this, as after nearly three weeks together, she could see right through him—and she braced herself for whatever pestering question or impetuous conclusion he was about to throw her way.

"We could do something, Eve."

"No, we couldn't."

"Do you really believe that?"

Again, the room was quiet. Eve ignored Jason's gaze and stared out the window, which was all the answer he needed.

"Look, Eve, we're *powerful.* You know that a hell of a lot better than I do. Haven't you even thought about it?"

"Yes, I've thought about it—a lot, actually. I've thought about how I'm only nineteen years old. How I have no money, no experience, no weapons."

"I don't buy that. I *know* you. You know your strength." He leaned in closer to her. "You can't deny what you're capable of. And you shouldn't be afraid of it, either."

"I'm *not* afraid."

"Then why are you brushing this off?"

"Because it's *too much*, Jason," she spat. "I can't save myself *and* the world at the same time."

"Save *yourself?*"

"Just," she mumbled, resting her forehead in her hands, "just forget about it."

Eve could see Jason's face out of the corner of her eye. His look of disappointment was almost too much to bear. She breathed in deeply.

"Look," she began, this time much more calmly, "what I'm trying to say is that... I prefer to fly under the radar."

"Really? With a gift like yours?"

"People here don't know I'm a chimera. They can't." She picked at her cuticles anxiously. "Alien fighter isn't exactly the best cover for someone like me."

"It's not like you'd be doing it alone, you know. You have me."

Their eyes finally met, and Eve felt as if she was exposed and unarmed before him. Jason's stare was aching, like a heavy weight on her weakened back, and *God* was it unfair of him to look at her like that.

"Can we just drop this for now?"

He frowned, defeated. "Fine, but this isn't over."

A stream of vile words flooded Eve's mouth, begging to be spoken, but she swallowed them down like vinegar. She was frustrated—with Billington, with the Interlopers, but mostly with herself. But before she could ruminate on the subject any longer, something else caught her attention.

"Jason, is that *blood* on your neck?"

"*Shit*," he muttered, immediately barreling toward the sink.

"What happened?"

He rolled his eyes. "I think you know what happened."

After washing the blood spot from his neck, he turned to face Eve. She was scowling at him, not out of irritation or disapproval, but out of worry.

"I was trying to see if I could melt two things at the same time," he explained. "It worked with the small stuff—silverware, balled-up socks—but once I tried something bigger... well, you get the idea."

"What were you melting?"

"The bed and the desk."

"*God*, Jason—"

"I had to see if I could do it, Eve."

She sighed; she could feel his aggravation festering in his tense shoulders and rigid jaw. It was a frustration she had felt many, many times before.

"It's a *really* complicated melt. Give it time. I don't know of any chimera who can melt multiple things at once except—"

"You?" He smirked.

He was right; after all, it was the hardest melt to conquer, an unpredictable task with plenty of hazardous consequences. And with that, a new thought came to Eve's mind. She smiled and stood from the bed.

"We're doing something different today," she explained. "You're going to control a moving object."

"That sounds like a potential disaster."

"Oh, don't get me wrong, it's extremely dangerous," she grinned childishly, "but it's the most fun you'll have melting, *easily.*"

"All right, Teach, so what am I working with?"

She didn't answer; instead, her eyes spoke for her, glowing with anticipation as her feet bounced with restless excitement.

Jason stared back with confusion, and then it hit him. "Oh, no, not again," he insisted, waving his hands in disagreement. "We're not doing it this way."

"What? I haven't even said anything."

"It's you, Eve. You're the moving object."

She cocked her head innocently. "So what if I am?"

"You just got through saying how dangerous this is—"

"*And* how *fun* it is!"

"I'm not going to risk your safety over some stupid trick."

"Stupid *trick*?" she gasped playfully. "I'm going to pretend you didn't say that."

"We can practice with something else. Not you."

"Come *on*, Jason. You obviously wanted a challenge. I'm giving you one."

"I said no, Eve."

She folded her arms and pouted. "Look, I wouldn't recommend this if I didn't think you were capable."

He didn't respond.

"Now it's your turn to trust *me*, Jason."

He sighed. "God, Eve, way to back me into a corner."

She pranced to the opposite side of the room, delighted with her conquest. "You're welcome!"

"So, how are we doing this?"

"Well, I figured I'd just run across the room and jump, and then you can take it from there."

"That's a horrible idea," he groaned.

"Oh, please." She winked. "Don't be such a scrote."

"Oh, so now we're name-calling?" He laughed. "Fine, you win. I'll do it."

Eve stretched her legs, preparing for her short sprint across the room. "Now, this might take a few attempts. You won't have time to relax, so you'll have to melt instantly." She took her stance. "Just, please, whatever you do, don't get distracted. I don't want to be like your snow globe and end up in pieces all over the floor."

"Wow. No pressure, huh?"

The teasing stopped as they stood facing one another, bracing themselves for the task at hand. Every possible outcome played through Eve's mind, both the compelling and the unfortunate, but she felt fearless and confident.

With a deep breath, she dashed across the room and leapt into the air, and all the while Jason stared at her with intense, focused eyes. Then, less than half a second later, her feet smacked against the ground, and she stumbled along the linoleum floor.

Nothing had happened. Jason scowled at Eve, his eyebrows raised in that *I-told-you-so* fashion she absolutely loathed.

"What?" she scoffed. "Did you expect to get it on the first try? Please, you're good, but you're not God."

Without a single hesitation, Eve flung herself across the room for a second time, bouncing into the air with even more height than before, and again she landed on the floor with a thud.

"Again," she commanded.

She sprinted past the hospital bed once, twice, three more times, again and again, each time without any improvement or even the slightest levitation.

"Look, I can't concentrate," Jason moaned. "I don't want to hurt you."

"You're not going to hurt me."

"You don't know that—"

"I do," Eve interrupted. "I really do."

Jason looked back at her; she was smiling, her eyes sparkling with a level of optimism he wasn't used to seeing in her. With a nod, he took his place on the opposite side of the room and waited for her launch.

Again Eve bolted across the room, her stare fixed directly on Jason. With a grunt, she jumped into the air—this would be the eleventh time—but for whatever reason, this attempt felt different: she felt powerful, her spring so high that she thought, just for a moment, that she could almost touch the ceiling, and before she knew it, she was doing just that. With a light thump, her entire back was pressed against the ceiling as if ungoverned by the laws of gravity. She looked down at Jason, who was standing beneath her, laughing loudly with wide, excited eyes.

"You're right, this *is* fun," he beamed. "How do you feel?"

"Like a superhero," she chuckled, still floating high above him. "Come on, don't just leave me here—make me fly."

At her request, Jason sent Eve dipping down from the ceiling and gliding through the room, soaring like a small, delicate airplane in what little space was available. She swerved low to the ground and then high into the air, looping in circles and all the while laughing hysterically at the carefree nonsense of it all. She spun her arms and kicked her feet as if she were swimming, flying across the space and even circling Jason for a brief moment until she decided anything further would leave her feeling sick, and so he gently lowered her to the ground.

"I told you," she cheered, scurrying back toward her starting place. "We're doing *that* again for *sure*."

But before she could reach the opposite wall, her body was once again torn from the ground and launched into the air. She felt weightless, as if guided by an invisible hand, but she didn't stay aloft for long this time: soon her feet were scraping the linoleum beneath her, heading for an awkward and uncontrolled landing. She thumped clumsily to the ground and stumbled, trying to regain her footing but instead crashing into something firm and steady, something that scooped her up in its arms. Her hair was messily strewn across her face and her limbs felt limp and disjointed, but something was holding her, stabilizing her—and as she caught her breath, she realized that the something was Jason. They stood nose to nose, their eyes locked, their hands tightly clutching one another.

"Sorry for the rough landing," he said, sweeping the tendrils from her face. "Guess I got distracted."

Eve felt small in Jason's arms. He held her close, as if at any moment she might slip away, and though her breathing had now steadied, her heart began to race.

"It's—" She stopped, suddenly very aware of the situation. She backed away from Jason, breaking his hold and nervously straightening her blouse. "It's okay. You're doing great."

"Eve, I wasn't trying to—"

"Jason, it's fine." She didn't bother to let him finish—she knew what he was going to say. It was all becoming too easy. Too wonderful. Too much. She forced a smile.

"Let's get back to work."

***

"MURDERER!" he screamed.

The stone smacked against her face, and Eve fell to the ground, her hands and cheek sliding along the gravel. She could feel the sting of dirt forming a crust over her open wounds, and her palms were pink and bloody like raw meat. She tried to hoist herself onto all fours, but the boy kicked her in the ribs, and again she collapsed to the floor.

"CHIME!"

Her classmates encircled her, chanting the obscenity with their fists held high. They were impassioned, consumed with some deranged power, an authority that commanded them to hurt Eve—to kill her.

Eve's hands ached, and she gripped at the ground beneath her, struggling to lift her heavy body onto her knees.

The world went black; Eve felt a heavy pounding against her temple, one that reverberated through her skull and centralized in her brain. A rock thudded to the ground beside her, and she felt the cool rush of blood dripping down her neck. Her chest lurched forward, landing in a flat, feeble pile in the middle of the playground. She tried to breathe, but blood gurgled in her throat, and with a pitiful hack, she coughed out a tooth, which fell to the ground in a splatter of the reddest blood she had ever seen. The chanting of her classmates grew louder and louder until their words were imprinted on her brain.

"KILLER!"

"DIE, CHIME! DIE!"

Eve mustered every ounce of strength she had and flopped onto her back. The sky was so beautiful and blue above her, without a cloud in sight, and the sun shined brightly. It was such a lovely vision to enjoy before she died.

"STEP ON HER!" a girl shouted. "STOMP ON HER FACE!"

Eve's view of the sky was blocked by the bottom of a boot. It seemed to approach in slow motion, gradually inching closer until she could smell the dog feces and bubblegum wedged in the crevices of it's sole.

Just as the lining of the boot grazed the tip of her nose, her hand suddenly came to life, springing up and grabbing the boy's ankle. She hardly knew what was happening—her arm acted on its own, as if independent from her body, and without warning, she tossed the boy forward, throwing his body into the air and sending him tumbling to the ground beside her.

The crowd of children shrieked with terror. Eve leapt to her feet, amazed by her sudden power and newfound strength. Her clothes and skin were practically soggy with blood, yet she felt revitalized and restored. Adrenaline flowed through her veins like fuel, and the sound of the crying children became nothing but white noise, drowned out by the heavy thumping of her heart.

"KILL HER!" they screamed. "SHE'S A MURDERER!"

A boy picked up a rock beside his foot, tossing it back and forth between his hands as an evil grin spread across his lips. He wound up and, with a grunt, flung the rock at Eve as hard as he could, aiming for right between her eyes. The rock flew toward her like a bullet—then stopped inches from of her face, where it quivered slightly as it hovered in the air.

The children gasped, mesmerized by the floating rock. Eve watched it bob in front of her, then turned her gaze to the boy who had made her his target. Their eyes met—his body froze, and she could see sweat trickle down his forehead. Eve relaxed her shoulders as the pain in her body subsided into numbness, and through the sheer force of her mind, she sent the rock hurtling back at the crowd.

The students screamed and scattered. The rock hit no one and fell harmlessly to the ground—just as Eve had intended—but the kids ran, saving themselves from the filthy chime, the *monster* they had stoned.

Eve was free from their torment—at least, for the remainder of the day. It was likely to continue tomorrow.

Suddenly the terrible pain in her body reemerged, and the reality of her situation hit her: she was dying. No, not literally dying, but she knew that the life she had lived was dead, never to be resurrected. Evelyn Kingston was no more. She was now *chimera*. Chime. Monster. *Murderer*. And with that last thought, Eve burst into tears, the salt stinging the scrapes on her cheeks.

"How sad," a familiar voice whispered in her ear.

Heather stood beside Eve as she watched her eight-year-old self grieve in the middle of the playground.

"It's really quite a shame," Heather said. "I mean, look at you. So pitiful."

"What do you want, Heather?"

"I just have a message for you. That's all."

"And what's that?"

"It's all going to happen again." Heather smiled sadistically. "I think you should be prepared for that. We're going to stone you. We're going to eat you alive."

Eve stared helplessly at her childhood self, who had crumbled into a ball on the ground, sobbing uncontrollably, crying out for the parents who would never come to rescue her.

"You need to know, Eve—it's all over."

Eve's eyes flicked open, and she gasped aloud at the sound of her alarm clock. With a deep breath, she sat up in her bed and cradled her head in her hands. It felt like a cruel punishment, to be tormented by Heather both during the day and while she slept.

She glanced to her side—Madison's bed was empty, as it had been when Eve fell asleep the night before. In fact, she couldn't remember the last time she'd seen Madison. Had Eve been deprived of Madison's shimmering diamonds and vapid drivel all weekend? She shrugged and began her morning routine.

It was refreshing, walking to class on her own for once. Monday morning had never felt so good, so *invigorating*. She was so pleased to be rid of Madison and Hayden that she almost didn't notice the eyes following her. Almost. It became painfully obvious after the fifth time someone's eyes locked with hers and then darted away. Eve stopped for a moment; she fiddled with her tie and adjusted the waistline of her trousers. Was her blouse unbuttoned? Was her hair astray?

Another girl in the distance stared at Eve as she waited for the elevator to arrive. Clearly, Eve was imagining things. She was letting her nightmare get to her. No one was looking at her. Without Madison and Hayden by her side, flipping their hair and loudly ranting about shallow nonsense, there was nothing to look at anyway.

The business building was visible off in the distance. Clusters of students congregated on the front steps, and Eve expected to find her two comrades standing among the rest, but still they were missing. Instead, her eyes landed on a small group of girls—Rutherfordians; she had seen them in the tower—whispering to one another. And staring back at her. At Eve.

Eve looked away; she was allowing her nightmare to consume her, a horrible habit she used to have as a child and certainly not one she cared to reacquire.

Eve continued on to class, where she took her usual seat toward the back of the lecture hall, only to see that Madison and Hayden still hadn't arrived. It was strange, really, their sudden absence. She didn't mind it, of course, though as class continued, she couldn't help but stare at the door, waiting for the two blondes to barge through unannounced. The time never came though, and as class ended and Eve headed for the exit, she found herself completely baffled.

"Miss Kingston?"

Eve jumped, jolted by the voice behind her, and turned around to find the kind face of Professor Clarke.

"Sorry, Eve, didn't mean to startle you." He smiled.

Eve breathed a sigh of relief. "It's okay, I'm just a little edgy this morning, I guess. Did you need something?"

"I just wanted to see how you're doing."

"Oh," she stuttered, "well, to be honest I'm a little behind on my homework..."

"No, no," he looked to either side and lowered his voice. "I wasn't talking about that."

"Oh..."

"I just want to see how you're holding up," he continued. "When someone is given so much responsibility at such a young age, it can take a toll on them."

Eve smiled awkwardly. "I'm okay."

"You sure?"

"Yeah. It's nice of you to ask, though."

Professor Clarke crossed his arms, his brow twisted as if puzzled. "No one's giving you any problems?"

Eve thought back to Heather's deceit and Madison's endless array of questions. She remembered their constant badgering, and then she thought about their complete disappearance over the past few days.

"Everything's fine."

"Well, if that changes, you can talk to me."

"Thanks, Professor, but I don't think that's necessary—"

"I'm serious," he maintained, his voice suddenly firm. "If there's any trouble, you let me know."

Eve's nerves softened the slightest bit. With a quick nod, she hurried from the room and into the hallway, only to be stopped immediately outside the door. Her path was blocked by a barrier of girls—the three girls she hadn't seen all day.

"There's about to be some trouble," Hayden giggled.

Before Eve stood Hayden and Heather, both wearing menacing grins, and wedged in between them was Madison, her face twisted into a wicked glare.

"You little *bitch*," Madison snarled.

Her words felt like a bus barreling into Eve's chest.

"Did you just call me—"

"Shut up!" Madison snapped. "You don't get to talk!"

Eve's mouth gaped open. "What the *hell* has gotten into you?"

"You *sicken* me, do you know that?"

"Madison—"

"I told you to *shut up!*" she barked. The hallway traffic slowed to a halt as students turned to watch the scene unfolding before them.

"You're a filthy, repulsive *parasite*. Your existence is a *disgrace* to the rest of the world. I'm almost *embarrassed* for you."

Eve felt her blood bubbling within her like a seething cauldron. Her chest burned and her throat tightened as she tried to remain calm and apathetic, but apathy was the last thing she felt.

"Do you think I'm *stupid*? That I'd never find out?" Madison face was just inches from Eve's. "You're a *joke*, Eve."

"So what am I, Madison? A parasite, a disgrace, or a joke?" Eve sneered. "You've used a lot of colorful terms to describe me during this lovely conversation."

"*Screw you, bitch.*"

"Oh, yes, I forgot—I'm a bitch, too."

Without warning, Madison slapped Eve across the face, the impact so fierce that Eve's neck spun violently in the opposite direction. Eve took a second to contain herself, certain that her shock was written across her face. She stared into Madison's hateful eyes and then at the dozens of classmates who stood like statues, gawking at her public lynching.

"YOU'RE A GODDAMN *CHIMERA*, EVE!"

It was here: the day she had feared. The day she had been running from since she'd first walked through Billington's gates. The words cut deeper than any blade, but all she could feel was the pounding in her chest and the aching of her cheek. The onlookers gasped and whispered. Her secret was out.

"I can't *believe* I've been sharing my room with a *chimera*. It disgusts me. *You* disgust me."

"Hit her again, Maddie!"

"*Shut up*, Hayden," Madison hissed, her eyes still fixed on Eve's face. "You tried to fool me, Eve. You lied to me about *everything*—about who you are, about tutoring Jason—"

"I *am* tutoring Jason—"

"Oh *please*, that's a load of bullshit. You're probably *breeding*."

"*Breeding*? God, I'm not some *animal*—"

"You're not human either, you *freak!*" She leaned in close enough for Eve to feel her heavy breathing. "Let this be a lesson to you, *chimera*: you do not *lie* to Madison Palmer. You do not *screw* with Madison Palmer." She brought her lips toward Eve's ear. "I will make your life *miserable*."

Madison flipped her hair across her back and stormed down the hall with as much finesse as she could muster. Hayden scrambled behind her, pausing for one moment to look back at Eve.

"I always *hated* you," she jeered before scurrying off.

The onlookers slowly dispersed down the hallway, all wearing the same critical glare. Most muttered to one another or growled slurs in Eve's direction, and one man even spat at her feet, then wiped his lips triumphantly. Eve stood with her back to the wall and lifted her chin high as if it would somehow help her rise above the verbal sewage that had been spewed in her face. She resisted the urge to cup her cheek—the pain had subsided to a numbness that felt heavy on her jaw—as such an action would symbolize weakness, vulnerability, or worse, defeat.

Eve shot a resentful glare at Heather. The redhead still stood in front of her, tapping her heel against the floor with an air of cheer and self-contentment. She offered Eve a smile—the same smile she had worn the day they'd met.

"Are you happy?" Eve asked through gritted teeth.

"Oh, more than words can express."

"Tell me, Heather, *why?* Why waste your time on me? How does my suffering benefit you in any way?"

"Eve, darling, it's not personal—it's politics." She nestled up to Eve's side, glancing across the hall to make sure no one else was listening. "We both came to this school for a reason: to be powerful."

"That's not why I'm here."

"You don't expect me to believe that, do you?" she smirked. "The strongest leaders on this planet ruled through force. They captured their supporters through the most basic, primal emotion that mankind has to offer: *fear*. If I'm going to be someone, if I'm going to leave a mark on this world, I need to be feared. I feed off of the terror." She blissfully closed her eyes. "It's like candy to me."

Eve grimaced. "You're sick, do you know that?"

"Maybe I am. Or maybe I'm just a realist."

"Why are you telling me this? Why reveal your 'master plan' to the person you just buried?"

Heather lightly rested her hand on Eve's shoulder and gave it a squeeze. "What does it matter? After today, no one will be talking to you anyway." She dug her nails deep into Eve's back. "You'll have no one to tell."

With one last patronizing grin, she began to walk away. Compelled by pure impulse, Eve grabbed at Heather's wrist and yanked her back.

"One last question, *darling*," Eve scoffed.

"And what's that?"

"How did you find out? Medical records? Talk in the ward?"

Heather giggled and pulled her arm from Eve's grip.

"Silly Eve, I knew the whole time."

Eve felt her heart sink with Heather's words. They replayed in her mind over and over again—she'd known the whole time. The *whole time*. The phony friendships, the shameful stifling; the secrets, the suppression, and above all else, the lies. None of it had been necessary; she'd been discovered before she'd even set foot on campus.

"You knew this whole time... and you waited until *now*?"

"Well, I could've said something sooner. Actually, I was planning to, to tell you the truth. That day, back in the medical ward. But there was an unforeseen complication."

Eve clenched her jaw. "Jason."

"Yes, right, your student. His arrival at the ward made a mess of my plans. But you know what? I'm glad that it happened. I'm thrilled, actually, that he was rushed through the ward at the exact moment I planned on exposing you. Because this way was *so* much more fun. Better than I could have possibly imagined!"

Heather finally turned away, her frilly A-line skirt twirling around her as she shimmied down the hall. As the other students hurried along, their faces distorted with repulsion, Heather turned back once more, her smile still intact.

"Welcome to your nightmare, Eve."

CHAPTER 7: DEEP BREATHS

Deep breath.

Eve's lungs expanded slowly, smoothly, as she pinned her hair to the side. Today was a very important day—a thought that she pushed to the back of her mind. It was too somber to think about, and besides, she had other worries. She adjusted her collar and stared at her reflection. She looked pretty: her outfit was simple yet charming, and somehow her hair fell into perfect placement for the first time in years. It seemed so ironic, how lovely and almost angelic she looked on a day such as this. No blouse or hairstyle would convince anyone that she was an angel—in the eyes of the masses, she was nothing but a villainous monster.

She turned from her mirror and faced her dorm room. A blood-red strip ran down the middle of the floor—Madison had taped the room, dividing it in half, as if to create a protective barrier from Eve and her belongings. The heiress had snuck in while Eve was away and stacked her mountain of suitcases on her own side, forming what looked like a bright pink fort next to her bed. The whole thing was so childish; but then again, the past few days had felt like one long flashback from Eve's childhood.

Deep breath.

Eve left her dorm room and strolled down the hallway as if it were any other day—as if everything were normal. Unfortunately, her composed demeanor was a façade. Everything was *not* normal; everything had changed. Her back straightened as she sauntered past the other Rutherfordians, who watched her with eyes filled with hate, or fear, or curiosity. She pretended not to notice.

The elevator dinged as it arrived at the twelfth floor, and Eve entered—alone. She stood in silence as she listened to the soft hum of the moving cables, her shoulders rigid and her fingers tight. She had to prepare herself for what she was about to face that day; there was no room for surprises.

As she stepped out into the lobby, the other Rutherfordians stopped dead in their tracks, but she paid no attention to them. She looked straight ahead without so much as a blink or a flicker of her lashes. It was a trick she had learned years ago, a technique that, for whatever reason, made the attention feel less perverse.

The doors to the courtyard were just a few yards away, and she knew that if she were to maintain her indifferent front, she would have to exit the lobby without the slightest hesitation. With expressionless eyes, she shoved the doors open and coolly made her way outside.

"THAT'S HER!"

Deep breath.

The protestors surrounded her, shoving her back and forth like rabid dogs fighting over a kill. She could sense herself drowning, sinking deeper into the endless pit until all she could see were countless screaming mouths and bloodshot eyes. They thrust their signs in front of her—*KILL THE CHIMES* and *YOU ARE NOT ONE OF US*—while barking smutty slurs, which faded into white noise in the back of her mind. *You don't have to take this,* she thought to herself. *You can silence them with the slightest melt.* She suppressed the thought, as tempting as it was, and pushed her way through the horde until she reached the other end of the courtyard.

Her formerly perfect hair now fell messily across her face, but otherwise Eve had escaped the crowd unscathed. She did her best to shake her locks back in to place as she continued toward the business building, quickening her stride until the protestors were far behind her.

Unfortunately, the animosity didn't disappear with them—Eve was now the center of attention no matter where she went. Since her true identity had been revealed just one week ago, her peers no longer saw her as Evelyn Kingston, or a Rutherfordian, or even as that-tall-girl-who-lives-with-Madison-Palmer.

She had been reduced to *chimera.* Nothing more.

The stairs at the front of the business building felt steeper with each passing day. The climb was so mentally taxing that Eve failed to even notice the slips of paper blowing down the steps with the breeze. Students walking out of the building muttered and gawked as she approached, but this was already so familiar, so ordinary. She opened the doors and made her way inside.

Deep breath.

The hall was a sea of white and grey; papers lined the walls and doors from floor to ceiling, and countless more slips were spilled across the ground. Clusters of students cluttered the walkway, their hands eagerly gripping the pages, their lips flapping with gossip. As the doors closed behind Eve, all eyes turned to her in unison, and suddenly the hallway went dreadfully silent. Eve's limbs became heavy and her throat tightened; she knew what was happening. She yanked one of the pieces of paper from the wall and observed the slander for herself.

It was a photo of her—from where, she didn't know, perhaps the face database Heather had raved about—but it was the writing that she was most concerned with. *EVELYN JANINE KINGSTON* the page read, and beneath it was a phrase that sent her heart sinking into her stomach.

CHIMERA BITCH.

The words were dense and black, much like the soul of whoever had hatched this sickening scheme.

Deep breath.

Eve crumpled the slip of paper into a ball and let it drop to the ground. She considered removing each and every flyer from the walls, the doors, the floor, but it was a futile effort—more slanderous material would surely be gracing the business building soon after anyway. Instead, she swallowed her pride—and the lump in her throat—and went to class.

A hush fell over the classroom as soon as Eve entered. Nothing out of the ordinary there—Eve's presence was usually met with uncomfortable silence. As she took her seat, the nearby students rose from their desks and scurried off to sit elsewhere; she ignored them, pretending to fiddle with her scratchpad in order to evade their stares.

"Hey, I think you dropped this." A boy walking by slapped a piece of paper onto her desk—it was her *Chimera Bitch* photo, of course. His friends laughed as he strutted proudly back to his seat, muttering "*dumb chime*" under his breath. Eve offered no reaction; she simply let the paper fall to the ground.

The classroom door flung open, and Madison and Hayden waltzed through the entrance, their arms linked together as they giggled like young schoolgirls. They sashayed to the opposite side of the room—far away from Eve's desk—and whispered what she could only assume were catty remarks into each others' ears. Not far behind them was Professor Clarke, and Eve breathed a sigh of relief as he took a stand at his podium; at least now, maybe half of the class's attention would be directed at someone other than herself.

"Leadership," Clarke began without preamble, "is about standing firm in the face of adversity. It means being unpopular, maybe even ostracized. But a leader will persevere with conviction. A leader will meet resistance with courage. And if people start slinging mud or throwing stones, a leader won't falter. They will only grow stronger. Better.

"And what about everyone else?" he continued, his voice reflecting a hint of scorn. "The mudslingers—those who blindly follow the norm without question. They're misguided. Impressionable. *Weak*. Because, you see, it's easy to stand back on the sidelines and criticize. It's easy to throw stones. But more often than not, that target you're aiming for is a *leader*. They just may not know it yet."

An unlikely hand shot up from across the room: Madison's.

"Yes, Miss Palmer?"

"Professor Clarke, I was under the impression that sometimes," she paused and shot a fierce scowl in Eve's direction, "certain people *deserve* to be stoned."

"And what determines that, Miss Palmer? What makes one person condemned to a life of judgment? Is it because they're truly evil? Subhuman? Or is it simply because they're different?"

"I think it's because they're a barftastic bitch," Madison answered.

The class erupted into laughter, and Eve felt the room shrink around her.

"Miss Palmer, that's enough—"

"I think someone like that—a repulsive, suckgasmic slophole—should just fall off the face of the Earth."

"MISS PALMER—"

"I mean, isn't it our duty? Isn't it our moral obligation as students—no, as *leaders* at Billington—to rid the campus of such disposable *shit*? After all, we'd be better off if chimeras like *Eve* weren't around—"

"MADISON PALMER, GET THE HELL OUT OF MY CLASSROOM!" Clarke roared, his voice booming across the lecture hall.

It was too late; the damage had been done. The entire room was in an uproar, their cheering undoubtedly echoing far beyond the confines of the lecture hall. Madison rose from her seat, bowing to her fans as she cavorted across the classroom. At the door, she stopped, turned to Eve, and, with a devious smile, blew a kiss in her direction.

Eve flinched, as if she could feel the girl's lips on her skin, and turned her attention to Clarke—he was frantically waving his arms as he struggled to control his students, shouting demands that were completely drowned out by their applause. With a visible sigh, he glanced over at Eve, his face long, his eyes pleading for her forgiveness. His intentions were good—she knew that—but all she could hear was the cheering that surrounded her—the sound of jubilant, triumphant hate.

The rest of her day would only get worse; it was an unfortunate truth she had come to accept. And she was right, for each class that followed seemed to be a little bit more miserable than the last. At least Hand-to-Hand Combat had the potential to be uplifting—or so she thought, until Ramsey made a surprise announcement.

"Drills are over," the captain barked. "We're sparring today."

Eve sighed. She knew this would happen—the class *was* Hand-to-Hand Combat, after all—but she was hoping that the timing wouldn't be quite so terrible.

"This is full-contact sparring, so things *will* get messy," he continued, pacing across the gymnasium. "You will get hurt, and you will bleed. That's the whole point of fighting: to make your enemy *bleed*." He cocked his head toward a line of mats behind him. "You'll be paired up alphabetically. You and your partner will fight using the techniques you've learned. If you're down for more than ten seconds, you're done. If you tap out or step off the mat, you're done."

"Captain Ramsey, permission to speak?"

"Granted."

"Captain, while the rest of us are fighting, do we have any dolls for the girl to play with?"

The other students stifled their laughter and Eve rolled her eyes. Of course it was Chin Dimple—only *he* would be brazen enough to ask that.

"Well, look who's a goddamn clown!" the captain sneered, unamused with his student's quip. "You think you can beat Kingston?"

Chin Dimple smirked. "I'm sorry, I'm assuming that's not a serious question, right?"

"You watch your tongue, *boy*."

Ramsey glared at the footballer and grumbled to himself, his face red with irritation. Then he turned back to face his class.

"Do you know why Billington offers a series of *combat* courses? Why I'm standing here, teaching you to fight?" He began pacing the floor yet again. "It's 'cause the world we live in right now is a *shit show*. People are being taken. Tortured. *Murdered*. All from right under our noses. We need *soldiers*. People who can protect. People who can *kill*. People equipped to handle *surprises*—the kind of surprises that leave behind mangled, bloody corpses just so we can *piss 'n' shit ourselves*."

He stopped pacing and stared at his students, his eyes slowly panning over each and every one of them.

"That's what you all signed up for. You're here to become soldiers—to learn what it takes to handle any hazard those ugly alien shits throw your way. And so you'll face surprises in this class." His eyes landed on Eve. "Surprises like Kingston. Because Kingston is not a defenseless little girl."

Eve held her breath; she knew what he was going to say next, and even though the secret was already out, a part of her prayed to God that he wouldn't.

"Kingston is a chimera."

The class stirred only slightly, and still Eve's gut churned with chagrin.

"She's someone you might initially misjudge. You may come to regret that judgment later."

"Yeah, we've seen the flyers, Captain," Chin Dimple said matter-of-factly. "Not much of a surprise if everyone already knows."

Eve glanced at the footballer—he was so smug, so confident, with his stupid chiseled jaw and his nauseatingly pronounced cleft chin. Ramsey, too, was watching him; she had expected him to react with fiery anger like he usually did, but instead his demeanor was cold and rigid.

"Never underestimate your enemy." The captain turned his attention to the rest of the group and reached for his clipboard. "Once I call you and your partner, you'll grab a mat and prepare to spar. When I blow my whistle, it's game on." He went through the list, reciting each name until he reached the letter "K."

"Keller, you're with Kingston."

A long, irritated sigh sounded from across the room. Eve looked down the line and spied the source: a boy, roughly six feet tall with caramel skin, wide shoulders and a defined chest. He shook his head as his friends poked at his ribs and slapped his back, teasing him for his terrible luck of the draw. Eve could see in his eyes that he was humiliated, and she knew at once that this was Keller, her sparring opponent.

Once all the pairings had been read aloud, Eve approached the mat, facing

Keller's miserable scowl. She took her stance, preparing to fight—but Keller just crossed his arms, annoyed.

"So sorry to inconvenience you," she barbed.

"Let's just get this over with," he mumbled.

The whistle blew, and the two fighters began pivoting on either side of the circle. While Eve was comfortable and focused, Keller appeared anxious, breathing heavily from his nose. She almost pitied him—the stress of fighting her was written all over his face. She was nearly positive she knew what he was thinking at that moment—*To hit her, or not to hit her*—but even after a full minute had passed, he remained stationed on the opposite side of the mat, shuffling from side to side while buckets of perspiration gushed down his forehead. With a heavy sigh, Eve dropped her fists and impatiently tapped her boot against the mat.

"Are you going to fight me, or are you just going to stand there?"

"Shut up," he spat, his fists inching closer and closer to his face.

"Look, you don't have to be easy on me just because I'm a girl—"

"I SAID *SHUT UP.*"

Eve glanced across the room; her other classmates were well into their matches—some had already been won in that short period of time. She looked back at Keller and rolled her eyes.

"*Seriously*? I'm confused. Are you scared to hit me because I'm a girl, or because I'm a chimera? Or both?"

"Girl, you're really testing my patience."

"Well, maybe if I piss you off enough, you'll finally muster the courage to make a move."

Keller lunged toward her, now visibly enraged. Eve dodged his jabs, weaving effortlessly from side to side, evading every attempt he made to strike her. Suddenly, and with overwhelming speed, she pounded her fist into his prickly jaw, sending his entire body lurching to the side of the mat.

He steadied himself, gripping his chin as he stared back at her in disbelief.

"Pissed now?" she scoffed.

He adjusted his jaw, trying to hide his surprise. "You hit like a man." He paused. "A really, *really* big man."

"Well, that should make it easier for you to pretend you're fighting one."

He charged toward her yet again, his lungs heaving and his neck red with fury. Eve ducked, her body twisting gracefully around his, and struck him across the temple with a powerful right hook. He fell to his knees and clung to his ear.

"*Jesus*, woman," he growled.

"Want me to back off? I can if you want. I'll probably still win though."

Keller let out a war cry and bolted forward, completely consumed by his own embarrassment. Finally, the real fight had begun. He pounced toward her, attempting to roundhouse kick her across the face, but Eve ducked easily below his foot and kicked out his anchoring ankle, sending him dropping face-first onto the mat like an enormous domino.

Keller immediately leapt back onto his feet and hurled his fists at her face, and with each miss he swung harder, faster, only to swat futilely at the air in front of him. Eve was elusive and, much to Keller's dismay, still unscathed, and she could see in his eyes that his need to defeat her had escalated into a genuine longing for her death. Just as he prepared for his next move, she punched him once in the pit of his stomach and again across his face, sending him staggering backward, his eyes clenched shut in pain.

Eve stopped for a second, watching him fight to catch his breath. But instead of Keller's face, she saw Madison's hateful glare. Suddenly, she too felt a swell of rage inside of her, and as Keller finally summoned the strength to swing, she evaded his jabs and struck him hard, first in his right cheek and then his left, and then, with one last deep breath, she bashed him in the center of his throat. He crashed to the ground, and Eve hopped onto his thrashing body, holding him firmly against the mat for eight, nine, ten seconds.

The match was over, and Eve was victorious. She bounced to her feet and dusted off her knees while Keller pulled his aching body from the floor.

"Good match. Sorry about your throat," she mumbled. She extended her arm for a handshake, but he refused, muttering under his breath as he made his way to the loser's bench.

Eve glanced across the gymnasium—about twenty other students remained beside their mats, their heads held high in triumph. The losers' bench was already half full; tired, discouraged young men slumped across the bleacher like pouting children, and Eve realized that all of their bitter, glaring faces were pointed directly at her. She looked away—should she have feigned failure? No, what a stupid thought; after all, they already knew what she was, and there was no need to pretend otherwise. Still, the way her classmates watched her—their eyes filled with resentment—left her feeling uneasy.

"I know what you're thinking, Kingston."

Ramsey stood by her side, his hands on his hips as he took note of the winners and losers. He turned to face her.

"Do *not* back down. Remember: if you slack off, you fail my class."

"People are talking about me."

"Do you really give a shit what these sons-a-bitches think of you?" he scoffed. "If you do, you're not the woman I thought you were."

He blew his whistle and cocked his head at the mats. "Round two: winners against winners."

Eve reluctantly took her spot in front of a new mat and a new opponent. This boy was bigger than Keller—in fact, he might have been the largest student in the class, with muscles bulging from his chest, arms, and thighs, and thick veins lining every exposed inch of his body. He looked down at her as if she were a toy for him to play with—and laughed.

Still, Eve was hardly concerned, as she had greater issues to worry about. As he studied her, licking his lips like a hungry animal, she contemplated her next move—would she channel her strength, or would she restrain herself?

"Screw you, *chimera*," he hissed, wiping the sweat from his brow.

Eve smiled. "You just made my decision a hell of a lot easier."

The whistle blew, and Eve immediately barreled forward, aiming straight for her beastly rival like an arrow shooting toward a target. Before he could even raise his fists, Eve dropkicked him across his face, pounding her boot into his jaw and sending his massive body flying from the mat. He landed on the hard gymnasium floor with a thundering boom that shook the entire building and sent clouds of dust billowing up from the wooden planks.

Silence. The gym was still, the other fighters frozen beside their mats. Eve peered at her opponent's body; he was out cold. She looked up from his fallen frame and back at the rest of her classmates. They stared at her, their mouths gaping open in astonishment.

"What the hell are you waiting for?" Ramsey snapped. "Get to sparring!"

The other fighters reluctantly continued, and Ramsey wandered to Eve's side and looked down at the sleeping giant.

"Is he going to be okay?" she asked.

"He'll be fine."

"I don't know. It was a pretty bad landing."

The captain slapped at the boy's cheek, and he snorted abruptly, finally waking. Ramsey turned to Eve and smirked. "The bigger they are, the harder they fall." He patted her on the back. "Keep up the good work, Kingston."

The sparring continued throughout the remainder of class. Eve fought and won her matches one after the next, much to the dismay of her overconfident opponents and the losers who observed from the bench. Their skepticism turned into shock, their shock into awe, and soon their awe morphed into objection.

Eve's latest partner staggered from the mat, brushing the dust off of his pants after his embarrassing loss. He cursed under his breath and growled at her before stomping toward the losers' bench.

"Captain!" he shouted, refusing to take a seat among the defeated fighters. "We shouldn't have to fight her. She has an unfair advantage!"

Ramsey glowered. "An advantage is always unfair—that's why it's called an advantage, son. It's your job to make the best of that short straw you just drew."

"Ah, come on, Captain. You can't expect us to win against her!"

Ramsey folded his arms. "If you're in the heat of battle, are you allowed to bow out just because your opponent has an *unfair advantage*? Do you get to tell your enemy, 'hey, tone it down, will ya?'"

The boy hung his head low, his brow still heavy with scorn. "No, Captain."

"I'm not gonna give you all a gold star for participating. You'll face obstacles in this class. Today, your obstacle is one another, and if someone is better than you, you'll have to try that much harder to beat 'em."

"But—"

"But nothing! Goddamn bunch of whiney scrotes." Ramsey quickly looked over at the final remaining fighters. "You two—final showdown."

Eve glanced at her opponent—the last man standing—and immediately grimaced. It was Chin Dimple, of course: the obnoxious, nameless, perfectly coiffed footballer.

"The Betty and the ball player," Keller mumbled from the bench. "Who would've thought *they'd* be the final two?"

"I thought he didn't have any fighting experience?" another classmate added.

"Man, screw that guy. He may not fight for real, but that hammer fights dirty."

Eve wasn't amused by their conversation, nor was she entertained by the stupid grin gracing Chin Dimple's face.

"Hey, Sweetie." He blew her a kiss. "It's time for Daddy to *spank* you."

Before she could even shudder with revulsion, her attention was diverted to a rustling at the gym's entrance. The doors opened, and Armaan scurried inside.

Ramsey sighed. "Looks like duty calls. Kingston, time for you to hit the road."

"That's probably for the best," Chin Dimple smirked. "I'd hate to ruin that pretty little face."

Eve's patience was wearing thin, and the burn of resentment pumped through her veins. She took one look at Armaan—his eyes were wide and anxious as he glanced back and forth at the bodies towering over him—and then she stared at her opponent, his smile dripping with arrogance.

"No. I'll stay."

"Kid, you don't get to call the shots here," Ramsey countered. "Your session in the ward starts *now*."

"Then I'll be late."

"It's okay, Captain," Chin Dimple winked. "This won't take long anyway."

Ramsey looked at the two fighters and then down at the very timid Armaan.

"I can wait..." he croaked, sheepishly.

A glimmer of excitement sparkled in Ramsey's eyes. "Well then, in that case, take your positions."

Eve waited on her side of the mat, her body tense and eager to be engaged. As he meandered to his starting point, the ball player stopped behind her, leaning his jaw close enough to her ear that she could feel his hot breath tickle her neck.

"Listen," he whispered, "just a quick word of advice: when I get you down on the ground and I'm lying on top of you, pinning you to the floor," he grinned and licked his lips, "try not to enjoy it too much."

He slid his fingers down her arm and she quickly pulled away from him.

"Pig," she muttered, disgustedly.

At the sound of the whistle, Eve immediately began circling the outer edge of the mat, studying her opponent closely. He smiled at her—it was sickening, the sheen of his perfectly straight teeth and the patronizing look in his eyes—but she stifled her animosity and concentrated on the task at hand. Fighting came naturally to her. Her genes were programmed for it, and with immense power coupled with years of experience, she could almost predict her contender's next move. She could see it in his stance, his body language, his technique—and instantly counter whatever he had in store for her. This fight would be no exception.

With incomparable confidence and little grace, the footballer viciously sprang toward her. *How typical,* Eve thought to herself. She bobbed and weaved, preparing to dodge his uninteresting hooks, but at the very last second the boy altered his attack, his diversion so quick that it hardly registered with her. Before she knew it, it was too late: a harsh, burning pain pulsed through her cheek. She staggered backward and shook her head in disbelief.

He slapped me?

He *had* slapped her. Hard.

What is it with people slapping me lately?

Before she could react, another sharp sting burst through her cheek, this one so severe that her neck spun to the side and her hair swung across her face.

He slapped me AGAIN?

Eve swiftly ducked her head, dodging his next attempt. With her fists balled tightly and her face bright red, she shot him a scathing glare and continued to sidestep across the mat. Ramsey was shouting *"Bad form"* in the background, but all she could hear was the loud pumping of blood in her ears. It was deplorable: she had allowed him to strike her. Hell, she had allowed him to strike her *twice.* He wasn't fighting as she had imagined—no, he was taunting her, picking and prodding at her with his spasmodic behavior. He could sense her contempt—she knew it, and the harder she tried to conceal it, the bigger his smile grew.

He winked. "You got a lil' somethin' right here," he sneered, and flicked the tip of her nose.

Eve's mouth dropped open. "Did you just *flick* me?"

Before the words fully escaped her lips, Chin Dimple pounded her square in the eye, the force of his blow knocking her to her knees. Her classmates gasped. She tried to open her eyes, but all she could see were flashing lights and several spinning football players standing before her with foolish smiles painted across their faces. She watched as they brought their elbows back, slowly and in unison, and then punched her again in the same eye, sending her neck jerking to the side. Bright, shining stars consumed her vision; she blinked once and winced as an intolerable surge of pain shot through her skull. Her opponent laughed.

"Pathetic."

She hated him—she could feel it in her bones. It was what he wanted, after all: for her to despise him, to loathe him so much that every subtle irritant he threw her way would knock her off balance.

No more, she thought to herself.

Eve got to her feet and struggled to open her eyes. Her vision was still hazy, but she could make out the line of students sitting on the losers' bench, the tiny Armaan nestled in the middle, their faces all wearing the same expression of shock. With a resounding sense of conviction, she raised her fists and regained her fighting stance.

Chin Dimple dove forward, his grin still cocky as ever, but Eve quickly darted from his path and punched him in the jaw, finally making contact with his revolting cleft chin. He stumbled backward, and for a moment, Eve took pride in beating the smile right off of his face, but she immediately regained her focus. He glared at her, tilted his head over the mat, and spat blood onto the gymnasium floor.

"Bitch."

She leapt toward him, pounding him across the chin once more, again and again as if the dimple itself was a target for her fists. He swung wildly at her, his coordination faulty and clearly compromised, but she easily eluded his jabs and kicked him straight in the gut with such power that she could hear his ribs crack beneath her boot. She swung at his face, this time aiming for his mouth, sending blood shooting from his lips and throwing his exquisitely styled hair out of place. Again she kicked him in the stomach, then punched him across the face, her knuckles numb from the impact and the adrenaline. She wanted to make him pay. She wanted him to feel pain. And more than that, she wanted to be the cause of it. With one last surge of hatred, she jumped into the air and hit him across the nose with a sweeping roundhouse kick, sending him tumbling onto the mat in an instant.

Chin Dimple lay still, his arms and legs sprawled across the mat in an erratic fashion. Eve crept toward his side and stood over his defeated body. *One*, she thought to herself. *Two. Three...*

Chin Dimple's eyes snapped open like a corpse suddenly brought back to life. He grabbed at Eve's ankle and yanked it forward, pulling her from her feet and sending her toppling to the ground. He flipped her onto her back and pushed her body into the mat, crushing her with his weight as he stretched across her. She writhed beneath him, but he pinned her down, digging his knees into hers and forcing her arms to her sides. With a laugh, he lowered his red, bleeding face inches from hers and smirked.

"Does it feel good?" He dug his pelvis into her hips. "I knew you'd like it."

Time moved slowly. One second passed. Two seconds. He was going to beat her. How pitiful—to lose to an obnoxious footballer, a cowardly meat-head with no fighting experience, a boy who *flicked* her just to get his jabs in. She could have died in that moment; it was his blatant unpredictability that had smothered her. His sporadic movements and his nonsensical methods had gotten the best of her.

And that's when it hit her. Unpredictability. It was his only asset. If he was going to be unpredictable, she would have to be the same.

Five seconds. Six seconds.

Eve gasped for one last shallow breath and clenched her jaw. It had come to this.

Seven seconds. Eight seconds. Nine seconds.

Eve flinched as the footballer's grasp was torn from her body. He flew into the air, his arms and legs flailing, until at last he stopped, hovering ten feet from the ground. Eve's classmates gasped in shock, but she was unaffected; she hopped up from her spot on the mat and wiped the dust from her cloth-ing, taking the time to crack her back and stretch her legs.

She stared up at the boy—he was pointed face-first at the ground, his eyes wide with fear. There was no point in gloating or tormenting him any further. She spent the last few seconds of her melt gracefully lowering him to the mat, setting his boots down just a few steps in front of her.

He forced a feeble grin, shaking his hair into place. "That all you got?" He faked a laugh. "Did you put me down so I could continue dominating your fine ass?"

It was Eve's turn to smile, though hers was genuine.

"No," she answered. "I put you down so I could do this."

With all the brutal, untamed strength she could rally, she snapped her leg forward and pounded her boot straight into his groin. He gasped aloud and dropped to the floor with a thud, cupping his crotch as he rolled from his back to his side. There was no need to count down—he was going to be there for a while. Eve had won the match, and she had her unpredictability to thank for it.

With the stride of a winner, Eve made her way to the football player's side and crouched down beside him, lowering her chin to his ear.

"Does it feel *good*?" she hissed with pleasure. "I knew you'd like it."

The satisfaction came and went. Eve stood up and headed straight for the gymnasium doors. She didn't look back—not at Armaan, who was most likely trailing behind her, nor at her classmates, for she could already predict the dumb, stunned expressions on their faces. In that moment, all she could see was the exit: her escape. Her heart thumped within her chest, and she hurried her stride, wanting nothing more than to be alone.

She darted into the locker room and frantically fiddled with her combination, her fingers still shaking with adrenaline and anger.

Deep breath.

With the gradual simmering of her nerves came the pain; she had forgotten about it, but there it was, suddenly magnified and pulsating behind her eye. She tried to ignore it as she continued getting dressed, pulling her hooded sweatshirt over her head and wincing as the cotton rubbed against her tender cheek. The ache was spreading and intensifying, so much so that she could practically feel it surging through her skull and into her brain. To disregard it seemed impossible, and so with great apprehension, she slid her palm-sized mirror from her pocket and took a look at her beaten reflection. The bruise was already forming, thanks to her immune system being so quick to respond, and she knew that within minutes her entire eye would be black and blue.

Eve sighed. It was the perfect accessory to wear on such a terrible day.

Armaan was waiting for her in the hallway. They walked together in silence, Eve blankly staring at the emptiness in front of her, while Armaan watched in awe at the morphing colors of her rapidly bruising face.

"You okay?" he asked.

"I'm fine."

"Are you sure—"

"I'm *fine.*"

Again they were quiet, Armaan not knowing what to say and Eve not wanting to say anything at all. Instead, she listened to the sound of the soft autumn breeze that stung the raw skin around her eye. She thought of San Francisco; back home, the weather was hot, and the sun shined brightly late into the evening. Back home, it was Indian summer.

Armaan finally spoke, though reluctantly. "You seem upset. You should be happy. You won, after all."

"It's been a bad day."

"People still down on you now that they know your secret?"

"It's more than that..." Her voice trailed off as her mind wandered. "It's just a bad day."

When they arrived at the medical ward, Eve headed straight for the isolation wing. She should have felt relief; the wing had become somewhat of a sanctuary, the only place with no flyers, no whispers. A place where she could, at least to some extent, breathe easily. A place where she could maybe, possibly, be herself. And yet, no matter how much she told herself to be happy, she couldn't do it, not even when she saw Jason waiting for her in his room.

He rose from his desk, eager to greet her, but his large smile quickly faded, replaced by a look of grave concern.

"Eve, what the hell *happened?*"

"What are you talking about?"

"What do you mean what am I talking about? Your *eye!*"

Eve dashed to the sink and peered into the mirror. Various shades of purple and yellow decorated her swollen lid—it wasn't the worst black eye she had ever worn, but it was definitely gruesome.

She turned to Jason, forcing her cringe into a half-smile. "It'll be gone by tomorrow. One of the many perks of being a chimera."

"Did someone *hit* you?"

"Relax, it happened in class—"

"Someone hit you in the middle of *class?*"

"Jason, it was Hand-to-Hand Combat. We're *supposed* to hit each other."

He took a step back, his jaw clenched and his hands balled into fists. "Who did this to you?"

"Chin Dimple," she grumbled, flopping into her usual seat.

"*Who?*"

"I don't know his name. I just call him Chin Dimple because—"

"He has a chin dimple?"

She smirked. "I see you were able to decipher my complex code. Well done."

"This isn't funny." He grabbed a fistful of ice from the refrigerator and wrapped it in a hand towel. "And why the hell are you taking Hand-to-Hand Combat anyway?"

"I like a good workout—"

"The *truth*, Eve."

She sighed. "I was an outed chimera by the time I was eight years old. People *hated* me." She rested the makeshift icepack against her eye and cringed from the pain. "I've been fighting for years now. I had to learn to defend myself."

Jason turned away from her, pressing his fists into his desk as he breathed deeply and angrily. His shoulders were rigid, his back taut, and she could see a hint of red creeping up the nape of his neck. "You've been stressed lately—preoccupied, or something. Then you come here with a *black eye*? Something's not right, I can tell."

A lump had suddenly found its way into Eve's throat. She hadn't told Jason about her untimely reveal—of her run-in with Madison, Hayden, and Heather. And as for the *Chimera Bitch* flyers? Well, he didn't need to know about that, either. After all, what good would it do? If anything, she was protecting him from the stress of knowing what sort of hatred faced someone like her. Someone like *him*.

"You're being ridiculous, Jason. And the black eye—"

"God, I could kill him."

"Jason—"

"The guy laid his hands on you, Eve. I can't let him get away with that."

Again, Eve found herself at a loss for words. She was accustomed to black eyes, to cuts and scrapes and deep wounds, but she wasn't accustomed to explaining them—nor was she familiar with anyone giving a damn, regardless. It was a foreign situation derived from very un-foreign circumstances, and with no idea how to act, she did nothing at all but watch Jason furiously pace the floor.

At last he stopped and knelt before her, peering up into her eyes.

"Can I see it?" he asked, his voice now calm and tender.

With a hint of reluctance, Eve lowered her icepack and revealed the grisly bruise beneath it. Jason lightly caressed her cheek as he assessed the injury.

"Does it hurt?"

"No," she replied unconsciously. She paused and reconsidered her answer. "Yes. A little." She paused again. "A lot."

"That Chin Dimple guy... he's a dead man."

"Yeah, well, I think he already got what was coming to him. Let's just say he won't be walking the same for a long time."

Jason said nothing and simply stared back at her battered face.

"It'll be gone before I wake up tomorrow morning."

"That's not the point, Eve. Someone hurt you. That's all I care about."

He gently pressed the hand towel back against her cheekbone, his eyes now overflowing with an odd blend of anger and affection. She looked away uncomfortably and tried to change the subject.

"Want to start melting?"

"No."

"Oh?" She hesitated. "So, what did you have in mind?"

"Interlopers," he said, taking a seat on his bed. "I want to talk about the Interlopers."

Eve sighed. "Jason—"

"I know, you're not into it, I get it. But they're *evil*, Eve."

"Do you think I disagree?" she said. "Look, what they're doing—it's beyond words. It *sickens* me. But we're two people, and there are God knows how many of them. What could we possibly do about it?"

"I don't know." Jason cast his eyes down to the floor. "But we have to do *something*. And if we work together—"

"What? We'll figure it out along the way?" Eve scoffed. "This is life or death, Jason. We can't exactly wing it."

"You don't have to be on board, Eve. I'm doing this with or without you."

"You're insane."

"I have to do this."

"Why? Why does this have to be *your* responsibility? Why *you* of all people?"

"Because they cut me *open!*" he barked with sudden ferocity. "They strapped me down and carved me up like a goddamn *animal!*" His chest heaved as he spoke. "I want them to *pay* for what they did to me. For what they did to Woodgate. All of them. I *need* to make them pay."

The room became quiet and still. Eve felt stupid for pressing him; she had known the answer all along. The top of his scar protruded from the V-neck of his t-shirt—it was staring her right in the face—and yet she hadn't seen it for some reason. Hesitantly, she joined Jason on the edge of his bed.

"You know, I can't understand..." She stopped short and bit her lip, struggling to find the right words to say. "I mean, I want to. I want to understand."

"Is that your way of asking me to tell you what happened?"

For the first time since the start of their sessions, it was Jason who avoided Eve's gaze; he kept his eyes pointed at the window, pretending to watch the yellowing sky, but really lost in thought—in memories.

"I went for a walk that night," he began. "It was stupid. I knew about the attacks. I knew it was dangerous to be out alone. But I figured I was safe"—he chuckled, amused by his own naivety—"because I thought I was human."

Eve listened quietly, studying him as he spoke. His eyes were cold, almost empty, but she could hear something raw and visceral in his voice: a repressed pain.

"It happened suddenly. Something pounded into my back, knocking the wind out of me. I fell to the ground, and I tried to get up, but someone—some*thing*—was pushing me down, shoving my face into the dirt. At first I thought I was getting mugged. Then they tossed a bag over my head, and I assumed it was some stupid fraternity prank." He grimaced. "I felt something *wet* dripping onto my back—something slimy. I could only imagine what it was, but every disgusting possibility crossed my mind. Everything went black after that. I took a huge blow to the head, and I was out cold.

"When I woke up, I was already strapped down to the table. They had metal cuffs on my wrists and ankles. There was something attached to my forehead—I couldn't see what it was, but it was ringing. Maybe that was just in my mind, I don't know. My head was throbbing."

Jason's hands gripped the edge of his mattress tightly, and the veins in his forearms bulged.

"Have you ever seen an Interloper up close?" he asked, finally turning to Eve.

Her breathing became shallow. "Just once," she said.

"His eyes were so black, like polished stones. He looked frail; I can't believe something so damn skinny could be so strong. But the worst part was his teeth—hundreds of long, silver needles. They were the sickest things I had ever seen in my entire life... until I saw the inside of my own body.

"He called me *chimera*. He said my death would be their salvation—that I didn't deserve my power. I didn't even know what he was talking about. All I knew was that he *hated* me. It was written all over his ugly face."

Jason finally released his grip on the sheets and raised his hands, measuring out a length of about two feet. "His blade was this long," he explained. "He showed it to me and laughed. He wanted me to be terrified. He was enjoying every second of it. And then," his voice trailed off and he lowered his hands, "he just started cutting."

"Jason—"

"I've never felt anything like it. It was indescribable—a pain you could never, *ever* imagine. I could *feel* my skin, my muscle... *separating* from my bones. I could feel... everything."

"Jason," Eve repeated, "you don't have to keep going if you don't want to."

Jason shrugged. "There's nothing left to tell, anyway. I don't remember much else—I was in and out of consciousness, I guess. But there's one thing I'll never forget." His eyes became fiery, and his lips curled furiously. "That *freak*—he kept licking my blood off of his talons, like it was chocolate syrup or some shit. One of his talons, on his left hand, was broken—cut in half, like a jagged stump. He'd soak it in my blood and then suck on it like it was *candy*. I'll remember that forever."

Eve was quiet, captivated by the strange feeling of nothing and everything at the same time. The hairs on her arms stood up straight; every sense within her was piqued and ignited, and yet her body was cold and paralyzed. It took her a moment to finally realize she was holding her breath, and even longer to notice that she was also holding Jason's hand. It felt instinctive, almost natural, and yet so very unlike her. With a surge of conviction, she leaned closer to him and nodded at the incision line peeping from his shirt collar.

"That scar doesn't define you, Jason. I know it feels like it does—like they took something from you—but they didn't."

"You sure about that?" he scoffed. "Because every night, I see his eyes and fangs and that damn blade. I hear him laughing and that god-awful ringing in my ears, and sometimes I think I can even smell the blood. Do you know what that's like? To have nightmares every single night?"

"Yes." The word left her lips before she could stop it. "I do."

Jason studied her face, searching for answers. "You do?" His eyes widened. "Because of your parents?"

"Look, we're talking about *you* right now, not me—"

"Do we have to do this?" he asked. "The back and forth. I'm going to keep asking, and after some kicking and screaming, you'll tell me."

"You seem awfully confident," she grumbled.

"Am I wrong?"

Eve let out a deep, aggravated breath and pulled her hand away from his. For the first time in so many years, she felt weak, breakable, and defenseless, as if every wall and every guard she had built up was now crumbling around her. She had never told anyone about her parents, about the beginning of the end of her normal, happy life. Back home, everyone assumed they knew the story, but only Eve knew the truth; she carried it with her always, like an arduous burden that weighed her down. In this moment, the burden felt heavier than it ever had before.

"They died today, eleven years ago." She finally spoke. "Today's the anniversary."

"Eve, I had no idea—"

"Don't—" she cut in, forcing a smile. "It's okay. It really is."

Her smile quickly faded as she recalled the evening that had changed her life forever.

"The drunk driver came out of nowhere. Before I knew it, the whole thing was over. It was so *loud*, the crash. He *destroyed* them."

Her eyes were distant as if watching the accident play out before her.

"I just stood there. The bastard got out of his truck—asshole had the nerve to *threaten* me. The whole scene, it was so foul, so awful.

"Something happened inside of me. I felt this horrible pounding in my head, and then suddenly—everything stopped. I couldn't see or hear or feel *anything*. That split second felt like hours of just... nothing.

"When I could finally see again—when all of my senses came flooding back—I felt, I don't know—different. I felt strong. Too strong. I couldn't handle it. The first thing I saw was that beast of a truck. I looked at it, just for a moment, and," she paused, her voice wavering, "it *flew* into the sky, like the ugliest damn bird you've ever seen. And then it fell to the ground, flat on top of the drunk driver."

She raised her chin as if to brace herself. Jason remained silent.

"CSI had to hose his body off the pavement. It killed him instantly—*I* killed him instantly."

"My *God*—" Jason murmured.

Eve grimaced. "The police tried to say that the truck—my emergence—was intentional. I was charged with second-degree murder. They were going to try me as an adult due to the '*gravity*' of the situation." She paused and shook her head. "My face was all over the local news. Everyone thought I was a killer."

"What happened?"

"They stuck me in juvie during the court proceedings."

"Juvie? For how long?"

"Six weeks." She closed her eyes and cringed as an icy chill ran through her. "Look, things happened. I—"

"Don't want to talk about it?"

She ignored Jason's interruption and quickly moved on. "I was eventually acquitted. The whole case was dismissed. People were calling it the greatest failure of the judicial system in years." She turned to look at him briefly. "You know, San Francisco is a big city, but once everyone there wants you dead, it really starts to feel so small. So *suffocating*.

"I was sent to live with my aunt. God, that was the worst part—seeing your own family look at you like you're some kind of monster. She couldn't stand the sight of me. We didn't speak."

Eve cast her eyes down to her hands and angrily picked at her nails.

"I was tormented every day. They beat me, they broke my bones. When I started fighting back, they kept their distance, but the hate never went away." She scowled disgustedly. "My aunt—she'd *see* me come home covered in my own blood. And she didn't say a *thing*. She'd look at me with the most pathetic, lifeless eyes, like *she* was the victim... and then she'd just walk away.

"I got out of there when I turned sixteen—made some money, got an apartment, and filed for emancipation." She finally rested her hands on her lap and stared blankly at the wall in front of her. "I've been on my own ever since. Not like I wasn't when I lived with her. I've been on my own since I sent that truck flying.

"And the nightmares—they're consistent. Every single night, it's the same thing. I used to wake up screaming. Now... now I'm just so used to it. It's like some sort of twisted lullaby."

Finally, her story was out in the open. It seemed to hang in front of her like a third body in the room, and for the first time in years, she was overwhelmed by a feeling she thought she had learned to abandon: fear of judgment. She could feel Jason watching her, but he didn't speak, and his silence sounded like the loudest, most agonizing scream she had ever heard.

"I didn't kill that man," she declared. "Well, I *did* kill him, but I didn't do it on purpose, like they said I did. I'm not a *murderer*."

"I know that."

She picked at her nails yet again. "I know what you're thinking—it explains a lot, right? How I've lived. It explains why I am the way I am."

"I wasn't thinking that."

"Then what were you thinking?"

"That you're amazing."

Eve froze. "What?"

"That you're the strongest person I know," he continued. "That despite all the bullshit you've been put through, you're still good. You're not filled with hate."

"You don't have to say that, Jason."

"I don't have to say anything I don't want to." His voice was stern, almost reprimanding. "I mean what I say."

There was no way for Eve to respond. A weight had been lifted from her shoulders, and though she couldn't look at him, she felt herself begin to relax the slightest bit.

"So, are you glad to be out of San Francisco? You can't miss it much."

Eve hesitated. "There's one thing," she began. "It's kind of stupid. Sometimes at night I'd head south, toward the mid-peninsula. There was this park that had a beautiful view of the bay. I'd lie down on one of the picnic tables, stare up at the sky and just *think*." She took in a deep breath. "It's cheesy as all hell, I know that. But the sky was always pitch black, and the stars were so perfectly clear. It was the only time I felt peaceful—like all of my problems were insignificant."

"You can do that here, you know. We've got picnic tables."

"I tried once." She smiled ruefully. "That was the night I found Marshall Woodgate's body."

"Jesus Christ..."

"I came here to get away from all of that: the chaos, the blood. My past, more than anything." Her mind wandered to her first day at Billington, and to how drastically things had changed since then. "I had a goal in mind. A purpose. It sort of consumed me."

"And that was?"

Eve was quiet, refusing to look Jason in the eye.

"You're not going to tell me."

"It doesn't matter. It didn't work out. I failed."

He shrugged. "Maybe you didn't."

"Trust me," she chuckled, "I really, *really* did."

"Maybe it wasn't meant to be. Maybe it was never your true purpose in the first place." He leaned forward, inching his way closer to her side. "Sometimes you want something so badly, you get caught up; you lose yourself in that hunger. But then, once it's gone, you have a chance to reassess—to decide what it is you're truly after. Half of the time, it's not what you originally thought it would be."

Jason's words repeated in Eve's mind; they had awakened something inside of her, a powerful surge of energy that now ached to be released. In an instant, every single function within Eve's body stopped—her breath was stifled inside her chest, her hands were frozen at her sides, and her eyes were dilated. It was there, right in front of her—an answer to a puzzle she didn't know she was trying to solve—and suddenly everything had become so simple, so clear. She turned to Jason.

"I changed my mind."

Jason wrinkled his brow. "What do you mean?"

"I want to do it."

"Do what?"

Eve was intoxicated with a new sense of purpose: a new desire born inside of her in that very moment. Her carriage became strong, almost austere, and her eyes lit up with a passion and fervor that glowed through her like a burning fire.

Deep breath.

"The Interlopers—I want to fight them."

CHAPTER 8: STARRY NIGHT

The classroom was nearly empty. Eve sat alone at her desk, hurriedly slaving away over her exam; it was the fifth unannounced test they'd had already, and they were barely halfway through the semester.

Eve looked up from her papers and made eye contact with Professor Richards—he sat at the front of the room, scowling at her from his desk—and she tightly gripped her old-fashioned pencil until it snapped in half. Richards chuckled to himself; *God*, he was a dick.

This was the second time Eve had taken this test. During the normal class hours—which, for the record, had long since ended—Richards had pointedly scanned the room looking for *cheaters*, or so he had claimed. And then, just as Eve had reached the last page, the final stretch of this nightmare of an exam, Richards had appeared at her elbow, torn the exam from her grasp, and ripped it to shreds. "Caught her eyes wandering," he'd announced to the room, though they both knew it wasn't so. "How selfish, and to think such behavior from the top student—the only 'A' in the entire class." And so he had made her take the test again, all sixteen pages.

Eve slapped her packet onto Richards's desk. It was complete—again—and she would undoubtedly receive an 'A,' and the entire class would object and shout and hiss obscenities at her. And Dr. Dick, all the while, would smile.

Before the professor could make one of his usual snide remarks, Eve stormed from the classroom and headed down the hallway. The corridor was quiet, almost eerily so; classes were in session, and thanks to Richards's little stunt, she was nearly twenty minutes late to Strategic Communication. Still, something about the silence of the hall, the sound of nothing except her heels clicking against the floor, made her uneasy. Something wasn't right.

Another sound punctuated the stillness: footsteps, and not her own. They were flat and clomping—the footsteps of a man. Two men. Now three. She quickened her stride, and soon realized that the footsteps quickened, too. She could see their shadows bobbing along the floor now, growing larger and larger as they came up behind her. She ran, and they did too, though she knew their efforts were futile—none of them would ever catch up to her. Her skirt whipped back and forth across her legs, and her heart pounded within her chest, and as she turned the corner yards ahead of them, she felt as if she could breathe the slightest bit easier.

But around the corner, a fourth man was waiting for her. He blocked her path and sent her nearly toppling to the ground. She recognized this one: his perfect hair, his arrogant smile—and the pitted cleft of his chin.

"Hey, Sweetie," Chin Dimple sneered.

Her body suddenly lurched forward as someone grabbed her from behind, one hand securing her wrists and the other yanking her hair, shoving her face-first into the wall. As her cheek was pressed against the cool surface, she felt Chin Dimple hovering beside her, his lips close to hers.

"You didn't think I'd just let it go, did you?"

The other boy spun her around and thrust her back against the wall. She remembered him; she had fought him the day before. She couldn't recall his name, but she knew his size, his massive build, and the way he'd fallen to the ground after mere seconds in the ring with her.

"There's four of us now," he grunted. "Won't be so easy for you this time."

Two more boys stood behind him. Their sleeves were rolled up to their elbows and their fists were clenched; they were prepared to fight. Chin Dimple folded his arms and faced her, though he didn't dare stray from his burly comrade's side.

"I hope it was worth it—making a fool of me."

"You made a fool of yourself."

He lunged forward and grabbed her face, squeezing her cheeks until her lips puckered together like those of a fish.

"Who's the fool now, *chimera*?"

He released her face, his hand now trembling with rage.

"My friends here—they're going to do a number on you. And when they're done, well..." He paused, eyeing her up and down, a sickening grin spreading across his lips. "I'll do my *own* number on you."

She looked down at her shoulders—at the huge hands that pressed her against the wall—and then up into the eyes of the face they belonged to.

"If you know what's good for you, you'll let me go," she said.

The boy laughed loudly and ignored her command. He leaned in closer to her, examining her face.

"Looks like your shiner's gone. Guess I'll have to give you a new one."

He pulled his arm back, flexing his muscles as if to prolong the anticipation. Then, with a deep breath and a menacing smile, he sent his fist barreling toward her eye.

Eve's hand sprang from its resting place and grabbed the giant fist, halting it inches from her face. Her long, skinny fingers barely wrapped around his knobby knuckles, but still she overpowered him, forcing his entire arm still. The other boys gasped, and her captor stared back at her with fearful eyes. She was cool and inexpressive, but inside her chest burned a fiery, overpowering hate.

"I told you," she said, calmly. "You should've let me go."

She tightened her fingers, curling them around the boy's fist, and then she twisted—snapping his wrist. The crack of his bones breaking was muffled by his shrill, pained howl. His knees buckled, and with one swift movement Eve swung her elbow forward, smashing it into his nose and sending blood spouting from his nostrils.

The boy staggered backward, trying to clutch his broken nose with his broken hand as he bellowed in agony. The other three boys just stared at her, their mouths gaping open in shock.

"Anyone else want to do a *number* on me?" she asked.

They bolted down the hallway, leaving her alone with the wounded beast.

Eve looked at the injured boy; he cowered on the ground, still crying and cursing as blood coursed from his nose. And then she felt eyes on her from down the hallway. She turned, and her body went numb; someone was watching them from a distance, his arms folded as he leaned casually against the wall.

Professor Richards. Had he been there the entire time?

With a disappointed scowl, he turned the corner and walked out of sight.

Eve waltzed into Strategic Communication class nearly twenty-five minutes late. Her mind was still shaken, and she hardly noticed the stares of her peers as she took a seat in the back corner of the room. She breathed deeply and looked down at her hands. They quivered with anger, and she quickly dropped them to her sides. The elbow of her blouse was spotted with blood, and she hoped no one noticed.

Class debates had begun. One by one, students approached the front podium as if part of an assembly line, each arguing theatrically until someone won in a fit of false, meaningless glory—and someone lost, covered in their own shame and humiliation. Eve thought the entire arrangement seemed ostentatious: a platform for students to belittle one another and chalk it up as a learning experience. She ignored the display, still attempting to calm her restless nerves.

Gupta raised his baseball cap high in the air. "The next topic will be chimera repression." He reached into the cap and pulled out a slip of paper: a name. "Representing the pro side: Travis Braverman."

A boy with brown, gelled hair and a blue blazer stood up, his like-minded friends shaking his hand as if he had been nominated for some great achievement.

Gupta continued, his face glowing with excitement. "And representing the con side..." He shuffled through the cap, finally grabbing a piece of paper and unfolding it before the class. His smile dropped suddenly, his face draining of color.

"...Evelyn Kingston."

The entire room hushed, and Eve cursed under her breath. What luck— what absolutely unfortunate, shitty luck. Eve looked at her opponent, who folded his arms arrogantly and laughed. *What a total jackass*, she thought to herself as she lugged her body toward the front of the room, finally facing Travis and her misfortune.

"Human beings have always been the apex of the planetary ecosystem," Travis began, his voice booming with over-dramatic eloquence. "We are the top of the food chain, the most fearsome predator in the world. That is, until chimeras came along. Some believe that chimeras are the next step in our evolution—the new apex predator. But I'm here to tell you that they're wrong." He glanced at Eve. "Just as a chromosomal abnormality can cause disability or mutation, this malfunction—this *flaw*—created chimeras. They are not *evolved*. They are *defective*."

Eve couldn't restrain herself. "While your lack of insight is impressive, your argument is shit."

"Miss Kingston," the professor interrupted, apprehensively, "it's still his turn to speak, and I must ask you to please keep the cursing to a minimum—"

"There's no *chromosomal abnormality*," Eve continued, ignoring Gupta. "Scientists can't even find a genetic difference between humans and chimeras."

"Just because they can't pinpoint the genetic source of the gift doesn't mean we're all the same. Chimeras are *dangerous*. Everyone knows that."

"*Everyone* is capable of being dangerous," Eve said. "Humans and chimeras alike. No group is more prone to violence than the other. Just because chimeras are stronger doesn't mean they'll use their strength with evil intentions."

"Says the girl with blood on her shirt."

Eve hesitated. She looked down at her sleeve—at her elbow spotted with patches of bright red blood, now dried and stiff. The scene from the hallway flashed before her eyes, and her entire body became rigid and cold.

"Chimeras have brought nothing but chaos to this planet," Travis sneered, not waiting for Eve to respond. "They show up, and look what happens: Interlopers. Abductions. Death. Why should we accept them?"

Eve winced. "Because it's the right thing to do. Because anyone with any moral fiber—"

"What do you know about *morals*, chimera?"

Eve took a step back, physically moved by his retort. "Excuse me?"

"Is there even any proof that chimeras are capable of moral comprehension?"

She glared back at him with disgust. "Are you *joking*?"

"Chimeras aren't human, and thus, one can argue that we must classify them as animals. Animals, after all, bear some similar features to humans, but they lack one very important quality: a higher level of comprehension. The intelligence to wonder, to think, to believe in right and wrong." His eyes pierced through Eve as he spoke. "If chimeras are animals, which logic would dictate is so, then they're incapable of moral awareness. They're ignorant."

"Wait, you can't possibly be serious."

Travis tried to conceal his grin. "Professor Gupta, I'd like to dismiss this debate on the grounds of incompetency: *Eve's* incompetency."

Eve wasn't sure whether to feel shocked or enraged. "INCOMPETEN—"

"Simply put, you can't expect me to have a rational, fair debate with a subhuman creature. A *thing*."

Eve angrily swung her arm up in protest.

"Professor, you and I both know that I'm *more* than capable—"

She stopped; out of the corner of her eye, she could see Gupta hunched over into a round, cowering ball. He cringed and shielded his face, his entire body trembling with fright. Eve became still, almost numb, and slowly lowered her arm to her side.

"Professor Gupta, are you *scared* of me?"

Gupta hesitantly regained his composure, rising from behind the podium and straightening his sweater vest almost shamefully.

Travis snickered. "I think that answers your question, chimera."

Eve couldn't move or speak. To know that her very existence was enough to terrorize a grown man—to cripple him with fear—was like a knife to the chest. The classroom around her disappeared, and all she could see was the horror lingering in Gupta's eyes.

The only visible escape was the doorway, and she took it. She rushed from the classroom, slamming the door behind her and barreling down the hallway with no destination in mind. She needed to get away, far away, wherever her legs could take her, and with each step she felt a little voice inside of her dying to scream louder, and louder, and louder. Complete humiliation and rage consumed her, so much so that she didn't even hear the voice calling her name.

"Eve! EVE, *wait!*"

Eve turned around and sighed loudly.

"What do *you* want, JJ?" she snapped. "You want to take a shot at me, too? I'll be here for four years, so you'll have plenty of time to get your digs in."

"No," JJ stuttered, "that's not why I'm here."

"No *Rutherfordian* comments today? Are you fresh out of clever insults?"

"Eve, I—"

"Because you usually have an arsenal of abuse, so lay it on me, JJ. Go for it. I *insist.*"

"Eve," JJ lowered her chin with chagrin, "I just wanted to see if you're okay."

Eve froze. She crossed her arms and squinted her eyes. "*Excuse* me?"

"I just thought you might need someone to talk to."

Suddenly, Eve burst into laughter. "You're cute, JJ. Really cute."

"Eve, come on—"

"*Stop it.* Stop pretending to give a damn. You treated me like shit for *weeks.*"

"Yeah, but that was before I knew—"

"Knew what?" Eve hissed. "Knew that I'm not a 'princess'? Knew that I'm a *chimera*? You know, for someone with such great *observation skills*, you sure screwed up on that one."

"Eve—"

"Tell me, are you so anti-establishment that you only want to talk to me once the entire school *hates* me? Is this part of your attempt to march to the beat of your own damn drum? Is that it?"

"Look, I'm trying to apologize. I'm trying to be friends."

"You can keep your apology and your goddamn friendship, JJ." Eve turned her back and continued down the hall, leaving the girl far behind her. "I've gotten along perfectly fine without them, as you can see."

***

"We need to kill them. All of them."

"*What?*"

"We take them out, one by one—"

"Eve—"

"Weapons would be nice, but we could make do without."

"Eve, please, stop for a second."

Eve ignored Jason as she paced across the hospital room, staring at her hands and rambling tirelessly. Her mind was consumed, producing incoherent thoughts on top of thoughts, all of which meshed together into one massive knot. She couldn't breathe or rest or do much of anything except think, endlessly, about the Interlopers.

"I mean, we're chimeras," she continued. "If anyone could kill them, we could."

"*Eve—*"

"I'm really strong, you know. I gave a guy twice my size a concussion with a single dropkick the other day—"

Jason grabbed Eve's shoulders, halting her. "*Stop,* Eve. You have to *stop.*"

"Isn't this what you wanted?" Eve spat, tearing her arms from his grasp. "To fight the Interlopers?"

"Yes, but not like this."

"Not like what?"

"Something's wrong."

"What's wrong?"

"*You*, Eve!" he barked. "You're worked up. Something's going on, I can tell."

"It's nothing."

"It's *always* nothing."

"Jesus, Jason, just back *off*—"

"God*dammit*, Eve, will you just let me *help* you for once?"

She glared at him. "I'm not a child, Jason. I don't need your help."

"Yeah, well, you've made that pretty clear."

"What's *that* supposed to mean?"

"What do I have to do, Eve?" he snapped, waving his arms in the air. "What do I have to do to get you to finally trust me?"

"For *Christ's sake*, Jason, I TRUST YOU!" she cried. "Don't you get it? I let you melt me twice! I trusted you with my body *twice*! I *trust you*, Jason. I trust you and I'm terrified. What more do you *want* from me?"

Eve stopped in the center of the room, cradling her head in her hands as if her neck alone couldn't support the weight of her thoughts. She breathed in deeply, trying to subdue herself, to just *relax*, but still her hands were shaky. Jason watched her, puzzled and distraught; it was so unlike her to lose control, to be anything but unbreakable, and yet there she stood, desperately trying to hold herself together. Without warning, he scooped her up in his arms and held her tightly, wrapping her in a warm, firm embrace. She resisted, pushing at his chest like a defiant child until she finally gave in and rested her head against his shoulder.

"I'm sorry," she mumbled as her breathing slowly returned to normal, her chest rising and falling with his.

"You're fine."

They stood together in silence. She could feel the faint pulse in his neck, beating rhythmically like a soothing lullaby. She pulled away from him, awkwardly picking at her cuticles as she stared at the floor, and they took their usual seats—Eve in her folding chair and Jason in his bed. He watched her drag the frayed edges of her lounge pants back and forth across the floor almost hypnotically.

"Are you going to tell me what happened?"

She wasn't going to answer him—he was sure of it—but before he could feel secure in his defeat, Eve looked up at him, her eyes bright and oddly forthcoming.

"Have you ever felt like your life was just a series of the same events happening over and over again? Like you're a hamster running on a wheel—just the same shit day after day, and no matter what you do or how you try to change it, despite how much you think things will be different, you're still running on that same damn wheel?"

"Yeah. I know what you mean."

"I just thought fighting the Interlopers would—"

"Get you off the wheel?"

She didn't respond.

Jason studied her. She looked tired; drained. Yet even in her weary state, her underlying strength was undeniable. It was as if she was vulnerable and indestructible at the same time.

"Come here."

Eve wrinkled her nose. "Huh?"

"I have a surprise for you."

"A surprise?"

He shuffled to the side of his bed and patted the empty space beside him. "Get over here."

Eve's eyes widened and her nostrils flared. "You want me to get in *bed* with you?"

"God, Eve, it's not like that at all."

"Some 'surprise,' pervert."

"*Eve*," Jason laughed, "come *here*."

Eve sulked and tromped toward the bed, finally taking a seat next to him. "*Fine*," she mumbled.

"Okay, lie down."

"*What?*"

"Eve!" Jason groaned. "Just trust me."

She plopped her head onto the pillow and sighed. "You sure are bossy today."

"Only because you're especially stubborn today." Jason fidgeted with his end table, pulling a small brown box from the drawer and resting it on his lap as he lay down beside her. "I'll get the lights."

"Oh, God—"

"*Eve—*"

"I know, I know. I trust you." She blushed. "We covered that already, remember?"

Jason melted briefly, long enough to flip the light switches. The room was filled with darkness aside from the slender streams of moonlight that poured in from between the window blinds. Eve wiggled uncomfortably, finally resting her hands on her stomach as she waited for something to happen.

"You ready?"

"I was born ready," she teased.

He chuckled. "Okay. Watch the ceiling."

Jason opened the small box, exposing a faint glow from within. He took in a deep breath and melted, keeping his eyes focused on the blackened ceiling above them.

One by one, small, bright flecks danced out of the box, encircling the room like glimmering beads of light. Hundreds of glowing speckles scattered into the air above them, shooting back and forth before finally settling into position. In an instant, the room had been transformed into a magical night sky.

"They're stars," he explained. "Well, it's actually glow-in-the-dark glitter, but they're *supposed* to be stars."

Eve smiled, captivated by the provisional starry night. "It's beautiful." She looked over at Jason, who was still gazing at the ceiling. "Why'd you do this?"

"Yesterday, you said you liked looking at the stars—made you feel peaceful. So I just thought I'd bring you some. No dead bodies included."

Eve laughed and looked back at the twinkling dots, some of which were now streaming across the ceiling like a cluster of shooting stars.

"And you just happened to have glow-in-the-dark glitter lying around?"

Jason smirked. "Got some help from my nurse. She has a little girl."

"Well, I'm impressed. This is..." She paused. "This is incredible."

"Glad you think so, because I was pretty nervous about it."

"Why? It's just me."

"Yeah. I know."

Eve glanced at Jason. The light reflected off of his eyes like sparkling diamonds. It was perfect, the moment. The rest of her day disappeared; all she needed was this very instant. She looked back at the starry sky and sighed.

"Thank you," she whispered. "This is the most thoughtful thing anyone has ever done for me. And I mean that."

She couldn't see him, but she could feel him smile.

"Just wanted to do something nice for you."

They stared at the ceiling in silence. Jason tapped his finger against his chest every so often as if orchestrating the movement of the glitter, sending it bursting into various shapes and soaring through the room like fireflies.

"Can I ask you something?" Eve turned to Jason. "Aren't I supposed to be tutoring you right now?"

He chuckled. "Yeah, we kind of stopped doing that a while ago, didn't we?"

"There's really nothing left for me to teach you. I mean, look at you—look at *this*. You're melting multiple things at once, you know."

"What, the glitter?" He rolled his eyes. "They're little. I can do little. It's the big things that give me trouble."

"Give it time—you'll get it. With a gift as strong as yours, I'm guessing a year, tops."

"So soon?" he asked, sarcastically.

"Everything you know now, you learned in one month. That's *amazing*, Jason." Her words were firm but kind. "As far as our little tutoring arrangement goes, I think it's safe to say you've graduated."

"So, what does that mean?"

"It means"—she hesitated, her throat suddenly tight, her voice soft and unsure—"I don't think you need me anymore."

Jason was quiet.

"I think I do," he said.

Eve bit her lip, trying to suppress the deep, wavering breath she desperately wanted to take. Her body relaxed into the mattress as if in that instant, everything was different—as if for the first time in years, she wasn't alone. She smiled the slightest bit and delicately rested her cheek against Jason's shoulder.

"You need to know something," he began, anxiously. "When I first found out I'm a chimera, I thought my life was over. They stuck me in this room— they said it was for *safety*, but I know better. They're hiding me." He stopped for a moment, searching for the right words to say. "Then I met you, and everything changed. You make me feel powerful, like I'm just now really living. And suddenly, this place feels like the best thing that's ever happened to me. It's all because of you."

Jason turned to face Eve, finally forcing himself to look her in the eye, only to find her lying by his side, fast asleep. He watched for a moment as her chest slowly rose and fell with each breath, her body so still and peaceful.

With a quick melt, he sent the glitter cascading from the ceiling and back into the small box. Eve stirred slightly and nuzzled her chin closer to him as he slowly reached for a blanket and lightly rested it over her body. He stared at her for a while, admiring her wavy hair, the light sprinkle of freckles on her shoulders, the way her usually worried brow now looked so soft, so calm. He slid his fingers through a loose strand of hair resting against her cheek and placed it behind her ear. Then, compelled by impulse, he leaned in close to her and gently kissed her forehead.

Eve flinched; she awoke with wide eyes that locked onto Jason's as he quickly pulled away. They stared at one another in complete silence. Eve wanted to speak, to say or do something, *anything*, but her body was paralyzed, and her thoughts were racing. Suddenly, her heart was beating rapidly with incredible strength, and her senses were heightened and very aware; she could see the nervous energy in Jason's eyes, hear the sound of his shallow breathing, and even the slightest touch of his skin against hers sent shivers down her spine.

Eve lifted her chin and closed her eyes. Without a moment of hesitation, Jason leaned in and kissed her, savoring the sweet taste of her lips as he combed his fingers through her hair. The moment was shocking, like a burst of electricity coursing through her, illuminating every cell within her body. He kissed her again, slowly and smoothly as he ran his hand down her arm, lightly grazing her skin and causing every goose bump on her body to stand at attention. He wrapped his arms around her waist and brought her in closer, and in turn she slid her hands down his neck to his chest, the tips of her fingers gliding over his tender, raised scar. She could feel his heart pounding beneath his skin and lost herself in the moment.

Jason held her tightly against him, kissing her softly, and in that instant she knew that this was something she wanted—something intangible, but so much more real than any other feeling she had ever experienced. As her nerves began to simmer and her body became heavy, Jason took her chin and gave her one last, long kiss, resting her head against his shoulder as they drifted to sleep in one another's arms.

* * *

Eve opened her eyes. Sunlight poured through a crack in the window blinds and streaked across her face, and she squinted against the brightness. She yawned, wrinkling her nose and stretching her toes as she squirmed beneath the sheets.

Jason was lying beside her, sleeping soundly, completely undisturbed by her awakening. Eve exhaled, taking a moment to enjoy the serene atmosphere. She couldn't remember the last time she had felt so revived in the morning, so energized and uplifted, and then it dawned on her: there were no nightmares, no horrific scenes or miserable memories lingering in the back of her mind. For the first time in over eleven years, she had had a dreamless sleep.

Her eyes darted toward the wall clock, and suddenly, the delight of the moment was ripped away from her like a rug being pulled from beneath her feet. It was nine thirty-seven in the morning, and she was in the medical ward with Jason.

Still.

Panic set in as Eve tiptoed out of bed. She had missed her first class, and her second one was already in session. Would Madison and Hayden notice? Of course they would. Madison also surely realized that Eve never came back to the dorm last night. She cringed; the last thing she needed was more speculation about her behavior. She slipped on her hooded sweatshirt and headed for the door, still racking her brain for worst-case scenarios. She looked back at Jason, letting herself be captivated by his steady breathing for just a second before her frenzied state took over once more. As she reached for the door handle in front of her, her body froze.

What if Heather was volunteering today?

Eve lowered her shoulders as she plodded through the isolation wing. A nurse passed her, shooting her a judgmental grimace and rolling her eyes. Eve blushed with chagrin and made her way to the door, peering out of the one small window and shuddering over the anticipation of maybe, possibly seeing a redheaded bloodsucker waiting at the clerk's desk.

And sure enough, there she sat in her scrubs, her auburn hair pulled into a delicate bun at the top of her head. Eve cursed under her breath as she watched the Rutherfordian fiddle with her scratchpad, hard at work and appearing so utterly innocent. Eve could see it now: the look of sinister excitement on Heather's face as Eve came waltzing through the ward twelve hours after her session with Jason first began. No, it wouldn't happen. She would make sure of that.

Her eyes landed on a stack of paper at Heather's side, and suddenly a plan was born. She melted instantly, sending the paper flying from Heather's desk, each sheet blowing across the hallway as if swept by a sudden breeze. Heather shrieked aloud, chasing after the papers as they scattered in every direction until they spilled around the corner, far past the clerk's desk.

As Heather rounded the corner, Eve bolted from the isolation wing and headed straight for the elevators. She pounded at the buttons, frantically looking over her shoulder while she waited impatiently for the doors to open. Finally, the elevator arrived; she hurried into the metal box, letting out a sigh of relief as she traveled down to the lobby and hoping with every fiber of her being that her escape had gone unnoticed.

As her nerves calmed and Heather's face faded from her mind, a new face made its way to her thoughts: Jason. She reminisced over the taste of his lips, the warmth of his hands, the ease of waking beside him. It was so unlike her to feel this way—to be happy and scared at the same time.

Pressed for time and hardly presentable, Eve dashed to her dormitory, changed into a simple pantsuit, and headed for the business building. Before she knew it, the door to the Strategic Communication lecture hall loomed before her, and she grimaced at the sight of it. All eyes would be on her. She imagined Travis, proud and smug with his head held high, and Professor Gupta cowering in her presence. She sighed, her eyes pointed at the ceiling as if begging for some sort of divine intervention to save her from the humiliation she would surely endure.

The classroom immediately silenced when she walked in. She rolled her eyes at the dramatics, taking her usual seat in the back, pretending to be unaware of the awkward tension. She caught a glimpse of Travis out of the corner of her eye and tried to mask her repulsion. As heads at last turned away and the students continued with their chatter, Eve pulled her scratchpad from her shoulder bag, thankful to be left alone.

The moment didn't last. A small body plopped itself in the seat next to hers.

"You going to bite my head off again?" JJ asked, carelessly resting her feet on the desk in front of her.

Eve didn't respond.

"I think you should reconsider my offer."

"Your *offer*?"

"Yeah. You should forgive me, and we should be friends."

Eve scowled. "Are you really trying to *negotiate* a friendship with me?"

"Look, I judged you prematurely. I can admit that. But we have similar interests, parallel agendas—"

"And you know this *how*?"

JJ winked. "I just know."

"Well, you've been wrong before, so you're probably wrong now."

"Hey, I'm not the *enemy* here."

Eve furrowed her brow. "And who *is* the enemy, exactly?"

JJ offered a sly smile, ignoring Eve's question and instead eyeing the hunk of junk on her desk. "Your scratchpad is a piece of shit, by the way. I could fix it for you—*if* we were friends." She stood from her desk and made her way across the room. "I'm good with computers, remember?"

After what felt like an eternity of valueless debates, class finally came to an end. Eve hadn't really paid attention—she was flustered, consumed with thoughts about the night before, so much so that even the perverse glances and mutterings of her classmates had gone unnoticed. She packed her things and left the room, remarkably with most of her dignity intact, and tried in vain to push the distractions from her mind. And now, she saw them—the hateful looks of the passersby. Each face she encountered was twisted into a disparaging glare. That is, all but one.

"Armaan!" Eve chirped, almost too enthusiastically. "Are we off to the ward already? Feels like I was just there."

"Oh, hey Eve," he replied, seemingly surprised to see her. "No, not today."

"Oh, really?" Her stomach churned. "Is something wrong?"

"No, quite the contrary. Wait, you didn't hear?"

"Hear what?"

"Jason was released this morning. He's back at school. Should be around campus somewhere."

"Oh..." Eve faltered. She thought of Jason, of his desperation to be free from the isolation wing. She thought of the time they shared together, the kiss...

"That's great."

"Yeah, I guess," Armaan muttered, casting his eyes down to the floor.

"Why the long face?"

"We'll probably never hang out again. No more walks to the ward. No more talks about melting." He frowned. "It's depressing."

"Armaan, we're friends. We'll still talk." She squeezed his shoulder. "I promise."

Armaan's face lit up immediately, and she smiled. There was something different about him today—he looked especially small in his oversized, boxy suit, like a little boy playing in his father's closet. It was an unusual outfit choice for him, and he fidgeted with his cufflinks nervously.

"What are you doing here anyway?" she asked. "I didn't expect you to have any classes in the business building."

"Oh, I don't. I have an interview with the med school board somewhere in this building. I'm applying for early admission to the medical program."

"Planning on skipping another grade, huh?" She chuckled. "Good for you."

"Yeah, well, it's super competitive." Beads of sweat began to form on his forehead, and he took a deep breath. "Wish me luck?"

"Luck is for idiots." She winked. "You're the smartest guy I know. You don't need luck."

Armaan grinned and wiped his hot, sticky face with his giant sleeve. But as his eyes made their way from Eve to the hallway behind her, his childlike smile disappeared, replaced with a perplexed scowl.

"Armaan, you okay?"

"Those girls over there." He paused, pointing behind her at whoever had captured his attention. "They're staring at you."

"Everyone stares at me, Armaan."

"Not like this."

A terrible tingle crawled up Eve's spine, and her shoulders became rigid. She could almost feel them behind her, lurking like awful shadows. There was no doubt in her mind—she knew exactly whom he was talking about.

"Are they blond?" she grumbled. "Is one of them especially—"

"Hot? Enticing? Chesty?"

"I was going to say angry, but thanks for the superlatives. And *chesty? Really?*"

"They're headed this way."

"God help us." She grimaced. "You should get out of here. I can handle them."

He ignored her, still gawking at the blond duo, when suddenly his expression changed yet again, this time into a shrewd smirk.

"Looks like you won't have to. Your knight in shining armor is here to save the day."

"Knight in shining armor?"

Eve finally turned, daring to see who loomed behind her. Madison and Hayden were only a few yards away, but they remained still, their bodies frozen, their mouths hanging open in surprise—it was Jason who now walked toward her. He wore a crisp white shirt and black tie—a stark contrast from his usual t-shirt and lounge pants—and as he made his way down the hall, Eve could've sworn that the sun glimmered through the windows a little bit brighter.

"He looks awfully happy to see you."

Eve slugged Armaan in the arm before he scurried away, leaving her to talk with Jason alone—or as alone as they could be in a crowded corridor.

"Hey," he said, shoving his hands into his pockets almost bashfully.

She smiled. "You look—"

"Stuffy? Boring?"

"I was going to say great. Debonair, even." She picked at her cuticles. "So, you're finally free. How does it feel?"

"It feels weird, honestly. People keep staring at me. Some whisper, some look scared."

I know the feeling, she thought to herself.

"Where did you go this morning?" he asked.

She glanced nervously behind him. Madison and Hayden were still watching them, and she prayed to God that they were out of earshot.

"I overslept. Missed my first two classes, left in a hurry."

"Oh, sorry about that. Kind of my fault, I guess."

She hesitated. "I'm not," she finally managed to say. "Sorry, that is."

Jason grinned and relaxed his shoulders. "I was hoping you'd say that." He fiddled with his pocket. "Hey, I have a question for you." He pulled out a slip of paper and presented it to her. "What is this?"

Eve's heart stopped. It was her flyer—her infamous *Chimera Bitch* photo. She could hear Madison's victorious laugh in the distance but ignored it. There was nothing for her to say, so she just stared at the flyer, her eyes empty and her lips silent.

"What's going on, Eve? Are people giving you a hard time?"

"I thought those would be gone by now."

"Is this why you've been so stressed lately?"

A wave of dread flowed through her, festering in her stomach until she could've sworn she was going to be sick. She looked apprehensively into his eyes.

"They know I'm a chimera."

"Who?"

"Everyone."

He glanced around at the passersby as if searching for answers. "Is this because"—he paused, his face dropping instantly—"is this because of *me*? Because you were tutoring me?"

"Jason, it's not your fault."

"God, if you hadn't met me, this would've never happened."

"That's not true. Heather knew since day one. It was inevitable."

"And the flyers? Who was behind that? Was it Madison?"

"I can only assume."

"You sure everyone knows?"

"Positive. I'm the juiciest piece of gossip this campus has to offer."

Jason took in a long, deep breath, still eyeing the passing students as he anxiously ran his fingers through his hair. Finally, he crumpled the paper in his hand and leaned in toward Eve, lowering his voice to a soft whisper.

"Why didn't you tell me?"

A sharp pang of guilt pierced her ribs, but she tried to remain firm. "Jason, I was trying to protect you. You had enough to deal with—"

"Eve," he interrupted, clenching his jaw, "I like you. I like you *a lot*. I thought last night proved that." He leaned in even closer to her, his once kind eyes now stern and focused. "I want you to be honest with me. I *want* to be there for you."

"I'm a big girl, Jason. I can take care of myself."

"I know that, Eve. But you shouldn't have to do it alone."

Eve bit her bottom lip and picked at her cuticles, her mind racked with frustration. She told herself that he was wrong—that he was being unreasonable and demanding—but it was an unconvincing lie. He cared for her, and regardless of how foreign it was for her to feel this way, she knew that she cared for him, too.

Jason smiled slightly, sensing her inner conflict. "I want to see you tonight."

"Wow, you don't waste any time, do you?"

He laughed. "Friday night is poker night with the boys. We all get together, have a few beers, shoot the shit. I want you to come."

"To *guys'* night?"

"I want you to meet my friends. What do you say?"

His voice was steady, but she could see in his eyes that he was nervous. The situation felt surreal, like an excerpt from someone else's life—anyone's but Eve's.

She raised her eyebrows assuredly. "Prepare to lose all your money."

"Prepare to eat your words," he laughed. His smile was a relief to see, and for a second, Eve felt as if nothing had changed—as if they were still in the isolation wing, just the two of them. He reached out and wrapped his hand around hers, caressing her palm with his fingers, and just as she was about to relish in the moment, she stopped herself. Behind Jason's shoulder only a few yards away stood Madison and Hayden—still. They were unapologetic in their gaping, their faces dripping with hatred and rage, and suddenly she realized that things were very, *very* different. Jason and Eve were on display for all to see.

"Is something wrong?"

Eve nodded at the two girls. "They're watching us."

He glanced over his shoulder at the twosome, who in turn quickly looked away. A confident smirk graced his face; he took Eve's hand and brought it to his lips, kissing it softly as he stared into her eyes.

"Let them watch."

Eve's heart thumped loudly in her chest, beating so forcefully that she felt as if it could move her entire body. She heard the girls gasp aloud, but she ignored it, feeling almost entertained by their reaction. With one last nod, she turned from Jason and headed for her next class, passing Madison and Hayden along the way and giggling at their expressions of uncontained shock. Before she had made it too far down the hall, she stopped and turned toward Jason one last time.

"Jason," she called. "You said there'll be beer tonight?"

"Yeah, why?"

"You do know chimeras can't get drunk, right?"

He hesitated momentarily and then chuckled to himself.

"No, I didn't... but that explains a lot."

***

Eve pulled her blouse over her head and tried to fluff her hair into place. As she stared at herself in the mirror, applying the last bit of blush to her cheeks, she couldn't help but notice an ugly scowl in the corner of the reflection. Madison was lying on her bed, idly flipping through the digital pages of her scratchpad magazine, but her eyes were focused on Eve, glaring resentfully. Eve ignored her, continuing to play with her thick locks and attempting to stifle her uncharacteristic excitement.

An abrupt knock at the door startled both girls. It was Jason, his eyes bright and his hand clasped around an economy-size bag of chips. He smiled at Eve, hardly noticing Madison's horrified face in the background.

"Hey," he said, softly. He peered over her shoulder into her room. "Need a minute? I can wait—"

"*No*," Eve blurted. She glanced back at Madison, who was now angrily grumbling under her breath. "Let's just get out of here."

As she closed the door behind her, Eve thought she could hear Madison mutter *"bitch"* under her breath. It didn't matter—she had a night of poker and ineffective beer ahead of her. Jason glided his hand down her wrist, tightly wrapping his fingers around hers, and in that moment she forgot about Madison completely.

They took the elevator down to the lobby and waltzed out into the courtyard. It was late into the evening, and aside from the light of the streetlamps, the entire university was covered in darkness. A sense of calm lingered in the cool, autumn air—the protestors were nowhere to be found, and most students were tucked away in their dorm rooms—and Eve took in a deep breath, relishing the rare moment of peace. Jason pressed his free hand against the small of her back, guiding her as they rounded the student union and shuffled across campus.

"Where are we headed?" Eve asked.

"The law and ethics building."

"So, we're about to gamble—in the law and *ethics* building. Tell me you see the irony in this."

Jason laughed. "The place has been under renovations for over a year now. They're adding a wing or something, I don't know."

"It's empty?"

He nodded. "No faculty, no patrolmen—just a bunch of dumb guys losing their parents' money."

Soon, the building was only a few yards ahead of them. Its courtyard was littered with rows of scaffolding and piles of dirt, and Eve could see the unfinished skeleton of the additional wing jutting from the building's side.

"You could lose your parents' money in your dorm room, you know," she teased, following Jason to the back of the building.

"Not enough space for everyone. Besides, they're all pretty rowdy, and *loud*—none of us are trying to get busted for drinking and gambling."

"But breaking into school property is totally fine," Eve quipped.

Jason stopped in front of a grey door labeled "Staff Only" and jiggled its handle. The door promptly creaked open, and he turned to Eve and winked.

"I'd hardly call this *breaking in*."

Eve chuckled, taking one last look across the campus before quickly ducking through the entrance with Jason. The door closed behind them, and immediately they were surrounded in a thick veil of black. Eve could hear the slight rustling of Jason's clothes as he retrieved his phone from his pocket and then illuminated the space ahead of them with its screen. Finally she could see where they were: the back of a hallway, its walls covered in loose plastic tarps, the floor coated with dust and lined with buckets and equipment.

"This is kind of—"

"Creepy?" Jason interrupted.

Eve smiled. "Dynamic."

They headed down the hall, laughing childishly as they clumsily maneuvered around the debris in their path. Rows of doors sat along either side of them, each one marked with an empty nameplate, and Eve assumed they were in the office wing of the building. Soon she noticed a door, slightly ajar, with a stream of light pouring from the opening. Jason cocked his head in its direction.

"So, it's kind of a big group. They can be obnoxious at times—a little snarky and sarcastic—"

"Jason, do you realize who you're talking to?"

"I just don't want you to feel uncomfortable."

"God, you make it sound like there's a horde of barbarians in there," she scoffed. "Come on, they can't be *that* bad."

Jason opened the door, only to reveal a nearly empty room. Three boys—one small and scrawny, another tall and slim, and the last round and portly—sat on the opposite side of a makeshift plywood-board-turned-poker-table, sipping beers in total silence.

Eve scanned the room, her nose wrinkled with confusion. "This is your 'big group'?"

Jason was even more perplexed than she was. "Where is everybody?"

The smallest one hesitated, his face visibly apprehensive. "They... couldn't make it?"

"Come on, we're all adults here," the tall one chimed in, rolling his eyes. "They weren't exactly *feeling* the whole chimera thing."

Jason paused. "Oh."

"I think one even dropped the abbrev," the tall one continued. "Called you a chime."

Jason shrugged his shoulders. "Oh well," he mumbled, pulling a seat out for Eve and taking one beside her. "Screw 'em."

"Amen to that."

Eve glanced at her surroundings once more. She could tell the boys had been using the room for quite some time—the entire space was dimly lit with portable lamps, and all of the remaining loose tools had been carelessly pushed toward the walls—and then she noticed the line of extra folding chairs neatly stacked in the corner. She turned to Jason, who offered her a reassuring smile.

"Eve, this is my band of bastards. Everyone, this is—"

"Evelyn Kingston," the tall one cut in. "We've seen the flyers."

Eve grimaced and sank lower in her chair.

"Relax." The boy took a swig from his beer before he continued. "At least it was a good photo—never mind being vilified across campus."

"This is Percy LaFleur," Jason explained. "We've known each other since we were in diapers."

"Yeah—same nanny. Same silver spoon."

Eve took a good look at Percy: he was long and lean with chiseled features, sharp cheekbones, and a handsome face. His eyes were a deep brown, practically black, which matched his black fitted thermal and dark designer jeans. His entire look was one of immaculate grooming: his skin was flawless and smooth, and his jet-black hair was styled into a perfectly coiffed pompadour. The only hint of disorder in his appearance was the mess of steel rods that hung from his heavily pierced ears.

"We grew up together," Jason added. "My folks are friends with his grandparents."

"Friends with benefits—money and power, that is. Not the other kind of benefits." Percy winked. "My grandparents founded LaFleur Fusion Power, so they're all in the same pretentious New York social circle."

"LaFleur..." Eve murmured. "Isn't your mom pretty famous?"

Jason chuckled under his breath. "That's an understatement. She's—"

"Alicia LaFleur: heiress. Socialite. Single-handedly kept the tabloid industry afloat with her drunken party girl antics for sixteen years." Percy casually shoved a fistful of chips into his mouth and spoke between loud crunches. "But don't get me wrong, I love my mom. She's like the baby sister

I never had."

Jason grabbed a beer for himself and slid one to Eve. "Heard of his dad? He's a Puerto Rican telenovela star."

"What does she care who my parents are?" Percy scoffed. "I don't even care. I'm bored already." He turned to Eve and flashed a smug grin. "Look, all you need to know about my folks is that I'm their incomparably attractive, exceptionally magnetic, gay spawn. That's what really matters."

"He's humble, too," Jason smirked.

"Honest. The word you're looking for is honest."

Jason pointed his beer bottle at his smaller friend, who was busy distracting himself with a lighter, apparently mesmerized by the tiny, flickering flame.

"This is Michael Sanchez. He's my roommate."

"Everyone calls me Sancho," the boy explained, his gaze parting from the lighter for only a second.

Eve liked him instantly; he was a shorter, skinny boy of Filipino descent, with large black eyes that twinkled with delight as he spoke. What he lacked in size he more than made up for in energy—everything about him oozed animation, from his spiky black hair to his flaming orange sweatshirt. His mind seemed to be racing just as swiftly as his small golden-brown hands, which continued to manipulate the red lighter that had him so entranced.

Jason chuckled, "He's kind of a pyro."

"I love fire," Sancho proudly proclaimed.

"He loves explosions."

"I LOVE EXPLOSIONS."

"He's majoring in mechanical engineering."

"I want to make things that make other things *explode*." His eyes grew larger and larger as he spoke.

Percy rolled his eyes. "Sanch, tell her how you got expelled from high school."

"You mean *accepted* into Billington?"

"Whatever. It's the same story."

Jason stepped in as if to mediate their bickering. "Sancho built a pipe bomb and entered it into his high school's science fair."

"It *wasn't* a pipe bomb," Sancho insisted, frantically waving his hands. "It was a highly sophisticated, mildly destructive explosive device."

"Still a bomb."

"Percy doesn't understand my genius," Sancho added with his nose in the air.

"They say there's a fine line between genius and insanity."

Sancho scowled. "My high school didn't appreciate my pioneering ways, but Billington did. That highly sophisticated—"

"Bomb," Percy interrupted. "He's talking about a *bomb*."

"That *bomb* got me into Billington—full scholarship, living in Rutherford Hall with a *celebrity*."

Jason laughed. "*Celebrity?*"

"Yeah man, you're on HV all the time!"

"For being kidnapped by aliens. That doesn't make me a celebrity, Sanch."

"Well, I'm using it. Girls love friends of celebrities."

Jason rolled his eyes and refocused his attention on their third, strangely quiet comrade. "This is..." He paused and looked at his other friends. "Um, who is this?"

"Oh! This is Gary. He's in my drafting class," Sancho chirped, leaning in toward Jason. "When I told him we were all playing poker tonight, he was dying to come. I think he's a big fan of yours."

Gary sat still, his chubby hands clasped together as he stared at Jason. His curly brown hair was like frizzy springs, and his skin was pale and oily. He began sniffing loudly, his nose wiggling with each inhalation, and he suddenly turned his attention to Eve.

"You smell."

"Wow," Eve muttered. "That was... tactful."

"You smell good," he added.

"...Thanks?"

"Really good."

Eve forced an awkward smile and turned her attention to the other three boys. "So, are we going to play poker, or what?"

"My kind of woman," Percy quipped, grabbing the deck of cards and slapping it against his palm.

"Wait, not yet!"

Percy sighed. "Sanch, I'm half drunk and we haven't even dealt the cards yet."

"Jason has to show us something."

Jason furrowed his brow. "Something?"

"The gift!" Sancho chirped, his eyes wide and fiery. "You're a chimera now—"

"I was *always* a chimera, Sanch. I just didn't know it," Jason corrected.

"You know what I mean. Do a trick."

"Come on, man, no one cares."

"I care! Percy cares! Right, Percy?"

Percy shrugged. "I'm seeing shit float anyway, might as well be real."

"Gary cares, too, right?"

Gary remained silent, his blank stare still locked on Eve.

"See? He totally cares."

Jason shook his head and took another swig of his beer, ignoring Sancho's request.

Sancho turned to Eve. "Have you seen it? Have you seen him use his gift?"

A small smile spread across her lips. "Actually, I have. Quite a few times."

"Jason, stop holding out on us!"

"That's different," Jason maintained. "She taught me how to melt."

Sancho stared at Eve in awe. "*You* taught him?"

Eve hesitated. "It's really not that big of a deal—"

"Not a big deal?" Jason interrupted. "This girl is *incredible*."

"Oh God, here comes the mush."

"Shut up, Percy."

"What about you?" Sancho asked Eve, his eyes still hungry for entertainment. "Got any tricks?"

"What a stupid question," Percy moaned. "She *taught* Jason how to melt, of course she has tricks."

"Do something!" Sancho begged. "Please?"

"Guys, leave her alone." Jason turned to Eve and rested his hand on hers. "Look, you don't have to do anything you don't want to."

"Eve, do your thing," Percy said, waving his bottle around like a magic wand. "There aren't any chimera-haters in this room. Right, Gare?"

Gary was expressionless, his eyes unblinking, his hands resting in his lap.

"Do it," he commanded.

"See, even Gary wants to see," Percy smirked.

Eve took in a deep breath and relaxed her shoulders. She glanced around the room for a toy to play with and immediately found the perfect thing. With a quick melt, she sent the perfectly stacked deck of cards sliding across the table, stopping directly in front of her. Sancho gasped, and she laughed. She focused her gaze on the deck, and the cards began shuffling in midair, jumbling and arranging themselves over and over again. The entire table was spellbound. She sent the cards flying through the room, dancing and diving in the air like cars on a roller coaster zipping across an invisible track. They spun through the empty space, racing across the walls and onto the ceiling, and then they fell like snowflakes from the sky, twirling with impeccable precision. Finally, the cards darted back to the table, forming a neat stack in front of Eve, and she dealt them properly to each player.

"HOLY BALLS!" Sancho squealed, hardly able to contain his excitement. "That was the most *dynamic* thing I've EVER SEEN!"

"Now, the real question is, can *you* do that, Jason?" Percy chuckled.

"Not as good as she can, that's for sure."

"Well, our new friend Gary doesn't seem impressed." Percy grabbed a fistful of chips and kicked Gary's shin under the table. "You've been awfully quiet."

Gary didn't move. He stared at Eve, his gaze almost haunting and grim.

"You're very powerful," he said.

"We already covered that, Gare—"

"Your power," Gary continued, ignoring Percy. "I can smell it from here."

"Sanch, this guy is weird," Percy jeered. "Why'd you invite him again?"

"I've been watching you, you know," he added, his gaze morphing into a frightening glare. "We've *all* been watching you."

"Okay man, you're freaking us all out," Jason said.

Gary stood from his seat, hovering ominously over the group. "Your power is undeserved," he intoned, his voice suddenly loud and forceful. "You have done *nothing* to earn such a gift."

"Jesus, what is your *problem*?" Eve spat, now glaring back at him.

Jason rose from his seat and folded his arms. "I think it's time for you to *leave*."

Gary didn't waver; his body began to quiver as sweat poured down his colorless face. Clearly, Sancho had invited a fanatic—a maniac who wanted nothing more than to torment Eve. She was familiar with the kind, though something about Gary—about his unblinking eyes and booming voice—made her uneasy.

"You are unworthy. Both of you." Sweat gushed down his forehead; his hair was now plastered across his face. "*We* deserve it," he howled, now walking steadily toward the pair. "*We* deserve what you have been so frivolously handed, and you use it like a *toy*."

The entire group stood to their feet and backed away from the table. Only Jason remained firm; Eve saw that his hands were balled into tight, trembling fists.

"Get. The *hell. Out*," Jason growled.

Gary flung his head back and forth, spraying the entire room with his profuse perspiration. Eve gasped as the beads of sweat splattered against her face and chest, the putrid smell perforating her nostrils. She wiped her hands across her cheeks and flicked the thick, disgusting liquid from her fingers and onto the floor. It was strange how slimy and viscous his sweat felt against her fingertips. Then she looked down at her hands, and her heart stopped.

She was covered in creamy, liquefied skin.

"Holy shit!" Percy bellowed. "What the hell is wrong with your *face*, man?"

Eve looked at Gary and felt her stomach drop to her knees. His entire face was dripping like gooey syrup, pouring down his body and exposing a grey, rubbery substance underneath: a second skin. He breathed heavily, his chest throbbing with each inhalation, so much so that his knitted sweater began to tear at the seams.

"Oh, God." Sancho pressed his shaking body against the wall behind him. "He's exploding. He's literally exploding."

Gary let out an earsplitting roar, his mouth opening so widely that his lips tore at the edges. He swatted at the table in front of him, sending it crashing against the wall, and then he stretched his arms and back until his sweater ripped into shreds. With a sinister grin, he shook his now naked body, sending his loose skin splattering across the room in every direction.

Gary—this creature—lifted his hands, which were now adorned with talons, and wiped the excess liquid from his legs and chest—and from the wings that had suddenly sprouted from his angular back. His once plump figure was now frail, grey, and much taller than before, easily reaching seven feet, and his teeth were long, silver, and dripping with strings of flesh. Eve couldn't believe her eyes—there before her, instead of a paunchy college student, stood an enraged Interloper.

"SONOFABITCH!" Jason shouted. "This is NOT happening!"

The Interloper crouched low to the ground and raised one long, sharpened talon, pointing it at Eve.

"YOU," he growled. "My mission was for the male, but *you* are a far greater prize." His claws curled, and he let out a deep growl. "Fairon will be pleased with my offering—with your power. He will be *pleased* with your inevitable *death.*"

Without another word, he lunged toward her, his teeth and talons bared. There was hardly any time to react, to think, to *breathe*—and just as her mind began to digest what was happening, Jason sprinted forward, charging at the Interloper.

"JASON, DON'T!"

It was too late—Jason flung his weight into the monster and tackled him to the floor, their bodies flopping in a pile of limbs and wings. Jason swatted at the alien, pounding him across the chin and sending his teeth flying from his mouth like metal raindrops. Without relenting, the Interloper grabbed at Jason's shirt and slammed him into the ground, pinning him with his incomparable strength. As Jason struggled against his opponent, the creature smiled and laughed.

Suddenly, the Interloper lurched backward, pulled from Jason's body by an invisible power—by Eve's gift. She stood at the front of the room, her eyes focused on her target as he barreled through the air and collided into the back wall. She picked him up once more and thrust him across the room, smashing him into either wall over and over again, until the sheetrock was littered with massive craters.

Percy and Sancho ducked as Eve melted the Interloper at the wall one last time, and then, with all the strength she could summon, she launched the creature straight into the ceiling and then blasted him back down onto the floor with a resounding thud. The Interloper's body crumpled and settled in a heap.

"*Jesus Christ*, woman," Percy said, his eyes wide with shock.

Stillness. The room was quiet, and for a fleeting moment, Eve thought that the fight was over. But before she could breathe a sigh of relief, the Interloper leapt up from the floor and let out a guttural roar, startling her and sending her stumbling to her knees. He then shot into the air, soaring like a torpedo, and landed on top of her, pinning her against the floor.

Eve stared up into the creature's black, glossy eyes; she could see her own frantic expression reflected back at her as if she were being forced to watch her own death. With a dip of his chin, the Interloper buried his face in her neck, taking in her aroma as he dragged his nostrils across her skin.

"It is true, what they say—your power is superior. Far more divine than the others." He smiled sadistically, bearing his teeth like trophies. "I will kill your male, and then I will bring you to Fairon." He let out a cackle. "And he will kill you *himself.*"

The creature suddenly jerked to the side, twisting and turning as if possessed. His entire body was ripped away from Eve and pulled into the air, only to be flung into the wall once again, crashing against the surface and then collapsing onto the splintered remains of the poker table. Eve scurried to her feet and looked over at Jason, who quickly ended his melt and rushed to her side.

"You okay?"

There was no time to answer. The Interloper marched toward them, undeterred and uninjured, each step heavy enough to shake the entire room. Without warning, Percy jumped onto the creature's back and wrapped his arms around the thing's neck, sending the Interloper stumbling across the room like a massive wrecking ball. The alien roared loudly, beating his wings and flinging his body from side to side, but still Percy hung on, dangling from his shoulders, his face reddening as he tightened his grip. With a growl, the Interloper staggered backward and rammed his back into the wall, crushing Percy into the sheetrock. He stepped forward, then again he thrust Percy against the wall, finally breaking the boy's hold and sending him dropping to the floor.

The alien looked frantically from side to side, searching for Eve and Jason, only to find the very small Sancho standing before him, his hands gripping a large plywood shard. With a grunt, Sancho smacked the board against the creature's face and watched helplessly as it shattered into a million small pieces. The Interloper was unaffected; he looked down at Sancho, his lips curling into an amused grin, and then he swatted at the boy with his wing, sending him flying across the room.

Again, his eyes darted across the space and then locked on to his target—Eve was huddled beside Percy, hoisting him to his feet. But before the Interloper could make a move, Jason dove on top of him, slamming him into the floor. Jason pummeled his fists into the creature's face, the sheer impact of his blows knocking more long, silver teeth from his mouth. Blinded by fury, Jason slammed his fist directly into the creature's mouth, slicing his knuckles open as they skidded across the needle-like fangs. As blood gushed from his shredded hand, the Interloper threw him to the ground, effortlessly shaking him off and sending him rolling into the corner of the room. Jason staggered to his feet, but it was too late; the alien approached him, cornering him by the wall, his chest swelling with rage.

"I will especially enjoy killing *you*," he sneered.

The creature suddenly lunged toward him, bellowing the loudest, most shrill cry Jason had ever heard. Jason cringed and pressed himself against the wall, holding his breath while anticipating the worst: either indescribable torture or sudden death. He could feel the Interloper hovering by his cheek, could taste the foulness of his dripping skin—but to his surprise, no attack was made.

Apprehensively, Jason opened his eyes. The alien was leaning against his shoulder, his talons gripping at a crowbar protruding from his stomach. Looking over the creature's shoulder, Jason saw Eve, clinging to the other end of the tool she had thrust through the creature's gut.

Eve gritted her teeth and yanked at the crowbar, ripping it from the creature's flesh. The Interloper howled and stumbled away from Jason, clutching at the gaping hole in his stomach, which now oozed a cloudy, mustard-colored pus.

The alien turned to face Eve. She had expected to see him fall to the ground, his eyes glazed over until they closed shut with death, but instead he growled and stomped toward her, reenergized and seething with rage.

"HOW IS HE NOT DEAD?" Eve cried, staggering backward.

The Interloper raised his claw and backhanded her across the jaw, sending her toppling to the ground. Jason dove forward, ready to melt the beast right off of his feet, when suddenly he stopped; the creature grabbed Eve from the floor, yanking her by the hair and pulling her close to his body.

Jason watched helplessly as the creature wrapped his arm around her, shielding himself with her body and tugging at her hair. She looked back at Jason.

"Do it," she demanded. "Melt him. Blow him away."

"I can't," Jason answered, his eyes darting back and forth from Eve to the Interloper. "If I melt him, I melt you."

"Do it anyway."

"I'll *hurt* you."

"*Do it anyway.*"

"I will not kill her—not yet." The creature smiled, stroking Eve's chin with a single talon. "Fairon needs her alive."

Abruptly, the Interloper pounded Eve's skull into the wall, knocking her unconscious. As he let her body collapse to the floor, Jason barreled toward him and swung at his face, beating him with his bloodied fists and toppling the alien face-first to the ground. Powered by aggression, Jason pounced atop the Interloper's back, but the creature quickly expanded his wings and sent Jason flying across the room.

The alien jumped to his feet, cracking the floorboards with his jagged talons, but before he could make another move, Percy and Sancho hurtled toward him and forced him to the ground. The two boys fanned across his flailing body, each securing a wing to the floor with their weight, though they knew they could only hold him for a moment.

Just as the wings began to slip from their grasp, Jason leapt onto the Interloper and shoved him against the floor, pinning his writhing body with his legs and clasping his hands around the alien's neck. He squeezed the creature's throat until his fingernails dug into the grey flesh, creating moon-shaped punctures that oozed yellow pus. Jason's veins bulged from his arms as a raw hatred pulsed through him, and with each movement the Interloper made, Jason tightened his grip even more. The Interloper gasped, choking on nothing as all three boys held his gaunt body to the ground.

Finally, the thrashing stopped; the alien went limp, and his wings slapped against the floor with two loud thuds.

Jason gave the creature's neck one last, firm squeeze before dropping it to the floor. He took a step back, his breathing laborious. The body was still, its lips slightly parted, its eyes empty. Percy and Sancho got to their feet and stared down at the body in silence.

Suddenly, as if awakened from a trance, Jason turned to Eve, who remained on the floor in the corner of the room where the Interloper had left her.

"*Eve!*" he gasped. He grabbed her shoulders and shook her frantically.

Her eyes opened—just barely. Her vision was hazy, and a horrible ache pulsated behind her temple. She glanced at her surroundings—at Jason sitting before her, at Percy and Sancho standing by his side, at the pieces of plywood and drywall that littered the floor, at the gaping holes in the walls and ceiling. She cradled her head in her hands, still struggling to focus, and suddenly her eyes widened. She looked at Jason, through Jason, and in an instant she was awake.

"Eve, *please*, say something."

"Duck," she answered.

"What?"

"*DUCK!*"

Behind Jason stood the Interloper, his gut dripping with pus and his body fueled with a newfound strength. Just as Jason dropped to the ground, the crowbar exploded from the floor and shot through the air like a missile. It was aimed to kill—Eve made sure of it, as she couldn't risk failure, not now. In the blink of an eye, the tool hurtled straight for its target, piercing the alien right between the eyes and lodging itself deep within his skull. The room quaked as the creature fell to the ground with a loud boom, the sound of defeat—of death.

The foursome hovered over the body, staring in shock at the alien, at the hole in his stomach and the crowbar jutting from his face. Eve grabbed the tool and ripped it from the Interloper's head.

"What are you doing?" Jason asked.

Without hesitating, Eve slammed the crowbar back into the creature's face, creating a second, though equally vile, gushing hole.

"I'm making sure the little shit is *dead* this time."

"That was NOT a *little shit*," Sancho asserted. "That was an ALIEN. A giant, ugly, ALIEN."

"*You* invited him here," Percy snapped. "*Brilliant* idea, by the way."

"Shut up, both of you," Jason ordered. "We're all right—that's what matters."

"I can't believe it," Sancho muttered. "An Interloper. We *killed* an Interloper. And what you did, Eve," he stammered, staring at her with awe-struck eyes, "sending him flying like that—God, you're like a superhero!"

Eve didn't respond; her eyes were still fixed on the Interloper's lifeless body. Jason tried to steer her away from the corpse, but she remained rooted to the spot, completely unwilling to leave the creature's side.

"Eve," Jason began, "are you okay?"

"I just..." she stuttered, still staring at the remains. "I just can't get over it."

"Get over what?"

The words were so hard to utter, and yet she couldn't stop herself. Nothing could have prepared her for this—it was worse than she had ever imagined, even in her darkest nightmares.

"Interlopers," she mumbled, finally looking back at Jason. "They're people."

CHAPTER 9: THE LIST

"Thanks for helping us out on such short notice," Eve cooed, giving Armaan's shoulder a comforting squeeze. She could feel him shaking and wondered if he was frightened or excited.

"Are you kidding me?" Armaan chirped beneath his surgical mask. "This is huge—bigger than huge, actually. This is *monumental*."

Sancho glanced nervously back and forth across the room. "Are you sure we should still be here?"

"The alien's dead, Sanch. God, of all people, you'd think the guy who builds pipe bombs would have a little backbone."

"It wasn't a pipe bomb, *Percy*, it was a highly sophisticated—"

"WE KNOW."

"Will you both be quiet?" Jason hissed. "Armaan is trying to concentrate."

The five bodies hovered around the makeshift operating table—a line of desks, stolen from a nearby classroom and pushed together in the center of the room. The entire space was a shambles, as the walls were littered with gaping holes, and scraps of plywood were strewn across the floor. Armaan paid no mind to the destruction and fiddled anxiously with his tools: a few shoddy instruments from a pilfered fetal pig dissection kit. The air stank of seething adrenaline and rotting flesh—the flesh of the dead Interloper that lay on Armaan's table.

Percy elbowed Eve in the ribs. "Who is this guy, again?"

"He's my friend," she answered, trying her best to breathe through her mouth. "He knows what he's doing. He's a medical student."

"Actually, I'm not," Armaan muttered.

"What? What happened to your interview?"

"They rejected me. Some guy named Lionel Vandeveld got the spot."

"Lionel Vandeveld?" Eve scowled. "Who the hell is that?"

Armaan shrugged. "His parents are friends with one of the deans. I never stood a chance."

Eve sighed. "That's not fair."

"Whatever. I bet *Lionel* isn't dissecting an alien right now." Armaan smirked. "You win some, you lose some."

"All right, can our mad scientist explain what we're looking at?" Percy cut in, gagging at the horrible stench. "Because all I see are soggy alien parts."

Armaan gazed up at the foursome, his eyes wide and eager. "Its fascinating, really. I mean, there are similarities to humans, definitely, but they're so... different."

Eve strained her neck over the body. "Can you tell us anything important? Anything of value?"

"I most certainly can. At least, I think so. Probably."

"Loving the confidence, Armaan."

Armaan ignored Percy's retort. "Let's start with the second skin," he began, pointing to a tray filled with leftover, slimy flesh. "It's a liquid coating that hardens to form the appearance of the human epidermis. It's nothing more than a disguise, really—a very convincing disguise. I think they can control it—though how, I'm not sure." He spun his gloved finger in the mixture. "The craziest part is what the fluid does. When applied, it can reshape the Interloper's body. Basically, it acts as kind of a shrink-wrap. Whatever shape the Interloper wants to take, this stuff will do it."

"So, what you're saying is, anyone could be an Interloper?" Eve asked.

"Yeah. Pretty much."

The room became oddly still. Eve's eyes wandered to Jason, who was staring at the dead body, his face twisted with disgust.

Sancho looked back and forth at his friends. "What if someone in this room is an Interloper?" he whispered.

"Oh, for God's sake, no one here is an alien," Percy groaned.

"That sounds like something an alien would say..."

"Okay, let's cut to the chase," Eve interrupted. "How do we kill these things?"

"A great question. But in order to answer it, you first need to know what *doesn't* kill them." Armaan plunged his hands deep into the creature's abdomen, stirring up new, foul aromas. "This is where you initially stabbed him, right in the stomach—or, at least, where one would *assume* the stomach would be." He pulled apart the grey flaps of flesh, revealing a pit filled with pulpy film.

Eve wrinkled her brow. "There's nothing there. Well, nothing but... mush."

"Exactly—they don't have stomachs. Their digestive tract is up here." He pulled at a long pink tube that ran from the neck through the abdomen. "This tube—it looks more like a filtration system than anything else." With a scalpel, he sliced a small tear alongside it, sending a thick, reddish-brown liquid pouring into his cupped hand. "See this stuff? It's mostly blood. Chimera blood."

"*Jesus,*" Jason muttered.

"Holy balls," Sancho gasped. "They're *vampires.*"

Percy rolled his eyes. "Don't be a dick-squeeze. Vampires aren't real. They only exist in teenage romance novels."

"Oh, so you're telling me *aliens* exist, but *vampires* are too farfetched?"

"They're not vampires," Armaan corrected. "They just can't digest solid foods. They feed off of liquids. They drink whatever they can get, whatever is... drinkable."

"Chimera blood," Jason growled. "That explains why the one who cut me open was licking his claws." He turned away, cursing under his breath.

"Wait," Eve interjected. "If they can't eat solid food, then why do they have—"

"Teeth?" Armaan smiled. "I was wondering the same thing." He parted the Interloper's lips, exposing countless fangs. "These teeth look more like bayonets than anything else. They're not designed for chewing—they're weapons. Look." He yanked at a tooth, breaking it off at the root and revealing a silver bud growing beneath it. "There's another fang ready to take its place. It looks like they shed their teeth as easily as animals shed fur. It's a never-ending supply of weaponry."

"But why would they need such heavy-duty hardware in their mouths, of all places? For combat? For intimidation?"

"That, *and* protection." Armaan grinned. "This is the best part."

He tugged at the Interloper's jaw and shined a small flashlight down its throat. A pale pink pouch protruded from the back wall of the creature's mouth, directly above the esophagus. The fleshy sack was covered in hundreds of tiny tubules, each one branching across the mouth and throat like a spider's web.

"You're looking at kill zone number one: an Interloper heart."

"*That's* a heart?" Jason asked.

"Well, maybe not a heart per se—a heart is the closest human equivalent I can think of. But it's the central hub in their anatomy—their life source, if you will. Those tubes branch across their entire body, stretching to every limb and every organ, like veins or arteries." Armaan made a tiny incision in the center of the sack, and a stream of yellow fluid oozed from the cut. "Interloper blood," he said.

"*God*, the smell," Percy gagged.

"So, let me get this straight," Sancho said. "You're telling us that this thing's *heart* is in its *mouth*?"

"Well, the back of the throat if you want to be precise, but, yes, basically." Armaan casually closed the creature's mouth. "If you think about it, it actually makes sense. The teeth act as a shield—just as our ribs enclose our heart, their teeth protect their life source. The good news is, the heart is fragile, so you can probably kill these guys with one laceration. The bad news is, you have a forest of fangs to fight through first, as Jason has already discovered."

Eve looked down at Jason's tattered hand—it was bandaged in thick surgical cloth and spotted with patches of blood.

"Is there any other way?" she asked. "I mean, not to be pessimistic, but there's a hell of a lot of teeth to dodge."

"That brings me to kill zone number two: the brain." Armaan fumbled with the Interloper's head, pulling the skin back to reveal a thick, black skull that was cracked down the center. He delicately removed the pieces of bone and pulled out a small grey sphere; it was spongy and light, covered in dimples and craters, and it fit easily in his hand.

Eve studied the brain, curiously. "It's so... small," she mumbled.

"Size doesn't matter," said Armaan.

"That's not what I've been told," Percy smirked.

Armaan spun the sphere in his hands. "There's really no way for me to analyze this. There are too many differences. I mean, the size is different, the color, the texture, not to mention the hemispheres: we have two, they only have one."

"Which hemisphere houses all of the crazy? Because that's the one the Interlopers got stuck with," Percy quipped, chuckling at his own joke.

"What I *can* tell you is that perforating its brain *will* kill it. And I know that, because that's how *this* one died." He turned the brain around, exposing a pit in the spongy wall. "See? A hole, right through the center of the brain."

"That's a good thing, right?" Eve asked. "Stab the brain. Sounds easy enough."

"Yeah, well, it's not." Armaan plopped the brain back into its cavity and pulled out a large slab of bone. "The problem is getting through the skull. This stuff is practically impenetrable. It could be a weapon all on its own."

"But it's in pieces right now. That means something broke it," Sancho added.

"Yeah, and I still can't figure that one out." Armaan fitted the bone slabs together like pieces of a puzzle. "His skull—and brain—was perforated by this crowbar." He held up the tool, examining it as if it were more alien to him than the specimen on his table. "*This* shouldn't have done the trick—not unless some epic force was used, or it was moving really, *really* fast. I'm talking lightning speed."

Jason, Sancho, and Percy turned to look at Eve; she was the one who had maneuvered the rod. She was the one who had killed the Interloper.

"Well, I melted it as fast as I could," she explained. She turned to Jason. "There wasn't a lot of time. He was right behind you."

Sancho looked back at Armaan, his eyes bulging excitedly. "You should've seen it. It was like a rocket," he gushed. "*So* dynamic."

"Well, you'd better hope that every single blow is rocket-fueled, because that's the only way you're getting past this bone." He folded the Interloper's skin back over its skull and reopened its chest. "Which brings us to the final kill zone: the spine."

Armaan waded through the creature's chest with his hands, pushing clumps of pulp to the sides and revealing a long, angular structure: black and glossy, crooked like the trunk of an old tree. Skinny, twisted bones jutted out from it, reaching up the neck and down to the abdomen like knotted branches.

"That's one gnarly spine," Percy mumbled. "Guy must've had scoliosis."

"It doesn't look like ours, but it appears to serve the same purpose. It's just as thick and sturdy as the skull, and equally hard to penetrate, but—"

"Break it," Eve interrupted, her eyes still fixed on the spidery branches.

"Yeah. The back. The neck. If you don't kill it, you'll at least paralyze it."

"I'd rather kill it," Jason grumbled.

Armaan looked back and forth between his new comrades and his specimen. "Well, you get the idea. You know the three kill zones. Same as humans, just different locations. And, well—" He paused and raised one long, sharp fang. "Booby-trapped. Beware the teeth, and beware the bone."

"Is there anything else?" Eve asked. "Anything we should know?"

"Not that I can see." He fiddled with his tray, scooping up a handful of metallic shards and a single blue button. "I found this attached to the back of the Interloper's head, toward the neck. It looks like it was some kind of mechanism at one point. It's completely destroyed, smashed to pieces. Could be nothing."

As Eve surveyed the dismembered specimen lying in front of her, an overwhelming sense of ownership coursed through her. The Interlopers were *not* indestructible—their fight had proven that, and Armaan's examination had further solidified the fact. They could be defeated. They had *kill* zones. Her body tingled at the thought of viable victory, however farfetched it appeared to be, because she at least knew that it was the slightest bit possible.

A rustling at the side of the room caught her attention. Jason was pacing back and forth by the wall, his hands balled into fists. She watched him for a moment—he was raw, exposed like a reopened wound—and she felt a sharp stab deep in the center of her chest.

Armaan chuckled. "I knew you liked him."

Eve playfully slugged him in the arm.

"You know, you're stronger than you think. Those punches hurt."

"You be nice to me. I brought you an alien, remember?"

Eve made her way to Jason's side and lightly rested her hand on his back—she could feel the tightness of his muscles beneath her fingertips.

"How's your hand?"

He tucked his bandaged fist under his arm. "It's fine. How's your head?"

"Probably a lot more *fine* than your hand."

Jason didn't respond; he just stared blankly at the wall.

"Tell me what's wrong, Jason."

He clenched his jaw. "His talons. They were all there."

"What do you mean?"

"They were all there. They were... perfect."

"Jason, I—" She stopped herself, suddenly very aware of what he was getting at. "That wasn't him. The one who..."

"The one who cut me open had a broken talon on his left hand. This one..." Jason's voice trailed off, and his eyes became distant. "It's not him."

"Were you hoping...?"

"I don't know. I don't know what I was thinking."

Eve looked at Jason, but he didn't meet her gaze. There was nothing for her to say, so she grabbed his unscathed hand and squeezed it tightly.

"That *thing* knew I'd be here," Jason grumbled. "That *thing* wanted to kill us."

"That thing is dead, Jason," Eve said, firmly. "*Because* of us."

Jason shook his head. "Seeing him ripped open and lying on that table, just like... just like *me*. I hate them, Eve. God, I hate them more than I can even explain." He fidgeted anxiously. "If we're going to do this—if we're going to fight them—we have to be smart. Today, we were caught off guard. That can't happen again."

"I know."

He finally turned to face her. "I couldn't live with myself if we made a stupid mistake and something happened to you."

"Then we won't make mistakes. We'll be prepared. We'll find out everything we need to know about the Interlopers before we make a move."

"I don't even know where to start."

"I do."

Jason tilted his head, perplexed, and Eve smirked.

"I know someone who has access to the kind of information we need. Someone who could point us in the right direction."

"And what makes you think this person will actually be willing to help us?"

Eve glanced back at the others. The whole scene was practically comedic: five misfit students dissecting a murderous alien, attempting to solve some of the greatest mysteries the human race longed to uncover. She looked at the Interloper's once terrifying body, now pathetic and lifeless, then turned back to Jason.

"Because we have something he wants."

* * *

"You can't keep showing up like this!" the receptionist cried.

Eve ignored her; she burst through the office door and brazenly approached the mahogany desk before her.

"This time, you're going to tell me *everything*," she growled.

Furst removed his glasses, seeming, as always, unruffled by her presence. He nodded at his frazzled receptionist. "You may go."

The woman exhaled loudly and stomped off, muttering to herself as she shot one last glare in Eve's direction. Furst cleaned his lenses, his demeanor poised and at ease. His tone, however, was laced with aggravation.

"Miss Kingston, are you going to make this a habit? Do I need to station some patrolmen outside of my office?"

Eve folded her arms, raised her chin, and hoped to God that she looked the slightest bit formidable. "You can be as patronizing as you want, but I'm *not leaving* until you give me some answers."

"Miss Kingston, I will not play this game with you."

"You *will* tell me everything you know about the Interlopers, Furst."

"And why is that? Why do I need to oblige your request, let alone give you an ounce of my attention?"

"Because I know how the Interlopers are invading the campus. I know how they're abducting students, right underneath our noses."

The dean smirked. "A tale of fiction, I'm sure—"

"*Fiction*? Why would I *lie* to you?"

"It's human nature to lie. Especially in order to get something you want."

"Then it's a good thing I'm not human," she scoffed.

Furst sighed, unimpressed with her sarcasm. "Miss Kingston, I'm not going to continue having this conversation with you. You will not be getting any assistance from me in this regard. There is absolutely nothing you can do or say—"

"I have a body," she interrupted. "An Interloper."

Furst stopped; he stared at Eve, his lips parted as if searching for the right words to say. After a brief moment of stillness, he adjusted his tie nonchalantly.

"You have a body? In your possession?"

"Yes. Do you?"

"Of course not. Not even the government has access to an Interloper specimen." He stopped short. "I probably shouldn't have told you that."

"Well, you'd better get used to talking. You're going to be doing a lot of that really soon."

"It's impossible. They're like cockroaches, the Interlopers. They're extremely difficult to kill."

"Yeah, I've noticed. But I can tell you from experience that they're not invincible. And I can tell you even more, *if* you agree to help me."

Furst stared at his desk, refusing to look her in the eye. Each second of silence crept by at a glacial pace, and Eve's thoughts screamed for him to speak.

Finally, he looked up. "Miss Kingston, what *exactly* are you proposing?"

"I'll tell you their methods. I'll tell you how they're sneaking into Billington undetected. I'll even tell you how to kill them. And you can keep the body—do what you want with it."

"And in return?"

"I want to know *everything*. Everything you know."

Furst took in a deep breath and stared down at the pen he twirled between his fingers. He was pondering the offer—she knew it—and she could hardly stand the anticipation. It had to work. There was no other option.

"I don't believe you. There's no evidence—no proof."

Before he could finish his thought, Jason charged into the office, his sudden presence a surprise only to the dean.

"Here's your evidence," he said, tossing a slimy grey object onto Furst's desk.

Furst looked down at the strange item in front of him. It was an Interloper claw, severed at the wrist, its fingers curled and stiff with rigor mortis.

Furst scanned the talons, his nostrils flaring from the stench, and then glanced at Jason and Eve, who hovered above him, anxiously awaiting his response.

"Well, I wasn't aware that *you* were involved in all of this, Mr. Valentine," Furst replied with a hint of annoyance. He peered at the two chimeras above his glasses. "I presume your many sessions together brought you awfully... close."

"I should probably thank you for that. It was really generous of you to allow me a tutor during my month-long solitary confinement," Jason quipped.

Furst stared down at the claw, completely underwhelmed by Jason's retort. "And you cut off its hand. Good God, I can only imagine how badly you've mangled the rest of it. I expect it's beyond recognizable at this point."

"At this rate, you'll never know," Eve snapped, her patience waning. "Not unless you give us some answers."

Furst glanced back and forth between the hand and the two students, his face drooping to a miserable glower. He had lost the battle, his authority suddenly reduced to an empty title. Reluctantly, he stood from his desk and approached his younger, much taller collaborators, his face pointed at the floor as if he knew that, at that moment, he'd be forced to sacrifice a fraction of his command to them.

"Follow me," he muttered, making his way out of his office.

Jason and Eve looked at one another, their eyes wide with shock.

"Holy shit," Eve whispered. "I think that actually worked."

They scurried behind the dean, following him to a nearby elevator and hurrying inside. As the doors closed in front of them, Furst pressed the basement button, sending the elevator gliding slowly downward. Seconds later, he struck the red emergency button, bringing their vessel to a sudden halt.

Jason glanced nervously at Eve. "You sure we can trust him?"

"Relax, Mr. Valentine," Furst responded. "You wanted answers, did you not?"

Furst checked his watch and then pressed the emergency button once more, this time holding it down at the same time as the basement button. The elevator shook slightly, coming to life for just a moment, and Furst ran his fingers across the button panel, pressing a variety of numbers as if completing a complex code. Suddenly a blue stream of light swept through the crevice of the elevator doors, scanning Furst's face, then moving on to Jason's and Eve's. An intercom buzzed overhead.

"State your names," a male voice boomed.

"It's Dr. Furst, and I've brought two guests."

"Under what security clearance?"

"*I* am clearing them for entry."

The voice paused, the room silent aside from the humming of the intercom.

"I am not permitted to accept visitors into the Shelter."

"And who created that rule, Cadet?"

The voice hesitated. "You did, sir."

Furst smiled. "He who forges it can most certainly break it."

"Is there foul play?"

"You're good to ask, but no, their accompaniment is of my own choosing." He paused and looked back at the two chimeras. "More or less."

"Prepping for three bodies to enter the Shelter. Sending you down."

The elevator lurched once more, sending Eve stumbling into Jason's side. Furst chuckled slightly, keeping his eyes in front of him as the elevator continued past the basement level. The drop felt endless, and the air in the room became dense and stifling as they plunged deeper and deeper beneath the surface.

The doors finally opened before them, and Eve's eyes lit up with awe. They had reached a large, open space with bright white walls and silver tables, filled to the brim with uniformed patrolmen and women. The room—this Shelter, as the intercom voice had called it—stretched far into the distance, the entire location rounded like a giant circle. Technicians huddled around holo-monitors, debating tactical procedures and warfare approaches, and patrolmen analyzed holographic Interlopers, studying their anatomy and debating combat strategies. To the right was a line of offices and conference rooms, each one stuffed to the seams with prominent commanders.

"Welcome to the Shelter," Furst said, though his tone was less than inviting. "Conceptualized and developed when the attacks first began. The school officials realized we needed a secure place to strategize—to meet in complete seclusion, away from the prying eyes of students such as yourself." He glared at his unwanted comrades and continued. "If it's answers you want, you will find them here."

Furst led the twosome to the conference rooms, their every step met with a string of curious stares. They stopped at a sizable office in the back of the Shelter, and Eve could tell by the rich conditions and copious awards that the space must be reserved for whoever commanded the Shelter. Behind the desk stood a vaguely familiar figure: a tall, fair-skinned man with light blond hair. He turned to face his company, and Eve immediately recognized the weathered scar that lined his jaw. This was the man she'd seen arguing with Furst in the medical ward.

"Colonel Eriksen, I'd like you to meet two of our most notorious students." Furst nodded at the twosome. "Evelyn Kingston and Jason Valentine."

The colonel glanced back and forth between the two students, his brow furrowed, first with uncertainty and then, undoubtedly, with anger.

"Why are they here?" he growled.

"We are going to show them around. A guided tour, if you will."

"Are you *crazy*?"

"It is an order."

"Furst, I will *not* allow you to destroy this operation over what I can only assume is a temporary moment of *insanity*—"

"They have an Interloper body," Furst interrupted, calmly folding his hands together. "They know how they're occupying the campus, and they agreed to cooperate with us if we provide them with some... insight."

The colonel froze, taken aback by Furst's statement. He glared at Eve and

Jason, his lips curled with aversion.

"How the *hell* did you two get an Interloper body?"

"We killed one?" Jason answered.

"It's a simple business transaction, really," Furst interrupted. "We trade information, and then we go our separate paths. Now, Colonel, please show this young man and young lady around our facilities." He leaned in toward Eriksen, resting his hand on the man's back. "Again, that is an order."

The colonel grumbled under his breath and trudged from his office, cocking his head as if instructing the twosome to follow him. They made their way past the conference rooms and headed back to the hustle and bustle of the Shelter.

"We'll make this quick. Get your questions ready, because this is a one-time deal," he groused, keeping his eyes straight ahead of him.

The colonel led them to a row of table displays surrounded by studious technicians in white lab coats. They slid their fingers across the screens, generating holographic diagrams of Interlopers, weapons, and other things—odd mechanisms, most likely warfare-related, that Eve was unfamiliar with. They studied the images, murmuring to one another as they jotted notes on their scratchpads.

"This is our strategy sector, where we gather pertinent data regarding the Interlopers' tactics and motivations. It's important in any warlike setting to study your enemy—how they think, how they feel, how they operate." The colonel slid his fingers along one of the monitors, pulling up a holographic image of a chimera with marks noting common dissection locations: chest, back, throat. He turned to his guests. "Their objective is clear: they want you—chimeras. We assume they're interested in absorbing your gift."

"Wait, you *assume*?" Jason interrupted. "So you don't know for sure."

"It's not like we can just *ask* them," Eriksen growled. "Logic dictates that the gift is their prime focus. And for whatever reason, they think they can find the key to your power by tearing you guys apart."

Eve scowled. "That's ridiculous. No scientist has ever found any sort of chimera gene, or trigger, or whatever else. It doesn't exist."

The colonel shrugged. "Maybe. Maybe they don't trust our science. Or maybe they know something we don't."

His ominous tone sent Eve's heart racing, though she tried to appear unfazed. Eriksen cleared his throat and continued.

"We've got some of the top psychoanalysts in the country studying the

Interlopers' behaviors, and if there's one thing they agree on, it's that these freaks are smarter than we ever gave them credit for. Their technology is staggering. Their methods are complex. And yet despite their advanced intelligence, their emotional capabilities are stunted—primitive, even. Remorse, compassion, empathy: all nonexistent within the Interloper culture. Something's missing in them. It's almost like they—"

"Only have half a brain?" Jason muttered.

Eriksen sneered. "I take it that's more than a figure of speech." He glanced over at the technicians and lowered his voice. "Look, these things *will not stop*—not until they get what they want. There's a madness—a desperation—in their endeavors. We want to know why. We want to know what motivates them to such an acute degree."

With a quick flick of his wrist, he minimized the projection and continued through the Shelter; Jason and Eve hurried to keep up. They weaved between the sectors, passing groups of armored patrolmen practicing drills and buzzing technicians with scratchpads in hand, all of whom stopped to stare at the two chimeras that had invaded their space.

Eve staggered to a halt, nearly colliding with the colonel's back. He had led his guests to a vast array of small, framed monitors, each one displaying a very recognizable Billington location: the Rutherford Hall lobby, the back corner of the Billington Library, the barred campus gates. Several uniformed workers sat in front of the live video feeds, watching them intensely.

"This is the surveillance sector," Eriksen stated. "When the attacks first began, we had only twenty cameras. Now we have over one hundred checkpoints stationed across campus."

"And have you seen anything?" Jason said. "Anything suspicious? Anything at all?"

The colonel hesitated, visibly embarrassed. "I know how it sounds, but I've played the footage myself again and again, searching for clues." He shook his head. "We've never caught an Interloper on our feed. Not once."

Eve thought of the creature she had battled the night before and remembered when he'd looked like a simple college student. "Not a single alien," she mumbled, glancing at Jason. "I wonder how that could be."

They approached the next sector: a large space filled with swarming bodies and strange noises. Sizable computers displayed zigzagged images of sound waves, each one projecting the most unusual symphony of sounds Eve had ever heard. Technicians scrutinized the waves, pinpointing specific clicks and twangs in the rhythms. The colonel stopped and cocked his head at the odd display.

"Here we have our communication sector, the heart of the Shelter. Our team works day and night tracking and translating the Interlopers' transmissions."

"You've hacked their communications?" Eve asked.

The colonel nodded and pulled up a hologram of a circular device, palm-sized and metallic, with a glowing blue button in its center. He expanded the image, making it large enough to see the intricacies of the design.

"Each Interloper has a device," he explained, rotating the image. "We call it the beacon. They're surgically attached to the backs of their heads, just beneath their skulls. This mechanism allows them to transmit orders, data, and even images to one another in the most quick and efficient manner possible. It's a level of innovation we've never seen before." He minimized the hologram. "Fortunately, we've managed to decrypt their language, but that's only half the problem."

"What's the other half?"

"There's a delay," he grumbled. "The signals are only traceable by our systems hours after they've been transmitted. We never know about an attack until well after it's occurred."

"How do we fix that?" Jason asked.

"*We* won't be fixing *anything*," the colonel snapped. "It's up to us at the Shelter. This does not involve you two."

Eve stared at the hologram, studying the image. "I think I've seen this before," she said. "Our Interloper—he had one of these."

Eriksen's eyes lit up with intrigue. "Do you still have it?"

"It was destroyed in the fight. It's in pieces now."

The colonel growled. "The only way to eliminate our handicap—to receive the signals in real time—is to gain access to a working beacon. The problem is, in order to get one, we need a body." He turned off the projection and scowled at Eve. "Looks like your specimen won't be all that useful after all."

"Sorry to disappoint," Eve mumbled.

They wandered toward the last sector, which was easily the most cluttered of them all. Countless patrolmen, all of seemingly high rank, hovered around rows of intricate maps—Eve recognized a map of Billington and a couple others of various cities in Southern California. The soldiers conferred with one another while analyzing the various locales.

"We've reached the locator, our final sector," Eriksen explained. "Here, we track and log all of their dissection sites. They never use the same spot more than once, so they're piling up fast. But more importantly, we're trying to identify a meeting place—a hub. In almost all of their transmissions, the Interlopers mention a central location. We call it their lair." He crossed his arms and glowered. "Trouble is, we can't find it."

Eve sighed. "Well, that's not very encouraging."

"We looked at their dissection sites for common themes. At first we noticed they chose locations near pipelines, sewer systems—places with access to water. We weren't quite sure why—"

"They can only digest fluids," Jason interrupted. "I'm giving you that one for free."

The colonel continued. "Pretty soon, the trend disappeared. Their locations became random and varied, without a water source nearby."

"That's because they'll drink *any* fluid," Eve added. "Doesn't have to be water. We found chimera blood in their digestive tract."

"Good *God*—"

"So you really have *no* idea where their lair is?" Eve asked.

"The signals are rejecting all of our tracking methods. We'll keep trying."

Eve glanced toward Jason, only to discover that he was gone. Her eyes darted frantically across the sector until she finally spotted him standing before a holographic map, roughly ten feet tall and just as wide, covered in bright blue lights. He was still, almost hypnotized by the projection.

"That's a map of all the dissection sites," Eriksen explained, making his way to Jason's side. "Each blue light marks—"

"A chimera," Jason interjected. "Someone you've saved."

He nodded. "You'll find your light among the rest."

Jason's eyes scanned the map, stopping for a moment in front of an anomaly—a small, red glow.

"The red light," he added. "That's Marshall Woodgate, isn't it?"

Eriksen hesitated. "The red light represents—"

"Death."

They stood in silence: Jason staring at the lights, and Eve and Eriksen staring at Jason. Finally, Eve noticed her surroundings; they had come full circle, and the offices where they had started were only a few short yards away. The colonel impatiently cleared his throat.

"Look, you've seen the Shelter. We accommodated your demands. I think we're done here—"

"Who's Fairon?" Eve interrupted.

The colonel took a step back, startled by her random firing. "Excuse me?"

"I want to know who Fairon is."

"That wasn't part of the trade—"

"The trade was for *everything*. Everything you know in return for the body."

Eriksen's back straightened, his frame visibly tense. He grabbed both Jason and Eve by their shoulders and forced them forward.

"My office. *Now*."

Jason and Eve charged ahead, goaded by Eriksen's heavy hand and assertive demand. He shoved them into the room and locked the door behind him.

Furst turned in his chair and offered the threesome the slightest, most unnatural smile he could have possibly mustered. "Back from your tour already?" he asked. "Well, I hope you found everything you were looking for."

"We're not finished yet," Eve snapped, shooting a scathing glare at Eriksen.

The colonel's pale white face had turned a deep shade of red. "They want to know about Fairon."

Furst exhaled softly, and his body sank into his chair. He offered the colonel a slight nod.

"Well, then, by all means, Colonel. Tell them."

Eriksen faltered, his entire demeanor in a perceptible state of conflict. He bit at his lip, but reluctantly submitted to the dean's orders.

"Fairon is their leader."

"*Christ*," Jason sighed. "Of course there's a leader."

"We have yet to find an Interloper of higher command," he continued. "He's unique in strength, esteem, and appearance, though we're not sure how. But we know he has power over the others—immense power. He's the one to beat."

"Beat how?" Jason grumbled. "If you can't take down *one* Interloper, how do you expect to defeat their kingpin?"

"*You* of all people should know what we're up against," Eriksen fired back. "The Interlopers aren't beneath us. They're an intelligent and capable species—a species led by a cruel, calculating leader. The sooner you realize that, the better."

Eve and Jason were quiet. Eriksen glanced back at Furst before continuing.

"Look, he's leading their entire mission at Billington. He's ordering all of the dissections, and now, apparently, the deaths." His voice had suddenly become firm and commanding again. "He's smarter than the rest and twice as evil. The head of the beast, like a sick, twisted God for the rest of 'em to blindly obey. And they *will* obey him, without a second thought. We've been searching for that piece of shit for months now. If we get *him*, we've got them all by the balls."

And if they didn't get him, Fairon would have Eve, Jason, and the rest of the chimeras killed. Butchered. Torn apart. Unless, of course, the patrolmen found a way to grab him by the proverbial *balls*.

Do Interlopers even have balls?

"How did they find me?"

Jason broke the silence, interrupting Eve's thoughts. He was staring out the window, his eyes fixed on something off in the distance: the glowing map.

The colonel furrowed his brow. "'Scuse me?"

"I didn't even know I was a chimera until they abducted me." He turned toward Eriksen and Furst, his jaw rigid with anger. "How did *they* know if I didn't?"

Eriksen looked away, and for a moment, Eve noticed something different about him—something weak.

"I *said*, how did they *know* that?"

Eve recalled the moment she first saw the colonel. She glanced at Eriksen. "'*Fairon has everything.*' You said that in the medical ward."

"Miss Kingston, are you still fretting over that conversation?"

"What do they *have*, Furst?" Eve hissed, glaring at the dean. "This time, you have to tell me. You know you do."

The friction in the room was palpable and heated. Furst looked up at the colonel, his eyes brimming with defeat, and took in a long, deep breath.

"Billington University didn't earn its unprecedented reputation without reason," he began. "We only accept the best of the best. Thus, it was determined early on that we needed to acquire as much relevant information about our candidates as possible. So we did just that: we gathered information. Every detail we could find about our students is here in our academic databases. We have very important records. Records that cannot be tampered with without... significant damages."

Eve's stomach twisted into a knot. She had the most awful feeling that he was about to say something terrible, and she prayed that somehow she was mistaken.

"As you both know, students are required to report some basic medical history to Billington upon admission. Vaccinations, family history, any relevant health scares. It's standard procedure." He fiddled with his cufflinks as if to avoid her cutting glare. "But what our students do not realize is that we dig much deeper than that. Past illnesses. Blood tests. Abnormalities. We have our medical ward study these records vigorously, and thus we were able to determine which of our students were, well..." He stopped for a moment, finally meeting Eve's gaze. "Unique. Exceptionally healthy—too healthy for the average human being, whether they knew this or not."

"Jesus Christ," she said, finally realizing what he was implying. "You didn't."

"We generated a list," he declared, his words razor-sharp. "A list of all of our chimera students. Every last one of them." He looked back at the colonel, who was standing, petrified, by his side. "This list is the most valuable asset this institution had in its possession. Now... it seems as though the Interlopers have stolen it."

"*ARE YOU OUT OF YOUR DAMN MINDS?*" Jason roared. "*DO YOU HAVE ANY IDEA WHAT YOU'VE DONE?*"

"How is that *possible*?" Eve asked. "How could they just take it from you?"

"It was heavily guarded and highly secure—"

"They *stole* it!" Jason barked. "How *secure* could it have been?"

"We have no idea how they were able to locate it—"

"You're responsible, do you know that?" Jason glared at the dean, his veins bulging from his neck. "You have *blood* on your hands."

"Have they"—Eve stuttered, almost too stunned to speak—"have they had it the *whole time*? Is that why they targeted Billington in the first place?"

Furst hesitated. "It appears so."

"A *list*," Jason snarled. "You compiled a goddamn *list*. How could you be so *stupid*?"

"We're handling the matter as aggressively as possible. All we need to do is find the list, destroy it, and move past the charade. It's all very manageable—"

"They're disguised as *people*, Furst," Jason spat. "That's why your *cameras* aren't catching them, that's why the victims don't notice their attackers beforehand. It's because they look *just like us*. They can be *anyone*. They are *everywhere*."

Furst's eyes widened. "Are you telling me they're masquerading as *humans?*"

"I'm telling you that you've screwed up more than you can *possibly* imagine."

Eve was speechless, her body stiff and unmoving aside from her shallow breathing. It wasn't true, it couldn't be—and yet no matter how many times she told herself as much, she knew it was a lie. Furst and Eriksen looked at each other, their faces drained of all color. With what little composure he had left, Furst cleared his throat and turned toward Eve.

"If what you're telling us is true, then it's best that you know one last thing—"

"Dr. Furst—"

"It's all right, Colonel," the dean insisted. "She deserves to know."

"*What* do I deserve to know?" Eve grumbled.

Silence. Both Furst and Eriksen opened their mouths to speak, and yet they said nothing. Eve thought back to her fight with the Interloper—his sinister sneer, his exceptional strength, and the words he uttered tauntingly in her ear.

"The Interloper that attacked us," she began. "He said I was a *great prize.* That he was going to offer me to Fairon." She paused. "What was he talking about?"

Still the room was silent.

"*Answer me, Furst.*"

Furst fiddled with his glasses, pushing them up the bridge of his nose. "I didn't think it necessary to tell you. I had nothing but faith in our patrolmen. But, after this... unforeseen complication, I feel it needs to be said."

"Oh, God," Jason growled. "How could this possibly get any worse?"

Furst dipped his chin. "There was one additional note on the list. One key element that stood out from the rest."

Eve closed her eyes. She knew exactly what he would say next—it was almost as if she had known all along.

"It was you, Miss Kingston. Your name was the pinnacle. It was the most important name on that list, because it specifies you as what you already know you are: the strongest chimera in the world."

"You *sonofabitch*—" Jason hissed.

"They know, Miss Kingston. And I can guarantee they've been watching you." His voice was stern, but he continued with the same intensity. "You are in danger, more than anyone else at Billington. More than anyone else in the world. You are, and will forever be, their most prized mark. You're the one Fairon wants."

Eve didn't speak. She didn't breathe, or make a sound, or move an inch, and yet in her complete stillness, her mind was racing feverishly. It was all too much to take in, and so she did nothing but stare blankly at the floor.

"Miss Kingston, do you understand what I'm saying?"

Eve parted her lips slowly, still searching for the right words to say. "Find the lair, kill Fairon, and destroy the list," she said. "That's what needs to be done."

"Oh, I see what's going on here," the colonel interrupted. "Look, this is *our* responsibility, not yours."

Jason sneered. "Yeah, and you're doing a hell of a job of it."

"You're so confident, aren't you?" Eriksen snapped. "You kill one Interloper, and what? You can take 'em all? You can take on *Fairon*? Let me tell you right now, you *can't*. Fairon is far more dangerous than you can possibly imagine. If you go after Fairon—if you fight him—he will *win*. And he won't just kill you—he will *obliterate* you."

"The colonel is right," Furst interjected, turning to Eve. "You do understand that, although we agreed to exchange information, you are not to act on any of this?"

Eve didn't respond.

"Miss Kingston, do you hear me?"

"Yes." She finally looked back at the dean. "The lair. Fairon. And the list."

Again, there was silence. Eve's frantic thoughts had suddenly coalesced into one clear, concise sentence: *Find the lair, kill Fairon, and destroy the list.* She hadn't noticed that the entire room was staring back at her, Jason with worry, the colonel with apprehension, and Furst with conviction. Were they staring at a dead woman?

Furst brushed the pleats of his trousers and rested his hands on Eve's and Jason's backs. "Well, it appears you two have been brought up to speed, yes?" he said almost lightheartedly. He gave their shoulders a hard squeeze and flashed a smile.

"Now, show me that *damn alien*."

* * *

"HOLY BALLS," Sancho squealed, dashing through Percy's dorm room like an overexcited child. "This place is dynamic!"

Eve eyed the private pad—room 1502, one of the exclusive luxury suites atop the fifteenth floor of Rutherford Tower. It was impressively large with a marble kitchen, modern dining nook, and a comfortable living room complete with a state-of-the-art entertainment center and a sumptuous seating area in rich, black leather. Percy's bedroom was toward the back—locked, as he claimed, *to keep out the manic pyro*—but Eve imagined that it was just as lavishly styled as the rest of the apartment. As she and Jason grabbed a couple of barstools and took their seats, Sancho flung himself onto the plush couch, and Percy took root in the kitchen.

"Hey, how come we never play poker *here*?" Sancho whined.

"Because I have nice things, and I'd prefer if said things weren't set on fire," Percy scoffed. "I designed this place myself, you know. Everything's custom."

"You had your dorm room custom built?" Eve asked. "Why?"

"Trust me, it was necessary." He pulled a bottle of booze from his liquor cabinet and raised it in the air. "Scotch, anyone?"

"Yes, *please*."

"Not for you, Sanch. You'll probably use it as lighter fluid."

"The drinking can wait," Jason interjected, turning toward Eve. "We have a lot to discuss, and the first line of business is you, Eve."

She wrinkled her nose. "Me?"

"We have to get you out of here. Away from Billington."

"What? Why?"

"Didn't you hear Furst? Fairon is coming for *you*."

"There's no point in running," she countered. "If he wants me so badly, he'll follow me wherever I go."

"Look, this is serious. You're not safe here."

"I'm not safe *anywhere*, Jason."

"*Jesus*, Eve, if you stay here, Fairon *will* find you," Jason snapped. "He's not going to stop, not now that he knows you're the strongest chimera in the world."

Eve cringed. She glanced at Percy and then at Sancho, who looked back at her with wide, intrigued eyes.

"You're the strongest chimera in the *world*?" he asked.

Eve sighed loudly and scowled at Jason.

"Sorry," he muttered, sinking in his seat. "Forgot they didn't know already."

Percy chuckled. "Relax, your secret's safe with us," he said, swirling the alcohol in his glass. "Though it wasn't much of a secret, at least not after you beat the shit out of Gary. And what did he say to you, again? Something about being divine or magical or whatever else? It doesn't take a genius to put two and two together."

Despite his words, Eve felt little relief. Jason was still watching her, his eyes pleading for her to listen to him—to abandon Billington. She met his gaze.

"I'm not leaving," she repeated. "We fight."

Percy laughed. "Fight who?" He downed his drink and poured himself a double. "Have you forgotten that your enemy has a major camouflage advantage?"

"God, we don't even know who we're looking for," Jason grumbled.

"Come on guys, it shouldn't be *that* hard to come up with Interloper candidates, right?" Sancho flashed Eve an encouraging smile. "Can't you just think of everyone who really, *really* hates you?"

"*Everyone* hates me. Way to narrow the playing field." She rolled her eyes. "Look, we can't find the lair because we don't know where to search. We can't find the list because we haven't found the lair. And we can't find Fairon because, well," she grimaced, "he probably looks like everyone else."

"Well, we can't just do *nothing*," Jason growled.

"We'll focus on self-defense." Her voice was self-assured, but inside she felt meek. She turned to Jason. "If they're watching us—or watching *me*—they'll attack again. We just have to make sure that when they do, we're ready for it."

"But what about us?" Sancho asked, innocently pointing to himself and Percy. "What are we supposed to do?"

Jason furrowed his brow. "What do you *mean* what are *you* supposed to do?"

"We want in on the action!"

"Oh, no," Eve rebutted. "You two can't get involved. This is really dangerous."

"God, Eve, stop being so maternal," Percy quipped. "You can't tempt us with an adventure and then yank it away. Don't be such a tease."

"She's right, guys," Jason added. "It only makes sense that we do this alone. We're faster, we're stronger, we heal better than you do—"

"I can design weapons!" Sancho blurted. "Come on, Jason, you know I can!"

Percy slid his now empty glass toward the sink and smirked. "He has a point. Disaster and mayhem are sort of his bread and butter."

"And it's not just bombs—I can build anything. When I was thirteen I built a flamethrower out of soda cans and the dismantled pieces of my cousin's bicycle."

Jason paused and glanced at Eve.

"We do need weapons," she mumbled.

He sighed. "Fine. You're in, Sancho."

"Dynamic!" The newest addition to their team pulled his scratchpad from his sweatshirt pocket and immediately began flipping through digital drafting plans.

Percy folded his arms and leaned casually against the kitchen counter. "So, when do we start?"

The room became quiet. His three guests froze in place, their eyes darting back and forth at one another, their lips firmly shut.

"What? What did I say?"

Eve and Sancho stared at Jason, silently willing him to say the words they dared not speak. His face flushed and he cleared his throat.

"You see, Percy, we were kind of thinking it would be, you know... just the three of us."

Percy laughed. "You're kidding, right?"

Again, no one spoke. Instead, the threesome gazed awkwardly at the floor.

"Oh, God, you're *serious*?" he spat. "The *pyro* gets to join the crew, but *I* can't?"

"It's not personal. Eve and I have the gift, Sanch is an engineering genius—"

"And you think I'm—what? Useless?"

Sancho hesitated. "Well, I mean, look at your place. Look at your clothes. Your lifestyle doesn't exactly scream 'survival of the fittest.'"

"*Really*? After I *vouched* for you? God, Sanch, you're a real scrote."

"Come on, Percy, don't be like that," Eve said.

"We just don't want you to get hurt, that's all," Jason added. "Having you around could be a liability."

"Wow, so now I'm useless *and* a handicap?"

Eve shot Jason a glare and attempted to clean up his verbal mess. "We just want to make sure that everyone can contribute equally. If you've got something to bring to the table, by all means let us know."

Percy grumbled to himself. "If I've got something to bring to the table, huh?" He turned away from his traitorous friends and headed to his bedroom, pouting.

"Wait, Percy—come back!" Eve groaned as she and the others hurried behind him.

Percy flung his bedroom door open, revealing a sleek king-size bed, mahogany furniture, and crisp walls covered in black-and-white paintings. The heir stood in the doorway and shoved his hands into the pockets of his designer jeans.

"Percy, don't just run away from us," Sancho pleaded.

"I'm not *running* away from you guys. *God.*"

"Then what are you doing?"

Percy smirked, still fiddling with his pockets. Finally, he pulled out a small remote control and held it in front of him.

"Showing you what I *bring to the table.*"

With a single click of the remote, Percy's entire bedroom came to life. The cabinets and shelves of his wardrobe and dresser swung open, revealing secret compartments lined in black crushed velvet. His paintings swiveled out from the walls and folded into grooves hidden within the frames, displaying rows of drawers divvied into multiple sections.

Eve, Jason, and Sancho stared in shock at the newly exposed gems before them: guns. Guns in all shapes and sizes, guns in every make and model, guns from every country and era. Percy strolled toward one of his hidden compartments and retrieved a small firearm, admiring the craftsmanship and gently stroking the grip.

"Mother of balls," Sancho gasped. He wandered around the room, eagerly inspecting the firearms like a child in a toy store.

"I'm a collector," Percy explained smugly. "These are just my favorites. The rest of them are at my mom's place not far from here."

"There's *more?*"

"Of *course* there's more." He looked down at Sancho and sneered. "How's my lifestyle looking now?"

"You own *guns?*" Jason asked. "Since *when?*"

"God, Jason, what an observant friend you are. I've been shooting since I was *twelve.*"

"You can *shoot* these things?"

"Jesus Christ! You never noticed my shooting awards?" He pointed to a stack of medals and plaques sitting on his desk.

Jason lowered his head sheepishly. "I thought they were for photography."

Eve stood in front of the wardrobe, her eyes dancing across the firearms. "Billington allows you to keep these here?"

Percy winked. "What they don't know won't hurt 'em."

"Wow. What an ironic statement."

"Can you show us how to use them?" Jason asked.

"Does that mean I'm in?"

"You are *so* in," Sancho gushed. "Right, guys? I mean, he *has* to be in."

"Yeah, yeah," Jason smirked, playfully punching his friend in the shoulder. "You're in."

Percy grinned. "Then I can definitely teach you how to shoot. And fortunately, I have the perfect place to do it."

***

The sound of gunshots reverberated in Eve's eardrums. She held her firearm with both hands, her stance solid, her mind at ease. She stared at her target—a sloppily drawn Interloper tacked to a haystack—and imagined it was real, that a monstrous alien stood before her, his chest heaving and his mouth salivating. The hairs on her arms stood on end, and she fired once, twice, again—until before she knew it, her magazine was empty and a thin trail of smoke glided from the barrel of her gun. This was really happening— the gun in her hand, the pull of the trigger, and the ten silver bullets buried in the center of her target.

"You're a natural," Percy said, slapping her across the back. "But then again, you chimeras are good at *everything*, so what else is new, right?"

The foursome had traveled to Percy's "third home," as he had described it—a stately Calabasas mansion only a short distance from campus. They had navigated their way through the manor's endless backyard to the makeshift gun range: a row of haystacks covered in paper aliens and tables lined with delicate trinkets just waiting to be blown to insignificant bits. Jason and Percy stood by Eve's side, each aiming a firearm at one of the targets, and Sancho sat on a patch of sod behind them, fidgeting with his scratchpad with such intense concentration that he had managed to ignore the shooting entirely.

"Hey, Percy," Eve asked, flinching at the sound of another gunshot. "If your house is so close to school, why even bother living on campus?"

Percy laughed. "Please, and live with my *mom*? No way. Sometimes she's here for as long as a *week*. I need my space." He raised his firearm and eyed his target. "So, what are we aiming for?"

"Hard to say," she answered. "I saw a horde of cops shooting at an Interloper once, and the bullets did nothing but piss the damn thing off."

"But we know the kill zones," Jason added, firing at a broken dish. "I'm sure the cops didn't."

Eve sighed. "There's no way bullets will break through their bones, and the life source is protected by their teeth."

"What if you knock the fangs out?" Sancho added. "You know, like that old-fashioned carnival game, the one with the giant clown face with the wooden teeth?"

"God, the only thing creepier than Interlopers." Percy shuddered. "*Clowns.*"

Eve glanced at the heir and smirked. "That's not a bad idea. Shoot out the teeth, then destroy the life source. Could work."

Percy nodded and loaded his gun. Eve watched as he took aim at one of the many Interloper drawings and then fired a slew of bullets into the center of the faux victim's mouth. His technique was fluid and natural, as if the weapon were simply an additional part of his hand. He grabbed a second firearm, now holding one in each hand, and fired them consecutively, launching a blaze of bullets into the target and ripping the paper into dangling shreds. He reloaded both weapons and fired again, fanning the bullets across the other targets until each dish, vase, and soda can had been reduced to shards. Finally, Percy spun his guns in each hand, twirling them on his trigger fingers before lowering them to his sides.

"*Balls*," Sancho whispered from his spot on the ground. "You're like a cowboy. Is it weird that I kind of want to be you right now?"

"Everyone wants to be me," Percy quipped.

Jason turned toward Sancho. "What the hell are you doing back there anyway? Shouldn't you be shooting with us?"

"I don't need practice. I've killed plenty of aliens in my day."

"Hologames don't count, Sanch."

Sancho scowled at Percy and continued. "I'm doing research—looking up our old friend Gary. Apparently, he went missing six months ago."

Eve perked her head up. "Missing?"

"Yeah, I'm reading an article all about it." He waved his hand over his scratchpad, projecting an image of the news headline. "The police found bones and everything—with Gary's DNA."

"*Goddamn*," Percy muttered.

"The weirdest part is, the guy just miraculously reappeared a few days later. The DNA lab was accused of evidence tampering. Everyone there lost their jobs."

"Holy *shit*," Jason muttered. "That means—"

"The real Gary is dead." Eve crossed her arms, her body suddenly tense. "That Interloper had been posing as him for the last six months."

"Who knows how many others they've done this to?" Jason growled.

"Marshall Woodgate wasn't the first human they've killed. They've been doing this for months and no one's noticed." Eve turned to Sancho. "You need to look for other articles like that one."

"I already did, and came up with nothing." He minimized the projection and slipped his scratchpad back into his pocket. "Gary must've been their only slip-up."

"Then where are all the other bodies?" Jason asked.

No one answered. The entire yard was suddenly silent aside from the faint whisper of the wind.

Eve's muscles tightened, and she spun toward her comrades. "Look, whatever bonds we have outside this group, they're gone." She glanced at each of the boys one by one and hoped they couldn't sense her fear. "No one at Billington can be trusted, no matter how long we've known them."

Sancho nodded, the hood of his sweatshirt bobbing atop his head. Jason stared back at her; he was worried for her, she could tell, and she forced a smile to alleviate his fears. Percy remained still, his eyes distant as if deep in thought. Finally he sauntered to his gun kit and grabbed two firearms and stacks of ammunition.

"A gift for you," he said, tossing both Eve and Jason a weapon. "Never know when an Interloper will pop up."

Eve looked down at the piece resting in her hands. "Thanks, Percy, but you don't have to do this."

"Actually, I think I do. Don't want you two to die, after all," he teased. "But I have one rule for the both of you: don't kill anyone. At least, anyone who isn't an alien. If it's an alien, go to town on his ass." He tilted his head toward his humble mansion. "Look, the cleaning crew will be here soon, and the less eyes on us, the better. Just make sure you take care of your guns. Don't leave 'em lying around."

"Speaking of guns, can I have one?"

"*No*, Sancho."

"Why not?"

"*Why?*" Percy scoffed. "Because I wouldn't trust you with a butter knife, let alone a firearm, that's why."

Sancho scurried behind Percy as they made their way to the car, bickering and shoving one another all the while. Eve watched as they disappeared in the distance, her heart heavy and her thoughts consumed with battles to come. She felt a hand press against the small of her back; Jason stood beside her, his eyes reflecting the light of the setting sun.

"Been an interesting weekend, huh?"

"It's been an interesting semester," she muttered, forcing another insincere smirk. "But nothing the *Chimera Bitch* can't handle, right?"

Jason didn't respond; instead he stared back at her, his eyes scanning her face, her hair, her shoulders. For the first time in weeks, Eve hadn't the slightest clue what he was thinking.

"We should practice, you know." She glanced down at her gun. "Shooting, fighting, even melting. We need to be prepared for anything."

He hesitated for a moment. "Are you free tonight?"

"You don't mess around, do you?" she teased. "You must really be nervous."

"Actually, I was hoping I could take you on a date."

Eve stopped, her body suddenly hot, her boots like blocks of lead weighing her down. "A date?"

"Yeah. You seem surprised."

"No, I mean, it's just," Eve stuttered, the heat rising from her chest to her neck and face, "a date?"

"Yeah, a date." He anxiously ran his fingers through his hair. "Are you free?"

"Yes," she answered, a little too enthusiastically. "I'm free."

A faint cry rang in the distance—it was Percy, shouting obscenities as he impatiently urged the two of them to get moving. As they began their trek across the yard, Jason looked back at Eve and smiled.

"Well, not anymore," he chuckled. "Now you have plans with me."

***

Eve stood in the elevator, her eyes pointed at the ceiling. The only sound she could hear was the soft beep that marked each passing floor. Thirteen. Fourteen. Fifteen. The doors opened, and with what felt like the first breath she had taken in hours, she entered the hallway of the top floor of Rutherford Tower.

She ventured through the corridor, her knees stiff, her fingers fidgeting at her sides until she finally shoved them into the pockets of her jeans. She cursed to herself, irritated by her own anxiety. It was just Jason. She had spent nearly every day with him for over a month already, and there was no reason to treat this meeting any differently. He *liked* her. Hell, they had already kissed—and God, was it a good kiss. Actually, if she was going to be honest with herself, they technically *made out*, but never mind the specifics. He liked her, and she liked him, and thus there was no need to be nervous. But no matter how many times those words repeated in her mind, she was still terrified. Whether she wanted to admit it or not, this meeting *was* different than all of their previous meetings, because this one was a date.

A real, honest-to-God *date*.

She knocked at the door of room 1502 and then rammed her restless hands back into her pockets. It wasn't too late; she could still make a run for it. She was certainly fast enough to get away without being seen. But she wanted to be there—she truly did. She had just hoped that at some point between the primping in her dorm room and her arrival at the fifteenth floor, her nerves would have finally settled. Unfortunately, that hadn't happened.

Jason opened the door, his smile childlike and innocent. Perhaps he was nervous, too.

He ushered her into the room. "Come inside, have a seat."

Eve took a look around at the familiar, lavish dorm. "I have to admit, I was a little confused when you told me to meet you at Percy's room," she said.

"I figured, but I had good reason. You see, Percy has a kitchen."

Jason made his way toward the kitchen nook, which was cluttered with pans, dishes, and various other utensils. Eve's eyes moved from Jason to the dining table, which was perfectly set with china for two.

"You're cooking for me?"

"I thought it might be a little more personal than taking you to some restaurant." He looked up from the sink as he washed his hands. "Besides, I figured you could use some privacy—a break from people staring at you. At us."

Eve walked past the counter, her fingers trailing along the marble as she studied the vast array of food. "Wow," she smiled, finally taking a seat on one of the bar stools. "This is... wow."

"Double wows, huh? That's a good thing, right?"

She felt her nerves settle just a touch. "It's a *really* good thing," she said, watching Jason fiddle with ingredients like a true chef, or at least like she assumed a true chef might. "So, you actually know *how* to cook?"

Jason laughed. "Don't sound so shocked."

"Hey, I'm not judging. I can work a microwave like a fiend, but that's as far as my kitchen knowledge takes me."

Jason paused. "What's a microwave?"

"It's retro. Never mind."

Eve looked around the room once more, spotting Percy's bedroom door in the distance, securely shut, and most likely locked and double-bolted. "Percy's okay with us seizing his dorm like this?"

"He's a good friend. He's spending the evening in my room with Sancho." Jason chuckled. "They're probably already arguing about something stupid by now."

Eve studied the spread in front of her: chicken breasts, cheese, spices, garlic, butter, and flour were partitioned into separate bowls and pans along the counter. "So... what are we eating tonight?"

Jason raised his eyebrows confidently. "Chicken marsala over angel hair pasta with sautéed mushrooms and garlic parmesan bread."

"Damn... Where did you learn to cook like this?"

Jason looked down at his cutting board, focusing on the small cloves of garlic as he chopped them into tiny pieces. "Growing up, I had a nanny."

"The one you shared with Percy?"

"Right," he answered. "Her name was Esmeralda—we called her Essie. My parents were never around, so she was the closest thing I had to a mom. Most days it was just me and her for hours and hours, and she would always cook these big, elaborate dinners for the two of us." He smiled slightly as he reminisced. "I'd sit and watch her—I had nothing better to do—and finally one day she told me to make myself useful." He stopped to brush the garlic flecks into a bowl and looked up at Eve. "I cooked with her every day after that. It was kind of our thing, I guess."

Eve grinned, enchanted by his story. "Do you still talk to Essie?"

"No. I haven't seen her in years."

"Oh." Eve's face dropped. "What happened?"

Jason moved to the stove, lighting the burners and seemingly keeping his gaze as far from her as possible. "My parents fired her."

"Why?"

Jason hesitated. "Don't know. They wouldn't tell me."

Eve couldn't find the words to say, and so she sat in silence, her head low as if she were in some way guilty for having asked in the first place.

Jason continued, forcing a half smile. "Now cooking kind of makes me feel like, I don't know... like I'm home. Puts me at ease, I guess."

She studied him as he chopped and sautéed, his hands quick and artfully precise. She noticed that her nervous energy had finally subsided; in fact, she was completely calm. It baffled her, how in the midst of such chaos and uncertainty she had managed to find an unfamiliar comfort—a sense of peace—with Jason.

"So," she chirped, "are you going to let me help, or what?"

"Oh, no, that's not how this arrangement works."

"What?" Eve sprang to his side, squeezing her way into the small kitchen nook. "I told you all about my microwave skills. Were you not impressed?"

"You know, I still don't know what that micro-thing is."

"That's not the point. The point is, I'm helping."

He laughed. "I'm treating *you*. Sit down and relax."

"Jason, if you don't tell me what to do, I'm just going to wing it."

He sighed. "Fine. You can boil the pasta."

With a smug grin, Eve filled the large pot with water and placed it atop the burner. Jason continued with his duties while keeping one eye on her. He watched her just as she had been watching him, gazing at her brown hair, her slender hands, her simple clothes. He took a deep breath and smiled.

"Thank you."

Eve chuckled. "You planned everything. The least I can do is help you boil some damn noodles."

"No, I meant for showing up in the first place."

Eve wrinkled her nose. "What are you talking about?"

"I know you don't trust people." He leaned against the counter, gripping the marble edge. "It's written all over your face. Sometimes, when we talk, I can literally see you battling yourself, debating whether or not to let me in."

Her cheeks flushed. "God," she mumbled. "Didn't realize it was so obvious."

"We've spent a lot of time together. I think I know you pretty well by now."

Eve exhaled. She didn't want to look at him—she wanted to stare at the floor, for all eternity if she could get away with it—but she forced herself to face him, her eyes communicating a level of vulnerability that she was hardly comfortable with.

"It's not easy for me—all of this," she began. "Truthfully, I can hardly remember what it feels like to be... *somebody*, to someone else. I've always been alone. I'm *good* at being alone. But... I feel like you're different. And I'm trying."

Jason leaned in toward her. "I've never met anyone like you, Eve. You need to know that." He ran his fingers over the palm of her hand as he spoke. "I don't know what changed—what made you decide to give me a chance—but I'm glad you did."

A hissing noise sounded behind the two. Eve jumped abruptly, knocking over a bowl of flour and sending a cloud of white billowing up from the counter. She sighed; her pot had boiled over, spilling bubbling water across the stove.

Jason hovered close to her ear. "Mood killer," he whispered.

Eve shot him a phony glare. Without hesitation, she grabbed a handful of flour and smacked it across his chest, leaving a messy handprint on his t-shirt.

Jason looked down at the mess on his chest. "Wow," he laughed, "really mature."

Before Eve could react, he flung a fistful of flour at her neck, the white flecks spilling down the front of her shirt. She gasped, her mouth hanging open in shock.

"In my *hair? Really?*" She plunged her hands into the bowl and cupped two handfuls of flour, smearing one on each of Jason's cheeks. He laughed aloud, reciprocating with a cloud of flour aimed directly at her face.

The war had begun. Flour sprayed through the kitchen, spattering across them both, leaving them white and dusty. Their laughter turned into an uproar, both of them coughing over the powder that now covered the space like a blanket of fog. Just as Eve tried to slap Jason with yet another fistful of flour, he grabbed her wrist and held it tightly, stifling her attack. The two stood together, their laughter simmering until they were out of breath. They were a mess, as was the entire kitchen, and as they finished assessing the damage they had done, their eyes finally met.

Jason tugged at Eve's arm, pulling her up against his body. Her breath caught, and he leaned in closer, lingering for just a second before kissing her, the touch of his lips awakening every nerve inside of her. He wrapped his arms around her waist and squeezed her tightly, sparking competing feelings of both weakness and security within her, and she ran her hands from his chest up to the nape of his neck, combing her fingers through his hair. She allowed herself to let go, to feel weightless in his arms as they kissed again, his hands on the small of her back and his heart beating against her chest. Her lips hovered on his for a moment before she kissed him once more, so engrossed in the experience that she almost didn't hear the sound of the door opening behind her.

Jason's lips abruptly tore away from hers as he shot an angry glare at the door. "Dammit, Percy, have you heard of knocking—"

He stopped suddenly, his eyes wide and his body frozen. "Oh, God."

Eve turned; a man and woman stood at the front door, both easily in their mid-fifties and superbly dressed. They seemed vaguely familiar—perhaps she had met them before, though she couldn't quite remember.

The woman scornfully pursed her lips and crossed her arms. "Sorry, we didn't realize you were... busy."

Jason kept his arm around Eve and brought her close to his side. "What... why..." he stuttered. "How'd you even know where to find me?"

The woman tugged at her cashmere gloves and folded them into her purse. "Well, we went to your room first, looking for you, of course. Instead we found that little Filipino boy and Percy. Percy said you were here with a date."

"And that didn't give you the idea that I was *busy*?"

"Yes, well," her eyes moved to Eve, shooting a judgmental scowl in her direction, "nothing important, I assume."

Eve recognized the couple then—it came in an instant, sending a horrible tremor down her spine. She quickly wiped the flour from her cheeks, suddenly very aware of her messy appearance, and felt herself blush beneath the white powder.

Jason's stern demeanor didn't falter. "What are you *doing* here?"

"What kind of question is that?" the man chimed in, flashing a sparkling white smile. "Do we need a reason to see you?"

Jason looked down at Eve, his stare both cross and apologetic. With a loud sigh, he uttered the words she was hoping he wouldn't say.

"Eve," he mumbled, "meet my parents."

CHAPTER 10: ONE OF US

Eve awoke the next morning with a sickening feeling in the pit of her stomach. She thought of her date with Jason and its abrupt ending—thanks, of course, to his parents' interruption—and wished that the whole thing had been an embarrassing nightmare. She cringed as she recalled the looks of pure, unadulterated criticism on their faces. The memory was almost unbearable, and as she rushed to get ready for class, she prayed for a potent distraction.

Eve trudged through Rutherford Hall, her mind still racked with anxiety. She glanced at her fellow Rutherfordians as they scurried by; they stared at her and whispered, but that was to be expected. And then she saw it: a crisp, white envelope resting in the palm of one of her towermates' hands. Make that two envelopes, as yet another student buzzed past with the stationery tucked in his back pocket. Three envelopes. Six. Eleven. One by one, the students tore open the black seals and read over the pieces of parchment inside. Then, like clockwork, each student's eyes left the embossed paper and made their way to Eve, staring at her as she walked by.

Shit, she thought. Could it be another slanderous flyer? Had someone concocted a new method of torture? She quickened her pace, eager to rid herself of the pestering glances and escape the prison that Rutherford Hall had become. The door to the courtyard opened before her, and for a second she felt free.

"SHE'S BACK! THE CHIMERA IS BACK!"

Eve groaned. How could she have forgotten the protestors?

With a glower, she forced her way through the mob. Countless hands grabbed at her hair and clothing, nearly ripping her blouse at the seams and yanking her from side to side. She growled and tore her body from their grasps as she shoved her way to the opposite end of the courtyard. She didn't even bother to adjust her disheveled clothes or comb her tousled hair; instead she focused on her anger, her deep, pulsing resentment, and the slow, steady blackening of her vision.

"Eve!"

Armaan hurried toward her, his cheerful smile enough to thaw her icy animosity. But as he reached her side, his face dropped to a perplexed frown.

"What happened to your face?" he asked.

Eve had hardly even noticed the stinging of her cheek. She quickly wiped her face and looked down at her hand—blood. She pulled out her pocket mirror and eyed the three oozing scratch marks that graced her cheekbone.

She sighed. "You know the drill. People *love* me."

"Sorry, Eve."

Eve lowered her head. "I heard the patrolmen confiscated the Interloper body." She looked back at Armaan, her eyes brimming with guilt. "We had to offer Furst *something*. It was our best bargaining chip."

"I know. I get it. Besides, they didn't take *everything*." He fumbled with his shoulder bag and pulled out a small container filled with a dull, beige-colored slime.

Eve grimaced. "You saved the *skin*?"

"I had to keep *something*. They were so distracted with the body, I just swiped it while they weren't looking."

"But why are you carrying it around with you?"

"You can't be too careful." He anxiously glanced from side to side and shoved the jar back into his bag. "I'm keeping this baby on me at *all* times. It's never leaving my sight."

"Do you even think we can learn anything from it? I mean, it's just goo."

"Who knows?" He shrugged. "But I'm going to keep running tests on it. I've got nothing else to do with my free time." He pouted. "It's not like I'm going to be in the medical program any time soon."

"Screw the medical program." Eve offered him a sympathetic smile. "*We* need you: Jason, Percy, Sancho, and me. Billington's loss is our gain."

Armaan blushed as he headed off to class, grinning the entire way. Eve chuckled to herself, enchanted by her friend's innocence, but her good spirits vanished when she entered the business building; her gut churned at the sight of even more white envelopes, tucked into shoulder bags and pockets, their owners all looking at her with the same curious gaze. In the distance she spotted Jason and Percy strolling down the hallway, and in Percy's hand was yet another envelope.

"Hey, Eve," Percy called out, urging her to join them. "I hear you met Mr. and Mrs. Dick-squeeze."

She furrowed her brow. "Huh?"

"Jason's parents. They're about as pleasant as a root canal, am I right?"

"Percy," Jason muttered, nodding his head at Eve, "can we have a minute?"

"You got it." He shuffled off to class with a smirk, pausing for a second at Eve's side. "By the way, that look they have—you know, the one where they look like they smelled piss? They give that look to *everyone*. Don't worry."

"Percy, leave. *Now*," Jason groaned. As Percy strutted away, he rolled his eyes.

"Eve—" He stopped short, squinting. "What's on your cheek?"

Eve ran her hand across her cheekbone; she had forgotten about the scratches, which were now tender, swollen scabs.

"Got caught up in that mob outside Rutherford Hall. Someone left me a souvenir."

"*Assholes*," he hissed.

"Jason, I'm fine."

He sighed. "Look, about last night, I am so, *so* sorry for what happened. I don't think I can apologize enough."

"It wasn't so bad." Eve forced a smile. "Better than an Interloper interruption, right?"

"Hardly," he muttered. "I just can't believe them—the nerve they have. They practically disown me while I'm stuck in the medical ward, and then they show up here without the slightest warning."

"Do you know why they came?"

"Unfortunately." He sifted through his shoulder bag and pulled out something very familiar—a single white envelope. He handed it to Eve. "Open it."

Eve glanced hesitantly at Jason once more before tearing at the paper and unfolding the stationery within. With relief, she saw that the contents were far from slanderous, but she quickly found herself perplexed as she read and reread the text:

You are cordially invited to
Jason A. Valentine's 21st Birthday Celebration
A Night Best Spent in Black & White

"It's a black-and-white ball," he explained, his words dripping with irritation. "God, I don't even know how my parents come up with this garbage. 'A *Night Best Spent in Black and White'*—it's enough to make me puke."

Eve looked up at Jason. "I don't understand. Is this their way of apologizing?"

"Not even. More like damage control. A lot of important people will be there, not to mention the press. Everyone's dying to know how the senator's chimera son turned out." He crossed his arms and leaned against the wall. "This whole thing is my parents' attempt at proving to the world that I'm just like the rest of them—that I'm normal and presentable, even though I'm a chimera." He scowled. "It's pathetic."

"Then why do it? Why agree to this party?"

"It's already done. These invitations were printed weeks ago." He chuckled, almost amused by the repugnance of the situation. "The only thing left on their to-do list was to tell *me* about my own damn party."

Eve grabbed his hand and squeezed it affectionately, and in response, a series of gasps sounded behind her. A small group of students had congregated nearby, observing them like visitors gawking at animals in a zoo.

"I don't get it," she mumbled. "All the people you invited—"

"Hold up—*I* didn't invite them."

"That's not the point. Your *guests* keep staring at me. I mean, even more than usual."

Jason hesitated. "Well, that's probably because I'm expected to bring a date." He paused and looked her in the eye. "I was hoping that could be you."

A wave of heat washed over Eve's face, and her cheeks flushed a bright shade of pink. She glanced over the invitation once more and sighed.

"It says black tie."

"Yeah. So?"

She grabbed the tie around her neck and frowned. "Well, unless they literally mean *a black tie*, I'm totally screwed."

Jason laughed. "You can wear a black trash bag for all I care. Or a white one. Just be there."

"I don't know. You bringing another chimera—and not just any chimera, but *the Chimera Bitch*... What will your parents say?"

He smirked. "Do you really think I care what my parents have to say? Look, I don't want this party. I don't want the press or the attention, and I certainly don't want my parents or their friends there. All I want is for *you* to be my date. Having you by my side would make the evening a hell of a lot less miserable."

Eve looked down at her invitation once more, in part to escape Jason's gaze. The whole thing was detestable—the party, its purpose, and the look of sheer dread on Jason's face—and yet, despite it all, Eve found herself the slightest bit excited.

"Fine," she finally said. "You twisted my arm."

"Good." He smiled. "Save the date: November tenth in the Rutherford Ballroom. It'll be the most stuffy, boring twenty-first birthday party you'll ever attend." He backed away and winked. "I have to run, but I'm sure I'll see you later."

Jason sauntered down the hallway, leaving Eve alone with her flurry of nerves and the cluster of onlookers still gaping from afar. She shoved the invitation into her shoulder bag, and as she turned away from the spectators, she discovered a new hurdle before her: a small girl with large, grey eyes.

"Look at you lovebirds," Hayden mumbled. "It's gross, watching the two of you. I feel nauseated already."

Eve ignored the girl, walking right past her as she headed for class. Undeterred, Hayden scuttled behind her.

"Hey! I'm talking to you!" She scampered to Eve's side, finally managing to keep pace with her long-legged stride. "Have you seen Madison lately?"

Eve rolled her eyes. "Why would *I* have seen her, of all people?"

"Well, you do *live* together," she scoffed. "God, you're dumb."

Eve sighed, already growing impatient with the pint-sized lackey. "We're hardly ever in our dorm at the same time. She makes herself scarce."

"So you didn't see her last night?"

Eve shook her head. "I just assumed she was with you. You're attached at the hip, after all."

Hayden flipped her thin hair over her shoulders. "We had plans. A slumber party, actually. Facial masks, gossip—you know, *best friend* stuff." She pouted. "But she didn't show... I waited for hours. I haven't seen her all morning either."

"Maybe she found a new best friend. *Again*," Eve smirked.

Hayden grimaced. "Your face looks barftastic, by the way." She wiggled her nose and stormed into their classroom, promptly slamming the door in Eve's face.

Eve muttered to herself and started to open the classroom door, but a small hand jutted forward and slammed it shut yet again. It was JJ who now blocked Eve's path, leaning against the door with a stony glower plastered across her face.

"We need to talk." She paused. "You know, you got somethin' on your face—"

"I *know*," Eve groaned, "and for the love of *God*, JJ, leave me alone. I don't want to be your friend."

"I don't give a shit about your friendship anymore. It's bigger than that now."

"What are you *talking* about?"

JJ glanced around the hallway. "We should discuss this in private."

"No, JJ. I'm not going anywhere with you."

JJ crossed her arms. "Fine." She scowled. "We can talk about the *Interlopers* right here, right now."

Eve's eyes widened and darted from side to side. "*Jesus*, not so loud!"

JJ leaned in closer and lowered her voice to a whisper. "I know what you're doing, Eve. I know you're trying to track them down."

"You *what?*"

"I want in."

"No," Eve barked. "Absolutely not."

"You need my expertise—"

"Your *expertise*? God, you're cocky—"

"I'm a *hacker*, Eve!" JJ spat, her face red with anger.

Eve paused. "A hacker?"

"Yes. A computer hacker. God, how else could I have found out about your plan? Not like you made it difficult. I mean, *really*? Doing research for a covert mission on your unprotected, piece-of-shit scratchpad? What is this, amateur hour?"

"You *hacked* my scratchpad?"

"And Jason's. Wasn't hard to connect those dots."

"And I'm supposed to want to work with you now?"

"Look, I can access Billington's files and get any information we need. I could even hack through the Interlopers' systems if I had the right tools. I just need—"

"Me?" Eve scoffed.

JJ sighed. "Yes. I need you. But *you* need *me*, too."

"How could you possibly expect me to trust you?"

"Eve, our past differences aside, shit is really getting serious. I don't think you realize—"

"You don't think I *realize?*" Eve hissed. "I was attacked by an Interloper a few days ago. Did all of your hacking tell you that? Did it also tell you that I was the one who discovered Marshall Woodgate's body?" She stopped for a moment, attempting to regain her composure. "You should go, JJ. My answer hasn't changed."

JJ glared back at her. "Fine. I'll leave," she grumbled, "but know this: you haven't seen the worst of what the Interlopers can do. I've seen the recordings. I know what they're capable of. And I hope to God that you're prepared for what'll happen next, because they're coming for you, too."

With one last growl, JJ released the door and marched down the hallway, leaving Eve alone at last. Eve watched the girl for a moment, cursing under her breath before she finally opened the door to the classroom.

She stopped in the doorway, her body paralyzed, her eyes vacant as they stared at the scene in front of her. Thick black soot had been smeared across the walls of the classroom, smudged deep into the plaster. Eve's throat became tight, her lungs like lead weights in her chest.

DIE CHIME.

This was more than a simple act of vandalism. The words covered the walls, written over and over again like a terrible echo, a sinister message scrawled in ash.

DIE CHIME. DIE CHIME. DIE CHIME.

Eve didn't even see the other students. They wandered through the lecture hall, gaping first at the threat and then at Eve, waiting for her reaction, but she gave none. Professor Clarke was in the corner of the room, barking into his phone.

"I *said* we need campus security here *immediately,*" he snapped. His eyes darted toward the doorway and locked onto Eve. "*Shit.*" He glanced at his other students. "Look, class is canceled. Everyone go," he ordered. "NOW."

The students flooded from the lecture hall, bumping into Eve as they spilled into the hallway. With the room emptied, Eve finally moved, slowly making her way toward the wall and the giant, ashy words. She trailed her hand through the letters and stared down at her blackened fingertips. Clarke approached her side, the two of them now alone in the classroom.

"It's an empty threat, I'm sure," he said softly.

"They're never empty threats."

"They'll find who did this, Eve."

"Will they?" she scoffed. "In my experience, the higher-ups don't usually waste their time helping the poorly connected chimeras."

Clarke sighed. "I know things are rough," he began. "These are complicated times." He hesitated and shook his head. "Never mind that. *I'll* do what *I* can, okay?"

Eve looked at Clarke, tearing her eyes from the message for the first time since she'd entered the room. "Can I ask you a question, Professor?"

"It's my job to answer questions."

"Why are you so nice to me?"

"Why wouldn't I be nice to you?"

Eve rolled her eyes and folded her arms. He knew the answer without her needing to speak it aloud, and so she remained quiet.

"Not all of us are afraid of people who are different, Eve."

"Most are."

His eyes were dark and warm, filled with a sense of wisdom and contentment that comes only with age, or perhaps experience. "I see a lot of potential in you. And I think one day, what makes you an outcast will instead make you... very powerful."

"I'm already powerful. Haven't you heard?" she quipped.

"You know very well what I meant by that, Eve."

The tension had taken its toll on her. She took one last look at the writing—*DIE CHIME*, the letters screamed—and then headed for the door.

"Eve," Clarke called out, "I could pull a few strings with Furst—see if I can get a patrolman or two to escort you around campus, if it would make you feel safer."

Eve stopped at the doorway, gripping the doorknob tightly. "I'll be okay," she murmured. "I can take care of myself."

"Eve, there's no shame in accepting assistance—"

"*I can take care of myself*," she repeated, firmly. "And you know very well what I meant by that, Professor."

***

The day moved at a glacial pace, as if Eve were watching it unfold in slow motion. Her mind was elsewhere, far from her studies, and even farther from the curious glances cast her way. Her entire focus was on two words:

DIE CHIME.

The more she repeated it, the heavier it felt in her chest. She wandered into the empty locker room, which provided her some solace, at last, though the silence couldn't save her from the noise of her pestering thoughts. She knew her hands were moving—knew they were unbuttoning her blouse, lacing her boots and suiting up for Combat class—but she felt nothing.

As she entered the gym, her mind was still hazy. The hateful message had consumed her, enveloping her thoughts in its black ash. It would take a miracle to break her spell; it would take an absolute shock, a sudden jolt to the senses.

"We have a new recruit joining the class," Ramsey announced, slapping the back of the young man at his side. "Valentine, get in line."

Eve's mouth fell open in disbelief. Before her stood Jason, dressed in the same black uniform as everyone else, his thick scar protruding from the neckline of his tank top. He took his place beside her in line, struggling to stifle his amusement over her obvious shock.

"What the *hell* are you doing here?" she whispered.

"Nice to see you, too."

"The talking stops now," Ramsey snapped, glancing over his clipboard. "Everyone—laps." He looked straight at Eve. "And no slacking."

With a quick chirp of his whistle, the captain sent his students sprinting onto the track. Eve and Jason effortlessly sped past their much slower classmates, weaving around their burly bodies and leaving them in a cloud of dust. As the others disappeared into the background, Eve looked over at Jason and scowled.

"What's going on?"

"I dropped Political Inquiry and took up Combat," he answered nonchalantly.

"I gathered that. But *why*?"

Jason laughed. "Are you *mad* that I'm in your class?"

"You don't have to keep tabs on me, if that's what you're doing."

"Keep *tabs* on you?" he chuckled. "Look, Eve, I know you can take care of yourself. You don't have to remind me. But we were attacked this weekend. We could've been killed. And that won't be the last time it happens." His tone became somber as he stared at the endless track ahead of him. "I need to learn how to fight."

Eve glanced over her shoulder to make sure that no one was within earshot, but her peers were trailing far behind them. "You seemed to do a pretty good job of it."

"Pretty good isn't good enough."

"So, you're not here because of me?"

He winked. "Of course not. Seeing you is just an added bonus."

Ramsey's whistle sounded from across the field. "If you can talk, you're not working hard enough!" he shouted. "Move your lazy asses!"

"God, Eve, you really have to stop holding me back in class," Jason teased, sprinting ahead of her.

Eve grumbled to herself and charged forward, competing against Jason for the remainder of the run, the two of them eventually lapping the rest of their classmates.

Sprints were soon over, and the students hurried back to the gym, each of them sweaty and achy—except, of course, for Eve and Jason. The others watched them as they walked by; it seemed that Eve was no longer the center of attention, as Jason's celebrity and visible scar had sent the entire class into an awkward stir.

"It's funny," Jason said. "I actually know some of these guys. And now they won't even talk to me. They just… stare." He turned to Eve. "But you're totally used to this, aren't you?"

"I never get used to it."

"Get used to what?" A voice from behind startled Eve, and she turned to see Chin Dimple's arrogant grin. "Being the shit stain of the human race?" He stopped and cocked his head at Jason. "Looks like you called in some backup. Too weak to take on the pressure alone? Couldn't handle it?"

Eve smirked. "I handled myself just fine when I had my foot lodged between your balls."

"You should be careful. That mouth of yours is going to get you into trouble."

"*Hey*," Jason snapped, stepping forward. "That's enough. Walk away."

The footballer ignored his demand. "You're the guy from HV, right? The one they dissected?" He approached Jason, staring him up and down until his eyes landed on his scar. "They carved you up like a goddamn turkey. How'd that feel?"

Jason stood firm and stared back at his newfound adversary. He examined the boy's face: his combed hair, his chiseled jaw, and his cleft chin. He turned to Eve.

"*This* is Chin Dimple?"

"Chin Dimple?" The footballer turned to Eve and winked. "You got a pet name for me?"

"I think *Ass Face* might've been more appropriate," she scoffed.

"Oh, I can think of plenty of names for you, *baby.*"

"She's not your *baby—*"

"You mind your own, chimera. I've got a message for her, that's all." Chin Dimple put his face just inches from Eve's and stared her in the eye. "What happened in the business building? That was nothing. We let you off easy." He leaned in even closer, his gaze fixed and perverse. "Next time, I'm going to make you scream like the little *bitch* you are."

Jason lunged toward him. "You better watch what you say, or I swear to God—"

"You'll what?" he jeered. "You trying to play hero now?"

"Stay *away* from her," Jason growled.

"Why? Is she your *girlfriend?*" He laughed. "Is *that* what this is about?"

A single vein bulged from Jason's neck as he stared at Chin Dimple, his eyes furious and his jaw clenched. *"Don't touch her."*

"Don't touch her, huh? Funny you should say that." A smile spread across his lips. "Did you see the shiner I gave your girlfriend, *chime?*"

"What the *hell* is this shit?" Ramsey spat, entering the gym and interrupting the confrontation. "This ain't a tea party. Line up, *now.*"

Jason glared at the footballer, his blood boiling as he took his place in the formation. Eve stared at Jason: his arms were stiff at his sides, his fingers curled into tight, red fists.

"What was he talking about?" Jason muttered. "What happened in the business building?"

Eve sighed; she recalled the threat and quickly shook it from her thoughts. "It was all talk."

"*What* was all talk?"

"Jason, I took care of it."

He looked down at her, his eyes stony and cold. "Apparently you didn't."

Ramsey cleared his throat and flashed the twosome a critical frown. "Just because we have a new recruit doesn't mean we're going to take things easy today," he began. "We're picking up where we left off: full-contact combat drills. Two will square off at a time, and the class will observe for takeaways and tactical education."

"Permission to speak, Captain?" Jason brazenly interrupted. Eve cringed; she had the terrible feeling that whatever he had to say couldn't be good.

"Yes, Valentine?"

"Captain, it seems only fair that I go first, seeing as everyone's had a chance to fight except me."

The captain smirked. "Glad to hear you're so *just* and *honorable*," he said, his words riddled with sarcasm.

"And Captain," Jason continued, cocking his head toward the end of the line. "I want to fight *him*."

Eve froze in place, her eyes wide and mortified—he had challenged Chin Dimple. *God DAMMIT,* she thought to herself. She spun toward Jason.

"What the hell are you doing?" she hissed.

Ramsey chuckled. "You don't get to pick your opponent, kid—"

"I'm in," the football player interrupted, confidently strutting forward.

The captain hesitated. He glanced back and forth between the athlete's smug grin, Jason's cross glare, and Eve's exasperated gawking. Suddenly, he smiled.

"You know what? I'm feeling obliging today." He tossed his clipboard to the floor. "To hell with the rules. Keller, Samson, set up the mats."

As the ring was assembled, the sound of mutterings and whispers filled the room. The other students stared at Jason, curious for the fight in store, but Eve didn't share their intrigue; she stormed toward him, her eyes bulging lividly.

"Are you *crazy?*" she spat. "What do you think you're doing?"

"Look, the guy's a hammer. He was asking for it."

"Jason, you don't even know how to *fight*."

"So? I'm a chimera."

"It's not that simple, Jason."

He looked back at his opponent, who was busy boasting to his friends. "We're supposed to be good at all things athletic, right?" he asked. "I mean, I've always been good at basketball."

"This isn't *basketball*, Jason. This is beating the *shit* out of someone."

"Well, shouldn't it just, I don't know... come to me?"

Eve sighed. "It doesn't work like that."

"Then how *does* it work?"

"Look, you're in *way* over your head—"

"I'm doing this, Eve, whether you help me or not."

Eve growled under her breath. She knew it was no use, that Jason was stubborn and meant what he said. She cursed his resolve and bit her bottom lip.

"Your muscle memory, reflexes, and speed are impeccable. That comes with the territory. But there's more than that inside of you—more that you haven't experienced yet."

"What do you mean?"

She looked around before continuing. "Emergence doesn't just bring about your gift. It sort of... heightens everything else, too. Including your strength."

"So I should be fine, right?"

"Not necessarily. You have to work for it. You have to find that *fire*."

Jason furrowed his brow. "*Fire?*"

"Yes. Adrenaline. It's like jet fuel for us. Whatever triggers your strength—your passion—find it."

"That doesn't sound so hard."

"Jason," Eve groaned, "you're not taking this seriously."

He smirked. "Are you *worried* about me?"

"I'm trying to help you *win*."

"You're worried. It's cute."

Eve let out a long, irritated breath. "Just find the passion. Okay?"

Jason glanced at the mat, which was now fully assembled. "Passion. Got it."

Eve followed Jason to the center of the gym and reluctantly joined the onlookers, wiggling her way to the front of the crowd. She fidgeted nervously, first resting her arms at her sides and then ultimately deciding to fold them across her chest. As Jason took his stance on the mat, Eve held her breath and dug her fingernails into the palms of her hands.

Ramsey nodded his head at the fighters, instructing them to enter the ring and take their marks.

"Remember," he said, "this is full contact. Keep it clean and stay within the ring." He fiddled with his whistle, swinging the cord around his thumb. "The match begins at the sound of this whistle."

Just as the words left Ramsey's lips, Chin Dimple slugged Jason across the jaw, sending his neck whipping to the side. Eve gasped aloud as Jason stumbled backward, his legs nearly bending under the force of the blow. Eve could barely hear Ramsey's cry—"*Bad form, bad form!*"—as if it were miles away, because her head was filled with the sound of her rapid breathing and the thumping of her heart.

The footballer strolled casually to his opponent's side; Jason was hunched over, clutching his knees for support.

"Sorry," he said, his tone patronizing. "Thought I heard the whistle. Guess I was wrong."

With a quick kick, he slammed his heel into Jason's ribs. Jason dropped to his hands and knees, gasping for air and coughing up blood, and again Chin Dimple kicked at his gut, this time even harder, sending Jason's body collapsing onto the mat.

"This is too easy," he gloated, proudly standing above Jason and playing to the crowd. "Give me a real fight."

With gritted teeth, Jason kicked at his adversary's boot, knocking his legs out from under him and sending him onto his back with a loud thud. Jason lugged his heavy, beaten body off of the mat and regained his footing; he dragged the back of his hand across his mouth, wiping the blood from his split lip and flicking it against the ground. As the bright red drops splattered onto the floor, Eve felt her heart leap into her throat.

Chin Dimple leapt to his feet, undeterred by Jason's advances. He cracked his neck and flashed a pompous smile.

"That it?"

Jason jabbed at the footballer, first at his nose and then his mouth, and for a second Eve felt the slightest hint of relief. But Chin Dimple just adjusted his jaw and spit onto the mat before striking Jason with a roundhouse kick across the face, sending him flat onto his back in what seemed like an instant.

"Jackass," Chin Dimple muttered, his voice thick with bloody saliva.

Jason regained his feet and swung his fist at his opponent's eye, but the footballer blocked his blow and immediately pounded him across the nose. Jason staggered to the side of the mat and wiped the blood from his mouth, smearing it like red paint across his face.

"You're worse than your girlfriend," Chin Dimple sneered.

Jason struck him with a right hook to the temple and an upper cut straight to the jaw, and blood spewed from the footballer's lips like a sputtering faucet. Driven by fury, Chin Dimple smashed his boot into Jason's cheekbone;

blood gushed from Jason's mouth, staining his chin a deep shade of red. Eve felt her pulse beating in her throat; she wanted to intervene, to end the fight herself, and yet she was paralyzed, her feet rooted to the floor as she watched the primal display in shock.

Chin Dimple pounded Jason's jaw yet again, aiming for the bloody mess as if it were his only target. Jason struggled to guard himself; he was determined but weak, visibly lacking the energy to fight. Again he was struck in the jaw, and then once more, his body swaying from side to side as the blows came one after the next. The footballer kicked Jason in the gut, and his chest curled forward as he helplessly gasped for air. Every ounce of power had been drained from Jason's body, and Eve knew that the match would soon be over: Jason was going to lose. Just when he appeared to have had enough, Jason's jaw lurched to the side yet again as his rival jabbed at his already battered nose, sending blood gushing from his nostrils.

Eve winced; Jason was still standing, but barely, his body broken and debilitated, his face bruised and streaked with blood. One or two more strong blows and he would be finished. Chin Dimple circled Jason like a vulture over a carcass, evidently overjoyed by his soon-to-be-conquest.

"This was fun, wasn't it?" he crowed in his typical, arrogant fashion. "But you know what was even more fun? Fighting your girlfriend."

"Shut up," Jason spat, drawing his fists closer to his face.

"Oh, you want to hear this," Chin Dimple went on. "You see, she may have won that fight, but I'm the one who really left a winner. You want to know why?"

"I said, *shut up.*"

The footballer punched Jason in the face, silencing him instantly.

"I'm going to tell you anyway." He leaned closer to Jason, utterly confident in his dominance. "When I had her pinned to the ground and I was lying on top of her—God, it felt *so* good just to feel her sweet ass underneath my body." He smiled, his teeth red with blood and his stare cutting like razor blades.

"Even if she's nothing more than a dirty, whorish *chime.*"

Something flashed in Jason's eyes, and out of nowhere his fist flew, pounding the footballer across the chin so hard it sent his body spinning in a complete circle. The entire room gasped in unison. Jason struck again, this time in the nose and then again across the jaw, sending a spray of blood from his mouth.

Jason was rejuvenated, recharged with a new, overwhelming power that surged in his veins like gasoline. He grabbed at Chin Dimple's shirt, nearly tearing the fabric with his grip, and punched him across the jaw again and again with a strong right hook. The football star wobbled from side to side, but before he could even attempt to regain his footing, Jason sprang forward and kicked him in the center of his chest.

Chin Dimple staggered off of the mat, nearly tripping off the edge as he stumbled across the gymnasium floor. He was out of bounds, and technically that meant the match was finished, but Jason wasn't stopping. He had a fire burning in his eyes—a seething strength that couldn't be stifled until he was satisfied. Jason followed his opponent off of the mat and hooked him across the jaw, first from the left and then the right until his knuckles were spattered with the footballer's blood.

"OUT OF BOUNDS!" Ramsey barked. "MATCH IS OVER!"

Jason ignored the captain and slugged his adversary straight in the eye. Chin Dimple teetered backward, his eyes clenched shut and his arms flailing, but Jason yanked at the footballer's torn shirt and head-butted him with savage aggression. Chin Dimple crumpled to the ground, his body crashing to the floor with a heavy thunk.

It was over. The crowd was silent, awed by what appeared to be the gruesome end to an epic match—but Jason melted, lifting Chin Dimple's feeble figure off of the ground and back onto his feet, his eyes wide with terror.

Jason grabbed at the neckline of the boy's tank top and pulled him in closer. *"I'm not finished with you yet,"* he sneered through gritted teeth.

Jason struck the footballer across the nose once more, sending blood jetting from his nostrils and spraying across the ground. Chin Dimple hobbled backward, the two fighters now far from the mat, approaching the opposite end of the gymnasium. Jason jabbed his adversary in the stomach and hooked him across the chin, his moves fierce, swift, and unbelievably strong. Ramsey continued to scream and blow his whistle, and the students cheered barbarically, but Jason didn't hear any of it. He felt adrenaline pulsing within him, numbing his beaten face and revitalizing his weakened body. His breathing was rapid, charged with an anger that could only be stifled by the defeat of his opponent. As Chin Dimple stumbled into the gymnasium wall, Jason melted him off of his feet and pinned him there, forcing the footballer to look him in the eye.

Chin Dimple forced a smirk on his bloody, trembling lips. "Screw you," he hissed, his eyes nearly swollen shut. "Screw you, you damn *chime*."

Jason pounded him in the chin with as much power as he could summon, and the footballer's unconscious body dropped to the ground. Jason's chest heaved as he stared down at his conquest—his victory. His classmates cheered like spectators at a sporting event, and he slowly made his way back toward the group, his brow furrowed and his lips and chin still covered in drying blood. He glanced at Eve, whose jaw had fallen open in utter shock.

"Sorry," he muttered. "Guess I found the passion."

"VALENTINE!" Ramsey shouted. "COMPLETE DISREGARD FOR THE RULES! BAD FORM AND POOR CONDUCT!" He pointed to the gym doors. "LAPS! NOW!"

"Yes, Captain," Jason mumbled. He looked over at Eve one last time, her eyes still wide with disbelief, and then ran out of the gym toward the field.

The gym buzzed with excitement. The young men gawked and guffawed, and a handful of them helped Chin Dimple to his feet, but Eve was silent, her body numb to her surroundings, her eyes staring blankly at the blood-sprayed mat. She felt Ramsey standing beside her.

"I don't know what to say," she managed to utter.

Ramsey watched as the football star struggled to make his way to the locker room. "Don't need to say anything," he huffed. "The boy's got ego. Too big for his britches. If he gets anything outta this class, I'm hoping it'll be a sense of humility."

Eve wrinkled her nose. "What do you mean?"

"I mean the boy needed an ass-whoopin' more than anyone else. You know, I kept tellin' him not to underestimate his enemy. Guess his ears aren't workin' right."

Eve sighed. "Well, regardless, this scene," she paused, shuddering at the sight of the pools of blood, "it can't be good for you—for your position here. And I can't help but feel somewhat responsible."

Ramsey chuckled. "The only thing you're responsible for is helping an old soldier achieve a personal goal."

"Excuse me?"

He stared off into the distance—out the double doors at the track, where Jason was running—and for a brief second, he smiled.

"I've always wanted to train a chimera. Thanks to you, now I get to train two."

***

The campus was dark and dreary, the black night sky a shadow that cloaked Eve as she made her way toward Rutherford Hall. She shivered—the air was colder than usual, a subtle reminder of home—and she pulled her jacket closer to her body. She walked with Jason in silence; he stared at her, waiting for her to say something, but still she was quiet, her eyes distant as she gazed at the dormitory ahead of them.

They entered the building together and headed straight for the elevators, ignoring the night owls who whispered as they passed. As the metal box took them up to the twelfth floor and their prospective rooms, Jason's patience waned, his body antsy and his nerves on edge. He turned to Eve, and still she said nothing, her eyes pointed blankly at the silver doors in front of her.

"Thanks for waiting for me while I ran laps," he finally said. "And while I did drills. And then while I ran laps again."

"You're welcome," she answered, flatly.

"You know, you haven't spoken to me since class."

Eve faltered. "I just have a lot on my mind."

The elevator doors opened. Eve headed down the hallway, and Jason followed.

"Like what? Like the fight?" he continued. "Look, I know it got out of hand, but that guy was a dick. The whole thing was—"

"Reckless? Impulsive?"

Just as Eve reached her dorm, Jason grabbed her hand, halting her in front of her door. She turned, finally looking him in the eye. The bloody mess on his face had long since been washed away, but his bruised cheekbones and swollen, scabby lip were enough to make the terrible fight flash before her eyes once again.

"I lost control. I can admit that. But I'm not going to apologize for caring about you. I'm not going to pretend that what he said and what he *did* to you didn't affect me."

"He was *trying* to get a rise out of you, Jason."

"Well, it worked," he spat. He leaned in closer to her. "Every last bruise on his body was deserved. You and I both know he had it coming—"

"They *all* have it coming, Jason," Eve snapped. "Do you know how many Chin Dimples I've met in my life? How many people have given me black eyes? How many guys have *threatened* me?" She fidgeted anxiously with her cuticles. "Look, I'm not saying he didn't deserve what he got. Lord knows he did."

"Then what *are* you saying?"

"That I get it, okay? No one gets it more than I do. But when you're defending yourself—or defending *me*—they don't see a guy fighting for honor or integrity. They see a *chimera*. A chimera who's beating the shit out of a *human*. Do you understand? That's all they see."

Jason looked down the hallway; girls in their pajamas scurried to their rooms, giggling to one another as they observed the twosome. He turned back to Eve and lowered his voice to a whisper.

"I don't care what they see. I'm not going to sit back and do nothing."

"I'm not asking you to do nothing," she said. "I just want to make sure you know what you're up against, being who you are." She looked down at the floor. "Being with me. I just need you to be prepared for whatever comes next."

Jason stared at her and, for a moment, detected a hint of fear in her eyes. "I'm not going anywhere, if that's what you're getting at."

Eve exhaled loudly, still picking at her fingernails. "Look, what happened today—it won't be the last time. But I fight when I *need* to, not when I want to. If I fought when I wanted to... I'd never stop."

Jason ran his fingers through her hair and lightly cupped her cheek. Eve sighed and wrapped her fingers around his, bringing his hand forward and examining it. His knuckles were scratched and scabbed, and again she saw the powerful jabs replay in her mind.

"I was *horrified* for you, you know." She grimaced. "All that blood..."

"I'm fine, Eve."

She hesitated, her eyes still focused on his bloody knuckles. "You're really strong, Jason." She paused. "I've never seen anyone fight like that."

"You weren't kidding about that jet fuel."

She ran her fingers gently along his palm. "How did it feel?"

"It felt... intense."

"How do you feel now?"

"Like hell," he chuckled.

She was quiet for a moment as she stared at him—at his black-and-blues and swollen scrapes. With a look of worry, she smoothed her hand across his face, her fingers delicately grazing his skin until they fell to his neck. Finally, she leaned in close and softly kissed his lips, lingering only for a moment before she pulled away.

He smiled. "What was that for?"

"You know what it was for." She smirked.

Jason moved a single tendril of hair from her face and placed it behind her ear. His eyes wandered from hers and then stopped, his body suddenly tense with discomfort. Reluctantly, he backed away from Eve and gave her hand a quick, comforting squeeze.

"See you tomorrow," he said with a wink as he made his way down the hall.

Eve looked to her side: Heather was shamelessly watching her from her doorway. She might have appeared almost angelic in her white silk nightgown, if not, of course, for her devilish grin.

Eve rolled her eyes. "Haven't seen you in a while."

"Oh, I've seen *you*. Think of me as having eyes and ears everywhere."

"How long have you been standing there?"

"Long enough," she answered. "Aren't you two precious? Madison will be *thrilled* to find out about your budding romance. She says he's number ten on her list, but it's just a front. He's been number one ever since you started tutoring him."

"Yeah, well, that *list* is the dumbest thing she's ever come up with."

"Maybe so, but it doesn't matter what you or I think," Heather rebutted, her voice unusually cold. "All that matters is that Madison Palmer cares. When she finds out, she'll hate you even more than she already does, if that's possible. And when that girl *really* hates you, she won't rest. She will hunt you down like an animal."

Eve let out a patronizing laugh. "Terrifying, I'm sure."

"She *will* find out, Eve. I'll make sure of that."

"Sounds like a threat."

"Oh, I wouldn't call it that," she simpered. "I'd say it's a *promise*."

"And this is all part of your plan, for what? For power?"

The Rutherfordian brought her perfectly manicured index finger to her lips. "Hush, Eve, that's our little secret."

"God, you're really screwed up."

"You shouldn't be so complacent. You have no idea what's in store for you."

Eve yanked at her doorknob and trudged into her room. "I hate to disappoint, but Madison doesn't scare me, and neither do you."

"You know, Eve, you *should* be scared," Heather interrupted, stopping Eve in her tracks. "When Madison Palmer holds a grudge, she doesn't just *let it go*. She'll never forget—not until there's blood on her hands."

Eve shot one last glare in Heather's direction before locking the door behind her and tossing her key on the end table. She looked around; the dorm room was empty as usual, and Madison was nowhere to be found. Eve prepared for bed quickly, hoping to be fast asleep before her roommate returned, if she ever did. Heather's words lingered in the back of her mind, and she chuckled to herself—*blood on her hands.* She thought back to only a month ago, when Madison considered her a friend, when she insisted on eating dinner together, and gave her an Everlasting Diamond. Eve grabbed her shoulder bag and dug through the front pocket; there it was, still sparkling and beautiful, and for a moment she wondered if she should return it to her roommate. But just as she debated the idea, the diamond slipped from her fingers and rolled across the floor, disappearing underneath Madison's bed.

Eve growled to herself, stumbling through the maze of suitcases, daring to trespass into Madison's territory. She crawled onto her knees, fanning her hands beneath the heiress's bed until she finally found the gem. As she examined it, holding it up toward the light, she suddenly stopped—her hands were filthy, covered in dust or powder or something else. Something black. She looked down at the floor and saw a film covering the panels of wood. A chill ran down her spine, sending goose bumps across her skin. She got to her feet, her eyes panning from the dirty ground to Madison's bed; the pink sheets were covered in the same thick layer of black. Eve's fingers curled into shaking fists, her gaze still focused on the sight below—the streaks of ash that were smeared across Madison Palmer's sheets.

* * *

Clarence Hall appeared lifeless, completely and utterly average. The walls were beige, drab, and bare, the wooden floor was scratched and dull from abuse and neglect, and Eve couldn't help but notice the monotony of the brown doors lining the corridor. It was a typical college dormitory, as mundane and standard as any other, and absolutely incomparable to the extravagant Rutherford Hall.

Eve sighed; no wonder JJ resented her.

The other students—perhaps they were called Clarencians, though it was doubtful they would broadcast such a label—stared at her as she passed by, and she wondered if it was because of her reputation or her unexpected appearance in the building. She kept her eyes forward, searching for room

3013, though the bland uniformity of the hallways made her feel as if she were walking in circles through a never-ending maze. Finally, she found it and tapped lightly at the door, hesitant to create a sound and draw any more attention to herself than she already had.

The door swung open, and Eve was met with a crazed smile.

"What took you so long?" Armaan asked, pulling her into his room and slamming the door behind her.

As Armaan dashed to the corner of the room, Eve took a moment to observe her surroundings. The dorm was small, barely half the size of Eve's, though still built for two. One of the twin beds was covered with test tubes, petri dishes, and even a Bunsen burner, and she knew right away that that bed belonged to Armaan.

"So, why did you ask me to stop by?" she asked, carefully weaving through the cramped space. "You said you wanted to show me something important? Did you want me to call Jason and the rest of them?"

"No time," Armaan quickly answered, his back facing her as he fiddled with his equipment. "My roommate is supposedly 'at the library,' which is his code for doing the deed with his girlfriend. We only have fifteen minutes."

"How do you know that?"

He rolled his eyes. "The guy doesn't even know where the library is. And knowing his track record, it usually takes him about fifteen minutes to get the job done, if you know what I mean."

"Wow," Eve muttered. "I don't know if I should question his stamina or why you know so *much* about his stamina."

Armaan turned to face her; he wore a silly grin and held his arms out in front of him, his sleeves rolled up past his elbows. In one of his hands was a dish filled with cream-colored goo—a platter of second skin.

"Watch this."

Before Eve could protest, he flipped the dish over his opposite hand, dumping the slimy liquid onto his palm and letting it slide down his arm.

"Armaan! What are you *doing*?" she gasped.

He ignored her, coating his entire arm in the fluid until it was completely covered. He finally looked up at her, his eyes wide with excitement.

"Just pay attention."

After a moment of stillness, the second skin began to expand and bubble as if it were breathing. Suddenly, a cracking noise punctuated the silence; it was loud and harsh, and Armaan cringed, his knees buckling under his body.

"Armaan, you need to stop—"

"It's almost done," he quickly rebutted.

The noise turned into a loud chorus of snaps and pops. Armaan's arm continued to breathe and pulse, the liquid fizzing as it blended into his skin, morphing from cream to brown to a familiar color—a light shade of olive. His fingers bent and curled in every direction, cracking and quivering until they appeared longer, thinner, and unusually feminine. He was panting, his eyes clenched shut in obvious pain, and just when Eve thought she couldn't bear the sight of it any longer, everything stopped.

Eve stared down at Armaan's hand—which no longer appeared to be his at all—and was stunned into silence. His arm was now much longer, his fingers slender, and the palm of his hand was marked with a thin scar.

"Holy shit," Eve mumbled. "Your hand—"

"It's *your* hand. And arm." He wiggled his fingers and admired his new appendage. "Pretty dynamic, huh?"

"How did you *do* that?"

"I figured out how the second skin works."

"I gathered that. Please, enlighten me."

"It's mind-controlled. I imagine the form I want it to take, and like that, it's done." He stuck his arm out before her. "Touch it. Go ahead. It feels totally real."

Eve hesitated, then lightly grazed her fingers along his forearm, sending chills running through her body. She flipped his wrist and compared his palm with hers—the scars were identical, as were the fine lines, even the fingerprints.

"This is..."

"Amazing?"

"Creepy." She shuddered. "Like something out of a sci-fi movie."

Armaan laughed. "There are limitations, though. The second skin relies on memory, so I can only change myself into someone I know—someone I've seen face to face. I can't just invent a persona out of thin air."

"Which explains why the Interlopers are taking over people's lives instead of just creating new ones."

Armaan held his hands in front of his face and analyzed the dissimilarities. "It's remarkable. The transformation itself is unpleasant—"

"It sounded like your bones were being crushed."

"And it felt like it, too," he grumbled. "But once that part is over, it feels completely natural, as if I've always been this way."

Eve eyed his arm—or rather, *her* arm—and again felt a tremor of nervous energy race through her. She shoved her hands into her pockets and tried to appear unaffected.

"How do you remove it? How do you go back to normal?"

"I just *will* the fluid to release itself from my body, and like that, it's done." He paused, his smile suddenly wide as if he had a secret. "But there *is* another way—a way that could work in your favor."

"What do you mean?"

He fiddled with the equipment on his bed, his hands working in perfect synchronicity as if there were no difference between the two.

"Each time I removed the second skin, I noticed that I became hot—like, *really* hot, almost as if I had some sudden, overpowering fever."

Eve thought back to her run-in with the Interloper in Jason's dorm. "When Gary attacked us, he was sweating like crazy before his skin came off."

Armaan smiled. "Exactly." He grabbed his Bunsen burner and opened the air hole until a blue flame surged at the burner. Without hesitation, he thrust his faux hand into the fire.

"ARMAAN!" Eve screamed.

"Relax, Eve," he reassured her, "it doesn't hurt. And look." He nodded at his hand, which was now dripping like candle wax. The second skin trickled down his fingers, exposing his tan, knobby knuckles. Finally, he lifted his arm, removing it from the flame and exposing what appeared to be his own, normal hand emerging from the gooey Eve-hand. He turned to her and grinned.

"Extreme heat—it does the trick. It melts the stuff right off without damaging the body underneath."

"So, if we want to expose an Interloper, we just have to light the bastard on fire," Eve said.

"Which isn't exactly a great option. You can't just run around with a flamethrower igniting anyone you suspect is an alien." He wiped his hand clean and gathered the remaining liquid in a small petri dish. "But I figured it's a starting point—something you could work with."

Eve looked at Armaan's messy bed—the array of supplies, the slime-filled dish—and then gazed at his arm, now back to its original form, perfectly intact and unscathed.

"You're making history, Armaan. You know that, right?"

He smiled bashfully and glanced at his watch. "You better get going. My roommate will be back any second."

She cocked her head toward the door. "Did you want to come with? You can show the guys your discovery."

He shook his head. "I have to head to the medical ward anyway."

"Of course. The volunteer work never ends," she barbed.

"Actually, I'm not a volunteer. Well, not anymore, at least." He lifted his chin with false confidence. "I'm an assistant now."

"An assistant?"

"It's really just a fancy term for *personal servant*." He shrugged. "I'm working for the ward's only humanovus surgeon—Dr. Dzarnoski. Have you heard of him?"

"Vaguely. Furst was telling me about him a while back. He's one of the best in the country."

"Yeah, one of the best and a real hammer. I've gone from fetching you to fetching *coffee*."

Eve sighed. "Let me guess, being his assistant will help you get into medical school?"

"It will if Dzarnoski writes me a letter of recommendation." He beamed. "But just having the opportunity to learn from him, maybe even discuss his research..." He stared off across the room as he daydreamed about the possibilities. "For that, I'd get his coffee forever. It would be worth it." He glanced back at Eve and rolled his eyes. "Hope that Lionel Vandeveld guy is enjoying his new spot in the medical program. Some of us actually have to *work* our way up."

Eve chuckled to herself as she left Armaan's room and made her way out of Clarence Hall. She was headed to Percy's suite in the Rutherford Tower, where her comrades were waiting, undoubtedly stewing over flimsy strategies and unsound theories, and so for a moment she felt the slightest bit excited that she had something to offer. As she waited in the tower elevator, the memory of Armaan's arm flashed before her eyes, bubbling and bending until it took the form of her own hand. She closed her eyes, trying to rid herself of the disturbing vision, and when she opened them again, she had reached Percy's room. She opened the door and hurried inside.

Before she could utter a word, she stopped short, her eyes wide as she gaped at a new, equally disturbing sight: the sight of Jason, Percy, and Sancho surrounding a fourth figure sitting at the kitchen counter.

"Oh, hey Eve," Jason smiled. "We met your friend. How come you didn't tell us about her?"

Eve's throat tightened. *Friend,* she thought to herself. The word almost sounded offensive. As if choreographed, the girl swiveled around on her bar stool and flashed the most self-satisfied grin Eve had ever seen.

"Hey, *friend,*" JJ chirped with a wink.

Eve growled. "What is *she* doing here?"

"She's showing us all of her different programs," Percy answered, nodding at her sleek, polished scratchpad.

"Yeah, she's *incredible.*" Sancho turned to JJ, his eyes bulging. "You're incredible, did I tell you that yet?"

She rolled her eyes. "A few times, actually."

"She said you two discussed this already," Jason added.

"We *discussed* this?" Eve snapped. "God, you're a real piece of work, JJ."

"Wait, am I missing something?" Jason looked back and forth between the two girls. "Aren't you two friends?"

Eve scoffed. "Hardly."

"But wait a second," Sancho said. "You have to be friends. She knows all about our research."

"That's because she hacked my scratchpad!"

"Hey, in my defense, I begged her to get me involved," JJ chimed in. "Desperate times call for desperate measures."

Eve turned to her comrades and crossed her arms. "Look, she can't be here." She lowered her voice. "We don't know anything about her—"

"Well, apparently I'm *incredible,*" JJ quipped. "You don't need to know much else."

"She could be an *Interloper* for Christ's sake!"

JJ laughed aloud. "That's the dumbest thing I've ever heard! I mean, really, do I *look* like a damn alien?"

Eve and her friends stood in silence, sharing awkward glances as JJ's laughter trailed off into an uncomfortable hush.

"What?" she finally asked.

"She doesn't know," Jason mumbled. He looked over at Eve, perplexed. "You didn't tell her about the second skin?"

"Of *course* I didn't tell her. We're not friends. She's not in the group."

"Wait, what *second skin*?" JJ questioned. "What are you guys talking about?"

Again the group was quiet. Eve muttered under her breath, irritated at

JJ's gall. The boys stared at one another sheepishly. They had been infiltrated, outwitted by a small girl wearing purple sneakers, and the embarrassment was written across their faces. Percy cleared his throat, breaking the stillness.

"Okay, JJ, what's the real story?"

JJ flashed a complacent smile. "Look guys, my methods may be questionable, but my work speaks for itself. Yes, I hacked into Eve's and Jason's scratchpads—"

"Wait," Jason interrupted, "you hacked *my* scratchpad too?"

JJ sighed and continued. "But that's besides the point. I have access to Billington's database. That's how I found out about their underground Shelter and the colossal mess they've created. I know all about Fairon and the infamous *list*—the list that Billington lost. Haven't seen it myself, but damn are they shitting themselves over it." She turned to Jason. "I know *everything*. Well, everything except for this 'second skin' bull you keep rambling about."

"The Interlopers are disguising themselves as humans."

"*Jason*," Eve hissed.

"They're wearing a liquid coating—a second skin—that makes their true identity undetectable."

"Why are you telling her this?"

"She deserves to know," he answered, firmly. "At least for her own safety."

Eve scowled. "Well, now that you've been brought up to speed, you can leave."

"Ease off, princess, I'm just trying to help you."

"Why? Why the sudden interest in what we're doing?"

JJ shrugged her shoulders. "I have my reasons."

"And they are?"

"My reasons are none of your business."

"Great," Eve groaned, turning to her comrades. "So we're supposed to trust her, but she can't even trust us."

JJ laughed. "God, with your level of paranoia, you'd think someone was lookin' to kill you."

Eve opened her mouth to speak, but no words came out. Her face reddened; she thought of Gary's ominous message, Furst's dreadful warning, and the ashy letters that had decorated her classroom walls.

"Wow," Percy muttered. "Talk about putting your foot in your mouth, JJ."

"Eve is Fairon's number one target," Jason explained.

"It's not just that," Eve muttered. "I received a death threat: '*Die Chime.*'

It was written all over the classroom walls... in ashes."

"Good *Lord*," Percy said.

"Do you have any idea who did it?" Jason asked.

Eve glanced at JJ, still perturbed by her presence, and reluctantly continued. "I found ashes all over Madison's bed."

"You were threatened by your own *roommate*?" Sancho gasped.

"When did this happen?" Jason cut in.

"Yesterday."

"And you're just telling us *now*?"

"Well, I would've said something sooner, Jason, but I was a little distracted by your *ass-kicking rampage—*"

"Hold on, let me get this straight—the king of the Interlopers wants to dissect you, and the queen of diamonds wants to kill you?" Percy cringed. "Sucks to be the Chimera Bitch."

"Do you think she means it?" Sancho asked. "Do you think she'll follow through?"

"I don't know." Eve shook her head. "It doesn't make sense. I thought she was just upset about Jason."

Percy shrugged. "Maybe she is."

"Upset enough to want me *dead*?"

"Hell hath no fury like a woman scorned."

"So, what are we going to do about it?" Jason asked.

"Nothing," Eve asserted. "Ambushing her will only fuel the fire."

"Eve—"

"She's *my* roommate. She's *my* problem," Eve maintained. "We have more important things to worry about."

"I couldn't agree more," JJ brazenly interrupted. "The soap opera can wait." She leaned back in her seat and smirked. "Look, you're barely treading water with the Interlopers as it is. It's time to face facts: you *need* me."

Eve grumbled. "Is that so?"

"Still not convinced?" JJ activated her scratchpad. "Fine, I'll prove it to you."

She hunched over her computer and ran her hands along the screen. Eve and the others hovered above her, watching as rows of numbers clouded the display. JJ dragged her fingertips across select digits, plucking them from the screen until they floated in front of her in holographic form. She rearranged the numbers, creating long, complex formulas that Eve didn't understand, then sent them back into the display of her computer.

"What are you doing?" Sancho asked.

"Hacking into the Shelter's mainframe."

His eyes widened. "*Balls.* You're like a computer goddess."

JJ continued, reorganizing row after row of numbers and symbols with unremitting focus. Finally, an image appeared on her screen, and she waved her hand above it, projecting it as a three-dimensional display.

Eve stared at the hologram—it was a small device with a single blue button in its center, a mechanism she had seen before.

"They call this the beacon," JJ said.

"Right, the Interlopers' communication device," Eve said.

"You're familiar with it?" She minimized the hologram. "Good, then I can skip the tedious explanations and get straight to the point. If you guys can get your hands on one of these things, I can crack it for you. That means you'll have the inside scoop on the Interlopers' agenda, and on top of that—"

"We'll know about an attack before it happens," Jason added.

"Precisely." She turned to Eve. "And who knows? Maybe it'll help you track down your best bud, Fairon."

Eve grimaced. "The beacon is alien technology. How can you be sure you'll be able to get it working?"

"I can't be sure," JJ scoffed, "but let's face it, I'm a hell of a lot more qualified to do the job than any of you."

Eve rolled her eyes and glanced at her friends; they stared at the ground, avoiding her critical gaze, and immediately she felt a horrible twinge in her stomach.

"Oh, shit," she said. "You guys are buying into this, aren't you?"

Percy offered JJ a pathetic pat on the shoulder. "Would you excuse us for a moment?" He nodded at the remaining three. "Team—assemble. Living room. Now."

The foursome headed to the living room and huddled together. Eve was seething, her hands planted firmly on her hips.

"Look, I hate to point out the obvious, but the girl's a liability. She lied to our *faces*, she hacked our scratchpads—"

"But she also hacked the *Shelter*—and, in what? *Seconds*?" Percy argued. "Liar or not, she's got *skills*. Can *you* operate a beacon? 'Cause I can't."

"He's right," Jason concurred. "You and I have the gift. Percy and Sancho have the firepower. JJ has the technology. It's a natural fit."

"I agree," Sancho cut in. "She's amazing. She's perfect. She's totally in."

"You guys can't tell me you actually *trust* her, right?"

Jason hesitated. "Honestly, no," he answered. "But in this case, I think we have to push our apprehensions aside."

"And besides, Eve, I'm pretty sure she's my soulmate." Sancho's face lit up as he spoke. "A technical genius with a naughty side? *Please* don't mess this up for me."

"Um, guys?" JJ interrupted. "You're only, like, ten feet away from me, and I can hear everything you're saying…"

Jason looked at Eve, his eyes pleading for tolerance. "If she can help us, shouldn't we give her a shot?"

"Yeah, like a trial run—a probationary period?" Percy added.

Eve paused, and the room became uncomfortably still. Finally, she cradled her head in her hands and let out a long, defeated sigh.

"God, I can't believe this is actually happening."

"Good!" JJ chirped, leaping from her stool and strolling toward the group. "So it's settled." She slapped Eve playfully across the back and gave her shoulder a firm squeeze. "Don't worry, darlin', I've been on probation before."

Eve's eyes panned across the other members of the group: they were distinct, idiosyncratic, even dysfunctional, yet they fit together like the pieces of some bizarre puzzle. It was a collaboration she never would have assumed possible, and yet there they stood, all with the same goal in mind for whatever motivation. With a pained expression, she turned to her newest, unwanted ally.

"All right, JJ," she muttered bitterly. "I guess you're one of us, now."

CHAPTER 11: A NIGHT BEST

SPENT IN BLACK AND WHITE

It was early November, halfway through the fall semester, and autumn was officially in full swing in Calabasas. The air had become cool and breezy, and the sun set earlier and earlier with each passing day. A sea of coats stretched across campus as students meandered to their classes, discussing midterms, group projects, and Jason Valentine's fast approaching twenty-first birthday party, the hot topic of the school.

Oddly enough, the one subject that seemed to be missing from every conversation was the Interlopers—because there simply was nothing new to discuss. There hadn't been a single abduction or any other alien-related disturbance in over two weeks. Furst chalked it up to the work of the patrolmen, and others speculated that the Interlopers had lost interest, but Eve was unconvinced. The longer the Interlopers remained out of sight, the more she dreaded their inevitable return.

Eve's first class of the day was finished. She lingered by the door for a while, staring at the white walls, imagining the ashy stains that had long since been scrubbed away. With a deep breath, she left the room, only to be stopped at the doorway. Madison was waiting for her, her lips curled into a hideous frown.

"Tomorrow's Jason's birthday party," she sneered.

Eve rolled her eyes. "Is that so?"

"I know you're his date."

"You're quite observant."

Eve continued down the hallway, but Madison bolted in front of her with unexpected speed and stopped her dead in the center of the corridor.

"Jason was off limits," she barked. "He was *mine*."

Eve laughed. "*God*, are you really trying to pick a fight with me over a *boy*?"

Madison's eyes narrowed into scornful slits. "You knew I wanted him—"

"No, Madison, here's what I knew: when you found out he's a chimera, you said it was gross. You said you were disappointed—that he was *tainted*."

"Oh, don't be such a self-righteous dick-squeeze, I was just talking—"

Eve shouldered past her. "And *I* was just leaving—"

"I'm invited, you know," Madison called out. "And let me tell you, my boyfriend and I will be leaving a lasting impression."

Eve turned back, her brow wrinkled. "You have a *boyfriend*?"

"His name is Lionel Vandeveld. He's an all-conference athlete, the newest addition to the Billington medical program, and next in line to inherit his family's multimillion dollar practice—though I'm guessing you haven't heard of him since you're so unfamiliar with the upper echelons of society."

"Oh, I've heard of him," Eve answered, making her way to Madison's side, "but what I'm failing to comprehend is why you give a single *shit* about what I do with Jason if you have a *goddamn boyfriend*."

"You were never *supposed* to end up together. You're *supposed* to be alone." Madison folded her arms. "Now, you're encroaching on my property—"

"Your *property*?"

"You're getting in my *way, chimera*," Madison hissed. "I get what I want. I *always* get what I want. And you know what I want more than anything right now? Your *head*." She leaned in closer to Eve, her nostrils flared. "Do you understand me?"

Eve hesitated. She stared at the heiress's shiny hair, her piercing blue eyes, her flawless skin, and again she saw the piles of soot underneath her bed.

"I *said*, do you understand me?" Madison repeated.

Eve took a step back, taking one last moment to eye the girl up and down. "I got your message, Madison," she muttered. "Loud and clear."

DIE CHIME—the words repeated in her mind all throughout her next class, the lecture itself nothing but a distant buzz. At the front of the classroom, Professor Richards paced beside his projection, rambling mathematical nonsense as he flipped back and forth between charts and diagrams.

"Kingston," he barked, "what's the answer?"

Eve raised her eyes slightly, glowering at him as he tapped his foot impatiently. He was trying to catch her off guard—to humiliate her. His efforts were so slimy, she could hardly stand it.

"Forty-seven-point-two-six."

"Units? Dollars? Inches? This is a math class—be specific."

"Dollars. Forty-seven dollars and twenty-six cents."

He sneered. "Another correct answer from Kingston, the only student with an A in this class, thanks to her *unique* situation." He leaned against his desk, beaming with satisfaction. "If you want to know who's setting your curve, look no further."

Eve sighed and stared down at her scratchpad, ignoring the grumblings of her classmates. She could see Dick watching her out of the corner of his eye, along with her peers. They all hated her, unanimously and with fiery passion, and for once the detested professor seemed to have garnered favor among his students. Still, despite his glare, it was hard for Eve to shake her earlier encounter, to imagine anything but the loathsome look on Madison's face, and while she tried to concentrate on Richards' words, she found her mind wandering. *DIE CHIME*—was it merely an empty threat, or was Madison more dangerous than she appeared?

"KINGSTON!"

Eve's head shot up in an instant. Professor Richards was standing right in front of her, red-faced and furious. He looked down at her scratchpad textbook, which was open to a page they had passed fifteen minutes ago.

"Are you even *paying attention*?"

Eve's classmates giggled as she gripped the corners of her desk. No kind or courteous words came to her mind, so she remained silent.

"You *dare* to disrespect *me*? You think you're above us all, don't you?" He leaned in, his oily nose uncomfortably close to hers. "Your kind can be so *arrogant*."

"My *kind*?"

Richards slammed his hands onto her desk. Her classmates jumped, but Eve flinched only slightly, too stubborn to show any sign of weakness.

His lips quivered with rage. "*You disgust me.*"

With one quick sweep, Richards slapped Eve's scratchpad off the desk, sending it crashing to the floor. Eve gasped aloud, staring in shock at the sparking, broken remains of her archaic computer.

"You dropped something," he muttered.

Eve crawled to the floor, examining the computer that held all of her homework, textbooks, and notes—the computer she could not afford to replace. The mangled pieces and cracked screen looked like something she had seen before—no, something she had felt. She breathed in deeply, clinging to what was left of her pathetic scratchpad as if it were the remains of her messy life.

***

"FIRE!"

Sancho launched the clay disk into the air, and with the finesse of an expert, Jason pulled his gun from his belt and fired, shattering the disk into tiny pieces that scattered like hail to the ground. The group had traveled to the LaFleur gun range, as they often did after classes were over; JJ and Eve sat in the sod while Percy lounged in a lawn chair, watching as Jason shot one disk after another from the sky.

"Lookin' good, Valentine," Percy praised halfheartedly. "Not as good as me, but still workin' it like a pro."

Jason sighed and shoved the gun into his belt. "Well, that's probably because this is all we've been doing for the last two weeks."

"Isn't that a good thing?" Sancho asked. "If the Interlopers haven't made a move in a while, couldn't it mean they've called it quits?"

"It means they're planning something—something big," Eve said, discouraged. "They're just waiting for the perfect opportunity to act."

"While I do enjoy speculating *so* much, don't you think it'd be a lot easier to actually *listen* to their communications so we know for certain what's going on?"

Eve grimaced. JJ's request for a beacon had turned into a persistent complaint, one that was rapidly whittling away at her patience. She bit her lip.

"We get it, you want a beacon. Unfortunately, it's not that simple."

"I'm not asking for simple, I'm asking for a *beacon*. We *need* one if we're going to get anywhere."

"Look, we're all on the same page," Jason interrupted, "but that doesn't change the fact that we don't know how to find one."

JJ folded her arms. "I say we track down an Interloper and take it."

"Oh, really?" Eve scoffed. "Just like that?"

"I don't hear *you* coming up with any ideas," JJ snapped. "Are we just supposed to sit around and wait for one to fall into our lap?"

"All right, people, let's play nice." Percy stood from his seat and playfully wrapped an arm around Jason's shoulders. "We've got a birthday tomorrow. And not just any birthday—it's a twenty-first, the holiest of all birthdays, a gift from the gods of inebriation."

"Some of us weren't invited," Sancho grumbled under his breath.

"For the millionth time, I didn't get to pick the guest list," Jason groaned.

"Whatever." Sancho scooted toward JJ and flashed a debonair smile. "If I was invited, I would've totally asked you to accompany me. I look quite dapper in a suit, you know."

JJ rolled her eyes and turned to Jason. "Is he always going to be like this?"

"God, I hope not." Jason shoved his gun into the back of his pants and tossed his shoulder bag over his arm. "Look, I've got to run. I have my last tux fitting tonight."

"Yeah, I have to get going, too." Sancho shot Jason a dirty look. "Got a big project to work on, one that's *way* more exciting than some stupid *party*."

JJ gathered her things as well, then stopped suddenly when her eyes wandered to Eve's lap. "Holy mother of *suck*, what happened to your scratchpad?"

Eve had been fussing with the computer, trying to fix its splintered pieces to no avail. "It's nothing," she growled.

"Nothing but *crap*, you mean." JJ yanked the device from Eve's grasp and examined it. "What did you do, drop this thing into a wood chipper?"

Eve snatched the computer from JJ's hands and quickly deactivated it, ignoring the loud sputtering as she thrust it into her shoulder bag. Without another word, she sprang from her resting place and headed toward the firing range.

Jason watched her for a moment; her hands were swift, her movements sharp as she loaded her gun. He could see the stress in her stance and her jaw, and he delicately rested his hand on her back.

"You coming with us?"

"I think I'll stick around for a little while longer," she mumbled.

"You sure?"

She eyed her firearm. "To be honest, I just really feel like shooting something right now."

Jason nodded and joined Sancho and JJ, and they slowly made their way from sight. Eve turned to face her target, immediately taking aim.

Percy stood in the background, observing Eve as she fired her weapon. He cocked his head, studying her rigid frame and agitated face as she continued to shoot over and over again, her target now riddled with holes. After a brief silence, Percy wandered to her side and cracked a half-smile.

"You still mad about JJ?"

Eve sighed. "No. Kind of. I don't know."

"Well, you're mad about something."

"Gee, how could that be when I have so much to be thrilled about?"

Percy laughed. "That's why I like you, Eve—you're a smartass, just like me."

She ignored his quip and reloaded her gun, her eyes still fixed on her target. Before she could fire, Percy plucked the gun from her hands and spun it across his wrist, then shoved it into his belt. He smiled.

"I don't know if you know this, Eve, but I don't think of you as Jason's... date. Crush. Romantic interest? What the hell are you two, anyway?"

Eve paused. "I don't really know what we are."

"Okay, well, I don't just think of you as Jason's *whatever*. I think of you as a friend."

Eve felt her back loosen the slightest bit. "Well, the feeling is mutual."

"All right then, shit-dick," he smirked. "For the record, that's what I call all my friends. It's a term of endearment, I promise."

"How sweet," she mumbled.

"As I was saying, I know something's grinding your gears. You never put up with JJ's mouth."

"It's nothing you don't already know. The people at Billington—"

"Hate you." He nodded toward her shoulder bag. "And the scratchpad?"

Her eyes darted to the ground; she could see her computer poking out of her shoulder bag, its deformed paneling clearly visible. "Look, things are—"

"Complicated?"

"Are you going to keep doing that?"

"Sorry, nasty habit. But you should look at the bright side: your complications are over, at least for the weekend. Instead of dodging protestors and hunting aliens, you'll be sipping champagne and rubbing shoulders with high society at Jason's party."

As the words left his lips, Eve let out a loud, irritated groan and cradled her head in her hands.

"What? What did I say?"

"I haven't even thought about the party," she groused. "God, I don't even have a *dress*. I'm so screwed."

Percy became still, his eyes faraway as if deep in thought. "You don't have a dress?"

"No, nothing. I haven't worn a dress since I was eight years old."

Suddenly, a devious smile spread across Percy's lips. "I can get you a dress."

Eve let out a cynical chuckle. "Yeah, I'm sure you've got a closet full of 'em."

"I do. Several closets full, actually. And these closets are a lot bigger than the kind you're used to."

Eve glanced sidelong at Percy. She expected him to burst into laughter at any moment, but instead he stood firm, his grin widening as he waited for her reaction.

"Wait—you're serious?"

"As a heart attack. So soon you forget that my mother is *the* Alicia LaFleur, infamous socialite with a coveted wardrobe to die for."

Eve's mouth gaped open. "You want *me* to wear one of your mother's gowns? I... I can't."

"You can, and you will."

Without warning, Percy snatched up Eve's shoulder bag, yanked at her arm, and charged up the field toward the mansion. Eve stumbled behind him, awkwardly lurching from side to side as he dragged her along.

"Where are we going?"

"To see my mom."

"Wait, you're taking me to *meet* her?"

"Of course! How else are we going to get the dress?"

"Percy, this is a bad idea—"

"On the contrary, it's a *brilliant* idea. I am prone to moments of brilliance, after all. It's pretty common."

"What will your mom say?"

He laughed. "She'll probably say that any friend of mine is a friend of hers. Then she'll ramble on about her glory days, back when she was our age, and then she'll insist that the two of you look like sisters." They had reached his car, and he held the passenger door open for her. "You getting in or what?"

"Percy, you don't have to—"

"Oh God, Eve, just get in the damn car before I run you over with it," he moaned, flopping into the driver's seat and revving the engine.

Eve reluctantly took the seat beside him and sat in silence as they drove off together. A surge of anticipation swelled within her, and she anxiously fidgeted in place. The drive felt long and intolerable, and just as her nervous energy became too much to bear, she began to notice the scenery outside of her window. The busy streets, tall, dilapidated buildings, and overpasses covered in spray paint were unfamiliar to her. Before she knew it, they were deep in the heart of Los Angeles, far from the Billington campus or any other place she was accustomed to. She glanced over at Percy, who wore a smug smirk.

"Where exactly are we going?" she asked, skeptically.

"To see my mom, duh."

"I know that, but where *is* she?"

He smiled. "Home."

"We were just *at* your home."

"No, she's *home* home."

"What do you mean she's *home* home?"

"She's at our condo—in Manhattan."

"WHAT?" Eve shrieked. "We're going to *NEW YORK?*"

"Yeah. Where did you think we were going?"

"I don't know, not across the entire *country*, that's for damn sure."

"Relax," he answered, trying to stifle his spreading grin. "We're taking my mom's private jet. It's not like you have to fly commercial or anything."

"It's not the flight accommodations that I'm worried about, Percy."

"Then what's the problem?"

"What's the *problem*?" she snapped. "We're flying to the east coast, and the party is *tomorrow*."

"We'll fly in, snag a dress, stay the night, and fly back tomorrow morning. With the time difference, we'll be back *way* before the party even starts."

Eve sucked in a deep breath and watched as a small private airport appeared in the distance. She cursed to herself and picked at her cuticles.

"I don't have anything. No toothpaste, no change of clothes..."

"My mom has toothpaste *and* clothes," he scoffed. "Where do you think I'm taking you? A desert island?"

"This is crazy."

"Live a little, Eve." He punched her in the shoulder. "The plan is foolproof. What's there to worry about?"

Eve stared at the rows of jets; they were sleek, lined up like prized ponies on display.

"I've never even been on a plane before."

"*What*? Are you *serious*? Where are you from, the nineteen hundreds?

Does your car run on gasoline, too?"

Percy hauled Eve from her seat and dragged her through the lot like a parent with a stubborn child. His plan was completely absurd, but for whatever reason, be it desperation or the hint of elation buzzing inside of her, Eve decided to surrender to his will. She boarded the private jet behind Percy, admiring the luxury of the plush leather seats and ruby-red floors. The cabin was lit with a faint glow, the walls and ceiling the color of champagne and lined with a gold trim. She sat down in the seat across from Percy, who had already made himself comfortable, and just as she was getting acclimated to her surroundings, a well-groomed steward squatted beside her.

"Good afternoon, Mr. LaFleur, Miss Kingston," he began, his words breathy and cool. "Can I interest you in a beverage?"

"Scotch on the rocks for me," Percy chimed in. "And a hot towel, please."

The steward looked at Eve, his eyes warm and almost hypnotic. "For you, Miss Kingston?"

"Um," she stuttered, "water is fine."

"Seltzer, flavored, mountain, holy, or spring water?"

Eve hesitated. "The regular kind?"

Percy laughed, leaning back in his chair like a proud king. "Enjoy the ride, my dear. You'll thank me for this later."

Despite her apprehensions, Eve quickly adjusted to the comfort and opulence of the LaFleur private jet. The flight was smooth, and time seemed to pass in an instant, as there were plenty of entertainments to occupy their time. A large HV and gaming system adorned one of the cabin walls, and at Percy's insistence, Eve allowed herself to partake in the frivolous hologames. They battled ninjas, zombies, and ninja zombies, and they cheered and laughed until they were tired and out of breath. For that short period of time, Eve was free from any hint of anxiety—she and Percy were just friends engaged in a foolish, thoughtless adventure.

Upon landing, Eve followed Percy through the airport, trying to catch quick glimpses of the city through the windows. It was hard to believe she was actually in New York, and while she wasn't typically easily excitable, she felt a rush of childish delight within her. Before she could relish in the moment, Percy stopped just short of the exit and beckoned her to his side.

"You ready?"

"Ready for what?"

"Two things: one, it's going to be colder than shit out there."

Eve looked down at her light hooded sweatshirt and frowned. "Thanks for the warning."

"Two," Percy continued, "be prepared for bright lights. *Lots* of bright lights."

"Is this some type of metaphor for the lights of New York?" she quipped. "Cute, Percy. Really cute."

He laughed. "Actually, forget that last part. I think I'm going to enjoy this."

Without another word, Percy led her outside, exposing them to a frenzy of flashing lights and incoherent shouting. Eve gasped, her eyes practically blinded by the incessant blinking of the shining, white lights.

Percy smirked. "Having fun yet?"

Eve squinted, straining to discern the chaos in front of her. A horde of photographers surrounded the duo, snapping pictures and barking the most inane, mindless questions she had ever heard.

"PERCY! WHERE'S YOUR MOTHER?"

"PERCY, IS THAT YOUR GIRLFRIEND?"

"OVER HERE, PERCY! LOOK OVER HERE!"

Eve clung to Percy, who appeared confident and poised, completely unfazed by the mob of paparazzi. She looked past the crowd, deep into the darkness of the street, and saw a stretch limo waiting only a few yards away.

Percy elbowed her in the ribs. "Let's keep it moving, lady."

He grabbed at Eve's wrist and tugged her through the crowd, and the flashing lights and witless shouting surged around them. Eve thought the mayhem felt vaguely familiar, as if she had been there many times before, and then she remembered the angry protesters at Billington, with their painted signs and deranged chanting. The paparazzi, though equally unyielding, seemed innocent in comparison; they smiled as Percy passed, almost completely uninterested, for once, in the chimera at his side.

Percy shoved Eve into the limousine and slammed the door behind him, quickly repositioning his hair and adjusting his leather coat at the seams. Eve shook her tousled locks from her face and wrapped her arms around her shivering body, trying her best to shield herself from the blistering cold. Amid all of the insanity, she almost didn't notice the woman sitting across from her.

"Oh, dear, you're shaking like a leaf," the woman cooed. She turned toward a small speaker in her headrest. "Aleksander, please turn on the heater immediately."

A rush of heat pulsed through the vents, and Eve sighed with relief. Settling into her seat, she took a good look at the strange woman in front of her.

Her face was beautiful and oddly youthful with rosy cheeks and plump, pink lips to match. She had shoulder-length, silky brown hair that shimmered like gold under the faint light of the limo. Her emerald-green eyes were sparkly and bright, offset by the rich ebony wrap that hung over her milky shoulders. Eve could see hints of Percy in her features—they had the same almond-shaped eyes, the same pointed chin and high cheekbones—and she knew immediately that this stunning woman was his mother.

"Thank you," Eve muttered shyly. "Not just for the heat, but for picking us up—for everything."

Percy smiled. "Eve, this is my mother, Alicia. Mom, this is Eve."

"Ah, yes, the one you've told me so much about. Well, let me tell you, darling, any friend of Percy is a friend of mine." She giggled to herself and glided her fingers through her hair, exposing several jeweled bracelets that hung around her wrist. "So, tell me about this party you're attending. I hear you're in a bit of a pickle, yes?"

Eve glanced back and forth between Percy and her hostess before continuing. "Well, Jason Valentine is having his twenty-first birthday party tomorrow, and I'm supposed to be his date, except I don't have a dress."

"Oh, you two are absolute dolls. I remember what it was like to be your age—so young, so full of adventure. Flying across the country on a whim, just for a simple gown." She sighed, her eyes distant as she reminisced. "When I look at you, Eve, I see so much of myself in you. I mean, really, Percy," she turned toward her son and pointed at Eve, "don't we look alike? I swear, people could mistake us for sisters."

Percy chuckled, glancing at Eve as if to say *I told you so.*

Alicia scanned Eve, studying her appearance. "You're a vision, darling. Very statuesque, and such elegant features." Her eyes lowered, landing on Eve's simple grey and blue wardrobe. "Love the ensemble, by the by. Minimalism is so in right now. Tell me, what inspired you?"

Eve hesitated. "Poverty?"

"Poverty is on *fire* this season. Way to be on point with the trends, darling."

The limo glided through Manhattan, swerving past bustling New Yorkers and yellow taxicabs. It was just as it appeared in the movies, the buildings stretching like giants into the night sky, looming overhead in a way that made Eve feel small. It was as if she had been transported to another time and dimension, away from Billington and its theatrics. Just hours ago she had been firing guns in Calabasas, and now she was sitting in a limousine with Alicia

LaFleur, a simple woman with not-so-simple taste, discussing a passion for fashion that Eve wasn't entirely sure she had in the first place.

The driver pulled over to the side of the street, parking the car in front of the double doors of a massive tower. The building reminded her of Rutherford Hall, though it was at least three times as tall and far more luxurious. The grounds were lit with spotlights that flickered against the large black windows, making the building sparkle like a beautiful gem in the heart of Manhattan.

Before Eve could admire the architecture any longer, her window was blocked, the view covered by a very strange sight—a crotch, or rather the zippered fly of a pair of jeans, worn by yet another nagging paparazzo. In moments, the entire car was surrounded. Eve glanced at Percy, who was fiddling with his sunglasses, unconcerned with the situation.

Alicia wrinkled her nose and pouted. "It looks like they've cornered us again, haven't they?" She turned to Eve and nodded her head at the blocked door. "Go ahead and open it, darling. They'll make room for you—eventually. And if they don't, well"—she winked—"feel free to be a bit *aggressive.*"

"Oh, okay," Eve stuttered. She reached for the handle and gave it a forceful push, knocking it against the photographers that crowded around the limousine.

"ALICIA!" they shouted. "ALICIA, LOOK OVER HERE!"

Alicia stepped onto the pavement and flashed a gorgeous, toothy smile at the cameras. Eve reluctantly stumbled out after her, followed by a much more graceful Percy, and Alicia eagerly grabbed both of their hands before steering them toward the high-rise.

"WHAT ARE YOU DOING TONIGHT, ALICIA?"

Mrs. LaFleur giggled. "Spending time with my handsome son and his *delightful* friend."

"ALICIA, WHAT IS YOUR FRIEND WEARING?"

"Poverty," she smiled, wrapping her arm around Eve and squeezing her tightly. "She's wearing poverty."

The threesome shuffled into the lobby of the building, sauntering past uniformed workers and wealthy residents, and all the while Eve gawked at the lavish conditions. They filed into a glass elevator that shot up like a bullet to the LaFleur family condo on the thirty-first floor, and when the doors opened, her eyes lit up with awe. The entryway was amazing: vanilla-colored marble floors reflected the lights of the colossal chandelier hanging overhead, and beyond that, ivory staircases sat along either side of a single hallway, itself lined with a crimson rug intricately stitched with flecks of gold and bronze. A massive, hand-painted family portrait adorned one of the walls, and beneath it stood a line of tuxedoed servants.

Alicia scampered toward one of the servants and plopped her wrap onto his outstretched arms. "Follow me, darlings," she trilled before heading up one of the staircases, leaving Eve standing in the middle of the entryway, still awestruck.

Percy nudged her shoulder. "What are you waiting for? We've got dresses to sort through."

Eve and Percy scurried up the staircase and down the hallway, following Alicia to a large, open room lined with rows and rows of the most beautiful shoes, purses, and jewelry Eve had ever seen.

"What is this?" she asked, strolling past a tier of glittering necklaces. "Is this your bedroom?"

Alicia chuckled. "Don't be silly, darling. This is a closet."

"Your closet is bigger than the apartment I lived in for three years."

Alicia's chortle turned into an uproar. "Percy, you're right, she *is* hilarious."

Just as the heiress's laughter began to ebb, three more servants came barging through the doorway, pushing racks stuffed with more gowns than Eve could have possibly imagined, all perfectly color-coordinated and over-flowing with glittering appliqués, voluminous skirts, and rich fabrics.

Alicia delicately ran her hand across the dresses, admiring her collection. "So, where would you like to start? You have such a lovely skin tone—eggplant or coral would look absolutely *remarkable* on you."

"It's a black-and-white ball, Mom," Percy muttered. "I think you can gather from that what her color options are."

Alicia turned to Eve and frowned. "What a shame. Cherry red would really suit you." She turned to her servants. "Gentlemen, please remove the colored gowns."

The workers scuttled through the room, reorganizing the racks with the speed and efficiency of an assembly line. Finally, only one rack remained, displaying the finest black and white chiffon, satin, and lace that money could buy. Alicia flipped through the gowns like they were pages of a book, trying to find the perfect look for her protégé.

"So, my dear, how would you like to look?" She pulled out a white ball gown with a fluffy tulle skirt. "Belle of the ball? The princess alongside Prince Valentine?"

"God no," Eve blurted out. She blushed. "I mean, I'm not exactly the 'princess' type."

"Hm." Alicia continued to search through the selections, landing on a sexy number with panels of black sequins and a plunging neckline. "How about the dark, seductive temptress?"

Percy rolled his eyes. "Eve needs all the likeability points she can get. Parading around as a villainous femme fatale will hardly help her cause."

"Oh, I've got it," Alicia chirped, grabbing a long, lace gown in ivory. "A delicate pearl—a damsel in distress, yes?"

"Mom, *please*," Percy moaned. "A *damsel in distress?* The girl's a chimera; she's genetically programmed to be an ass-kicking *machine*."

Eve winced, as if Percy's words were daggers piercing her skin. Alicia looked up, her eyes suddenly bright with astonishment and intrigue, and Eve felt a pang of dread in her gut.

"You're a chimera, dear?"

"Not just any chimera, Mom. She's the strongest chimera in the *world*, which makes her a mega, über, *super* chimera—"

"Percy," Eve grumbled, "I can speak for myself."

"Sorry. Told you it was a bad habit."

Alicia was silent, still staring at Eve with the gentlest eyes Eve had ever seen. Eve held her breath, anticipating the storm to come, waiting for Alicia to snarl with disgust, or to banish her from her home never to return again. The quiet felt endless, and with clenched fists and a straightened back, Eve braced herself for the verbal assassination she was sure would take place.

"The strongest chimera in the entire world," Alicia repeated. "Well now, that changes everything, doesn't it?"

With one fluid motion, Alicia reached up and tucked a strand of hair behind Eve's ear. She smiled.

"A woman with such power needs a powerful dress—a statement piece."

Eve's eyes widened; she opened her mouth to speak but couldn't find the words.

"The strongest chimera in the world should command attention and admiration. And I know *just* the dress." Alicia beamed with delight and dashed toward the rack, pulling out a strapless gown in jet black with a heart-shaped neckline. "It's a vintage piece from the twenties—twenty-twenty-seven, I believe. One of my absolute favorites—a gown fit for a queen."

Alicia pressed the gown against Eve's body, comparing the size versus Eve's shape. "I wore this when I was around your age, and it looks like you're practically the same size I was back then. Of course you're much, *much* taller—but that's of no concern, we can have the tailor add some length." She circled Eve, eyeing her body. "Yes, you have a lovely figure." She paused, her eyes landing on Eve's chest. "Your boobs are much smaller than mine, though. We're all blessed in different ways, I suppose. You with your gift, me with my perfect breasts."

"*Mother*," Percy groaned. "Focus, please."

"Well, we can get the bust tailored anyhow." She sighed, admiring Eve as if she were staring at her own daughter. "I'll have the alterations completed tonight. Tomorrow morning, you will have a gown that fits like a glove, revamped especially for you. And when you go to that party, you will be the most *beautiful* girl in the room. Do you feel it?"

Eve furrowed her brow. "Feel what?"

"Beautiful!"

"Beautiful?" Eve hesitated. "Honestly, it's not something I think about."

"Oh but you *should* think about it, darling," Alicia corrected. "*Everyone* deserves to feel beautiful. It's your God-given right to look in the mirror and love what you see. Never mind the imperfections—we're all imperfect, after all. But people tend to get so caught up in what they're lacking, they forget to appreciate all that they have." She pranced toward one of her many servants and tossed the dress across his shoulder. "To alterations, please." She turned back to Eve once more, her eyes shining with enthusiasm. "You are *so* beautiful, Eve. And tomorrow night, you're going to be an absolute *gem*."

Eve couldn't help but love Alicia; her vitality was contagious, her sweet disposition a breath of fresh air. Eve smiled back like an impressionable child.

Alicia rested her hands on her hips and gave Eve a playful wink. "And I'll tell you one thing: if seeing your sexy self in this stunning gown doesn't give our Mr. Valentine a raging boner, then he's about as gay as my darling Percy."

"MOTHER!" Percy shouted. "God, the mouth on this woman."

"What? What did I say?"

***

Eve awoke the next morning on a cloud—a soft, shimmering cloud that was the color of red wine and smelled of warm vanilla sugar. She opened her eyes, her senses hazy until she finally recognized her surroundings: the cream walls with their golden crown molding, the rich hardwood floors, the massive canopy bed draped with burgundy silk sheets—she remembered it now. Alicia LaFleur had so many guest rooms to choose from, but she had insisted that this one was the best, a bedroom fit for a queen, and Eve had to agree. She breathed in deeply. The room was so peaceful, she could hardly find the will to pull herself from her pillow. And then she recalled Jason's fast-approaching twenty-first birthday party.

With a grunt, she hoisted herself from her sheets and tromped out of the bedroom, heading through the hallway and down the winding staircase in search of any sign of humanity. She followed the red and gold rug until she at last reached the kitchen, where Percy and Alicia sat at the counter giggling like best friends.

"Eve, darling!" Alicia squealed, rushing to her side and squeezing her tightly. "I suspect you slept well, yes? You look rested."

Percy snickered before biting into a shiny green apple. "Nice ensemble," he teased through munches.

Eve looked down; she was wearing a pair of Alicia's pajamas, made from burgundy silk to match the bedsheets.

"What? They're your mom's."

"Yeah, well, it's also two o'clock in the afternoon."

"*Son of a—*" Eve stopped herself, blushing as she glanced over at Alicia. "This time zone thing has me all messed up."

"Oh, ignore Percy. He forgets that not everyone is used to the constant traveling. Your body thinks it's the a.m., and so we should get you some breakfast," Alicia chirped, scurrying through the kitchen.

"Oh, that's not necessary. We probably have to get going soon anyway—"

"Nonsense," Alicia smiled. "You have plenty of time. I'll have the chef prepare you a plate. Until then," she grabbed a crystal flute and two bottles of juice, "how about a morning cocktail? Cranberry and vodka? Or maybe pineapple and rum?"

"Um," Eve stammered, "isn't it a bit early for that?"

Alicia shot Eve a blank, confused look, then quickly masked it with yet another picturesque smile. "You're right. I'll go fetch you a bottle of champagne." She pranced from the room, teetering in her six-inch heels.

The room went quiet. Percy studied Eve, watching as her face dropped and her gaze became distant, as if she was preoccupied with something.

"Don't you dare."

"What?" she asked.

"You've got that look in your eye," he said, taking one last bite of his apple. "The one that says you're thinkin' about aliens."

Eve frowned. "The Interlopers aren't going to take the day off just because we're going to some *ball*."

"Eve, we're in *Manhattan*," Percy declared, spreading his arms wide. "We're getting ready for a top-drawer party tonight—*Jason's* party. And we're going to eat, dance, laugh, and get drunk—well, *I'll* be getting drunk. Not you two." He tossed his apple core into the trash and took a swig from his afternoon cocktail. "I promise we'll get back to alien hunting tomorrow."

Eve slumped over the counter and rested her cheeks in her hands. "Fine," she pouted, "but we can't stay here much longer. We've got a flight to catch."

"Don't be silly," Alicia cooed, startling Eve as she waddled into the kitchen with a bottle of champagne in hand. "We have so much to do before you leave."

"We do?"

"Of course!" She popped the cork and promptly poured two glasses of champagne, one for Eve and another for herself. "The beautification process takes time. It's an art form—a ritual, even—and you absolutely *have* to slow down and savor every last bit of it." She grabbed Eve's chin and examined her face. "Tell me, when was the last time you had a facial?"

"A facial?" Eve asked. "I washed my face this morning, if that's what you mean."

Alicia let out an adorable giggle and turned to her son. "Isn't she a riot?" She released Eve's chin and strolled toward the hallway. "I'll call my beauty team. They'll be over within the hour. You've waxed, yes?"

Eve hesitated. "Um..."

"No worries, I'll add it to the itinerary. Afterward we'll have lunch—well, brunch for you, thanks to our pesky time zone debacle—and then we'll finish off with nails. It's going to be such a fabulous day—us girls doing our girl thing, and Percy, too, of course. He's such a good sport." She let out a tiny squeal of delight before bustling down the hallway, her hips swaying with every step.

Percy slapped Eve across the back. "Guess we're going to be here for a while." He winked. "Hope you don't mind being fashionably late."

The next few hours flew by like a tornado—except this tornado was filled with scented candles, moisturizers, and soothing botanicals. Eve sat back, passive and helpless as several bodies hovered around her, ripping hair from her flesh, painting fruity paste across her cheeks, and buffing her nails to glossy perfection. It was the strangest ambush she had ever been subjected to, and despite all of her ranting and protesting, Percy insisted on watching the spectacle and reveling in her torment. Time came and went, and soon Eve's stomach was full, her nails perfectly polished, her skin glowing, and her legs silky smooth, all thanks to the LaFleurs. Before she knew it, the process had come to a close, and she stood with Percy and Alicia in the building's lobby.

"All right, darlings," Alicia said, "if you want to get to your party on time, you should probably leave"—she peered at her watch—"twelve minutes ago." She smiled and shoved Eve's dress bag into Percy's chest. "Give or take a few minutes, of course."

"Shit," Eve mumbled. "We'll be late for sure."

"Don't think of it as being late—think of it as *making an entrance*," Percy said, tossing the bag over his shoulder. "I'll load up the car."

As Percy filed from the lobby, a line of people followed suit, each wearing an all-black ensemble and dragging a silver suitcase. Eve looked back and forth between the troop and Alicia, who casually sipped her evening cocktail.

"Where are all those people going?"

"Oh, that's your hair and makeup team," Alicia responded nonchalantly, swirling her drink in her hand much like Percy always did. "You can't forget about the hair and makeup. They're just as important as the dress itself."

Eve smiled; as ridiculous as the whole charade seemed, she knew that Alicia had planned it all just for her. It was an act of selflessness and care that Eve hadn't experienced in so many years.

"Thank you." The words felt feeble and almost inadequate. "You've been so kind—*too* kind to me."

"Oh, you stop it," Alicia cooed, sauntering toward Eve's side and grabbing her hand tightly. "It was my pleasure."

Eve looked down at her hand and then up at Alicia. "Percy is really lucky," she stuttered, awkwardly. "You're a great mom."

Alicia giggled. "God, that makes me sound so old, doesn't it? I'll never get used to being called *Mom*." She cupped Eve's hand and brought it close to her.

"Please, don't be a stranger, darling. You're part of the family now."

Without another word, Alicia flung her arms around Eve and hugged her firmly. Her embrace felt warm and loving, and Eve couldn't help but hope and pray that her words were authentic and true—that they were family.

Knowing there was no time to spare, Eve made a mad dash to the limousine. Cameras flashed and paparazzi barked inane questions—it was still just as terrifying as the first time—and she hurried past them, diving into the car and parking herself alongside Percy. As the limo drove away, she sat in silence, her eyes glistening, and a strange, unfamiliar stir of emotion surfaced within her.

Percy glanced over at his friend and smirked. "Need a tissue?"

"Shut up, dick-squeeze."

"Atta girl," he chuckled, wrapping his arm around her.

They continued on their trek to the airport and, upon arriving, eagerly boarded the LaFleur jet. Eve had expected a smooth, carefree journey, much like her initial flight to New York, but their flight back to Billington felt exponentially longer and even hectic. There were no hologames to distract her—instead, she sat less-than-patiently as makeup artists dusted her cheeks and glued her lashes and hairstylists tugged and wrapped her locks around burning hot irons. She tried to keep track of the time—she even asked Percy on multiple occasions, but he proved to be utterly useless, too busy directing the finishing touches on his tuxedo jacket. The entire flight was a chaotic blur—a random flurry of colored powders, harsh-smelling hairsprays, and seemingly needless accessorizing—and when the captain signaled that the jet would be landing shortly, Eve breathed a sigh of relief.

Just as Eve relaxed in her seat, Percy grabbed her by the shoulders and hoisted her to her feet.

"All right, woman, take off your clothes."

"*Excuse me?*"

"Oh, don't be such a prude. We have to get changed, and we have to do it *now.*"

"Now? While we're *landing*? Can't we do it back at Billington?"

"The party starts in exactly six minutes and thirty-two seconds."

"*What?*"

"The second we land, we have to bolt to the Rutherford ballroom. Now," Percy ripped off his shirt, exposing his svelte chest, "get naked, and do it *fast.*"

Eve glanced at the hair and makeup team, who sat only a short distance away and watched the pair with curious eyes. Eve sighed and glared at Percy.

"Fine," she groused, unzipping her sweatshirt and pulling her top over her head, "but you should know that I *hate* you a little bit right now."

Percy stood in nothing but his boxer briefs, fiddling with his white dress shirt as if time and nudity were of no concern to him. He eyed Eve's gangly figure and smirked.

"Black bra *and* panties? *Someone* has a naughty side—"

"*Shut up,*" she spat, stumbling as the plane shook slightly. A light flicked on above them—it was the fasten seatbelt sign, and Eve glanced over at Percy.

"Ignore it," he ordered, grabbing her dress from the rack. "Lift up your arms—you're going to need all the help you can get maneuvering into this monstrosity."

The cabin shook once again, this time much more severely. Eve tumbled forward, colliding into Percy's chest, and the two of them toppled to the floor in a pile of tangled limbs. As she pushed herself up, she realized that he was sprawled beneath her, nearly as naked as she was, and her eyes widened with horror.

"This *never* happened," she barked.

"I don't know, Eve. Is it weird that I find this strangely sexy?"

"Ugh!" She pushed herself off of Percy's body and staggered to her feet.

"You're fun to screw with, did you know that?"

"DRESS. NOW."

Eve stretched her arms into the air, and Percy slid the gown over her head, dragging it down past her hips until the skirt touched the floor. He tugged at the back, pulling both sides of the zipper close together.

"Suck in."

"I *am* sucking in."

"Not enough."

"I thought this dress was tailored to fit me?"

"It *was* tailored to fit you. Just not while you're breathing," Percy scoffed. "Suck in, *now.*"

Eve emptied her lungs, most likely for the last time that evening, and winced as Percy forced the zipper up her back, sealing her into her dress. She shoved her feet into her strappy black stilettos, teetering across the jet just as the wheels touched down. Percy took a second to admire his jacket—solid white with a thin black lining across the lapel—then quickly slid it over his arms and shoulders. The jet finally slowed to a stop along the runway, and

Percy stepped away from Eve, eyeing her from head to toe.

"Yup. That'll do." He cocked his head toward the door. "Time to get our asses out of here."

"Wait," Eve interrupted. "I almost forgot."

She rummaged through her pile of clothes and pulled out a sleek black gun—the gift from Percy. With little grace, she shimmied her dress up her leg and strapped the firearm to the inside of her upper thigh.

"You're bringing your *gun*?"

"I bring it with me everywhere. Never know when I'll need it."

Percy opened his jacket, exposing one of his pistols tucked in the inside pocket. "My kind of woman," he quipped. He took one last look at Eve before heading for the door. "Hope you can run in heels."

The two of them tore from the jet and raced to Percy's car, fueled by an anxiety that only formal occasions could bring about. Eve sat anxiously in the passenger seat, bouncing her knee up and down and picking at her perfectly manicured cuticles. She groaned aloud, hoping that time would slow down just a bit, but with each passing minute she found herself more and more restless.

The car peeled onto the Billington campus, screeching to a stop behind Rutherford Hall, and Percy and Eve flew from their seats and raced up the dormitory stairs. They barged through the lobby—heads turned, but they paid no attention—and piled into the elevator, and with a deep, exhausted breath, Percy slammed at the button for the third floor and watched with relief as the doors closed in front of them.

"Twenty-three minutes late," he panted. "Not too bad, right?"

Eve was silent; for the first time all day, she didn't feel rushed or panicked. Instead, she was nervous. She turned to Percy.

"How do I look?"

He smiled. "Like a tall glass of water."

Whatever that means, she thought to herself, and suddenly she realized she truly had no idea how she looked. Nervously, Eve turned toward the shiny wall of the elevator and gazed at her own reflection.

Her hair was parted to the side and cascaded down her shoulders in loose, voluminous waves; her eyes were elegantly lined in black to offset the sweet, supple appearance of her full red lips. A large diamond necklace hung from her neck, a perfect match for her teardrop earrings and the glittery bracelet adorning her wrist.

And then there was the dress. *God*, the dress was *perfect*. It was simple yet stately with a heart-shaped neckline that plunged ever-so-subtly between her small breasts. The material followed the shape of her body, accentuating her narrow waist and delicate curves, then flowed away from her figure at the mid-thigh, creating a short train that trailed behind her.

Eve could scarcely believe the reflection staring back at her was her own.

The elevator dinged, signaling their arrival at the third floor. Percy scrutinized Eve's ensemble one last time and then nodded at the opening doors.

"I have to run to my room for a minute, so this is where I leave you."

"But—"

"*Go*," he urged, "crotch-breath."

And with that, Percy shoved her out of the elevator just before the doors closed again. Eve cursed to herself as she stumbled down the hallway, nearly tripping over the lining of her dress before regaining her balance. She tugged the fabric from underneath her heel and smoothed her hair into place, and just as she recovered a hint of confidence, she looked down the seemingly infinite hallway and immediately felt faint.

Waiting for her at the end of the corridor was Jason.

Their eyes met; Jason froze, his lips slightly parted as if he had been stunned into silence. Eve took one step forward, and then another; the walk down the hall felt endless, like a perilous journey, and all the while Jason watched her, his stare sincere and penetrating. Finally, his chest rose with one long, deep breath, and he smiled the biggest, most joyful smile Eve had ever seen, and she couldn't help but smile back. She made her way to his side—he looked handsome and dignified in his black tuxedo and matching silk tie—and before she could nervously squirm or fiddle with her bracelet, he took her hand and brought it to his lips for a soft kiss.

"Sorry I'm late," she murmured bashfully.

"Don't be sorry. Good parties never start on time." His eyes danced across her, and again he smiled. "You look... incredible."

She blushed. "Thank you. It was Percy—"

"No, it's you, Eve," he interrupted. "Percy has nothing to do with it."

He stared at her for a moment longer, then cocked his head toward the double doors. "You ready?"

Eve apprehensively linked her arm with his and stared at the doors with wide, fearful eyes, as if she were looking at the gates of hell.

"I have no idea what I'm doing."

He offered her a playful wink. "Neither do I."

"You're lying."

"I know."

Eve held her breath as the doors opened in front of them, revealing a large, grand ballroom. Long sheets of ivory silk were draped across the windows, secured with thick golden tassels that matched the gold place settings. Crystal chandeliers hung from the ceiling, reflecting twinkling lights across the floor, and lush bouquets of white roses adorned every table. A large, hardwood dance floor lay in the center of the room, accompanied by a well-dressed string quintet. And at the back of the room shuffled a line of reporters and photographers, all vying to get a glimpse of the man of the hour—the man at Eve's side. As the two of them walked into the room, arm in arm, a sea of exquisitely dressed guests, all in black and white tuxedos and gowns, rose from their seats and applauded the guest of honor.

Jason assumed a half-smile—Eve could tell right away that it was contrived—and humbly nodded to his guests. As he did, Eve noticed two figures in her peripheral vision—Jason's parents, headed straight toward them, both wearing toothy grins that reeked of artificiality. Mrs. Valentine glided across the dance floor like a ghoulish demon and nudged her way between Eve and Jason, breaking their hold and wrapping her son in an embrace that made his body go rigid with discomfort. Mr. Valentine patted Jason on the back and raised his glass of champagne to his guests.

"Tonight, we celebrate the coming of age of a fine young man." He paused, turning to look at Jason. "A good, hardworking member of society. A man I am *proud* to call my son. Jason, do you have any words for your guests on this very special day? A speech, perhaps?"

Jason looked out at the crowd: cameras flashed, and small clusters of reporters inched their way closer to the dance floor, eager to hear what the now infamous chimera had to say. He took his glass of champagne from his father's hand and raised it slightly and with little enthusiasm.

"Thank you all for coming."

And with that, he shouldered past his parents, stepping out of the spotlight. He hurried toward Eve—she had made her way to the side of the dance floor, as there had seemed to be no place for her beside his parents—and grabbed her hand, escorting her to their seats at the central table a short distance in front of them.

"How you holding up?"

"I should be asking you the same thing," Eve answered out of the corner of her mouth.

Jason leaned in to her, whispering into her ear, "God, did you *hear* him? 'A good, hardworking member of society.' I swear, if there was one night where I wish I could get drunk, tonight would be the night."

Eve's eyes panned across their table. They had been seated alongside two other couples, both much older and clearly uninterested in Eve and Jason's company. They arrogantly lifted their chins and turned to one another, mumbling most likely about the scandalous senator's son and his undoubtedly classless date.

"Hello, mutants," Percy interrupted, approaching Jason and Eve from behind with a glass of champagne in each hand. He kicked out a chair beside Eve and took a seat. "What are *you* two doing here? I thought this party was for humans *only*."

"Thank *God* you're at our table," Jason sighed. "I thought it was just going to be my parents and their horrible friends."

"And it is, because this isn't my seat. I'm just stopping by to let you know I won't be staying long."

"What? Why?"

"You know, this wasn't really what I had in mind. Stuffy parties filled with half-dead, elitist butt plugs aren't exactly my thing," he scoffed. "I'm skipping out early to hit up the Meltdown."

Eve wrinkled her nose. "The Meltdown? What's that?"

"It's an underground chimera club downtown, in the alley across from the new Pier Lorent Hotel."

"A chimera club?" Jason asked. "Those exist?"

"Of course they do. God, shouldn't you of all people know these things?"

"But, why are *you* going?" Eve pried. "You're not a chimera."

"I want to peruse the selection of chimera men. They're brooding and damaged with daddy issues." He glanced at Jason. "Like you, except you're kind of a boy scout."

"So you're going to bail on my birthday? Come on, you can't leave us with these people—"

"Then come *with*."

"I can't."

"Says who?" Percy looked from side to side and got up from his seat. "Look, the king and queen of misery are headed this way, so I'm going to make myself scarce. I'll stick around for a little while longer, but if you can't find me later, you know where I'll be."

Percy sauntered away from the table, jokingly waving at Mr. and Mrs. Valentine as they passed him. Eve couldn't help but study their perfect poise and phony grins. They seemed so animated and even cheerful, but as they neared her and Jason, the air in the room became chilly and tense.

"Was that the LaFleur boy?" Mrs. Valentine asked.

"Good God, the kid has so many balls and hooks in his ears, he looks like a damn Christmas tree," Mr. Valentine muttered.

Jason rolled his eyes. "Eve, you've met my parents, Cynthia and Donald."

Jason's mother pursed her lips. "You may call me Mrs. Valentine."

"And you can call me Senator," Jason's father ordered. He looked down at Jason, his grin never wavering, though his eyes were scathingly critical. "What the *hell* was that all about?"

"What was *what* about?"

"Your speech," he hissed through gritted teeth. "Look, every goddamn news station on HV is here, plus half of Congress. They *want* you to *speak—*"

"I don't *care* what they want," Jason growled.

"They're expecting you to fail—"

"*You're* expecting me to fail."

"And you're doing a hell of a job of it."

"What your father is trying to say is that you should try and make an impression," his mother added coolly. "A positive one, preferably."

"Show 'em nothing's changed. Show 'em you're still—"

"*Human?*" Jason interjected. "Is that what you want?"

The senator glanced at the press, trying to keep his smile intact as they observed from afar. "There are a lot of important people here, son. Go *talk to them.*"

"I'll get around to it."

"Are you deliberately trying to humiliate me?"

"I'm actually trying to show my date a good time, something you're making extremely difficult."

Cynthia looked over at Eve, her eyes squinting into a glower. "You're the *tutor,* aren't you?" she asked, her words as toxic as venom. She turned to Jason. "An interesting choice, son. You know, Madison Palmer looks beautiful tonight. It's a shame she's here with her boyfriend."

"What an unfortunate hammer," Jason mumbled under his breath.

Donald grabbed Jason's shoulder and squeezed it tightly, digging in with his fingers. "Mingle. *Now.*"

Jason ripped his shoulder from his father's grasp and stood from his seat, not bothering to hide his frustration. He turned to Eve and extended his hand to her.

"Come on, Eve," he said, still scowling at his father. "Let's mingle."

Eve hurried alongside Jason, making her way through the ballroom and weaving through the swarms of guests. When she looked back over her shoulder, she saw Jason's parents still watching them, their expressions cold and critical.

"God, your folks are *awful.*"

"You remember when you said my parents were assholes? You were right on the money." Jason led Eve to a quiet place in the corner of the ballroom, far from the socialites and politicians that drank and fraternized with one another. He ran his fingers through his hair, his expression heavy and drained. "This whole thing was a terrible idea. I never should've forced you into this. It's not fair to you."

Before Eve could respond, camera flashes popped around them as photographers and reporters inched closer and closer, desperate for a sound bite or shocking photo. Unfortunately, the press wasn't the only nuisance in close proximity—Madison Palmer was also headed their way.

Cynthia was right: Madison looked beautiful, almost angelic, her white, off-the-shoulder gown a complement to her generous breasts and ivory skin. Her golden hair was tied to the side in a low ponytail and fastened with diamond pins to match the lavish diamond necklace that hung across her décolletage. As she sashayed across the floor, she paused to pose for the flashing cameras, then turned to Jason, folding her arms across her chest and squeezing her cleavage.

"Hello, Jason. You're looking awfully tasty in that tux." She glanced at Eve and sneered. "And you, Eve—how *appropriate* of a black sheep to choose a black dress."

Eve rolled her eyes. "Where's your boyfriend? Did he come to his senses and leave?"

Madison pouted. "He's here, just a bit shy, that's all. He's not looking his best and is trying to keep a low profile, because unlike *some* people, *he* has a reputation to uphold. Would you like to meet him?"

"Not especially."

"Lionel, sweetheart," Madison called out. "Come meet the guest of honor and his... *sheep.*"

A tall man with broad shoulders trudged toward them, dragging his feet as if they were bricks hanging from his legs. His suit was distinguished, his tawny hair stylishly gelled, but his hazel eyes were tired, resentful, and bruised. Eve gasped. His face was badly beaten, covered in yellowed contusions and thick scabs, all the way from his heavy brow to the bridge of his broken nose—and even down to his cleft chin.

"Ass Face?"

"*Chin Dimple?*" Jason laughed. "*You're* Lionel Vandeveld?"

Madison glanced back and forth between Jason and her glaring boyfriend. "Have you all met?"

"Never." Jason squinted his eyes and sardonically examined Lionel's injuries. "Wow, someone really went to town on your face."

"Come on Madison, this party's a suckgasm. Let's get the hell out of here," Lionel groused.

"We're *staying*. Get me champagne, *now.*"

Lionel walked off like an obedient puppy with a wounded ego, and Madison turned to Jason, wiggling her hips and flashing a gorgeous white smile.

"Did you see his ring?" She nodded her head in her boyfriend's direction.

Eve looked over at Lionel; a massive diamond ring adorned his pinky finger like a gaudy, miniature dog collar.

"A gift from me to him," Madison gloated. "I treat my men well—did you know that, Jason?"

Jason ignored her, still snickering to himself as he watched Lionel from afar.

"*Jason,*" Madison repeated, "can I speak with you privately?"

"Um," Jason finally tore his eyes from the footballer and glanced at Eve. "I don't know about that—"

"It's okay," Eve reassured, taking a step back. "I'll... mingle."

Jason reluctantly walked off with Madison, glancing back once more at Eve before weaving his way through the crowd of reporters. Eve's eyes darted from side to side: there wasn't a single soul in the entire ballroom who was interested in her company, and so she stood by herself and watched as Jason disappeared from sight.

"You see that? That's Madison Palmer getting what she wants."

Heather made her way to Eve's side and folded her arms, staring at the spot where Jason once stood. Her red hair was tied into a tight, knotted bun at the top of her crown, and her fitted dress was two-toned: a panel of white down the center and two strips of black running along her sides.

Eve sighed. "I don't think so, Heather. You assume the worst in people."

"And you don't? When did that change?"

Eve tried not to meet Heather's gaze, as if such action would render her vulnerable. "I trust him. He hasn't given me a reason not to."

"That's adorable, truly, and you probably have every reason to trust him, but that won't stop Madison. In fact, it'll just fuel her fire. She's only begun to make you suffer."

"And you're just brimming with excitement over the whole thing, aren't you?"

"I am, actually. It'll be like a Shakespearean tragedy, I imagine. I'm absolutely delighted to watch it all unfold." She leaned toward Eve and whispered into her ear.

"You need to remember that, Eve: I *am* watching you. Always."

***

Jason followed Madison through the grand ballroom, trudging behind her until she parked herself behind a marble pillar. She turned to Jason, her face suddenly distraught and consumed with emotion.

"All right," Jason sighed, "what's going on?"

Madison leaned against the pillar, apparently too overcome with feeling to stand on her own. "Have you ever felt like you were in so much pain you just wanted to *die*?"

Jason looked down at his chest—at where his scar sat beneath his clothes—and laughed under his breath. "Madison, do you realize who you're talking to?"

She rolled her eyes. "Oh please, Jason, I'm not talking about the stupid dissection."

"I figured."

"What I meant was, have you ever wanted someone so badly that, I don't know, you could *feel* it? Like, in your chest and in your bones—you *ache* for them. Do you know what I mean?"

Jason didn't respond; instead, he stared out at the party, his eyes scanning the room as if he were searching for someone. For Eve.

Madison's face dropped. "Barf," she groaned. "*Please* don't even bother answering that."

"Look, what's your point?"

"You should be with *me*, Jason."

"God, Madison—"

"We have history, you know. We've known each other since we were kids. We're practically family already."

"Madison, you just introduced me to your *boyfriend*."

"Lionel is replaceable. But you," she tugged at his sleeve, her eyes pleading for attention, "you're one of a kind. And I can learn to look past the revolting scar on your chest. It *is* revolting, isn't it? I mean, I can only assume—"

"Why are you doing this? All of a sudden, after all these years?"

"Because *she doesn't deserve you*."

"Jesus *Christ*—"

"I love you, Jason."

"Madison, you need to stop, okay?"

"But—"

"I don't want you," Jason blurted. "You're shallow, you're mean, and the worst part is, you only want to be with me because you *hate* the fact that I'm with Eve. That's not real, Madison. What you *think* you feel for me—it's a lie."

Madison took a step away from Jason, glaring at him with eyes as piercing as daggers. Her bottom lip quivered, and her fingers clenched with a rage that turned her fair skin a potent shade of red.

"You're a stupid shit-sack, Jason, do you know that? You should *want* me. I'm *Madison Palmer*. And you choose *Eve*? A freakish, Amazonian *whore*?"

Jason stared back at Madison, his gaze lifeless except for the slight curl of his upper lip—the subtle hint of disgust.

"I thought you were better than this," Jason said. "I guess I was wrong."

Jason left Madison by the pillar and ventured back to the party. His eyes darted back and forth until they finally landed on the one person he was searching for. He hurried to Eve's side and wrapped his arm around her waist.

"I'm done mingling," he said. "This party sucks."

"Are you okay?"

"I will be." He tilted his head at the dance floor. "Dance with me?"

Eve nodded, and he led her toward the wooden paneling alongside the string quintet, veering around other couples until they found an empty spot.

Gently, he took her hand and drew her in close, and they swayed slowly to the soft music. Jason watched Eve as they danced and found himself calmed by her presence.

She rested her cheek against his. "Happy birthday," she whispered. "I probably should've said that earlier. Today has been overwhelming, to say the least."

Jason chuckled. "I know the feeling."

"I was in New York this morning."

"Percy took you on the private jet, huh?"

"How did you know?"

"Not his first time pulling a stunt like that, that's for sure." He was quiet for a moment and breathed in deeply, pausing to savor this brief feeling of peace.

"You make me forget—about my parents, about this train wreck of a night, about the Interlopers. You know what to say to take my mind off things."

Eve smirked. "I don't know about that. I've never really had a way with words."

"You're better than you think."

"What I really am is an ass," she said. "I was so preoccupied with flying across the country and hunting for a stupid dress that I didn't even have time to get you a present. I have nothing for you."

"That's not true. You're here—that's all that matters." He hesitated. "Being with you is a gift. Always."

"See, *you're* the one who's good at talking. You're practically a poet, for God's sake—"

"Be my girlfriend."

Eve stopped, frozen in place by his words. She pulled away from him slightly so she could look him in the eye.

"What?"

"I want you to be my girlfriend. And I want you to want it, too." He looked away uncomfortably. "I know this stuff is hard for you, but I want you to feel like it's easy with me—like it's right. Because it feels right to me."

Her breath caught in her chest, her lungs suddenly tight. She stared up at Jason as if she were seeing him for the first time. His eyes were cast off to the side, his face stressed yet kind—he always seemed so warm to her, no matter the situation—and even though her body felt hot and weak, her thoughts were simple.

"Okay."

"Okay what?"

"I'll be your girlfriend."

His eyes shot back toward hers. "You will?"

"I will."

"You sound certain."

"I am."

He smiled, running his fingers through her hair and sending shivers down her spine. He cupped her cheek and brought his lips close to hers, lingering for just a second before dipping his chin and—

He stopped, distracted by the sound of cameras flashing and guests murmuring, all of them staring at the couple without a hint of subtlety.

"People are watching," Jason said.

Eve leaned into him. "I'm starting to care a little bit less about that."

Jason closed his eyes and kissed her, his lips like an electric shock that revitalized every sense in her body. Eve ran her hands up his chest to the back of his neck, holding him tightly and relishing the moment. She opened her eyes, and for a second she thought she saw fireworks, but quickly realized it was the flashing cameras. She almost didn't even mind, and Jason hardly seemed to notice.

His eyes lit up. "I have to get you something."

"What?" she asked, perplexed. "No, no you don't."

"Of course I do. You're my girlfriend now."

"Jason, it's *your* birthday, not mine—"

"Flowers," he interrupted. "It's not official until there are flowers."

Jason pointed his wrist toward their dining table not too far from the dance floor. A single, white, long-stemmed rose floated from the center vase and sailed through the air, drifting above the dance floor, then landing in Jason's hand.

The sound of horrified gasps and shrieks echoed through the ballroom; guests jumped from their seats, their faces twisted with repulsion and offense, and the quintet dropped their instruments, which clanged loudly against the floor. Reporters immediately swarmed the two chimeras, and Eve shielded her eyes from the blinding lights of their cameras, but even in the midst of such chaos she could still see the hundreds of wide, petrified eyes that stared back at her, consumed with terror.

Jason's father tore through the throng of photographers and charged toward them, his wife trailing right behind him. No longer did he emanate poise or dignity; he displayed no charming grin, no pleasant façade. All that was left was pure, unadulterated rage.

"*WHAT IN GOD'S NAME DO YOU THINK YOU'RE DOING?*"

"Dad—"

"Don't you *dare* call me that! You are *no* son of mine!" the senator snarled.

"Do you understand the severity of what you've just done?" Cynthia cried.

"What I've *done*?" Jason repeated, scornfully. "You mean using my gift? *My* gift? Being *who I am*? I'm a *chimera*, Mom. Whether you like it or not, I will *always* be a chimera!"

Donald pointed a trembling finger at Eve. "This is *her* fault," he growled. "She's a bad influence on you. You would've *never* behaved this way before."

"Is that so?" Jason sneered. "And how the *hell* would you know?"

"*Excuse me?*"

"WE DON'T KNOW EACH OTHER," Jason barked. "You are a *stranger* to me. Hell, you didn't even come to see me when I was in the *hospital*—"

"You know very well that was—"

"BULLSHIT, Dad. That was *bullshit*."

"Don't try to make this about *me*—"

"It's *always* about you. You and your precious *image*." Jason backed away, glaring at his father. "You're right, I'm not your son. Not anymore." He turned to Eve. "Come on, let's get the hell out of here."

Before Eve could follow him, someone grabbed at her wrist and yanked her back to the dance floor. She turned to see Donald Valentine's distraught face.

"For God's sake, talk some *sense* into the boy."

Eve stared back at him—at his clammy skin and panicked eyes—and ripped her forearm from his grasp.

"I'm sorry, I thought I was a bad influence, *Senator*."

She pushed past him and shoved her way through the horde of reporters, ignoring Madison's and Lionel's shocked faces and Heather's Cheshire grin as she hurried for the doorway. Jason was waiting for her at the end of the hall, angrily pacing in front of the elevator doors.

"Jason?" she stammered. "*Jason*. Where are we going?"

He looked at her, his eyes suddenly wide and energized, almost hopeful.

"To the Meltdown."

They walked for nearly an hour, arriving at the Pier Lorent Hotel just as the sky faded from purple to black. The hotel stood like a beam of light in the darkness, its white walls and blue windows sparkling with newness, though Eve and Jason were hardly interested, their sights fixed on the alley-way across the street. They hurried across the road hand in hand, dodging honking cars and laughing like children until they reached the sidewalk and ventured into the alley.

The air felt thick and damp, as if stifled between the two buildings, and the deeper they headed into the narrow passage, the darker their surroundings became. It couldn't be much farther, and so they continued forward, trekking past rows of reeking dumpsters, stumbling through puddles of God knows what, and all the while keeping their eyes open for anything that resembled the entrance to a nightclub.

"Lost?"

Eve jumped, caught off guard. She glanced from side to side, searching for the source of the voice, but no one could be found.

"Down here."

The voice seemed to be coming from the ground, though it couldn't be so. Eve's eyes darted across the brick wall of the neighboring building and down to the floor, and then she spotted it: an opening at the foot of the building, practically hidden in the darkness. She crouched beside the hole, which she soon discovered was the entrance to a cement stairwell, and peered down at the foot of the stairs, where two bouncers stood in front of a heavy black door.

"When Percy said the Meltdown was an underground club, I didn't realize he *literally* meant underground," Jason chuckled.

"You looking for the Meltdown?" One of the bouncers cocked his head at the door. "You found it."

Eve and Jason headed down the stairs, ducking their heads to clear the low ceiling, and apprehensively examined the grimy surroundings.

"Looks structurally sound," Eve mumbled, sarcastically.

"The goal is secrecy—seclusion from protestors." The first bouncer, thick and muscular with dark skin and a heavy brow, eyed the chimeras critically. "Aren't you two a little overdressed?"

"Save it," said the second bouncer, a smaller man with multiple piercings. "They're not the first ones to show up looking like this." He shoved his hand forward. "IDs. Now."

Jason and Eve fished their driver's licenses from their pockets and tossed them into the man's palm. He stared at the small photos for a split second and immediately did a double take.

"Holy shit, you're Jason Valentine!"

"I *knew* you looked familiar!" the first bouncer chimed in.

"Looks like we've got a celebrity in the flesh. And it's your twenty-first birthday. Well, you've come to the right place."

He flipped over to Eve's license, glancing back and forth between her and the thick piece of plastic. After a few moments, he let out a loud, irritated sigh.

"'Fraid I have bad news: I can't let you in, not with her."

"Why not?" Jason asked.

"She's not twenty-one. Didn't even think to bring a fake ID?"

"Why does it matter anyway? Neither of us can get drunk," Eve added.

"Rules are rules. Can't have anyone underage in the club, even if they're a chimera. Sorry Miss Kingston, but you've got to go."

"Hold on," the larger bouncer interrupted. "Your name's *Kingston?*"

Eve hesitated. "Yes?"

"*Evelyn* Kingston?"

"How do you know my name?"

"I'm from San Francisco."

Eve felt her stomach drop like a bag of cinderblocks. It was inevitable—she had known a moment like this was bound to happen—but did it have to be tonight of all nights? The bouncer stared back at her, his eyes quizzical, and then, after a long, agonizing silence, he yanked open the door, unleashing the suppressed sound of thundering music and the strange stench of sweat, candy, and sex.

"What are you doing?" the smaller bouncer hissed.

"Letting her in."

"But—"

"You think *he's* a celebrity? Well, *she's* a legend." He glanced back at Eve and Jason and offered them a wink. "Have fun, you two."

Eve gazed curiously at the bouncer, but only for a moment, as Jason quickly pulled her into the club, eager to get inside before the bouncers changed their minds.

The door slammed behind them, shaking the ground and sending dust falling from the cracks in the ceiling. Eve and Jason glanced at one another and then at the long, dark corridor in front of them. Far into the distance, they could faintly make out a flicker of pink and purple lights pulsing with the beat of the music. With apprehension, they made their way down the corridor, going deeper into the building where the air became ripe and stale. The music grew louder, and as the passageway finally ended, Eve and Jason found themselves immersed in bright, streaming lights.

They were standing at the top of a rusted spiral staircase that plunged deep underground, leading to the pit of a massive, concrete warehouse. Eve could feel the stairs vibrate with each thump of the bass. She peered down over the side, where an ocean of bodies, some chimeras and some human sympathizers, surged and swelled, dancing and drinking and doing whatever else they pleased.

Eve and Jason climbed down the stairs, spiraling in dizzying circles until they finally reached the dance floor. To their left was a somewhat neglected bar with a lone bartender leaning against his vintage register, bored and aloof as he stared at his nails. A sign hung above his head—*Water: Seven Dollars, Soda: Ten Dollars, Beer and Alcohol: One Dollar*—a pricing system that would be preposterous at any other establishment, but not at a chimera club. At the back of the room sat a makeshift wooden stage, swarmed by people who watched the performers in awe. A seven-piece band was playing, though each musician seemed to look surprisingly like the next one, and Eve soon realized that the band was actually only one man reflected into multiple holograms, each one fading in and out of view based on its relevance to the performance.

"My little deviants!"

Percy charged toward the couple and wrapped his arms around them, nearly spilling his tequila shots onto their clothes. He laughed and gave them each a big, wet kiss on the cheek. "You came! This sure as hell beats your boring-ass party, huh?"

Jason smirked. "I wouldn't say the party was *boring*—"

"Well, this is better, trust me."

They stared out at the throng of bodies—at the profusely sweaty humans and the boundlessly energetic chimeras—and gawked at their outlandish ensembles. Everyone seemed to wear the same minimalist clothing in ripped denim, leather, and latex, if they wore anything at all, as the vast majority were practically nude. Mini-skirts, bathing suits, shorts, and thongs were the ensemble of choice for both men and women, and breasts and butt cheeks were plainly visible throughout the club. Percy turned to his friends and laughed.

"Looks like we're the best-dressed folks here. I win top honors, of course, but you two take a close second and third."

Jason smiled. "I don't know, Eve looks pretty spectacular."

"You should see her in her underwear, if you haven't already," Percy added.

"Wait, *what?*"

"No questions. You didn't come here to talk, did you?" Percy downed his shots and tossed the glasses behind him before pulling his two friends onto the dance floor. "I'd offer you a drink, but that would just be a waste."

Eve noticed a long red ribbon hanging from Percy's neck, tied into a sloppy bow. Another ribbon, this one yellow, was tied across his wrist, and three more in pink, orange, and blue were wrapped around the arm of his white jacket.

"Hey Percy," Eve yelled over the music, "what's with the bows?"

"It's called gift-wrap. It's the gimmick of the chimera club scene. You're free to melt here, and if you impress someone with a trick, they give you a ribbon."

"So why do you have so many? You can't melt."

"I may not have the gift, but I still have plenty of tricks, if you know what I mean." He smirked, stumbling drunkenly to his side and nearly crashing into a shirtless woman. "Hey, when you blow this joint, do you think I could ride back with you guys? I tried checking in at the Pier Lorent, but the front desk troll said there wasn't a *single* room available. I told her money was no object. I even threw out the whole 'Don't you know who I am?' spiel, and still no dice. Either that place is the hottest spot in SoCal, or that lady was full of more shit than a public toilet."

Jason shrugged. "We walked here."

"You two are useless, did you know that?" Something caught his eye, and he nodded at the crowd. "Look."

A group had formed beside them, all circling one man; he was skinny and feeble, with his balls practically hanging out of his skimpy shorts, but his arms and neck were covered in ribbons, laced across his body like rows of rainbows. As Eve looked on, the man stared at a penny resting in his hand, his eyes lazy and relaxed; slowly, the penny levitated from his palm, gliding through the air and floating high above the crowd until it disappeared somewhere in the warehouse. His audience applauded excitedly and tied their ribbons across his already-decorated arms.

"You two would smoke that hammer," Percy scoffed. "Look at him with his damn penny. What a joke."

Eve was hardly concerned with the level of talent in the room and simply watched as other chimeras melted shot glasses and jewelry and maybe even the occasional shoe if they were especially daring. After a moment of quiet observation, she felt herself smiling. There was a place for people like her, however tacky and rundown it may be—a place where her gift was seen as a good thing. An actual *gift*.

Jason approached her from behind, sliding his hand down her neck, across her shoulder and around her waist. He whispered into her ear. "You want to dance?"

They nudged their way through the mass of people as Percy trailed closely behind, his focus split between them and whoever else caught his attention. They picked a spot—just a slight opening in the crowd, hardly room for one, let alone three—and began dancing with the rest of the misfits, their bodies pressed against one another as they swayed to the pulsing sound. The purple and pink lights shined through the crowd, illuminating each and every dancer with the same fluorescent glow until the horde of bodies blended together into one massive, growing life form.

Percy coolly bobbed his head as he danced alongside a beautiful man with a chiseled build. Eve looked up at Jason who stared back at her with caring eyes; he reached into his jacket and pulled out the rose from his party, now flattened.

"I believe this is yours." He looked at it and laughed. "It's seen better days."

She plucked the rose from his fingers, broke it at the stem, and placed it behind her ear. "It's beautiful," she smiled.

Jason wrapped his arms around her, bringing her close and dragging his fingers down the center of her back. He leaned into her, his lips brushing against hers until—

"Jason Valentine?"

Eve pulled away, her cheeks flushed with embarrassment. A portly man with a round belly and an ear-to-ear grin had approached them.

"Sorry, I wasn't trying to... er, interrupt. You're Jason Valentine, right?" Jason nodded. "Yes, that's me."

"I *knew* it!" the man shouted, gleefully. "I *knew* it was you!" He grabbed Jason's hand and shook it vigorously. "It's an absolute honor to meet you."

"Pleasure's all mine, I'm sure," Jason chuckled.

Soon the man was joined by other patrons—friends of his or strangers, Eve wasn't sure, but one by one they encircled Jason, their eyes large and curious.

"I've never met a celebrity before," the man continued.

"I'm not a—"

"And you're here in a tux, like a true superstar. God, I feel so underdressed."

"Actually, I was at my—"

"Mr. Valentine, it would mean the *world* to me if you'd melt for me."

Jason hesitated. "Oh, I don't know—"

"*Please*," the man pleaded. "I think everyone here's dying to see it."

The other spectators chimed in, nodding their heads in agreement and slapping Jason across the back as if they were old buddies. Percy ruffled Jason's hair.

"Give the public what they want, *Mr.* Valentine."

Jason smiled bashfully. He stared at his newest fan, calming his senses within a fraction of a second. With a cock of his head, he sent the man floating smoothly into the air, his feet dangling as he spun in soft, fluid circles until he was high above the crowd. The man's eyes bulged and he laughed aloud, over-joyed by his sudden flight, the absolute most impressive melt the Meltdown had ever been exposed to.

"My *God*," he cried. "This is AMAZING!"

The horde cheered; many tossed ribbons in Jason's direction while oth-ers scuttled toward him and tied them along his arms. Jason turned to Eve; he was illuminated with a fire she hadn't seen since their tutoring sessions together.

"If you guys want to see something *really* amazing, you have to see what my girlfriend can do."

"*Girlfriend?* God, I missed a lot when I left that party," Percy muttered.

Jason grabbed Eve's hand. "Do it, Eve. You deserve to show people just how powerful you are—how good you are at what you do. You deserve to be celebrated."

Eve looked at Jason, at Percy, at the countless other faces that watched her with intrigue. No one here knew who she was. That's exactly what she had always wanted, after all—to be anonymous and unimportant. Here was a room filled with people who, for once, saw her as nothing more than Jason's girlfriend—the tall, spindly girl who was incredibly overdressed for an under-ground warehouse club. She could keep that image, hold on to it like it was all she had, and relish her fleeting affair with secrecy. Or, for once, she could be *somebody*—be who she truly was.

The decision was easier than she had expected. She lifted her hands—only slightly, just at the wrists—and her vision faded from purple and pink to black. One by one, the people in front of her began to levitate, their feet slowly leaving the ground and hovering above the floor. One body, seven bodies, twenty-seven, thirty-five—she sent everyone in her line of vision rising higher into the air like colorful angels flying up to the ceiling. They cried out in awe; some wore silent tears of joy, others shrieked with excitement. Soon, nearly the entire club was floating high above the ground, and Eve watched from below as hundreds of ribbons in every color of the rainbow fell around her. She ran her hand along the floor and picked up the ribbons —gifts from the misfits just like her.

Jason rested his cheek against hers. "They love you."

"Not everyone." Percy pointed across the dance floor. "Looks like you've got a hater."

The floor was nearly empty, thanks to Eve; only a few patrons remained standing, their gazes fixed on the bodies floating above them. Yet one man seemed to have no interest in the floating crowd—he was, instead, staring directly at Eve. He was tall and thin, cleanly dressed in a black fitted shirt and tie, and his eyes expressed a searing glare that sent a shudder of dread running through Eve. She tried to ignore him, but for whatever reason, she couldn't help but study his rigid jaw, his stoic frame, and the beads of sweat forming along his hairline.

"What a creeptastic flesh stick. That's an evil eye if I ever saw one—he could rival the kids at Billington, I'm sure," Percy quipped. "And *damn* is that boy sweaty."

Eve choked. "Oh God."

Jason grabbed her wrist, his face frozen with fear. "Put them down, Eve."

"If I put them down, we'll lose him—"

"What are you guys talking about?" Percy asked.

Her breath caught short as she stumbled over the words.

"He's an Interloper."

"SHIT—"

"Put them down *right now*," Jason repeated.

The patrons floated slowly down to the floor, blocking Eve's view of her latest foe. They crowded around her, showering her with words of praise, desperate to meet or even just to touch the most powerful chimera they had ever seen.

"You need to leave," Jason shouted, frantically pleading with the crowd. "You have to get out of here, *NOW!*"

Eve strained to see over the mass of people, but it was no use; they grabbed adoringly at her wrists and dress and hair, pushing her farther and farther away from the man she was so desperately searching for.

"YOU'RE NOT SAFE!" Jason yelled. "YOU HAVE TO LEAVE!"

"He's gone," Eve cried, her voice laced with panic. "I can't see him!"

A shrill scream sounded in the back of the club, followed by a loud rumble—the sound of running, of terrified patrons stampeding toward the stairs. People shoved past one another, fighting their way through the horde, a mass of tangled limbs pressing urgently toward the exit.

Boom. The ground shook, and dust spilled from the ceiling. Then another boom, louder and heavier than the one before. Eve braced herself, standing firm as patrons jostled her, waiting for the inevitable to come. Finally, she saw it—the massive wings that spread high above the crowd, the thrashing talons, the large, inky eyes that stared at her, and her alone. With a long, guttural roar, the Interloper charged straight toward her.

"EVERYONE, OUT OF THE WAY!" Eve commanded. "*NOW!*"

She thrust her arms forward and melted the creature, slamming him into the concrete wall like a massive, flailing wrecking ball. The Interloper toppled to the floor, falling to his knees and struggling to regain his balance.

Eve knew there wasn't much time. She hoisted up the skirt of her dress, fumbling with the fabric until she found the gun she had strapped to her thigh. She looked up at the creature, who was now staring back at her, wearing a sinister smile that made her blood run cold. She pointed the gun and fired, aiming directly at his silver teeth, the needles spilling from his mouth and clanging to the floor. The alien staggered backward and let out a primal howl, and with one quick swoop, he whipped his immense wing forward, knocking Eve, and her firearm, to the floor.

Jason reacted immediately, melting the Interloper from the ground and pounding him against the wall, ramming the creature's back into the surface until mustard-colored fluid oozed from his flesh. Jason channeled his power again and flung the alien across the warehouse, slamming him into the bar countertop and sending broken glass flying across the room like shrapnel.

Just as he fell deeper into his melt, Jason felt a tug at his wrist. He looked over to see Eve pulling herself from the floor, her lip bloody and eyes panicked.

"Don't," she pleaded. "You have to stop."

"Why?"

She pointed to the Interloper as he stumbled from the bar. Attached to the back of his head was a small, metallic device with a glowing blue button.

"The beacon. We need it. We can't risk it getting destroyed."

Just as the words left her lips, the Interloper shot up into the air, beating his wings and hopping from wall to wall, his movements sharp and erratic. Suddenly, he bolted down to the ground once more and grabbed Jason's shoulders with his clawed feet, yanking his body from the floor and dragging him up toward the ceiling. Eve cried out in horror as she watched them soar overhead, and she screamed again when the creature released his hold on Jason, sending him tumbling downward.

Jason's arms flailed as he fell, but before Eve could act, his hand found the staircase railing and held on—just barely—stopping his descent. A swarm of patrons immediately raced to his aid, working together to hoist him over the banister and onto the safety of the steps, while the Interloper continued to fly through the air, eyeing the happenings below.

Eve turned to Percy. "We need to get him grounded."

Percy reached into his coat pocket and grabbed his pistol. His eyes panned over the room, finally landing on Eve's gun, which sat in a pile of rubble in the corner. He smirked.

"I'm on it."

With one fluid movement, Percy slid across the concrete and plucked Eve's gun from the floor, swiftly pivoting in place before firing a torrent of bullets straight through the creature's wings. The alien flapped uncontrollably, desperate to remain in the air, but buckled in the relentless hail of gunfire and plummeted to the ground in a messy heap.

The Interloper stumbled to his feet, shaking the bullets from his flesh before turning to Percy, his eyes fierce with loathing. With a grunt, he lunged at his new target, whipping his talons back and forth, but Percy ducked beneath his swinging arms and pistol-whipped his foe across his face. The Interloper lurched to the side and, with an irritated glare, struck Percy in the jaw, sending him flying.

Eve's eyes darted to Percy—he was conscious at least, pulling himself from the ground and realigning his jaw—and then she looked back to the beacon. She bit her lip, kicked off her heels and frantically hiked her dress up her legs.

"What the hell are you *doing*?" Jason yelled, fighting his way down the staircase to the warehouse floor.

Eve took a deep breath. "I'm getting that damn beacon." She glanced at Jason. "Don't kill him until I say so."

Before Jason could object, Eve pounced on the Interloper from behind, wrapping herself tightly around his neck and waist. The creature howled and thrashed his arms, desperate to shake her from his body, and in a fit of rage he plowed across the floor and leapt onto the wall, nearly trampling Jason and Percy in the process. He scaled the concrete surface, digging his claws into the cement until he had reached the ceiling, and even then he clambered onto the rafters, where he hung upside down high above the club, Eve still clinging desperately to his back.

Eve's breathing became shallow; she could feel the blood rushing to her head, and her fingers were slipping down the alien's slick skin. The floor was easily four stories beneath her, and chimera or not, a drop like that would kill her.

The entire room gasped as the alien expanded his tattered wings, pushing Eve's legs from his body and sending her wildly swinging from his neck. She dug her nails deep into his throat, ripping at his skin until yellow blood oozed between her fingers and dripped down her arms, making her grip that much more tenuous. Her hands were slipping, faster now; she tried to adjust her grip, but the creature shook, and her fingers could hold on no longer—

Eve fell.

The patrons screamed in terror as Eve plummeted toward the ground. The nightclub whirled in her vision as the hard floor raced up to meet her.

Then suddenly, she stopped. Eve glanced from side to side, expecting to find herself in a bloody pile on the floor, but instead she was suspended in midair, floating twenty feet above the ground as if caught in an invisible net. She looked below her and saw Jason's face, his eyes wide and petrified.

"I got you," he said, his voice wavering. "I got you."

A roar sounded beside her—the Interloper was climbing down the wall, his talons scraping at the concrete and sending rubble spraying across the room. He dropped to the ground, landing on his feet with a quaking boom, and immediately set his sights on Jason and Percy. Percy raised his guns, but Jason stopped him, pointing briefly at the beacon, and they braced themselves as the creature barreled in their direction.

Eve's heart pounded in her chest. "TAKE ME TO HIM, NOW!"

She torpedoed toward the ground and collided with the Interloper's back, sending the beast stumbling forward, his face slamming into the floor. Eve wrapped her limbs around the Interloper as she had before, shimmying up his body and heading straight for the glowing beacon.

The Interloper reacted quickly; he pounced to his feet and scrambled to the wall yet again, and Eve knew it was only a matter of time before they were hanging from the ceiling once more. She climbed up the creature's back and yanked at the beacon, only to find that it was stuck, attached to his head almost as if it were a part of his body. The Interloper flailed and pulsed his wings, trying to break Eve's hold; and just as had happened only moments before, one leg slipped, and then the other, and the only grip she had was one arm around the alien's neck and one hand that tugged at the device.

Eve clawed at the beacon, her nails digging into the flesh beneath, the muscles in her arm screaming from the force of the effort. Gritting her teeth, she mustered one last surge of strength, and pulled.

With a bloody rip, the beacon tore loose from the creature's skull, bringing with it a thick chunk of grey flesh and a flood of pus. The alien let out a piercing shriek, and Eve released her grasp, falling to the floor below, landing on her back with a painful thud.

But she had the beacon.

"DO IT!" she screamed. "KILL HIM!"

Jason melted instantly, pulling the Interloper from the wall and sending him pounding against the opposite side of the warehouse. Again he bashed the alien into the wall, cracking the foundation as dust billowed over the ground below. Finally, Jason sent the creature hurtling up toward the ceiling. For a moment, he left him there, floating limply, looking down on the tiny, though far from feeble, chimeras beneath him. Then, with all of the power he could summon, Jason thrust the alien to the ground, blasting him downward at incredible speed, sending him crashing directly into the concrete floor.

The entire warehouse was still, enveloped in a cloud of dust that floated from the ceiling and hung in the air. A handful of patrons were frozen on the staircase, clutching one another, struggling to catch their breath. Percy stood in the center of the club, wiping the blood from his brow, and Jason stared at the fallen creature with fixed, hateful eyes.

It was Eve who ended the stillness. She hoisted herself from the ground, dusting the dirt from her ruined gown, and hobbled to the alien's side. Its body was limp—bones jutted from its flesh, and yellow blood oozed from each contusion onto the floor—and Eve knew without a doubt that the creature was dead. She knelt down beside him, running her fingers through the debris until she found what she was looking for: her white rose, now grey and filthy. She placed it in her hand next to the glowing beacon and stared at the destruction before her.

The club began to stir just the slightest bit. Jason rushed to Eve's side, scooping her up in his arms and squeezing her tightly. Eve gaped at the lumps of concrete, the broken glass, the pools of yellow blood, and then she saw it—something out of place. She pulled away from Jason's grasp and crouched down, tugging a single piece of parchment out from beneath the Interloper's body.

"Oh my God."

"What?" Jason asked. "What is it?"

Eve read and reread the calligraphy, but no matter how much she wished it would change, the raised, embossed characters remained the same:

A Night Best Spent in Black and White.

"He was at your party, Jason. He followed us here."

CHAPTER 12: FLORENZA GALLO

Eve slapped the beacon down on the kitchen counter.

"Here you go," she muttered. "Have at it."

JJ stared wide-eyed at the device; she gracefully picked it up and examined the intricacies of its design.

"You *actually* got one!" she gasped. "How the *hell* did you manage that?"

Eve rolled her eyes. "An Interloper fell into our lap."

The entire group had agreed to reconvene in Percy's suite the day following Jason's birthday disaster. They all huddled around the kitchen counter: Percy sipped his Bloody Mary and cursed his hangover, JJ stared in awe at the beacon while Sancho stared in awe at JJ, and Eve sat beside Jason, still struggling to digest the chaos from the night before.

"Can you work it?" Sancho asked. "Can you figure out how it functions?"

"Of course I can, don't be stupid," JJ scoffed. "There's a reason I'm wanted in four countries. I worked hard for my bad reputation."

"Speaking of bad reputations..."

Percy slid his scratchpad in front of Jason. A digital magazine graced the screen, splashed with the headline *CHIMERA LOSES CONTROL* and accompanied by a photo of Jason, his arms wrapped around Eve as a single rose hovered in the air.

"Congratulations, Jason, you've officially graduated from newspapers to tabloids." Percy smirked and flipped through the pages. "Once you become gossip fodder, you *know* you've made it to the big leagues."

Jason shook his head. "I don't need to read this garbage."

"You sure? Because I've got at least thirty others to show you."

"It's not so bad," Eve added. "Really, it could be a lot worse."

"I don't know, man—you melted in public." Percy raised his eyebrows. "That's pretty damn gutsy. Maybe you're not as big of a boy scout as I thought."

"Can we just drop this?" Jason moaned.

"No way, this is too juicy to pass up!" Percy snatched his scratchpad and began reading from the article. "'The entire night, the senator's son appeared uninterested, disenchanted, and aloof,'" he read aloud. "God, Jason, they make you sound like a real ass."

"I'd be *aloof* too if my parents were such hammers," Sancho teased.

"'Valentine committed several bold acts of rebellion, including open displays of affection with an unnamed woman and public use of his gift for the entire party to witness. Guests were reportedly shocked and disturbed, speculating that his recent emergence may have warped his sense of decency.'" He laughed. "Hey Eve, at least you've been promoted from '*Chimera Bitch*' to '*Unnamed Woman*.' That's an improvement."

"Okay, Percy, you've had your laugh. I think we're done now," Jason mumbled.

"'Chimera repression activists theorize that his melting of a single long-stemmed rose was part of a ritualistic mating call, thus symbolizing his desire to copulate with his dancing partner—'"

"*Enough.*"

"Later in the night, Valentine, the unnamed woman, and their unbelievably attractive associate saved a packed nightclub from a savage, violent alien."

The entire group turned to look at Percy, their faces twisted with skepticism.

"Okay, it doesn't really say that, but it should."

Eve sighed. "This is terrible."

"I know! Not a single article mentions me once!"

Again, the group stared at Percy in silence.

"What? What did I say?"

"Look, we killed another Interloper, and we have a beacon," Jason said, eager to change the subject. "Let's just count last night as a success and move on."

"We also know why the Interlopers disappeared for so long," Eve added. "They were waiting for your birthday party. Probably knew we'd both be there and figured it was the perfect time to attack."

Sancho pouted and slumped in his chair. "Some of us missed all the action..."

"For God's sake, Sancho, let it go," Jason groaned.

Percy took a swig of his drink. "Man, talk about a killer guest list, right?"

"No kidding," Eve scoffed. "The world's worst parents, an army of press, and on top of all that, a goddamn *alien.*"

"You're forgetting about our favorite homicidal heiress, Madison Palmer."

Eve cringed; the name alone sent her body stiff with discomfort.

"Has she mentioned anything?" Sancho asked, poking Eve in the ribs. "You know, about the death threat?"

"Not specifically," Eve muttered. "But I did speak with her before the party."

"What did she say?"

"That she wants my *head.*"

"And you're still rooming with her?" JJ tore her eyes from the beacon long enough to cast a critical stare in Eve's direction. "How do you sleep at night?"

Percy chuckled. "With one eye open, I'm sure."

"She's irrelevant," Eve grumbled. "Just a thorn in my side."

"A crazy thorn with murderous tendencies," Percy corrected.

"She probably already has a lock of your hair hidden in her purse," JJ added.

"And an Evelyn Kingston voodoo doll—"

"I SAID she's *irrelevant.*"

Eve stopped herself. Her words were bitter, *too* bitter, and her cheeks reddened with chagrin. She gazed down at the palms of her hands, but instead of her olive skin, she saw piles of ash sifting through her fingers. She quickly shook the image from her mind and glanced at the others, only to see that they were all staring at her. She cleared her throat and turned to JJ.

"How quickly can you get the beacon working?"

"Hell if I know. It *is* an alien device, after all."

Eve bit her bottom lip. "Fine. Let us know when there's progress." She nodded at the others. "Until then, we stay armed. We stay prepared." She fiddled with her fingernails and let out an aggravated sigh. "Look, I have to go."

"Me too," Sancho added. "I've got that project to finish up."

"All right then, meeting's adjourned." Percy eagerly filed toward the door and swung it open. "Now get your asses out of my dorm. I have a hangover to nurse and an afternoon nap to take."

The door slammed shut behind Eve and the others. JJ scuttled down the hallway with Sancho trailing behind her, leaving Eve and Jason alone in the middle of the corridor. She could feel him waiting by her side, and though she sensed there was something on his mind, she remained silent.

"You don't have to pretend that Madison doesn't bother you," he whispered.

"She doesn't."

"She does." He turned to face her. "I can talk to her."

"*Don't*," Eve insisted. "I'll handle it."

"You can stay with me and Sancho—"

"Jason, I'm not scared of her."

Jason sighed. "Look, just tell me what you need."

She looked up at him—his eyes were warm and caring, pleading for her to be the slightest bit forthcoming—but she forced a transparent smile.

"What I *need* is a shower."

Eve hurried down the hallway to the elevators, leaving Jason standing in front of Percy's dorm room. A shower *did* sound refreshing, possibly even cathartic, a chance to wash away her anxieties, to clean her body of tension and worry—and thick, black ash. She groaned. The words *DIE CHIME* flashed before her once again, forever on her mind, just as Jason had feared.

When she reached the washroom on her floor, she angrily shoved open the silver doors and stomped past the shower stalls. The room was empty, with only the sound of a dripping faucet to accompany her, and she welcomed the seclusion. With a relieved sigh, she plopped her belongings onto the center bench and shimmied her hooded sweater from her shoulders, adjusting her shirt at the hemline.

She stopped herself. The room had suddenly become warm, stale, and full. She wasn't alone. Eve lowered her shoulders and slowly turned toward the doors behind her.

Madison stood by the entrance, her arms folded and her lips pursed into the nastiest scowl Eve had ever seen. Hayden stood by her side, mimicking Madison's body language with her chin held high and her eyes bright with excitement. Seven other Rutherfordian girls hovered around the pair—girls Eve had seen many times before, loathing her from afar. All told, nine girls stood before her, a line of soldiers with hate in their eyes. She was being ambushed.

"Wow," Eve muttered. "You're certainly taking a page out of your boyfriend's playbook, aren't you?"

Madison ignored the remark. "I heard you and Jason are official now."

"We are. Maybe sometime we can double date."

"You think you're so damn cute, don't you?" Madison spat, approaching Eve and leaning her neck forward. "But what you don't realize is that Jason just feels *sorry* for you. You're cute like an injured puppy is cute—pathetic and sad."

Eve forced a smirk. "I happen to like puppies, injured or not."

"You're an impoverished *orphan*. You shouldn't feel so good about that."

Eve's chest became hot, as if suddenly lit with a flame. She cocked her head. "And what about you, Madison? Are you *proud* of yourself?"

"Oh *absolutely*, because unlike you, I don't drag people down in the gutter. You're Jason's girlfriend for, what? Thirty seconds? And already he turns into a complete embarrassment?" Madison leaned in close to Eve, her blue eyes like shards of glass as sharp as her words. "You're like sewage, Eve. Everything you touch turns to *shit*."

"So, that's it. This is all about Jason? Everything you've said, everything you've *done* to me, is because of him?" Eve stared back at her foe, looking deep into her eyes as if searching for something. "I just don't buy it."

"No, Eve, this is about *you*. This is about how much I *hate* you. I hate your ugly face, your cheap clothes, your stupid comebacks, and your god-awful presence. Everything. You and your kind can all go straight to *hell*."

Eve glanced at the other girls for the first time since their ambush began. They glared at her, fueled by an animosity Eve had long since grown accustomed to. She turned her gaze back to Madison, and her body tightened with repugnance and hate. Her vision became foggy, her mind slowly engulfed by a pulsing blackness—

She blinked, and her vision cleared. Madison stood in front of her, her perfectly glossed lips quivering with rage. Eve turned, weaving through the Rutherfordian girls as she headed for the door.

"We're done here."

"Running away?" Madison sneered. "Are you afraid? You should be, you know. I told you I would make your life miserable." She lunged forward, hovering behind Eve like a shadow. "I keep my promises, Eve. I will *destroy* you."

Eve lingered by the door, turning to look at her nemesis once more. "I see you, Madison. I see who you really are."

"Well I can see you too, and you're nothing but a worthless *CHIME*—"

Darkness surged through Eve in an instant. The group of girls shrieked as Madison's body flew across the room and slammed against the back wall. Eve's lungs heaved, her entire being immersed in a power that radiated through her like heat. The other girls scattered to the sides of the room, nearly tripping over one another as they clung to the shower curtains and porcelain sinks. Eve paid no attention to them; all she could see was a swelling black-ness—and the blond Rutherfordian helplessly pinned to the tile wall. She charged forward and thrust her red, furious face just inches from Madison's.

"Did you really think I wouldn't *find out*?" she hissed, bringing her face in even closer. " You're not so good at hiding *secrets*, Madison."

Madison's jaw dropped open and her eyes widened with horror. There was nothing left to be said; her expression was the only confirmation Eve needed. In that moment, Madison's face had spoken more truth than her lips ever had.

Eve ended her melt, sending the heiress tumbling to the floor and scram-bling into a ball at Eve's feet. As the rage inside of her waned, Eve bolted for the silver doors, stopping for just a second to look back at her roommate.

"Never underestimate your enemy," she growled. "My combat professor taught me that. And you know what? I haven't lost a fight since."

***

"WAKE UP!"

Sancho pounced atop Eve's sleeping body, jolting her awake.

"Sancho!" she barked, pushing him from her bed and onto the floor. "What the *hell* do you think you're doing?"

"You've got to come, *quickly—*"

"How'd you even get in here? I always keep the door locked."

"I picked it open."

"Where'd you learn to do that?"

"Jason taught me."

"*Jason* taught you?" She scowled. "You know, you could've just knocked."

"I know, I'm sorry, it's just all so exciting—"

"*What's* exciting?"

"The *beacon*," he yelped, nearly bouncing with glee. "JJ's done it! She got it working!"

Suddenly, Eve's entire being buzzed with energy. It had been nearly two weeks since they had found the beacon, and the wait for progress had felt agonizingly slow. JJ had locked herself in her dorm room, skipping classes and avoiding all human contact, slaving away over the alien device. Now, finally, a development. And deep in her gut, Eve knew that everything was about to change.

"It works?"

"*Yes*, Eve!" Sancho yanked her from the mattress and tripped over the sheets that had spilled onto the floor. "That's why you need to get up! We've got work to do!"

"All right, all right, but can I at least brush my teeth?"

"*No.*"

She folded her arms. "Can I get dressed?"

Sancho paused, eyeing her flannel pajama bottoms and faded t-shirt. "Yeah, okay, I guess you should probably do that."

Eve waited in silence, impatiently tapping her bare foot against the floor. "Can you turn around, please?"

"Oh, sorry." He spun around, staring at the door in front of him. "It's just, I'm—"

"So excited?"

"How'd you know?" He glanced at the side of the room and eyed Madison's empty bed. "Hey, where is," he hesitated, "you know."

Eve rolled her eyes. "She's avoiding me. Has been for weeks." She hastily tugged on a pair of blue jeans and tossed a white cotton tank top over her head before kicking on her combat boots. "Where to?"

"My dorm. Everyone's waiting."

The twosome scurried through the hallway, anxiously glancing down the line of doors to make sure no one was watching them. Sancho and Jason's room was just a short distance away, conveniently situated across from the washrooms, but the secretive nature of their operation made the journey seem long and precarious. As Eve tiptoed past the showers, Sancho flung open his dorm room door and pulled her inside, eager to show her their latest breakthrough.

The room was cozy and carelessly decorated in a manner that only young men could get away with. Sancho's bed was unmade, his walls covered in posters of hologames and big-breasted women, while Jason's side of the room was simple, monochrome, and mostly bare. Percy and Jason hovered over JJ, who sat at Jason's desk with three bright scratchpad screens propped in front of her.

Eve hurried to their side and peered over JJ's shoulder. The far left screen was covered in rows of blue audio waves, streaming across the monitor almost endlessly. The middle monitor displayed lines of text, appearing word by word just as quickly as the sound waves formed. The final and most lifeless screen showed a map of Billington and the surrounding neighborhoods.

"Pretty dynamic, isn't it?" JJ boasted. "This beacon is a million times more advanced than anything we have on this planet." She picked up the device, which was now dismantled and linked to her scratchpads through a tangle of wires. "This thing allows the Interlopers to transmit verbal commands directly to one another's *minds*. Someone speaks on one end, and the other Interloper hears it in his thoughts."

"That's incredible," Jason murmured, watching the sound waves in awe.

"And it's not just commands. They can transmit pictures, maps, instructions—anything—and the receiving party will see it as if it's right there in front of them."

"Fascinating," Percy muttered. "But am I the only one here who doesn't know what the hell we're looking at?"

"The waves are the different verbal commands being sent to the beacon. Each wave represents a different voice—a different Interloper—who's transmitting some type of information. Of course, they're all in some strange, alien language, which would've been a bitch to translate"—JJ turned to Eve and winked—"so I just stole the Shelter's translation system."

"Great," Eve muttered. "Now we're accessories to theft."

"*That's* what the middle screen is," JJ continued, ignoring Eve's remark. "All of the waves are rendered and converted to the English language here."

"Is there a delay?" Jason asked.

"Seconds at most."

"And the third screen?"

JJ rolled her eyes. "That one's a big fat waste of time. It's my global tracking system. I was hoping to locate where the voices were coming from, but so far, no dice. Instead, I've been using it to upload the pictures they're transmitting."

Eve folded her arms as she watched the text shoot across the middle screen. A random flurry of words caught her attention—*campus, chimera,* and *target*—and she grimaced at the sight of it.

"So, now that we've got their communications, what the hell are they saying?"

"Lots of crap. And let me tell you, those shit-sacks *hate* you guys. Especially you, Eve."

"Shocking."

"But I *have* picked up a few signals that were particularly interesting."

JJ fiddled with her scratchpads, sliding her fingers across the screens until a single picture appeared. It was a silver, cylindrical rod, long and lean with a curved head, apparently constructed of the same metallic hardware as the beacon. A thin groove wrapped itself around the device, and a small, spherical knob sat at the base. Across its entire shaft were rows and rows of blue buttons, glowing and flickering seemingly at random.

"The best English translation I could get for this thing was *torq*, although I'm pretty sure they said it with some sort of clicking noise."

Percy wrinkled his nose. "Does anyone else think this thing looks sort of..."

"Phallic?" Eve scoffed.

"I was going to say cock-like, but I'm glad we're on the same page."

"HOLY BALLS," Sancho gasped. "It's a *probe*."

Jason laughed. "The Interlopers don't probe people. *God*."

"Maybe they do."

"Well, they didn't probe me."

"How would you know? You were in and out of consciousness."

"It's not a *probe*," JJ said. "It's a personal computer of sorts—a scratchpad, if you will. Each Interloper has one, and it carries all of their data and missions."

"So if we had access to one of those, we could get an inside look at the life of an Interloper?"

JJ flashed a smug smile at Eve. "Darlin', you set your sights too low." She enlarged the image of the torq, pulling it from the screen until it hovered in front of her in holographic form. "From what I've read, there's a hub in their lair—a mainframe that holds all of their intelligence. They use their torqs to gather information and then download their findings to the mainframe." She turned to face the group. "That hub is pivotal to them: it's their lifeline."

Eve's eyes lit up. "We need to destroy it."

"Bingo, princess." JJ turned back to the hologram and ran her fingers through it, sending it spinning in a circle. "If we had a torq, I could try to booby-trap it with a virus. Then, once we find the lair, all we'd have to do is locate the mainframe, attach the torq, and activate the virus. We could wipe out *everything*."

"Including the list?" Eve asked.

"Especially the list."

"Great news!" Percy sang, slapping Jason and Eve across their backs. "We just need to nab ourselves one of those schlong-a-dongs and we'll be on our way."

JJ hesitated, glancing awkwardly at her computers. "There's one more thing."

"Well, judging by your tone, it isn't good," Eve sighed. "So, lay it on us."

"It's Fairon." JJ paused. "He's on campus."

"*Sonofabitch*," Jason growled.

"Wait, but he's the leader," Percy said. "Doesn't he have more important things to do? Like actually *leading*?"

"Apparently *this* leader likes to be on the front lines of the battlefield."

"How long has he been here?" Jason asked.

"Months. Probably the entire semester, if not longer."

Eve folded her arms almost defensively. "Well, it was to be expected. If he wants me so badly, he can find me himself."

"Oh, he's found you all right."

JJ minimized the holographic torq and swept her fingers across the third monitor, pulling up a file of photos stored in her scratchpad's archive. One by one, a series of images flooded the screen—images of Eve walking to and from her classes, sitting in the various lecture halls, toying with her scratchpad. Some of the pictures were distant and blurry, while others were straight on as if Fairon had been standing right in front of her, close enough to reach out and touch her face.

Jason's eyes widened. "He's *following* you?"

"I don't understand," Eve stammered. "If he's gotten so close to me, why hasn't he made a move yet?"

"Maybe he knows you're too strong," Jason reasoned.

JJ sank lower in her chair. "Or maybe he has a plan."

Eve stared at the last remaining image. It was a tightly cropped picture of her face, her eyes focused on whoever it was that stood before her. On Fairon. Before she could react, a tiny siren blared through the speakers of JJ's scratchpads.

"What's that?" Eve asked.

"I'm monitoring for pivotal keywords. Whenever one of them is mentioned, it triggers a noise alert. The name 'Fairon' triggers a chiming sound, 'abduct' triggers a bell—"

"And which keyword sounds off the siren?"

JJ glanced up at Eve, her eyes large and fearful. "Kill."

Her fingers fluttered across the scratchpads, dragging text boxes to the foreground as she frantically read the latest transmissions. Suddenly, she stopped; her body was still, practically frozen as she stared at her brightly lit screen.

"They have someone in custody. A female..." She hesitated. "Human."

"*Shit balls,*" Sancho gasped.

"They abducted her"—JJ paused, still reading the text as it appeared on her screen—"Christ, nearly *three hours* ago."

"Who was it?" Eve asked frantically.

"They're sending an image of her right now."

JJ pulled the screen closer to her, impatiently waiting for the image to appear, and when it did, her hands dropped to her sides and her jaw fell open.

"Oh, God."

"What? Who is it?"

JJ turned the third monitor toward the group, displaying a photo of a warm, smiling face. The girl had large teeth that seemed to overpower her mouth and perfectly straight, honey-brown hair that fell limply across her shoulders. She was vaguely familiar, as if Eve had seen her before once, maybe twice, and as she studied the girl's lightly freckled nose and bright hazel-green eyes, her mind became flooded with visions of her screaming in torturous agony.

JJ pointed her finger at the screen. "They've got Florenza Gallo."

"*Florenza?*" Percy scoffed. "Sounds like some sort of virus."

Sancho shrugged. "Never heard of her."

"Well, if you paid any attention to the news, you'd know that *Gallo* is the name of the Italian president," JJ groused, "which means Florenza—"

"Is his daughter," Eve said.

"She opted to study abroad." JJ frowned. "Bet she's regretting that decision right about now."

"I didn't even know she goes to school here."

"I used to see her in the political science building all the time," Jason said. "She's hard to miss. Doesn't speak much English, so she's got a team of translators with her at all times. Not to mention a ton of security, just like Woodgate."

"Oh my God," Eve said, her body suddenly cold. "They're doing it again—another Marshall Woodgate. She's the next human victim." She grimaced. "They've already gotten the United States to turn against chimeras, and now they're trying to do the same thing with Italy. They're starting a world war."

"So, what's the plan?" Sancho asked. "Do we tell Furst?"

"Um, guys, I have a *ton* of illegal shit on my scratchpads," JJ protested. "You're not telling *anyone* about this. *Ever.*"

"There's no time for that anyway," Eve rationalized. "Something has to be done *now.* She was abducted three hours ago. They're not going to keep her alive much longer."

"If they haven't killed her already," Jason mumbled.

Percy sighed. "All right then, what do you want to do?"

The room became quiet. Eve could feel everyone's wide, anxious eyes staring at her, waiting for her to formulate the plan, to issue the orders. It was all on her shoulders. For whatever reason, it was her decision to make, and hers alone.

Eve glanced at the photo of Florenza, trying to avoid the piercing gazes of her comrades; she had to concentrate, to *think*, and God, did they have to stare at her like that? The pressure was overwhelming, and though her thoughts raced in every direction, they always seemed to come back to the same uncomplicated conclusion.

She turned to JJ. "Did they list her location?"

JJ nodded. "About a half hour from here."

"Can you tell us how to get there?"

"Absolutely."

"Percy, can we borrow your car? And your guns?"

Percy grinned. "Yes and *hell* yes."

Eve took a deep breath. "Then I guess we're going to get her ourselves."

The room erupted into applause, though Eve didn't know what for. The enthusiasm was invigorating and even the slightest bit encouraging, but she couldn't help but remember Gary, and the Interloper at the Meltdown—their exceptional strength, their vast wings, their bayonet-like teeth—and wondered if anyone else remembered them, too.

Eve glanced at the clock. "If we're going to do this, we have to go *now.*"

"But wait," Sancho squealed, scurrying across the room. "We can't, not yet!"

"Sancho, there isn't any time—"

"Oh, you're going to want to see this." He hurried to his wardrobe and swung the doors open. "You have no idea how long I've been waiting for this moment."

Jason wrinkled his brow. "Are you going to tell us what's going on?"

"That project I've been working on?" he answered, flipping through a messy pile of clothes. "It's finished!"

Percy groaned. "Look, Sanch, no one cares about your project—"

"It's a *weapon*." With a grunt, he yanked at a sheet-covered object, dragging it from his wardrobe and onto the floor. "And not just *any* weapon: it's a trailblazing, alien-killing *machine*. Inspired by my favorite hologame—"

"Oh God, here we go..." Percy muttered.

"It's calculated, it's precise, it's brutal and downright *filthy*. It's—"

"Get on with it."

Sancho glared at Percy before continuing. "Ladies and gentlemen," he announced, ripping the sheet from his prized creation, "I call it the Dirty Sanchez."

It was the most unusual contraption Eve had ever seen—a cluttered mess of cords, bolts, and rods, practically robotic in appearance, though it included one key component that was entirely recognizable: guns. Several guns, in fact, each one attached to a retractable arm that was in turn attached to a single, wheeled platform. To the side of the device was a small controller lined with buttons and knobs, which Sancho plucked from its resting place and tossed back and forth between his nimble hands.

"Holy hell," Eve murmured, "how many—"

"Guns? There are ten, all of them controlled by a single remote device." He beamed with pride. "I can load, aim, and shoot each and every one of them with this controller. It's like a real-life hologame."

Percy stepped closer to the Dirty Sanchez, inspecting the creation. "Wait a second—are these *my* guns?"

"Well, I'd like to think of them as *our* guns now..."

"You little dick-squeeze, you stole my guns!"

"Enough. We need to get moving." Eve stormed past the group and headed for the door. "Percy, grab whatever's left of your guns. Sancho, pack your Dirty Sanchez. We're leaving, and we're leaving *now*."

JJ reached into her pocket and pulled out a handful of what appeared to be small plastic buttons. "Here," she ordered, tossing one to each of her comrades. "Take these."

Eve held the object up to the light: it was a tiny clear disc, about the size of a dime, but flexible in her hand. A red, thread-like cord was curled inside of it, and as she cradled the device in her palm, she could feel a slight prickling sensation.

"They're communication devices—earpieces. Not as advanced as the beacon, but at least we can keep tabs on one another."

Eve's stomach churned at the thought of trusting the hacker, but she pushed aside her reservations and reluctantly pressed the disc into her ear. She nodded at JJ. "Stay here. Use your tracking system to tell us how to get to Florenza."

She opened the door and waited as Jason, Sancho, and Percy filed out into the hallway. And as she stood there, watching the team assemble, the reality of the situation struck her: they were infiltrating the Interlopers. They were waging war.

As she turned to follow her comrades, JJ grabbed at her wrist and halted her. "The torq." Her voice was forceful. "Find one, and bring it back."

"We save Florenza first, and if there's time—"

"*Make* time," JJ commanded, squeezing Eve's wrist even tighter. Her usually facetious demeanor had turned grave and severe. She stared at Eve, her eyes fierce and intense, and let go of her wrist.

"Trust me, Eve. We need this."

* * *

The drive was quiet. All sense of excitement had vanished, replaced by the bitter taste of reality—the frightening realization that each of them was potentially walking into a death trap. Despite her stubborn cling to courage, Eve secretly hoped that the car ride would take much longer than it did, but it was practically fleeting, and her face drained of all color as Percy parked at the side of the dusty dirt road.

They had arrived at the Wilds of Los Angeles—an abandoned woodland, once a lovely state park with a pretty Spanish name that had long since been neglected and transformed into a deserted mess of greenery and garbage.

"*Drive through*," JJ ordered, her voice booming through Eve's earpiece. "*I'll tell you when you've found it.*"

Percy grumbled to himself as he steered his sleek black SUV through the wooded forest, maneuvering over fallen branches and wincing with each bump and thud that echoed off of his car's exterior. Eve glanced over at Jason and Sancho, who sat in the back seats, stabilizing the Dirty Sanchez; their eyes were distant, and she knew they were just as terrified as she was. It was an incredibly stupid idea, after all—coming to this place, an execution site filled with God knows how many Interlopers—and yet it was the only option, the right decision among an array of horrible alternatives. They had no other choice.

"Stop," JJ commanded. "It's right in front of you."

There was no need for her to say it, as Eve could see the site plain as day. It was unmistakable: a massive cave, clearly unnatural, sculpted by what had to have been unimaginable hours of labor. Eve thought of Marshall Woodgate, shuddered as she recalled his gouged eyes, and wondered if she would find Florenza in the same state.

The four of them stepped out of the car, closing the doors as quietly as they could manage. Eve looked back at Sancho and Percy, who were hastily unloading their weapons from the trunk.

"You two wait here," she instructed. "Jason and I will head inside. Stand guard, and be prepared, in case... in case something happens to us."

They nodded their heads in unison. Percy reached into his coat and pulled out Eve's and Jason's handguns, handing them over.

"You'll probably need these."

"Eve, don't forget—"

"I know, JJ," Eve hissed, fiddling with her earpiece. "I won't forget your precious torq."

Eve looked over at Jason. He was staring back at her, his posture strong, but his eyes were wide with fear. With a deep breath and a sharp pang in her gut, she made her way into the cave with Jason by her side.

The light of the outside world dimmed to black. They had entered a tunnel—a damp passageway made of mud or clay or whatever it was that extended almost endlessly into the distance. Eve struggled to focus, her eyes dilating as they adjusted to the dark, and she could faintly hear Jason's rapid breathing over the sound of her own beating heart. Together they ventured deeper and deeper into the cavern, their backs taut and their hands hovering over their guns.

A passageway branched off to the left, and Eve peered carefully around the corner. The cavern was empty, but here it split into three separate corridors that twisted in different directions. She looked down the tunnel directly in front of them and realized that it was punctuated with countless openings and junctions as far as she could see.

"This place... it's like a maze," she mumbled.

Jason hesitated. "It's a nest."

They continued ahead, moving farther into the darkness without the slightest notion of where they were headed. A few rats scurried past them, their presence almost comforting in the midst of such gloomy stillness. Eve felt her throat tighten; there was nothing, nothing but an infinite black tunnel, nothing but branches of passageways on either side of them.

As they advanced through the cavern, the air became damp and hot, the moisture clinging to their skin, and still they pressed on, venturing deeper into the humid stink. They reached another junction, and then another, each as empty as the last, and as the murky thickness became practically intolerable, Eve slid her fingers along the wall of the tunnel as if to help navigate her through it. The surface of the clay was gritty—a familiar texture, one that sent her blood running cold. She glanced down at her hands.

"Oh my God."

"What?" Jason whispered. "What is it?"

Eve stared at the tunnel in front of her; it was everywhere, collecting in mounds along the cavern floor. Reluctantly, she raised her hand in front of Jason; her fingertips were coated in a fine, black powder.

"Ashes."

"Ashes?" He gasped, "Wait, *ashes*? Like—"

"*Die Chime.*" The words flashed before her eyes, along with the ashes on Madison's sheets, and an overwhelming sickness festered within her stomach.

"Holy shit," Jason muttered, his eyes wide with shock. "You don't think—"

He stopped. A sudden noise rang in the distance: a clang, the sound of metal against metal. Eve froze in place, her body rigid with terror. Again the clang echoed down the tunnel. Again. Again.

Jason and Eve looked at one another. Despite how much they wanted to run, to flee from the cavern and never return, they trudged forward, forcing themselves toward the incessant clanging.

"*What's that noise?*" JJ mumbled.

Eve ignored her earpiece, afraid to utter a word as they followed the hypnotic pounding. Clang. Clang. Again and again, the sound resounded through the cavern until she could feel it in her bones. She could vaguely make out a light at the end of the tunnel—literally, as a faint glow shined off in the distance, possibly signaling the source of the noise. It was calling her, beckoning her forward, and soon she could see nothing but the small circle of yellow light.

A slight rustling caught her attention, releasing her from her trance. The sound was coming from a passageway only a few feet ahead of them. She glanced at Jason, who pulled his gun from his belt and released the safety, and she did the same. With one long, deep breath, the pair slowly approached the corridor and hesitantly peered into the dark, eerie cavern.

Eve's lungs froze within her chest; she was immediately met with a foul, overpowering stench, the smell of decay and death. The passageway was lined with rows of barred cages, each one empty aside from scant scraps of rotten human flesh and bits of ivory bone. Eve's nostrils flared and she gagged, barely able to control the nausea bubbling in her throat, when suddenly there was a new sound—not the ceaseless clanging, which still continued in the distance, nor the faint pitter patter of the scurrying rats, but a soft, familiar noise.

Whimpering.

Jason and Eve hurried into the passageway, frantically searching the line of cages until they finally found her—a petite girl, curled into a tight ball in the corner of her cage, her face buried in her knees and her body shaking uncontrollably.

"Florenza?" Eve whispered, crouching by the cage. "Florenza, are you okay?"

The girl looked up at the two of them. Her eyes were swollen from hours of crying, but even in her haggard state, Eve could tell that she was the Italian president's daughter. She cowered, pressing herself against the metal bars as tears gushed from her eyes.

"Dio mio," she stuttered. "Dio mio."

"We're here to help you," Jason added. "We're going to get you out of here."

"Dio mio," she repeated, her voice wavering. "Please, non voglio morire!"

Eve glanced at Jason. "What is she saying?"

"Hell if I know." He leaned closer to the cage and flashed what he hoped was a comforting smile. "It's okay, Flo. Can I call you Flo?"

"Please," Florenza moaned, "do not kill me!"

"We're not going to hurt you," Jason reassured her. Slowly, he reached his arm between the bars of the cage and extended his hand toward her.

Florenza cried out in terror, and Jason grabbed her mouth, silencing her as quickly as he could manage.

"*Quiet!*" Eve hissed. "Do you want them to hear us?"

"She thinks we're Interlopers," Jason explained, his hand still firmly covering her mouth. "She saw them change out of their second skin. That has to be it."

Eve leaned in toward the terrified prisoner. "We're, not, *aliens*," she whispered, enunciating clearly.

Florenza whimpered beneath Jason's hand, her eyes still flooded with tears.

"Think she understood me?"

"Nope."

"How do we tell her we're the good guys?"

"Know any Italian?"

Eve's eyes darted across the ground, desperately searching for something to work with, and landed on a small shard of metal, one that was sharp and pointed at the tip. She glanced back and forth between the fragment and Florenza, who squirmed beneath Jason's grasp, letting out a single, muffled yelp.

"Shh!" Eve hushed. "Just watch. *Please.*"

Eve pressed the metal shard into her forearm and carved a straight line deep into her skin. She winced; blood poured from the gash, spilling down her arm and dripping onto the ground beneath her.

"See?" she whispered. "I'm not an alien. My blood is red, not yellow."

Florenza's breathing slowed and body loosened as she stared at Eve's bloody arm. Apprehensively, Jason lowered his hand and let out a sign of relief.

"Per favore qualcuno mi aiuti, non voglio morire," the girl stammered as she choked on her own tears. "Please. *Please.*"

Jason shook the cage, searching for an opening or lock, something he could manipulate. A single silver bar rested along the edge of the cage's door, securing it shut. He tugged at the device until the entire contraption wobbled in place.

"Jason, I know you're super strong and everything, but I don't think that's going to work," Eve mumbled, glancing nervously down the tunnel.

"Dio mio," Florenza cried, gazing hopelessly at the ceiling. "Dio mio."

Jason let out a long, heavy sigh. He reached down the back of his pants and pulled his handgun from his belt.

"*Jason,*" Eve whispered. "Don't *shoot* the damn thing."

"That's not what I was planning on doing, *Eve.*"

He held the grip of the gun above the latch and waited—for what, Eve didn't know. The room became still, and all she could hear was the soft sound of Florenza crying, the distant clanging, and Jason's faint voice as he counted quietly to himself.

"One, two, three—"

The clang sounded in the distance, interrupting his count. Again, he began counting.

"One, two, three—"

Another clang echoed down the corridor. Eve glanced over at Jason; she knew what he was doing. She stared down at his gun, at the latch below it, and counted with him.

"One, two, three."

Right as the clanging erupted in the distance, Jason pounded the grip of his gun into the latch, the sound of the ceramic clashing against the metal construct hidden by the far off noise. Again, they counted.

"One, two, three."

Jason smashed the gun into the bolt again. The lock hung more loosely now from the cage, still attached but only barely, and Eve knew that one more blow would release Florenza from her prison.

"One, two, three."

Jason struck the latch one last time, sending the lock tumbling to the ground. Florenza burst through the cage and threw her arms around his neck, her entire body trembling.

"It's okay," he said, stroking her hair. "Nothing's going to happen to you."

Jason strained his neck past the opening of the passageway, peering down the long tunnel toward the entrance of the cave. He looked back at Eve.

"Let's get the *hell* out of here."

Eve hesitated; she peered down the corridor at the soft glow she had spotted earlier. The clang sounded again, and for a moment she thought she saw the shadow of someone—or something.

"Eve? Eve, we need to leave, *now*."

"I can't," Eve answered. "There's one last thing I need to do."

"*Eve*," Jason hissed, grabbing at her wrist. "Are you *crazy*?"

"I have to get the torq."

"*Screw* the torq—"

"Jason, just trust me." She tiptoed slowly toward the opening, sliding her body against the wall as she headed for the shining light in the distance.

"No no no," Florenza pleaded. "You will die. *We will die.*"

"Eve, what you're doing is *suicide*."

"Stay here," Eve ordered, dismissing their warnings. "Listen for me in your earpiece. Whatever I tell you to do, *do it*."

Eve stepped into the tunnel and moved cautiously toward the faraway glow. She timed her steps with the echoing clangs, afraid to make even the slightest sound. It *was* suicide—she knew it—but she also knew that her name, along with so many others, was on a list stored in the Interlopers' mainframe, and the only way to destroy that list was through the torq.

As Eve made her way down the tunnel, the light became brighter and brighter, and soon it was all-encompassing. She pressed her body against the wall, desperate to remain unseen, sidestepped her way to the end of the tunnel, and peered around the edge.

In front of her was a single room, the source of the light and the incessant clanging noise.

An Interloper stood in the middle of the room, his claws wrapped around a metal mallet. He swung his mallet into the air and thrust it down. Again, and then again; the clanging reverberated painfully in Eve's eardrums, so much so that she shuddered at the sound. The Interloper was pounding at a sheet of a metal, molding it into place against a second sheet. He was building something familiar to her—a giant "X," like the one used to display Marshall Woodgate's body. Eve felt a tremor of fear pulse through her, but she ignored it, her eyes feverishly panning across the space in search of anything that could possibly resemble a torq.

"*Have you found it?*" JJ whispered. Eve had almost forgotten that she was listening, as she had been remarkably quiet for most of their journey. Eve didn't respond.

"*Eve,*" Jason added, "*are you okay?*"

Still, Eve was silent. She had to be. As she glanced back and forth through the space in front of her, she lost the ability to speak, to move, to breathe. She was staring at an army of Interlopers—thirty, maybe forty, no, easily more than that—who bustled about the room.

"*Eve? Eve?*"

Eve remained quiet. She watched the Interlopers work, some piecing together the metal construct while others sharpened weapons. Still others barked orders across the room in a language she couldn't comprehend.

Suddenly, one of the Interlopers stopped, his body going oddly still and his eyes gazing off into the distance. He craned his neck and wiggled his nostrils, sniffing at the air. Another Interloper joined him, and then another; together they breathed in deeply, sniffing at the murky atmosphere like dogs taking in a scent. They muttered to one another in their alien language, basking in whatever aroma they had stumbled upon.

"Ey falep qerolian. Der falep raj *chimera.*"

Eve almost choked. Chimera—it was the only word she recognized, and the last one she was hoping to hear. What did it mean? She looked down at her body—at her jeans and her boots and her bloody arm. She stopped—could it be her? Could it be the blood? She grabbed at the wound, grimacing as she held it tightly, trying to close the gash.

The Interlopers continued their sniffing, tapping their comrades and alerting them to the smell. Eve cringed as she observed them, praying to God they would stop, that they would forget the scent and move on with their work, but still they remained, their eyes closed as if mesmerized by the intoxicating scent.

The rhythmic clanging stopped; the Interloper tossed his mallet to the floor, barking a string of unintelligible phrases at his comrades and immediately sending them back to work.

Eve's body loosened a bit, though she was far from relaxed. Her eyes darted across the room, searching for a silver cylindrical device, a torq, and soon she spotted one. It was close, so close that she wondered why she hadn't noticed it earlier, a mere one or two yards away, resting on a shelf carved into the wall. Just one quick grab—one smooth, controlled swipe—and the torq would be hers.

Eve inched forward, venturing just the slightest bit farther into the room, the light spilling across her shoulder. She took another step, and then another; the torq was within reach, and she slowly, very slowly, lifted her arm and wrapped her fingers around the polished device. Finally, she pulled it into her chest, breathing a sigh of relief.

She had retrieved the torq, and not a single Interloper had noticed.

A spine-chilling scream echoed off the walls behind her.

"SHIT!" Jason barked, his voice booming in Eve's ear.

"What? What happened?" JJ gasped.

"A rat crawled over Florenza's foot."

"She's screaming over a rat? In a nest filled with aliens?"

"Eve," Jason continued, ignoring JJ's ranting. "Eve, is everything okay?"

Not a single word left Eve's lips. She stood, paralyzed, staring directly at the room filled with Interlopers—Interlopers who were now staring back at her.

Every last one of them.

Eve bolted down the tunnel. She could hear the sounds of wings beating and feet stomping behind her—the sounds of thirty or forty Interlopers chasing after her on foot and in the air—and she pressed forward, her legs racing with a fiery speed she had never needed to utilize before. Her heart pulsed in her throat; far ahead of her, she could see her only escape from the cave, and even closer was the passageway where Jason and Florenza were waiting.

"RUN!" she screamed.

Jason and Florenza leapt from their hiding place and sped down the passageway. Jason's stride was much quicker than Florenza's, but he slowed, grabbing her hand and forcing himself to match her pace.

Eve trailed behind them, her feet pounding against the ground, and then her stomach lurched with horror—another horde of Interlopers poured from a junction ahead of her, their wings pulsing as they chased after Jason and Florenza. Eve charged forward, sprinting faster than she thought possible, until she was right behind the pack, close enough to feel their wings beating the hot air against her face.

Her vision blackened, and in that moment, time froze to a near standstill. With a surge of absolute conviction, Eve dropped to her knees and slid beneath the aliens, pointing her arms at the ceiling and then flinging them back down to the ground. Instantly the Interlopers parted above her, their bodies crashing into one another as they were thrust into the tunnel walls, slamming violently against the clay and then toppling to the floor.

Eve jumped to her feet, her jeans torn and her legs dripping with blood. Jason turned to look behind him; when he saw Eve and the horde of Interlopers that followed her, he yanked at Florenza's arm and threw her over his shoulder. Like a bullet released from the barrel of a gun, Jason hurtled forward, his feet moving with incomparable speed as he tightly gripped Florenza's body.

A single Interloper flew over Eve's shoulders, his sights set on Florenza, but Eve delved into her melt and thrust him against the wall. Another Interloper zoomed forward, and then another, and Eve sent them smashing into one another, their sharpened teeth impaling each other as they landed on the ground in a messy heap. One more Interloper darted toward her, his talons bared, and she melted him headfirst into the ceiling, the impact alone enough to snap his neck.

She forced herself to run faster; Jason was now only steps ahead of her, and the exit to the cave was just a few short yards away.

Eve's lungs expanded as she breathed in the cool, clean air of the forest. They were free of the cave, but not of the Interlopers, who were only seconds behind them. Percy and Sancho quickly prepared their weapons, and Jason plopped Florenza's shaking body behind Percy's car.

"Stay here," he ordered. "Close your eyes, cover your ears, and whatever you do, *don't move.*"

Eve dropped the torq into Florenza's lap. "And don't lose this!" she barked. She pulled her gun from her belt and glanced over at Percy. "They're coming."

Percy plucked two pistols from his waistband and aimed them at the cavern, flashing an overconfident grin in Eve's direction. "I'm ready."

"The Dirty is prepped for battle," Sancho chirped excitedly.

Jason took his place beside Eve and raised his pistol. "Whatever comes out of that cave," he commanded, "kill it. Kill 'em all."

Just as the words left his lips, they heard it—a steady rumbling, the sound of flapping wings growing louder and louder with each passing second. Eve's face paled as the Interlopers poured from the mouth of the cave, shoving past one another, a flood of slick grey skin, batlike wings, and silver teeth. Eve could see a thirst in their eyes—a genuine yearning for the task ahead of them, for the chance to kill—and as she watched them rush toward her, their sadistic smiles quickly faded into a pulsing blackness.

A series of shrieks resounded through the forest; the entire horde of Interlopers was thrown off course, their bodies lurching backward through the air as if pushed by an invisible force. Their limbs flailed as they were propelled high into the sky, and Sancho, Jason, and Percy gaped in awe as their adversaries disappeared from sight.

The forest became quiet. Percy turned to his side, staring wide-eyed at Eve, at her outstretched hands and her panicked eyes that blinked and fluttered as she ended her melt.

"God, I'll never get used to that," he muttered.

Sancho glanced from side to side and lowered his controller. "Are we done?"

Eve watched the sky. Tiny grey specks reappeared in the distance, and as they grew in size and number, she felt her heart race within her chest. She raised her weapon.

"No. We're not done."

Again, she heard the rumble of wings like a thundering storm. There were perhaps fewer Interlopers than before, but still Eve and her comrades were woefully outnumbered. Following Eve's lead, the others pointed their own weapons and braced themselves as the swarm of aliens hit.

All four of them opened fire, launching wave after wave of bullets until the air was spotted with black and stank of smoke. The Interlopers seemed to halt in midair, their bodies convulsing as they were saturated with lead, blood bursting from their skin. Several fell to the ground, their loose fangs dangling from their lips, but many others remained, undeterred and exceedingly agitated. A single Interloper, his chest dripping with mustard-colored pus, swerved away from the gunfire and dipped low to the ground, charging at Eve. Another one followed suit, and as the pair came near, their talons and fangs bared, Eve melted them away, parting their bodies and slamming them both into nearby trees.

Another Interloper broke from the pack, but his sights were set on a different victim. He grinned as he spotted Florenza's muddy, bare feet sticking out from behind the car, and he bolted toward her, swerving to dodge the hail of bullets. As the creature rounded the vehicle, Percy jumped in front of him in an attempt to shield Florenza, and the alien barreled right into him, knocking him to the ground.

The Interloper stared down at Percy, who was pinned beneath his talons. He leaned in closer, his ominous growl expanding into a furious roar—and then he abruptly shot into the sky, pulled from the forest floor as if caught on a fishing line. Percy looked to his side; Eve's arm was high above her head, her hand clenched into a tight fist as if she were holding the creature up by his neck, and Sancho, who stood beside her, swiveled his joystick until every last barrel of the Dirty Sanchez was pointed at the alien. With a deep breath, Eve closed her eyes, and Sancho unloaded his murderous creation, firing a torrent of bullets at the Interloper until all that remained of him was yellow blood and black bone.

Eve frantically scanned the forest. Nearby, Jason was firing his handgun over and over into the mouth of an Interloper, who ultimately collapsed at his boots amid a pile of teeth. Jason looked over at Eve, and his eyes widened with horror.

"EVE, BEHIND YOU!"

Eve turned just in time to see an alien headed toward her, shooting through the sky with great speed. Before she could react, the creature jolted backward, his body seized by Jason's gift. With as much power as he could summon, Jason forced the Interloper through the air and rammed his face into a tree branch, impaling him through the mouth.

Before Jason could recover, another Interloper headed straight toward him. There was a hatred in his eyes—a longing for Jason's death, a desire to rip out his jugular and wear his blood as a sign of victory—and with a single breath, he opened his mouth wide and let out a horrendous roar.

Then in the blink of an eye his life source exploded—sending golden custard spewing across Jason's face—and the alien's body dropped to the forest floor. Jason wiped the gunk from his mouth and glanced over at Percy, whose gun was still pointed where the alien once stood.

"Sorry 'bout the mess." Percy winked. "Good shot though, right?"

He had barely finished his sentence before he was hurtling through the air, his body torn from the ground by a single, enraged Interloper. Percy landed face-first against the forest floor, his limbs sprawled across the dirt, but again the creature picked him up, this time hurling him high into the sky, leaving him to meet his inevitable bloody fate when he smashed to the ground below.

But Percy felt nothing—no crash onto the turf beneath him, no breaking of bones or sting of open wounds. He opened his eyes and found himself floating in the air, hovering weightlessly just a few short yards above the ground, with the alien levitating at his side, gnashing his teeth in his direction. Below them both stood Eve, her hands raised, palms open as if supporting the weight of their suspended figures. With the slightest, most subtle flick of her wrist, she shot the creature through the air and then just as quickly sent him plummeting down to the ground. With a loud, startling boom, the Interloper's body smashed against the forest floor, his bones crumbling into pieces and his innards splattering across the sod.

A wing slammed into Eve's chest, thrusting her body into the air and sending her toppling to the ground. Stars flashed before her eyes, and she heard the thud of Percy dropping to the forest floor—she had lost her melt, interrupted by the Interloper who now stood before her. She hoisted herself onto her hands and knees and grabbed for her gun, looking up at the creature just in time to watch him kick her across the chin. Her gun flew from her hand, and again she fell to the ground and skidded across the dirt. A throbbing pain pulsed through her head, but she ignored it, scrambling toward her weapon while keeping one eye trained on her looming adversary.

The Interloper lunged for her yet again, but she quickly rolled away from him, plucked her gun from a puddle of yellow blood, and pounded the grip across his face. As she staggered to her feet, the creature dove forward and clawed at her ribs, digging his talons into her flesh and forcing her to the ground once more. A deep pain coursed through her—it was a sharp sting, intensifying with each subtle movement she made—but still she channeled what little strength she had and pulled herself to her knees.

The creature stared back at her; he was sure of his victory, so sure that he laughed aloud, his mouth wide enough for Eve to make out a very familiar sight—a small, pink heart. With one short, shallow breath, she raised her gun, held her arm steady, and fired a bullet into the creature's life source.

Meanwhile, Jason was cornered; he melted one Interloper after the next, throwing them against boulders and trees, yet no matter how many he thrust aside, still more charged toward him. He raised his empty hands, his mind consumed with his intoxicating melt, and forced his latest adversary high into the air, pounding him backward against the cave entrance and watching his limp body tumble to the ground. Another Interloper bore down on him, and he lifted the creature from his feet and tossed him against the side of a tree, the impact so strong that the tree itself cracked in half. Jason's sight faded to darkness—to nothing but black and rage and power—and just as a third alien made his advances, Jason melted the Interloper's body into the air, sending him shooting through the sky, never to be seen again.

Suddenly, two large feet pounded against Jason's back, forcing him face-first into the dirt. The Interloper stood on top of him, pushing him into the ground and clawing at his back, ripping his jacket to shreds and slicing deep into his skin. Jason howled from the shooting pain, and with clenched fists and gritted teeth, he melted the creature from his back and thrust him into a nearby tree. Jason clambered to his feet; as he watched the alien stagger toward him across the forest floor, he suddenly found himself overcome with anger and adrenaline. He slammed his fist into the creature's gut, then again across his face, and finally he kicked at the Interloper's jaw, sending him crashing to the ground. Jason hovered over his adversary, and as his rage overtook him, he stomped on the creature's mouth, breaking his teeth into pieces and sending a glob of pus oozing onto his boot.

Miraculously, the number of aliens was dwindling, and despite her haggard state, Eve allowed herself to feel the slightest inkling of hope. Four more Interlopers torpedoed toward her in perfect synchronicity, and with a single pulse of her gift, she sent them sailing far across the forest. Another one headed in her direction, but Jason immediately threw the creature off course, melting the alien's head against a jagged rock. Eve scanned her comrades; their bodies were filthy, broken, and splattered with blood, but they were alive, and again she felt a twinge of optimism in her chest. She turned to Sancho; he gripped the controller of the Dirty Sanchez, his eyes brimming with fear and excitement all at the same time. Suddenly, she heard Percy's loud cry.

"SANCHO, DUCK!"

It was too late; an Interloper flew down to the ground, grabbed at Sancho's shoulders, and plucked him from the forest floor. Eve watched in horror as he dangled from the creature's claws, helplessly trying to shake himself free.

Percy turned to Eve, his eyes frantic. "Can you give me a boost?"

Eve stared back, confused. "A boost?"

"My bullets." He pointed at his gun. "Can you give 'em a boost?"

Eve nodded; they had to act quickly. Percy aimed both of his guns at the Interloper, following the creature's movements as he dipped and looped through the sky. Finally, he made the move Percy had been waiting for—the alien swooped low to the ground—and Percy pulled both triggers, firing at the ugly creature.

For a moment, the bullets froze in place—hovering amid the smoke. Eve channeled her gift, letting it grow inside of her, and then released. The bullets resumed their course, shooting through the air with unparalleled speed, plunging right through the alien's thick skull and killing him instantly. Together, Sancho and the horrid creature fell to the ground, landing in a twisted pile.

Eve turned at the sound of more gunshots—this time from Jason, his sights set on an Interloper circling overhead. Just as the creature dove down toward him, Jason unleashed a stream of bullets that ripped through the alien's teeth until a single shot finally penetrated his heart. Percy, too, was firing at a small pack that soared high above them, and Sancho joined the pursuit, hurriedly wielding his contraption as sweat poured down his forehead.

One Interloper finally fell to the ground, and then a second, their mouths free of teeth and oozing with blood, and the boys whooped and chanted over their shared victory. Another Interloper darted in front of them, and again they aimed their weapons, unleashing twelve bullets in unison that once again froze in the air, completely motionless. They looked at Eve; she stood beside them, her eyes and gift focused on the bullets, and then with a smirk, she launched the ammunition straight through the Interloper with so much power that they carried right through the front of the creature's skull and shot out the back, tearing up everything in between as the alien collapsed, dead.

Only one Interloper remained. This one was larger than the others, though his body was littered with bullet holes and gaping wounds. Jason had already targeted him, punching his jaw and chest without reprieve, sending teeth spilling from his mouth and blood pumping from his lesions until he staggered feebly from side to side. With a grunt, Jason jabbed again at the alien's throat, sending him falling onto his back amid puddles of mud and pus. Jason dropped to his knees and hovered over the creature's weakened body, pausing for just a moment to remove his tattered jacket and toss it to the ground. The Interloper blinked, struggling to look back at his opponent, the man who would surely bring about his death. His eyes scanned Jason's face, his arms and blood-soaked fists, his chest and the thick dissection scar that was visible above the neckline of his tank top. A small smile formed at the corners of the Interloper's lips, spreading across his face like an infectious disease.

Then he laughed, softly at first, then with a thunderous cackle, and with the last ounce of energy he could rally, he pointed at Jason's scar with his talon.

His jagged, broken talon.

Jason looked down at the claw—cut at the base like the stump of a tree—and then back at the Interloper, his eyes wide with horror. His body trembled and his lungs raced, and he was suddenly overcome with a heated fury, a hatred that he couldn't control. He opened his mouth and let out a gut-wrenching roar that echoed throughout the forest, and with all his strength he pounded his fist into the creature's battered face—over, and over, and over again, until yellow blood sprayed in every direction. His jabs were sharp and unyielding, and then, with one quick movement, he plunged his arm right through the mouth of the creature, ignoring the teeth that sliced into his flesh, and ripped the life source from the alien's throat. As he held the heart in his torn, bleeding hand, he squeezed it, his fist quivering with rage until the organ burst between his fingers.

Jason stood and stared down at the Interloper carcass. He couldn't feel his torn hand, which hung limply at his side; the pulpy life source slid from his shredded fingers and splattered onto the ground. In that moment, nothing existed but the lifeless Interloper—the creature who had maimed him, had left him with a lasting scar on his chest and, worse, in his mind—and as he gazed down at his fallen adversary, he failed to notice his comrades standing by his side, watching him.

They were silent—Percy, Sancho, and Eve—their bodies still, worn and beaten, their eyes dead from shock. They ignored the graveyard that surrounded them, the stink that hung from the mangled corpses, and instead watched Jason. Finally, he turned to them, and looked only at Eve, his chest heaving with each laborious breath he took, his ragged hand dripping at his side. Still, he said nothing.

A sudden surge of emotion raced through Eve. She hurried toward Jason, throwing her arms around his neck and hugging him tightly. She pulled away from him and studied his face.

"You're hurt."

"You're hurt, too."

"Your hand..." Her voice wavered. "You need to go to the medical ward."

"*No.* I'm *never* going back there."

Percy sprang to life, pulling his shirt over his head and wrapping it around Jason's hand, the cotton quickly soaking up his bright red blood.

A familiar buzzing rang in Eve's ear. *"Can someone tell me what's going on?"* JJ asked. *"Is everyone okay?"*

Eve looked around at her comrades—at Percy's hunched back and bloodied forehead, at Sancho's gouged shoulders, at the gashes along Jason's back and her own slashed ribs.

"Yeah," she mumbled. "We're fine."

"We did it, guys," Sancho muttered. "We killed them all."

Eve turned toward Percy's car. For the first time since the battle had begun, she remembered Florenza, the girl who had sat through the whole thing with her hands clasped around her ears, her head buried in her knees, and the silver torq resting in her lap.

"All right, guys. Let's take her home."

* * *

Right foot. Left foot.

Eve dragged her boots across the concrete pathway, every step an arduous task. She took in a deep breath, a chore in itself, and a shooting pain raced through the gashes along her ribs.

Her comrades walked by her side. Sancho proudly pulled the Dirty Sanchez behind him, though his usually gleeful face was now worn and tired. A shirtless Percy hoisted a single firearm over his shoulder, and despite his limp and his dirty, bloodied face, he still oozed a level of badassery that only he was capable of. And then there was Jason—he stared blankly into the distance as he carried the shaking Florenza in his arms, his tattered hand gripping her so tightly that his own blood began to seep through his makeshift bandage onto her clothes. It didn't matter to him, or to Eve—the pain, the struggle they had all shared. None of it was important, because they had made it back to the Billington campus.

They were alive.

Alive, yes, but barely awake. Exhaustion settled over Eve, spreading through her to the point of debilitation. As she walked across campus, she thought nothing of her clothes torn to shreds, her body covered in blood. She didn't even see the passing students, nor did she hear their fearful gasps and cries. They parted before her as if scared to even cross the bloodied group, but Eve was deadened to their reactions.

She was so numb to her surroundings, in fact, that she hardly noticed the bodies running toward them. They were blurry in her vision, though all so very similar in appearance. Patrolmen—they poured down the pathway one after the next until she couldn't count them all if she tried, which she didn't. She could make out Colonel Eriksen's white-blond hair and scarred face from within the crowd, and jogging alongside him was an older man in a black suit, his arms outstretched and his eyes brimming with tears. It was Florenza's father—the president of Italy—and yet still Eve couldn't muster a reaction. She walked in silence.

Right foot. Left foot. Again. Again.

Florenza jumped from Jason's arms and ran toward her father, quickly wrapping herself in his warm embrace. The patrolmen were nearing Eve and her comrades, but still she was vacant and cold, even as the uniformed soldiers surrounded them, shouting something, some nonsense that she couldn't quite understand, for she could hear nothing at all.

Sancho was the first to fall, dropping to the floor like a tree chopped down at the roots. Percy was next, falling alongside his friend. Chaos surrounded the foursome, and still Eve heard nothing, not even Jason's shouting as the patrolmen forced him to the ground. Eve saw nothing, felt nothing. Not the hands that grabbed at the nape of her neck and the back of her skull. Not the hostile push, her ragged knees hitting the pavement, or her cheek slamming against the ground.

She felt nothing.

CHAPTER 13:

THE QUEEN OF DIAMONDS

"What were you doing with Gallo's daughter?"

Eve sat quietly in the dark, enclosed room—the same room she had been locked in for the past four hours. She could feel the dirt festering in her still-fresh wounds, though she knew they would heal regardless. The entire scene felt like a dream, like a piece of her past had been plucked from the pages of her life's story and randomly rearranged into the present day. Except that one key ingredient was inherently different—she wasn't afraid. Not anymore.

"How were you able to locate the girl's whereabouts?"

She stared back at Colonel Eriksen without a hint of self-doubt. The soldier tried his hand at appearing formidable, but Eve could see his pale white skin turn a bright shade of pink that suggested he was frustrated, even worried by her silence.

"I've got all the time in the world, Evelyn."

"Has Jason been taken to the medical ward yet?" When she finally spoke, her tone was lukewarm and steady. "Has his hand been treated?"

"*I'm* asking the questions here."

"And I'm not answering anything until I know my friends are safe—that their injuries—"

"They wouldn't *have* any injuries if you hadn't been so careless."

"We fought Interlopers and *won*. Florenza is safe because of *us*."

"Is that so?" the colonel sneered, rising from his chair and pacing across the room. "Because all we know is that Gallo went missing about seven hours ago. Then you four came on campus with her in your possession." He stopped and scowled at Eve. "Looks to me as if the Interlopers had nothing to do with it. In fact, I think I'm staring at her captor right now."

Eve snarled. "Are you *kidding*? Is this some kind of sick joke?"

"Did you kidnap the Italian president's daughter?"

"Oh, for God's sake—"

"Where did you take her?"

"We didn't take her *anywhere*—"

"What did you *do* to her?"

"We saved her *life*."

"*Then how did you FIND her?*" he snapped, his patience wearing thin. "Hell, how did you even know she was gone in the first place?"

Eve glanced across the room, and her eyes landed on the thick, dark mirror in front of her. She took in a deep breath as she stared emptily at her own reflection.

"Answer me, Evelyn."

"You really think that'll work? That I've never been interrogated before?" She glared back at the colonel. "I'm not talking."

The door opened, and Dean Furst entered the room. He rested his hand on the colonel's back and offered him an authoritative nod.

"Excuse me, I'd like a word with Miss Kingston."

Eriksen growled, bending to the will of the dean and reluctantly shuffling from the room. As the door slammed shut, Furst pulled out a metal chair and sat before Eve, clasping his hands together along the edge of the table.

"What do you want?" Eve mumbled.

"I've been watching this whole charade, and I must say, I'm not surprised by your reaction," Furst began in his typical cool manner. "I think by now I know you well enough to know that you do not respond to intimidation."

"And your point is?"

"I'm going to be honest with you. Brutally, as that seems to be your preference."

Eve laughed under her breath. "What a kind gesture. Turning over a new leaf, are we? How does *honesty* sit with you?"

"We need to know how you learned of Florenza's abduction and discovered her location."

"And what happens if I tell you?"

Furst leaned back in his chair. "If you were seeking her whereabouts—if you were infringing on the work of our patrolmen and what they have been trained and ordered to do—you face immediate expulsion and, possibly, criminal charges for reckless endangerment."

"Wow, what a generous reward for my cooperation."

"It is not up to me. It is how the system works—to protect people from—"

"The mess you created through your damn list?"

Furst pursed his lips with annoyance. "From risking the lives of themselves and others in the foolish pursuit of heroism."

Eve's eyes shrank to slits. "So it was foolish of us to save her? We should've let her die? Is *that* what you're saying?"

"I'm *saying* that you need to tell us what you know so our patrolmen can do *their* jobs and our students can do what they came to Billington to do—study. *Learn.* Harness a proper education. *Not* battle Interlopers."

"Except that, if I tell you anything, *I* won't be *harnessing* anything. I'll be rotting in a prison cell."

"There are patrolmen searching your rooms right now, as we speak. If there's anything to be found, they will find it." He leaned in closer, peering at Eve over his glasses. "Now, all that's left is for you to say your piece."

"What about my friends? I want to know if they're okay."

"You should care less about your friends' well-being and more about what they have to say. After all, if your stories don't align—if one person tells the truth, and you do not—well, that will pose quite a problem for you." The slightest, most understated frown graced his lips. "Obstruction of justice? You're a smart girl, I'm sure you're familiar with the term."

Eve let out a long breath. "So, let me get this straight. If I say I sought out the Interlopers myself—that I knew about Florenza, tracked down her whereabouts, killed thirty, maybe forty aliens and brought her back to safety—if I tell you all this *and* how I did it, you're going to expel me from Billington and lock me up. Is that it?"

"Yes."

"But you *want* to know, right? You want that sort of information for yourself. For your patrolmen."

"It would be a silver lining to an unfortunate situation."

"And if I don't, then what? Are you and Eriksen going to accuse me of kidnapping Florenza? Turn this whole thing into another rotten smear campaign against the chimera population? Am I going to be arrested for a crime I didn't commit?"

Furst hesitated, his body suddenly rigid. "Florenza already came forward and asserted your innocence. She insisted that you, Jason, and the others saved her life." He paused for a moment, looking Eve straight in the eyes. "She called you heroes."

"So if I don't admit to *infringing* on your patrolmen, or whatever the hell you said, am I free to go?"

"Theoretically."

Eve wrinkled her brow. "*Theoretically?*"

"You are an honest girl to the point of being curt. I am encouraging you to be so right now—to do the right thing. But if you say that your behavior was innocent—that you did not seek Florenza's whereabouts intentionally—you will be free to go." The man lowered his chin, his demeanor suddenly grave and severe. "However... if, at a later date, we discover that you were lying, and if such actions continue, expulsion will be the least of your concerns. You *will* be incarcerated, and so will your friends. It's not a matter of if—it's a matter of *when*, and for how many years."

Eve's eyes were distant. She stared back at her reflection—at her tousled hair, her mud-streaked face, and her torn, formerly white tank top, now soiled with blood of both the red and yellow variety. It was foul—*she* was foul—and yet in that moment, the stabbing in her ribs disappeared, and her dirtied face didn't seem so sullied anymore. In fact, she almost felt like smiling.

"Do you understand, Miss Kingston?"

"Yes. I understand."

"Good. Then I will ask you again: how did you come across Florenza Gallo's whereabouts?"

Eve shrugged. "Right place at the right time."

Furst grimaced. "I need an unequivocal answer from you, Miss Kingston," he ordered, his words uncharacteristically demanding. "Did you seek out Florenza Gallo and the Interlopers?"

Eve looked back at the dean. There was no more treading lightly, no more dabbling in the art of warfare. From this point forward, she would be bound to the new position she had chosen. She was committed.

"No."

***

The mood in the waiting room was uneasy. Jason sat in front of the doorway, anxiously bouncing his knee and eyeing his surroundings. He glanced at Percy and Sancho—they were slumped in their chairs, their bodies drained—and then he stared down at his wrists, which were shackled together in thick, silver cuffs. Finally, he gazed at the door in front of him, hoping that, at any moment, Eve would come walking through it.

Suddenly the door swung open, and a line of patrolmen barged into the room. Jason breathed a sigh of relief: Eve plodded behind them, followed by a glowering Colonel Eriksen. He begrudgingly unfastened their handcuffs.

"You're all free to go," Eriksen muttered.

Eve's eyes scanned her comrades and immediately narrowed with anger. "You *sonofabitch,* you didn't even take them to the medical ward?"

"It's fine, Eve," Jason said, rubbing his now-freed wrists. "We're fine. Let's just get the hell out of here."

They filed from the waiting area, finally realizing where it was they had been taken: they were in the Shelter, suddenly thrown into the mix of soldiers and technicians, some of whom worked tirelessly while others stopped to gape at their battered intruders. The patrolmen, rifles in hand, escorted the group back to the elevator and then through the dean's building, abandoning them only once they'd reached the front doors.

Sancho looked back nervously at the line of soldiers as he and his comrades hurried across the terrace. "You know, that wasn't exactly the warm heroes' welcome I had in mind," he mumbled out of the corner of his mouth.

Jason sighed. "That's because to them, we're not heroes. We're just a bunch of worthless bastards."

Percy grinned playfully. "Well, I've got to say, I think vigilantism suits us."

"*Quiet,* all of you," Eve whispered. "We can't talk about this, not now. They know what we're doing, and they'll be watching us."

"So, what do *you* think we should do?" Sancho asked.

"Lay low for a while. Let things calm down." Eve looked back at the patrolmen one last time; they were far away, but still she kept her voice low. "We'll figure out our next step later. Until then, not a word."

The group parted ways when they reached the center of campus. Percy decided to retreat to his room and relax in the comfort of his luxurious solitude— "*Nothing that a shot of bourbon and a painkiller can't cure*"—and besides, a few scars would only enhance his rugged good looks. Sancho headed to the medical ward, a decision that surprised everyone, as it was certainly the most mature option to take. But despite Eve's urging, Jason refused to accompany him. He claimed it was unnecessary, that Armaan was just as capable of stitching his hand as the nurses at the ward. Eve knew better—she knew that he was afraid, that he loathed the idea of being trapped in the ward for even one more day, and that nothing would ever make him feel any differently.

Eve headed for the Rutherford showers. She stumbled into the washroom without grace or caution, and the other girls froze where they stood—at the sinks, by the changing benches, in front of the mirrors, their eyes fearful as they stared back at the bloodied chimera. Quickly, they scurried from the room, pausing only long enough to gather their belongings and wrap their wet bodies in towels before dashing through the silver doors. Eve welcomed the isolation and dragged her feet to the now-empty changing bench; with a deep breath, she peeled her sticky shirt from her body, groaning as the fabric ripped from her scabbing wounds. She angrily tossed her shirt into the trash, along with her torn jeans, and looked at herself in the mirror. Her bloody knees and gashed ribs were grisly, enough to make any human cringe, but she had been beaten enough times to know that these injuries would be gone in a matter of days.

Yes, she had been here before, staring into a full-length mirror at the trauma that marked her body. But this time it was different.

Reluctantly, Eve forced herself into the shower, wincing as the water stung at her open flesh and rivulets of red and pink blood and brown and black dirt streamed down her body. Each droplet offered its own torment—cutting like a shard of glass as it hit her skin, burning like sandpaper against her ragged knees—and so she propped her hand against the wall, leaning heavily as her legs became weak. She let her wet hair hang over her face as she hunched forward, her eyes clenched shut as she endured the ironic torture of cleansing the filth from her body.

How familiar all of this was—the suffering. She felt the water pouring down her nose and lips and thought for a moment that she could drown, but instead she took in a single, shallow breath and opened her eyes. Dirt, now mucky and thick, accumulated by her feet as it slowly filtered through the drain, along with the red pool of water that swirled like silk between her toes. She was clean. And this time, unlike the others, she was restored.

Eve dug through the lost-and-found bin, nabbing a pair of lounge pants and a baggy sweatshirt and tossing them onto her body before leaving the washroom. The Rutherfordians stared at her—she told herself it was because of her wet hair and tired face, but she knew otherwise—and she continued past them, avoiding their gazes as she fiddled with the lock of her dorm room door.

She barged through the entryway and suddenly stopped—the room was empty, or practically so. Not a single suitcase, diamond, or couture garment was in sight. The floor was visible for the first time since the semester began, and Madison's bed had been stripped down to the mattress. The dorm room felt huge, open, and naked, and though Eve had often wished for such a sight, it suddenly seemed unsettling. She looked down at the end table beside her; there sat Madison's room key, its grip adorned with sparkly crystals.

"She moved out."

Hayden stood behind Eve, her arms folded over the buttons of her pea coat.

Eve rolled her eyes. "Thanks for clarifying. I wouldn't have been able to figure that out on my own."

"You're welcome."

Eve sighed. "So, let me guess, she moved in with you?"

"No."

"Really? But you're her shadow. I figured you'd jump at the chance to room with her."

Hayden gazed at the floor. "She's living with Lionel instead."

Eve smirked. "Back at the bottom of the totem pole, are we?"

Hayden didn't respond. Eve was surprised, as the girl was typically quick with a barb, but instead Hayden just shuffled through the room and plucked a small cardboard box filled with pink paraphernalia from the floor.

"I have to go," she mumbled. "This is the last of her stuff."

Eve stared at Hayden—at her downcast eyes, her uncharacteristically somber look—and for the first time, she pitied the girl.

"You know, you should maybe think twice about hanging out with Madison."

Hayden wavered. "What are you talking about?"

"She just may not be what she seems."

Hayden's large, grey eyes became small and focused. She took a step toward Eve, her nose wiggling as she studied each and every inch of her face. After a moment of silence, she sneered.

"I see what you're doing. You're trying to poison me against her."

"Look, I'm serious. You need to be careful—"

"I'm not *stupid*, you know. You think you're better than me, but you're not."

"Hayden, she could be *dangerous*."

"*Stop it,*" she growled. "I don't want to talk about this anymore."

"I'm just trying to *help* you—"

"I said, *STOP IT.*"

Suddenly the cardboard box flew from Hayden's grasp and crashed into the wall, sending its contents spraying across the floor. Eve gasped, glancing in shock at the random trinkets, now in pieces along the ground, and then at the limp box that had so abruptly come to life. There was only one explanation for its sudden movement, and it certainly wasn't Eve—no, Eve had total control of her gift. Slowly, she looked up at Hayden.

"Did you just—"

"Don't say it," Hayden spat. "Don't even think it."

Eve gazed blankly at the mess, still struggling to digest what she had just witnessed. "Oh... my God."

"You didn't see anything, okay?" Hayden maintained, her voice trembling. "You *didn't see ANYTHING.*"

Eve looked back at Hayden, her forehead wrinkled. "This *whole time?*"

"JUST GO, OKAY?" the girl cried. "JUST LEAVE ME ALONE."

Eve furrowed her brow. "This is *my* room, Hayden."

"Oh." She paused. "Right."

Hayden lingered in the room for a moment longer, attempting to gather up the broken shards of whatever-they-once-were from the floor before deeming it futile. She hurried to the doorway, seemingly eager to be rid of Eve's presence, then abruptly stopped beside the end table.

"Eve," she said, resting her hand along the table. "Please." She paused and looked back at Eve. Their eyes met.

"Please don't tell."

* * *

"I still can't believe they let us go!"

Sancho flung his body onto Percy's couch and sank into the folds of the rich leather. It had been over a week since their assault against the Interlopers and subsequent run-in with the patrolmen, and despite their better judgment, the group finally agreed to meet between classes in the privacy of Percy's suite. As they convened near the HV, circling a celebratory bottle of aged scotch and a bowl of salt-and-vinegar chips, a long-stifled sense of relief and victory swept through the room.

Sancho placed his hands behind his head and smiled complacently. "I didn't realize I was *that* convincing. Maybe I should be an actor."

Eve rolled her eyes. "They knew we were full of shit. Percy's car was loaded with guns."

"I told them we were on a hunting trip." Percy shrugged, kicking at Sancho's legs and freeing a spot for himself at the end of the couch. "If you think about it, it's not exactly a lie. We *were* hunting aliens, after all."

"They only let us go because, by the sheer grace of God, all of our stories matched up," Eve said.

"No one told the truth." Jason squeezed beside Eve on the loveseat and rested his arm around her shoulders. "I've never been so proud of you rotten little liars."

"We dodged a bullet this time, but they'll be watching us." Eve anxiously picked at her cuticles. "If Furst gets the slightest inkling that we're still tracking the Interlopers, you can bet your ass he'll send patrolmen to break down our doors."

As soon as the words left her mouth, there was a knock at the door. The group froze, their lips stunned to silence and eyes wide with dread. Percy inched slowly toward the entryway, stepping softly as if desperate not to make a sound, and with a deep, nervous breath, he gently turned the knob and opened the door.

"You're all under arrest," JJ teased, shoving past the heir and taking his seat on the couch. "Just kidding, you big babies."

"JJ, my divine, celestial creature, you're alive!" Sancho hurried toward her. "Where have you been?"

"We haven't heard from you since the Wilds." Eve glowered. "You didn't even come to class all week."

"That's because I was *trying* to appear inconspicuous." She winked at Eve and shoved a handful of chips into her mouth. "A little bit of distance from you guys didn't seem like the worst idea after all the trouble you got yourselves into."

Eve growled. "They raided all of our rooms. We assumed they found you in Jason's dorm. We thought you were expelled."

"*Please,*" JJ scoffed. "As soon as you guys were taken in, I bolted. Did you really think I'd stick around for that mess like a sitting duck? This isn't my first time dealing with the authorities—and don't be all high and mighty with me, because I know it's not *your* first time either." She shifted her attention from Eve to Jason and flashed a critical scowl in his direction. "Or *yours*. I know *all*, remember?"

Jason cleared his throat uncomfortably. "Well, I hate to be the bearer of bad news, but we've got nothing for you."

"Yeah, Eriksen confiscated everything—our earpieces, our guns, even the Dirty Sanchez." Sancho bowed his head somberly. "God rest his soul."

"And most importantly, they took the torq," Eve sighed.

Percy grinned, his eyes sparkling with self-satisfaction. "Or did they?"

With a single swoop, he threw his arm beneath the couch and pulled a small, concealed lever. Suddenly the middle cushion of his couch rose up with Sancho still on top of it, sending him toppling to the floor. Percy casually stepped over his friend and pulled a drawer from the cushion, opened the leather casing, and delicately removed a silver, cylindrical device. With a sly grin, he revealed to the others the secret he'd been keeping for the past ten days: he still had the torq.

"Geez, Percy," Sancho grumbled as he gathered himself from the floor. "How many secret compartments do you *have* in this place?"

"How the *hell* did you sneak that past the patrolmen?" Eve gasped.

"I have my ways."

"Seriously, how'd you do it?" Jason pried. "You had to have worked some magic, because they frisked me."

Eve nodded. "Me too."

"And me." Sancho eyed the heir suspiciously. "You know, a common method criminals use to smuggle contraband is to stick it up their—"

"For the love of God, *please* don't finish that sentence," Percy snapped.

"Well, how else could you have gotten away with it?"

"I put it down my *pants*."

"But they checked my legs, and my pockets—"

"*No,* Sancho," Percy groused, pointing at his groin. "I put it down my *under*pants."

Jason's jaw dropped. "*Excuse me?*"

"I did some... well, some *tucking,* if you will, and I put it in the crotch of my chonies."

"Oh... my God," Eve muttered.

"Hey, you and I *both* know that thing looks like a, well, *thing*," he spat. "I figured the patrolmen wouldn't fondle the family jewels. And if that didn't work, I hoped that the bulge alone would scare them off."

Jason laughed. "That's disgusting."

"It was *genius*. And by the way, you're welcome."

"Hell, I'm not complaining," JJ said. "Just remind me not to touch it with my bare hands."

Eve turned to JJ, eager to change the subject. "So, now that you have the torq, can you start coding that virus?"

"It's going to take some time. I have to figure out how it functions before I can even attempt to create a compatible virus."

"Well, whatever you have to do to get that thing working, do it."

JJ flashed a smug grin. "Yes, *Your Majesty*."

"And keep watching the beacon's transmissions. If something else comes up, we need to know about it."

"And then what?" Percy interrupted. "We can't do anything. Not with Big Brother breathing down our necks."

"No kidding." JJ pulled her scratchpad from her shoulder bag. "You're on Furst's radar in a big way. Over the last week, the Shelter doubled their cameras across campus, and I can tell you, they're not just looking for aliens."

Sancho's eyes bulged comically. "What if they're watching us right now?"

"Relax," JJ said. "There aren't any cameras in this room, or any other dorm room. Trust me, I've checked. Never mind the fact that that would be *illegal*, but regardless—"

"We have to watch our backs," Jason cut in.

JJ smiled. "Or I can watch them for you."

She turned her scratchpad to face the others. Hundreds of tiny video clips filled the screen, displaying live feeds from across campus. "You can't forget my arsenal of tech goodies. I have total access to the surveillance sector, so I can tell you when you're in their line of vision."

Sancho sighed adoringly. "You'll be like our very own personal guardian angel."

"And *you* can continue to be my very own personal pain in the ass."

"Speaking of pain in the ass, we need to discuss Madison," Jason added.

"God, *again*?" Percy groaned. "We get it, she's a possessive, psychotic mess."

"Yeah, well, she may be a hell of a lot more than that." Jason turned to face the group. "We found ashes all over that nest in the Wilds—the same ashes used to write *Die Chime* in Eve's classroom. The same ashes—"

"On Madison's sheets," Eve mumbled.

Jason cradled his forehead in his hands. "I can't believe that *Madison Palmer* could be an Interloper, of all people."

"No way, she's totally human," JJ countered. "What about all that lovesick puppy bullshit?"

"Maybe it was all an act." Eve glanced at Jason. "Hell, maybe she sent you her underwear just in hopes of getting you two alone together."

"Wait, an alien sent you his *underwear*?" Percy asked.

Jason's face reddened. "Don't ask."

"Have you tried talking to her?" Sancho asked. "You know, to feel her out?"

"Of course she hasn't." Percy rolled his eyes. "What the hell is Eve supposed to say? 'Hey Madison, I hear you want me dead. Is this for *human* or *alien* reasons?'"

"It doesn't matter," Eve grumbled. "Talking isn't an option."

Sancho wrinkled his nose. "Well, you have to talk to her one of these days. You do *live* together."

"Not anymore. She moved out."

"What?" Jason asked. "Why?"

"We sort of had a confrontation." Eve paused, sinking lower in her chair. "I might've melted her against a wall. Or something."

Sancho gasped. "*Balls*. Bet you're regretting that decision right about now."

"I didn't *know* she was an *alien* when I did it."

"And we still don't know for certain," Jason added. "The ashes thing could just be a coincidence."

"Pretty damn significant coincidence," Eve muttered.

JJ shrugged. "Well, the only way we'll know for sure is if we light the broad on fire—"

"*Or* we can just cut her open," Jason added.

"Really? You two are proposing we *shank* or *incinerate* a well-known heiress?" Percy laughed under his breath. "Enjoy your lawsuit."

"I'm just saying, Eve cut her arm open back at the Wilds in order to prove her humanity."

"Yeah, because I was *desperate*," Eve said. "I didn't know if it would actually *prove* anything. I still don't. Who knows what the second skin does internally?"

"So, what are we supposed to do, then?" Sancho asked.

"We'll keep an eye on Madison," Eve answered. "If she *is* an Interloper, we're at least clued into it. That puts us one step ahead of her."

Percy grabbed his bottle of scotch and poured himself a double. "Well, if we can't do anything about our blond basket case, let's talk about something we *can* do."

"What do you mean?" Eve asked.

"Weapons." He took a seat on the arm of Eve's chair. "We need new ones."

"Seriously," Jason mumbled. "We can't have a repeat of what happened at the Wilds. We came out alive, which means we did *something* right, but the whole thing was—"

"A shitstorm?" Percy finished.

Jason sighed. "We won, but barely. There were too many close calls."

"It took at least twenty bullets—and some *extremely* impressive shooting"—Percy raised his eyebrows smugly—"to kill *one* Interloper." He downed his drink before he continued. "And I can't ask Eve to give my ammo a boost every time I fire at them. We need something stronger—something more efficient."

"Like what?" Sancho asked. "Like brass-tipped bullets?"

"That's not going to cut it."

"What about carbine?"

"Even stronger."

Eve's eyes widened. She sat upright in her seat, struck by an idea she couldn't believe she hadn't considered long before.

"*Diamonds*," she declared, boldly. "We can use diamonds."

JJ laughed. "That's ridiculous. A diamond would shatter on impact—"

"This won't." Eve sprang from her seat and dug through her shoulder bag until she found it—the gift from Madison after their first week of school. She held the diamond between her fingers and displayed it for the others to see.

"It's an 'Everlasting Diamond.' Some synthetic crap, designed to be shatterproof."

"A shatterproof diamond?" Sancho snatched the jewel from Eve's hand, studying it closely. "If this is for real, then it's *exactly* what we need—something hard enough to cut through any surface, but tough enough to withstand any impact. It's perfect—that is, assuming the hype is valid."

Jason stood from the loveseat. "Well, there's only one way to find out."

Without explanation, he disappeared down the hallway, returning shortly with something dangling from his hand—a hammer. He plucked the diamond from Sancho's palm and rested it delicately on the coffee table, analyzing the jewel as if assessing a challenging opponent. He stopped and glanced at Eve.

"Do you mind?" he asked.

Eve shrugged. "Be my guest."

Jason turned toward the diamond and raised the hammer high above his head, squinting his eyes as he focused on the tiny, glittering target. With a deep breath, he pounded the jewel, sending flecks of wood spraying across the room as the hammer smashed deep into the paneling of the coffee table.

"You ASS!" Percy shouted. "That was a custom table!"

"Sorry, man, I'm still getting used to this whole super-strength thing." Jason yanked the hammer from the table and eyed the damage. "I'll pay to replace it."

"It was ten *thousand* dollars!"

"*Jesus Christ,* Percy!"

"LOOK!" Sancho crawled along the floor, sifting through the splintered wood before recovering the gem. "The diamond, it's in one piece!"

The entire group gathered around Sancho, staring in wonder at the spotless, immaculate jewel.

Jason shrugged. "Looks shatterproof to me."

"While I *do* hate to be a downer, I don't think a hammer's going to do the trick," JJ added. "We need to fire it from a gun in order to be sure."

"Well, thanks to the patrolmen, we don't *have* any guns," Percy whined. "The closest thing we have is—"

Before he could finish his thought, the diamond darted from the floor and shot across the room like a crystal bullet whizzing through the sky. With a loud crack, it burst through a cabinet in Percy's kitchen, disappearing from sight.

The entire group stared at the tiny hole in the center of the cabinet, then turned to look at Eve. She ended her melt and met their gazes.

"You *were* talking about me, right?" she asked, blankly.

The team dashed toward the kitchen nook, pushing and shoving at one another until they reached the cabinet door. Jason eyed the tiny hole before yanking the door open, revealing a shattered bottle sitting in a pool of whiskey. Behind the shards of glass, in the back of the cabinet, was a second hole; Jason peered through it and saw a pipe that extended past the shelves and down toward the kitchen sink, and through that pipe was yet another hole.

"Holy shit," Jason laughed. "The diamond—it cut through everything. It even cut through the piping."

Sancho dropped to the floor and climbed beneath Percy's sink, grabbing at the various nozzles and hoses. He yanked at the pipe and pulled it free from the duct, sending grey, murky water spilling across his lap.

Percy sighed. "I don't think my dorm is going to survive the day."

"It's here!" Sancho yelped, extracting the jewel from the piping and holding it above his head for his comrades to see. "The diamond—it's still perfectly intact!"

"I *told* you," Eve said. "If anything can break through the Interlopers' bones, it's this diamond."

JJ grabbed the diamond from Sancho's hand and studied it for herself. "Where the hell did you get this thing?"

"Madison gave it to me months ago. It's supposed to be the next big thing in jewelry or fashion or whatever."

"I don't care what Madison says," Jason added. "This isn't jewelry. It's a weapon."

"So, it's decided," Percy declared. "Diamond bullets—what a concept."

Eve glanced at Jason; he was staring at the gem, his gaze vague and distant as if he was deep in thought. Though he didn't speak it, Eve knew what was on his mind, and her stomach churned with discomfort.

"I want one," Jason finally said. "A knife, a sword, an axe, I don't care—just something I can use in hand-to-hand combat. Something made with this diamond."

Sancho furrowed his brow. "Why?"

"It's fine," Eve quickly interrupted. "We need bullets and a blade. The question is, where the hell are we going to get a stash of Everlasting Diamonds?"

"Percy's loaded," Sancho said. "Can't he just buy some and call it a day?"

Eve shook her head. "Madison said they're not for sale yet. She only has access to them because her dad holds the keys to the kingdom."

"Well, it's a shame none of us are on good terms with her—assuming she's human, that is." Jason turned to Eve. "That girl may be crazy, but she's generous with her friends. And if you date her—God, she *showers* her men with gifts. I mean, did you see the rock on Lionel at my birthday disaster? Getting Everlasting Diamonds from her would be a piece of cake."

The room fell silent. Percy and Sancho looked at one another and then at

Jason, their eyes wide as if they had suddenly come to the same conclusion. Eve groaned. She already knew what they were about to say—it was both painfully clear and dreadfully logical—and yet it sickened her to the core.

Jason looked back and forth between his comrades. "What? What did I say?"

Sancho cowered. "Jason, I think you need to take one for the team."

"What do you mean?"

"You have to take Madison on a date," Percy blurted.

"*What?*" Jason barked, standing upright. "*No.* Absolutely not."

"Come on," Sancho whined, "you're the perfect man for the job. She's *in love* with you."

"Or wants to kill you. The verdict's still out," JJ mumbled.

"But think of it this way," Sancho continued. "A date could be the determiner —the ultimate test to see whether or not she's an Interloper. If she's human, the date will unfold normally. And if she's an alien, she'll—"

"Cut me open? Dismantle me for parts? Impregnate me with alien babies?"

"Is *that* why you're so skittish?" Percy teased. "Don't tell me you're scared of a little interspecies saliva swapping."

"I don't *care* if she's an Interloper," Jason groused. "She can be an alien, or a human, or a goat or whatever else. My answer is still *no.*"

"Oh, don't be such a scrote," Percy said. "Take her out for dinner, whip out the chimera cock, grab yourself some diamonds, and be on your way!"

"I have a girlfriend, *dumbass.*"

"Eve doesn't mind," Percy insisted. "Right, Eve?"

"Look, I get it—the whole thing's a gamble," JJ cut in, acting as the voice of reason. "If she's an alien, you're shit out of luck in more ways than one. But if she's human, this could be our *only shot* at getting those diamonds."

"I'm not doing it," Jason maintained. "End of story. We're just going to have to find some other way to get the diamonds."

Eve eyed her friends—they all stared at her, waiting for her to weigh in— and she felt her cheeks flush with embarrassment. She cleared her throat.

"Well, as much as I'm loving the awkward turn this conversation has taken, we're already late for class," she said, anxiously heading for the door.

"Yeah, I was ready to leave at *chimera cock*," Jason muttered as he followed her out of the room.

Eve and Jason left the suite and hurried to the football field where their combat class was already underway. After a very loud and very public chastising from Captain Ramsey, they dashed toward the track and began their daily laps, weaving through their classmates with ease.

They sprinted alongside one another, their breathing steady and movements nearly synchronized, but despite the ease of the task, Eve felt strained and on edge. She tried to occupy her thoughts with distractions: it was December already, and in a few short weeks, the semester would be over. She attempted to think about her upcoming exams—about Ramsey's nagging expectations and even her inevitable "A" in Dr. Dick's class —but it was no use. While other students were fretting over their fast-approaching finals, Eve was worried about diamond bullets, Furst's watchful eye, and whether or not her boyfriend should take her possibly alien ex-roommate on a date. With a deep breath, she bit her lip and looked over at Jason.

"You know, if you want to go out with Madison," she began, stuttering over her words, "I mean, I know you don't *want* to, but if you *need* to, I'm okay with it."

Jason chuckled. "You've never been a good liar."

"Well, obviously it's not ideal, but I understand it's for the benefit of the team."

"Eve, I don't want to do it. It's not me. It's not worth it."

"What do you mean?"

The two broke apart for a moment as they veered around a straggling classmate, then met up again in the center of the track, once again matching pace.

"If she *is* human, then the date would be real. Regardless of the intention, it would mean something, at least to Madison." His voice trailed off as he stared out at the endless track. "I don't want to do anything to screw up what you and I have together—not even if it's for the team." He glanced over at her. "I know it wasn't easy for you to let me in. I don't take that for granted."

Eve smiled, looking first into Jason's eyes and then down at his hand. Though his injuries had healed within days, she could still see the countless pink scars that decorated his knuckles and wrist. She thought back to their experience at the Wilds—Jason plunging his fist through the Interloper's mouth, blood spraying from his torn flesh—and an unsettling chill ran through her body.

"I lost control."

Eve's eyes quickly darted away from his hand, but it was too late; he had noticed her staring.

"Excuse me?"

"Back at the Wilds." Jason refused to look at her, gazing emptily at the field instead. "I saw his talon and I couldn't help myself. I ripped his goddamn heart out... and the worst part is, I enjoyed it."

The two were silent; they ran together, both watching the track in front of them as if scared to look one another in the eye.

"I don't know if I can do it," Jason said, finally ending the awkward silence. "I don't know if I can restrain myself. I *hate* them, and in the moment— all that *rage*—it's too much. It's like I'm someone else."

"That's why you want the weapon. The blade."

"Sure in hell would beat tearing up my hand again. Because it *will* happen again. I'm sure of it."

Again they were quiet. The cool air had suddenly become hot and tense, and Eve could feel Jason's agitation as if it were a cloud surrounding the two of them.

"I don't want you to think I'm some kind of monster," he added.

"You know I don't, Jason."

"Well, I wish you'd say something."

She finally turned to look at him. "Do you feel better?"

His brow wrinkled. "*What?*"

"You killed him. You had your revenge. Do you feel better now?"

Jason bit his bottom lip and stared at the ground. "No."

Eve sighed. "I wish you did."

"You're not freaked out?"

"I know a thing or two about anger, Jason."

He looked back at her. Her eyes were thoughtful and kind, and suddenly the tension in the air turned into something else: a shared sadness, a longing for relief.

"I killed the man who murdered my parents," she said, her tone uncharacteristically revealing. "It was an accident, but I still did it. I wish it had made me feel—I don't know, avenged, maybe even happy. But it didn't." Her eyes became stern, almost angry for him. "That creature stole your peace of mind. You deserve to have it back."

"KINGSTON!"

A loud cry from across the field startled Eve, sending her skidding to a stop. She turned to see a red-faced Captain Ramsey pacing beside the bleachers.

"Get your ass over here!"

Eve offered Jason a quick smile before jogging toward the captain, bowing her head somewhat humbly as she reached his side.

"Sorry for the talking," she muttered. "It won't happen again."

"Bullshit," he grumbled, "and that's not why I called you." He took a moment to glance over his clipboard and lowered his voice. "I hear you an' Valentine are huntin' aliens. Is this true?"

Heat pulsed through her veins, and her frame became rigid. "No, Captain."

"Think I can't spot a liar?"

Eve fidgeted uncomfortably—she glanced over at Jason, who was close to lapping the other runners—and then turned back to the captain.

"I don't know what you've heard, but the whole thing was just a coincidence." She straightened her back, feigning an air of confidence. "Just bad luck I guess."

"Save the tall tales for the patrolmen. I don't give two shits about their damn rules and legal garbage. Truth be told, I want to congratulate you on a job well done."

Eve faltered. "Captain?"

"You're taking initiative—doing something no one else has the guts to do. Don't let some suit behind a desk tell you to quit. You're a fighter. A warrior."

"A warrior, huh?" Eve smirked and folded her arms. "You should tell that to Furst. The man treats me like I'm an incapable little girl."

"I see no gender. I just see power." He lowered his clipboard, finally giving Eve his undivided attention. "The next time you go out to fight them Interlopers—"

"I'm not fighting Interlopers."

Ramsey smiled and winked. "Good work, soldier. Trust no one."

With one sharp trill, Ramsey blew his whistle, summoning the rest of the students to the end of the field where he stood. As they gathered around, Jason ventured to Eve's side, eager to know what Ramsey had said, but the captain cleared his throat and immediately dove into his lecture.

"We're gonna do things a lil' different today," he said. "This exercise will involve the whole class in one combat simulation. Some folks call it defensive training, but I like to call it what it really is: your *worst nightmare.*"

He fiddled with his clipboard, pulling two red circles made of thick cloth from the back of his notes. He held them in front of the class. "These patches? They're targets. And if you end up with one of 'em on your back, then the odds have just been stacked against you. You're outgunned. You're outnumbered. And it's your job to fight for your life." He weaved through his students, pacing behind them in an ominous fashion.

"And as for everyone else? You're the enemy. Your job is to attack your targets—to *take 'em down*. Think of these soldiers as trespassers. They've *violated* you. They've infiltrated your territory." He paused. "Your *nest*."

Without warning, Ramsey slapped both Jason and Eve across their backs, firmly attaching the red cloth targets to their shirts. He smirked.

"Now *fight*."

***

Eve stood outside the lecture hall, fumbling with her shoulder bag and its contents. She glanced through the window behind her; Professor Richards was sitting at his desk and, unsurprisingly enough, staring directly at her, as if the thought of subtlety had never crossed his mind. He kicked his heels up onto his desk, smacking them down atop several sheets of paper—her finished test, another "A" to add to the list and another opportunity for resentment and ridicule.

Eve cursed to herself, hoping that the professor could read lips, and continued to shuffle through her bag. She found her scratchpad and tinkered with it; it sparked and sputtered when she tried to activate it, and so she angrily shoved it back into her bag and leaned her head against the window frame.

Deep breath. A slight sense of calm flowed through her, but it was immediately replaced by the feeling of eyes watching her. She lifted her head from its resting place and glanced down the corridor.

Madison stood at the opposite end of the hallway, glaring at Eve. Her rage was transparent—it was in her eyes, in the slight curl of her upper lip, and in the stillness of her body. Eve thought about her conversation with Percy and Sancho the day before; she recalled their "brilliant" idea and imagined Jason and Madison on a romantic date. And then her mind was flooded with images of thick, black ash.

Her eyelids fluttered, and again she saw the heiress glowering back at her. The light from the entryway window set Madison's blond hair aglow like the halo of an angel, but the look of sheer loathing on her face was practically devilish.

"She's staring into your soul."

Eve jumped, startled by the unwanted spectator now at her side. *"Jesus,* JJ, you scared the shit out of me."

JJ leaned against the wall, fiddling with her chain bracelets before playfully slugging Eve in the arm. "Loosen up, princess. You're always so goddamn tense."

Eve scowled, still peering at Madison out of the corner of her eye. "Yeah, well, I'm sure you can gather why."

JJ chuckled. "Don't be a scrote. She's not going to attack you in the middle of the business building."

"You never know," a second voice chimed in. Percy had joined them and carelessly wedged himself between the two girls. "Those Interlopers are gutsy. If one was willing to throw down in a packed nightclub, then a university hallway seems like fair game to me."

Eve rolled her eyes. "You guys are being ridiculous. This whole conversation is stupid."

"Come on, Eve, look at her." Percy squinted his eyes, unapologetically studying the heiress. "It's almost like she's taking a mental picture of you."

"Like the ones we found on the beacon," JJ muttered.

"God, the evil eye on her—it's creeptastic." Percy shuddered and backed away. "I'm getting out of here before I turn to stone."

Eve ignored Percy as he sauntered away, her gaze still focused on her former roommate's glare. Percy was right: Madison's face alone was ominous, and for whatever reason, be it the death threat or her now indistinct agenda, her presence had transformed from a mere annoyance to one of grave concern. As if summoned by Eve's pestering thoughts, the blond bombshell suddenly stirred to action, delicately flipping her hair across her shoulder and marching straight ahead.

"Oh Lord," JJ said, still attached to Eve's hip. "We've awakened the beast."

Eve groaned. "Sonofa*bitch...*"

"She's coming this way. *She's coming this way!*" JJ snickered.

"Will you get out of here?" Eve barked.

"No way, I need to see this."

Madison approached the two girls, her eyes scanning them as though she was scrutinizing their every imperfection. Her lips became tight, as if she had just tasted something bitter, and after a long, uncomfortable silence, she managed to speak.

"Hello," she grumbled.

Eve sighed. "What do you want?"

"I'm not talking to you," Madison spat. Her eyes turned to JJ. "I'm talking to your... weird, gothic, Asian friend." She pointed down the hallway. "Who is he?"

Eve and JJ turned, curious to see who had caught her attention. Percy stood in the distance, casually schmoozing with some other Rutherfordians before his class began. JJ glanced back at the heiress, her brow furrowed.

"Who? Percy?"

"His name is *Percy*?" Madison sneered. "God, his parents must *hate* him."

"Wait," Eve interjected, "*you* of all people don't know who Percy LaFleur is? Aren't you supposed to be some kind of expert on the social elite?"

"Look, I don't need your suckgasmic bullshit, all right? Just tell me who he is."

"Why do you want to know?" JJ asked.

"Well, I mean, look at him." Madison sighed. "He's tall, he's handsome, he oozes confidence. And do you know how hard it is to find a guy with some fashion sense? I can smell the high-quality designer material from here."

"Are you *attracted* to him?" Eve asked.

"God, you make it sound so *primal*."

"But I thought you and Lionel were official."

"Just because we're *official* doesn't mean we're *exclusive*."

"Um... I think that's exactly what it means, Madison."

"Save the lecture, *Mom*," Madison snarled. "Just tell me, what's his story?"

JJ laughed. "His story? Girl, you're barking up the wrong tree, because Percy LaFleur is one hundred percent—"

"*Single*," Eve quickly cut in. "Very, *very* single. *And* he has an affinity for blondes... and boobs!"

Madison wrinkled her forehead. "Are you serious?"

"Yes, *Eve*," JJ added, raising an eyebrow, "are you *serious*?"

"I can talk to him for you if you want," Eve continued, ignoring JJ. "Maybe set up a date?"

Madison faltered, staring Eve up and down suspiciously. "Why are you being so nice to me?"

"I—" Eve stammered, searching for a viable excuse. "I don't know."

JJ's scowl suddenly transformed into a duplicitous smile. "I do," she chirped, turning to Madison. "You see, deep down she wishes you two were still friends."

Eve's face reddened. "No, I don't."

"Yes you do," JJ countered. "It's basic psychology, really. She's hoping to win your affection through random and extravagant favors."

"That's really not it."

"Ah, there it is—textbook denial."

Madison straightened her shoulders and pointed her nose at the ceiling. "Well, you shouldn't be ashamed, Eve. If I were you, I'd want to be friends with me too." She flicked her wrist toward Eve like a master directing a well-trained dog. "Set me up on that date, and maybe I'll consider it."

"Gee, Madison, you're too kind," Eve muttered.

"I'm *kidding*, Eve. I hate you, remember?" the heiress jeered. "But still, the date—make it happen."

Madison scampered away from the duo, her hips swaying with each graceful step. Eve indignantly flared her nostrils and clenched her jaw.

"You're a real asshole, JJ."

"I know, right?" JJ laughed, patting Eve patronizingly on the back. "And the worst part is, I'm going to watch and laugh while you break the news to Percy."

Eve growled, shaking JJ's hand from her shoulder as she made her way back to Percy's side. He was still waiting in front of his next class, eyeing his reflection in the lecture hall window before turning to greet them.

"Back for more?" He winked. "Can't get enough of me, can you? It happens."

Eve's body became stiff. "Percy," she began reluctantly, "we sort of need to ask you for a favor."

"*We* don't need *anything*," JJ corrected. "I told you, you're on your own with this one."

Eve shot JJ a glare before turning to face Percy once again. "I need you to take Madison out"—she paused, clearing her throat—"on a date."

"Ha! Right," he scoffed. "What's on the itinerary? Some dinner, maybe a couple's massage, and then we finish the night off with a chimera dissection? Sounds like my kind of evening."

Eve was quiet; she fiddled with her cuticles as she stared back at him, and in that moment he sensed something unfamiliar in her eyes: a hint of desperation.

"Wait, you're serious?" His jaw dropped open. "You're *serious*?"

"*Please*, Percy," she moaned. "We *really* need those Everlasting

Diamonds."

"Why *me*, of all people?"

"Because she's interested in you. She thinks you're sexy and stylish. It'll be like taking candy from a baby."

"Or taking diamonds from a bimbo," JJ muttered under her breath.

Eve sighed. "Please, Percy. You *have* to do this."

"Did you forget the fact that I'm *gay*?"

"But you're Percy LaFleur!" Eve countered. "You can woo anyone, male or female!"

"Or *alien*?"

"The whole Interloper thing was just a theory—"

"Well, *forgive* me if I'm not interested in taking any chances with your *theory*."

"But you were so willing to let Jason go out with her."

"That was different."

"How?"

"*I'm not Jason*."

"If you think about it, even if she *is* an Interloper, you should be safe," JJ cut in, her gaze darting between an angry Percy and a surprised Eve. "I mean, you're not a chimera. What would she want with you?"

"Maybe she wants me *nailed* to a construct with *needles* sticking out of my eyes. Need I remind you about Marshall Woodgate?" His eyes widened. "Oh my God, that's it. *I'm* the next Marshall Woodgate."

"You're *not* the next Marshall Woodgate," Eve insisted. "You're Percy LaFleur, Billington's most eligible bachelor. A young heartthrob who just so happened to catch the eye of the very beautiful, and very *selective*, Madison Palmer." She folded her arms matter-of-factly. "You said it yourself: people can't get enough of you."

"You've got a little brown on your nose, Eve."

"Percy," she sighed, "please don't make me beg."

"Yeah, Percy." JJ elbowed him in the ribs. "She's kind of begging already, and, quite frankly, it makes me sad."

Percy glanced back and forth between the two girls. One stared back at him with heavy eyes and the other with a condemning scowl. He groaned loudly.

"*Fine*," he hissed, succumbing to their combined forces. "But I'm doing this because I'm the only man qualified to get the job done."

"You really, *really* are—"

"Save the ass-kissing, Eve, I already agreed to your little plan." He glowered. "But I am *not* happy with you right now."

Though she tried to suppress it, Eve couldn't help but smirk. "Don't be such a dick-squeeze, Percy."

He squinted his eyes and frowned. "*You* are a grade-A *slophole,* Eve."

"Hammer."

"*Ballsack.*"

With a childish pout, he stormed away from the duo, but his irate clomping morphed back into his usual confident strut before he reached Madison's side. Eve watched from afar as Percy worked his magic, and though she had no doubt in his abilities, she felt a swell of relief the moment she heard Madison giggle. Just as she began to relax, JJ approached her side and poked her in the fatty part of her arm.

"What's with all the name-calling?" she asked.

Eve shrugged. "They're terms of endearment. It's just what we do."

"Sounds almost like you two are siblings."

"I wouldn't know. Never had any brothers or sisters."

They watched as Percy and Madison disappeared down the hallway together, his hand resting on the small of her back. JJ cringed.

"Well, whatever you are to one another, the fact remains—" She turned to Eve. "We might've just sent your surrogate brother into an Interloper death trap."

***

"That was a lovely dinner," Madison mumbled, her voice flat and uninspired, "but I have to admit, when I asked if you wanted to go somewhere else for dessert, my daddy's diamond showroom wasn't exactly the place I had in mind."

Percy strolled into the showroom as if he were walking into his own dorm, casually meandering past the rows of glass-encased diamonds, rubies, and garnets without the slightest hint of awe. The location had closed hours ago, but that was hardly an issue; Madison had access to every showroom, a fact that Percy had researched ahead of time—along with many other pivotal details. Sure, it was awfully audacious of him to take his date to such a place, but this was no ordinary *date*—it was a business transaction, one that he aimed to execute as quickly and efficiently as possible. He turned to the heiress and winked.

"You don't think it's exciting? I thought you loved diamonds."

"I do," she countered, briefly eyeing the gems. "But there's a showroom near Calabasas. We could've just gone there... instead of flying to Maryland."

"What can I say? I'm full of surprises." He wandered toward a single display case, pretending to admire the ostentatious jewelry. "Besides, isn't this your largest, most impressive showroom in the country?"

She pouted. "Still..."

"Did I upset you, doll? My apologies. I just thought sneaking into your dad's showroom, late at night, just the two of us was... I don't know..." He paused, nestling up alongside Madison and running his fingers through her hair. "...kind of hot."

She blushed. "Well, when you put it like that—"

"So, tell me," he interrupted, eagerly straying from her side and glancing out across the rows of jewels. "Where do you keep the most exorbitantly priced diamonds—say, of the shatterproof variety?"

"I don't want to talk about diamonds."

He sighed. "Wonderful," he said through gritted teeth. "Want to talk some more about yourself? We've only been doing it for hours already."

"I want to talk about you." She took a seat on a pink velvet chair and crossed her legs. "Eve made out like you're some important guy, but I've never heard of you."

"You've never heard of me? Ever?"

"Nope."

"How about Alicia LaFleur?"

"Doesn't ring a bell."

"Wow," he grumbled. "Well, if you must know, my grandparents founded the country's leading distribution chain of fusion power."

"Oh, God, how dull," Madison whined, rolling her eyes. "No wonder I've never heard of you. I try not to pollute my brain with that science garbage."

"Clearly."

"So how do you know *Eve*?"

"Eve?" Percy chuckled. "Funny, I thought we were talking about me. How soon the conversation changed..."

"It just doesn't seem like you two would run in the same circles. Your circle being boring science money, and her circle being the cesspool of humanity."

"What an artfully cruel and specific metaphor."

"I've had practice."

Percy hopped atop one of the glass cases and took a seat facing Madison. "Meeting her was by chance, really." He shrugged. "Jason and I are good friends."

"Oh." She glowered. "So you met her through Jason."

"Yes."

The room became quiet. Madison glared at the floor, her thoughts suddenly preoccupied.

"And here I was worried this date would be awkward," Percy muttered.

"How are they?"

"Excuse me?"

"How are they... you know, *together*." She forced a laugh and lifted her nose in the air. "I mean, not that I care about their relation*shit*."

"Of course you don't. Why else would you pry?"

"Are they together a lot?"

"I think you already know the answer to that."

"And when they're not together," she began, her lips curled with repulsion, "does Jason say anything about her?"

"Well, he likes her legs." He smirked. "That guy has always been a legs man."

"I don't *care* about her stupid legs, *God*," Madison growled. "Does he say anything else? Anything about Eve? Anything specific, anything... personal?"

"Wow, Eve's *really* gotten under your skin." He stopped for a moment and mumbled under his breath, "Or perhaps your second skin."

"What?"

"Let's change the subject to something a little more lighthearted. Like, I don't know, diamonds?" He hopped down from the display case and cocked his head at its contents. "Those sparkly suckers really rev my engine, if you know what I mean."

"God, you and I have *so* much in common," Madison sighed.

Percy approached Madison, hoping his debonair refinement masked his true distaste for the girl. "You know, I've always been *so* impressed with your company."

"It's my daddy's company," she corrected.

"But *your* name is on the box," he answered, pointing at the twinkling *Madison* signage hanging from the ceiling. "So really, isn't it all about *you*?"

Madison faltered for a moment. "Well, I guess you could say that."

"I mean, look at this jewel." He clutched her shoulders and steered her toward a large diamond in a lit display case. "The cut is remarkable, as if it were molded with a delicate, gentle touch." He stood behind her, his voice airy as he lightly slid his fingers down her arms. "But in actuality, it takes a strong, *firm* tool to shape this diamond—it takes unrelenting *control*." He squeezed her wrists, leaning his chin over her shoulder until his lips hovered beside her ear. "This diamond is an image of *intense* power and perfection, and your name is written all over it."

She let out a long, wavering breath. "You are *so* speaking my language."

Madison spun around and shoved Percy against the wall. With a flirtatious grin, she ran her manicured fingers up his legs and grabbed at his upper thighs.

"Is that a gun in your pocket, or are you just happy to see me?"

She slipped her hand into his pocket and suddenly stopped short; reluctantly, she pulled a sleek, black firearm from his pants and dangled it in the air.

"Oh... it *is* a gun." Her eyes widened. "You brought a *gun*?"

Percy stuttered, "It—it's nothing, really."

"It's a *gun*."

"Yes, we've established that already." He snatched the weapon from her hands and shoved it back into his pocket. "But I bring it with me everywhere. So, really, who cares, right?"

"*I* care."

"You shouldn't. In fact, you should forget this ever happened—"

"No," she interrupted, forcing him against the wall yet again with an unexpected surge of aggression. "I think it's *sexy*."

He hesitated. "Sexy?"

"Yeah, almost like you're, I don't know," she brought her lips close to his, "*dangerous*."

"Oh," he mumbled, his body stiff. "So, you like danger. Care to elaborate?"

"Are you trying to talk *dirty* with me?"

"More or less." He paused. "Maybe less." He fidgeted, attempting to shake her hands from his body. "So, this danger you mentioned... Are we talkin' brooding-guy-from-the-wrong-side-of-the-tracks danger, or, say, cutting-people-open-and-digging-through-their-guts danger?"

"*Excuse me?*"

"Sorry, my ex's idea of dirty talk was pretty graphic. Guess it's hard to shake."

"Look, something's going on here." She backed away and folded her arms. "And I think I know what it is."

"Before you jump to any conclusions—"

"You're nervous."

Percy wrinkled his brow. "Come again?"

"I totally get it." She took another step back, giving Percy the opportunity to admire her. "I mean, look at me: I'm physically flawless. Everything you could ever want in a partner, I've got it."

Percy smiled. "You know me so well."

"And on top of my impeccable beauty, I have this winning personality."

"Don't forget about your humility and firm grasp of reality."

"Who could blame you for being nervous? You're probably shaking in your Italian leather boots." She let out a condescending giggle. "It's adorable."

"*Adorable?*" He cringed. "God..."

"First you're stylish and sophisticated. Then you're wealthy, like me—although your association with this obscure power company is kind of disappointing, but I guess I can live with that." She slid her hands along the lapels of his blazer. "Then you're some mysterious gunslinger. And now..." She stopped, gazing into his eyes. "Well, now you're shy. You're like every dream guy rolled into one. It's *intoxicating.*"

"Funny you should mention that, because I have the overwhelming desire to be intoxicated right about now—"

Before he could finish, Madison wrapped her hands around his neck, yanked him forward, and kissed him firmly on the lips. Instinctively, he grabbed her arms and pushed her away from his body.

"What? What's wrong?" she asked.

"Nothing," he stammered, his face white with shock. "Just feels like I'm kissing a girl for the very first time."

She sighed. "And now you're boyishly innocent." Her wholesome smile quickly morphed into a seductive stare. "I am *so* into you right now."

A lump formed in Percy's throat. He stared back at Madison, at her piercing eyes, flushed skin, and trembling lips, and despite how much the thought sickened him, he knew what he had to do. With a grumble in his stomach, he pulled the heiress close to him and kissed her, dipping her slightly as her body became weak in his arms. He sucked and nibbled on her bottom lip, trying to imagine the feeling of a prickly chin against his own and the taste of whiskey on her breath, but her smooth skin and glossed lips left him bored and even a little disgusted. With an arduous breath, he tugged at her soft, luscious locks—a stark contrast from the short, rough hair he was accustomed to—and gave her one last, forceful kiss.

Madison tottered away from him, her lips stunned to silence. She hastily adjusted her dress and fluffed her hair, and after she regained what was left of her composure, she looked back at Percy and smiled.

"I want to give you something."

"A gift? Well, gosh, I wasn't expecting anything."

She scurried behind the showroom desk, fiddled with the cabinets, and finally returned with a palm-sized buckle covered in sparkling white diamonds.

"It's a Feverish Heat Diamond belt buckle," she explained, placing it in his hand. "One of the best cuts we have in stock, and I have the sneaking suspicion that it'll really accent your"—she cleared her throat and cocked her head toward his groin—"you know."

He stared down at the buckle, his eyes heavy with disappointment. "Oh."

"*Oh?*" she hissed. "I give you an *unbelievably* expensive, limited-edition fashion accessory, and all you have to say is '*Oh*'?"

"It's beautiful, truly," he muttered, tossing the buckle onto the counter, "and I do appreciate the nod to my penis. But I'm not interested in *one* of the best. I want *the* best. I'm on a date with *you*, after all: surely that proves my standard for excellence."

Madison crossed her arms. "Keep talking."

"I heard a rumor about a very special, synthetic jewel." He leaned into her. "Is it true, what they say? Do you really have a shatterproof diamond in stock?"

"It's true," she answered, melodramatically. "The Everlasting Diamond—it's our greatest treasure."

"I want one," Percy commanded, squeezing her hands tightly. "No. I *need* one."

Madison's eyes darted back and forth across the showroom as a giddy smile spread across her lips. "You know, I'm not supposed to do this..."

"*Do it,*" Percy blurted. "For the love of God, *do it.*"

"You're so sexy when you're demanding." She bit her lip before scuttling across the room, disappearing out of sight into the back corner. "This is the only showroom in the country that carries these, you know."

"Really? I hadn't the slightest idea."

Madison returned, this time with a small box in her hand, adorned with a blue velvet "M". She opened the box and revealed a single Everlasting Diamond.

"For you." She beamed. "The most immaculate jewel you will ever lay your eyes on. It's all yours."

Percy stared at the twinkling gem and felt a swell of dismay in his chest. He was now the owner of an Everlasting Diamond—*one* Everlasting Diamond. Hardly enough to make a single bullet. But he wasn't yet ready to admit defeat. He looked up at Madison and offered her a playful wink.

"God, I love it when you talk diamonds."

She flipped her hair across her shoulder and raised her nose in the air. "My daddy says I'm kind of a marketing genius."

"You're a natural." He slid the diamond into his blazer pocket and casually took a seat atop a row of cabinets. "In fact, I don't think I can be satisfied with just *one* of these bad boys."

"Really? Just because of what I said?"

"Of course. Can you think of any other reason?" He fished his wallet from his pants and began fanning through his credit cards. "Honestly, I've never been more convinced of a purchase in my life!"

"Oh, Daddy says they're not for sale."

"*Daddy* says?" He hopped down from the showroom desk and pulled Madison close to him. "But this is *your* company. You can do whatever you want."

Madison hesitated. "Whatever I want?"

"Whatever. You. Want."

Madison wavered for just a moment before dashing behind the showroom cabinets. "There is one thing," she said, unlocking a small black safe beneath the register. "We have a club—a super-exclusive client list, completely unknown to the public. It's called the Crystalline Society. All members get priority access to our finest jewels." She delicately removed a leather box from the safe and hurried back to Percy's side. "Normally membership is reserved for only the most important people: foreign royals, A-list celebrities, the mafia," she rolled her eyes, "but since this is *my* company, I can make a special exception for you."

She opened the leather box and removed a sleek black card with a silver emblem in the shape of an old, European-cut diamond. She grabbed Percy's hand, separated his index finger from the rest, and pressed it against the diamond emblem. Suddenly the card's black pigment became translucent, and all that could be seen was a red fingerprint in the center of the clear plastic. Then the color and pattern of the card slowly returned to normal.

"Welcome to the Crystalline Society—member number nine."

Percy held the card up to the light, examining its surface. "So, how does this work?"

"Flash this card at any location, and the diamond world is your oyster. No wait, no limitations."

"Does this work for Everlasting Diamonds, too?"

"*Anything.*" Madison sashayed closer to Percy and squeezed his shoulders. "You can have whatever you want, *whenever* you want it."

Percy ignored the girl; he was transfixed by the card, admiring the emblem and the glossy texture. His feelings of disgust faded away, replaced by a surge of pride: the tediousness and humiliation of this night had all been worth it. He stared at the card for a second longer, hardly noticing Madison nuzzling against him, and for the first time since the night began, an authentic smile graced his lips.

"Can I order in bulk?"

CHAPTER 14: THE ALIBI

"Are you ready?"

"Of course we're ready, Sancho. We're all here, aren't we?"

Eve impatiently tapped her foot as she stared at the dining table, which was conveniently covered by a silk sheet, most likely for dramatic effect. Jason, JJ, and Percy were at her side—Jason's brow was furrowed, JJ feigned an air of indifference, and Percy casually sipped his bourbon while amusedly watching his friend's wide-eyed elation.

Sancho had called this impromptu meeting in Percy's dorm room much quicker than anyone had expected. In just a couple days shy of a week, he had managed to turn a hastily derived conjecture into reality.

"I've tested them out and, I have to say, they're even better than I anticipated." Sancho gripped the edge of the sheet, his fingers quivering with excitement. "Under this blanket is the *future* of weaponry—the ace up our sleeve. A development so powerful, the patrolmen could only *dream* of it. A tool so dynamic, Furst himself would bow down to our authority—"

"*Sancho*," Jason moaned, "just show us already."

Sancho cowered. "There's one thing you should know..."

"Oh God," Percy grumbled, "don't tell us you screwed something up."

"I didn't, I promise, it's just—" Sancho paused and forced an apologetic smile. "There was an unforeseen drawback—a minor imperfection."

JJ sighed. "And that is?"

Sancho yanked the blanket from the table, exposing a cluster of bright, reflecting light. Eve shielded her eyes as she looked down at the table; she was staring at a pile of Everlasting Diamonds, perfectly sculpted into bullets, and despite their very serious application, they glimmered and shined in the most beautiful, unintimidating way.

Sancho shrugged. "They're really sparkly."

"Goddammit," Percy groused. "Guess we should've seen that one coming."

Eve plucked a single bullet from the pile, studying its form and its pointed tip. "These bullets could be covered in glitter for all I care, so long as they *work*."

"Trust me, they'll work," Sancho said. "With this sort of technology, the Interlopers won't even know what hit 'em, and I do mean that literally."

Sancho and Eve glanced at Jason, who had remained silent during the reveal. His eyes were fixed on another weapon resting beside the pile—an axe, long and forbidding, and while the crystal clear blade shimmered slightly, it looked far more sinister than the bullets themselves.

"Go ahead, touch it," Sancho encouraged him. "It's yours, after all."

Jason lifted the axe from the table. It felt heavy in his hand, weighed down by the giant diamond blade and the sleek, black material that made up the handle. He turned to his roommate and pointed at the glossy grip.

"What is this?"

"Interloper bone." Sancho grinned, pleased with his creation. "I got it from our last fight. Figured it would come in handy. No pun intended."

Jason eyed the weapon for a second longer, swinging it in front of him as if to get a feel for it. With an approving nod, he squeezed his friend's shoulder.

"Good work, Sancho. You may be crazy, but you're also kind of a genius."

"We can't forget about Percy," Eve added, elbowing the heir in the ribs. "None of this would've been possible without his smooth, charming ways."

Percy rolled his eyes. "That's me," he muttered, "the team gigolo."

"I'd like to think of you as more of a supplier," Eve teased.

"Well, as our *supplier*, I was able to snag more than just a sack of diamonds."

With one sharp movement, Percy pounded on a black and white painting that hung on the wall beside him. Immediately—and by this point, unsurprisingly—the painting swiveled in place, extending out from the wall and then retracting into a hidden groove along its frame, revealing yet another secret drawer.

"Since the patrolmen confiscated all of my guns, I decided to go on a bit of a shopping spree. You know, load up on some new toys."

Percy opened the drawer, displaying a line of weapons much more threatening in appearance than the sparkling diamond bullets. Several guns with sleek finishes were evenly positioned in a row like toy soldiers lined up for battle.

"Holy shit," Jason mumbled.

"They're V-Class Anarch handguns. Street name is 'the executioner.' I sort of figured that with the new-and-improved bullets, we ought to have some firearms that are just as impressive."

Sancho nervously eyed the new weapons. "Aren't these things illegal?"

Percy winked. "Nothing's illegal when you're rich."

Eve delicately slid her fingers along the firearms, her eyes bright with anticipation. She cleared her throat, stifling her excitement, and turned to JJ.

"Any updates on the torq?"

JJ nodded at her scratchpads, which were propped up along Percy's new coffee table. "I've downloaded the torq's data, but it's still being converted, and I have *no* idea how long that'll take. I mean, we *are* talking about a computer from *outer space,* after all." She shrugged. "The good news is, I know enough about the device itself to start coding a potential virus."

"Well, at least we're headed in the right direction," Eve said, relieved. "We're on target with the virus, we have weapons, we've got plenty of ammunition—"

"I wouldn't say *plenty,*" Percy interrupted. "I bought out Palmer's entire stock, so what you see is what you get. Until *Daddy* gets his ass in gear, we have to make do with the ammo we have."

"Balls. I still can't believe you actually went on a date with *Madison Palmer,*" Sancho chuckled.

Percy winked. "Wasn't so bad. She tasted like bubble gum."

"But weren't you nervous?" Sancho added. "I mean, she's an alien, right?"

"I wouldn't be so sure."

"What do you mean?" Eve asked.

"I mean the girl's harmless," Percy laughed. "Sure, she's definitely obsessive—wouldn't stop asking about you, actually—but other than that, she was just a big jumble of self-directed delusions and hormones." He nonchalantly downed the last of his drink. "Either that alien is one hell of an actor, or Blondie is the real deal."

Eve sighed, her brow furrowed with confusion. "But the ashes..."

"Happenstance? An unrelated anomaly?" Percy shrugged. "I mean, don't get me wrong, she totally wants you dead. I just don't think she's an

Interloper."

The ringing of a bell sounded, grabbing everyone's attention.

"JJ," Eve began, her voice laced with trepidation, "was that the beacon?"

JJ rushed across the room, throwing herself atop Percy's couch and fiddling with her triad of scratchpads. "It's a trigger," she said, frantically tapping at her computer screens. "Someone's about to be abducted. A chimera."

It was a blow to the gut. They'd known this day would come, and yet Eve felt sickened by the news. JJ turned one of her screens to face the group and expanded a photo of a boy. He had a full head of strawberry-blond hair, blue-grey eyes, and a stubbly chin.

"Sam Remington, a Billington sophomore." JJ scanned the screens, reading the text as it appeared. "They're doing it today, in exactly twenty-two minutes."

"Can you tell us where?" Jason asked.

"They're sending the coordinates right now."

"Good. Then we have to go stop them."

"Wait," Eve blurted, grabbing at Jason's wrist. "What about the cameras? How the hell are we going to bypass all of them?"

"I can guide you," JJ added. "I have access to all of the Shelter's surveillance, remember?"

Eve said nothing. Instead, she stared at JJ, studying her face as if it could somehow ease the anxious knot coiling within her stomach.

JJ folded her arms and scowled. "Still don't trust me, huh?" She turned toward the others, but they were quiet as well. "Look, the Interlopers don't want to end up on camera either, so you know whatever location they choose to stage the abduction will be surveillance-free. All you have to do is find a clear path to that spot. I *know* I can get you there. Besides, you don't really have a choice—or a hell of a lot of time."

Eve sighed. "Fine," she grumbled. "Hand over the earpieces."

"No earpieces this time. The cameras will pick 'em up, no matter how camouflaged they are. So"—JJ dug through her pocket—"I made these."

JJ opened her hand, revealing a pile of small red tablets, each no bigger than the size of a bean.

"Pills?" Percy scoffed. "Is *dealing* on your list of illegal ventures?"

"They're communicaps—ingestible transmission devices." She tossed one to each of her comrades and shoved the rest back into her pocket. "Inside each capsule is a communication chip. Swallow the communicap, and I'll be able to talk with each of you as if we were in the same room. You can't use 'em to talk to each other, just to me—but you'll all be in the same location anyway."

Eve's lips curled with aversion. "You want us to *swallow* these?"

"Relax, it won't kill you. At least, I don't think it will. It shouldn't, anyway."

"Wow, that wasn't the slightest bit reassuring," Eve mumbled.

"It'll pass through your system in a few hours. Or days. I'm not sure, exactly."

"Hold it right there," Percy blurted. "We have to *shit* these out?"

"It's new technology. I haven't worked out all the kinks yet."

"Well, it's good to know that we get to be your guinea pigs," Jason muttered.

"Don't listen to them, JJ," Sancho said. "I think they're *brilliant*."

Eve stared at her communicap, twirling it between her thumb and index finger before looking back at JJ, who glared at her impatiently.

"It's your only option, whether you trust me or not."

Eve still hesitated. She glanced back and forth between JJ and the capsule one last time, and then, with a deep breath, downed her communicap, cringing slightly as it slid down her throat. The others reluctantly followed suit, swallowing their capsules one by one until they all wore the same expressions of dread.

JJ nodded in approval and fastened a headset over her ears, adjusting the microphone in front of her mouth until it was perfectly in place. She then dragged her fingers across her scratchpad screens until the words *ACTIVATE COMMUNICAP* flickered four times in bright red lettering. Four holographic buttons—red, to match the flashing letters—extended from the screens, and without a hint of delay or delicacy, JJ pressed them all.

A loud screech rang in Eve's ears, the noise so shrill that she grabbed at her temples and winced in pain. She opened her eyes, a struggle in itself, and saw Jason and the others doing the same, their mouths contorted into looks of torment. Finally the screeching stopped, leaving behind an unpleasant ringing in her ears.

"Dear Lord! What the *hell* was that noise?" Percy groused.

"You heard that?" JJ asked, underwhelmed by his complaint. "Good, that means it's working. The buzzing will subside in a few seconds. Hopefully."

Seconds passed, and nothing changed.

"There's one last thing you should know," JJ added. "Before I take you to the abduction coordinates, I have to plant you all in different locations throughout Rutherford Hall. You guys need alibis—visual proof caught on camera that pins you far from the abduction site."

"Sounds complicated," Sancho mumbled.

"That's because it *is* complicated, which is why I need you to *trust me*." JJ shot a quick glare in Eve's direction. "Whatever I tell you to do, do it. Look calm, be cool, and *please* act normal. Once you're off camera, I'll make sure you stay that way."

Eve nodded. "Okay then, let's gear up."

"Were you even *listening* to me?" JJ scoffed. "You're going to be on camera, at least for a few minutes." She cocked her head at the weapons. "If you can't hide it, you're not bringing it."

The foursome eyed the dining table and their sparkling new weapons. After a brief silence, Percy plucked two handguns from the drawer and tucked them into the back of his pants, making sure they were both completely concealed by his leather jacket. Sancho eagerly grabbed another gun, admiring the piece before shoving it inside his oversized sweatshirt. Jason quickly followed, snatching his axe from the pile and attempting to hide it in his pant leg.

"You're not taking that," JJ ordered.

"What? Why not?"

"I'm going to need you to get a little physical on camera—"

"What do you mean by *physical*?"

"The axe will get in the way," JJ insisted. "You don't want it on you. Trust me."

Jason stared at his weapon and frowned, disappointed. He turned to Sancho.

"Think you can make room for it?"

Sancho nodded and shoved the axe into his sweatshirt, awkwardly balancing it with the firearm. Soon, it was Eve's turn to select a weapon, but she immediately stopped short. She examined her outfit—her snug thermal, her fitted jeans and combat boots—and realized there was no place for her to conceal much of anything.

"Looks like you won't be taking anything." JJ laughed. "Kind of makes you rethink the whole tight pants ensemble, doesn't it?"

Jason leaned toward Eve. "I like your pants," he whispered.

"You have seventeen minutes," JJ interrupted, anxiously looking at her scratchpad clock. "Time to hit the road. Wait for your orders outside."

The foursome filed out of the dorm room and into the hallway, leaving JJ alone in Percy's suite. Eve nervously picked at her cuticles, trying her best to ignore the incessant buzzing of her communicap as she waited for some type of direction.

"Good God," JJ muttered, her voice fuzzy in Eve's ear.

"What? What happened?"

"Unexpected complication," JJ continued. *"I can hear all of your, well, insides. Your heart, your lungs, your stomach."* She gagged. *"Sancho must be starving."*

Without further delay, the hacker rattled off a list of instructions to her eagerly awaiting comrades. They engaged in fake conversation per her request—though they were awkward at best—and after a minute of phony laughs and uncomfortable ramblings, Sancho left the group, guided by JJ to his alibi location: the Rutherford dining hall. Percy was next, meandering down the hallway toward the tutoring center, an option he tried to argue with—he didn't *need* any tutoring, he claimed, though JJ was hardly concerned. A considerable amount of time passed, and all the while Eve stared at Jason, apprehensively awaiting their instructions.

"All right, Jason and Eve, it's your turn. Head for the elevator."

They obediently followed her request and made their way into the metal box. As the doors closed in front of them, Eve's limbs became restless and uneasy, and she clasped her hands together as if to suppress her nervous energy.

"There's a camera above you."

Both Eve's and Jason's heads darted up toward the ceiling, their eyes searching for the device.

"Don't look for *it!"* JJ snapped. *"Jesus Christ, act natural!"* She grumbled under her breath before she continued. *"Jason, push the button for the ground level. You're going to the lobby."*

Jason did as he was told, trying his best to appear casual. The elevator lurched in place and slowly began its trek down the fifteen stories. Immediately, JJ's voice once again rang in their ears.

"Okay, now make out."

"What?" Eve spat.

"Don't talk to me," JJ hissed. *"You're on camera right now, remember? Now, be a good boy and a good girl and start kissing—and make it really steamy."*

The elevator had suddenly become much smaller, the air hot and stifling. Eve glanced at Jason—his face was red as he stared back at her—and as subtly as she could, she fiddled with a strand of hair, making sure that her arm was strategically angled in front of her mouth.

"I don't see why this is necessary," she whispered.

"Come on, you're a couple. This should be the easy part."

Jason forced a cough, covering his lips with his hand. "Doesn't feel so easy when you know a million people are watching."

JJ sighed. *"Look, you're running out of time. Do it, and do it now."*

"But—"

"NOW!"

Eve slammed Jason against the wall of the elevator, gripping his shirt and kissing him deeply as if something within her—an animal instinct or a heated ferocity—had been released. There wasn't a single moment to think, to calculate or reassess, and so she acted, forced by JJ's words and the adrenaline pumping through her veins. She could feel Jason's breathing become heavy and rapid as she sifted her fingers through his hair and ran her lips down the side of his neck. Every nerve within her awoke with sensation as Jason's hands slid from her back to her shoulders, finally making their way down her arms to her hands. With one swift movement, Jason spun her around, pressing her back against the wall and pinning her wrists above her head.

Eve's breath caught short, frozen in her chest. He lingered by her lips for a moment before kissing her, and then again, this time harder and deeper, as if the camera above them was no longer a thought in his mind. Time had become infinite; Eve wrapped her arms around Jason's neck as he pulled her body against his, the firmness of his chest pressed against hers a stark contrast to his soft hands that slid into the back pockets of her jeans. The mission now seemed miles away, a mere memory in the thick haze of her mind, as she soaked in the feeling of Jason's lips kissing hers, and the sound of their heavy breathing, punctuated only for a second by the faint ding of the elevator.

The doors opened, the light from the lobby spilling across Jason's back.

JJ chuckled. *"All right, lovebirds, put those hormones on ice for now. Time to exit the elevator."*

Jason's face dropped. "Do we have to?"

A slight murmuring filtered into the elevator; Eve peered over Jason's shoulder. Eyes, too many to count, stared back at them, bulging with shock. The lobby was filled with Rutherfordians, all of whom watched the two chimeras that had suddenly appeared in front of them.

"Eve, take his hand and leave."

The order was hardly necessary. Eve yanked at Jason's wrist, pulling him from the elevator as she weaved through the crowd of onlookers, desperate to be rid of their whispers.

"Go straight to the rec room, and don't look back."

The rec room was so close, and yet through this mass of people it felt like a perilous journey. Each stupid, gaping face began to blend with the next. *"There's a supply closet in the back corner of the room."*

"You mean the nookie nook?" Jason asked. "Isn't that where everyone goes to have—" He stopped short, his eyes wide as if suddenly jolted awake. "Oh God."

"Don't question my methods. Do you see the closet?"

Eve could see the closet—it was right in front of her, and yet she couldn't move. An obstacle lay ahead of her, and while it was delicate and covered in dusty pink cashmere, it was easily the most dreadful sight she could possibly have imagined. There in front of the closet sat Heather, idly flipping through a scratchpad novel, her eyes focused on the two chimeras. She raised an auburn eyebrow and leaned back in her chair like a proud queen, and in an instant the room became dark, cold, and empty.

Eve breathed in deeply. "Yes."

"Good. Get in."

Eve glanced at the closet door and then down at her redheaded adversary.

Heather smiled, neatly folding her hands in her lap. "Going somewhere?"

The image of Sam Remington flashed before Eve's eyes—his round cheeks and angular chin like a caricature in her thoughts—and suddenly Heather's horrid grin seemed a little less formidable. In fact, she could hardly stand the sight of the Rutherfordian, much less her intolerable presence. The mission was clear and simple, and Heather—well, Heather was of little importance. With a smug sneer, Eve shoved past her adversary, swung open the closet door, and pushed Jason inside, quickly slamming the door behind them.

"Well done, horndogs, you're off camera," JJ quipped. *"Now the folks at the Shelter will assume you're occupied for the next fifteen minutes to an hour, depending on Jason's... performance."*

"So will the rest of Rutherford Hall," Eve mumbled.

"That was the point. You have countless eyewitnesses who think you're busy spawning. It's the perfect alibi."

"Yeah, *perfect*, except you led us to a dead end," Jason added.

"On the contrary, this is your escape route. Do you see a latch on the floor?"

Eve glanced around the tight space, really noticing her surroundings for the first time. The closet was pitch black aside from the small stream of light that poured underneath the door, illuminating the stacks of buckets, mops, and cleaning supplies strewn across the ground.

"I don't see anything on the floor. It's covered in junk," Eve griped, pulling a knot of cobwebs from her hair. "Seriously, how the hell do people have sex in here? This closet is filthy."

"Quit whining and look for the latch," JJ ordered. *"And while you're at it, make some loud moaning sounds—you know, to add to the façade."*

Eve growled under her breath. "No, JJ."

"Come on, be a good sport."

Eve balled her hands into fists. "I said *NO*," she barked, stomping her boot against the ground, or what she thought was the ground. Jason let out a long, awkward groan as he clutched at his throbbing foot.

JJ laughed. *"Geez, Jason, way to finish early."*

"Jason!" Eve yelped. "Are you okay?"

"Yeah." He hunched over, struggling to regain his composure and straining to stare at the grimy floor. "I think I found the latch, too."

"Good. Pull it open," JJ instructed. *"You'll see a stairwell leading to the basement."*

Jason yanked at the latch, knocking over buckets and tools in the process. Beneath them was a metal stairwell, just as JJ had described.

"Hurry, there isn't much time. The abduction is scheduled to take place in eight minutes and twenty-seven seconds."

Before Eve could head down the stairwell, Jason grabbed her wrist.

"Wait!"

He tugged her close to him and gave her one last, long kiss, pulling away with a smirk.

"Sorry, I had to."

"Eight minutes," JJ groaned.

They flew down the flight of steps and maneuvered their way through the basement. A damp heat emanated from the pumps and boilers, sticking to Eve's skin and settling in her throat, but she paid no attention to it. She was looking for another staircase, per JJ's nagging instructions, and at last her eyes locked onto the concrete steps that appeared in the distance.

"Exit through the blue door at the top of the stairs," JJ commanded. "You'll find yourself at the back of Rutherford Hall, toward the rear of the campus. Turn right, and follow the wall. So long as you stay close to the building, you'll remain off camera. And guys, you know that super speed you've got at your disposal? Now's the time to use it."

They reached the doorway long before JJ finished speaking, and immediately they began sprinting down the narrow pathway behind Rutherford Hall. The cool air felt like shards of ice clawing at their skin, but still their bodies were warm with adrenaline. Eve kept close to the wall, trailing her fingers along its surface, and pushed herself to run faster. Jason did the same, though he could see the end of Rutherford Hall looming a short distance in front of him.

"We're running out of wall here," Jason said.

"Don't stop," JJ ordered. "You're clearing all four dormitory halls. As long as you stay on that path, you'll remain off camera."

Jason and Eve raced between the two buildings, hoping to God that they had gone unnoticed. Discretion was key; Eve could hear Furst's harrowing threat repeating in her thoughts, and she suddenly felt her heart thumping in her throat.

"Where are we going?" she asked.

"The music building courtyard. That's where they're staging the abduction."

"Jesus Christ, that's all the way across campus!" Jason spat.

"And you have five minutes and fifty-seven seconds to get there, so I suggest you shut up and run," JJ groused. "I have to patch over to Sancho and Percy. Await my instructions at the end of Langley Hall."

The twosome passed Hutchinson Hall, and then Clarence Hall, all the while checking for the prying eyes of nonexistent passersby. They were consumed with paranoia, and though each step they took felt like a bigger mistake than the last, they forced themselves forward, their eyes focused on the back corner of Langley Hall.

Jason skidded to an abrupt stop; Eve grabbed at his shoulders, bracing herself as she caught her breath.

"We're here," she panted.

"Took you long enough," JJ muttered. "Do you see a row of trees ahead of you?"

They peered around the corner of the building. Beside the front steps of the dormitory was a line of lush palm trees that continued across the edge of campus.

"Yes," Eve answered.

"Good. Duck behind them and continue straight."

Eve obeyed, though it pained her to do so—she could see people meandering across campus, and the slim trees offered little coverage. But despite her apprehensions, she and Jason dashed behind the palms, trying to convince themselves they were hidden from view, while knowing that was hardly the case.

"Can you see the music building yet?"

Eve stopped, positioning her body behind a single palm tree. Ahead of them was a large, white building with a domed ceiling, sitting behind a circular courtyard lined with red and bronze tiles. It was most certainly the music building, and its courtyard was surprisingly empty. She breathed a sign of relief.

"Yes."

"Good. Go to it."

"But there's no cover," Jason retorted.

"It's all right, you're not on camera."

"People will *see* us," Eve added.

"They're meeting Sam here. You have no other choice."

"But—"

"Look, for every person who sees you here, there will be ten more who swear they saw you sucking face with Jason back at Rutherford Hall," JJ rationalized, her patience waning. *"Which story do you think everyone will believe: the one where you're heroes, or the one where you're the filthy chimeras they want you to be?"*

Eve glanced over at Jason; with a nod, they both stepped out from behind the tree. They moved quickly, suddenly feeling exposed and vulnerable.

"Your path will lead to the center of the courtyard. There's an area—a circle—that's completely out of any camera's view. That's where they're going to initiate the abduction."

"How the hell are we supposed to know where this invisible circle is?" Jason asked.

"Take note of the statue to your left, the tree to your right, and the steps of the music building in front of you," JJ answered. *"They're all on camera. The Interlopers won't go anywhere near those landmarks, and neither should you."*

Eve's eyes panned across the courtyard; she saw the statue, a bronze sculpture in the likeness of a former U.S. president, and then she noted the single maple tree on the opposite end of the tiled quad.

"Do you see anyone?"

Jason turned to his side; two figures were headed their way, coming from opposite directions, though each was equally familiar.

"Yes, Sancho and Percy are coming."

"Anyone else?"

They appeared as if out of nowhere. Four students: a tall boy with tanned skin, another one broad and muscular, then a girl with pin-straight black hair, and finally another boy with stark white skin and reddish-blond hair. Eve's body became taut.

"Four people: one girl and three boys. One of them looks like Remington."

"That's them—the Interlopers and their target. It's happening now."

"Got it." Jason turned to Sancho and Percy, who weren't too far away, and nodded. "We're going in."

Eve and Jason entered the courtyard, their hands clenched as they followed the foursome—the three convincingly disguised Interlopers and their unsuspecting target. Just as they were close enough to hear their pointless chatter, Jason grabbed one of the students, digging his fingers into the boy's shoulder and jerking him to the ground. The other three spun in place, surprised by the sudden intrusion.

Sam stared at Jason, his face dripping with shock and repulsion. "What the *hell* do you think you're doing?" he spat.

"You need to get out of here," Jason answered, his voice firm and commanding.

"Do you think I don't know who you are?" Sam sneered. He turned to Eve. "Both of you?" He backed away, forming a line with the other two students. "You stay away from me and my friends."

"They're not who you think they are, Sam," Eve warned.

Sam opened his mouth to speak but stopped short. "How do you know my name?" He turned his attention to Sancho and Percy, who had also drawn near. "And who the hell are *you*?"

Sancho and Percy were silent—Sancho fussing with his sweatshirt, running his fingers over the concealed weapons, and Percy keeping his hands above the guns tucked in the back of his jeans. Jason and Eve remained still, their gazes fixed on the two students by Sam's side—on their still bodies, their beady eyes, and the sweat that formed along their foreheads. Eve took in one last, long breath.

"Run, Sam," she ordered.

"What?"

"RUN!"

A startling howl sounded behind them. Eve and Jason spun around and gaped at the third student, who was now rocketing into the sky, propelled by grey wings that sprouted from his soggy back. He stopped and hovered in the air, skin oozing down his face like candle wax, and vigorously shook his body, sending the loose flesh raining down on the courtyard below. Then, with a hateful smile, he dove down to the ground once again, his sights clearly set on Jason.

"SANCHO!" Jason barked. "THE AXE!"

Sancho pulled the axe from his sweatshirt and tossed it to Jason, and without hesitation, Jason sprinted toward the Interloper, fueled by an un-contained aggression. Just as it looked as if their bodies might collide, Jason swung his axe at the creature, slicing him clear across the throat. The alien's severed head flew through the air and plopped onto the ground.

Jason froze in place; he stared in awe at the lifeless Interloper, at the decapitated head, and then at the diamond axe in the palm of his hand.

"Holy shit," he gasped.

There was no time to revel in the moment; the girl at Sam's side released her second skin, sending her flesh spraying from her body like an explosion of foul meat. Sam scurried in the opposite direction, his face pale with shock, but the newly exposed Interloper ignored him, instead focusing his attention on his four new opponents. He lunged toward the group, then abruptly his body lurched backward into the air, his limbs flailing as he shot higher and higher into the sky. Suddenly Eve sent him plummeting to the ground, hitting the surface so forcefully that the courtyard tiles shattered beneath his broken body and yellow guts.

The final Interloper had already targeted his opponent: he charged to-ward Sancho, smiling as he saw his prey fumbling with his firearm. Sancho glanced anxiously back and forth between the gun and his target, and then, with a surge of panicked energy, he steadied his hold and fired at the creature, nearly toppling over backward from the sheer power of the weapon.

The Interloper merely flinched. He looked down at the hole in his stom-ach and pulled the poorly aimed bullet from his flesh—and then with a sneer, continued forward, galvanized by a newfound anger. Sancho fired again and again, not once making contact with a single kill zone, and the alien dove in his direction, whipping him with his wing and sending him flying, hurtling toward the presidential statue and, more than likely, toward his death.

Suddenly, Sancho halted in midair. He hovered, weightlessly drifting above the ground mere inches from the statue. He looked down and saw Jason, his arms extended at his sides, his hands trembling as he struggled to support the weight of both Sancho and the Interloper, who was also suspended in the air—mid-lunge.

Jason's breathing was heavy, his brow twisted as he strained to control the two figures, and as his lungs tightened within his chest, he felt the cool tingle of wetness on his upper lip: blood was dripping from his nostrils, down his lips, over his chin. A throbbing pain surged behind his temples, and soon all he could see and feel was a blend of darkness, blood, and a recognizable agony. He gritted his teeth—the sensation was overpowering, crippling his body until his legs shook beneath him —and with a defeated cry, he dropped his arms to his sides. He had lost his melt, and Sancho and the creature promptly tumbled to the ground below.

Just as the Interloper clambered to his feet, a loud gunshot sounded, and the alien collapsed to the ground, face-first. Behind him stood Percy, his gun barrel smoking, his face wearing a satisfied smirk as he admired the gaping crater in his conquest's spine. He turned to Jason and winked.

"That was easy," he boasted.

Sancho hopped up from the ground and joined the others in the center of the courtyard. Together they admired their kills: three fallen Interlopers, dead in just a few short minutes. Their eyes met with Sam's, who was paralyzed by the front steps of the music building, and then made their way to the small crowd of spectators wandering toward them.

"You guys," Sancho mumbled, "people are watching us."

Eve looked toward the gathering crowd. Their stares seemed off—distant and oddly empty. They cocked their heads, eyeing the two chimeras and their human comrades, and one by one, their curious glances turned into loathsome glares. Then, as if Eve knew it was coming all along, their faces became slimy and moist. Eve clenched her fists.

"Don't think they're people, Sanch."

The crowd was expanding—five became ten, and ten became fifteen—and soon the group was surrounded by a whole host of wide-eyed students with vacant gazes and dripping skin. Jason stared at the swarm, nonplussed by their sudden appearance, then he noticed the wiggling of their noses as they sniffed at the air. One by one their eyes turned to him, and he instantly remembered his bloody nose.

"Did I—" Jason wiped at his face. "Did I *attract* them?"

"Wait, what do you mean, *attract* them?" Percy asked, raising both of his guns.

"The blood," Eve answered. "They can smell Jason's blood."

Percy groaned. "Then for God's sake, Jason, close your damn nostrils!"

Just as the words left his lips, two Interlopers bolted from the crowd and soared high into the air. They circled the group below and, with perfectly synchronized movements, they dipped their wings and barreled down toward the center of the circle. Eve halted them with a melt, then propelled their bodies in opposite directions, throwing one toward the statue and the other toward the maple tree on the other end of the courtyard.

"WAIT!"

Eve stopped, as did her two victims—they bobbed in the air, desperately attempting to free themselves from her invisible hold, and failing miserably. Eve turned to Jason, who pointed anxiously to the two landmarks.

"The cameras."

Eve glanced at the ends of the courtyard; the cameras were discreet but visible, and she sighed with annoyance. With a nonchalant flick of her wrist, she pulled both aliens back to the center of the circle and slammed them together, their conjoined bodies dropping limply to the ground. She turned to Jason and shrugged.

"Better?"

Three more Interlopers plowed through the pack, shoving their way toward their human and chimera foes. Percy chuckled, unconcerned with the threat; he quickly fired his guns, launching a sparkling bullet into each of their skulls and sending them toppling to the ground. A third Interloper barreled toward him, and he shot the creature in the throat, clear through the neck. He smiled as he eyed his marks and the glittering holes in their bodies.

"God, I love these bullets."

Quickly, Eve scanned her surroundings and spotted Sam, who was racing up the steps of the music building, his entire body shaking with fear. An Interloper was in pursuit, torpedoing through the air in his direction. Eve reacted immediately, delving deep into her melt, and before the creature could even reach the ivory steps, she had catapulted him high into the sky, where he disappeared among the clouds.

Suddenly a heavy wing plowed into Eve's shoulders, knocking her from her feet and forcing her to the ground. She flipped onto her back and stared into the eyes of an Interloper, but before she could even channel her melt, the creature convulsed in place, rocking back and forth as thick, yellow fluid pumped from scattered holes across his body. Finally, the alien slumped at Eve's side with a loud, anticlimactic thump. She glanced over her shoulder and saw Sancho standing behind her, firearm in hand.

"These things really should come with controllers," he said.

Jason was pivoting back and forth at the other end of the courtyard. Several Interlopers had targeted him, their nostrils twitching as they took in his intoxicating scent. One finally bolted toward him, and Jason swung his axe at the creature, splitting him across the middle and sending his innards spilling to the ground. A second Interloper hurtled in his direction, and Jason buried his axe into the creature's mouth, the slice so deep that he had to kick at the alien's chest just to dislodge the weapon from his skull. Jason glanced from side to side—his comrades were busy with their own battles—and soon spotted the last remaining Interloper.

They pounced toward one another, Jason wielding his axe and the alien waving his talons, both of them wearing expressions of hate and disgust. With his jaw clenched, Jason hurled his axe at the creature, aiming for the head but missing at the last second as the Interloper ducked beneath him and knocked the axe from his grip. The axe fell to the floor with a loud clang, and the Interloper swung his claws at the chimera, tearing through the back of his shirt and grazing his skin. Jason spun away from the creature and quickly stabilized himself. He eyed his axe, which sat on the ground behind the alien's feet, and then he stared at his opponent, who was cackling ominously.

"Your blood... It smells delicious. Like power and *hate*."

Jason pounded his bare fist into the creature's face, over and over again, consumed by an anger he was now growing accustomed to. The Interloper thrashed his wings, but Jason dodged his attacks, nimbly swerving to the side and ducking low to the ground. He could see his axe only a few feet away—its blade was glistening in the sunlight, begging to be engaged—and just as the Interloper charged at him, he slid along the floor, grabbed the weapon's handle, and hurled the axe at the creature. The alien dodged, but not enough—the blade slashed straight through his wrist with an assertive chop.

The Interloper staggered away from Jason, cradling his bloody stump against his chest as he roared and howled. He stared down at the severed hand that lay on the ground before him, and then finally looked back at Jason. His eyes narrowed into slits, and despite his gruesome injury, he began to smile.

"I have heard stories of your female," he began. "That her blood is intoxicating—that she will taste like paradise. Even now, with your redness dripping down your face, still I can smell her." He stood upright, seemingly unaffected by his trauma, and his smile widened into a full and detestable grin. "And when Fairon carves his blade into her flesh, we will all fight to taste her before she dies."

Jason barreled toward the creature, who in turn barreled toward Jason, and just as the two were nearly close enough to strike, Eve slid across the ground between them and thrust her hands forward, sending the Interloper hurtling against the nearby statue. He fell to the ground, landing face-first with an almost-comical smack against the tiles. Though he was far from defeated, he scrambled along the floor in a chaotic manner, his eyes wide and fearful. Anxiously, he glanced up above him—at the camera pointed in his direction—and he bolted high into the sky, flying away from the campus and far from sight.

"*Dammit,*" JJ growled, her voice ringing in Eve's ears. "*He was on camera.*"

"Better him than us," Jason muttered under his breath.

Eve stared at the courtyard, now covered in Interloper corpses, severed limbs, and pools of yellow blood, and then she glanced up at Sam. He was sprawled across the steps of the music building, his terrified gaze aimed directly at her.

"Please," he stuttered. "Please don't tell anyone what I am. No one knows, not even my parents."

"This *never* happened," Eve spat, ignoring his plea. "We were *never* here. Do you understand?"

"But—"

"DO YOU UNDERSTAND?"

Sam's eyes flitted between the foursome, ultimately landing on Eve once again. "Yes. I understand."

Quickly, Eve assessed her surroundings. A new crowd had begun to form, students come to gape at the slew of dead Interlopers. Instinctively, Jason raised his axe and Percy pointed his guns, and the onlookers gasped and cowered in fright.

"Shit," Jason hissed, lowering his axe to his side. "They're human."

"They've seen us," Eve added.

Jason leaned in toward her. "What do we do now?"

"Leave!" JJ shouted. *"Before more of them show up!"*

Sancho wavered. "But the bodies—"

"Are the patrolmen's problem now," JJ interrupted, her voice noticeably tense. *"Look, time is of the essence. Take the same paths you came in on. You need to get moving, and you need to do it now."*

With that, the foursome sprinted away from the courtyard, each of them returning the same way they came. Though they knew they had been seen, they could only hope that their alibis were much more convincing than the truth.

In what seemed like an instant, Eve and Jason found themselves in the Rutherford basement once again, scurrying up the metal steps and crawling into the supply closet. They had come full circle, and the dread of battle was soon replaced with the overwhelming excitement of victory. Eve turned to face Jason.

"How's your back?"

He ran his fingers along his torn shirt and shrugged. "Just a few scratches."

He reached for the doorknob, but Eve stopped him.

"Wait," she said, "your nose."

With a gentle touch, she wiped the excess blood from his upper lip, smearing it onto one of the loose rags at their feet. She chuckled.

"We're about to be labeled as perverts across the entire school. We don't need them thinking we're into crazy torture sex, too."

She stared into Jason's eyes. His gaze was calming as usual, but despite his disarming presence, a new feeling had taken hold of her: the fear of what, or who, was waiting for them just outside the closet. Jason nodded his head at the door.

"You ready?"

Eve hesitated. She thought of Heather and the other Rutherfordians, of the rumors that were sure to follow, and she realized that she didn't give a damn what they had to say. With a smirk, she playfully ruffled her hair, leaving it a disheveled mess.

"Now I am."

Jason smiled. He leaned in close to her, and with a firm squeeze of her palm, he delicately kissed her forehead. Hand in hand, they each took in a long, steady breath and opened the closet door.

There they were, yet again: eyes, most of them large and gaping, others fierce and beady, and all of them staring at Eve and Jason without a hint of discretion. They watched as the couple exited the nookie nook, their hands still clasped together as if their unity could somehow deflect the judgment now being cast in their direction.

Eve could clearly make out Heather from within the crowd—her fiery hair was hard to miss, as was her spiteful grin—but she paid her no attention. With each step she took—with each shoulder she pegged and slur she overheard—Eve felt stronger and better than she ever had before. She made her way from the rec room and out into the Rutherford Hall lobby, looking over her shoulder just in time to spot two girls whispering to one another, pointing at the back of Jason's shirt.

"Wow, he must've been good. Look at the scratch marks on his back!"

***

The lecture hall was filled with energy as the soft hum of whispers spread through the room. Professor Clarke had hardly noticed—either that, or he chose to ignore it, though neither seemed typical of him—and continued with his lecture, rambling endlessly about whatever it was that he was rambling about today.

Eve sat in her corner, alone as usual, but she could still make out the mutterings of her classmates. Many spoke of her—they thumbed through their scratchpad tabloids and snickered at the outrageous headlines: *The Insatiable Sexual Appetites of Chimeras. Public Debauchery: Chimera Edition.* Her romp in the nookie nook had been leaked, as she had assumed would be the case, but amid the talk of her supposed raunchy rendezvous was, for once, a rumor that piqued her interest: a story of Interlopers, some said ten, others said twenty, found dead on campus. They had been impaled, or decapitated, or ripped apart by diamonds sculpted into bullets. Some even said that it was a combination of all three, but most agreed that such a story was too far-fetched to be true. This rumor was the one Eve was most interested in, not because of its gory appeal, but because it was just that—a rumor.

Class finally ended, and one student after the next filed out of the doorway and into the hall. As Eve gathered her things, a boy spat at her feet, and another hissed something degrading under his breath. She just smiled—none of it mattered. A new calm had taken her, lifting her from her seat and filling her head with unusual thoughts of fulfillment—and even, dare she say it, hope—so much so that as she made her way toward the classroom exit, she was too distracted by her own contentment to even notice that Professor Clarke was summoning her.

"Eve," he repeated, this time a bit louder, "a word?'

Eve flinched, startled by the interruption, and made her way to the professor's side. He nervously eyed the door, waiting for his remaining students to scamper from the classroom. He didn't speak until they were finally alone.

"You haven't submitted your proposal yet." He fidgeted with his projection controller, his fingers restless, then shoved both hands into his pockets. "You're usually so prompt with your assignments."

Eve sighed. "Yeah, about that..."

She dug through her shoulder bag and pulled out her scratchpad cube, resting it on the professor's podium before activating it. Clarke jumped when sparks flew from the computer, and he raised his eyebrows when its sides awkwardly unfolded, revealing the shattered screen.

The professor swatted at the stream of smoke trickling from the sputtering scratchpad. "How did this...?"

"How do you think?"

He took a deep breath, his eyes filled with disappointment. "You know, if you tell me who's responsible, they could face corrective action. Harassment is a serious offense. They could be removed from campus."

"I don't think that's possible."

"Why?"

"Because he has tenure."

Clarke turned to Eve, his lips parted as if he was about to speak, and yet he said nothing. Finally, after a moment of silence, he exhaled deeply, cradling his head in his hand.

"A handwritten proposal is fine. I won't penalize you for turning it in late. I understand that the library has some scratchpads for rent. I'll arrange to have them waive the fee for you."

"Thanks, Professor." Eve deactivated her scratchpad, which shook and whined as it shrank back into cube form. "You really don't have to do that for me."

"No, I really do." The professor's eyes were distant, his hands planted on his hips. "Eve, there's something else I need to ask you."

Eve wrinkled her brow. "Yes?"

"Are you okay?" He paused. "Are you... safe?"

"Am I safe?" She faltered. "Well, there hasn't been a reported attack in weeks, if that's what you mean."

"They found Interloper bodies on campus two days ago, in front of the music building."

"Really?" Eve's chest became tight, but she feigned an unaffected front. "I didn't know that."

"They were killed—their spines shattered, their bodies mangled." He stared down at his podium. "One was even decapitated."

"Well, it's good to hear that the patrolmen are having so much success."

Clarke let out a long, frustrated sigh. "There were *witnesses*," he continued. "They saw *everything*." He chuckled cynically under his breath. "None of what they said can be proven, of course, but you probably already knew that."

"I'm not quite sure what you're getting at, Professor."

"Eve," he paused, finally making eye contact with her, "while I respect and admire your courage, what you're doing here... It's *dangerous*."

"I don't know what you're talking about."

"Look, I know you're not going to stop just because I say so, nor am I in any type of position to tell you how to live your life, but know this—" He leaned in closer to her, his hands gripping the edge of the podium. "There will come a time—a breaking point—when you will fail, not because you're incapable or weak, but because *everyone fails at some point*. And you have to ask yourself if you're ready for that—if you're ready to collapse. Because in a situation like this—fighting a battle like the one you're fighting—failure could be small, or it could be something much, much greater. Something tragic. Now, be honest: are you prepared for that? Are you prepared for tragedy?"

"Professor Clarke, I—"

"Answer me, Eve."

She eyed him apprehensively, reluctant to speak. "Yes. I'm prepared."

"Are you sure? Are you really, *really* sure?"

Eve stared at the professor, and while she saw conviction and care in his gaze, there was something else there: it was herself, her own reflection in each of his pupils, watching her as if they, too, were awaiting her answer. Finally, she spoke.

"I know what I'm doing. And I'm sure."

Without delay, she hurried from the classroom and barreled down the hallway, eager to get away from the most likeable professor at Billington. She tried to push his words from her mind, but his voice reverberated in her thoughts until all she could hear was his strict tone, and all she could see was his anxious gaze.

Preoccupied with her thoughts, she ran right into another student who had strayed into her path. With a grunt, Eve regained her balance and turned toward her most recent obstacle, only to realize that she had inadvertently stumbled into the very last person she was hoping to see.

"God*dammit*," Eve groaned.

Heather cocked her head. "You're not happy to see me? I'm hurt, Eve, truly."

"What a surprise. I didn't know you were capable of *feeling*."

The redhead ignored her barb. "How are you holding up?" she asked, eyeing Eve up and down. "You look a little pale. Perhaps some morning sickness? I imagine you're carrying a litter already."

Eve rolled her eyes. "Really clever, but then again, you *are* Billington's most accomplished mudslinger."

"I wouldn't call myself a mudslinger—too dirty." Heather wrinkled her nose with distaste. "I just prefer to lead others to the mud pile and watch as they roll around in it. You know," she smiled, "like pigs."

"Classy," Eve mumbled, "*and* deranged."

"I'm sorry to hear that your intercourse with Jason has turned into such an infamous incident."

"Yeah, I wonder who could've been the cause of that." Eve crossed her arms. "Feels like someone created a mud pile and then forced me to roll around in it."

"Eve, darling! Don't compare yourself to pigs. It isn't becoming—for the pigs."

"Heather!" a voice called from behind Eve.

Eve spun around, curious to see who had joined their conversation. An enthusiastic Hayden was running toward the pair, her arms filled with multi-colored thermoses that leaked onto her white collared shirt.

"Heather, I picked up your morning juice blend! I wasn't sure what you were in the mood for, so I just grabbed one of each." She leaned over a single thermos, sniffing it curiously. "This one smells like feet."

"Pomegranate blueberry sounds divine," Heather cooed, plucking one of the containers from Hayden's grasp. "You can have the rest."

Hayden's eyes lit up. "For me?" She grinned, still juggling her armload. "You're *so* generous. Like, really, *really* generous."

Eve glanced back and forth between the two girls. "What is this?"

Heather wrapped her arm around the pint-sized lackey and squeezed her tightly. "Hayden and I are best friends. Haven't you heard?"

"Since when?" Eve turned to Hayden. "What happened to Madison?"

"I took your advice," Hayden sneered as she guzzled down one of Heather's juice medleys. "But don't expect a thank you, because you're not getting one."

"My advice was to steer clear of Madison, not to replace her with someone equally unhinged."

"We should go," Heather cut in, steering Hayden down the hallway. "We have spring classes to enroll in, after all." She offered Eve a patronizing wink. "I trust you haven't selected yours—hasty, careless decision-making seems to be your forte."

The two girls scurried away, Heather with a delighted spring in her step and Hayden with a thermos straw lodged between her lips. Just when Eve thought she was finally rid of them, Heather suddenly swiveled in place.

"You know, a little birdie told me that some Interlopers were slain on campus—created quite a stir, apparently. It's a shame we missed all the action. I was engrossed in my novel, and you—well, you were busy in the nookie nook, right?"

And with that, the two girls made their way out of sight, leaving Eve standing in the middle of the hallway with her lips parted in a foolish manner. She couldn't help but gawk, dumbfounded by Heather's words, and even when she realized that she was no longer alone—Percy was now waiting beside her—she still said nothing.

"Hello, crotch-face," Percy barbed, playfully elbowing her in the ribs. "Or should I say, sexual deviant. Your phony libido is the talk of the town."

Eve rolled her eyes. "It's funny: so many people have screwed in that closet, but the minute Jason and I do, it's a scandal."

"That's because you're not *people*, you're chimeras," Percy scoffed. "And chimeras don't *screw*, they procreate—like animals. Don't you know these things?"

Eve didn't respond. Her eyes were still focused on the spot where Heather once stood. Percy gazed curiously down the corridor and then back at Eve.

"You okay? You look like you've just seen a ghost."

"Yeah, I'm fine," Eve answered. "Just had a strange encounter, that's all."

"Well, you better get used to that. The whole campus thinks you and Jason are exhibitionists." He lowered his voice. "You should be proud, though—our last hit was practically seamless. Regardless of what everyone thinks, Remington is alive because of us."

Before Eve could respond, a new sight caught her attention: Madison had just entered the business building and was sauntering down the corridor in an extravagant shirt-dress like a stunning model on a European runway.

"Look who's here," Percy muttered sarcastically. "My beautiful girlfriend, the apple of my eye."

"You mean *ex*-girlfriend, right?"

"Well... not exactly."

Eve furrowed her brow. "What do you *mean*, 'not exactly'?"

"I never formally ended things with her. I just sort of, you know, phased her out. I mean, for God's sake, it was just *one* date. It's not like we're actually *together*."

Eve critically eyed the heir. "Has she called you?"

"Maybe."

"How many times?"

"A few... dozen."

"So, basically, you've been spinelessly ignoring her for a week."

"Hey, I wouldn't call it *spineless*. I'm just keeping my distance. I mean, the girl threatened to kill you just because she likes your boyfriend. I don't want to be on the receiving end of her wrath. Unlike you, I don't miraculously *heal*."

Eve sighed loudly. "You need to dump her."

"What? *Why*?"

"Because she's a human being. You said so yourself: 'Blondie's the *real deal*.'"

"She's a *psychopath*," he hissed.

"It's the right thing to do."

"Oh, don't lecture me about right and wrong. We used the girl for diamonds, remember?"

Eve folded her arms. "Percy, dump her. Now."

Percy groaned. "You know, you can be a real pain in the cock."

"Do it."

"I know, I know. I'm going, *Mom*."

With the maturity of a moping child, Percy stomped down the hallway, quickly combing his hair into place before approaching Madison's side. She turned to face him, her lips turned up into a dazzling smile.

"Percy! My delicious red velvet devil, where have you been? I've been trying to get in touch with you for *days!*"

"Lost my phone," Percy muttered. "Look, we need to talk."

"Um, yeah, I know that. Why else would I be calling you?" she snorted.

Percy offered her a condescending smile. "I'll go first—"

"I'm breaking up with you."

Percy stopped short, aghast. "What?" he snapped. "*You're* breaking up with *me?*"

"It's nothing personal," Madison continued. "You're handsome, you have amazing style, and *God* are you a good kisser—a little shy, but still pretty tasty." She trailed her finger down the buttons of his shirt and sighed. "I just can't lead you on like this. It wouldn't be fair."

"What do you mean, 'lead me on'?"

"There's someone else." Madison stopped and considered. "Actually, there's a couple of them..."

"Look, I already know about Lionel—"

"But then there's Jason."

Percy wrinkled his brow. "*Jason?* You're not even *dating* him."

"I know, but I will be someday—someday very soon, once that *slophole* is out of the picture." She glared at Eve, who was still waiting in the distance. "Don't you see? I'm in love with Jason, and I'm in a relationship with Lionel. Two men at once is my limit—three's a crowd. You understand that, right?"

Percy was silent, his expression a mix of shock and shame. "I've never been dumped before."

"I know it hurts to lose me. It's a deep pain, I'm sure." She rested a hand on his forearm. "You can keep the diamonds, though."

Percy smirked. "Trust me, that part wasn't up for negotiation."

Madison gave his arm one last squeeze. "Goodbye, Percy," she cooed, slowly backing away from him. "If you see Jason, tell him that I love him?"

And with one last flip of her hair, the heiress disappeared around the corner, leaving Percy alone in the center of the hallway.

Eve made her way to his side. She stared at his bewildered expression, her brow twisted with confusion.

"How'd it go?"

"Don't ask."

"But—"

"Don't. Ask."

They walked together in complete silence. Eve glanced at Percy out of the corner of her eye; his back was taut and his cheeks were an unusual shade of red. She looked over her shoulder at Madison one last time and shrugged.

"She seemed to take it well."

"*Eve.*"

"Sorry," she mumbled, trying her best not to smile, "ass-sack."

* * *

The cool breeze brushed across her face, blowing her hair from her shoulders. Eve was accustomed to December in San Francisco—to the blistering wind and foggy haze—but the weather in Calabasas was only slightly chilly, and so she removed her coat and set it off to her side. Jason had insisted on their meeting this evening—"*I'm stealing you,*" he'd said with a wink—and so there she sat, on his faded quilt, atop the grassy hill that overlooked the entire campus. She fidgeted with her black tie and matching pleated skirt, adjusting them into perfect position, and then, deciding that perfection was simply unattainable, she allowed the fabric to flutter with each gentle gust of wind.

Jason was rummaging through his shoulder bag, but stopped for a moment to gaze down at the base of the hill. A cluster of photographers was gathering, their cameras flashing as they watched the two chimeras, and Jason's face became consumed with irritation.

"Someone's tipping them off," Eve said. She rested her hand on his. "They would've found us no matter where we went."

"Still, maybe a picnic wasn't the best move."

"I think it's romantic."

Jason's eyes flicked from the photographers to Eve. "Good." He smiled. "That was the idea."

He continued to dig through his shoulder bag and at last pulled out two glasses and a bottle of merlot.

"Wine? But why?"

Jason chuckled. "You know, some people actually drink it for the *taste.*"

He handed her a glass, and they clinked their crystal together.

"A toast," Jason began, "to us. To future success."

"To kicking ass," Eve added, downing her drink.

"We're doing it, you know. Little by little. We could actually win this."

"I know." She exhaled, relaxing her body into the quilt. "For the first time in my life, all of that"—she paused, cocking her head toward the paparazzi—"that *noise* seems insignificant. Like I can finally breathe."

"I can tell."

"What do you mean?"

He smiled. "You're different now."

Eve hesitated. "Different how?"

"More at peace, I guess." He stared out at the campus below. "There are some things—some *burdens*—that never go away. I get that now. But *Billington* shouldn't be one of them. Not the protestors, not the flyers, not even Madison—"

"She hasn't spoken to me. Not since her date with Percy."

"Good," Jason said. "Now you won't have to be bothered by all of her whining and daddy issues."

"*Daddy* issues?" Eve rolled her eyes. "Madison has issues, but I don't think her dad is one of them."

Jason furrowed his brow. "What are you talking about?"

"What are *you* talking about?"

"Mr. Palmer totally disregards Madison. They haven't spoken in *years*." He set his empty glass to the side. "Don't get me wrong, things were never great—he's *always* put work before her—but, I don't know, *something* happened. Something made everything even worse."

Eve looked over at him, perplexed. "I don't understand. He named his company after her."

"Is that what she told you?" Jason laughed. "Madison Diamonds was launched four years before Madison *Palmer* was even born. Which means—"

"He named his daughter after his company." Eve faltered. "But all the gifts—"

"Toys to play with, to keep her occupied." Jason shrugged. "Or quiet."

"Wow," Eve mumbled. "I'd almost feel bad for her if she hadn't *slapped* me."

"Why are we even talking about her?"

"What should we talk about?"

"How beautiful you look today."

"Oh, God," Eve chuckled, blushing the slightest bit. "Guess you brought some cheese to go with the wine, huh?"

Jason stared at her, studying the details of her skin, the dark flecks in her eyes, and the three, maybe four freckles on her cheeks.

"A lot has happened these last few months. The Interlopers, the team—" He glared at the photographers below. "The *press*. But I want you to know that, above all else, what matters most to me is this." He stopped and wrapped his fingers around hers. "What we have together."

Eve was quiet. She concentrated on the feeling of her palm resting in his, on how natural it felt. It struck her that only a few months prior, the very thought of such a thing would have been completely foreign and unfamiliar.

After a brief silence, Jason leaned in closer to her.

"Still cheesy?" he asked.

"Yes."

"You like it."

"I do."

Eve smiled as Jason brought her chin closer to his and delicately kissed her bottom lip. He dragged his hand up her back and to the nape of her neck, running his fingers through her hair as he kissed her again, this time firmly and passionately. Eve ignored the blinking lights of the faraway cameras and closed her eyes, opening her senses to the feeling of his prickly cheek against hers, the taste of wine on his tongue, and the sound of fervent shouting in the distance.

"GUYS! Hey, guys!"

Sancho was barreling up the grassy hillside, waving his arms. Jason pulled away from Eve and scowled.

"God, this *always* happens to us," he groused.

Sancho stopped at the edge of the quilt, eyeing the wine bottle and empty glasses. "Sorry," he mumbled, "looks like I'm interrupting."

"You think?" Jason hissed.

Sancho glanced back and forth between the couple and the photographers. "You do know there are people taking pictures of you, right?"

Jason rolled his eyes. "What do you want, Sanch?"

Sancho hesitated, lowering his voice to an unnecessary whisper. "We need you guys... you know, back at Percy's place."

Eve wrinkled her forehead. "Why?"

Sancho was quiet. Again, he looked at the paparazzi below.

"They can't hear you, Sancho," Eve said.

He turned to her, his eyes bright with excitement. "There's been a development."

Jason glowered. "Can't it wait?"

"Trust me, you want to see this."

Jason sighed with annoyance and offered Eve an apologetic glance. "Fine," he muttered, gathering their things before following Sancho down the hill.

The threesome traveled across the Billington grounds back to Rutherford Hall. Sancho opened the door to Percy's suite, and as he ushered the two chimeras into the room, Eve's eyes immediately landed on the unexpected visitor beside the kitchen counter. He sat on one of the barstools, his short legs dangling high above the floor, and though his back faced her, his shaggy, unkempt head of hair was instantly recognizable.

"Armaan?"

"Eve! Jason! You're here!" Armaan spun in his seat and hopped to the floor. He glanced at the two chimeras and blushed. "Sorry to intrude like this."

"You hear that? He's *intruding,*" JJ said, crossing her arms. "Are you going to yell at him like you did at me?"

Eve offered Armaan a reassuring nod. "Don't apologize. You're an invaluable part of our group." She turned to JJ and sneered. "Armaan's the first *friend* I made here at Billington. Did you know that?"

JJ grumbled. "Dynamic."

"So what's this new development we've heard so little about?" Eve asked.

"It's the second skin." Armaan raised a small jar, filled with creamy, foul-smelling flesh, and scurried toward the seating area, urging the others to follow. "Kind of embarrassing how it all happened, actually. I was running more tests and got a little careless—it was the excitement of it all, I guess. Anyway, I accidentally spilled the stuff all over my bedsheets."

"Well, that's a shame, I guess," Jason mumbled.

"*Hardly.* It actually led to my most surprising discovery thus far. Look."

Before anyone could object, Armaan popped the top from his jar and poured the beige-colored contents onto Percy's coffee table.

"Mother of *ass!* I *just* replaced that thing," Percy groaned.

Armaan didn't respond; instead, he focused intently on the ooze-covered table, his gaze fierce and his brow twisted. As he stared, the substance started to bubble and seethe as if heated by a burning flame, and then the coffee table began to bulge and contort into strange and unnatural shapes: the wooden legs expanded like lungs, the drawers shriveled into nothingness, and the blackened tabletop shrank in size, its surface morphing from hard and sleek to soft and textured. Soon, the coffee table was no more, having been replaced by a black velvet throw pillow identical to the others that adorned Percy's couch.

"Good Lord, it's magic slime," Percy said, staring in awe at the pillow.

"I told you you'd want to see this," Sancho grinned, plucking the pillow from the floor and tossing it up in the air.

"I don't know why it didn't occur to me sooner," Armaan added, pleased with his discovery. "The second skin works on *anything*, living or otherwise."

"But what's the point of it?" Jason asked. "I mean, I understand why they would want to disguise *themselves*, but what else are they trying to conceal?"

Eve's eyes suddenly widened. "The lair. It could be hidden in plain sight."

Armaan nodded. "My thoughts exactly."

Eve sighed disappointedly. "For all we know, we've walked right past it and didn't even know it."

"So we don't know who Fairon is *or* where he's hiding," Jason grumbled, anxiously running his hand through his hair. "God, what a mess."

"What about the torq?" Eve turned to JJ. "Have you found anything?"

JJ shrugged. "I'm still converting the information. It's incredibly complex. But I finished coding the virus, and it's ready to upload."

"So, we're ready to destroy the mainframe. We just have to find it first."

"And until then, what?" Sancho asked. "Keep killing aliens?"

"How about until then, no more nosebleeds," Percy added, shooting a critical glare in Jason's direction. "Keep those face periods under control. We don't need any more aliens suddenly *attracted* to us."

"It wasn't intentional," Jason said defensively. "I can only melt one thing at a time."

"There's only so much our gift can handle," Eve explained. "If you exhaust your gift, you bleed. And if you keep bleeding, you—"

"Die."

Eve stopped short—she turned to Armaan, who sat casually on the leather armrest, fiddling with his scratchpad and oblivious to her sudden silence.

"What?"

"Exhausting your gift—it'll kill you," he repeated.

"Where did you hear that?"

"From Dr. Dzarnoski."

Jason's eyes darted between the two. "Care to elaborate?"

"Your gift is a power source. When you push it past its capacity, the energy is depleted," Armaan recited. "The more you drain it, the weaker it becomes, until eventually it completely burns out."

"And then what?" Jason asked. "You're just giftless?"

Arman shook his head. "I wish it were that simple. If your gift kicks the bucket, it triggers a chain reaction. Every other function in your brain begins to shut down, one after the next, until nothing is left."

"That can't be right," Eve interrupted. "It doesn't make any sense—"

"Sure it does," Armaan maintained. "Look, think of your gift as a car battery. If the battery dies, the whole car stops working. Except that, unlike with a car, you can't just replace your gift with a new one." He turned to face both Eve and Jason. "Basically, when your gift dies, so do you."

A hush fell over the room. Eve and Jason stared at one another, their tension seeping through the space between them. Armaan glanced back and forth at the couple and cowered in his seat.

"Um, I take it you didn't know this," he mumbled. "I'm sorry, I wasn't trying to worry anyone."

A noise erupted in the corner of the room—a ringing that came from JJ's triad of scratchpads. Eve turned to JJ.

"Is that—"

"Another abduction," JJ answered, darting toward her computers. "This one's in Brentwood."

Jason furrowed his brow. "So soon?"

"And off campus?" Eve asked. "Why *Brentwood?*"

"Gee, I don't know, why don't you ask them when you get there?" JJ scoffed. "Look, the attack is going down in less than twenty-five minutes, and that's barely enough time to get to Brentwood." JJ turned to the others. "You need to leave *now.*"

And so they did, sparing only a minute for Eve to change her clothes— *"You can't possibly expect me to fight in a skirt,"* she scoffed when they protested—and as soon as they were able, they dashed to Percy's car and drove straight to Brentwood. JJ remained in Percy's suite, nagging the others via their communicaps, but despite her irritability, the car ride was calm and almost dull. They had killed Interlopers before—countless of them at this point—and though Eve questioned the location, she had faith in herself and her comrades.

She glanced at Jason, who was sitting with his axe in his lap. When he noticed her staring, he winked at her and smiled. She smiled back, and in that moment, any remaining shred of nervous energy she may have felt drifted away.

They arrived, albeit a bit later than JJ had hoped, and quickly filed out of the car. Night had fallen, painting the sky with a haze of black that made their unfamiliar surroundings even gloomier. JJ directed them to an alley, and for a moment, it reminded Eve of the alleyway to the Meltdown—but they were far from Calabasas, the Pier Lorent hotel, or the neighboring chimera club.

One by one, Eve and the others tiptoed down the alley until they finally reached its center—the exact location of the abduction, according to the beacon—and with their weapons raised, they waited.

Nothing happened.

Eve scanned her surroundings. They were completely alone, their soldierly stances almost silly given the situation. Jason, too, began to stir, his eyes flitting back and forth, perplexed by the glaringly obvious lack of action. After several minutes of silence, Percy let out an aggravated sigh and dropped his hands to his sides.

"Do you see anyone?" JJ asked.

"No," Jason muttered. "We're the only ones here."

Sancho fidgeted in place. "Give it a couple of minutes. Maybe they're late."

"You're the ones who are late. They probably finished and fled the scene."

"Please. You really think they completed the entire abduction in"—Percy looked at his watch—"four minutes? Give me a break."

"Look, no one's even walked by since we got here," Jason groused.

"Are you sure we're at the right location?" Sancho asked.

"They listed the longitude and latitude. It doesn't get more specific than that."

Percy shrugged. "Did you read it wrong?"

"EXCUSE me?"

"Shut up," Eve blurted. "Everyone just be quiet. They're not coming."

Sancho sighed. "But they said—"

"They changed their minds," she interrupted. "Or they chose a different location. Whatever it is, they're not here." She scowled, failing to conceal her disappointment. "Let's go back to Billington."

Percy and Sancho piled their guns into the car, grumbling under their breath. Jason made his way to Eve's side and rested his hands on his hips.

"I don't understand," he mumbled. "Why would they stage an attack and then bow out at the last minute? Did they know we were coming?"

"I don't know." Eve stared down the empty alleyway, and a sense of dread began to fester in her stomach. "Let's just get out of here."

The group drove back to Billington in silence. A cloud of chagrin settled over the car—Percy muttered about the traffic, Sancho pouted childishly, and Jason blankly stared out the window—but while the boys were preoccupied with thoughts of loss and inadequacy, Eve instead tried to ignore the grim feeling that gnawed at her gut.

They parted ways in the Rutherford Tower. Percy continued up to his suite, agreeing to manage JJ's wrath, while Sancho, Jason, and Eve sulked through the hallway of the twelfth floor, idly maneuvering toward their prospective rooms. As Sancho shuffled into his room, Jason lingered by Eve's side for a moment longer.

"We'll get 'em next time," he whispered, his fingers lightly grazing her arm before he pulled away, following Sancho's lead into their room.

Eve continued on to her dorm, tromping past the pajama-clad Rutherfordians and trying to stifle her persistent anxiety. With a growl, she thrust the door open, so consumed with worry that she failed to notice that it was unlocked.

As she stepped into the room, she froze, her feet fixed in place as if cemented to the floor. Her room had been ransacked. Both Madison's abandoned mattress and her own were ripped to shreds and tossed across the space. Her end table was in pieces, its paneling scattered along the floor in splinters, and her wardrobe was tipped on its side, its contents spilling from the opened doors. But it wasn't the mess that concerned her—she hardly even noticed the damaged walls, the scuffed floor or her torn clothes. What concerned her were the three Interlopers who were still digging through her things.

They stopped their rummaging and gazed back at her with glassy eyes. One of them snarled and kicked at the ground, scratching the floor with his sharpened talons. Another one pointed at her, or at least he attempted to, as his hand was nothing more than a scabbing stump. Eve recognized that one—she had fought him only days ago, and he had flown out of sight and out of mind—but she paid him no attention. It was the third Interloper that made her blood run cold.

He was huge: ten, maybe eleven feet tall, so tall that he had to hunch his shoulders just to fit inside her room. His wings were massive, easily large enough to break through either wall, but he kept them resting gently against his back, bobbing occasionally with his subtle movements. Like the other

Interlopers, he had deep black eyes, but his skin was unique—a cloudy, milky white that absorbed the light of the moon. His sharp teeth and talons were a gleaming gold, and two thick, golden horns jutted from his forehead and curled over the top of his skull. Though his body looked gaunt, his shoulders were broad, his legs were sturdy, and his presence alone commanded a power and fear that kept Eve rooted where she stood.

After what felt like an eternity, Eve finally parted her lips and let out the only word she could manage to utter.

"Fairon?"

"*WHERE IS IT?*" he roared. "THE BEACON—TELL ME WHERE IT IS!"

Finally, the spell was broken, and Eve was able to move again, to feel her body—the heaving of her lungs, the pounding of her heart, the tension in her muscles. She braced herself and let out a piercing scream.

"*IT'S A TRAP!*"

With a baleful glare, Fairon dragged Eve's wardrobe from the floor and hurled it in her direction. Eve threw herself to the side, barely dodging the wooden monstrosity as it smashed into the wall beside her. She pulled herself to her knees, her eyes wide and panicked. She knew without a doubt that her situation was dire.

The other two Interlopers charged toward her, their mouths spreading into sickening smiles. The first one swung at her with his single clawed hand and his useless stump, but Eve quickly plucked her gun from her jeans and fired at the creature, blasting the teeth from his mouth and sending his lifeless body collapsing to the floor.

Eve turned to aim at the second Interloper, but she was too late—he swatted the firearm from her hands, sending it skidding across the floor. He swung his talons at her throat, but Eve dodged his advances, and she pounded her fist into his face over and over again until he, too, toppled to the ground. As the Interloper paused to regain his balance, Eve forcefully melted him across the room and slammed him against the opposite wall. Again she rammed him into the sheetrock, and then once more, the wall now covered with yellow blood. Her melt grew in intensity, and this time she sent the alien flying right through her glass balcony doors and plummeting to the terrace below, where his body splattered onto the campus grounds.

And then only Fairon remained. He stared at Eve, his eyes vacant and his body unmoving, and even though he was silent, he exuded a formidable strength that sent a wave of terror down Eve's spine.

Suddenly and with no expression, he stomped toward her, snapping the floorboards beneath his feet, and Eve instantly lunged for the gun that now lay in the corner of her room. With trembling hands, she snatched the firearm from the floor and launched all of her remaining bullets at Fairon's face, knocking a flurry of golden teeth from his mouth and boring deep, bloody holes into his cloudy skin and blackened eye.

She waited—her hands were still raised, her gun still smoking—and hoped to God that Fairon would drop to the floor, dead, just like the others.

But he didn't fall, or even move. He simply stood in front of her, his body perfectly still, and then Eve noticed that something about him was different: his face was quivering, the skin rolling like boiling water. His flesh pinched together at each entry wound, pushing the bullets from his skin, spitting them onto the floor at his feet. His oozing eye glossed over, repairing itself so rapidly, it soon looked as if there had never been any contusion to begin with, and his bloodied skin did the same, regenerating with such precision that not a single blemish remained. Then Eve noticed his teeth: they, too, grew back, sprouting from his gums to replace the ones he had lost.

In seconds, it was over. Fairon was fully healed, his entire being in perfect condition, and he smiled at the look of horror in Eve's eyes.

"Killing me will not come easily for you," he explained, his voice chilling. "Killing *you*, however—it will be hard to avoid. I must be delicate with you."

Eve melted Fairon across the room, sending his colossal body crashing into the back wall with enough force to shatter the sheetrock behind him. Still, Fairon was unfazed. He jumped to his feet, casually shaking the debris from his shoulders, then charged at Eve yet again. Just as she began to channel her gift a second time, he struck her across her face with such power that she spun in a full circle and toppled to the floor. Her cheek screamed in agony, and the pain seemed to pulse through her entire body, yet she launched Fairon across the room yet again, slamming him against the frame of the balcony door.

Eve groaned and winced—every inch of her body ached, but still she dragged herself to her feet just in time to watch Fairon's broken arm snap miraculously into place. He turned to face her, his sinister grin still intact, and he barreled in her direction.

Before she could even move from his path, he whipped his claws forward, sinking his talons deep into the flesh of her arm. Eve shrieked in pain and clutched at the open wound. She stared down at the blood running between her fingers and then gazed back at Fairon.

"It is only the beginning," he declared.

Eve dodged his next advance, dipping beneath his sharp jabs while trying to ignore the stinging of her arm. With as much strength as she could summon, she threw her fist into the creature's jaw—only to immediately pull back and cry out in agony. The impact was excruciating, as if her hand had collided with a brick wall, and she doubled over, struggling to breathe through the shooting pain.

She forced herself upright, but there was no time to recover—Fairon grabbed her by the shoulders and tossed her against the wall, sending her collapsing to the floor.

Eve took in a short, shallow breath. Her mind felt dulled, a muddled haze that matched the thick blanket of fog consuming her vision. In that moment, all she could feel was the unbearable aching of her body—the throbbing of her skull, of her bloodied arm and her shattered hand—and through the pain, she faintly sensed the sinister presence of Fairon looming over her.

Above the ringing in her ears she could barely hear the commotion behind her door. There was frenzied running, panicked screaming, and through it all, a familiar voice shouting, "*MOVE! FOR GOD'S SAKE, GET OUT OF THE WAY!*"

And then she felt a gust of air as the door swung open behind her, and the feeling of one—no, two bodies standing in the doorway. She glanced up and saw Jason and Sancho, their eyes wide with shock as they stared directly at Fairon.

"HOLY SHIT," Jason gasped.

The words had hardly left Jason's lips before Fairon was charging toward him, fueled by a heightened aggression. In one fluid motion, he seized the front of Jason's shirt, pulled him high into the air, and slammed his back into the floor. Again, Fairon lifted Jason and hurled him to the floor, this time hard enough to crack the floorboards as well as his bones.

Jason winced; he struggled in Fairon's grip, trying to free himself, though his attempts were futile. And then he noticed his axe lying only a few feet away from him. With great effort, he pulled his arm from Fairon's grasp, seized the axe, and plowed it deep into the center of Fairon's face.

Jason yanked the axe from the creature's skull and breathed a sigh of relief as yellow blood poured from the open wound. Then suddenly his eyes grew large with horror; he watched in utter disbelief as the skin on Fairon's face rippled and restored itself to its natural state, as if the blow had never happened.

Fairon looked Jason in the eye and smiled.

With a surge of unimaginable strength, Fairon knocked the axe from Jason's hand and pulled him by his shirt from the floor, lifting him up until they were at eye level with one another. Then, with a triumphant roar, Fairon charged ahead, pounding Jason violently against the wall. He backed up, Jason's limp body still in his grasp, and then again he slammed Jason into the wall—no, *through* the wall, carrying both of them into the tower hallway amid a sea of debris.

Suddenly, Fairon lurched from his spot in the corridor; Eve pulled the alien into her room, channeling her gift as she slammed him against the back wall of her dorm. She desperately scanned the hallway, searching for Jason and Sancho, but all she could see was a horde of terrified Rutherfordians running for the elevators.

Again she turned her attention to Fairon. He stood opposite her, looking almost indifferent, completely unaffected by every assault that had been made against him. Yet despite the apparent futility of it all, Eve melted him again, tossing him first into the wall and then into the ceiling, praying that somehow he might become as weak as she felt.

But Fairon merely hopped to his feet, unfazed. She tried to dodge the attack she knew was coming, but he made it look effortless as he swatted at her and sent her crashing into the wall yet again.

Eve slumped to the floor, her eyes clenched shut and her body sprawled among the wreckage of her room. She felt like a rag doll, limp and defeated, and for whatever reason the bumps and collisions felt more torturous than ever before.

Two large, clawed hands roughly grasped her shoulders, pulling her from the ground and sitting her upright against the wall. She opened her eyes; Fairon was crouching low to the ground, his face only inches away from hers, and just as her lips parted to scream, he grabbed at her throat, clenching it tightly and lifting her until her entire body dangled above the ground. Then, with a curious nod, he pulled her from the wall and examined her closely.

"You *are* a magnificent creature," he growled.

Eve choked, and her face reddened as she hung from his giant curled fist. She coughed and gasped for air, and Fairon merely laughed at her struggle.

"Be calm," he cooed. "I will not kill you. You will fall into a deep sleep—a state of peaceful unconsciousness. And you should welcome this fate, because you *do not* want to be awake for what I have planned for you. You do not want to *feel* what I will do to you." He tightened his grip. "It is a gift, this sleep. It is an act of *mercy*."

Eve's heart raced with dangerous speed. Her legs flailed as if independent from her body, desperate to reach the floor beneath her, and her lungs weighed heavy in her chest, burning as they fought helplessly for air. Eve's hands sprang into action, clawing at Fairon's fist until her arms were wet with his blood—yet his wounds healed within only seconds of their affliction.

Eve stared into Fairon's eyes. She knew that he had won the battle, but still she dug her nails into his skin and wriggled and writhed within his grasp. And then at last her struggles slowed, as she felt his merciful sleep overtaking her.

The sound of gunshots brought her back to her senses. A hail of glittering diamonds burrowed their way into Fairon's flesh, and then just moments later were pushed from his repaired skin just as they had been before. A line of people stood at the doorway: Percy with his gun aimed; JJ, who stood by his side; Sancho, who had evidently retrieved the two; and Jason, his face lined with fresh blood. Eve could hardly see them, but she could hear Percy as he tossed a gun to each of them, even JJ, and she could sense it when they all raised their weapons in a synchronized fashion.

"*DON'T HIT HER*," Jason ordered.

A torrent of bullets flew past Eve, targeting Fairon's legs, his arms, any part of his body that wasn't conveniently blocked by her own. She felt a single bullet graze her already bloodied shoulder, yet she didn't care; not while she still struggled for breath, not while the yellow, gaping bullet holes in Fairon's body morphed immediately back into fresh, unblemished skin.

Percy maneuvered his way into the room and pointed his weapon at Fairon's raised arm, unloading a surge of bullets that tore at the Interloper's wrist, ripping apart the skin and bone until the hand itself fell to the ground, along with Eve, whose neck remained in its grip.

Eve tore the severed hand from her throat and drew in a long, gasping breath; she scrambled away from the stream of ammunition and glanced up at Fairon, only to see that a new hand was quickly regenerating from the stump of his arm. He laughed loudly and victoriously, and he expanded his wings as if he enjoyed the bullets piercing his skin.

As Eve struggled to regain her breath, her throat and lungs still burning from deprivation, her eyes lit up with unexpected hope:

The massive Interloper flinched.

His face dropped, and he looked down at his shoulder. A diamond bullet was lodged deep in his milky flesh—and there it stayed as a river of yellow pus oozed from the orifice.

"KEEP GOING!" Eve commanded.

The firing continued, and Fairon lurched and staggered across the room, his body now littered with bullets. He stumbled backward, crashing onto the balcony, his body strangely failing to regenerate. As he swatted at the bullets, trying to deflect them, they merely burrowed into his hands and arms, and he howled with annoyance.

Then, with one last breath, Fairon turned and stared directly at Eve, his eyes shrinking to slits. His lip curled up into the tiniest of grins, and he threw his body over the edge of the balcony, disappearing from sight.

Percy and the others lowered their guns. They stared in awe at the balcony, at the exact spot where Fairon had just stood. Eve pulled herself to her feet—the act alone was a struggle—and she, too, gaped at the mess her nemesis had left behind. Jason tore across the room, racing past the destruction to the balcony overlooking the campus.

"*Where is he?*" He turned to Eve. "Where the HELL did he go?"

Suddenly, a massive, clawed hand—the hand of Fairon—reached up from underneath the deck. Before anyone could react, it yanked at the back of Jason's shirt and flung him from the balcony.

"*JASON!*" Eve screamed.

It all happened so quickly. She ran to the balcony, her body electrified and her limbs forced into action. She extended her hands, trying to channel her gift in a split second, to pull Jason's flailing body from the air before he hit the ground. She didn't see nor did she care what had happened to Fairon, and with desperation, she thrust her trembling arms over the balcony ledge—

And then gaped with bulging, horrified eyes at the ground below.

At Jason's body.

Eve's stomach dropped. Jason was sprawled face-first over the ground, his arms and legs wildly outstretched above the pavement. An awful chill raced through her, starting in her chest and spreading through her entire body. Her lungs heaved until even the deepest breath felt shallow and fruitless, and though her thoughts were overcome with madness, her eyes remained fixed on Jason's body.

"*JASON!*" she screamed once more.

Down below, two bodies darted from Rutherford Hall and onto the terrace, both small in stature with jet black hair. Eve almost didn't recognize Sancho and JJ as they crouched down beside Jason and looked up at her.

"He's okay!" Sancho shouted. "You got him!"

"He's floating!" JJ added. "Just inches above the ground!"

Then a third voice chimed in—Jason's voice.

"Put me down, Eve!"

Eve was stunned. Her hands remained outstretched, her mind still deep within her melt. She refused to move, to obey their commands, or even acknowledge Percy, who had been standing at her side for God knows how long.

"Eve, he's fine," Percy said. "You saved him."

"No," she answered, her voice wavering.

"Eve, stop melting—"

"NO."

Percy lightly rested his hand on her arm, but she swatted him away from her.

"DON'T TOUCH ME!" she cried.

"*Eve*," he repeated, firmly grabbing her wrist. "*Please* let him go."

Eve still hesitated, staring down at Jason's body—his living, breathing body. Reluctantly, she lowered her hands, then watched as Jason climbed to all fours and, with the help of Sancho and JJ, pulled himself to his feet.

Eve ran from the balcony, jumping over the rubble and debris in her room and shoving past the gawking bystanders in her path. She flew down the stairwell, sprinting down all twelve flights, then burst through the doors to the terrace, stopping only once she had reached Jason's side.

He looked back at her with his familiar, warm smile.

"You caught me right before I hit the ground," he explained.

She approached him hesitantly, as if the slightest touch could break him. With an uneasy breath, she gently stroked his face with her fingers, staring at him as if he wasn't real. Suddenly, she backed away from him.

"I was wrong. I wasn't prepared for this."

Percy finally barged through the doorway and joined the others on the terrace, ignoring the spectators who watched them from afar. Jason delicately reached out and touched Eve's arm.

"Eve, everything's fine. We're all fine."

"*No*," she snapped, pulling her arm from his grasp. "I'm not doing this."

"Eve, what are you talking about?"

"We're not *doing this*," she repeated. She turned to face the others. "*Any* of this. The Interlopers, the mainframe, Fairon—it's all over. We're *done*."

"*What?*" Jason furrowed his brow. "Eve, what's *wrong* with you?"

"You could've died, Jason. *You almost died.*"

"But I *didn't* die—"

"IT'S ME, JASON!" she cried. "They want ME. You almost *died* because of ME. Don't you get it? As long as you're near me, you're all in danger."

Jason scowled. "That's not true, Eve. You *saved* me."

"I *cursed* you," she hissed. "I'm the goddamn angel of death. Anyone who gets close to me *dies*."

"Wait, *what?*" Jason hesitated. "Is this about your parents?"

"It's about *everyone*," Eve continued. "Everyone I've ever cared about— everyone who's ever cared for *me*—they're all gone." She glanced at the others. "Look, I wanted to do this because I thought I had nothing to lose. But now," her eyes panned back to Jason, "now I do. And I can't do it."

"But Eve, we're a team," Sancho stammered.

"Not anymore. Do you understand me? Destroy the beacon and the torq."

Percy's mouth hung open in shock. "You can't just tell us to throw away everything we've worked for."

"I can, and I *will*."

"Don't be so rash, Eve," JJ added. "We're your friends."

"For God's sake, JJ, we're *not* friends!" Eve spat, shooting a scathing glare in JJ's direction.

Jason took a single step forward. "Eve, if we stop now, they'll come for you."

"Then I'll face them. But I'll do it *alone*."

Eve marched back toward the tower, leaving her comrades in the center of the terrace. Crowds of people had formed, some weeping, others finally calling for the patrolmen, but Eve hurried past them, eager to be rid of their prying eyes. She could hear Jason running up behind her; he grabbed at her arm, pulling her close to him one last time.

"Eve!" he pleaded. "You don't want to do this. I *know* you."

Eve's eyes met his, then panned to the trail of blood dripping down his hairline. A horrible, sinking feeling festered in her stomach—it was the feeling of nothing at all, of loss and utter emptiness. She tore her arm from his grasp and continued to walk away.

"It's over."

CHAPTER 15: GO TO HELL

"Don't you tell anyone, little girl. Don't you tell a goddamn soul, y'hear me?"

Eve lurched awake in her bed; she was shaking, her body tense with fear, and so she rested her hand on her chest as if to calm the beating of her heart. As soon as her senses returned to normal, she took in a deep breath and cursed her own rusty endurance. She hadn't realized how accustomed she had become to her dreamless sleeping—that is, of course, until the nightmares had returned.

A loud clanging interrupted the stillness—if her dream hadn't awoken her, surely the hallway construction would've done the trick. She glanced across her disheveled room: the walls had been boarded up in a careless manner, and the floor was still a shambles.

She had fought Dean Furst for a new room—in a new dormitory building, away from the Rutherfordians altogether—but he had insisted that all dorms were filled. *"We will make the existing room as comfortable as possible for the time being."* Furst's words repeated in her mind, and she grumbled to herself at the thought of them. It didn't matter, anyway; the semester would be over in a few days, and soon she would be rid of Billington, at least for winter leave, if not forever.

A knock sounded at the door.

"Miss Kingston?" a voice called. "You okay in there?"

Eve groaned aloud. "I'm *fine*, Number Two."

"You asleep?"

Eve trudged to the door and yanked it open. Outside her room stood two patrolmen—affectionately known as Number One and Number Two, at least to her—and she offered them a condescending smile.

"If I were asleep, would I have answered you?"

Eve hurried through her morning routine and made her way down to the lobby below, her two trusted patrolmen following closely behind. Officially, they were her "bodyguards." Eve thought the very idea was comical, yet it was deemed mandatory by the Billington officials. *"Your protection is important to us,"* Furst had coolly explained, though with the extensive media coverage surrounding the recent attack at Rutherford Hall, Eve suspected the security had less to do with her own safety and more to do with the protection of the university's image. Still, the patrolmen accompanied her everywhere, as they had for nearly a week, ever since that horrible day in her dorm room.

Ever since she met Fairon.

The Rutherford Hall doors were only a short distance away, and behind them Eve could hear a muffled chanting—the familiar sound of protestors. Though she dared not look at them, she could sense her patrolmen tighten their grip on their firearms. She felt like screaming, but instead she bit her lip and said nothing, allowing her thoughts to do the screaming for her.

They reached the end of the lobby, and with a hint of hesitation, Number One pushed the doors open.

A hush fell over the courtyard. The protestors silenced, their fists and signs frozen in the air. Their eyes panned from Eve to the patrolmen, and then they reluctantly dropped their signs and trudged to the sides of the terrace, creating a pathway for Eve and her security.

Eve held her breath as she continued forward. She could see the hatred in the protestors' eyes, the absolute loathing in their forced compliance, but she tried to ignore their glares as she passed. A single protestor cursed at her, and another spat at her feet, but Eve and her patrolmen remained stoic. It was funny—the whole scene had become commonplace, as spitting and slurs had been a daily staple since her reveal, and yet over the past few weeks, she hadn't noticed. She had been too distracted by other things—things that were now no longer a part of her life.

It was finals week, and the business building was packed with students. Eve instructed her patrolmen to wait outside of her first class; the thought of them sitting behind her was simply humiliating, as if she were a child with two heavily armored babysitters. Still, even with them out of sight, she struggled to focus on her exam. She glanced around the lecture hall and saw Madison sitting on the opposite end of the room, glaring back at her as she usually did. Hayden was nowhere to be found—perhaps she was busy doing Heather's bidding, but Eve wasn't interested regardless. She looked out of the classroom window and scowled—Numbers One and Two were staring back at her, much to her chagrin. Finally, she turned her attention back to her tedious exam, though everything in her life had lately started to feel that way: monotonous and repetitive, the same shit moment after moment, just as it had been only a few months prior.

The exam period finally ended—*Thank God*, Eve thought—and she eagerly raced down the lecture hall stairs. Clarke was staring at her, his expression intense as if he had something to say, but Eve wasn't feeling especially social.

"Evelyn," he called.

She continued on her way, ignoring him.

"EVE," he repeated, this time louder.

Still she disregarded him, hoping that she appeared distracted or maybe even the slightest bit deaf.

"I'M SORRY," he shouted.

That stopped her. Eve turned to face the professor, her mouth twisted with confusion. "For what?"

He was quiet for a moment, waiting for his remaining students to leave the classroom. "I was out of line," he began. "When I spoke to you last week. It wasn't my place to say those things to you."

Eve approached the professor's podium and flashed a sardonic smirk. "With all due respect sir, you're being stupid. As it is, I should've listened to you in the first place."

He sighed. "Yeah," he muttered, "me and my wonderful advice."

Eve furrowed her brow. "Professor?"

"How are you holding up?" he continued. "You haven't seemed the same since," he hesitated and looked away, "the incident."

"I'm alive. The people I care about are alive too. We're all better off now."

Clarke chuckled to himself. "Better off, huh?"

"Excuse me?"

"The last couple of months have been good for you, Eve. For a while there, you actually exuded a sort of"—he stopped, looking for the right word—"a sort of *vitality*. You were a different woman than the one who walked into my class on the first day of the semester." He lowered his hands to his sides. "Now, it's as if that energy has been... depleted."

Eve forced a shrug. "Finals week isn't exactly my favorite time of the year."

"There are a few others who've been a little off, too." He eyed her curiously. "Mr. Valentine's in my next class. He seems especially dejected these days."

Eve clenched her jaw. "Professor Clarke, what exactly are you trying to say?"

"I meant what I said to you that day: that you needed to be prepared. But you also have to be able to live with yourself—with the decisions you make."

She bit her bottom lip with annoyance. "Look, we got cocky and careless. We thought we were unbeatable. And because of that, everything went to hell."

"And did you learn anything?"

"Did I what?"

"From the experience—from the failure. Did you *learn* anything?"

"I learned when to back down," Eve shot back. "You asked me if I was prepared for a collapse. Well, we collapsed—we collapsed *hard*—and I wasn't prepared for it."

Clarke shook his head, his eyes uncharacteristically sad. "You know, sometimes even leadership professors get the whole leadership thing wrong."

Eve offered him a sympathetic, though clearly contrived smile.

"And sometimes they get it right."

Eve left Clarke standing by his podium, not bothering to take a second look at him. She barreled into the hallway, nodding for Numbers One and Two to follow her, and just as she turned the corner to her next class, she smacked directly into another student, who was fumbling with an unwieldy mountain of paperwork. The student stumbled back, his papers scattering to the ground, and Eve turned to her patrolmen and grimaced.

"See? Now, how are you supposed to protect me from an alien if you can't even protect me from a stack of papers?" she teased.

She turned back to the mess of papers and the small, shaggy-haired student who scrambled to collate them.

"Armaan?"

He glanced up at her, trying to shake his ebony locks from his eyes. "Sorry, Eve," he murmured. "Didn't see you... for obvious reasons."

Eve crouched down and helped her friend sort through his pile. They worked together in silence. Eve quickly shuffled the pages into a messy stack, while Armaan worked much more slowly, his attention split between the task at hand and his friend by his side.

"I heard you quit the..." he glanced nervously at the patrolmen, "you know."

"Yeah."

"Do you want to—"

"Talk about it? Not even a little bit."

He frowned. "Well, I'm sorry it happened."

The stack was finally arranged, and Eve plopped the cumbersome heap into Armaan's arms, nearly throwing him off balance once again. He regained his footing and breathed a sigh of relief.

"What are you doing here?" Eve asked.

"Running errands for Dr. Dzarnoski, what else?" His voice was caustic. "The man's away on vacation, and I'm stuck making deliveries and doing his busywork when I should be in the medical ward learning, I don't know, *something.*"

Eve watched him for a moment. His usual plucky spark was gone, re-placed by a sense of resentment. She turned back to her patrolmen—*Leave,* she mouthed, and they obediently backed away—and then she returned her attention to the would-be medical student.

"You okay?"

"I just don't know how to escape this: this endless cycle of invisibility. I don't know how to get people to take me seriously." He leaned his head against the wall and sighed. "Maybe I'm just kidding myself."

Eve folded her arms in a reprimanding fashion. "Armaan, there are a lot of people in this world who are destined to be boring—to spend each boring day surrounded by other boring people at boring jobs for the rest of their boring lives. And they'll never do much of anything for anyone—or even for themselves. And then there are people who are destined for greatness: peo-ple like you. You're smart and ambitious, and people will try to shut you out or make you feel worthless, and do you know why? Because they're *boring,* but you... you're special." Her eyebrows narrowed, her expression one of kind criticism. "You were born to do big things. So stop being so goddamn *scared* and go *do those big things.* Jesus *Christ,* what are you waiting for? *Permission?* You don't need it."

Armaan chuckled. "Sounds like you're talking about yourself, Eve."

Eve's face flushed, and she instantly felt embarrassed.

"I have to get to class," she muttered.

With her cheeks still red, she rushed past the little assistant and down the hallway once again. Her patrolmen scurried behind her, struggling to keep pace, and just as they finally reached her side, all three of them suddenly halted.

Eve groaned. Another obstacle was in her path, one she should have seen coming.

"Saw your room," Hayden snorted. "You're messy."

Beside her stood Heather, her face bright with the most delighted, self-congratulatory grin Eve had ever seen on the girl.

"Eve, you're looking especially grim today," she cooed, eyeing her up and down. "It's almost as if you've been defeated."

"Good one, Heather," Eve mumbled, sarcastically. "You're so astute."

Heather pointed at the two patrolmen. "Are these your new friends? It looks as though you've abandoned your old ones." She tilted her head patronizingly. "Or have *they* abandoned *you*? That seems a bit more in keeping with your life story."

Eve felt her blood begin to boil, flowing through her like burning magma. She didn't need this—not today, not ever, and certainly not from Heather. She turned to the patrolmen at her side—they could see in her eyes the pique that had been ignited and quickly backed away—and with conviction, Eve turned back to Heather.

"Look, as much as I've enjoyed these hallway run-ins, I'm letting you know they end here."

Heather's lips pursed. "And what exactly does *that* mean?"

"I'm telling you to *stay away from me*," Eve hissed. "You can spread whatever rumors you want about my life—I honestly don't care—but if you *ever* come up to me with another one of your bullshit attempts at intimidation, I swear to *God* I will make you wish you never found my goddamn picture in that goddamn face database. Do you hear me?"

Heather stared back at Eve with the same complacent expression she always wore, though this time there was something more to it—something hard, almost challenging. After a brief hesitation, she smiled.

"Well, that was an awfully impassioned speech. Sounds like you've been meaning to get that off your chest for some time now."

"Get *what* off her chest?" another voice chimed in.

Eve turned, surprised and dismayed to see Madison approaching. She sashayed her way into the middle of the circle, her arms folded and eyes squinted.

"Madison!" Heather chirped, offering the heiress a hug. "I haven't seen you in ages. All is well with your new love muffin, I suspect?"

"Couldn't be better." She glanced at Eve. "Some people are calling us the *ultimate* Billington power couple."

Heather let out an insincere giggle that quickly faded into silence, and an uncomfortable hush fell over the girls. Hayden gazed at the floor while Heather and Madison attempted to be cordial, and meanwhile Eve made no effort to conceal her lack of interest in the whole thing.

"Well, isn't this like old times," Heather proclaimed at last. "The four of us, chit-chatting away."

"Yeah," Eve mumbled, "this isn't awkward at all."

"I was just curious what you guys were talking about," Madison paused and shot a scowl in Eve's direction, "with *her*."

"Nothing important," Heather answered. "Just humoring Eve's idle threats."

"She thinks she can scare us." Hayden glared at Eve. "She's wrong."

"What is this?"

The four girls jumped almost in unison; behind them stood Professor Richards, his hands on his hips and his face crinkled into a despicable sneer.

"Are you people *loitering?*" He muttered a handful of slurs under his breath. "This isn't a street corner. Get to class."

The girls scattered through the hallway, each one headed in a different direction. As Eve began her trek to class, her patrolmen on her heels, she heard Richards call her name.

"Kingston!" he shouted. He was crouched where Eve and the others had been standing, fiddling with a trinket he had found on the floor. He glanced up at Eve and thrust his hand in front of her.

"You drop this?"

In his hand sat a small key.

"That's not mine—"

Eve stopped herself—her body became numb, her once fiery veins now ice cold. She stared at the key, at its silver shaft, its intricate ridges, and the glittery crystals glued to its grip. She had seen it before: it was Madison's key to her dorm room.

"Something wrong, Kingston?" Richards snarled. "Looks like you just saw your life flash before your eyes."

Eve didn't respond. She slowly plucked the key from her professor's palm, examining it closely and skeptically. Its sudden appearance was odd—*too odd*—but she didn't have time to dwell on the matter. Richards snapped his fingers, drawing her attention back to him like a master training a disobedient dog.

"Final review starts in five minutes," he grumbled. "Don't make me castigate you for tardiness."

Eve watched as the professor plodded off to his classroom, and just as he slammed the door behind him, her heart dropped—Sancho and Percy were standing in front of the lecture hall, undoubtedly waiting for her, as there was no other reason for them to be there. She thought of what they might say, of what she might say to them, and then she imagined what would happen afterward, once she entered Richards' classroom—the hateful words of her professor and the resentful glares of her classmates. She was in no mood.

An idea sprang to her mind. She shoved the bedazzled key into her pocket and turned to Number One and Number Two.

"You know what? Screw Business Math. Who's hungry?"

The two patrolmen looked at one another.

"You're ditching class?" Number One asked.

"That's what I meant by *screw Business Math*."

Number Two hesitated. "But won't it affect your grade?"

Eve laughed. "Trust me, I'm getting an 'A,' whether I like it or not."

The three of them ate their lunch in silence, though Eve expected as much: Numbers One and Two were far from talkative, as their duties required them to be observant and, apparently, tight-lipped. For a second, Number Two offered Eve a slight smile; it was a look of compassion, though something about it made her feel more alone than ever. She remembered her life before Billington and how she used to covet her solitude, but suddenly the isolation felt different than it had before.

It felt lonely.

Strategic Communication would be starting soon, and though Eve considered ditching this class as well, her nagging conscience compelled her to attend. Leaving her patrolmen in the hallway, she took her usual spot near the back corner of the room, slouching in her chair as if hoping it would somehow diminish her presence.

Suddenly, the door swung open, and JJ barged through. Her appearance in the class was a rarity in itself, and she immediately locked eyes with her former comrade, sending Eve's stomach coiling into a knot. Neither girl said a word, and JJ stormed past her, taking a seat only three desks away from Eve, far enough to prevent their talking but close enough to leave them both with a palpable sense of tension.

This class had no final exam. Instead, Gupta required each student to deliver a persuasive speech, a task that many found considerably more painful than a simple test. Eve's speech was punctuated with awkward stares, as she knew would be the case, but she felt relief in having finished with her dignity somewhat intact. However, the comfort was fleeting; she grumbled to herself as the last presenter, the one classmate she had hoped would simply disappear into obscurity, approached the podium. Travis Braverman turned to the class and flashed his typical overconfident grin.

"My fellow scholars," he began, "Professor Gupta," he nodded at the instructor, "over the past few weeks, we have heard many speeches describing the good in our country: the charitable, the just causes, the heroes of this fine nation. And of course, we've heard the bad: the liars, the cheats, the criminals due for swift corrective action. However, we've yet to hear about the ugly." His face dropped into an expression of artificial concern. "That is what I'm here to discuss with you right now: the harsh ugliness of our society."

A stream of words was projected across the back wall, and Eve felt her heart drop in her chest.

Chimera: A Case Study in Humanity's Greatest Biological Failure

"Now, in order to help you fully comprehend this study, I decided to create a fictional character to help illustrate my points," Travis continued, pacing the floor. "She's a young, college-aged woman, who, while seemingly conventional in appearance, leads a life of debauchery, impropriety, and savagery due to her ill-fated birth as a chimera."

A caricature appeared alongside the text—it was a long, lanky girl with a wild mess of wavy hair. The drawing was primitive, but even with the crude animation, Eve immediately recognized the cartoon's likeness, as did the rest of her classmates. Travis smiled.

"The name of this completely *fictional* character is EmmaLynn Kingpin."

All eyes turned in Eve's direction. JJ was gaping at her, her mouth curled with disgust, but Eve instead glanced over her shoulder at Gupta, who sat in the last row of the classroom. He anxiously met her gaze and sank lower in his chair.

"*Scrote*," Eve groused under her breath.

"EmmaLynn Kingpin is the perfect example of why the chimera

population needs to be controlled—of course, hypothetically speaking, as she is, as I've noted, a fabricated character." Travis glimpsed in Eve's direction and shot her a quick wink. "And while it's not technically her fault that she was born into this species, it doesn't change the fact that her sheer existence has caused an outpouring of conflict and even interference from a world beyond this universe." He plucked a controller from his pocket and pointed it at his scratchpad, which was sitting on the podium in front of him. "Now, I don't know about you, but I certainly don't want creatures like EmmaLynn Kingpin destroying this beautiful planet."

A holographic image of the Earth was displayed from his scratchpad, rotating majestically. The words *"Save Our Planet"* wrapped themselves around the globe, complete with a pink heart. Eve swallowed the revolting lump in her throat, and out of the corner of her eye she could see JJ's face contort into an ugly, loathsome glower. JJ then pulled out her scratchpad and began tapping at the monitor.

"Now, while her peers are focused on their rigorous studies, EmmaLynn Kingpin chooses to center her attention on *reproduction*," Travis added, sending Eve into a state of sickness. Again the cartoonish representation flashed across the back wall, and the speaker cast a wicked grin in Eve's direction.

"You see, chimeras aren't mentally developed enough to understand the complexities of human intimacy. Instead, they breed whenever the urge presents itself. They're like animals in that sense, and EmmaLynn Kingpin is no different. She's a victim of her own raging sex drive."

Just as the caricature was about to do God knows what, though it was clearly suggestive, the figure froze. Eve and her classmates glanced back at Travis as the image flickered once and then disappeared completely. Travis tapped at his scratchpad, which seemed to be disagreeing with him, and smiled at the class.

"It looks like there's been some sort of malfunction. I can fix it."

He ran his fingers along the monitor, but still nothing happened. The classroom filled with the sound of whispering, but Eve found herself more interested in JJ, whose face was glued to her computer, her hands racing back and forth across the monitor.

A new sentence was projected across the front of the classroom:

THERE HAS BEEN A //GLITCH\\ IN THE SYSTEM.

The murmurings in the classroom intensified, and Travis became sweaty and nervous. "I'm sorry, I don't know what's going on here," he stammered.

An intense moan sounded in the lecture hall, the noise so loud that it surely could be heard all the way down the corridor. And with it, a holographic image appeared from Travis's scratchpad, life-sized and centered in the middle of the room: it was two women, both extremely well-endowed and completely naked, engaged in the most graphic act of cunnilingus that one could imagine.

The classroom erupted into gasps, shouts, and roaring laughter, but still the pleasured groaning of the pornography was much louder than the resulting reaction. Travis's face turned ghostly white, and he stared at Gupta in horror.

"I swear, I have *no* idea how this is happening!"

Suddenly, another hologram appeared beside the existing one: a man and a woman, screwing in the most obviously inauthentic manner, the woman's breasts jiggling with each thrust, the man donning a victorious smirk. Beside them appeared another couple, and then another, and then a threesome, until the entire front of the room was filled with so much porn that Travis struggled to find a place to stand that didn't leave him in the middle of some act of sucking, licking, or penetration. He stared in horror at the class.

"THIS ISN'T MINE!" he cried. "I SWEAR, IT ISN'T MINE!"

JJ laughed to herself, and for a moment Eve tore her eyes from the vulgar scene and instead watched the hacker at work. An instant later, all of the holograms disappeared, and the back wall of the room lit up with a screen shot of Travis's scratchpad. A small cursor toggled through various files until it pulled up a tiny folder that read, in all caps: *TRAVIS'S PORN—KEEP OUT.* The image was maximized, and then maximized again until the letters filled the entire wall. Travis glared at the classroom, his face changing from white to red.

"WHO'S DOING THIS?"

Again the wall went blank, but only for a moment. A video immediately appeared, this one of poor quality and obviously homemade, and within seconds it was clear that the star of the film was none other than Travis Braverman himself.

The boy looked awkward, his body sweaty and his face distorted into an expression of either lust or constipation—it was hard to tell, but judging by the uncomfortable female floundering beneath him, Eve settled on the former. A series of muffled grunts were uttered by both parties, and after a few intolerable seconds, Travis let out a long, relieved groan and flopped down onto the girl.

"*Three minutes?*" the girl griped, her voice stifled by his doughy body. "*Really,* Travis?"

The class was in hysterics. Gupta waved his arms frantically as he tried and failed to control his students, and Eve just remained in her seat, staring in shock at JJ's self-satisfied grin. With her chin held high, the hacker stood from her seat, casually strolled toward Eve's desk, and gazed down at her wide-eyed classmate.

"Oh, don't give me that look," she scoffed.

Without another word, she plopped a small box onto Eve's desk and left the lecture hall, leaving behind the pandemonium she had created.

Eve looked down at the box in front of her. She slowly removed the lid, and in an instant her eyes grew large once again. Inside was a brand new scratchpad cube—sleek, lightweight, fitting easily into the palm of her hand. Attached was a handwritten note, and she quickly unfolded it:

Here's one thing I know how to fix. Still working on everything else.

Eve activated the computer, watching with admiration as the jet-black paneling unfolded into a large, thin screen. She could tell that JJ had made it by hand, as Eve's initials, *EJK*, were engraved along the bottom of the monitor, and as the screen brightened, she noticed that the desktop itself was empty aside from a single folder, titled: *In Case You Change Your Mind.*

Eve clicked on the file and found a long list of documents: combat strategies, weapon schematics, and surveillance footage, all revolving around the Interlopers.

Class ended early, thanks largely to JJ, and Eve was soon headed for Hand-to-Hand Combat. She forced Number One and Number Two to wait outside the athletics arena. *"Don't tell me you're going to follow me into the locker room,"* she teased. *"Want to help me change my clothes, too?"*

Though her jibes were innocent, they were laced with rancor. She tried to deny it—to tell herself that everything was fine, that the day was almost over and thus her cares were few—but truthfully, she was dreading this class most of all. With trepidation, Eve dashed down the corridor, hoping to slip into the locker room unnoticed, but her attempts were in vain, as she knew they would be. Waiting for her beside the gymnasium doors was Jason.

He stared at her, his arms crossed and brow furrowed. Eve stopped for a moment, glancing involuntarily in his direction before refocusing her attention on the locker room. With a deep breath, she continued on past him.

"Eve!" he barked. She ignored him.

"EVE!" He hurried toward her. "I'm talking to you!"

She stopped in front of the locker room and immediately let out a loud sigh. Reluctantly, she turned around. Jason stood directly behind her, his gaze sharp and his jaw clenched with a transparent bitterness she had never seen in him before.

"What do you want, Jason?" she asked.

"What do I *want*?" he repeated, his words lathered with offense. "Are you *serious*?" He threw his hands into the air. "You've been ignoring me for almost a week now. What the *hell* has gotten into you?"

Eve picked at her cuticles. "You're angry."

"Yeah, great observation, Eve. I'm angry."

She looked over his shoulder at the gym. "We're going to be late for class—"

"You don't get to do this," he spat. "You don't get to just walk away without having the decency to let me say what I have to say."

"Fine. Say your piece."

"What happened that day..." He paused and leaned in closer to her. "That was *bullshit*. You got scared and you *bailed*."

"You're right. I *was* scared." She stared at him, her eyes brimming with both irritation and sadness. "You almost *died* because of me, Jason. I can't let you pay the price for the cross *I* bear."

"That's *my* decision. Not yours."

"I'm trying to protect you."

"By pushing me away?" He glared at her. "I'm a big boy, Eve. I can take care of myself."

Eve stared emptily at the floor, trying her best to think of something, *anything* to say, but she came up with nothing. She looked up at Jason, and again her thoughts became a convoluted mess, so warped with swirling emotions that she loathed the idea of even trying to sort through them. Jason stared at her, and suddenly his angry brow became softer, as if weakened by the look in her eye—the look that spoke whatever words she was failing to say.

"Look, I need to know," he said at last, quietly. "When you said it's over..." He paused. "Were you talking about us?"

"I..." she started, and for a second she thought that she might cry. She closed her eyes. "I don't know."

"I meant what I said that day, Eve. You and me—that's what I care about. We don't have to fight if you don't want to. We can forget about the Interlopers. But I don't want to lose you."

Her lips parted, but again she didn't speak. She looked back at Jason; his face was a deep shade of red, and she wondered if perhaps he was stifling the same swell of emotion that she was. Slowly he backed away.

"Promise me you'll think about it, okay?"

And with that, he disappeared into his locker room. Eve exhaled deeply, her breath wavering in a way that made her hope to God that no one heard it, and then she, too, ran into her fortunately empty locker room.

After taking a moment to still her nerves, Eve quickly changed into her uniform and headed out to the football field. Ramsey started class with laps, and though Eve relished the thought of releasing her stress through a formidable workout, the sight of Jason in her peripheral vision left her feeling hollow and overwrought. Though they were clearly at the head of the pack, they didn't sprint together—Jason trailed behind her the slightest bit for the entirety of their run. Perhaps he was making an effort to give her space, or perhaps he was simply too angry to share the path with her, but still she could feel his gaze, and that alone both pained and comforted her.

"KINGSTON!"

Eve flinched; Ramsey was pacing at the opposite end of the track as he often did. He crooked a finger at her, and she quickly trekked across the field to his side. When she arrived, his eyes were pointed at his clipboard, and he rustled through a series of wrinkled pages.

"Your times are good, Kingston. Looks like I won't be failing you after all."

"Thank you, Captain."

They stood together in silence, Ramsey's gaze still pointed down at his work. Eve fidgeted in place and anxiously shoved her hands into her pockets.

"Is that all, Captain?"

"Of course that's not all. You think I'd interrupt your run to tell you 'bout your goddamn grade?"

Eve waited for him to continue, but he remained unusually quiet. She took a quick peek at the clipboard in front of him and noticed that the paper he was staring at so intently was completely blank.

"You know, I took you for a lot of things, Kingston: A fighter. A warrior.

A hell-raiser. But a quitter?" He growled to himself. "That one caught me by surprise."

"It's complicated, Captain."

"It's *always* complicated, soldier." He finally dropped his clipboard to the ground. "But you muscle through it, 'cause you have to. 'Cause it's your *job*."

"With all due respect, it's *not* my job, Captain."

"Who else is gonna do it then?" Ramsey countered. "The patrolmen? Furst? Hell, what about Lionel-shitstain-Vandeveld? Want *him* to do it?" He spat on the turf. "No one else is gonna do it. No one else *can* do it. But *you* can—and that makes it your job. I know you know that."

Ramsey stopped abruptly; his clipboard, lying in the grass, trembled as if suddenly stirred to life. Eve felt it too—the shaking of the ground like an earthquake—and then she heard the distant boom and the hum of faraway screams.

She turned and stared in shock at the sight that met her from across campus. A massive cloud of grey and black smoke had erupted into the sky, billowing high above the buildings and spreading through the air. Then a series of shrieks sounded from afar, and her blood ran cold: one Interloper, two, ten, countless more were circling the distant destruction, their wings beating as they soared through the smoke and disappeared among the campus buildings.

Another rumble shook the field, this one followed by a thundering explosion, louder and much closer. Eve stumbled over the quaking ground and watched as the Billington gates were engulfed in roaring flames. A stampede of students poured from the nightmarish scene, their faces white with terror and streaked with ash, but Eve was transfixed by the swarm of Interlopers who followed them—the aliens who, one by one, dove down past the wreckage and plucked the students from the ground with their razor-edged talons.

The third eruption was a shock—a wall of fire tore through the football field bleachers, the explosion itself so powerful that Eve could feel the heat right down to her bones, as if it were only inches away. As she stared at the cloud of smoke and flames, a single body—a man in the same black uniform as hers—torpedoed through the air, propelled skyward by the force of the explosion. In an instant, Eve channeled her gift and raised her hands, catching her classmate with her melt and quickly lowering him to the ground.

Eve frantically surveyed the scene before her. The field was now packed with students, some in combat uniforms and others emerging from God knows where, all scattering in different directions. Nearby, an Interloper plunged to the ground and ripped a student from the field, lifting him high into the air until they both vanished from sight. Eve looked up at the sky, and her jaw fell open in disbelief: everywhere she looked, the clouds were spotted with flecks of grey. Aliens dipped and weaved above their heads, a swarm like she'd never seen, never imagined. It wasn't real—it *couldn't* be real—and yet despite how inconceivable it was, she couldn't deny the truth: the Interlopers had lowered their cloak of secrecy. For the first time ever, they were waging a very public attack.

Three Interlopers parted from the others and dove toward the field. Their sights were set on Eve, the ultimate prize in this chaos, but just as they neared her, she thrust them back into the sky, sending their bodies jetting past the clouds and fading into the distance. She spun in place and scanned the field. She was looking for only one person, but all she could see were waves of frenzied students scampering in every direction, tripping over rubble as they forced their way past one another.

Then, just when the task seemed utterly impossible, she spotted him: Jason was at the opposite end of the track, ramming his fists into the face of a bloodied Interloper. With a hateful glower, he melted the creature against the burning bleachers, watching as it thrashed within the flames. Then quickly, Jason turned toward the field, his face and chest streaked with ash, his eyes bulging as he frantically searched for something or someone.

His gaze fell on Eve, and their eyes locked; with a shared sense of relief, they immediately ran across the field, fighting their way through the crowd until they met in the center and wildly threw their arms around one another. Eve buried her face in the side of his neck, gripping him tightly, and then reluctantly pulled away and looked into his eyes.

"What's happening?"

"This is it," he panted, still holding her close. "They're coming for you. They're coming for *everyone*."

They swiftly broke apart as a monster headed in their direction—though this one was in the form of a cleft-chinned football player, his face white with fear, an Interloper right on his heels. Lionel grabbed Jason's arms and swerved around him, ducking behind the chimera as if to shield himself.

"What the *hell*?" Jason barked.

There was no time for explanations; the Interloper was right in front of him, swinging his talons, and so Jason kicked at the creature's chest and then his knee, forcing him to the ground. As the alien fought to regain his balance, Jason tore his arms from Lionel's grip and stomped on the back of the creature's head, spraying his needle-sharp teeth across the ground. With a growl, the Interloper shook free of Jason and staggered to his feet, his toothless mouth twisted into a bitter grimace. He lunged forward, roaring piteously, and Jason quickly melted the fallen teeth from the turf, launching them straight through the creature's life source like needles through a pincushion, killing him where he stood.

Another Interloper swooped down and landed beside Lionel, swatting his wing at the footballer and knocking him to the dirt. The creature pounced on top of him, but just as he bared his fangs and talons, he lurched from Lionel's body and hurtled through the air, smashing against the yellow goalposts at the end of the field.

Lionel looked up at Eve—she was ending her melt, and she met his stunned gaze with a scowl.

"Did you—" he stammered, "did you just *save my life*?"

"I didn't save your life," Eve hissed. "I simply ended *his*."

She started to storm off when a word caught her attention: *"Chime,"* it sounded like, spoken by none other than Lionel Vandeveld himself. Eve pivoted in place—she glared at the footballer and balled her hands into fists.

"God, I hate you," she growled.

She charged toward Lionel, her body trembling with rage, and with a furious swing, she pounded her fist into his nose. He stumbled backward, gripping at his face as streams of blood gushed from his nostrils and poured through his fingers.

"JESUS *CHRIST*, MY NOSE!" he cried. "IT'S BROKEN, *AGAIN!*"

"That's for using my boyfriend as a goddamn *SHIELD!*" she barked.

"You *stupid bitch*, I just had it *fixed!*" he squealed, dropping to his knees as he cradled his face. "Mother of *God, I just got it fixed!*"

And again Eve marched away, her body warm with satisfaction. Jason rushed to her side, glancing back and forth between Lionel and Eve.

"Did you just—"

"Yes."

He faltered. "I thought you only fought when you needed to."

"Oh, I needed to do that. Trust me."

The two of them sped across the field, instinctively looking for any sign of Interlopers, but finding none. Just as they reached the other end of the track, they were immediately halted; Ramsey grabbed at their shoulders, his calloused fingers digging into their backs as he steered them along the pathway.

"Come with me," he ordered.

"We can't," Jason said, resisting. "We have to find our friends."

"Like hell. You'll do what I say."

"Where are we going?" Eve asked.

"To Furst's office. He's called a meeting."

"What? Why?"

"Don't know and don't care, but orders are orders." Another explosion sounded in the distance, and the three of them flinched in unison. Ramsey nodded at the field behind them. "I've got shit to take care of here. Get to the dean's building."

"But—"

"*Now.*"

The captain scurried away, cursing at his class and ordering them back to the gymnasium. Eve and Jason hurried on, quickening their pace as the sounds of screaming and destruction surrounded them. Students ran past, their faces gripped with horror, and Eve couldn't help but stare at them as they so often did to her.

At last they approached the dean's building. Eve looked at Jason, but he instead stared toward the opposite end of the campus, his eyes focused on the faraway Rutherford Tower. He turned to face her.

"Go without me."

"Why?" Eve asked, panicked. "What are you doing?"

"I have to find Percy and Sancho. I have to make sure they're okay."

"But Ramsey said—"

"Go to the meeting," he urged. "You can meet me at Percy's dorm room and tell me all about it afterward." He clutched her hands tightly. "I promise."

Eve hesitated, her eyes nervously panning across Jason's face. "Can you make sure Armaan's okay, too?" she uttered finally. "And JJ?"

Jason offered a reassuring smile. "Of course."

"Please don't get hurt."

"I won't."

He took a few steps back, slowly at first, and then jogged away. As Eve watched him, her hands became fidgety, her heart beat heavily, and her body was suddenly consumed with nervous energy.

"WAIT!" she cried.

She raced toward him, and just as he turned to face her, she flung her arms around his neck so forcefully that he stumbled to his side, and then she kissed him. For a moment, she forgot all about the surrounding chaos and reveled in the feeling of his hands holding her close and his lips pressed against hers. Just before she lost herself completely, she pulled away from him and let out a long, relieved breath. He stared back at her, his eyes wide and hopeful.

"Does that mean you've thought about it?" he asked.

"Yes." She cocked her head toward the tower. "Go find our friends."

They reluctantly parted ways; Jason headed toward Rutherford Hall, and Eve continued to the dean's building. She charged into the lobby, slightly thrown off by how oddly quiet it was inside, and found the golden-haired receptionist at her usual perch, flaring her nostrils in distaste at the sight of Eve. With a grunt, the receptionist pointed down the corridor, instructing Eve to head to Furst's office, and she did, hastening her stride along the way.

When she opened the door to his quarters, she immediately halted. The room was packed, filled from wall to wall with students, some of whom were familiar though many were not. With a bit of authority, she forced her way through the crowd, finally settling into a spot within the thick of the throng where she had a somewhat compromised view of the dean.

Furst sat at his desk, sorting through his endless paperwork as if this were any other ordinary day, seemingly unconcerned with the madness raging just outside his office. Without the slightest acknowledgment of the students in front of him, he began to speak.

"I gather you're all wondering why you're here, especially in the midst of such unusual circumstances," he said, his voice laced with a hint of uncharacteristic humility. "As you know, our esteemed campus is being attacked—and destroyed—by the very same creatures that have haunted us for some time now. Despite the efforts of our brave and competent patrolmen, it seems we have lost this battle between man and trespasser."

He finally looked up from his desk, his eyes scanning the room with apparent indifference.

"Well, enough with the rhetoric. I'm sure you're not interested in my ramblings, and quite frankly, neither am I." He positioned a new stack of paperwork in front of him and began flipping through the pages. "You've all been summoned here for one very important reason: you're all chimeras."

A hush fell over the room. The students stiffened in terror, all except for

Eve, who chuckled over the dramatic display. Furst ignored the tension and continued.

"Some of you are aware of this already, while it may come as a surprise to others. For those who are unconvinced, believe me when I say that there is no mistake: you *are* a humanovus. I could prove that to you if time permitted, but, sadly, it does not."

Furst glanced at Eve, his eyes panning to the empty space beside her, and frowned. "Some are missing from this meeting, though I hope the message reaches them one way or another. You've been called here because the staff at Billington is asking you to leave our grounds immediately. The Interlopers know who you are, what you look like, where you live, your pastimes and behaviors. You are not safe here, not after this debacle, and while they ransack the campus, I ask that you quickly gather your things and take shelter elsewhere." Furst stared at Eve yet again, this time long and hard. "If you are even considering any other alternative, I insist that you dismiss it at once. If any brilliant dreams of heroism or martyrdom come to mind, banish them from your thoughts. Do as I say: *Leave Billington.* Take cover as far away as possible. And do so at once."

The room remained still. Some students hung their heads, while others anxiously eyed their fellow chimeras. Furst scribbled notes along his mound of paperwork, and after several tedious minutes of disregard, he looked up at the crowd as if surprised they were still there.

"You may go now."

The students hurried from the room, eager to be rid of the dean—perhaps eager to disappear completely. Eve hung back, not wanting to get caught up in the mad stampede of overwrought chimeras. And as she waited for the crowd to clear, her eyes landed on a very familiar face—the last face she was expecting to see. Her mouth fell open in absolute shock.

"*Are you serious?*" she spat. "*You* are *unbelievable.*"

Madison was tucked in the back corner of the room, failing to hide behind a filing cabinet. She saw Eve's disparaging expression and scowled.

"Oh, save it, Eve. Don't act like you didn't know already."

"Know? What are you talking about?"

"That stunt you pulled in the bathroom. You said you knew my secret." Madison straightened her neck and grumbled to herself. "Messed up my back, too."

"I was talking about the *death threat.*"

Madison faltered. "What death threat?"

"Don't play dumb with me. I saw the ashes all over your bed."

"*You* left them there!"

"Why the hell would I scatter ashes on your bed?"

"I don't know. Why would you steal my *husband*?"

"Oh, for God's sake—"

"I thought you were screwing with me!" Madison squealed.

"*Screwing* with you?" Eve glowered, her patience waning. "You were *missing*, Madison, on the same exact day that *I* was threatened—on the same day that those ashes *miraculously* appeared on your bed. How do you explain that?"

"I don't know a *damn thing* about your stupid death threat, *Eve*," Madison huffed. "And as for me going *missing*, I've been pretty busy with *Lionel* these days, if you know what I mean. And if you don't, I mean *sex*."

"Look, I talked to Heather right before I found those ashes, and *she* said—"

Eve abruptly stopped. She stared blankly ahead as her mind filled with images of Heather: on her first day at Billington, at her invasive reveal, in the hallway earlier that day. She thought about her shameless eavesdropping and her ominous warnings, and in an instant the room became black and stifling.

"Oh God," she mumbled.

"What?"

Eve dug through her pocket and pulled out Madison's sparkly room key. "Did you take this?"

Madison wrinkled her nose. "Why would I want my old room key? I don't even live there anymore."

A weight dropped in Eve's stomach, and her expression turned panicked. "Do you know where Heather is?"

Madison laughed condescendingly. "*God* no, nor do I *care*, for that matter—"

There was no need to wait for her to finish—Eve barreled through Furst's office and raced down the hallway, Madison scuttling frantically behind her.

"Where are you going?" she cried.

"To find my friends, and then to find Heather," Eve answered, coldly.

"Wait!"

Eve stopped, facing her former roommate one last time. Madison's lips were pursed as if she was trying her hardest to appear fearsome, but in her eyes was a very familiar weakness. She stared back at her fellow chimera and snarled.

"Don't you *dare* tell a soul, Eve. I'll make you suffer—I *swear*."

Eve eyed the girl up and down. *I'll make you suffer?* As if she hadn't done so already. Eve finally looked her in the eye, and despite the gravity of the situation, she couldn't help but smirk.

"Go to *hell*, Madison."

With an air of indifference, Eve marched through the lobby and out the double doors of the dean's building. Again, mayhem and disorder surrounded her, but her gaze was focused firmly on the grandiose Rutherford Tower looming in the distance. Just as she began her journey, she felt herself being pulled backward—two tall, stately patrolmen had appeared by her side, each one with a firm grip on her arms, and while their uniforms were familiar, their faces certainly were not.

"Come with us," one of them ordered, steering her with his grasp.

Eve wrinkled her forehead. "Who are you?"

"Number One and Number Two," the second patrolman proclaimed.

"No you're not."

"We're your *new* Numbers One and Two."

"What happened to my *old* Numbers One and Two?" Eve carped. "Don't tell me they went AWOL—they did disappear at the first sign of danger." She eyed the duo skeptically. "Great security program you've got here, by the way."

"They've been summoned for duty."

"And you two weren't?"

The first one wavered, but kept his eyes pointed straight ahead. "No more questions."

Eve tore her arms from their grasp. "Look, my parents may have been dead for a while, but if there's one thing I remember them teaching me, it's to not go wandering off with strange men."

"We're here to protect you," the new Number One explained, coolly. "The order came directly from Dean Furst."

"Okay, first of all, I don't *need* your protection," Eve rebutted. "Second of all, unless you get Furst to tell me *himself* that you're my new escorts, I'm not going anywhere with you." She chuckled. "For all I know, you could be—"

She flinched; her new Number Two was hovering awfully close to her, his face practically buried in her hair as if he was—oh, no, he wasn't *smelling* her, was he? With a grimace, she glanced down at his hands, which were clammy with sweat. She groaned loudly and quickly backed away from the duo.

"JESUS CHRIST, *COME ON!*"

The two men stood beside one another, cocking their heads in the same eerie fashion, and then together their bodies burst, spraying their second skin in every direction. They lunged for Eve, but she was unimpressed and short on time—with her typical precision she melted the two Interlopers from their feet and rocketed their bodies straight through the front wall of the dean's building. She waited for just a moment—she could hear Furst's receptionist shrieking and could see a limp wing hanging through the crumbled sheet-rock—and then she continued on her way to Rutherford Hall.

Suddenly, Eve tumbled to the ground, knocked from her feet by a power-ful blow to her back. A heavy weight pinned her to the cement, and just when she thought she would suffocate from the pressure, a single foot yanked at her shoulder and flipped her onto her back. She winced in pain and stared up at her attacker—her new Number One, or perhaps Number Two, his slimy skin punctured with shards of glass and jagged wood. He leaned in close to her and studied her face.

"You are powerful, but you are not invincible."

With one hand he dug his talons into her shoulder, and three slender streams of blood poured from the open wounds. Eve squirmed beneath him, fighting to wriggle free, but his grip remained firm.

"It is beautiful," he said, captivated by the reddish liquid. "The color. The consistency." He burrowed his talons even deeper into her skin. "The *mortality*."

With a look of disgust, Eve bit her lip and melted the creature from her body, gasping when his talons ripped free of her flesh. She cursed loudly—as if the words could somehow mitigate the pain—and slammed the creature against the wall of a distant building, watching with satisfaction as his lifeless body fell to the ground.

Eve hoisted herself to her feet and dusted the dirt from her combat uni-form. She ignored the passersby—some gawked at her, stunned by the sight they had witnessed, while most screamed and ran in the opposite direction—and once again headed to Rutherford Hall.

The campus was now a war zone: the pathways were covered in rubble, the buildings were blackened with ash, and it seemed as if every student and staff member was running across the grounds at the same time. Eve tried to stay calm, to tell herself that nothing had changed, but still she quickened her pace from a fast walk to a steady jog and then to a run. At last she reached

Rutherford Hall, and just as she entered the courtyard, she let out a long, aggravated sigh.

"SHE'S BACK! AND SHE'S ALONE!"

In front of her stood the usual pack of protestors, swarming the courtyard just as they had been the day before, and the day before that. Not even the utter destruction of the campus could deter them, and though they momentarily stopped their chanting to stare at her, a man from within the thick of the mob quickly ended the stillness.

"YOU!" he shouted, pointing at Eve. "YOU'RE THE CAUSE OF ALL THIS!"

His accusation was met with a thunderous roar of agreement, the protestors more outraged than ever. Eve continued forward; she didn't slow her pace, nor did she react to their unrelenting hatred. She was preoccupied—no, she was *pissed*—and in that moment, she decided she simply didn't have time for the protestors or their message, whatever it was. In fact, she had a message of her own for them, and just as she approached the edge of their horde, she rolled her eyes and flicked her wrist.

A chorus of gasps resounded across the courtyard, but Eve ignored it. She continued toward the dormitory hall, the walkway suddenly clear, not a single protestor blocking her path. When she reached the front doors, she turned to face the protestors once more—protesters who were now floating in midair, just high enough for her to walk beneath their feet but still low enough for her to gaze into their horrified eyes. With an apathetic shrug, she delicately placed them back on the ground, and then she folded her arms and scowled.

"GO HOME," she ordered.

With that, she raised her chin and strutted through the Rutherford Hall doors, leaving the protestors to stupidly gawk where they stood.

The lobby was packed. A swarm of Rutherfordians buzzed past, their arms filled with designer luggage, while others cowered along the walls with tears pouring down their faces. Eve shoved her way toward the elevators, which she soon learned were disabled, and then began what was sure to be a hellishly long sprint up the stairwell. Of course Percy had to live on the very top floor, and she growled to herself as she imagined him relaxing in comfort, a bottle of booze in hand.

She ran up the first three floors, though not quick enough for her liking, and so she pushed herself to move faster. Tenth floor, eleventh floor—she was almost there, and just as her thighs began to burn, she thought of Jason waiting for her, and her body became numb with power.

Eve burst through the doorway to the fifteenth floor and carelessly shouldered aside the other students in her path. At last she barged into Percy's suite and stumbled across the floor.

The room went quiet as she entered—each body froze in place, Percy by the kitchen nook, JJ and Sancho in the living room, and Jason near the entryway. They all gazed at her with wide eyes, which only added to the palpable discomfort. Finally, JJ let out a cynical chuckle.

"Look who's here," she said. "It's EmmaLynn Kingpin."

Jason glanced at her shoulder. "You're hurt—"

"I'm fine, Jason."

The others remained silent. Eve stared at her four former comrades, and before the awkwardness of the situation grew unbearable, she stopped and re-counted. Just four? Someone was missing.

"Where's—"

"I couldn't find Armaan," Jason explained. "I'm sure he's okay."

Again the suite was quiet, stirring only slightly from the occasional shaking of the walls. Jason cleared his throat, attempting to end the silence once and for all.

"So, what was the meeting about?"

"It was an evacuation notice," Eve said. "He wants all of the chimeras at this school to leave. He said we're not safe here. Not anymore."

"Like you guys were safe here in the first place," JJ mumbled.

"Seriously," Percy added. "It's like a goddamn termite infestation out there, except with much bigger bugs."

Sancho pouted. "It's so unfair. Why do we have to be stuck with creepy aliens? Why couldn't we have been invaded by super-sexy lady aliens with three boobs or something?"

Another explosion sounded in the distance, and all five students flinched in unison. They gaped first at the trembling furniture and rattling picture frames and then at one another, each waiting for someone to finally speak—to say what they were all undeniably thinking. Again Jason turned to Eve, his voice soft.

"So, what are we going to do, Eve? Are we leaving?"

Eve stared at the floor; she wasn't avoiding his gaze—though it undoubtedly seemed that way to him. No, she was just trying to think, to separate herself from Jason and the others, from the shaking of the dormitory and every other god-awful minute of this day. But she could still feel Jason's presence like a thick, warm coat, and she was sure he was trying *so hard* to appear at ease—that his face, his posture, and every fiber of his being were lying to her. She knew what he wanted her to say—what the entire room was dying to hear—but still her eyes were pointed at the floor, and still she said nothing.

And to her surprise, her thoughts, for once, were perfectly clear. They weren't wrestling in her mind: they were in her gut, firm and resolute. Her decision had been made before the question had even been uttered. And even though it was incredibly stupid, she knew it was right and unequivocally her own.

"Well, Eve?" Jason said, interrupting the stillness. "Are we leaving?" he repeated.

Eve had almost forgotten he was still waiting for her. With a deep breath, she looked up at the expectant faces of her comrades.

"No," she finally said. "We're going to kill some aliens."

The entire room erupted into a fit of cheering. Percy raised a shot glass in the air and guzzled the contents, and Sancho threw his arms around JJ—only to have her push him from the couch. Eve scowled and put her hands on her hips.

"I don't know why everyone's cheering. We're grossly unprepared. We still don't know where the lair is, and we haven't even uploaded the virus."

Jason and the others glanced back and forth at one another, smiling almost childishly as if they shared a secret.

"What?" Eve asked. "What's going on?"

Jason smirked. "Eve, we've still been working."

"We knew you'd come around eventually," Percy added, pouring himself another shot. "Just didn't think it'd take an apocalyptic experience to make it happen."

Eve frowned. "Did you know that all of this would happen today?"

"Of course not," JJ cut in. "Ever since they blindsided us the last time, the beacon has gone completely silent. They know we're listening."

"But we've been keeping busy!" Sancho jumped to his feet, his eyes lit with their usual fiery glow. "I made a new weapon!"

Before Eve could ask, Sancho was scurrying across the suite, shuffling through Percy's things and then dragging what looked like a black backpack from the bedroom. He threw it over his shoulders, stumbling for a second—whatever was in the bag was clearly heavy—and then he turned to face the group, grinning from ear to ear.

Two charcoal-colored tubes protruded from the backpack, resting on either side of his body like the arms of a chair. Sancho grabbed at the left cylindrical pipe and fiddled with a panel of buttons on its surface, and suddenly a series of firearms expanded from the top of the backpack and hovered above his head. He glanced up at the weapons and then looked back at Eve, beaming with pride.

"I call it the *Dirtier* Sanchez," he declared. "Assembled using Percy's guns—"

"But this time with my permission," Percy added.

"It's a shooting device *and* a flamethrower." He cocked his head at the cumbersome backpack, which Eve realized must double as a fuel container, and grinned. "You know, so we can light the lair on fire and release its second skin."

"And I uploaded the virus days ago," JJ said. "The torq is now a ticking time bomb."

It was Eve's turn to be quiet. She stared at Sancho's half-ridiculous, half-genius invention, and then at the torq, which sat on the coffee table. The team had been working; they had been waiting for her. She had told herself that she was the problem—that her absence was a blessing, that she was *protecting* them—and she had been wrong. A wave of shame flowed through her.

"Look, guys, about last week—"

"Oh God, Eve, don't do this," Percy moaned. "The mushy confessional—you're better than that." He rolled his eyes and poured himself a third, or maybe a fourth shot. "We get it, you're sorry. And we all solemnly swear not to die today, so you won't have any additional guilt to burden you."

Eve grimaced. "Wow. That wasn't even kind of funny."

"All right, people, we're running out of time," JJ interrupted, unamused by Percy's banter. "We need to get this torq to the lair, and we need to do it *now*. They're coming for Eve, and it looks like they're coming for everyone else as well."

"I don't get it," Jason added. "Is this a hostage situation? A mass dissection?"

"Or a mass *execution*," Percy grumbled.

JJ shrugged. "Whatever it is, the sooner we wipe out the mainframe, the more lives we save."

"But we don't even know where the mainframe is," Eve said.

"No, but we know someone who does." JJ activated her scratchpads. "I finally converted all the data from the torq. No mention of the lair, but I did get a ton of information on the Interloper in charge of this particular device."

"Like what?" Eve asked.

"Like his assignments, his mission, his dorm room, and, most importantly, his *name*."

She paused, swiveling one of her scratchpad screens around and expanding the image of a boy. He had flaming red hair and a collection of freckles splattered across his face, and Eve thought he looked vaguely familiar.

"Does the name 'Thomas Cooper' ring a bell?" JJ asked.

Eve thought back to move-in day at Billington; she recalled her very first conversation with Heather and smirked. "Heard he was a troublemaker."

"Well, apparently he's an alien, too."

JJ plucked a tiny, square chip from her pocket and held it out in her palm for everyone to see. It was flat and thin with a brownish surface and pitted ridges.

"This is a tracking device," JJ explained. "If we can find a way to attach this to Cooper's body, he'll eventually take us to the lair. I'm sure of it."

"And how the hell are we supposed to find him?" Jason asked.

"Well, according to his assignment, he should be..."—JJ paused as she scanned her scratchpad's text—"...*feeding* right now."

Sancho's nostrils flared. "*Feeding?*"

"He's in the dining hall," JJ continued. "Not sure why, since he can't even eat solid food."

"You sure he's going to be following his assignment on a day like today?" Jason folded his arms. "I mean, it's not exactly business as usual out there."

"Yeah, and even if he *is* in the dining hall, how are we supposed to get close enough to stick a tracking device on him?" Percy groused.

Eve's eyes widened; she looked at the tracking device one last time, and then her eyes darted down to the three gashes along her shoulder.

"I'm bleeding," she muttered.

Sancho's mouth contorted with disgust. "That's great, Eve, but we don't need to know the details of your monthly cycle—"

"*Jesus*, Sancho, she's talking about her *shoulder*," JJ groaned.

"He'll be drawn to me," Eve explained. "I can just go to the dining hall and wait for him."

"No way," Jason rebutted. "He'll *attack* you."

"Jason, I'll be fine."

"You don't know that," he maintained. "I'll go instead."

"We can all go together," Sancho cut in. "We can bring weapons!"

"Great idea, that won't look suspicious at all," Percy grumbled.

Eve backed away from the group. "I'm leaving now, and I'm doing this *alone.*"

"*Eve—*"

"If he tries to take me, I'll kill him. It's as simple as that." She raised her hand, commanding Jason to stay back. "Besides, my decision is final."

She waited by the entryway for a moment, taking one last look at her comrades. They were motionless, their faces full of fear and worry, especially Jason's—and Eve rolled her eyes at the display.

"Oh, don't look at me like I'm never coming back. This isn't my first Interloper encounter, remember?"

With a derisive grunt, she left her comrades in Percy's dorm room, making her way through the corridor and back down the Rutherford Tower stairs. The lobby was only slightly less chaotic than it had been before. The number of people seemed to have dwindled as they sought shelter elsewhere—or so Eve hoped, as she tried to push the all too plausible alternative from her thoughts.

She entered the dining hall and immediately scanned her surroundings. The hall was packed and raucous, as if every Rutherfordian had convened here, perhaps seeking safety in numbers. Many spoke frantically with one another or cried into their hands, while others gazed at the walls with empty, unblinking eyes. Eve saw students still in their classroom attire and others in pajamas, boys with ash-streaked clothing and girls with mascara dripping down their cheeks, tall Rutherfordians and short Rutherfordians with blond hair and black hair and brown hair.

And not a single redhead.

Shit, Eve thought to herself. She scanned the dining hall again, and then again, but Thomas Cooper was nowhere to be found.

Her neck and chest burned with anxiety. Perhaps Jason was right; perhaps he wasn't coming. After all, did his assignment really apply to days such as this? She shook her head as if to dismiss the speculations from her mind; he *was* coming. She would make sure of it. She would wait for him.

Eve caught sight of a handful of students huddling together and eagerly stuffing their faces with food. She thought it was silly to be eating at a time such as this, but then again, why else would they be in the dining hall? Then it occurred to her: *she* was in the dining hall, just standing idly in the dead center of everything, not doing much of anything except attracting the curious stares of passersby. If Thomas was coming—no, *when* he was coming—she would have to appear unsuspicious, as if her presence were nothing more than coincidental.

She made a snap decision. With an air of authority, she stomped toward a nearby Rutherfordian and plucked a slice of pizza and a glass of some purply-pink beverage from the place setting in front of him.

"What the *hell*—"

She ignored the boy and headed to the back of the dining hall, where she grabbed a seat and plopped her food down on the table in front of her. She glanced down at her stolen meal—sausage pizza and cran-grape juice, a terrible pairing—and then she looked straight ahead at her perfect, uncompromised view of the dining hall entrance. With a deep breath, she waited.

Nothing happened.

I'll give him fifteen minutes, she thought. If he still hadn't arrived by then, she would have to go and search for him. She would travel the entire university and open every door in every building until she found him. After all, how hard could it be to find a single faux-human in a campus filled with thousands of humans and faux-humans alike?

Well, at least he has that fiery red hair.

Again her mind was flooded with doubt. Maybe this was a dumb idea. In fact, maybe this was the dumbest idea she and her friends had ever concocted. Just as she became so distracted with indecision that she almost took a bite of her hand-me-down pizza, a boy entered the dining hall.

A boy with a freckled face and red hair.

He walked in her direction, his eyes dancing across her face, her clothes, and her wounded shoulder. Eve looked away, trying to appear casual, though failing miserably. Despite her slew of successful killings, this confrontation felt different, threatening—because she needed this alien alive. No matter how much her bones ached to be engaged, to end his life with a single melt, she would need to resist.

Before she could ruminate on her plan any longer, Thomas Cooper stood directly in front of her.

His stare was chilling, as if he hadn't the slightest clue about the impression he was leaving. Eve looked back at him, this time overtly, and thought of the tracking device in her pocket. She didn't know how she was going to plant it, and with no obvious ideas, she cleared her throat.

"Can I help you with something?" she began, scornfully. *Maybe I should be nicer*, she thought to herself. She nodded at the pizza beside her. "Want a bite?"

Eve cringed. *God, that was stupid.*

"No," Cooper finally answered, flatly. "I'm not all that hungry. Just..." He hesitated, his eyes drifting down to the slashes across her shoulder. "Thirsty."

A lump formed in Eve's throat, but she swallowed it down. She could see a line of sweat forming on Cooper's forehead and felt herself begin to panic. *He's going to attack*, she thought. She couldn't let that happen. She needed to avoid a confrontation, plant the tracking device, and send him on his way, none the wiser.

She plucked her cup of juice from the table and shoved it in his direction. "Have mine."

"I can get my own."

"I don't mind—"

"I do."

"But I *insist*."

She carelessly slammed the glass against his chest, splashing the purply-pink drink across his white shirt. He stumbled back, glaring at his ruined shirt.

"Well, shit, look at that." Eve pouted almost comically and sank her hands into her pockets, securing the tracking device in her palm. With another artificial smile, she pulled her hands from her pockets and began playing with Cooper's shirt collar. "Here, let me help you."

"Please don't," he grumbled.

"Hey, it's the least I can do after dying your shirt pink." She unbuttoned his collar and offered him a sarcastic wink. "Super masculine, by the way."

"Stop it."

"You know, most guys wouldn't complain about being undressed by a random girl—"

"You're no *random girl*," he hissed.

Eve froze; she stared at her mark, his once blank face now dripping with hate. Their bodies were close, so close that he could easily release his skin and tear at her throat, or she could blow him away with her gift, but instead they stood motionless, glaring at one another as if simultaneously considering the possibilities. With a hint of discomfort, Eve cleared her throat and gave his shirt collar one last tug, snapping the tracking device into place.

"You should get out of here, you know. Find a place to stay. Maybe," she hesitated, "somewhere off campus."

"What about you?"

She faltered. "Excuse me?"

He stared at her wound as if drawn to it. "You're hurt, and yet you're here. In the dining hall." He looked her in the eye. "Eating pizza."

Eve shrugged. "Flesh wounds make me hungry."

"Didn't Dean Furst order all chimeras to evacuate the campus?"

"He did."

"Why haven't you?"

"Guess I didn't feel like it."

He took a step closer, his nose now just inches away from hers. Eve could feel his breath against her cheek. Her body became tense, as if preparing herself for an attack, and yet despite the sweat forming on his brow, he remained still.

"How do you remain so calm in the midst of such anarchy?" he asked, his voice disturbingly emotionless.

"How do *you* know about the dean's evacuation notice?"

To Eve's surprise, Cooper flinched, but she tried to appear unfazed. His gaze had suddenly changed—there was something behind it now, an emotion she couldn't identify, and after a moment of awkward quiet, he wiped his now-drying forehead and took a step backward.

"I have to go."

With a slight wiggle of his nose, he spun in place and scurried from the dining hall just as quickly as he had come. Eve exhaled loudly; she hadn't the slightest clue what had happened or why he had opted to flee, but she took relief in his departure regardless. After taking a moment and several calming breaths, she dashed from the room and headed up the tower stairs to the fifteenth floor once again.

"How'd it go?" JJ asked as soon as Eve appeared in the doorway. Eve joined the others in the living room, flopping onto the couch and allowing her tired body to sink into the leather.

"Creepy and weird and disturbing," she muttered. "Remind me never to get into acting. I *suck* at it."

"Did you at least stick him with the tracking device?"

"It's on his shirt."

"His *shirt*? I told you to get it on his *body*."

"Well, unfortunately I couldn't seem to get him *naked*, so I guess his shirt will have to do." Eve nodded at JJ's scratchpads. "Start tracking him."

JJ immediately began fussing with her computers, plucking various codes from the screen and rearranging them into odd and complex patterns. The others waited with as much composure as they could manage: Jason paced the floor, Percy and Eve stared in awe at JJ's technique, and Sancho drummed his fingers against the coffee table.

"What if he takes his shirt off before he gets to the lair?" Sancho asked. "What if he finds the tracking device and destroys it? What if he releases his second skin and the tracking device gets lost in the goo pile?"

"What if you shut up and let me concentrate?" JJ growled.

"Balls, you're mean," he mumbled. "And I love that about you."

JJ ignored him, her eyes bright with the glow of her scratchpad screens. "He's leaving Rutherford Hall, heading south across campus."

"Wait, do you think he's going to the lair *now*?" Jason asked.

"He did leave in sort of a hurry," Eve said.

"Did he say anything?"

"Well, for starters, he knew about the evacuation notice."

"How is that possible?"

"See this?" She pointed to the darkened scabs along her shoulder. "I got it from an Interloper—disguised as a *patrolman*."

"The *patrolmen*? Infiltrated by *Interlopers*?" Percy's eyes widened. "Christ Almighty, Furst is really racking up some astronomical failures this semester." He let out a discouraged sigh and downed yet another shot. "I should've just gone to Yale."

"That's probably how they got the list in the first place," Eve said. "They've been on the inside the whole time."

"Well, it won't be long before we turn the tables on 'em and light their lair on *fire*." Sancho grinned, then paused and glanced at Eve. "We *are* going to light it on fire, right? Please tell me we're lighting it on fire."

"We'll light it on fire. Relax, Sancho."

He grinned again. "I can't believe we're doing this. We're going to take them out!"

"Don't get too excited," Percy cut in. "We don't even know who Fairon is yet."

"Yeah, about that," Eve muttered. "Has anyone seen Heather within the last hour or so?"

"No, why?" Jason stared at her, perplexed, and then his eyes lit up with understanding. "Wait—you think *Heather* is Fairon?"

"My room was unlocked the night we were attacked. I *never* leave it unlocked." She dug through her pocket and pulled out Madison's bejeweled room key. "I found this in the hallway today, right where Heather had been standing."

"Are you sure we can rule out Madison?" Sancho interjected. "I mean, Percy's word doesn't hold much value."

"Excuse me?"

Eve ignored Percy and casually shook her head. "Madison isn't an Interloper."

"How can you be so sure?" Sancho asked. "I mean, she threatened to kill you. All of the signs were there."

"She didn't threaten to kill me, and she's not an Interloper."

"And how do you know that?"

"Because Madison's a chimera."

Jason did a double take, and his jaw practically hit the floor. *"What?"*

"Holy balls," Sancho gasped. "Madison Palmer? *Seriously?*"

"God, that's rich." Percy laughed aloud and swirled his bottle in the air as if to give a toast. "The most bigoted hammer on campus—a *chimera*. I can't wait to see the looks on everyone's faces when they find out."

"They're not finding out," Eve commanded. "It doesn't leave this room."

The others looked at one another, puzzled.

"But why?"

"Yeah, after all she's done to you—"

"It doesn't leave this room," Eve repeated.

The three boys stared at Eve. They could see in her eyes that she meant what she said, that *nothing* could change her mind—and so they didn't try.

"Guys," JJ interrupted, her tone foreboding, "I think he's there."

Eve flinched. *"What?"* she asked.

"He's at the lair," JJ confirmed.

"Are you sure? Are you absolutely positive?"

"Yes. I'm sure. There's no other explanation."

Eve glanced at Jason; he was staring back at her, his jaw tight and his chin held high. He was already preparing—bracing himself for a fight.

"All right," he said, his voice low and steady. "Where is he?"

JJ tapped at the map on her screen, and a holographic image of a tall, white building appeared before them. Eve recognized it instantly: the bright blue windows, the crisp paint, the youthful elegance of its architecture and design. She had seen it before; in fact, she had walked right past the place and thought nothing of it. JJ maximized the image one more time and then let out a short, shallow breath.

"It's across the street from the Meltdown." She turned to face the others. "The Pier Lorent Hotel."

CHAPTER 16: LIGHT 'EM UP

"So, do we just walk in?"

Percy rolled his eyes. "No, Sancho, we're going to use our superpowers to scale the walls. Of *course* we just walk in."

Eve ignored the boys' bickering as she stared at the colossal building before her. The Pier Lorent Hotel—it was just as beautiful as she remembered. She eyed its clean lines and elegant construction, knowing all too well that it was just a façade—that the walls, the windows, and everything else were made entirely from some strange alien goo. She turned to face the others: Percy and Sancho were still prodding at one another, Jason was staring at the hotel in silence, and JJ was leaning against the side of Percy's SUV.

JJ caught Eve's gaze and held her hand out in front of her. "You ready?"

Eve looked down at JJ's hand; in her palm sat four small communicaps. Without any misgivings, Eve plucked a capsule and downed it in a single gulp, and the others followed suit. JJ immediately activated the devices—the ringing in their ears was much less intense this time; JJ boasted over having fixed some of the bugs in the programming—and then she fitted the headset over her ears. Together, the group took in a deep breath, and just as Eve regained a level of composure, JJ yanked at her arm and slapped a patch along her wrist.

"Jesus..." Eve mumbled, pulling her arm back to her side and glancing at her wrist. The patch was a slender black square, and flexible in design—it curved and moved with her arm—and in its center was a faint reddish glow that brightened as she neared Jason's side.

"These are heat sensors," JJ explained, attaching one to each of the boys' wrists. "They'll let you know when someone's nearby. They glow when you're in close proximity to other bodies. If they get *really* bright—"

"We're screwed?" Percy muttered.

"The brighter the glow, the greater the foe—well, in number, at least." She reached into her pocket and pulled out a handheld device that flickered with red and blue lights. "This is a tracker. It's designed to monitor your patches. I can let you know what to expect based on the sensors' readings."

Eve looked down at the sensor and then gazed up at the Pier Lorent. A chill ran through her body, one so severe that her knees nearly buckled beneath her.

Sancho cleared his throat, ending the brief silence. "So what's the plan?"

"JJ will stay in the car," Eve said. "She'll watch the tracker and keep us posted."

"And what about us? What's *our* plan?"

Eve avoided his gaze and focused on loading her gun. "Stay alive."

"No, seriously—"

"There *is* no plan," JJ interrupted, sensing Eve's tension. "Correct me if I'm wrong, but I'm guessing none of us have ever infiltrated an alien lair before."

Eve took in a deep breath, staring at her weapon for a second longer before finally looking up at her friends. "We find the captives and destroy the mainframe," she said, trying to sound authoritative. "And whatever happens in between, well"—she shrugged, stuffing extra magazines into her pockets—"we'll wing it."

"And what if we run into Fairon?" Sancho asked.

Eve's body went stiff at the sound of his name, and she looked Sancho in the eye. "We kill him."

"Look guys, I'm totally engrossed in this conversation, really, I am," Percy interjected, "but we're on a busy sidewalk in broad daylight, and we're heavily armed. People are starting to take notice in a *big way*."

Eve looked around. Percy was right: clusters of people had formed, some gaping from afar, others furiously tapping at their phones, most likely calling the police. Eve turned to JJ once again and extended her hand.

"The torq?"

JJ dug through her shoulder bag and pulled out the silver cylindrical device. She rested it in Eve's hand.

"Find the mainframe. I'll give you the instructions inside."

Eve nodded and tucked the device into the waistband of her pants. Percy shoved two guns in his belt, while Jason helped secure the Dirtier Sanchez along Sancho's back. Together, they headed through the hotel's revolving door.

The lobby was lavish and elegant. Three large, glittering chandeliers hung from a high domed ceiling, reflecting speckles of light across a polished marble floor. Gold leaf sconces lined the walls, and a stately fountain sat in the center of the room, its trickling water the only sound resonating through the vacant space.

"Balls," Sancho muttered. "This is one nice alien lair."

Eve took a step forward, gripping the torq with one hand and keeping the other on her gun, her eyes scanning the room. She could feel the others beside her: Percy was strutting in his typical nonchalant manner, and Sancho craned his neck as he gaped at the luxurious setting. Jason held his axe at his side, his entire arm flexed as if already prepared to swing, but at the same time his face was twisted with puzzlement. Something was on his mind—Eve knew exactly what he was thinking, for she was thinking it, too. He had noticed the eerie quiet and the emptiness of their surroundings. He had noticed that they were alone.

"Where is everybody?" he whispered.

Percy scoffed, "Probably off slicin' and dicin', doing what they do best."

They continued ahead slowly, not knowing where to go or what to look for, and the unnatural silence left them all feeling anxious. Sancho leaned in toward Eve.

"When do I get to light stuff on fire?"

Just as the words left his lips, Eve noticed a subtle movement out of the corner of her eye. She stopped in the middle of the lobby, glancing across the space before finally spotting the first sign of life they had encountered thus far: a woman.

She stood behind the guest services desk, her eyes fixed on the scratchpad in front of her. She was slight, almost delicate-looking, dressed in a crisp Pier Lorent uniform with her hair pulled back in a tight ponytail. Eve's entire body stiffened, and her fingers curled even tighter around the torq.

Suddenly, the woman turned toward them. She smiled at first, as if by reflex, but her lips quickly flattened. She stared at the foursome—at their faces, their weapons, and then the torq—and her eyes shrank into slits. Eve stood completely still, watching the woman as she exited her booth, making her way toward the intruders. Her steps were slow and graceful at first, but she hastened her stride, and soon her brisk walk turned into a full-on, combative sprint.

"SANCHO, NOW!" Eve shouted.

Sancho ran his fingers along the control panel of his device, and two roaring streams of fire gushed from the tubes at his sides. A wave of heat spread throughout the room—Eve and the others shielded their faces, while Sancho's eyes were wide with glee—and the woman's body was quickly engulfed in flames. Almost instantly her second skin exploded, spraying across the lobby like a flood of melted wax, and the newly exposed alien expanded his wings and soared high into the air. But just as he dipped down toward the ground, Eve sank into her melt and flung him against the wall with such power that he left a splatter of pus along the paint.

JJ's voice buzzed in her ear: *"TEN BODIES STRAIGHT AHEAD!"*

A "ding" sounded from somewhere nearby, followed by the ominous opening of an elevator door. Inside were indeed ten bodies—some in guest services uniforms, others dressed as servers or maids, but all of them wore the same hateful expression. They cocked their heads in unison and then spilled from the elevator.

Sancho reacted immediately, showering the creatures with a wall of flames. Their uniforms quickly burned and disintegrated into nothing, and their second skin formed puddles of sludge along the floor, revealing ten grey Interlopers in the midst of a blazing inferno. They continued forward, as if the fire was inconsequential to them, and Percy raised his gun and unloaded a surge of diamond bullets, each one sparkling like bits of sunlight before burrowing into the flesh of its target.

Three Interlopers separated from the group, shooting high into the air before dipping down toward their human and chimera foes. Eve was the first to act, lifting her hands and twisting her wrists, sending all three aliens colliding into one of the chandeliers. The chandelier wildly swung from side to side as the aliens' impaled bodies hung from its scrolls, and then the entire mess of lights and corpses crashed to the floor, landing atop yet another unsuspecting Interloper and smashing him into the marble.

Another alien ran toward Jason, his talons flailing as he let out two quick, piercing shrieks. Jason clenched his jaw, his eyes lit with a focused rage, and swung his axe straight at the creature's stomach, cutting the Interloper clean in half. As he came out of the swing, he spotted the last remaining Interloper at the far end of the lobby. The creature smiled, and just as he lunged toward the group, Jason launched his axe across the room, flinging it with such speed that it slammed into the alien's face and pinned him against the wall.

The lobby was silent. Eve and the others eyed the once elegant space, which was now decorated with yellow blood, broken bodies, and shards of shattered glass. Jason made his way across the room and yanked his axe from his victim's face, wiping the pus from the blade and ignoring the body as it slid down the wall to the floor. Percy remained by Eve's side, scanning the damage with a proud grin on his face.

"God, we are *so* good at this," he beamed, brushing a few flecks of dust from the shoulders of his leather jacket.

"*Guys,*" JJ interrupted, punctuating the stillness, "*there's one more.*"

Just as she spoke, another "ding" sounded behind them. A second elevator door opened beside the entryway, and inside stood a large, brawny man—a bellhop in an old-fashioned uniform. He stared at Eve, Jason, and their two human comrades, and then his gaze flicked to the ten Interloper carcasses in front of him. With wide eyes, he took one step out of the elevator, hesitated, then dashed across the lobby.

"He's getting away!" Sancho yelled.

Without a second thought, Sancho chased after the bellhop, his movement hampered by the weight of his flamethrower. The Interloper barreled across the open space, and just as Eve prepared to intervene, she stopped herself. The bellhop was headed for a dead end—a wall. Still, neither the hotel worker nor Sancho slowed their pace, and Eve watched in confusion as the bellhop ran straight into the wall—*through* the wall—and completely disappeared.

Sancho didn't stop either. He charged ahead, following the same path as the bellhop, until he, too, was inches from the wall.

"SANCHO!" Eve cried.

It was too late—Sancho smacked against the wall, his entire body ricocheting off the plaster and then collapsing to the floor with a loud thud that made Eve and the others cringe. He teetered atop his weaponized backpack, flailing his legs before finally rolling to his side.

"Mother of *balls,*" he moaned. "Didn't see that coming."

"You didn't see the *wall* coming as you *ran* into it?" Percy said.

"Well, *he* passed right through it—"

"It's the second skin," Eve speculated. "He was wearing it, the hotel is covered in it. It probably allows them to pass through without any issues."

Percy yanked Sancho to his feet and helped him regain his balance. As the pyro readjusted his device across his back, Jason made his way to his side and rested a hand on his shoulder.

"I guess that's your cue, Sanch. Light this place up."

Sancho looked up at Jason, his eyes bright with excitement, then glanced over at Eve, who nodded in agreement. With a look of conviction, he took one step forward and pointed his flamethrowers at the wall in front of him.

"*This*," he said, "is *definitely* the highlight of my *entire* semester."

Two blasts of fire jetted from his contraption, crawling up the wall until they bled onto the ceiling. Sancho slowly turned, running the flames across the guest services booth, the back elevators, and even the fountain, and soon the entire lobby was awash in flames.

Eve, Jason, and Percy huddled in the center of it all, practically numb to the blistering heat as they stared in astonishment at the walls—the walls that were neither charring nor smoking, but rather were dripping, like white, gluey syrup. Slime rained down from the ceiling, splattering atop their heads and forming puddles along the floor. The stately lobby was gradually morphing into something new—something dark and foreign.

As Eve watched, the walls began to move together, the spacious lobby rapidly closing in until it formed a tight circle around the group. The floor sank into the ground, devolving from marble into hard, compacted dirt. The ceiling, once bright and decorative, collapsed, reshaping itself into a mechanical dome only a few feet above Eve's head. In only minutes, the transformation was complete: the Pier Lorent Hotel was no more, and Eve and the others stood in the center of what was undoubtedly the alien lair.

"Holy shit," Jason muttered, his eyes wide with shock.

"*Christ Almighty*," JJ gasped. "*I don't know what you guys are seein', but the outside of the Pier Lorent just got a hell of a lot—*"

"Creepier?" Sancho interrupted.

Eve looked around at their unfamiliar surroundings. They were in a dark, enclosed room, circular in shape and stiflingly still. The rounded walls and ceiling were constructed from grooved panels of metal, pieced together and held with rivets. A single stream of light trickled in through the space; it was coming from the exit, now just a hole in the wall that opened out onto the sidewalk. Eve could see passersby gathering in the street, taking photos of the eyesore that had magically appeared before them.

She turned away from the exit and faced the opposite wall. Three separate openings were presented before her, each one dark and forbidding. The portal to her left was smooth, perfectly sculpted into the wall, and the portal to her right was its flawless mirror image. But the opening in the center was large and gaping, dripping with second skin and lined with sharp, silver needles, as if it were a weaponized mouth—the mouth of an Interloper.

The group stood in silence. Jason wandered around the rim of the room, trailing his fingers along its surface. Percy seemed unaffected by the transformation and took the opportunity to reload. Sancho's eyes danced across the three portals.

"Should we split up?" he asked.

"Are you crazy?" Percy groused. "Have you ever watched a horror movie? *Never* split up."

Jason finished his circuit of the room and made his way to Eve's side. "Which way do you want to go?" he asked, calmly.

She didn't respond. Instead, she took one last look at each opening—at the two unthreatening ones, and then at the one directly in front of her, its surface covered in teeth-like bayonets. Without a word, she headed for the ominous central portal.

"Oh, come on, not *that* one," Percy whined. "It looks like the mouth of *hell*."

"Which means it's probably *the right way to go*," she rebutted. "Besides, this is the direction the bellhop ran in."

Her three comrades reluctantly followed suit, ducking their heads to dodge the low-hanging spikes as they passed through the portal. Almost instantly, the light from the exit faded into darkness. Eve strained her eyes, trying to adjust to the encompassing black, and stretched her arm to her side, searching for a wall to guide her. Her fingers brushed against a hard, damp surface, one covered with fine grains of ash, and she realized that they were venturing through a tunnel much like the one in the Wilds. Behind her, she could hear a scuffle—the Dirtier Sanchez knocked against Percy, who in turn shoved Sancho into the wall—but she tried to focus on the path ahead, on putting one foot in front of the other and praying that nothing was lurking in the darkness.

Time seemed to pass slowly, and after a long stretch of aimless walking, she noticed that their path had taken a decline. They were heading underground, and with each step the air became muggier and even more stiflingly black. The only sight she could see was the faint glow of their heat sensors; Jason's brightened as he neared her side, and he rested his hand on the small of her back. She felt comforted, if just for a second, and then Sancho awkwardly bumped into her, effectively ruining the moment before teetering away. He coughed on the thick air and groaned.

"What are we looking for?" he whispered.

"The *mainframe*, obviously."

"I know that, *Percy*, but where *is* it?"

"For God's sake, *quiet down*," Jason growled. "You've been bickering this whole time."

"It's a legitimate question."

"We don't *know* what we're looking for," Eve hissed. She turned to Sancho and glowered. "Now *quiet*."

Sancho immediately went silent. It was so unlike him to take direction, but Eve soon realized that he was gazing behind her, transfixed by a muted light in the distance: a portal exiting the corridor. Jason grabbed his axe and took a cautious step forward, and Eve and the others followed suit, stopping only once they reached the side of the portal. Eve eyed her comrades, surprised to see that their faces were suddenly easily visible, each lit with a strong red glow. Reluctantly, she glanced down at her wrist—her sensor, along with the others, was shining brightly.

"JJ," she whispered, "our sensors are going crazy."

JJ hesitated. *"I... I don't think there are any Interlopers in there."*

"How is that possible?"

"The heat—it's all coming from one place—a concentrated source." Eve could hear the light tapping of JJ's fingers. *"It's not a body. It's something else. Something really, really hot."*

Eve glanced apprehensively at Jason. With their weapons raised, they slid around the corner and through the portal.

A wave of heat rushed over Eve's body, carrying with it a putrid stench. The room was faintly lit, and after she'd adjusted to the overpowering smell, Eve saw that it was just as lifeless as JJ had predicted. Percy and Sancho stepped into the room behind her, their faces immediately contorting with disgust.

"God, this places smells like a pile of old assholes," Percy muttered.

Eve maneuvered her way through the room. She could see it clearly now— the high ceiling made from sheets of metal, the small, glowing orbs that kept the space illuminated. The walls were lined with hooks and chains—for what, she wasn't sure, though the intention seemed sinister at best. Cages, much like the one that held Florenza, were stacked along one side of the room, their floors littered with bits of bone and rotting tissue. She noticed something in the distance—a small, square gate—but was quickly distracted by the sound of Sancho's voice.

"BALLS!" he yelped.

Eve turned just in time to see Sancho tumble face-first into a pit of ashes carved into the floor.

"Sancho!" she cried, rushing to the side of the ditch. "Are you okay?"

"Yeah, I'm fine." He hoisted himself to his knees and dusted the ash from his clothes. "Why did they stick a pile of ash in the middle of this dump?"

"Probably assumed people would watch where they're going," Percy quipped.

Eve began to roll her eyes but stopped herself. Again she noticed the gate at the far end of the room, only this time she thought she saw something moving behind it. She squinted, and realized the movement was a flickering fire: the source of the intense heat.

Eve approached the gate apprehensively, running her fingers along the handle and then instantly recoiling from the scathing heat. She cursed to herself and flicked her wrist instead, melting the handle and sending the gate swinging open with a loud squeak. The fire crackled higher, as if angered by her meddling, though Eve was unconcerned. She peered inside the opening, through the flames, and saw a long, black drawer, thin and narrow, the perfect size for one thing, and one thing only. A wave of nausea festered in her stomach.

"Oh. My. God."

"What?" JJ asked. *"What is it?"*

Eve's eyes panned over the hooks, the cages, and then once again made their way to the burning fire. She took in a short, shallow breath.

"It's a crematorium."

"A crematorium? Why would the Interlopers need a crematorium?"

"To burn humans," Jason added grimly, turning to gaze at the mound of soot behind him. "The humans whose lives they've taken over."

Sancho stared at Jason, perplexed, and then glanced down at the ashes— at the pit where he still sat. His mouth hung open.

"Oh, God. It's dead people. I'm *sitting in a pile of dead people.*" He scrambled out of the pit, spitting in every direction. "IT'S IN MY MOUTH! THERE ARE DEAD PEOPLE IN MY MOUTH!"

Eve ignored Sancho and stared at the waves of black that covered nearly half the floor. She turned to face the others.

"We're looking at *hundreds* of bodies here. There can't be that many Interlopers at Billington. It's impossible."

"Maybe they're not all at Billington," Jason said. "Maybe they're everywhere."

Percy let out a long, throaty sigh. "*God*, I wish I had a drink," he groused.

The group became quiet. Eve's eyes were cast down at the mounds of ash; she imagined the countless abducted humans and wondered if they had been killed instantly or perhaps held for days—or if maybe they were burned alive.

"We should get out of here," Sancho declared, "before *we* end up in this pile."

"You were just *in* that pile, Sanch."

"You know what I *mean,* Percy."

"Sancho's right," Jason grumbled. "I can't take this damn smell anyway."

Eve lingered for a moment longer, still staring at the sea of soot—the lives that had been reduced to ash. She shuddered and quickly left the room.

The foursome continued to make their way down the corridor. Eve waited for her eyes to readjust to the pitch black, but soon there was no need—she spotted a green light in the distance, and before long it was right in front of them.

The light came from a square panel along the tunnel wall, its glow casting a sickly green hue on each of their faces. Jason slid his hand over the panel, then dragged his fingers along the wall until they touched something hard and metallic. He knocked on the surface and angled his heat sensor across it, illuminating a giant slab that blocked their path, sealing the entire tunnel shut.

"Shit," Percy groaned. "We're at a dead end."

Jason hesitated. "I don't think so," he began, still running his hand along the metal sheet. "I think this is a door."

"Well, there aren't any knobs," Sancho said.

Jason turned back to the green-lit panel. It was a screen of some kind, made from a pliant, plasma-like material. He poked at its surface, and a small, blackened fingerprint remained, then quickly dissolved into nothing. He furrowed his brow.

"I think this is a palm scanner. Or a... claw scanner. Something like that."

Eve frowned. "I doubt any of *our* hands will work. I'm guessing we're not exactly the right *species* for this device."

"Try it out anyway," Percy suggested. "No harm in taking a stab at it."

"What if it triggers an alarm?" Sancho asked.

"And what if it *opens the door?*" Percy snorted.

"*Enough*," Jason hissed. He turned to Eve, who shrugged.

"It's your call. Thanks to our bellhop friend, I'm sure they know we're here regardless."

Jason stared at the scanner, practically scowling with disdain, and reluctantly pressed his palm against the screen. The device emitted a soft hum, and he quickly pulled his hand away. A blackened handprint remained on the panel, then faded until there was nothing left but a green light.

Jason let out an aggravated sigh. "Now what?"

"*FOURTEEN BODIES RAPIDLY APPROACHING*," JJ warned, causing each of them to jump at the same exact moment.

"It's an alarm," Sancho cried. "We triggered an alarm!"

"Where are they coming from?" Eve asked.

"*BEHIND YOU!*"

Together, they raised their weapons—Eve and Percy their firearms, Jason his axe, and Sancho his Dirtier Sanchez—and turned to face whoever, or whatever, had suddenly joined them in the corridor.

"Jesus *Christ!*" Eve gasped. She found herself staring down the barrel of a rifle, and as their sensors intensified and lit up the tunnel, she realized there were actually fourteen rifles in total, all of them pointed her way, each one in the hands of a patrolman.

A single patrolman in the front, the apparent leader of the group, snarled at her. "YOU ARE UNDER ARREST!" he shouted.

"*What?*" Sancho snapped, his mouth gaping open.

"You have the right to remain silent. Anything you say or do may be used against you in a court of law—"

"Oh, *HELL* no," Percy groused.

"You have the right to consult an attorney—"

"Are you *serious* right now?" Percy rolled his eyes. "We're in an *alien lair.* You do realize that, right?"

"Ignore them, Percy," Eve ordered, gripping her gun even tighter. "They're not patrolmen. They're Interlopers."

"Oh." Percy glanced over the soldiers and flashed a smug grin. "You sneaky little shits had me goin' for a second there."

"Interlopers?" The lead patrolman faltered. "We're not Interlopers."

"They're *lying*," Eve spat.

"Seriously," JJ scoffed in Eve's ear. *"I've never heard of a patrolman reading off Miranda rights, and I watch a TON of Crime HV."*

The patrolman clenched his jaw. "We're taking you into custody. You need to lower your weapons—"

"Like *hell* we are," Jason barked.

"Sir, you need to drop your weapon *right now*—"

"You do it first!" Sancho cried, trying his best to appear intimidating.

"This isn't a negotiation."

"It is now," Eve countered. "We're in a lair filled with aliens—aliens that can disguise themselves as *humans*. If you want us to lower our weapons, you have to prove you're human first."

The man sneered. "And how the hell are we supposed to do that?"

Jason nodded at the man's sleeve. "Cut open your arm."

"Excuse me?"

"You heard me."

"Look, we're not playing this game with you—"

"Cut your goddamn arm."

"Sir?" A patrolman from the back of the group interrupted the confrontation, nodding in Eve's direction. "She's got something in her belt."

The leader's eyes darted toward Eve, noting the torq tucked neatly inside her waistband. He grimaced.

"That a weapon?"

"It's none of your business."

"Hand it over."

"Abso*lutely* not."

"Look, I say we shoot 'em," Percy interjected. "They're Interlopers, plain and simple." He cocked his gun. "Let's just get the job done and move on—"

Suddenly, all fourteen patrolmen pointed their rifles at Percy.

"DO NOT MOVE!" the leader shouted. "DROP YOUR WEAPON! NOW!"

"What if we lowered our weapons at the same time?" Sancho suggested, glancing back and forth between the patrolmen and Percy.

Percy laughed. "Sounds like a brilliantly *stupid* idea, Sanch."

"That'll work," the patrolman said.

Percy's eyes shot toward the patrolman. *"What?"*

"You lower your weapons, and we'll lower ours," the man explained, still holding tight to his rifle. "Then you willingly hand yourselves over to us."

Percy let out a patronizing chuckle. "Great! So we can either be arrested or dissected. What a perfect way to end the day."

"You have no choice. You're outnumbered. If you don't lower your weapons, we *will* be forced to fire." He pointed his gun at Percy's forehead. "Starting with *you*."

"Why *me?*"

"Maybe I just *don't like you*."

"Fine," Eve interjected, anxiously. "We'll lower our weapons."

"*Eve!* What the *hell?*"

"It's okay, Percy," Eve said. "No one's shooting anyone." She turned to the patrolman. "Do you hear me? You will *not* shoot him."

"So long as everyone cooperates, I think we'll all be just fine."

The foursome eyed one another—it was a decision none of them wanted to make, and yet there were no other obvious alternatives. The lead patrolman, though still stern and formidable, seemed to relax the slightest bit.

"On the count of three," he began, and as he counted, Eve, her comrades, and the fourteen patrolmen gradually lowered their weapons. "One... two..."

A gunshot reverberated through the cramped space, echoing across the clay walls. Eve flinched and looked to her side at the slender stream of smoke oozing from the barrel of Percy's shotgun. He had lowered his weapon, just as he was told, but it had somehow found itself pointed at the patrolman's boot—the boot that was now seeping with yellow pus.

"See? He's totally an alien!" Percy cried, pleased with his own disobedience. "And you guys were going to surrender. I swear, you'd be lost without me."

In an instant, the patrolmen burst into individual clouds of creamy skin, exposing their true Interloper forms. They quickly shook the remaining tissue from their bodies and snarled at the foursome before lunging forward in unison. Percy smirked, unimpressed by the display, and fired a round of diamond bullets at the pack, injuring two and killing more, including the former lead soldier.

The two wounded Interlopers were only vaguely visible in the darkness— one had a gushing cavity in his neck, while the other's eye was reduced to a crater of pus. With a glare, the first creature shot toward the ceiling, gliding above the foursome, where his body suddenly lurched from side to side, spewing gobs of blood across the floor. Sancho had pointed every firearm of the Dirtier Sanchez at the alien, inundating him with bullets until his limp body plummeted to the ground.

Eve heard a grunt behind her; a decapitated alien flopped beside Jason's feet, and Jason glared down at the creature with a mixture of pride and hate. Seconds later, another Interloper was flying toward her, and she quickly swerved to her side, dodging the creature at the last possible instant. With a glower, she lifted her hands, catching the alien with her melt, and then thrust him into the tunnel wall. The creature toppled to the ground and then tottered to his feet, and as he attempted to regain his balance, Eve fired a single bullet into the back of his skull.

Silence. Eve stared down the tunnel, which faded from light green to darkness only a few feet in front of her. Sancho approached her side, his forehead wrinkled with confusion.

"Are we done?" he asked. "Seemed almost too easy."

Eve stared at the ground and counted six alien corpses. Only six. Hadn't there been fourteen patrolmen? Again she gazed down the tunnel, but still she saw nothing but blackness.

Hesitantly, Eve lifted her wrist and pointed her heat sensor at the corridor, trying her best to illuminate the space. Jason joined her, as did Percy and Sancho, brightening the tunnel with their glowing red lights, and yet they saw nothing but a long stretch of dirt. It was impossible—eight Interlopers couldn't have just disappeared. Eve leaned in toward Sancho and whispered into his ear.

"Your turn."

She could almost feel the excitement pulsing through him. An instant later, two streams of fire roared in front of them, illuminating the long, empty tunnel. Suddenly, Eve noticed something: a droplet that splattered on the floor. Two drops. Her body became cold; she gazed up at the ceiling and saw an Interloper, his claws burrowed into the clay surface, his eye-socket dripping blood.

Then she saw seven more, all hanging from the ceiling.

With one quick swoop, the Interlopers dove from the ceiling and zoomed through the tunnel. Eve instantly melted an alien off course and slammed his body against the metal door, while Sancho angled his firearms, obliterating two separate creatures with a surge of bullets. Jason set his sights on his own target, harnessed his gift, and flung the alien into another Interloper standing just a few yards away; together the two aliens crashed to the floor in a heap of broken bones. Jason glanced around the tunnel and caught sight of Eve, his eyes suddenly wide with terror.

"EVE, BEHIND YOU!"

There was no time to act. The Interloper pounced on top of Eve, knocking her to the ground and pinning her against the dirt. She groaned, squirming beneath the creature and frantically eyeing her surroundings. She spotted one of the patrolmen's rifles lying only a few yards away and reached for the weapon, her fingers barely grazing the grip. The Interloper dipped his face closer to her, dragging his nostrils along her skin, and just as he bared his fangs, Eve grabbed the rifle and shoved the barrel straight through the creature's open mouth. With a grimace, she pulled the trigger and blew out the back of his throat, sending hunks of flesh spilling in every direction, and the dead Interloper collapsed on top of her.

Jason ducked low to the ground, dodging another Interloper that flew overhead. The creature dipped through the tunnel in a chaotic manner, disappearing into the darkness, then reemerging again with his talons slashing at Jason's throat. With a surge of anger, Jason whipped his axe at the creature, slicing off his wing and sending him crashing to the floor. The Interloper roared, flapping his one remaining wing in a fit of rage, and just as he scrambled to his feet, he lurched forward and dropped face-first to the ground. Percy stood behind him, his shotgun smoking, and he smiled at the bloody hole in the back of the creature's head.

But before he could revel in the moment, Percy toppled to his knees, forced down by a heavy blow from the last surviving Interloper. The creature flipped Percy onto his back, glaring at him with his one remaining eye—the other had been reduced to a hollow pit of discharge. The creature grinned, admiring his target for just a moment, but it was a moment too long—Jason slammed the butt of a fallen rifle into the alien's face, knocking him to the ground with a thud. Jason pounced on the Interloper, and again he thrust the rifle into his skull, this time blinding his one good eye. Without relenting, he beat the creature's face until it was a mess of battered flesh and blood, and with one last surge of strength, he pounded the rifle through the alien's mouth, shattering his teeth and smashing his life source.

Jason backed away from the corpse, joining Sancho and Percy in the center of the tunnel. They counted the bodies—fourteen this time—and together, they breathed a sigh of relief.

"That was messy," Jason mumbled.

A slight rustling in the corner sent all three boys turning, their weapons raised. Eve was on the floor, pushing a hefty alien carcass off of her body. She looked up at the threesome and glowered.

"I'm fine, by the way..."

"Jesus, sorry Eve," Jason said, rushing to her side and helping her to her feet.

Sancho glanced at Percy. "I can't believe you shot that patrolman in the foot!"

Percy shrugged. "What? He was an alien. Who cares?"

"What if he was human?"

"He *wasn't* human."

"But what if he was?"

"No one's ever died from a gunshot wound to the foot."

"I'm sure *someone* has."

"Name *one* person."

"Guys, we're in an alien lair, remember?" Eve interrupted, shooting a critical glare at the twosome. "Keep your voices low."

Together, the group turned and stared at the locked metal door ahead of them. Jason furrowed his brow as he glanced back and forth between the palm scanner and the dead bodies a short distance behind him. Then, with an air of self-assurance, he sauntered over to the heap, kicked at the limp bodies, and swung his axe down onto one of the corpse's arms, severing it at the elbow. He plucked the arm from the pile and approached the plasma panel once more, flattening the talons against its surface.

A soft hum resonated through the space, and the door opened before them. Jason turned to his comrades, cocking his head at the detached arm still in his grasp.

"I'm keeping this," he said.

Without another word, he ventured through the opened doorway, casually holding the severed arm at his side.

Eve followed Jason through the doorway, immediately stopping at his side and staring out at their new surroundings. They had entered a massive room, one easily the length of a football field, with a lofty ceiling that loomed stories above them. The entire space was brightly lit with the same glowing orbs Eve had seen in the crematorium, and while she welcomed the visibility, the sight before her puzzled her: the floor was covered in long, silver racks, each one packed with rows and rows of clothing.

"Is this—" Eve stammered. "Is this a *closet*?"

"God, my mom would have a field day in here," Percy joked.

They continued through the space, weaving around racks as if navigating their way through a maze. Eve ran her fingers along the silver bars as she eyed the alien disguises—for that's undoubtedly what these were. There were suits, t-shirts, and gowns, all organized into sets of like ensembles. In the distance sat a row of military fatigues—she thought of the faux patrolmen they had just encountered and shuddered—and in another section she spotted scrubs from the medical ward and professorial sweater vests.

She stopped in front of single rack that looked out of place, as the clothing it held was scanty at best. Jason and the others joined her and gazed at the line of skimpy clothes: latex bikini tops, denim shorts, neon thongs. Beside the garb hung streams of colorful ribbons—the same ribbons that were passed out as favors at the Meltdown.

"I guess it only makes sense," Eve said, ending the uncomfortable hush. "This place *is* right across from the Meltdown."

"Do you think they took people from the club?" Sancho asked.

"Of *course* they did," Percy said. "We're looking at the evidence right here. I'm sure you've got bits of dead club hoppers all over your clothes right now."

Sancho frowned. "Then why would they even bother with Billington?"

"Because of the list," Eve answered, her jaw tightly clenched. "Because of me."

Eve quickly abandoned the rack, unable to look at it any longer. She hurried through the lavish closet, steering through the infinite lines of clothing until she found herself in a thicket of polished shoes, trousers, and ties, all perfectly in compliance with the Billington dress code. She slowed her pace and eyed the racks more closely: pastel shirt dresses, crisp, patterned blouses, and structured blazers in every size and style were waiting to be worn. Eve wished that at least one ensemble was recognizable, that she had seen it before on campus.

And then, her wish was granted—a white collared shirt had been carelessly tossed atop a single rack, and her fingers trembled as she slid her hands across the large, pink stain on its front.

"*You guys,*" JJ interrupted, confirming Eve's fears, "*you're not alone.*"

Eve released the shirt and glanced at Jason, Sancho, and Percy, who had each frozen behind her.

"How many?"

"*Six.*"

Eve sighed. "That's manageable."

"*Wait,*" JJ said. "*Ten. No, twelve. Seventeen.*"

"Dear God," Jason mumbled.

"*Twenty-four.*"

"Are you serious?" Percy chimed in.

Sancho anxiously eyed the room. "I don't see any..."

"*Thirty-one,*" JJ continued. "*Thirty-eight. Guys, they just keep coming.*" Her voice began to waver. "*I—I can't even count them all. They just keep coming.*"

"Where the hell are they coming from?" Eve snapped.

"*Can't you see them? They're all over! They're everywhere!*"

Eve wrinkled her nose. "What do you mean *everywhere?*"

Suddenly, an explosion of dirt and grime erupted behind her, and as she spun in place, she saw the head and wings of an Interloper protruding from the ground, his sharp, curled talons digging their way to the surface. Another Interloper burst through the floor, and then another, and soon others were burrowing out of the walls and the ceiling, and even more spilled from the opened doorway. A cloud of them flew overhead, swarming like insects, while countless others gathered along the ground, closing ranks from all corners of the room. A wave of dread washed over Eve; she and her comrades were surrounded.

"*What the hell are you waiting for?*" JJ shouted. "*RUN!*"

They bolted down the aisles. Eve could hear the sound of beating wings and stamping feet behind her, and so she pushed herself to move faster until the racks of clothes were a mere blur in her peripheral vision. An Interloper burst through the ground in front of her, pushing past the mud and clay with his wings, and she quickly swerved into another row. Again, an Interloper popped up through the floor directly in her path, thrashing his talons and gnashing his teeth, and she slid to a halt and scrambled down a neighboring aisle.

A chorus of shrieks sounded overhead, and Eve looked up to see a mass of Interlopers circling above her. With one quick movement, a single alien separated from the pack and plunged to the ground, snatching Percy up in his claws and carrying him up into the air. With a triumphant roar, the creature flung Percy at the wall, but before he made impact, Eve caught him with her melt, jolting his body in the opposite direction and pulling him back to the floor.

Eve continued racing through the closet, speeding past the racks as she searched desperately for an escape. Finally, she caught sight of something off in the distance: a darkened portal, leading to God knows where, but it was her only option, and she charged toward it.

A gust of hot air poured across the back of her neck—she looked over her shoulder and found another Interloper zooming behind her, his wings pulsing and his face twisted into a psychotic grin. Suddenly a river of bullets ripped through the creature's face, tearing the smile right off his lips, and his lifeless body crashed to the floor. Sancho was scurrying through the aisle beside hers, his guns protruding from the top of his backpack and his eyes wide with excitement.

"Is this thing a beast or what?" he chirped. "Look, I can even operate it with one hand!" He immediately held one hand in the air and ran the other along his control panel, and sure enough, his guns swiveled in place and unloaded a flurry of bullets at four fast-approaching Interlopers.

An earsplitting boom sounded overhead as a pack of aliens burst through the ceiling, sending chunks of dirt raining down on the room below. An unending swarm of Interlopers spilled out of the massive hole, and Eve barreled ahead, praying that she could somehow outrun the countless aliens now gathering above her.

An Interloper exploded from the ground just a few paces ahead. With no time to stop and nowhere to turn, Eve gritted her teeth and leapt over the creature, only for him to effortlessly swat at her boot and send her tumbling to the ground. She rolled once, twice, then staggered to her feet.

But something felt wrong. She patted her waistband.

The torq was gone.

Panic set in. Eve frantically scanned the ground around her feet, ignoring the surrounding chaos. She could feel the Interlopers bearing down on her, could hear the pounding of their wings, but still she searched. She couldn't leave without the torq.

There! She spotted it sitting beneath a rack just a few feet away. But before she could even take one step in its direction, an Interloper tore through the ground behind her and yanked at her ankle, sending her face-planting into the dirt. She lifted her head—the torq was so close, and she reached for it, barely touching it with her fingertips—but the Interloper tugged her backward, dragging her body along the ground. She clawed at the dirt, trying to free herself from her latest foe, but he grabbed at her waist and plucked her from the ground, pinning her arms to her sides.

Eve squirmed within his grasp, but he tightened his hold, squeezing her until she could feel the bones of his chest digging into her spine. With a grunt, she swung her legs backward, kicking at him over and over again, but to no avail; he laughed at her attempts, his body shaking with his caustic cackle. With few options, Eve clenched her jaw and slammed her head against the creature's face. He stumbled to the side, and though her own skull was throbbing from the impact, Eve managed to wriggle her arm free and jab her elbow into the center of the creature's throat.

Finally, the Interloper released his hold, and Eve dropped to the floor, immediately rolling onto her back and melting her adversary into a wall. She sprang to her feet and turned toward the last place she had seen the torq.

It was gone. Her eyes darted from side to side, and then she spun in a complete circle, but still, nothing. Instantly her stomach dropped, and the reality of the moment set in. *Oh God*, she thought. *I've lost it.*

Just then, an Interloper dropped down in front of her, landing with enough force to shake the ground. She staggered away from him, but not quickly enough—the creature backhanded her hard across the face, sending her toppling to the floor. She looked up at the Interloper, and her heart stopped.

In his hand was the torq.

He examined the device, turning it over in his claws, then looked back at Eve, a toothy smile spreading across his face.

"You are very clever, Female."

Suddenly, an eruption of thick, yellow pus sprayed from the creature's throat, and his head popped off of his neck like a golf ball hit from a tee. The headless body stood in place just for a moment, then limply toppled to the floor. Behind it stood Jason, his axe at his side, dripping with blood. He pried the torq from the creature's lifeless claws and tossed it to Eve.

"Looking for this?"

Another howl rang through the room. Even more Interlopers were soaring overhead, if that were possible, as if the number had grown exponentially. Eve stared at Jason, then pointed at the portal at the back of the room.

"We need to get the hell *out of here*," she ordered.

Just as the words left her lips, an alien tore through the ground between them, sending them stumbling in opposite directions. Again they dashed through the closet, keeping the portal in sight.

The Interlopers were in close pursuit. Three more dipped from the ceiling and hovered above Eve, but she channeled her melt and sent them crashing against the walls. Another pack pursued her on foot, shoving past the racks and leaving behind a trail of destruction. Gunshots echoed through the space, followed by the sound of bodies tumbling to the floor, and she turned to see Percy running behind her, his guns drawn. Again she focused on the portal, now only a short distance away, but yet another Interloper burst from the ground in front of her, clambering to his feet in an instant. Before she could react, Jason lunged from the opposite aisle, hurling a rack on top of the creature and shoving him to the ground. The two disappeared into a tangle of limbs and hangers, and then Jason resurfaced, slamming his axe into the pile beneath him until pus seeped through the fabrics.

At last Eve reached the portal, stopping beside it and frantically searching for her comrades. Jason was quickly by her side, and Percy, too, was fast approaching, still shooting at a handful of aliens that trailed behind him. Anxiously, Eve eyed the closet one last time—the toppled racks, the dead bodies, and the hordes of Interlopers still remaining—and just as she felt a hint of relief, a heavy weight suddenly dropped in her stomach.

"Wait," she muttered, "where's Sancho?"

She glanced back and forth between Jason and Percy—their mouths opened stupidly, but neither spoke. Again she gazed out at the room, past the ravenous aliens, but saw no black, spiky hair, no unwieldy flamethrowers. Her eyes widened.

"WHERE THE HELL IS SANCHO?"

"Oh my God," Percy spat. "We lost him. WE LOST SANCHO!"

"When did we lose him?"

"I haven't seen him since we got here," Jason said.

"OH MY GOD, WHAT IS *WRONG* WITH US?" Percy barked.

Two Interlopers lunged toward them, but Eve immediately channeled her gift and smashed their bodies into one another. Another Interloper headed their way, but Percy shot him in the throat and continued searching the empty space in front of them.

"SANCHO?" Eve shouted, pausing to melt yet another Interloper into the wall. Again she desperately scanned the room. "SANCHO!"

A guttural roar echoed from above, bringing Eve's attention back to the conflict at hand. Seven Interlopers were flying toward her, their bodies aligned like winged soldiers preparing for battle. Before she could even channel her melt, a gunshot echoed through the space, and the first creature plummeted to the ground.

Eve stared at the alien's body; the back of his head had been blown to bits, his flesh and skull lying in pieces beside him. Then, one by one, each of the other six attacking Interlopers dropped to the floor, collapsing into pools of their own blood. Eve stared in disbelief, first at the defeated corpses, and then at the figure before her: Sancho stood in the center of the pathway, his guns pointed in every direction.

"*Balls,* calm down, Eve," he mumbled.

The threesome gazed at him in shock. Eve peered around his small frame and saw a string of bodies lying behind him, each one with a bullet lodged in its skull.

"Did you—" Eve stuttered, "did you do all of that by yourself?"

"Told you this thing was a beast!" Sancho lovingly patted his device.

Eve gasped aloud; an Interloper was torpedoing toward them, his sights clearly set on Sancho. Without even turning his head, Sancho coolly ran his fingers along his controls, and one of his many guns swiveled in place and fired a single, precisely aimed bullet straight through the creature's mouth. Instantly, the lifeless alien dropped to the ground.

Sancho glanced down at the dead body and then looked up at the huge mass of Interlopers still looming.

"Go on without me," he said. "I'll hold 'em off."

"Are you *crazy*?" Eve snapped.

"Relax, I got this."

"Don't be an *idiot*, Sancho," Percy snarled.

Sancho fired at another Interloper and rolled his eyes. "Seriously, does it *look* like I need your help?" He smiled. "This is just like playing *Space Donkeys.*"

"But Sanch—" Jason protested.

"Go!" Sancho repeated, realigning his weapons. "I'll be fine!"

Eve stared at Sancho, who was already launching a stream of bullets at a new pack of Interlopers. Dozens of aliens remained, crawling along the walls and soaring below the ceiling, but Sancho was calm, even joyful, wielding his device with the utmost confidence. Eve hesitated; she couldn't just leave him there, and yet despite how much the thought sickened her, she knew she had no other alternative.

Percy stormed toward Sancho, his brow furrowed with disapproval. "Look, this isn't some goddamn *hologame*, Sanch. You're coming with us *right now—*"

Sancho turned to Eve and scowled. "Will you just take him with you already?"

"But—" she faltered.

"GO!"

Eve and Jason grabbed Percy's shoulders and yanked him backward, dragging him toward the exit. He fought their coercion, kicking his legs and spewing profanities, but his efforts were in vain, and he ultimately gave in to their force. Together, the three of them dashed through the portal and raced down the tunnel, running as far from the closet as possible, until Sancho and the entire war zone disappeared from sight.

After what felt like hours of aimless running, Eve finally slowed her pace, resting her hands on her knees as she waited for Jason and Percy to catch up. The two boys joined her in the center of the tunnel, nearly colliding with one another as they skidded to a halt, and then they each took a moment to catch their breath.

Eve tried to remain calm. She could feel Percy by her side, his labored panting slowing to a painful silence. A bitter lump formed in Eve's throat, quickly followed by a sense of self-loathing. She knew Jason felt it too, as she could hear him anxiously running his fingers through his hair. Percy was now pacing, kicking at the ground, and muttering the most vile curse words he could fathom.

"I'm sure it was necessary," JJ whispered, interrupting the silence. She knew exactly what they were thinking—that they despised themselves. Whether it was at his insistence or not, they had left one of their comrades behind. They had abandoned Sancho.

Eve swallowed the lump in her throat and approached both Percy and Jason, affectionately squeezing their shoulders before leading the way down the tunnel. They walked in silence, clearly distracted, shaken by Sancho's absence.

"You think he's okay?" Percy asked, his voice uncharacteristically fearful.

Eve didn't hear his question. Her eyes had adjusted to the darkness, and at last she could see the tunnel in front of her.

A series of portals stretched far into the distance.

"Shit," she muttered.

"Dynamic," Percy sneered. "They can literally attack us from any angle now."

Jason wrapped his arm around Eve's waist and brought her to his side.

"Stay close," he whispered. He turned to Percy, his axe in hand. "Be *cautious*."

The group continued on, walking as slowly and quietly as they could manage. Eve's eyes darted between her sensor, her comrades, and the tunnel ahead, making her dizzy and wrought with paranoia. Percy pointed his gun at the portals to his left, and Jason kept his sights on the portals to his right, but each opening they passed was dark and empty.

Soon they were nearing the end of the tunnel, and a large, closed door loomed just a short distance ahead of them. But just as Eve began to feel hopeful, she caught sight of a reddish glow in her peripheral vision. She looked down at her illuminated sensor and then eyed the few remaining portals to her left, quickly focusing her attention on one just a few feet away. She pressed her back against the wall, as did Jason and Percy, and as she slid closer and closer toward the opening, her sensor brightened until her entire face was lit with red.

"JJ," Eve whispered.

"I know. I'm counting."

They stood in silence, waiting for JJ to speak.

"Must be a big number," Percy mumbled, unenthusiastically.

"Forty-one," JJ finally answered. *"Forty-one bodies."*

Jason groaned. "God*dammit*."

Eve cocked her gun and took one last look at Jason and Percy. "You ready?"

The two boys nodded, their brows heavy, their jaws rigid as if they were grinding their teeth in anticipation. Together, the threesome sprang from the wall and barged through the portal, weapons drawn.

A series of gasps and shrieks sounded through the space. The room was small and dank, filled from wall to wall with rows of cages stacked one on top of the next—and sitting inside each cage was a human, their bodies curled into tight balls or pressed against the bars, some even sprawled on the floor in despair. They stared at Eve and her friends with petrified expressions, their eyes darting between the three new faces and their weapons.

"What's happening?" JJ asked, frantically. *"What's going on?"*

"Nothing." Eve lowered her weapon and breathed a sigh of relief. "We found the captives." She turned to Percy and Jason. "Come on, let's get them loose."

Eve ventured toward one of the cages, running her fingers along the frame as she eyed its design. These were the same cages she'd seen at the nest in the Wilds. Eve thought of Florenza, and then she noticed the captive staring back at her: a boy she didn't recognize, his hands shaking as he gripped the metal bars.

"I'm human," he stammered. "I'm not a chime—er, a chimera. I don't know what they want with me. I don't know why I'm here. You've got to *help me.*"

Eve ignored his ramblings and examined the latch hanging from the cage door. She remembered the effort it had taken to break into Florenza's cage, but that was before they had the diamond weapons at their disposal. Jason stepped up beside her, staring at an adjacent cage; he pointed his axe at the latch, and Eve followed suit, angling the barrel of her gun at the latch in front of her. Jason paused and turned to Eve, his voice soft and steady.

"This is going to be really, *really* loud," he said. "We need to work fast."

Eve nodded, as did Percy, who took aim at yet another latch. Eve tightened her grip on her firearm and took one last look at the prisoner.

"You may want to cover your ears."

And with that, the escape began. The sound of diamond crashing against metal echoed through the space, over and over, until Eve could feel it reverberating in her bones. Jason climbed up the stacks of cages, hacking at latches, while Percy and Eve continued along the bottom, and soon hordes of bodies were spilling from their cells and clustering together in the center of the room.

Eve hurried her pace; each shot she fired sent a wave of terror through her chest, as she knew they could be discovered at any moment, and so she flew through the congested room, opening the cages, compelled by her adrenalized fear. At last, only one locked cage remained, and just as she pointed her gun at its latch, she caught sight of the face staring back at her—his round cheeks, quivering lip, and familiar, terrified gaze. Eve shot a scowl at the prisoner—at Professor Gupta.

"Still scared of me, *Professor?*" she grumbled.

Before he could respond, Eve fired at the latch and turned away, paying no attention to the shamefaced professor as he crawled to safety. She fought through the throng of newly freed prisoners and joined Percy and Jason, who were waiting in the tunnel, just outside the portal. Jason turned to Eve, his concern visible.

"It doesn't make sense," Jason whispered. "They're not chimeras."

"So they claim..." Percy mumbled.

"They're not important, either," Eve added. "Florenza, Marshall—they came from powerful families. But these people... it almost seems like they were selected at random."

A loud clang sounded behind them. They quickly turned, only to see one of the captives tottering away from a tipped over cage. Jason sighed with annoyance.

"We need to get them out of here," he muttered.

"Well, we can't just let them wander free like a bunch of squirrels in traffic." Percy chuckled to himself. "Wouldn't end well."

Jason folded his arms. "They need protection. An escort."

"Right." Eve glanced at Jason. "Someone has to take them to the surface."

The couple stared at one another, their eyes locking as if coming to the same conclusion. Together they turned to Percy, who was busy reloading, oblivious to their penetrating gazes. Finally, he caught sight of them—and the looks on their faces, the looks that made their decision all too clear.

"What—*me*?" He waved his hands in disagreement. "*No.*"

"Percy—" Eve groaned.

"I'm not a babysitter. I am *not Armaan,*" Percy hissed.

"It's an important job—"

"Then *you* do it, Jason!"

"Maybe you'll run into Sancho," Eve added, her eyes bright and optimistic. "You'll see if he's okay."

Percy opened his mouth to speak but immediately stopped himself. He stared at Eve, pouting almost childishly, though his eyes were lit with hope. At last he sighed and turned toward the prisoners.

"All right, people, listen up, because I'm only saying this once! You're all a bunch of ducklings, and I'm your devilishly handsome daddy duck. That means you're following my ass out of this place, you hear me?" He cocked his head toward the exit. "No talking. Let's go."

Jason and Eve watched as the prisoners followed Percy, some clinging to the back of his jacket while others hovered close beside him. Just as the remaining humans made their way from sight, Eve heard one last voice calling her name.

"Evelyn," Gupta whispered. "*Evelyn!*" He waddled toward her, his stomach bouncing with each hurried step.

Eve sighed. "Look, Gupta, you need to go with Percy—"

"There are others," he said, his eyes bulging fearfully.

Eve flinched. "What?"

"There are other prisoners. They took them... they took them—"

"Where?" Jason interrupted.

Gupta pointed a trembling finger at the last remaining portal, near the end of the tunnel.

"I could hear them through the walls," he whispered. I could... I could hear them *screaming.*"

Without another word, the professor plowed passed Eve and Jason, racing to catch up with Percy, until he, too, vanished into the darkness.

An eerie silence fell over the tunnel. Reluctantly, Eve and Jason peered at the path ahead of them—at the large, metallic door and the darkened portal along the neighboring wall. Gupta's words repeated in Eve's thoughts; she glanced at Jason, who seemed to be thinking the same thing. Together, they slowly inched their way closer and closer to the last remaining portal.

Suddenly, the tunnel door slid open; Eve and Jason instantly sprang from the wall and scurried through the nearest portal, trying to stifle their nervous breathing. They could hear the sound of heavy feet clomping through the tunnel, stopping just a few feet shy of where they hid. A deep, gravelly voice interrupted the quiet.

"Ey falep qerolian."

"Frum humans," a second voice added. Eve turned to Jason—she couldn't help but wonder just how many Interlopers were in the tunnel at that moment.

"Fas," the first voice continued. "Ey falep chimera. Frum *kallas* chimera."

Eve's entire body tensed. She bit her bottom lip and waited.

"Frum kallas ka rash querasha." The second voice stopped, and Eve could hear the stomping of feet once again. "Tus tava den."

"Fas—"

"Tus tava den ar FAIRON!" the second voice roared.

A scuffle ensued. Eve could hear the sounds of wings flapping and talons scraping the floor, and a boom sounded amid the brawl. Eve nearly yelped aloud, and Jason threw his arms around her and pulled her into his chest, trying to keep her still. An Interloper scrambled to his feet—Eve speculated that he had been tossed against a wall—and he hissed loudly before joining the others somewhere in the tunnel. Eve clung to Jason and listened intently as the sound of footsteps slowly faded.

At last there was nothing but silence. The aliens had disappeared—to where, Eve wasn't sure—and she and Jason reluctantly peered out into the tunnel.

The space was empty, the metal door to the tunnel closed shut once more. Eve and Jason slowly slid past the portal and tiptoed through the tunnel. Silver teeth were scattered across the ground, and Eve instinctually tightened her grip on her firearm. Again they made their way to the last portal—the supposed site of the remaining prisoners—and Eve took a quick look inside.

In front of her was another passageway, this one punctuated with even more portals. Eve sighed—she had been hoping for a simple room like the one she had already found, for a quick rescue and an even quicker escape.

Suddenly, an Interloper came scuttling down the adjoining passage, casually making his way between the rooms, and Eve and Jason recoiled, immediately flattening their bodies against the wall. Eve could see Jason clench his jaw—it was more than clear where the Interlopers had disappeared to. Again, they peered around the corner, only to find the passageway empty this time, as the alien had presumably passed through one of the portals. Jason let out an aggravated sigh.

"There are dozens of portals. The prisoners could be in any one of them."

Eve grimaced. "Yeah, well, same goes for the Interlopers."

"Guys," JJ interrupted, "I'm not trying to sound like an asshole here, but whatever rescue attempt you're considering, you need to put it on hold."

"What?" Jason whispered. "We can't just leave them here."

"Time is critical. The Interlopers are looking for you. They know you're there. I mean, for Christ's sake, weren't you just ambushed?" JJ's voice was firm. "There's only two of you now. You've got to find the mainframe before it's too late."

"And what about the rest of the captives?" Eve asked, speaking as softly as she could manage. "We're supposed to just let them rot?"

"You can get them on your way back. I mean, shit, they're not going anywhere."

Eve took another look at Jason. She could tell that he was angry, that every fiber of his being wanted to reject JJ's command, but he glowered and said nothing. Eve cursed to herself and sighed.

"Fine," she muttered.

Together, they glanced around the corner one last time and then quickly sprang past the opening, moving instead toward the large metal door at the end of the tunnel. Jason eyed the door nervously, then pulled out the severed alien hand and pressed it against the glowing palm scanner. With a muffled clunk, the door slowly opened, revealing yet another tunnel, this one lit with glowing orbs.

Eve hurried through the doorway, eager to continue on, while Jason fumbled with the alien arm, tucking it under his bicep. Suddenly he stopped; a horrified scream sounded from somewhere behind him, one that was unquestionably human, and Jason's body became taut and on edge. He paused for a moment, then faced Eve, who was still waiting on the other side of the doorway.

"Go on without me," he said.

"*What?*" Eve hissed. "Jason, no—"

"Find the mainframe and destroy it."

"*No,*" she repeated, her face draining of color. "We do this together, Jason."

"Eve, I have to help them."

"We *will*. We'll come back for them."

"Who knows how much longer they have?" Jason's voice was confident, but his eyes were pleading with her, begging for her understanding. "Find the mainframe and destroy it. You can do it, Eve."

Eve was quiet, her body shaking, overcome with a crippling fear. She told herself that she wouldn't leave him—she couldn't—but deep down in her gut, she knew it was a lie.

"Okay," she finally said, her tone soft though surprisingly sure.

Jason forced a smile. "See you soon."

"Really soon," she answered, trying her best to smile back.

Eve turned away from him, her shoulders rigid and chest tight, but she forced herself to take the smallest step forward. The walk felt impossible, as if her legs had become faulty and inoperative, but still she pressed on, trying to ignore her lingering worries. She heard Jason's voice behind her once again.

"Eve," he called.

She spun in place. "Yeah?"

Again he smiled, but this time it was different—it was neither forced nor scared. Something about him had changed, as if he had found an unexpected sense of calm. Finally, he spoke.

"I love you."

Eve stared back at him, her eyes wide, her body overcome with a sudden paralysis. Every function within her had frozen into stiff placement, leaving her numb, dazed, and unbearably hot and cold all at the same time. After an agonizingly long half-second of silence, she took in a deep, much-needed breath.

A rumbling tore through the space—a mob of Interlopers poured from one of the portals and into the tunnel, their talons thrashing and bodies swarming with such heated rage that they nearly crashed into one another. Jason swatted at the creatures, instantly impaling one and wounding another, and looked back at Eve.

"GO!"

"JASON—"

He didn't wait for her to finish and slapped the detached alien arm against the control panel. "FIND THE MAINFRAME!" he ordered.

"JASON!" Eve dashed back to the doorway, but she was too late—the door promptly slammed shut, separating her from Jason and the horde of Interlopers. "JASON?" she screamed. "JASON!"

She pounded at the door, consumed with panic and hysteria. In a fit of rage, she rammed her fist into the metal slab and staggered backward, staring at the blocked exit as if it were more evil than any Interloper she could ever face. Her lungs heaved with her labored breathing, and though she tried to calm herself, she couldn't shake the horrible aching in her chest. She stared down at her hands—they were trembling, her knuckles split and bloody—and she suddenly noticed the stinging in her eyes and the rawness of her throat.

"He'll be okay, Eve."

"*Jesus,*" Eve mumbled, her face turning red. "I forgot you were there, JJ."

"*I'm trying to keep quiet—let you guys concentrate. I'm only chiming in when necessary.*"

Eve forced a laugh. "Must be a hard role for you to play," she said, her voice wavering despite her efforts.

The two girls were quiet. Eve stared down at her feet and tried to steady her breathing.

"*He'll be okay,*" JJ repeated.

"You don't know that."

"*I'm monitoring all four of you, remember?*"

Eve's eyes flicked forward. "Tell me when it's over. Tell me if he's all right."

"*I will.*"

Eve sighed. "For now... I guess it's just you and me."

Eve headed down the tunnel, holding her gun close to her chest. There were no doors in sight, no rooms or corridors or racks of clothing, and though the solitude should have been welcome, she instead felt overwhelmed by the stifling quiet. She thought back to just a moment before—Jason's face flashed before her eyes, as did the mass of Interlopers that surrounded him—and the vision tore a hole through her, one so tender that she could've sworn it was real.

"JJ, I know you're trying to keep your mouth shut and all, but can you say something?" She faltered, her voice weakening. "I really need you to say something."

"Sancho's here. He's back. He's fine."

Eve exhaled, relieved. "Good. Keep going."

"There's a mess out here. People are coming from all over, taking pictures of the giant monstrosity in the middle of downtown Calabasas. You should see their faces. It's like they've never seen an alien lair before."

Eve didn't respond. She could tell that JJ was trying to be lighthearted, even funny, that it was forced and contrived. She appreciated the gesture, but still she felt hollow, her chest heavy.

"I didn't say it back," she finally said. "He said he loves me, and I didn't get to say it back."

"You will. Later today. You'll tell him when all of this is over."

"What if I don't get the chance?"

"You will, Eve."

Eve exhaled slowly. She was racked with anxiety, but JJ's words, while hard to believe, were somewhat soothing.

She ventured farther down the corridor, hoping to see something new, something different, but still the walls were their familiar blend of ash and clay, and still she saw nothing but the brightly lit orbs that sat in perfect placement along the floor.

"People are coming out," JJ added, ending the silence.

"Of what?"

"The lair. Tons of people."

Eve stopped for a moment. "The captives. Do you see Percy?"

"Not yet. Everyone's swarming them."

"Tell Percy to try to go unnoticed. Tell him to get back to the car."

"On it."

Eve continued ahead, moving quickly down the long stretch of sameness. And then she noticed the slightest change: the tunnel was expanding, its walls spreading farther apart until, eventually, it grew vast and spacious. She hurried her footing, her steps keeping time with her racing pulse.

"*He's—*" JJ began, but suddenly her voice cut short.

Eve wrinkled her brow. "JJ?"

"*—here.*"

"JJ, you're cutting out."

"*Hello?*" JJ said, her voice now garbled in Eve's ear.

"JJ?"

"*—interference. Can you hear—*"

"I'm only getting bits and pieces."

"*—the mainframe. You're getting closer.*"

Eve stopped. "The mainframe?"

"*—interference—blocking the signals.*"

Eve pressed on, restive and alert. She walked swiftly, and then her walk turned into a run, the orbs now just a blur of light whizzing past her. In the distance, she could see something—a white glow peppered with yellow and blue—and her throat tightened with competing fervor and trepidation. As the glow grew in size, she soon realized that she was approaching an opening in the tunnel—an entrance to another room. She slowed herself, pressed her body against the wall, and slid closer and closer to the portal until she was right up against its frame. She could hear noises coming from within—frenzied movement and a strange, incessant drone—but she dared not look inside. Apprehensively, she glanced at her heat sensor, which was blood red and shining vibrantly.

"I think I'm here," she whispered.

Eve could barely hear JJ tapping at her controller. Suddenly, she stopped.

"*Oh God,*" she gasped.

"What?"

"*—fifty.*"

"Fifty what?"

JJ's next two words came through loud and clear. "*Fifty bodies.*"

Eve's legs became weak. Ahead of her were *fifty* Interlopers—fifty hungry, powerful, crazed aliens—and there was only one of her. The odds were so terrible it was almost comical, and she chuckled to herself.

"Guess this is it, then," she said.

"*Good luck, Eve.*"

"Thanks, JJ." Eve hesitated. "You're a good friend."

JJ was quiet, but the silence felt freeing, as if a weight had been lifted from both their shoulders.

Eve took a deep breath, resting one hand on her firearm and the other on the torq.

"Hey, princess." JJ finally said. "—some ass."

"What?"

"I said, kick some ass."

Eve smiled and cocked her gun. "You got it."

She leaned into the wall, trying to subdue the violent pounding of her heart and the racing of her thoughts. For God's sake, RUN AWAY. The words repeated in her mind until she felt as if they would pour from her mouth, so she bit her lip almost hard enough to draw blood. There was no use in thinking, no point in trying to stifle her nerves—and so against her better judgment, she waltzed right through the portal and stood directly in its center.

For a moment, Eve could only stand there, awed by the sight in front of her. The room was tight and enclosed but immensely tall, its walls stretching far above her, reaching all the way to the earth's surface. Most of the space was primitive in design, its floor and ceiling molded from ash and mud much like the rest of the lair, but one dissonant wall stood apart from the rest— the wall directly facing Eve. Its surface was a giant slab of hardware, pieced together with protruding blocks and panels, and covered in dials, buttons, and narrow, sculpted holes. A jumble of wires and cloudy tubules cluttered its front, climbing the surface until they disappeared somewhere within the machinery. Every so often, a light would flicker from the device, sometimes in yellow, other times in blue, typically brief and seemingly synchronized, as if transmitting some type of signal.

Eve was transfixed, her feet like bricks weighing her to the ground. She had found the mainframe.

And an army of fifty Interlopers, all of them staring directly at her.

The aliens were spread throughout the space—some on the floor, others crawling the walls, still others flying high above—but each one of them stopped and froze the moment she entered the room. They appeared calm, untroubled by her appearance—and then they smiled, as if they had been expecting her all along.

"Good Lord, here we go..." she muttered.

The thrashing of wings and the stomping of feet rumbled throughout the room as the Interlopers stampeded toward her. She knew they were rapidly approaching, that some were now only inches away—yet in that moment, time seemed to pass so slowly that their manic movements appeared almost graceful. Soon, the roar of their charge faded until all Eve could hear was her own steady breathing.

One breath.

Two.

It was time.

With her third breath, Eve delicately lifted the palms of her hands and watched as her vision faded from fifty ravenous aliens to a cloud of black.

Howls sounded across the room as all fifty Interlopers were ripped from the floor, the walls, the air, and thrust backward, slamming against the mainframe with sickening force. A loud crack reverberated through the space—the sound of shattered bones and broken machinery—followed by the sizzle of electricity bursting through the mainframe lines.

The Interlopers convulsed and writhed, their bodies lit with strings of white fire like lightning pouring over their skin. Some were killed instantly, and a few others flailed until their tissue melted from their bones and their life sources exploded. The survivors fell to the floor and scrambled to their feet—they appeared mangled and cadaverous, their ragged flesh littered with pockets of pus and exposed bones—yet they were alive and undeterred. Again they stormed toward Eve.

Eve pulled her gun from her waistband and immediately fired at the army of aliens. One Interloper fell after another, each with a yellowed pit in the center of his skull. An amazing power had overtaken Eve—it was the adrenaline rushing through her veins, a physical strength paired with cerebral prowess—and the trembling of her hands had been replaced with a steady grip and resolute control.

She pivoted, firing at three more Interlopers that approached her from behind. One swatted at her face, but she nimbly spun away from him and launched a bullet through the back of his head. Bodies were piling at her feet, but so many more remained—perhaps thirty, maybe fewer—and soon she was out of bullets and completely surrounded.

She took a half-second to eye her opponents—they closed ranks as they encircled her, grinning as if utterly confident in their victory—and then, with no other options, she covered her head and crouched low to the ground, forming herself into a tight, compact ball.

A blast erupted in the center of the room; the Interlopers were thrown against the walls, blown away by Eve's melt like debris scattered by a bomb.

Several of them dropped into lifeless piles on the floor, while the others scurried to their feet, their bodies deformed but their determination unwavering.

Eve reloaded her gun, quickly stuffing the magazine into place before firing at the remaining aliens. Another handful tumbled to the ground; the number of dead aliens was finally surpassing the number still living, and for the first time since she'd entered the room, Eve could feel a sense of hope growing inside her.

She reloaded her gun once more, fumbling with the clip for just a second before it was abruptly swatted from her hands. An Interloper stood before her, his stare piercing and malicious, and Eve could only watch in horror as the gun fell to the floor, the bullets scattering across the room.

Before she could react, the alien slammed his foot into the pit of her stomach, knocking the air from her lungs. She stumbled backward, clutching her gut, and again the creature kicked her, this time hard enough to send the torq flying across the room. Eve fell onto her back with a thud, gasping for breath, and the alien pounced on her, pinning her arms to the floor.

The creature stared into her eyes, his gaze blank and unfeeling, but Eve ignored his looming presence and instead eyed her gun, which sat only a few feet away. She wriggled beneath her attacker, trying to reach for the firearm, but the Interloper plucked it from the ground and dangled it above her face. Eve's eyes went wide as the alien crushed the gun between his talons, letting the broken pieces fall to the floor. He looked down at Eve, a satisfied smile on his face, and dragged his talons through her hair, slicing her skin until blood trickled down her scalp and onto her neck.

"You have no weapon, Female," he said, his voice deep and grating.

Eve glared at the creature, her body shaking with fury. She brought her face closer to his and gritted her teeth.

"*I* am the weapon."

Suddenly, the creature lurched up from her body, his limbs flailing as he soared higher and higher through the air until he hovered just inches below the ceiling. Eve staggered to her feet, her mind consumed with her melt, and with a hateful grimace, she propelled the Interloper to the ground, where his body splattered into a million pieces, spraying across the dirt like a cracked egg.

Eve raced across the room, sliding along the ground and grabbing the torq from its resting place. An Interloper flew toward her, and she effortlessly tossed him into the wall, still deep in her melt. A second Interloper followed closely behind, and just as he lunged toward her, she melted his nearby comrade to a spot directly in front of her, using him as a shield. The attacking Interloper plunged his claws deep into Eve's alien cover, and before either one of them could even make sense of what had just happened, Eve sent them both crashing against the mainframe, their bodies reduced to puddles of flesh and black bone.

Another Interloper batted Eve across the cheek, sending her neck jerking to the side and a sharp sting pulsing through her skull. He swiped again, this time slicing her temple, and then once more, clawing three deep gashes across her stomach, and Eve reeled back, crying out from the piercing pain.

Weakness settled in her bones. She could feel herself slipping, bending beneath the physical torture, but she rallied what little strength she had. As the creature made his next move, she dodged his swing and then punched him in the face, sending teeth spilling from his mouth. A surge of energy rushed through her then, rejuvenating her, and she pounded her fist into his nostrils again and again, harder and faster with each blow, and then kicked at his chest, knocking him to the ground. She stormed toward the fallen creature and slammed her boot into his mouth, over and over again until her sole was covered in blood and the creature's life source popped beneath her foot.

Eve scanned the room. Dead bodies were plastered to the mainframe and sprawled across the floor, and only a fraction of the Interlopers were left standing.

Three flew above her, circling overhead menacingly, and Eve quickly melted a flurry of teeth from the floor, sending them shooting at her looming adversaries. The teeth tore through the creatures' wings, shredding them into rubbery strips, and the aliens crashed to the floor. One broke his spine in the process, while the other two immediately sprinted in Eve's direction, but she promptly melted them into one another, slamming their bodies together over and over again until they were mangled and destroyed.

Only three Interlopers remained. Eve's heart began to race, and she tried to control her excitement, but still her knees shook so furiously that she had to lock them into place. Two of the aliens staggered in her direction—they were haggard and beaten, one with both eyes reduced to craters and the other with his arm twisted backward—and Eve hurled them against the mainframe wall, their bodies sizzling and frying until they were indistinguishable from one another.

Eve turned to the center of the room, her eyes darting across the space in search of the last remaining Interloper, but he was nowhere to be found. She spun in place, frantically looking for the creature, but still she saw nothing but corpses.

Suddenly, Eve felt a heavy weight smash into her back, the blow so powerful that she collapsed face-first to the ground. She gasped for air—a sharp pang shot through her chest, and she knew she had a broken rib or two—and then she gaped in horror at the sight of the torq rolling away from her across the floor.

Eve hoisted herself onto her elbows, dragging her body toward the device, and with what little strength she had left, she managed to bring herself to her hands and knees. But again she fell to the ground, as a massive foot smacked against her back, pressing her into the clay and magnifying the pain in her ribs. She cried out in agony, and the creature rested his other foot against the back of her head, shoving her bloodied cheek into the dirt. His talons curled around her crown, digging through her hair and into her flesh, and he shifted his weight until she felt as if her skull was being crushed. The Interloper laughed.

"I will not kill you," he proclaimed. "Fairon needs you alive. You know this, yes?" He leaned in closer, forcing even more weight onto her head, and brought his mouth to her ear. "But I will make you suffer. You will cry out for mercy, but I will not give it. I show no mercy, Female. None."

Tears flowed from Eve's eyes as if forced from her tear ducts by the sheer pressure of his foot. She wriggled beneath his body, but it was no use—he was stronger than her, and in that moment she felt exhausted, worn, and worthless. Every inch of her body was drained, and she could hardly muster the strength to even struggle. Again the Interloper increased the pressure on her skull, his claws raking deep gashes in her scalp, and she screamed in anguish.

Just as she felt herself give in to defeat, a glimmer of hope caught her eye: the torq was lying only a few yards away from her, and beside it sat a single diamond bullet. In an instant, she felt a tremor stirring within her—the familiar feeling of power, faint but not gone.

With the most shallow breath she could manage, she channeled what was left of her energy and allowed her vision to fade to darkness.

The Interloper flew from her back, pulled by the force of her gift, and hovered weightlessly above the ground. Slowly, Eve pushed herself from the floor—clenching her teeth as she grabbed at her ribs—and somehow made her way to her feet, brushing the hair from her face and wiping the dirt from her wounds. She turned to face her adversary, who floated only a few feet in front of her, and though she could tell he was trying to break free from her hold, her melt held him still, practically petrified. Eve took a step closer, staring at the creature with empty eyes.

"No mercy, huh?" She cocked her head as the Interlopers often did. "Funny, I guess we have that in common." Coolly, she leaned forward and plucked the diamond bullet from the ground, tossing it back and forth between her hands. Again she eyed the creature—there was now something different about his gaze, something timid and feeble—and calmly, she took a step back.

"The difference is, I don't need you alive."

The bullet flew from her palm and plowed straight through the center of his skull. His body dropped to the ground, flopping pathetically across her feet.

Eve breathed in as deeply as she could manage. The aching of her body subsided, replaced with a sense of authority and control. She eyed her surroundings.

Fifty broken alien bodies decorated the room, displayed like trophies.

She had won the battle.

"*Eve?*"

"JJ," Eve gasped, stirred by her friend's voice.

"*Eve, you—*"

"JJ, I can't hear you."

"*—you okay?*"

Eve looked over the graveyard before her once again. "Yeah, JJ. I'm okay."

"*The torq, it's—*"

"What?"

"*It's time. —the virus—activate the virus.*"

Her voice cut out for a short period, leaving behind nothing but garbled static. Finally, she became the slightest bit clear again.

"*—See a hole? In the mainframe. Do—see a hole?*"

Eve glanced over the massive wall and frowned. "There are a thousand holes. Which one do I choose?"

"*Any.*"

Eve plucked the torq from its resting spot and hurried toward the structure, stepping over corpses until she was standing directly in front of the giant computer system. With a look of disgust, she pushed a mutilated body from the mainframe and ran her fingers over the intricate wiring and mechanics.

"Click—button," JJ continued. *"On the torq—blue button."*

The torq was shaking in Eve's grip. She pushed the blue button, and the device became warm in her hands, its ridges glowing brightly.

"—in the hole."

"What?" Eve asked.

"Put the torq in the hole."

Eve stared down at the mechanism and grimaced. "God, this really does look like a penis," she muttered to herself, and then shoved the torq into one of the many cavities. "Okay, it's in the... hole."

"—knob at the end? Turn it clockwise."

Eve fiddled with the knob, her hands shaking so severely that she had to stop herself, cursing aloud as she stretched her palm. Again she grabbed at the knob, this time grasping it firmly, and twisted it until a loud *clank* sounded from the device.

"This is it," JJ added. *"This is the moment. You're—you're activating the virus."*

Eve took in a shaky breath. "I'm ready."

"Push down on the knob. It'll—release the virus."

Eve hesitated, just for a moment, and then grabbed at the knob, her grip so tight that her knuckles turned from pink to white. She clenched her jaw and, with more power than necessary, slammed the knob down until it clicked. Eve backed away from the device and the mainframe, her heart racing with exhilaration.

"It's done."

Eve could vaguely hear JJ laughing on the other end. *"Holy shit, Eve, you did it."* Her voice cut out for a moment. *"—finally over."*

Eve stared at the torq, her eyes wide with intrigue. The glow of the device brightened slightly and then faded into darkness. Suddenly, the tubules surrounding the torq illuminated, their once clear casing filling with a blue light that flowed through the wiring like water coursing along a stream.

"What's happening?" JJ asked. *"What does it look like?"*

Eve watched the blue travel from one tube to the next, leaving the torq and dispersing throughout the mainframe. It was beautiful, she thought: color circulated across the hardware like thousands of veins pumping blood through a body. And suddenly, it hit her—the virus was just that, a poison coursing through the mainframe, infecting each and every knob, dial, and panel that it touched. Eve backed away from the computer system.

"Death," she answered. "It looks like death."

She stood in the center of the room, still transfixed by the bluish light. A part of her thought she should leave—that the job was done, that she should find Jason and head for the surface—but still she waited, as if she needed to see the mainframe destroyed with her own eyes. Finally, the blue trickled through the last remaining inch of the mainframe, and the entire computer system was lit with a brilliant glow. The mainframe began to emit a muted hum, which quickly intensified in volume.

"Eve?" JJ said. *"Eve?"*

Before Eve could respond, a boom sounded through the space, the noise so powerful that it shook the ground beneath her feet. She regained her balance just in time to see hundreds of sparks ignite across the face of the mainframe, filling the wall with flickering yellow lights that sizzled and snapped like firecrackers. The blue light of the wires brightened until it was a rich shade of indigo, and in a matter of seconds, the entire room was tinted by the glow.

Eve knew it was happening: the mainframe was dying, and the list would die with it. And just as she predicted, another boom echoed through the room, this one violent enough to blow back her hair and send her stumbling to the side. A half-second later, a blast of light poured through the space, quickly morphing from blue to a blinding white. Eve shielded her eyes as her entire body was engulfed with the blazing light, the rumbling still quaking in her bones. A harsh ringing pierced through her head, bouncing back and forth between her ears before finally coming to rest behind her brow. The moment was surreal; her body was consumed with fear, power, and pain, all competing for her attention, but still she closed her eyes and shielded herself, standing her ground in the face of this uncontained strength.

Abruptly, the light dimmed to darkness, the thundering faded to silence, and the pain ebbed away until all that remained was a pestering ache.

Eve opened her eyes.

The mainframe was black and stagnant, its surface just as lifeless as the corpses at her feet. It was done. She had destroyed the mainframe—she had destroyed the list.

"JJ?" Eve said quietly. There was no response. "JJ?"

The room was dark and overwhelmingly quiet. Eve peered down the long corridor behind her and saw that the once glowing orbs had shattered, now reduced to mere shards and puddles of some strange, alien fluid.

"JJ?" Eve repeated. "Are you still with me?"

Still there was silence. Eve rubbed her aching head; she thought of the sharp pain she had experienced, and wondered if perhaps that was the communicap, if it had somehow been affected by the detonation. She looked down at her wrist—her heat sensor was solid black, clearly deactivated as well—and a rush of anxiety ran through her. She took one final look at the sabotaged mainframe, at the slew of bodies surrounding her, and then, as if awakened from a trance, she barreled from the room and into the tunnel.

Eve ran with all the energy she could muster, passing rows of broken orbs and not giving a second thought to who or what might hear her footsteps. The job was done—the list, and every possible variation of it, was gone—and in that moment, the only thought on her mind was reaching the surface and reuniting with her comrades.

Suddenly, Eve lurched to a halt. Ahead of her was a doorway, the last place she had seen Jason, except that, for whatever reason, the door was now wide open. She took the smallest, most hesitant step forward, afraid of what might be waiting on the other side, and then finally forced herself to make her way through. She glanced at the palm scanner, which was now black instead of green, a dull, sludgy plasma leaking from its lining. Eve dragged her hand through the fluid and smeared it between her fingers. The destruction of the mainframe must have disarmed the entire lair, just as it had compromised her communicap.

Apprehensively, she stared down at her feet, deathly afraid of what—or whom—she might find. But all she could see was an array of Interloper parts: heads, wings, arms, and legs severed from their bodies.

A spark of hope surged through Eve: Jason had done this. But before she could analyze the situation any further, she heard a familiar sound: a high-pitched, terrified scream. Instantly, she sprinted through the corridor, leaping over the scattered body parts and following the sound to a small, dark room.

Three Interlopers hovered around a long silver table, and Eve instantly melted them from their feet, slamming them into the walls with such force that their spines snapped. Anxiously, she ran toward the table, only to abruptly stop at its side, her nose and brow wrinkled.

"Hayden?"

The Rutherfordian was lying on the center of table, her wrists and ankles shackled with large silver cuffs.

"Eve, thank *God!*" she cried. "Please, you have to help me!"

Eve rolled her eyes. "God*dammit*," she muttered.

"They're going to kill me!"

"Yeah. I can see that."

"Please, Eve, you can't just leave me here—"

"I'm not going to leave you here, calm down," Eve said, making her way to the corner of the table. She toyed with the cuff, pulling at Hayden's wrist as she attempted to figure out its mechanics.

"Ow!" Hayden yelped. "That *hurts*."

"The complaining stops *now*," Eve snapped. "I'm saving your life, remember?"

Hayden pouted. She nodded at a panel on the wall, its face covered in buttons. "That thing over there? It controls the table. I saw them use it."

"It's not going to work, Hayden. I cut off their power."

"It will," she insisted. "It's manual, or something. I saw. I watched them." Again she nodded at the device. "The lever at the top? Pull it down."

Eve grumbled and trudged toward the panel. A long rod protruded from the top of the dashboard, its surface covered in various claw-shaped markings. Eve pulled on the lever, and yet it didn't move. Again she tugged at the rod, this time harder, and still nothing happened.

"Hurry up," Hayden hissed.

"Jesus, have some patience. I've never worked an alien torture device before."

With an aggrieved grunt, Eve yanked at the lever one last time, finally pulling it down until it clicked into place. The table lifted from the floor, slowly tilting forward until Hayden's body was perpendicular to the ground.

"There's a wheel at the base of the table," Hayden continued, her nose wiggling with excitement. "It'll loosen the cuffs."

Eve slid onto the floor. The wheel was small and just as stiff to maneuver, but she spun the dial until four clanks sounded overhead. She stood to her feet; the cuffs were looser, but still closed shut, and Hayden scowled in disapproval.

"What are you waiting for? *Undo* them!"

Eve groaned and crouched beside the girl's ankle. The lock was composed of three bars that were fastened together like puzzle pieces. She twisted the bars, pulling them apart in three quick movements, and then she moved to the second ankle, her hands working quickly and efficiently.

"FASTER!" Hayden barked.

Eve hopped to her feet and glowered. "Okay, I hate to sound like Madison, but I'm going to have to insist that you *shut up.*"

Hayden opened her mouth to speak but stopped short—Eve was glaring at her, her arms crossed and jaw clenched, and the small blonde looked away and said nothing. With a sigh, Eve fiddled with the girl's left wrist, while Hayden watched her out of the corner of her eye.

"Madison is—"

"A chimera. I know." Eve released the cuff and moved to Hayden's right wrist, still avoiding her gaze.

"And Heather is—"

"An Interloper." Eve unlocked the final cuff and helped Hayden to her feet. "I know."

Suddenly, Eve's entire body lurched to the side, her arm nearly yanked from its socket. A sharp click sounded by her ear, and she turned, bewildered, only to find her wrist now locked inside one of the silver cuffs—which was held shut by Hayden's tiny, frail hand.

Eve looked back at Hayden—at her once terrified eyes, which were now empty, lifeless, and cold. Hayden cocked her head and smiled.

"You know nothing."

CHAPTER 17: NEVER

UNDERESTIMATE YOUR ENEMY

Eve stared into Hayden's unblinking eyes, and the entire room seemed to shrink around her.

"*You?*" Her eyes widened. "No way. *No goddamn way.*"

With a rush of energy, Eve swung her free arm at the girl, but Hayden suddenly grabbed her fist and slammed it against the table. Eve let out a piercing cry—she could feel her wrist snap, the pain pulsating through her entire forearm—and Hayden effortlessly locked her hand into place.

Hayden then dropped to the ground, cuffing Eve's right ankle, and despite her kicking and flailing, Hayden yanked at her left ankle and forced it into the last metal cuff. She stood and gazed at her prisoner, her empty eyes igniting a burning rage within Eve. With gritted teeth, Eve head-butted the girl, but still Hayden was unaffected, and she clasped Eve's forehead and shoved her against the table.

Eve groaned and went limp, crippled by the pain swelling in her skull. She could vaguely feel Hayden's fingertips gliding across her forehead, pressing something into her skin: what felt like two small metal disks that sent a sharp ringing noise bouncing back and forth between her ears. Eve opened her eyes—which only seemed to magnify the ringing—and tried to make out Hayden's hazy figure before her. With her jaw clenched, she balled her one good hand into a fist and channeled her melt, directing all of her power at the girl in front of her.

Nothing happened.

Eve's lips parted in disbelief. Again she delved into her gift—yet there was no tingling of her spine, no darkness clouding her vision. Hayden still stood in front of her, eerily unscathed. She casually flicked at the buttons on Eve's forehead.

"Stifles the gift," she said. "A necessary precaution."

Eve growled. She tilted her head back and closed her eyes, trying to suppress the ringing, but it only worsened. Her breathing was now reduced to short, shallow pants, as anything more sent waves of pain through every inch of her body.

She opened her eyes again, though only slightly, and watched as Hayden strolled across the room to a shelf carved into the clay wall. A row of sharp, silver devices were laid out in front of her: tools. *Knives.* She snatched a pair of scissors from the shelf and marched back over to Eve, yanking at the hemline of Eve's ragged tank top.

"Don't touch me," Eve hissed.

Hayden ignored her and proceeded to cut the shirt from Eve's body. She roughly ran her hand down Eve's chest, past her bra and over her shredded stomach, and Eve recoiled from her touch. Hayden cocked her head.

"This will suffice," she mumbled, flatly. She eyed the table—it was still tilted perpendicular to the ground, just as Eve had left it—and crossed her arms. "I like you at this angle. Yes, almost at eye level."

Without another word, the girl scurried back to the shelf once more, where she polished her tools with her shirtsleeve. Eve concentrated on her breathing, trying to stifle the aching of her body, the sting of her wrist, and *God,* that *ringing.* She glanced at her captor and bit her bottom lip.

"What did you *do* with *Hayden?"* Eve spat. "Where is she?"

"The human female died six months ago," Hayden answered, still polishing her knives. "I killed her myself. She suffered greatly."

Eve's chest tightened. "This whole time—"

"I've been watching you. Since the day you moved to Billington. Since I sat on Madison's bed, and you and I—we spoke."

Eve stared at this small girl, this Interloper who had fooled her for months. "How—" she stammered, "how did you—"

"It is not difficult to learn the language of humans." She finally turned to face Eve. "Your language is simple. Your language is cruelty."

Eve hesitated. "And Heather—"

"The orange human?" Hayden turned back to her tools. "You think she is of my kind. You are wrong."

Eve closed her eyes again; she felt stupid. Shamed. And in an instant, the aching of her body was replaced with something even worse: a devastating sense of despair.

Reluctantly, Eve opened her eyes. Hayden had nearly finished preparing her tools, and Eve could clearly see the long stretch of sinister, sharp devices, each one more foreboding than the last. Her heart sank into her gut.

"Are you taking me to Fairon?"

Hayden put down her last tool and stared back at Eve, tilting her head almost inquisitively. "He is here. Would you like to see him?"

"Not especially," Eve muttered.

For the first time since their encounter began, Hayden smiled. Suddenly, her face became dewy, and Eve knew that the moisture forming along her flesh were beads of second skin, rolling down her neck and dripping from her fingertips into puddles on the ground. Within moments, her face was an oozing mess of wetness, her nose, lips, and eyes sliding down what used to be her chin, like a doll melting above a flame.

Two bulges protruded from her skull, pushing at her scalp and finally tearing through her second skin—horns. Her shoulders expanded, forming an angular hump that burst free of her clothing, revealing large white wings that flapped and flailed until they settled into place. She was tall, so tall that Eve had to strain her neck just to see her face. Soon, Hayden was gone, a mere pool of sludge on the floor—and in her place stood a towering Interloper with milky skin and golden teeth.

Fairon.

Eve's heart pounded in her chest, but she forced a stoic front. Fairon eyed her up and down, trying to stir anxiety within her, but still she offered no reaction. Finally, he spun away from her and returned to the shelf, where he ran his talons along the tools before plucking one device from the rest: a long silver blade. He slowly made his way back toward her, being sure to display the blade for her to see.

As he loomed over her, a low cackle left his lips, and with a grin, he touched the blade to her stomach, grazing the skin just above her navel.

"WAIT!" Eve barked.

Fairon stopped. He stared at Eve, surprised by her interruption.

"Ey falep ta reign, kallas *chimera*," he grumbled, his voice gravelly and deep.

Eve rolled her eyes. "Look, I don't know what the hell you're saying, Fairon."

"You lie here, strapped to my table, and yet *you* give *me* orders?"

"You're supposed to—"

He lunged toward her, pointing his blade at her throat. "You do not tell *me* what I am *supposed* to do."

"You're *supposed* to tell me your *plan*."

Fairon leaned in closer, pressing the blade deeper into her skin. "My plan?"

"Yeah," she continued. "Your *ingenious* method. You're supposed to tell me all the *bullshit* you did to get me to this point. The bad guys do it in all the movies." Her eyes darted down to the blade and then back up at Fairon. "So, spill."

Fairon's eyes shrank into thin, black slits, but Eve didn't waver. She could feel the air puffing from his nostrils and taste the mugginess of his skin, but she lifted her chin and feigned control. She had no other options.

Fairon lowered his blade. "You stall for time." He nodded at the doorway behind them. "You hope your male will come for you. It is irrelevant. If he does come, I will kill him." He placed the blade atop a nearby shelf. "Time is unimportant. If stalling brings you comfort, I will grant you an explanation. I am merciful, Evelyn. You need not fear me. I know that you do, but I am merciful."

Eve wanted to breathe a sigh of relief or possibly spit at his feet, but she resisted both urges. She kept her chin high, trying to disregard the aching of her body and the incessant ringing in her ears. Fairon was now pacing the room, his movements graceful, almost regal. He kept his eyes on the silver blade.

"We have been here, on this planet, much longer than you realize."

"I know," Eve interjected. "I saw the ashes."

Fairon turned to her and smiled. "Those ashes—they are young. However long you are thinking, we have been here *longer*."

Again he approached the blade, lovingly stroking it with a single talon.

"The Meltdown—it was not enough. We needed more. You understand, yes? Your species is consumed by avarice. No kind should understand more than yours.

"Billington was an obvious choice. And the list—we located it quickly." He looked back at Eve, his eyes large and filled with awe. "Thus we discovered you—you and your glory. Your *power*. We were destined to find you. This moment, it is bigger than us. It is fate."

"I don't believe in fate," Eve muttered.

"You assume I care about your lack of conviction. I do not." He took a step toward her. "I would study you myself. Hayden was an ideal host: she was aligned with the yellow female, your roommate. An unorthodox decision, to associate with a chimera, but the yellow one did not belong on my table. Her gift is weak—hardly a worthwhile pursuit. Her only value to me was her link to you."

Eve pursed her lips with revulsion, though the movement only amplified the ringing in her skull. Fairon continued, his nostrils wiggling as he spoke.

"The day we met—I could smell your power before you entered the room. It is potent, your gift—much stronger than I had imagined. And so I delayed my advances. I could not have you, not yet. I would fail. You had to be diminished first."

"Diminished?"

"The goal was alienation," he explained. "I worked to expose you—to make you a target among your own people. It was easier than I had anticipated. Your humans were very instrumental." He leaned in closer, and Eve realized that he was smelling her. "*Chimera Bitch*—such crude, simple wording. Your language is primitive, but effective."

"*You* made those flyers?" she spat.

"No. I did not." He pulled back. "I was a shadow. I coaxed your exposure to fruition. It was *your* people who spread the revelation. Your human race—they shamed you." He crouched down again, until they were at eye level. "These Earth people: they hate one another, attack one another, *kill* one another. They are blinded by their biases. They do not see our infiltration. It is to our benefit, your kind's preoccupation with one another. It is a flaw in your culture that works in our favor."

Eve smirked. "You're pretty long-winded once you get going, aren't you?"

"Your words—they carry rancor."

"Well, you *did* follow me for months," she muttered, her voice exhausted and bitter. "You strapped me down to this table. Pretty sure you broke my wrist—"

"It is none of those things. You have a high tolerance for physical pain. I caused you emotional torment. I made you suffer."

Eve clenched her jaw. "What the *hell* was the point of all that?"

"To prey on your resolve. To ensure you would be alone—that you would be vulnerable to our attack." He stepped away from her, pacing the room yet again. "And still, you found a male. It was a disturbance I did not predict. Your kind is so quick to feed off the weak. It was not to be expected."

"Maybe you're just not as smart as you think you are."

Fairon backhanded her across the face, sending her head smacking against the table. She groaned, her eyes clenched shut, her head consumed by a combination of throbbing, aching, and ringing. Fairon resumed his pacing, unconcerned with her suffering.

"I tried to kill your male. I sent my people—several times. They never returned." He looked back at her, though she was still reeling from the pain. "You aligned with more than one, yes? A logical choice. Your kind is a social race."

Eve opened her eyes. She could vaguely see Fairon, though her vision was peppered with darkness. She felt something trickling down her forehead, past her nose, and then it settled in the corner of her mouth. The taste was unfamiliar—was it salt water? Then she realized what it was.

She was sweating.

Oh God, she thought to herself.

Fairon continued. "Your mind had to be weakened, if not through isolation, then through pollution. And so I implemented a distraction: *DIE CHIME.*"

"The death threat... it was you," Eve replied, her voice barely a whisper.

"And yet you believed it was Madison for some time. I told you she was missing. You found the ashes. It was enough."

She grimaced. "Why even *bother*?"

"Did she contaminate your thoughts? Were there days when you saw nothing but her—but her supposed longing for your death? Did she distract you when you could have been thinking of me? When you should have been *seeing* me?" He came in close to her, his eyes fiery with passion. "Your episode in the washroom—it was magnificent, the validation. The knowledge that your mind was polluted."

Again he pulled away from her, looking back at the entrance of the room.

"You infiltrated one of our nests. It was courageous. It was *stupid*." He lowered his head, his back rigid. "The *beacon*—that is what your people call it. You *stole* it. So that very day, I went to your room."

"Jesus, *that's* why you were there?" Eve hissed. "You piece of shit, *you* stole Madison's key."

He spun toward her. "I NEEDED MY EQUIPMENT!" he roared, his voice echoing off of the walls.

Eve's heart raced. She straightened her back, pressing herself deeper into the table, away from Fairon. Again, he paced the floor.

"Your attack by the music building confirmed my suspicions. You were listening to us. And so I came for my equipment—and for you." He looked back at Eve, his stare alive with pleasure. "That night in your dormitory, when I threw your male into the sky... It broke your spirit. It was beautiful to see."

Eve thought of Jason falling from the balcony and felt a pang deep in her chest. Again her vision grew hazy, as if covered in a blanket of smoke.

"When Madison relocated, she was no longer useful to me," Fairon continued. "I aligned with the orange female. An appropriate choice—she was watching you as closely as I was. The key was constant visibility. To keep you in my sight. Always.

"I then realized the flaw in my method: I was working to destroy the very facet that drew me to you. To exhaust your unparalleled power. It was a mistake." Finally he stopped his pacing and stood in front of her. "All attempts against you were futile. The only way you would end up on my table was through your own free will. I would make your power my weapon."

"You knew I had Cooper's torq," Eve mumbled. "You *wanted* me to follow him here."

Fairon's eyes narrowed. "You operated the beacon. You would operate the torq." He rested his hands behind his back. "The prisoners—an added incentive. A chance to use your morality against you."

"You knew I'd save them. And you knew I'd save Hayden."

Fairon tilted his head. "You are so... ethical."

Eve was overwhelmed with feeling: with pain, with self-loathing, and that *god-awful ringing*. She looked back at Fairon, her eyes filled with hate.

"But I destroyed your mainframe. I destroyed the *list*."

"An unfortunate fact, yet you are on my table. The mainframe, the list: replaceable. Worthy sacrifices for your blood."

The ringing intensified until it was all Eve could hear, and soon her blackened vision began to pulse with the noise.

"I *killed* your *men*," she hissed. "You're their leader, and you let me *slaughter* them. Do you even care?" Her voice was laced with abhorrence. "You're their *leader*."

Fairon looked back at her, his face blank, almost confused. Then his lips parted, and a rich, sonorous chuckle escaped his mouth.

Eve grimaced. "You're *laughing*?"

"You think I am their leader?" he cackled. He thrust his face in front of hers. "*I am their OWNER*," he snarled. "They are *slaves*. Your strongest men struggle to defeat our most *inferior* species." He pointed at the gashes across her stomach. "Those marks on your body? The marks of *worthless creatures*."

Eve's mouth gaped. *Slaves.* The word repeated in her mind, while Fairon laughed at her ignorance. After a brief disorientation, she finally mustered the strength to speak.

"If they're just slaves, then who the hell are *you*?"

Fairon brought his lips closer to hers and bared his teeth. "*I am Fae,*" he growled. "A soldier. One of many. And if you had defeated me, you would have won but one small battle in a long and treacherous war." He backed away slowly. "But you did not defeat me."

Eve's body slumped, hanging loosely from the metal cuffs. She had been wrong. Everything she had learned from the Shelter, everything she had believed to be true, had been reduced to fiction. She thought of Fairon's words: *you know nothing.* He was right.

"Why are you doing this?"

Fairon looked back at Eve. She was staring at the floor, her head dipped as if in defeat.

"You still stall for time?"

Eve shrugged. "Maybe I'm enjoying our talk. You're a great conversationalist."

"Your questions—they are futile. But I will answer you—"

"Because you're so *goddamn merciful,*" she sneered.

"Perhaps it is good if your male comes. I will take pleasure in killing him in front of you. You will have nothing left to live for. You will submit yourself to me with ease."

"Answer. My. *Question.*"

Fairon stopped in front of her, looking into her eyes. "It is what we do."

"It's what you *do? That's* your answer?"

"We visit worlds. We procure resources. It is in the blood. We absorb what we need from the blood of a living specimen. Always living. Life—it is key." His eyes panned from her face to the gashes below her ribs. "The blood of the Earth people—it is the most beautiful we have ever seen. The color is different. *Vibrant.*" He dragged his talons along her stomach, creating three long, thin lacerations. "And you—your blood will taste delicious. Like sweet ambrosia."

Eve winced from the pain, biting her lip to prevent herself from crying out. She watched Fairon, who was staring at the blood dripping from his talons.

"So, what are you trying to procure here? The gift?"

"Everything," he answered, still gazing at his claws. "The gift—it is useful. But we've come for the strength. The health. The *immunity.*"

"But you *have* strength. You *have* health. Jesus Christ, I saw you regenerating. I *saw* it."

Eve stopped herself. Her eyes went wide.

"Oh God."

Fairon gazed back at her curiously. "You are coming to a realization."

Eve hesitated. "You melted," she finally said. "In my room, the day you took Madison's key—you *melted.*" She looked back at Fairon, shocked. "The melting, the regenerating... you've *already* figured it out, haven't you?"

Fairon grinned, pleased by her discovery. He brought his hand to his lips, and a long, forked tongue slid between his teeth and licked at the blood along his talons. He turned toward the distant shelf, his eyes locking onto the sharp blade, and it levitated into the air, gliding through the room until it stopped in front of him. He looked at Eve and laughed.

"The melting—it was no accident. You would think me of your kind. You would pity me. Then, when I deemed it so, you would save me." The blade hovered above the ground, and Fairon stared into Eve's horrified eyes. "*Never underestimate your enemy*—you said that once. Did you underestimate me, Evelyn?"

Fairon abruptly grabbed the blade and sliced it across his own arm, severing his hand at the wrist. Immediately, his yellowed stump began to bubble and expand, quickly reshaping until a new hand appeared in its place.

"Pairing the chimera strength and immunities with our own renders us all-powerful. Indestructible." He stared down at his new, perfectly formed hand, and released his grip on the blade, letting it float in the air for a while longer until it abruptly fell to the ground. With a glower, he plucked the blade off of the floor.

"Alas, it is temporary," he explained. "The gift, the restoration. That is why *you* are here: permanence." He looked back at Eve. "You are the strongest of your kind. There is something inside of you—something in your blood—that will grant us permanence. That will make us immortal—make us gifted, like you. Forever."

"And what if there isn't?" Eve snapped. "What if my blood is just as useless and *impermanent* as the rest of them?"

"YOU WILL GIVE US WHAT WE WANT!" Fairon pushed his blade against her neck. "I will *open* you, I will *study* you, and I will *drain* you until *I have what I want.* It will take time. It will take research. But I will find it in your blood. Only then will you die. And all the others—they will die too." He dragged his lips toward her ear. "Your annihilation will be our salvation. We will be *GODS.*"

He pulled away from her, admiring his weapon once more. Eve took in a shallow breath; her eyes were pointed at the ground, her gaze distant and foggy. She could still hear the ringing in her ears, the sound so acute now that she felt its resonance down the nape of her neck, and as it intensified, her vision grew hazy, spotted with patches of black.

Fairon looked down at his blade and again at Eve. "I have told you what you want to know. It is time to begin."

Still Eve gazed at the ground, too weary to look him in the eye. Fairon took a step toward her and cocked his chin.

"You are not going to beg? You are not going to plead for me to spare you?"

"Would it work?" she muttered.

"No. It would not."

"Then why bother?"

He chuckled. "You remind me of your male. I was told he did not beg. But when we carved into his chest, his scream could have woken the dead." He ran the side of his blade along her stomach, sending a chill through her body. "They all scream eventually. You will too, Evelyn. I promise you this."

Eve ignored him, still concentrating on the torturous ringing, on her blurred vision that faded from light to darkness. Fairon gestured toward the entrance of the room.

"Your male did not come. You waited for nothing."

He took a step back and raised his blade, pointing its tip at the center of her stomach. He paused, savoring the moment, soaking in the sight of his victim—she was drained, her body torn and broken, her eyes hardly open. Then, with a triumphant smile, he thrust his blade forward.

The blade stopped, halting inches from her stomach, as if blocked by an invisible wall. Fairon looked down at the tool and then at Eve, who was suddenly staring back at him, her eyes fierce and no longer weary.

"I wasn't waiting for my male, *dumbass*," she hissed. "I was trying to *melt*."

Fairon's eyes darted across Eve's body. He could see that she was shaking, her back taut, her forehead wrinkled. He leaned on the blade, pushing it forward with all his strength, but still it didn't budge. He laughed.

"Your gift is strong. You impress me. Still, you will tire. And when you do, I will have your blood."

"You'd be surprised by how stubborn I can be," Eve panted, her voice labored.

She locked her gaze on the blade, willing it to obey her. Her entire being was overwhelmed with a pain so magnified she was convinced it was more torturous than anything Fairon could possibly do to her. But still she melted, channeling what little remained of her gift, holding the sinister blade at bay.

Just as she sensed the slightest hint of power within her, she felt something wet dripping down her upper lip. *Sweat*, she thought to herself, but then she tasted it: warm and metallic. A tremor of fear raced through her. *Blood.*

Fairon stared at her bloody nose and grinned.

"Your gift is stifled. You are weak." His nostrils wiggled excitedly. "Your redness—it comes much quicker than you are accustomed to. It is beautiful to see."

Eve could feel the blood gushing from her nostrils and see it splattering onto the ground beneath her—bright red puddles, so much more blood than she had anticipated. For a moment, her hearing became muffled—she thought it a blessing, that it would suppress the insufferable ringing—but the noise grew louder, and hot, crimson blood began to trickle from her ears.

Fairon scowled. "You still push yourself?" He forced even more of his weight onto his blade, but it didn't move. "You are *wasting blood*."

"It's my blood. I'll do whatever the hell I want with it."

"You will *kill yourself*," he snarled.

"And what a shame that would be, since you need me alive." Her eyes flitted from the blade to Fairon. "That's what you said, right? *Life* is the key."

Fairon gripped his blade even tighter, his fists now shaking. "You are willing to kill yourself just to *thwart* me?"

"I certainly don't *want* to die," she answered. "But I also don't want you to annihilate my species. And call me bitter, but I have a personal problem with you, and I just really, *really* want to see you fail."

Suddenly, she choked; blood sprayed from her mouth and spilled to the ground like red raindrops. Still she delved deeper into her melt, and all the while Fairon's eyes flitted between his blade, her stomach, and her flowing blood.

"Your entire planet *abhors* you," he barked. "They *mock* your existence. And you will *die* to save them?"

"It's a tough call, but I guess I'm going with the greater good on this one. You'll kill me eventually anyway. At least now, my death will have a purpose. My death will save *billions*."

Fairon could see the conviction in her eyes. He grabbed the blade with both hands, pushing with all of his might, and yet still it didn't move. His body began to quiver with fury.

"TU KATH KALLAS!" he roared. "TU KATH CHIMERA!"

Eve stared into Fairon's eyes—eyes now consumed with wrath, humiliation, and hatred. She smiled, her teeth pink with her own blood.

"*Fuck* you, Fairon."

The moment was satisfying but fleeting. She instantly remembered the ringing, the sound alone like needles piercing through her brain. Her arms and shoulders trembled, and her eyes were so focused that she swore she was seeing things—the haze of black was punctuated with crimson, and soon she realized that blood was dripping from her tear ducts.

Still she melted, until her cheeks, her lips, and her chin were all stained red; until the blood was trickling down her neck, between her breasts, and across her stomach, where it soaked into the waistband of her pants. The ringing was palpable, like a wrecking ball pounding against the walls of her skull, but she melted despite all of it—she melted, because suffering was better than defeat.

Soon the pain was so unbearable that she couldn't help but scream, her eyes clenched shut as she endured the torment. She screamed louder, though she hardly noticed it—she was consumed by the ringing, the loudest, most excruciating sound she had ever heard. And suddenly, the moment was punctuated by something else, something soft and familiar: a voice.

"Oh God."

Eve opened her eyes. Jason was standing in the doorway, his face drained of all color.

Suddenly a new pain tore through her, ripping deep into her gut and spreading through her body. She looked down at her stomach—at the silver blade now lodged in her flesh.

She had lost her melt.

Jason's eyes widened. "EVE!" he cried.

Fairon looked over his shoulder at Jason, at his appalled expression and the axe in his hand. With one quick movement, Fairon yanked the blade from Eve's stomach. She cried out in agony, and Jason screamed her name once more.

Blood crawled down Eve's abdomen, slowly oozing from the open wound. She looked down at the gash and then up at Fairon, who was holding his blade close to his lips.

"Good." He nodded in Jason's direction. "Now you can watch him die."

Without another word, he ran his tongue along the blade, lapping up every last drop of blood from its surface. He turned to Jason and grinned, his golden fangs now smeared with red, and Jason's body became rigid with hate. Eve knew what would happen next. She wanted to scream in protest, but the words failed to escape her lips, and she watched in horror as Jason barreled toward Fairon.

Suddenly, Jason was ripped from the ground and soared through the room, his arms flailing wildly until he slammed, hard, into the back wall. He fell to the floor, his body riddled with breaks and tears, each one providing its own hellish torture. Reluctantly, he looked up at Fairon. The Interloper's back was straight, his stance stately, and in his eyes was a look of crazed intoxication. The alien had *melted* him—Jason knew it was true, and yet he couldn't believe it.

As he tried to make sense of the situation, he caught sight of Eve, hanging from the table, her body limp and her face covered in blood. An immediate rage flowed through him, and he pulled himself to his feet and sprinted in Fairon's direction once more.

Again, Jason's body was flung across the room, crashing against the wall and toppling to the ground. He groaned; a sharp pang shot through his chest, and he could feel broken ribs pulling at his skin. He coughed for air, struggling to normalize his breathing and ignore the aching of his body, but before he could even begin to recover, the ground began to shake beneath him.

Fairon was headed in his direction, his pounding footsteps moving at a slow, sinister pace. He stopped at Jason's side, hovering right above him.

Jason hoisted himself to his hands and knees, wincing in pain, and Fairon laughed at his expense.

"Your bones—they break with ease. They crumble at my *will*."

Just as Jason staggered to his feet, Fairon backhanded him across the jaw, sending him collapsing to the floor for a third time. Fairon's laughter became an uproar, and Jason faltered along the ground, his hands shaking as he struggled to lift his battered body.

Then Jason spotted it: his axe, lying only a few feet away. Wrath boiled inside of him, and with a growl, he grabbed the weapon, jumped to his feet, and swung the blade at Fairon's throat, severing his head from his shoulders.

Jason took a step back. He eyed Fairon's headless body, expecting it to drop to the ground, but it remained upright and unyielding. A yellowish bubbling foamed at the neck, seething until the surrounding skin became waxy and pliant. Black, glossy bone sprouted from the bloodied stump, shaping itself into a narrow jaw and a large, rounded skull, and then a web of flesh climbed across its surface, lining the entire exterior with tissue. Finally, two golden horns protruded from the creamy head, growing like the branches of a tree. In a matter of seconds, it was over: Jason stared in disbelief at Fairon's regenerated face.

Fairon studied the axe in Jason's grasp. A smile graced his lips, and he flicked his wrist, tearing the axe from Jason's hand and causing it to hover in the air. Fairon rotated the weapon with his melt, examining its diamond blade and polished handle—the grip made entirely of Interloper bone—and then, with a sneer, he hurled the axe in Jason's direction.

Jason dove to the ground, dodging the axe at the last possible second. Fairon lunged toward him, his own blade in hand, and though Jason dipped and swerved around the weapon, each jab was sharper and closer than the last. Someone was going to die—Jason could feel it in his gut—and no matter how many times he told himself otherwise, he knew it would most likely be him.

Again Fairon leapt in his direction, and with a deep breath, Jason pressed himself against the wall and melted the Interloper from the floor, sending him smashing into the opposite side of the room.

Fairon landed on his feet with a thunderous boom that shook the entire space. He glanced at his torn shoulders, watching with satisfaction as the lesions quickly faded, and then he roared triumphantly. Jason scrambled toward his axe, yanking its blade from the wall, and just as he turned to face his adversary once more, he abruptly lurched into the air, dropping the weapon to the floor.

Jason floated weightlessly above the ground, trying to break Fairon's hold, but his attempts were fruitless. Resigned, he watched and waited as Fairon approached him, his steps slow and regal, until they were finally face to face. Fairon cocked his head.

"Your gift is strong." He smirked as he surveyed Jason's body, stopping at his scar. "But not as strong as your female's. Not strong enough to be of any use to me."

With a nod, Fairon sent Jason hurtling across the room and smashing face-first into the ground. Eve screamed in horror; Jason's cheek was buried in the dirt, his body crumpled, limp, and still.

The room was quiet. Fairon made his way to Jason's side, lingering over him as if waiting for something to happen, but Jason remained motionless. Eve whimpered. *Please move*, she thought to herself. *Move, Jason. Goddammit, MOVE.*

And still, there was nothing.

Then suddenly, Jason's arm shot out from beneath his body, his palm pointed at Fairon, and the alien hurtled across the room, smashing into the back wall so hard that the clay cracked and splintered. Just as Fairon began to hoist himself to his feet, the fragmented wall disintegrated, spilling atop his body in chunks and pinning him to the ground. Jason ended his melt, immediately clambering to his feet and racing toward Eve, undeterred by his limp and the blood spilling from his scalp. He stopped in front of her and cupped her cheeks.

"*Eve.*" He examined her frantically. "Eve, stay with me. I'm getting you the hell out of here."

Eve's eyelids fluttered, her attention split between Jason and the incessant ringing. "The disks," she answered, weakly.

"What?"

"On my head," she mumbled, shutting her eyes. "The disks. Take them *off.*"

Jason tugged at the two metal disks, snapping them off with little effort and tossing them to the floor. Instantly the ringing in Eve's head disappeared, her mind cleared, and she took in a long, much needed breath. She opened her eyes, this time with ease, and nodded at the base of the table.

"There's a wheel on the ground, beneath the table," she said, her voice strong and whole. "Turn the wheel."

Jason crouched down and spun the wheel until all four cuffs unlocked. He hopped to his feet and began unfastening each shackle, his hands racing and his eyes filled with panic. Finally, he pulled the last cuff from her wrist, and Eve collapsed into his arms, too worn and frail to stand on her own.

"You're going to be okay, Eve." He pulled her to his chest. "I've got you."

Just as the words left his lips, Jason was yanked in the opposite direction, his body ripped from Eve's and thrown once more into the wall. Eve fell to the floor and groaned, debilitated by the shooting pain that coursed through her. She lifted her chin, a struggle in itself, and stared at Jason, who was lying on the opposite side of the room, gazing up at the newly freed and fast approaching Fairon.

Jason dragged his body through the dirt, trying to escape Fairon, though his efforts were clearly futile. The creature was only paces behind him, toying with him, his head tilted in an inquisitive and almost irritated manner. Jason's eyes panned across the room—he spotted Eve, and then he noticed his axe just a few feet away—and he turned his attention back to Fairon, who was now looming over him ominously.

"This has gone on long enough," Fairon declared. He nodded at Eve. "She has witnessed your suffering. She has seen you bleed. It is time to end things." He crouched low to the ground, bringing himself to Jason's eye level. "I grant you one final act of mercy: a choice." He leaned in closer. "How would you like to *die*?"

Jason grimaced, his lips trembling with disgust. *"Go to hell."*

Fairon scowled. "You choose not to answer. A foolish decision."

Without warning, Jason grabbed his axe and swung it at the creature's face, but Fairon swerved to the side, dodging the diamond blade. Jason quickly scrambled to his feet, wielding his axe with as much strength as he could muster, but still Fairon was untouched; he easily ducked and dipped between the jabs, seemingly entertained by his opponent's pitiful display.

Just as Jason took another swing, Fairon melted the axe from his grasp and guided it into his own palm. He stared at Jason, grinning maniacally, and snapped the handle between his talons, tossing the pieces to the ground. Then, with a single, powerful movement, Fairon struck Jason with his wing and sent him toppling over.

Eve watched helplessly as Jason's bloodstained face smacked against the ground. Jason pulled himself to his hands and knees, and Eve tried to do the same—she pushed at the ground, shrieking in pain as her broken wrist collapsed beneath her. Again she pressed at the floor, this time with her good hand, and a river of blood poured from the gash in her gut. Eve faltered, dropping to the ground once more. She caught a glimpse of Jason, who was battling Fairon with the little strength he had remaining, and then her vision went dark, fading underneath a hazy black fog.

Jason's neck swung to the side, his head throbbing from the force of Fairon's blow. He stumbled, barely managing to stay on his feet, and just as he turned toward Fairon, he was greeted with the tip of his long silver blade. Staggering backward, he melted the blade from Fairon's hands, sending it skidding across the ground.

Fairon growled and reached a clawed hand toward the weapon as if to summon it back into his possession. The blade teetered in place, floated up from the dirt—and then it stopped, wobbled, and fell to the floor with a clang.

Fairon's eyes shrank to slits. Again he thrust his hand forward, and again the blade did not move. He turned back to Jason, who stared at him in shock, his gaze flitting between his alien foe and the fallen blade.

Then, without a second thought, Jason melted the creature from his feet and rammed him against the wall.

Fairon pulled himself upright and quickly glanced over his shoulders, now marked with fresh lesions and tears, all failing to heal. He looked back at Jason, who waited at the opposite end of the room, his frame lopsided and his arms covered in pink abrasions, but his gaze was lit with confidence. Fairon smiled.

"There is hope in your eyes." He walked calmly in Jason's direction. "Still, you will fail. Our rise is foretold. You cannot stop us. And you cannot kill me."

"No one is invincible. Not even you," Jason said. "You can be killed."

Fairon sneered. "Yes, but not by *you*. Not by *your kind*."

Fairon bolted into the air, beating his wings before diving down toward Jason like a flash of white light. Jason slid to the ground and rolled away from the creature, and with his hands thrust forward, he melted Fairon up toward the ceiling and then sent him smashing into the ground below.

The entire room shook from the impact. Eve could feel bits of clay sprinkling along her back, barely discernible over the sting of her gut, but she kept her gaze focused on the fight in front of her.

Fairon climbed to his feet and turned to Jason. His flesh was dripping with pus, and a single, brass-colored bone protruded from his chest, but he maintained his air of cold indifference. Before Jason could delve further into his melt, Fairon swatted him with his wing, knocking him to the floor without care or concern. Jason pulled himself upright only for Fairon to backhand him across the jaw, and again Jason tumbled to the ground.

A deep, throbbing pain coursed through Jason's body. He glanced across the room, first at Fairon and then at Eve, whose eyes were pointed fiercely in his direction. She was bloody and beaten, her body shaking, and the vision alone sent a swell of adrenalized anger flooding through him. With a hateful roar, Jason bolted from the ground and hurled himself at Fairon, swinging his fists as if heedless of the consequences.

Fairon dipped and weaved between his jabs, smiling almost tauntingly, but still Jason continued, overcome by rage. He pounded his fist against Fairon's nostrils, and though his knuckles tore and bled from the impact, he was numb to the pain. Again, he punched the creature, and again, and each blow felt more satisfying than the last.

But Fairon merely cocked his head, bemused, seemingly unaffected by the beating. And as Jason lunged at him once more, he dipped to the ground, plucked his blade from the dirt, and thrust it deep into Jason's leg.

Jason howled, staggering away from Fairon and clutching his wounded thigh. Slowly, he removed his hands—they were covered in blood, the vision so ominous that he hardly noticed the shaking of his palms. Again Fairon dove in his direction, swiping his blade across Jason's stomach and then his chest, creating two deep cuts that sprayed bright red blood.

Jason fell back into the wall, sliding down its ashy surface and landing in a piteous pile on the ground. His eyes clenched shut; his breathing was fast and arduous, which only amplified the sting of his injuries, and he held his hands against his gashed chest and abdomen, trying to slow the bleeding.

Reluctantly, he opened his eyes; Fairon loomed over him, leaning in closely as if to examine his prey, and with one sharp movement, he grabbed Jason by the throat, pulled him from the ground, and pressed his back into the wall.

"A valiant effort," Fairon uttered flatly. "But you are incapable. Your battle was lost before it began." He leaned in closer. "*You* are not my nemesis."

Jason grabbed at Fairon's talons, struggling to pry them from his neck, but they remained locked and secure, the claws digging into his skin. He tried to melt, but instead a spurt of blood shot from his nostrils and dribbled down his face. Fairon raised his blade, slowly sliding the sharp edge up Jason's leg and across his stomach before finally positioning the tip directly over his heart. He gazed at Jason's scar, his eyes lit with a perverse hunger, and then plunged the blade into Jason's chest.

Jason's hands sprang to action, flattening around either side of the blade and forcing it still just as the tip pinched at his skin.

Fairon glanced at his weapon and at Jason's hands, and he chuckled.

"You fight to live?" He pushed on the blade, grinding it into Jason's chest. "Your death is fated. You cannot stop it. You fight for *nothing*."

Jason stared at the blade, watching as it slowly and painfully pierced his skin. A raw power pulsed through him, one he had felt before, but he knew it wasn't enough. Fairon was stronger than him, and though he had been able to slow the blade's progress, his arms were shaking so vigorously that the weapon began to do the same. The tip of the blade slid deeper into his flesh, and with no other options, Jason wrapped his fingers around the sharpened metal, using all of the strength he could summon to force the knife still.

Blood spilled from Jason's hands, trickling between his knuckles and coating his fingers. Fairon stared at the liquid, and a grin spread across his lips.

"Do you feel that?" His eyes met Jason's. "The *pain* in your body. In your shattered bones. In the blood that pours from your opened flesh. That sensation—that *feeling*—it is your *weakness*. It is your human fragility." He brought his lips to Jason's ear. "*FEEL IT.*"

Jason looked down at his bloodied hands, which were slowly slipping along the blade. He could feel the metal tip digging past his ribs, could see the blood seeping through his shirt. He gritted his teeth, trying to block out the competing torture of his throat, his hands, his wounded leg, and now his chest, focusing only on the power within him.

Though he stared at the blade, he could still see Fairon's victorious smile out of the corner of his eye. Jason knew what Fairon was doing—that he was taking his time, that he was *enjoying* the anticipation, and that the only reason he was still alive was for Fairon's twisted amusement. And though Jason could feel adrenaline flowing within him, he knew he couldn't withstand Fairon's force for much longer.

He was going to die.

A strange noise interrupted the moment: a soft cracking, like the sound of ice splitting along a frozen lake. A long, thin break spread through the blade, starting at the handle and climbing to the tip, splintering every which way until the entire weapon shattered into tiny pieces.

Jason's hands fell to his sides. He gazed, stunned, at the shards of metal, and then at Fairon, whose eyes were filled with something unfamiliar: confusion. *Fear.*

Another noise caught Jason's attention—a steady rumbling—and he noticed flecks of gold falling from above. Fairon's horns were dissolving, crumbling into tiny fragments, until all that remained were two pathetic stumps.

A loud crack echoed in Jason's ears as Fairon's talons shattered into pieces, disintegrating around Jason's neck and spilling down his chest. Frantically, Fairon released Jason and stared at his hands, watching in horror as his once daunting talons became mere piles of rubble.

Jason slumped against the wall, struggling to catch his breath, though not once tearing his gaze from Fairon. And just when he thought that the spectacle had ended, Fairon's eyes bulged with a new terror—his lips were spreading apart, slowly expanding, as if pried open by invisible hands.

Fairon grabbed at his jaw, trying to force it closed, but his mouth opened even wider, until the corners of his lips ripped and each and every one of his fangs was exposed. Suddenly, his jaw snapped into place, and after a brief stillness, a tooth popped from his gums; then another tooth fell, and then another, and soon all of his teeth were springing from his mouth and clinking against the ground like golden hail until his mouth was completely empty.

Jason stared up at Fairon in disbelief. The creature was practically unrecognizable, his most formidable features reduced to broken bits, his face ravaged and barren. Jason's gaze darted from Fairon's panicked eyes to his opened mouth, and he immediately spotted the small, pink life source sitting at the back of his throat. Suddenly, Fairon whimpered—he batted at his neck, as if trying to fight something within him, and then his groans turned into horrified howls.

Jason's eyes widened. The life source was swelling like an inflating balloon, growing so large that it tugged at the lining of his throat. Fairon fell to his knees, his wailing sharp and raspy, and before Jason could even absorb what was happening, Fairon's life source exploded, spewing gobs of flesh and blood in every direction.

Fairon collapsed to the ground, limp and broken.

Dead.

Jason froze. He stared at Fairon, at his lifeless body and the pieces of metal, bone, and teeth scattered across the ground, and his thoughts swirled with shock. It was impossible—everything he had just seen was beyond comprehension—and as he tried to consider the possibilities, it hit him.

He immediately turned to Eve. She was lying on the floor, her body trembling, her arm outstretched, and her eyes locked on Fairon, still channeling her melt. Then, after a second of silence, her arm dropped and her head collapsed to the ground, landing with a hard slap in the redness that surrounded her.

The pool of blood.

"EVE!" Jason cried. He ran toward her, sliding through the sticky pile and then kneeling at her side. He flipped her onto her back and instantly felt ill: her cheeks, chest and abdomen were saturated with blood, the gash in her stomach still oozing. Jason quickly pressed one hand against the wound and shook Eve with the other, urging her to open her eyes.

"EVE!" he repeated. "EVE, LOOK AT ME!"

Slowly, her eyes fluttered open. She stared at Jason, who seemed to be moving in slow motion, his figure hazy and dim. She tried to reach out and touch him, but her arm refused to budge. Jason was shouting—she could only vaguely hear him—and though she wanted to speak, she said nothing. Finally, a wave of exhaustion hit her, one so powerful, so *peaceful*, that she couldn't help but comply. With one last, shaky breath, Eve gazed up at Jason—his skin was pale, his voice now completely inaudible—and closed her eyes.

"EVE?" Jason screamed. "EVE!"

He shook her shoulders, this time much more aggressively, but still she didn't move. His eyes flitted from her face to her hand, once open and trembling and now limply curled at her side. His heart pounded in his throat.

"Oh my God. No," he stammered. He cupped her face. "EVE? Oh my God, EVE!"

Jason pushed at the center of her chest once, twice, over and over again, until he felt a rib snap beneath his hands. He tilted her chin back and breathed into her mouth, pausing for a moment to see if her chest had risen, which it did, and then he breathed once more. Again he pushed at her chest, and again he filled her lungs, but Eve was still motionless, and her eyes remained shut. Jason anxiously scanned her body, running his bloody hands through his hair.

"No... NO..."

An intense heat coursed through him, boiling so severely that his entire body began to shake. He stared down at Eve for what felt like hours, and the most horrible combination of feelings enveloped him: desperation, helplessness, and rage. His breathing became heavy, his lungs pounding in his chest with such force that he felt as if they could break past his ribcage, and soon his entire being was lit with a fire, one that took hold of him and urged him to obey—to act.

Jason scooped Eve up in his arms and bolted from the room, sprinting with as much speed as he could rally. The pain of his broken bones and gaping wounds was smothered beneath a deep burning, one that fueled him to run faster. Eve flopped limply in his grasp, her head slumped forward and her body bobbing against his chest, and he gripped her tighter. He flew through the lair, past the long series of portals and into the massive closet, swerving around the alien corpses that littered his path.

Time was of the essence, and soon all he could see was the path before him, and all he could feel was his own feverish power. As he sped past the crematorium, a hint of hope crept through him: he could see the light of the outside world ahead of him, and with one last surge of strength, he burst through the exit and barreled onto the busy Calabasas sidewalk.

Shrieks sounded all around him, but Jason didn't notice. He shoved through the throng of bodies, as packs of people had gathered around the alien lair, and forced his way toward Percy's car.

Percy was sitting in the driver's seat. JJ was flopped beside him, her feet resting on the dash, and Sancho was nestled between the two, anxiously peering out of the windshield. As the back door opened behind them, they all flinched in unison.

"Jesus, way to be inconspicuous, Jason," JJ muttered.

They turned to Jason, only to find him plopping Eve's limp body across the bench seats.

Percy's eyes widened. "*Holy shit—*"

"The medical ward!" Jason ordered. "NOW!"

"Is she covered in *blood*?" Sancho gasped.

"I said *NOW!*"

Percy slammed on the gas, sending the car charging forward and his passengers lurching in their seats. He glanced back and forth between the road and Jason, who was squatting on the floor, steadying Eve's body.

"What the hell happened to you?" he spat. "What the hell happened to *Eve?*"

"She exhausted her gift."

"*What?*" JJ shrieked.

"She's dying."

"Oh God," Sancho murmured.

"She's *dying?*" Percy repeated.

Sancho stuttered, "How is this possible?"

"It's *not* possible," JJ cut in. "Eve is a pro. She has *total* control of her gift—"

"All of you, just *SHUT UP*," Jason barked. "There's no time to explain."

"Did Fairon do this to her?" JJ persisted.

"Oh my God, it was Fairon, wasn't it?" Sancho moaned. "Did he follow you? Is he coming after us?"

"He's not coming after us," Jason growled.

"How do you know that?"

"Because he's DEAD."

"He's dead?" Sancho wrinkled his nose. "How—"

Suddenly, the car became quiet. JJ, Sancho, and Percy exchanged glances, each of them wearing the same bleak expression. They looked back at Eve, at the bloodstains along her cheeks, neck, and chin, and in an instant, it was more than clear what had happened. Jason breathed into Eve's mouth and pushed at her chest, and upon noticing his comrades' silence, he turned to face them once more.

"Look, she doesn't have much time."

"Well, that's a problem, because we're in rush-hour traffic, and it's going to take us at *least* a half hour to get back to Billington," Percy said.

"She doesn't *have* a half hour, Percy."

"Mother of balls, she's going to die," Sancho whimpered. "She's going to die right here in *Percy's car.*"

"She's not dying in this car," JJ insisted, pulling her scratchpad onto her lap. "And it's not going to take us a half hour to get to Billington."

Her hands flew across the screen, sorting through maps and satellite images of nearby roads. Sancho hovered over her shoulder, watching as she worked.

"What are you doing?"

"Finding a shortcut."

"Dynamic—the computer goddess saves the day!" Sancho beamed. "Are you going to hack the stoplights? Make 'em all turn green for us?"

"Not exactly. This may surprise you, but I'm not a secret agent, and this isn't a goddamn *movie*." JJ pulled one of her maps from the screen until it was floating in front of her in holographic form. "I'm looking for the quickest route based on current traffic conditions."

Percy rolled his eyes. "Great, my *car* can do that. Some computer goddess."

The vehicle lurched to an abrupt stop, throwing all of its passengers forward. Jason stabilized Eve and shot an angry glare in Percy's direction.

"*Goddammit*, Percy, be *careful!*"

"I can't *help* it! I *told* you there's traffic!"

"It's a parking lot up ahead. We're never going to make it." Sancho glanced at the road in front of them and then at Jason. "*Balls*, Jason, there's a *hole* in your leg!"

"Okay, everyone needs to QUIET DOWN," JJ barked, silencing her comrades in an instant. "If you want Eve to have any shot at living, you'll do as I say." She turned to Jason and nodded at Eve. "Jason, does she have a pulse?"

"Barely."

"Buckle her in. Do thirty compressions, two breaths, and repeat." She paused to make sure Jason followed her instructions, then she turned toward the driver's seat. "Percy, follow my direction. Whatever I tell you to do, *do it*. And Sancho," she shrugged, "just buckle up."

Sancho promptly scurried to the back row of the SUV, stumbling over Jason's legs and quickly buckling himself into place. JJ took one last look at Percy, whose stare was focused intently on the congestion ahead.

"You ready?"

Percy nodded, and JJ took in a deep, calming breath.

"Okay. Reverse."

"*Reverse?*" he repeated.

"That's what I said."

"You're not serious, are you?"

"There's an intersection behind us," Sancho added, looking over his shoulder out the rear window.

"Reverse, and don't stop until I say so," JJ repeated.

"We'll get hit!" Percy protested.

"I *said*, REVERSE!"

Percy yanked at the gearstick and pounded on the gas, sending his car speeding backward through the intersection. The sounds of horns blaring and brakes screeching sounded through the car, but Percy continued, keeping his foot on the pedal and wildly spinning the steering wheel as he tried to evade the obstacles in his path. Jason clung to Eve's body, Sancho gripped at his armrests, and JJ kept her eyes on the map in front of her.

"STOP!" she shouted.

The car skidded to an abrupt halt. Sancho let out a long, relieved sigh.

"Balls, that made my butt cheeks pucker up," he muttered.

Percy's shoulders hunched. They were sitting in the center of a busy street, surrounded by honking cars and angry drivers with their middle fingers in the air. JJ cocked her head at a side street.

"Sharp left, *now.*"

Percy obeyed, veering down the narrow road as quickly as he could manage. The atmosphere in the SUV had become tense and frantic: Sancho was anxiously bouncing in his seat, Jason continued to shove at Eve's chest, and Percy tightly gripped his steering wheel, but JJ was blind to the ensuing anxiety and kept her eyes focused on her hologram.

"Left again," she ordered.

Percy swerved the SUV around the corner and growled under his breath. "*Jesus,* JJ, a little warning would be nice."

"Turn right, and *punch it,*" she added, ignoring his complaint.

Percy sighed and spun the car down the side street, rolling his eyes at the echo of car horns and curse words that faded into the distance. A trail of sweat lined his forehead; he glanced at his speedometer—he was going triple the speed limit—and then he looked back at Eve, whose bloody arm was dangling over the side of the bench seat. With his brow furrowed, he faced the road and put all of his weight on the gas pedal.

JJ nodded at an upcoming intersection. "Left," she commanded.

"*Left?*" Percy asked, shooting her a perplexed stare. "It's a one-way street."

"I told you I'd find a shortcut."

"A shortcut that will get us all *killed*?" he snapped.

JJ bit her lip with annoyance. "Turn left, Percy."

"JJ—"

"TURN LEFT!"

At the last possible second, Percy yanked at the steering wheel, sharply spinning into oncoming traffic. Jason toppled across the floor, and Sancho and JJ awkwardly lurched back and forth in their seats, but still Percy plowed ahead, staring in horror at the line of vehicles in front of them. Some dodged him with ease, while others swerved into neighboring lanes and barreled onto the sidewalk, and Percy jerked his steering wheel from left to right, desperately trying to maneuver his way through the chaos.

"OH MY GOD!" he cried.

Sancho clutched at his armrests. "Oh shit oh shit oh shit OH SHIT—"

"Jesus *Christ*, calm down!" JJ shouted.

"Calm *down*?" Percy barked. "There are cars HURTLING toward us, and you want us to *CALM DOWN*?"

"Need I remind you that you just got through battling *aliens*, and yet you're scared of a little *oncoming traffic*?" JJ hissed.

Without another word, JJ grabbed at the steering wheel and spun it to the side, quickly veering the car down one of the main city roads.

Percy relaxed into his seat, but only for a moment—a chorus of sirens sounded in the distance, and he turned to see a line of police cars following behind him.

"Shit," he groused. "We've got pigs on our ass."

JJ peered around her seat, first taking note of the fast-approaching police and then staring down at Eve. Jason was breathing into her mouth, his movements frenzied, and she could see that, beneath the streaks of blood, Eve's skin was completely white. JJ turned to Percy once more.

"Don't stop," she ordered, firmly.

"Guys," Jason added, finally ending his silence, "her pulse is getting weaker."

"Keep going." JJ's voice was strong and assured, but her scratchpad was now shaking in her hands. She pointed at a nearby junction. "Percy, LEFT."

"It's not working." Jason shoved at Eve's chest, this time more aggressively, and pressed his fingers against her neck. "God*dammit*, it's not *working*!"

JJ's heart began to race; she eyed her map and glanced at Percy. "Turn right."

"It's another one way street, JJ!" he cried.

"For Christ's sake, Percy, do what she says!" Jason snapped.

Percy swerved down the neighboring street, once again launching the car directly into the mayhem. The street was packed with cars, all headed in their direction. The blaring of horns and the screeching of brakes rang through the SUV so loudly that he could hardly hear the police sirens.

A crash sounded behind them; Percy ignored it, instead slamming on the gas and plowing even faster into the thick of oncoming traffic, veering to the right around a sports car and to the left around a minivan. And just when he thought the worst was over, a semi truck suddenly appeared before him.

"TRUCK!" JJ screamed.

"WE'RE GONNA DIE!" Sancho wailed.

"OH MY GOD!" Percy shouted.

He swung his steering wheel in a circle, spinning his SUV into the opposite lane with so much force and speed that it skidded out of control. Time froze—the smell of smoke and rubber pervaded the car, as did the sound of squealing tires and shrill screams. JJ and Sancho whipped to the side, their bodies slapping against their seatbelts, and Eve's limp figure came to life, jerking forward and then collapsing against the bench seat. Jason was thrown from the floor and smashed against the car door, but Percy remained steady, clinging to his steering wheel with his eyes shut and mouth open, producing a long, infinite howl that harmonized perfectly with the sheer pandemonium of the moment.

The car screeched to a stop, and an unfamiliar silence filled the space. Percy's breathing was labored, his eyes bulging as he stared at the somewhat open road in front of him. JJ sat at his side, her cool demeanor stripped away, replaced by an obvious state of shock.

She shimmied her shoulders, as if to shake off the experience, and peered through the rear window. The semi truck was long gone, and instead a sea of smoke, tar, and metal scraps sat behind them. The police cars were now strewn wildly about the road, most in minor fender benders, and the officers congregated in the street, examining the damage. JJ turned to Percy and forced a shrug.

"See?" she said. "No more pigs. Happy?"

Percy leaned on the gas, still trying to calm his breathing. He pulled onto the highway and glanced back at the other passengers.

"Is everyone okay?" He turned to Jason. "Jason, are you okay?"

Jason was already hovering over Eve's body, once again pounding at her chest. "Just keep driving," he spat.

"I'll take that as a yes." Percy glanced at the back row. "Sancho?"

Sancho didn't respond. He sat completely still, his lips slightly parted and eyes vacant.

"I think he needs a minute," JJ muttered.

The group continued down the road, the interior of the car finally quiet aside from Jason's grunting. Soon the remnants of the Billington gates were visible in the distance, surrounded by a cloud of thinning smoke. A sense of relief flooded over JJ, though it was quickly accompanied by something else—an unsettling dread.

"Jason, just so we're clear," she began, "when we show up at the ward, we're going to be arrested. You know this."

Jason didn't bother to meet JJ's gaze. Instead, he glanced at the speedometer.

"Faster," he commanded.

JJ nodded. "That's what I thought."

"It's fine," Percy interjected. "We survived Billington, we'll survive prison."

"I like orange," Sancho croaked, finally ending his silence.

Percy peeled onto the Billington grounds and pulled alongside the medical ward entrance. The entire campus was still in a state of disarray—debris littered the pathways, and entire landmarks had been reduced to rubble—but the foursome paid no attention as they charged into the ward. Immediately they were immersed in a new chaos—injured students and medical personnel scrambled through the lobby—but Jason barreled through the crowds with Eve hanging in his arms.

"WE NEED A DOCTOR, NOW!"

The noise of the lobby lowered to a hum as everyone turned to stare at the two blood-soaked chimeras. A trio of nurses ran toward them—a man with sable skin and grey scrubs, and two women, one short with black hair and the other tall with freckles—gaping with shock.

"Oh my *Lord*—" the short woman gasped.

"SOMEONE GET A GURNEY!" the man ordered.

"Did this happen on campus?" the freckled nurse asked. "Were you involved in the attack?"

Jason ignored their questions and lowered Eve onto the newly arrived stretcher. "Look, none of that matters—"

"Sir, you're bleeding." The man examined his chest and leg and nodded at the corridor behind him. "We need to get you to the Emergency Room."

"Get your *hands* off of me," Jason growled.

"Sir, your wounds are serious—"

Jason grabbed at the man's shirt and pushed him away. "I *said*, get your hands OFF ME!"

The man stared wide-eyed at Jason and tugged his scrubs from his grasp. We're just trying to help you," he muttered.

Jason pointed at Eve. "You can help me by helping *her*."

"Where is all this blood coming from?" the shorter woman asked, pressing her stethoscope against Eve's chest.

"She exhausted her gift."

"Her gift?" The freckled woman paused and gazed at Jason, perplexed. "She's a chimera?"

"Look, her gift is dying, and *she's* dying," Jason cut in. "She doesn't have a lot of time. She needs a humanovus doctor. Get Dr. Dzarnoski, and get him *now*."

The man in the grey scrubs shook his head. "I can't do that, sir."

"What do you mean *you can't do that?*" Jason spat. "She needs Dr. Dzarnoski. He's the best humanovus surgeon in the country—"

"Dr. Dzarnoski isn't in the hospital."

"Well call him up and tell him to get his ass over here!"

The man hesitated. "He's on vacation."

"He's on *vacation*?" Jason barked.

"Your friend is in good hands." The man grabbed hold of the gurney. "We'll take care of her."

"Are you a humanovus doctor?"

"There are no other humanovus doctors on staff—"

"Jesus *Christ*!" Jason groaned.

The man pushed at the gurney with one arm and raised the other toward Jason. "You need to stand back, sir."

"I'm *not* leaving her."

"Sir, *stand back*."

"She's *dying*! Do you *hear me*?" Jason charged forward, his face red with frustration. "Now get her a goddamn *CHIMERA DOCTOR*!"

"SIR—"

"Patient's exsanguinating," the freckled girl interrupted, fastening a breathing mask over Eve's face. "Call the blood bank. We need to initiate a massive blood transfusion protocol. Let's get her to the ICU."

The man nodded and turned to Jason, scowling with annoyance. "Stay here."

"I *said* I'm not *leaving her*."

"Stay *here* and let us do our job."

Without another word, the threesome shoved Eve's gurney through the lobby and down the ICU corridor. Jason followed stubbornly behind with JJ,

Percy, and Sancho on his heels. The nurses wheeled Eve into a secure room, and though Jason tried to jostle his way inside, the door promptly slammed in his face.

Jason peered between the window blinds, desperate for a view of Eve, but she was surrounded by a swarm of doctors and nurses. He turned from the window, anxiously running his fingers through his hair, and just as he felt himself succumb to despair, a familiar figure scuttled down the hallway, clumsily juggling a large stack of documents.

"Armaan!"

Armaan jumped, instantly dropping his papers and sighing as they floated to the ground. He turned to Jason, gaping at the sight of his bloodied, beaten body.

"*Jason?* What—how—"

"Armaan, where the hell have you *been?*" Jason asked. "I was looking all over for you a few hours ago."

Armaan wrinkled his nose. "What are you talking about? I was here—I'm *always* here."

The sound of muffled shouting interrupted them. Armaan's eyes darted toward the noise, and through the window he could just make out Eve's body.

"Is that—" he stuttered, "is that *Eve?*"

Jason sighed. "Armaan—"

"What *happened* to her?"

"It's her gift." Jason faltered, struggling to get the words out. "She's bleeding out. She's dying."

"*Shit,*" Armaan hissed. He blushed. "Pardon my French."

Jason lowered his voice. "Look, you're Dr. Dzarnoski's assistant, right?"

"DON'T MOVE!"

Armaan and Jason spun in place, watching with chagrin as a bevy of patrolmen headed their way. Sancho, Percy, and JJ were clumped together in the distance, their jaws dropped and expressions bleak.

"PUT YOUR HANDS ON YOUR HEAD!" a patrolman shouted.

"Wait," Jason began, extending his arms as if to keep them at bay. He glanced at Armaan. "Wait, I need to talk to him—"

"PUT YOUR *HANDS* ON YOUR *HEAD!*" the patrolman repeated.

"Look, I'll cooperate, just please let me talk to him for a *second*—"

The patrolman pointed his rifle at Jason. "YOUR HANDS, NOW!"

"DAMMIT, YOU'RE NOT EVEN LISTENING TO ME!" Jason shouted.

Sancho glanced nervously between the patrolmen, Armaan, and Jason, who was slowly resting his palms behind his head, his panicked face compelling Sancho to act. He inched out of the patrolmen's line of vision, situating himself beside an artificial plant and a set of low-hanging curtains, and with as much subtlety as he could muster, he pointed his flamethrower at the plant and delicately tapped at the control panel. A sharp burst of fire spread across the faux leaves and up the drapery, and Sancho scurried toward the line of patrolmen and cleared his throat.

"Um, guys?" he croaked. "Hey guys!" He nodded at the flickering flames and shrugged. "The building is sort of on fire."

The patrolmen froze. "Ah, *Christ*," one of them groaned, and together they raced toward the fire, scrambling to put out the flames.

Sancho took one last look at the bumbling soldiers and turned to Jason. "What are you waiting for?" He pointed to Armaan. "*Talk* to him!"

Jason nodded at Sancho and hurried to Armaan's side once more. "Dr. Dzarnoski—you work with him," he began.

Armaan bobbed his head. "Yes. Almost every day."

"So you know his practices. You've learned his procedures, read his research."

"Yeah, I guess. I mean, I tried to, when I could."

"Then how do we stop it?" Jason asked. "How do we stop her from shutting down?"

Armaan sighed. "We can't, Jason."

"There has to be *something*, Armaan."

"There isn't."

"There *is*."

"Jason—"

"*Think*, Armaan!" Jason spat. He grabbed at the boy's shoulders. "There *has* to be a way to keep her alive. There has to be a way to save her—to save her gift."

Armaan opened his mouth to speak, but stopped himself. His eyes flitted from Jason to Eve's room, and immediately his face turned pale and clammy.

"What?" Jason said. "What is it?"

Armaan hesitated. "There's been research," he explained, "about a treatment. Dzarnoski's been conducting case studies on it for months now."

"A treatment?" Jason's eyes brightened. "What, like a cure?"

"Research suggests that the gift is controlled by the pairing of the cerebellum and the temporal lobe, and thus triggering these areas may in turn galvanize the gift." Armaan lifted his hands, waving them as he spoke. "This stimulus, in theory, will energize the coordination associated with the cerebellum as well as the visual memory of the temporal lobe, and if we focus our impetus specifically on the *right* side of the brain—"

"*Armaan*, time isn't exactly on our side right now," Jason cut in.

"It's an electroconvulsive treatment. It sends an electric current to the brain, which stimulates the relevant lobes and supposedly activates the gift."

"All right, so we need to get in there and tell her doctors to do this treatment."

Armaan shook his head. "Jason, it's *highly* experimental. I mean, it's still just a theory—"

"It's worth a shot."

"We're talking about *shocking her brain*, Jason," Armaan retorted. "And this isn't some negligible electroconvulsive therapy. These are powerful, potentially *lethal* currents. And even if it *does* activate her gift, there's no way of knowing if it'll reverse the damage done to her entire system. Not to mention, all of the equipment is stored in Dzarnoski's office, which is completely locked and secure."

Jason glanced back at Eve's room. Countless doctors and nurses were hovering over her, their faces white and panic-stricken. A horrible fear ran through Jason's body, and he turned to Armaan once more.

"Whatever it takes to save her—"

"This could *kill* her, Jason. You understand that? She could *die*."

"SHE'S ALREADY DYING!" Jason barked. "Look, does she have any other options? Anything?"

Armaan paused. "No."

"Can you do it?"

Armaan did a double take. "Wait, *what*?"

"Can you do the treatment?" Jason repeated. "Can you save her?"

"Hold on—"

"If I got the equipment, could you operate it—"

"Dammit, Jason, I'm an *assistant*, not a *doctor*!" Armaan hissed.

"This is *Eve* we're talking about, Armaan!" Jason spat, his patience waning. "Do you understand? She's your *friend*, and she's *dying*." He leaned in closer, his eyes pleading for cooperation. "Now, let me ask you again: if I got the equipment, could you do it? Can you do the treatment?"

Armaan hesitated. Again he glanced down the corridor, as he could still hear the muffled commotion coming from Eve's room. He turned to Jason.

"Yes."

"Do you think it'll work?" Jason asked.

"I—" he stuttered, "I don't know. But it's the only chance she has."

"HANDS ON YOUR HEAD!"

Jason groaned. The patrolmen were once again headed his way, and he slowly placed his hands on the back of his head.

"Where's Dzarnoski's office, Armaan?" he asked.

"Jason, it's locked!"

"Just tell me where it is!"

Armaan's eyes flitted between Jason and the patrolmen. "Fourth floor, down the corridor, and on the right. Look for the small black box with two white buttons."

"No more talking," a patrolman muttered. He yanked at Jason's arms, clasping them together with metal cuffs. "Stand *still*."

As the soldier dragged Jason down the corridor, Armaan scurried behind him, stopping only at the insistence of yet another patrolman. He stood on his toes and peered around the soldier's body.

"Jason! There's one last thing!" he shouted.

Jason glanced over his shoulder. "What?"

"Get a razor!"

Jason wrinkled his brow. "A *razor*?

"Just trust me!"

"*Sit down*," the soldier sneered, plopping Jason into an empty seat at the side of the hallway. Across from him sat Percy, Sancho, and JJ, their wrists shackled and their heads dipped in defeat. The patrolman glared at the four-some. "Don't move, none of you."

"Goddamn bunch of bastards," a second patrolman muttered. He pointed at Sancho. "This one lighting the damn hospital on fire."

They sat in silence. Jason fidgeted in his seat as he gazed down the hall at the staircase in the distance. Percy glanced between the patrolmen and Jason and cocked his chin at the spot where Armaan once stood.

"What did he say?" he whispered.

"There's an office on the fourth floor—"

"NO TALKING," one of the patrolmen growled.

Jason looked at his shackles and then at Percy. "I *need* to get to that office—"

"I SAID, NO TALKING."

"You're all going to jail. You realize that, right?" another patrolman chimed in. "Police are coming right now to take you into custody." He scowled at Jason. "And if your girlfriend lives, she's going to jail, too."

Jason ignored the patrolman and stared down the hall. Eve's room was only a short distance away, but the blinds were now closed. Armaan hovered beside the door, pressing his ear against its surface, and he looked back at Jason, his face awash in fear. Anxiously, Jason looked toward the far stairwell and then at the patrolmen in front of him, each one idly pacing the corridor with a rifle in his hands.

Finally, Jason turned to Percy, and their eyes locked as if they had come to the same unspoken conclusion. Sancho observed them skeptically, and as he realized what was about to ensue, he grabbed JJ's hand and held it tightly.

Percy subtly cocked his head at the patrolman standing in front of him, and Jason clenched his fists and nodded. With a deep breath, he counted down in his head:

Three. Two. One.

Suddenly, Percy slammed his foot into the patrolman's back. The soldier lurched forward, and Jason kicked at his chin, sending him toppling to the floor. Jason winced; his leg was throbbing, and blood poured from his injured thigh, but he pushed past the pain and staggered to his feet.

Another patrolman rushed his way, and Jason swung his shackled fists at the man's face, punching him once, twice, three times, until a torrent of blood shot from his nostrils. A third patrolman lunged toward him, and Jason head-butted the soldier, who fell to the ground with a thud.

Jason turned to Percy, who was fumbling with one of the fallen rifles; he steadied the weapon and fired at Jason's cuffs, snapping the chain in two, and without a word, Jason barreled toward the stairwell.

The last patrolman standing sprinted after him, but JJ stuck out her foot and tripped him, cringing as he smacked face-first to the ground. The soldier clambered to his knees, growling, but Jason had already fled far down the hallway.

"WAIT!" he cried. "STOP RIGHT THERE!"

Jason ran even faster, his weak body now infused with adrenaline. A gunshot sounded behind him, and his entire body jerked forward, but he regained his footing and continued on ahead. Soon a torturous ache pulsed through his arm, and blood splattered onto the linoleum—he had been shot, the bullet lodged somewhere in his triceps—but the pain was masked by a tingling numbness, one that spread from his arm to the gashes on his chest and stomach, to his broken ribs and his thigh, and in that moment he felt stronger than he ever had before.

With his brow furrowed, he slammed at the stairwell door and bounded up the steps, moving so swiftly that the world around him became a blur. He passed the second floor, and then the third, and when he reached the fourth, he swung open the door and tore down the hallway.

Gasps and cries sounded up and down the hall as patients hurried away from Jason, but he was too distracted to notice. Armaan's directions repeated in his mind, and he sped down the corridors, finally stopping in front of Dzarnoski's office door.

He tugged at the handle—the office was locked, as Armaan had said it would be—and with gritted teeth, he took a step back and threw his body against the door. A sharp pain ripped through his arm and chest, but the door didn't give. Again he hurled himself into the door, and then he kicked at the handle with the sole of his boot. Jason stumbled away from the door, now gripping his profusely bleeding arm. He could feel it now—the pain of each and every one of his wounds, the blood and dirt that clung to his skin, the weakness that he was so unaccustomed to.

But just when he felt himself yielding to his own fragility, he thought of Eve, of her smile and laugh, and then he saw her pale body covered in blood. A potent resilience coursed through him, and he slammed and kicked at the door over and over until it shook at the hinges. He screamed and roared, reclaiming his pain as motivation, and at last the door cracked at the latch and swung open, smacking against the opposite wall with a loud crash.

Jason darted into the office and scanned the space. He rifled through papers and tore through cabinets, searching for a small black box with two white buttons. Finally, he spotted it—it was the size of a scratchpad cube except rectangular in shape—and he immediately grabbed it and headed for the door. Suddenly he stopped himself; he caught sight of an electric razor sitting on the end table, and again he remembered Armaan's words. With a shrug, he plucked the razor from its resting spot, plopped it into his pocket, and barreled out into the hall.

A crowd of people had gathered by the office, gaping at the belligerent chimera, but Jason plowed past them and headed for the stairwell. He flew down the steps, his boots pounding against the stairs until he finally reached the ground floor and charged through the hallway once again.

Sancho, JJ, and Percy were still seated in the waiting area, the bloodied patrolmen now aiming their rifles at them, and Armaan was pacing in front of Eve's door, his hands fidgeting nervously at his sides.

"ARMAAN!" Jason shouted.

Armaan spun toward Jason. "Wow," he breathed. "That was *really* fast—"

Jason skidded to a halt, nearly stumbling into Armaan, and promptly shoved the equipment and razor into his hands. He nodded at Eve's door.

"Get in there. Do the treatment."

Armaan reached for the handle but stopped himself. "JASON! You're shot!"

"Armaan..." Jason growled.

"You need a doctor." He gazed at Jason, his eyes wide with horror. "There's a *bullet* in your arm."

"*Do the treatment, Armaan*," Jason repeated, quietly but firmly. "And please, for the love of *God*, save her."

Suddenly, Jason felt something press against the back of his head; it was hard and narrow, like a metal pipe, and he knew it was the barrel of a gun.

"*Don't move.*"

Jason took in a long breath. He stared at Armaan, who was trembling with fear. Hesitantly, he lifted his hands into the air.

"Step away from your friend, and *slowly* turn toward me."

"Jason..." Armaan whimpered.

"It's okay," Jason insisted. "We're okay."

Jason pivoted in place until the barrel was pointed at the center of his forehead. He stared at the patrolman, whose lips and chin were dripping with blood, thanks to their earlier brawl. The soldier scowled at Jason and peered over his shoulder at the terrified Armaan.

"Kid," he barked, "move away from the door."

"Don't do it, Armaan," Jason ordered.

"I said, move *away* from the *door*."

"I've got you, Armaan." Jason lifted his chin. "Stay right where you are."

"I'm kind of getting conflicting information here, Jason," Armaan said.

A second soldier joined the group, this one just as unyielding as the first. He pointed his rifle at Armaan.

"Sir, he's holding something. Could be a weapon."

The first patrolman glared at Armaan. "Move away from the door, and hand over the weapon."

"*Don't do it,*" Jason snapped.

"STOP GIVING HIM ORDERS!"

"Armaan, do you trust me?" Jason asked.

"Um," Armaan faltered, still eyeing the two soldiers. "Yes?"

"IF YOU RESIST, I WILL BE FORCED TO SHOOT YOU," the first patrolman barked.

Jason could feel the blood trickling down his arm and dribbling onto his boot. He looked back at the soldier, and then at the line of patrolmen now assembling by his side, and while their posture was proud and steady, their eyes revealed their fear.

A muted clamor erupted behind Jason—it was the sound of doctors shouting, and it was coming from Eve's room—and again, he turned to face the patrolman before him, his gaze piercing and severe.

"Look, man, I don't want to hurt you again, I really don't." He walked forward until the rifle's barrel was pressed against his forehead. "But I will if I have to."

The patrolman wavered, and for a moment Jason could feel his gun shaking. The man bit his lip.

"I'm going to count to three."

"Oh God, he's counting to three," Armaan stuttered. "He's *counting to three.*"

"Whatever you do, Armaan, don't move until I say so," Jason instructed.

The patrolman cocked his rifle. "ONE."

"JASON!" Armaan gasped.

"DON'T MOVE," Jason repeated.

"TWO—"

Before the soldier could continue, Jason grabbed the rifle barrel and thrust it forward, pounding it into the soldier's nose with a loud crack.

In that instant, a war began—soldiers came at him from every angle, but Jason stood firm, determined to shield Armaan. He hurled his fist at the nearest soldier, punching him once in the jaw and again in the throat, and then he melted another patrolman against the wall, sending him flopping onto a row of chairs. Two more patrolmen dove toward him, and Jason quickly grabbed one by the shoulders and threw him into his comrade, sending both to the ground in a tangled heap. Out of the corner of his eye, he saw another soldier at the end of the corridor, his rifle cocked and aimed, but Jason melted the weapon from his grasp and launched it across the room. With a growl, the patrolman bolted toward him, but Jason slammed his fist into the man's temple and kicked him in the gut, sending him staggering backward and toppling to the ground.

Jason pivoted in place just in time to find one last patrolman at his side, his gun pointed at Armaan. Without hesitation, Jason ripped the weapon from the soldier's hands and smacked him across the face with the rifle's butt.

Anxiously, Jason eyed his surroundings. The first handful of soldiers were all reeling at his feet, but even more were now sprinting down the hallway, headed in his direction. He spun toward Armaan, his eyes wide and frantic.

"DO IT!" Jason yelled. "GO, NOW!"

Just as he spoke, the entire horde of patrolmen lunged at Jason, pushing him to the floor and burying him under the dog-pile. But Jason had done what he needed—he'd cleared the way for Armaan—and through the thick of limbs, he saw Armaan dart into the hospital room and slam the door behind him.

Armaan stopped beside the doorway, staring in awe at the scene in front of him. At least ten doctors and nurses congregated around Eve's body, their scrubs covered in blood and their faces dripping with sweat. A single doctor hovered over Eve, pressing the electrodes of a defibrillator against her chest.

"Clear!"

The medical team looked on in dismay as their patient convulsed with the energy and then collapsed against the table—still limp, white, and lifeless. The lead doctor sighed and stared at the cardiac monitor, which displayed nothing but a flat line and produced a long, drawn-out beep.

"Enough, guys. I'm calling it," he muttered. "Time of death, seventeen forty-three."

A lump formed in Armaan's throat. He stared at Eve—her eyes peacefully closed and her face streaked with drying blood—and a surge of determination swelled within him. He tightened his grip around his small device and shoved his way through the medical staff.

"What the—?"

"Who the hell is *this* kid?"

"Will someone remove him?"

Armaan ignored them, fighting his way to the front of the room and situating himself beside Eve's body. There was no time to waste, so he moved quickly, taking advantage of the medical team's moment of shock. He pulled

Eve's head to the side and ran the electric razor across her scalp, shaving a large, rounded strip beside her ear.

With trembling hands, he pressed at the two white buttons on his device. They promptly released themselves from the mechanism, and he situated them along the bald patch on Eve's head, where they firmly adhered to her skin. He tugged at the ends of the black box, expanding it into a large screen, which projected a holographic image: a dial with various electrical frequencies, an impulse monitor, and a flashing red button.

Hesitantly, Armaan glanced up at the medical staff—they were scuttling toward him, moving almost in slow motion—and then he spun the dial and slammed the red button.

A thunderous boom sounded through the space, one so strong that it nearly knocked Armaan from his feet. Eve's head lurched forward, and in the same instant, the doctors and nurses were flung into the air, their bodies thrown to the back of the room as if blown away by a powerful force.

Armaan remained at Eve's side, his eyes frantically darting between her and the cardiac monitor, which continued to produce the same long, steady beep. With his jaw clenched, he spun the holographic dial to a higher setting and again pushed the red button.

Another rumble ripped through the space. Eve's head jerked forward yet again, and the tangled bodies rose from the floor, floating almost demonically, only to topple back into the same piles. The lights flickered, casting an eerie darkness through the room, but Armaan paid no attention to it; he gazed at Eve, his heart racing as he searched for some sign of life, but still there was nothing.

Again he raised the voltage, and again he pressed the button.

The third boom was punctuated by the sound of broken glass; the window into the hallway shattered, and even the blinds were ripped from the paneling and fell to the floor. Through the empty window frame Armaan could see a pile of patrolmen, presumably still pinning Jason underneath them, and behind them sat Sancho, JJ, and Percy, their eyes wide with shock. Instinctively, they grabbed hold of one another and wrapped their ankles around the bolted legs of their chairs, bracing themselves for whatever was to come next.

Armaan looked back at Eve. She was motionless, and the long, incessant beep of the cardiac monitor began to gnaw at him. He spun the holographic dial to its highest setting, and just as he positioned his finger above the button, he hesitated. Uncertainty and fear crept through him, threatening to cripple his resolve. But he looked once more at Eve, wan and lifeless on the table in front of him, and with his shoulders back and chin held high, he pushed the button one last time.

A shock wave roared through the room, tearing the door from its hinges and bursting into the hallway. JJ, Sancho, and Percy were thrown back in their chairs as if struck by a pressurized blast, and they clung desperately to one another as they tried to resist the impact. Patrolmen flew through the air and scattered across the hallway, leaving Jason alone in the center of the floor, gripping the legs of a chair.

The initial blast was just the start of it. An unrelenting energy had been unleashed, ripping at Armaan's clothes like a turbulent wind, but he stood firm, somehow impervious to it. The gale force intensified, first sending the lights blinking on and off and then crushing the bulbs altogether, and Armaan slammed his hands over his ears and closed his eyes, praying for the energy to dissipate. Power overwhelmed the ICU, surging through the room like a living entity, emanating directly and exclusively from Eve. The roar of her gift grew louder, the force of it stronger, and just when the pressure became too much to bear, it abruptly disappeared, leaving the room in a state of ghostly stillness.

Armaan opened his eyes and took in a long, much-needed breath.

Jason released his grip on the chair and glanced across the hallway at the piles of patrolmen and broken glass that littered the floor. Sancho, JJ, and Percy were still sitting behind him, awkwardly holding one another, though they too loosened their grasps. A second passed, and suddenly Jason's eyes widened. *Eve.* He jumped to his feet and charged into the hospital room.

"STOP! DON'T MOVE!"

A patrolman, recovered from the blast, grabbed at Jason's shoulder and yanked him backward. Jason growled and ripped his arm from the man's grip.

"Jesus *Christ*, you guys don't quit, do you?"

"YOU'RE GOING TO JAIL!"

"You can take me to jail in *five goddamn minutes—*"

"SHUT UP, BOTH OF YOU!" Armaan barked.

The two men froze, taken aback by Armaan's outburst. They turned and stared at the pint-sized assistant, whose gaze was firmly locked onto the cardiac monitor. Finally he spun toward them, his eyes large and bright.

"Listen."

The entire hall went quiet. Jason's eyes panned from Armaan to Eve, who looked calm and almost serene in the aftermath of such mayhem. Then, between the pounding of his heart and his hurried breathing, he heard it—the single most comforting sound he could've hoped for.

One beep. Two beeps. Three. Four.

CHAPTER 18: GOING HOME

The intersection was still, without a single pedestrian or moving vehicle in sight. The entire block was in a state of static permanence; it had been this way since Eve's arrival, however long ago that was, she couldn't remember—though it felt as if she had been there for an eternity. She sat in the center of the road, her legs folded and her chin in her hands, her eyes pointed directly in front of her—at the small blue car, totaled and wrapped around the telephone pole. At her parents' grave.

Her eyes surveyed the car's demolished frame, balding tires, and smoking hood. She could see the backs of her parents' heads poking from above their seats, and while a part of her longed to see their faces, she dared not venture any closer.

The street and sidewalks were completely empty. There were no nosy neighbors, no aunt to scoop her in her arms. There was no massive red truck, nor was there a blood-soaked drunk driver. In that moment, there was only Eve and the little blue car—the twisted metal, the shattered windows, and the calming silence. For the first time since she had arrived, Eve climbed to her feet, propping her hands on her hips, her gaze not once straying from the car.

"It's strange," she said, finally ending the quiet. "Usually when I'm here, I spend all my time fixated on that drunk driver and his stupid truck." Her lips twitched, as if debating whether or not to smile, though they quickly flattened. She sighed. "It's nice, having them gone."

And then, Eve was no longer alone. Someone was standing behind her, watching her. Waiting. Still, she stared at the wreckage, and an unsettling swell of emotion stirred within her.

"My parents *died* that day. Most people get to grieve when they lose some-one, but I didn't." She bit her lip and clenched her fists. "I didn't get to be sad, or bitter, or *pissed.* I had to adapt. I had to survive." Her fists began to shake, and she tried to hold them still. "I don't even know if it ever really set in—the reality."

She paused, and her shoulders finally relaxed.

"My parents are dead. I'm an orphan."

Silence. A slight breeze ran through the nearby trees and swept her hair across her back. She felt her visitor take a step toward her.

"Do you miss them?"

It was Jason—she knew it immediately, even before she heard the sound of his voice. She could feel him.

Eve took in a deep, unsteady breath. "Every day," she answered.

Jason was quiet. They stared at the car wreck, or rather Eve did, while Jason in turn stared at her. After a brief stillness, he ventured to her side, finally making his way into her line of vision, but Eve offered no reaction. Her eyes were locked onto her parents' car, as if nothing could pull her from that moment.

"It's time to go home, Eve," Jason finally said.

Eve laughed under her breath. "I don't *have* a home, Jason."

"Yes you do. It's with your family."

Eve's eyes flitted across the car, once again landing on her parents' heads. Her breath caught short, and her chest felt tight and weak.

"But what about—"

"They'll understand. I promise."

Eve felt her eyes brim with tears. This was the end, the moment she had feared, and yet something about it felt soothing, even cathartic. She was leav-ing. She was starting anew.

She relaxed her fists, allowing her hands to drop limply at her sides. Reluctantly, she tore her eyes from the blue car and turned to Jason.

A sense of serenity flowed through her. Jason's presence was both com-forting and radiant, though she expected as much, but what surprised her was that he wasn't alone. Behind him stood a row of familiar faces: Percy, JJ, Sancho, and Armaan were waiting along the sidewalk, each grinning at her warmly. Eve's eyes darted between her four friends and Jason, who took another step forward, this time extending his hand toward her.

"Come on," he winked.

Eve hesitated. She thought of taking one last look at the accident, then immediately dismissed the idea. There was no need; she had been there long enough. It was time. With a deep breath, she placed her hand in Jason's and held it tightly.

Darkness surrounded Eve in an instant. Her body felt heavy, hot, and weak, as if the slightest breath was a laborious task, but she forced herself to breathe regardless. Her eyes fluttered open, and soon she realized that the darkness had been of her own doing. Her vision was hazy, but after a few strenuous breaths and an uncharacteristic moment of patience, she began to see things more clearly.

She was in a dimly lit room, one much larger than her dorm, with an HV, a compact refrigerator, and a long desk covered in beautifully wrapped gifts. Suddenly, Eve realized that she had been here before: this was Jason's hospital room, neatly tucked away in the isolation wing of the Billington Medical Ward. She must have been summoned for her tutoring duties—and yet, somehow, she knew that wasn't so.

A line of twinkly lights adorned the desk, and a small, liberally decorated Christmas tree sat beside the gifts. She looked down at her feet and saw only a thick white sheet, one that stretched from the end of the hospital bed all the way up to her chest. Then she turned to her right and saw Jason, sitting in a flimsy folding chair, his head resting on his arms, which in turn rested on her bed.

She stared at him for a long moment—he was fast asleep, his shoulders peacefully rising and falling—and then she looked down at his hand, which lay delicately in hers. Suddenly, everything was clear: there was no tutoring session, nor was she in Jason's room. Eve was lying in her own bed, in her own hospital room, in the isolation wing.

A slight rustling caught her attention. Her door was ajar, and the light of the outside wing poured through the opening; bodies scurried by, and shadows bobbed along the floor. Suddenly, a nurse pulled the door open and poked her head into the room. She glanced at Eve, who shrank back from the light—and the nurse's eyes bulged in disbelief. With a sense of urgency, she tapped at her earpiece.

"Page Dr. Dzarnoski. She's awake."

The nurse quickly scanned Eve's monitors and jotted a few notes onto her scratchpad. Again, she looked at Eve, cocking her head in Jason's direction.

"You'd better wake him up. That boy has been by your side for days.

Hardly eats, rarely sleeps." She smiled. "Only gets up to use the restroom."

Without another word, the nurse retreated back into the hallway, closing the door behind her.

Eve turned toward Jason. He looked calm, and a part of her didn't want to disturb him. But after a brief hesitation, she squeezed his hand—or at least she tried to. Her hand remained still, unresponsive to her bidding, and the faintest scowl graced her lips. Again, she squeezed his hand, this time summoning all of her strength, and her fingers finally curled around his. Even so, her grip was nothing more than a light, airy touch.

As she stroked his palm with her fingers, Jason finally stirred. With a yawn, he grabbed her hand, his grip much tighter than hers—and then he lifted his head and met her gaze. Instantly, his eyes widened.

"Eve," he gasped. His lips parted, but he said nothing. Finally, he exhaled. "Hi." He smiled.

Eve smiled in return. "Hey, you," she whispered.

Jason stared into her eyes, his body frozen, his face turning a bright shade of pink. She could feel his fingers tighten around hers, and he lightly caressed the back of her hand with his thumb. He leaned in closer and delicately kissed her forehead, and as he took his seat, she could see that his face had gone from pink to red. He fidgeted in place and cleared his throat, finally tearing his eyes from hers and glancing at the door.

"I should get the doctor—"

"Nurse already covered that," Eve murmured with a half-smirk.

Jason grinned. He cupped her palm with both of his hands, bringing it to his lips for a soft kiss. "How are you feeling?"

"Tired." Eve paused for a breath. "How are you?"

"Dynamic. Today might be the best day of my life." He laughed, but she could see in his eyes that he was sincere. His voice shook. "I can't believe you're awake."

"How long have I been asleep?"

"Seven days." He nodded at the ornamented tree. "Merry Christmas Eve."

"It's Christmas?"

"No, it's Christmas Eve," Jason corrected. He chuckled. "I guess that's kind of confusing—it's Christmas Eve, *Eve*. December twenty-fourth."

Eve examined Jason, starting at his face and then making her way down his chest to his arms. His bicep was wrapped with surgical cloth, and a thick white bandage was peeping out of the neckline of his shirt.

"You're hurt."

Jason glanced at his arm and shrugged. "Just a few cuts and scrapes. Nothing major."

Eve sighed, knowing all too well that he was lying. Gradually, she was beginning to feel her strength and awareness resurface. She nodded at the stacks of gifts on the opposite side of the room.

"Who are those from?"

"Everyone. You're famous now."

"I was *already* famous, Jason," she scoffed. "I'm the *Chimera Bitch*, remember?"

Jason chuckled. "Well, they're not calling you that anymore. You're a hero."

"Hero, my ass. Furst will have me locked up as soon as I'm out of bed."

"You're not going to jail. None of us are." His eyes brightened. "We've been pardoned."

Eve furrowed her brow. "Pardoned? What for?"

"For saving everyone. For destroying the list. For killing Fairon."

Suddenly, Eve's blood ran cold. "Fairon," she repeated. Her eyes bulged. "Jason, you didn't tell anyone, did you?"

"Tell them what?"

"That I killed Fairon. *How* I killed Fairon." Her voice was panicked, and she squeezed his hand, this time with more strength. "If people find out..."

Jason sighed. "Eve—"

"They can't know, Jason. Promise me you won't say anything."

"Eve, I won't. I didn't." He glanced at the doorway and lowered his voice. "Look, people know... enough." He leaned in closer. "They know Fairon's dead—that you killed him—but nothing else. Not how. I promise."

"There are others, Jason," Eve continued, her voice laced with anxiety. "Fairon is just the beginning. I mean, he's *nothing*—just a soldier, or a Fae, or whatever it is—"

"Eve, please, just relax."

"Jason, this is *important*—"

"Yeah, well, so is your health. You *just* woke up." He lightly ran his fingers through her hair. "Please, try to relax. We'll talk about this later. I promise."

Eve faltered. She stared back at Jason, at his kind though compelling gaze, and despite her obstinate resolve, she knew he was right. She allowed her body to sink back into her mattress.

"Okay."

Jason smiled. He was still gliding his fingers across her forehead, and she could feel his palm begin to tremble. He quickly pulled his hands to his lap.

"God, you've missed a lot," he said. "I have so much to tell you."

"Like what?"

"Well, for starters, I got your grades." He fiddled with his scratchpad and expanded her holographic scorecard. "All A's, of course. Don't know how you do it. Maybe you should tutor me in more than melting." He winked. "It's weird though: Richards gave you an A-plus but wrote in some terrible comments."

Eve rolled her eyes. "Figures."

"Also, Armaan told me to tell you he's sorry."

"Sorry? For what?"

"For shaving your head."

Eve's eyes bulged. "HE SHAVED MY—"

"*Eve*, calm down," Jason laughed, grabbing her arm before she could clutch at her scalp. "It's just a little strip. Here, feel." He lifted her hand and ran her fingers over the bald patch, and then through the remainder of her long, wavy hair. "See? Looks kind of badass if you ask me."

Eve relaxed into her bed, more comforted by Jason's touch than by that of her hair. He placed her hand back at her side, and though his movements were gentle, she could still feel him trembling. His nervousness was palpable. She smiled.

"Jason—"

"He's going to want to know you're awake," Jason interrupted, pulling his phone from his pocket. "They all are."

"Jason..." Eve paused, watching as Jason hurriedly tapped at his phone. She furrowed her brow. "What are you doing?"

"I'm calling everyone, what do you think?" Four separate holograms appeared from his screen, each one a different color and assigned a different name. "Armaan's somewhere in this building. Percy's at his mom's place down the street, so he'll probably be here soon. JJ and Sancho are home for the holidays, but I'll get 'em on holoview."

Eve sighed. "Jason—"

"God, they're going to be juiced." He looked up at her, his eyes glistening and his hands still shaking. "You're awake. I just can't believe you're awake."

"Jason."

"Jesus, the reception here is shit—"

Eve swiped her hand through the four holograms, minimizing them from view. She grabbed Jason's hand and scowled.

"*Jason*," she groaned.

"What?" he asked.

She was silent, just for a moment. He stared back at her with anxious eyes, and though it was clear that he felt weak and overwrought, she felt peaceful. Strong. Happy.

Again, she smiled.

"I love you, too."

Made in the USA
Lexington, KY
01 January 2016